T0405713

K. J. Parker

This special signed edition
is limited to 1000 numbered copies.

This is copy 705

UNDER MY SKIN

UNDER MY SKIN

STORIES BY

K. J. PARKER

Subterranean Press 2023

See page 673 for individual story copyrights.

First Edition

ISBN
978-1-64524-079-2

Subterranean Press
PO Box 190106
Burton, MI 48519

subterraneanpress.com

Manufactured in the United States of America

Table of Contents

The Return of the Pig

[Nostalgia: from the Greek, νοσтου ἀλγεα, the pain of returning home]

It was one of those mechanical traps they use for bears and other dangerous pests: flattering in a way, since I'm not what you'd call physically imposing. It caught me slightly off square, crunching my heel and ankle until the steel teeth met inside me. My mind went white with pain, and for the first time in my life I couldn't think.

Smart move on his part. When I've got my wits about me, I'm afraid of nothing on earth, with good reason; nothing on earth can hurt me, because I'm stronger, though you wouldn't think it to look at me. But pain clouds the mind, interrupts the concentration. When it hurts so much that you can't think, trying to do anything is like baling water with a sieve. It all just slips through and runs away, like kneading smoke.

Ah well. We all make enemies. However meek and mild we try to be, sooner or later, we all—excuse the pun—put our foot in it, and then anger and resentment cloud the judgement, and we do things and have things done to us that make no logical sense. An eloquent indictment of the folly of ambition; one supremely learned and clever intellectual does for another by snapping him in a gadget designed to trap bears. You'd take the broad view and laugh, if it didn't hurt so very, very much.

WHAT IS STRENGTH? Excuse me if this sounds like an exam question. But seriously, what is it? I would define it as the quality that enables one to do work and exert influence. The stronger you are, the more you can do, the bigger and more intransigent the objects you can influence. My father could lift a three-hundredweight anvil. So, of course, can I, but in a very different way. So: here comes the paradox. I couldn't follow my father's trade because I was and still am a weakling. So instead I was sent away to school, where what little muscle I had soon atrophied into fat, and where I became incomparably strong. The hell with anvils. I can lift mountains. There is no mountain so heavy that I can't lift it. Not bad going, for a man who has to call the porter to take the lids off jars.

The mistake we all make is to confuse strength with security. You think: because I'm so very strong, I need fear nothing. They actually tell you that, in fourth year; once you've completed this part of the course you should never be afraid of anything ever again, because nothing will have the power to hurt you. It sounds marvellous, and you write home: Dear Mother and Father, this term we'll be doing absolute strength, so when I see you next I'll be invincible and invulnerable, just fancy, your loving son, et cetera. We believe it, because it's so very plausible. Then you get field assignments and practicals, where you levitate heavy objects and battle with demons and divert the course of rivers and turn back the tides of the sea—heady stuff for a nineteen-year-old—and at the end of it you *believe*. I'm a graduate of the Studium, armed with *stricto ense* and protected by *lorica*, I shall fear no evil. And then they pack you off to your first posting, and you start the slow, humiliating business of learning something useful, the hard way.

They mention pain, in passing. Pain, they tell you, is one of the things that can screw up your concentration, so avoid it if you can. You nod sagely and jot it down in your lecture notes:

avoid pain. But it never comes up in the exam, so you forget about it.

All my life I've tried to avoid pain, with indifferent success.

My head was still spinning when the murderers came along. I call them that for convenience, the way you do. When you know what a man does for a living, you look at him and see the trade, not the human being. You there, blacksmith, shoe my horse; tapster, fetch me a pint of beer. And you see me and you fall on your knees and ask my blessing, in the hope I won't turn you into a frog.

Actually they were just two typical Mesoge farmhands, thin, spare and strong, with big hands, frayed cuffs and good strong teeth uncorrupted by sugar. One of them had a mattock (where I come from, they call them biscays), the other a lump of rock pulled out of the bank. One good thing about the murderer's trade, no great outlay on specialist equipment.

They looked at me dispassionately, sizing up the extent to which pain had rendered me harmless. My guess is, they hadn't been told what I was, my trade, though the scholar's gown should have put them on notice. They figured I'd be no bother, but they separated anyway, to come at me from two directions. They hadn't brought a cart, so I imagine their orders were to sling me in a ditch when they were all done. One of them was chewing on something, probably bacon rind.

The thing about *stricto ense*—it's actually a very simple Form, they could easily teach it in first year, except you wouldn't trust a sixteen-year-old freshman with it, any more than you'd leave him alone with a jar of brandy and your daughter. All you do is concentrate very hard, imagine what you'd like to happen, and say the little jingle; *stricto ense ruit in hostem*. Personally, I always imagine a man who's just been kicked by a carthorse, for the simple reason that I saw it happen to my elder brother when I was six. One moment he was going about his business, lifting the offside rear hoof to trim it with his knife. His concentration must have wandered because quick as a thought the horse slipped his hold and hit him. I saw him in the split second before he fell, with a sort of semicircular dent a fingernail deep directly above his eyebrows. His eyes were wide open—surprise, nothing more—and then he fell backwards and blood started to ooze and his face never moved again. It's useful when you have a nice sharp memory to draw on.

If they'd come along a minute earlier, I'd have been in no fit state. But a minute was long enough, and *stricto ense* is such an easy Form, and I've done it so often; and that particular memory is so very clear, and always with me, near at hand, like a dagger under your pillow. I tore myself away from the pain just long enough to speculate what those two would look like with hoofprints on their foreheads. Then I heard the smack—actually, it's duller, like trying to split endgrain, when the axe just sinks in, *thud*, rather than cleaving, *crack*—and I left them to it and gave my full attention to the pain, for a very long time.

TWO DAYS EARLIER, we all sat down in austerely beautiful, freezing cold Chapter to discuss the chair of Perfect Logic, vacant since the untimely death of Father Vitruvius. He'd been very much old school, a man genuinely devoted to contemplation, so abstract and theoretical that his body was always an embarrassment, like the poor relation that gets dragged along on family visits. Rumour had it that he wasn't always quite so detached; he'd had a mistress in the suburbs and fathered two sons, now established in a thriving ropewalk in Choris and doing very well. Most rumours in our tiny world are true, but not, I think, that one.

There were three obvious candidates; the other two were Father Sulpicius and Father Gnatho. To be fair, not a hair's weight between the three of us. We'd known each other since second year (Gnatho and I were a year above Sulpicius; I've known

Gnatho even longer than that), graduated together, chose the same specialities, were reunited after our first postings, saw each other at table and in the libraries nearly every day for twenty years. As far as ability went, we were different but equal. All three of us were and had always been exceptionally bright and diligent; all three of us could do the job standing on our heads. The chair carries tenure for life, and all three of us were equally ambitious. For the two who didn't get it, there was no other likely preferment, and for the rest of our lives we'd be subordinate by one degree to the fortunate third, who'd be able to order us about and send us on dangerous assignments and postings to remote and barbarous places, at whim.

I don't actually hate Sulpicius, or even Gnatho. By one set of perfectly valid criteria, they're my oldest and closest friends, nearer to me than brothers ever could be. If there'd been a remotely credible compromise candidate, we'd all three have backed him to the hilt. But there wasn't, not unless we hired in from another House (which the Studium never does, for sheer arrogant pride); one of us it would have to be. You can see the difficulty.

The session lasted nine hours and then we took a vote. I voted for Gnatho. Sulpicius voted for me. Gnatho voted for Sulpicius. In the event, it was a deadlock, nine votes each. Father Prior did the only thing he could; adjourned for thirty days, during which time all three candidates were sent away on field missions, to stop them canvassing. It was the only thing Prior Sighvat could have done; it was also the worst thing he could possibly do. For all our strength, you see, we're only human.

So there I was, a very strong human with a bear-trap biting into my foot.

I've always been bad with pain. Before I mastered *sicut in terra*, even mild toothache made me scream out loud. It used to make my poor father furiously angry to hear me snivelling and whimpering, as he put it, like a big girl. I was always a disappointment to him, even when I showed him I could turn lead pipe into gold. So the bear-trap had me beat, I have to confess. All I had to do was prise it open with *qualis artifex* and heal the wound with *vergens in defectum*, fifteen seconds' work, but I couldn't, not for a very long time, during which I pissed myself twice, which was disgusting. Actually, that was probably what saved me. Self-disgust concentrates the mind the way fear is supposed to but doesn't. Also, after something like five hours, judged by the movement of the sun, the pain wore off a little, or I got used to it.

That first stupendous effort—grabbing the wisp of smoke and not letting go—and then fifteen seconds of total dedication, and then, there I was, wondering what the hell all that fuss had been about. I stood up—pins and needles in my other foot made me wince, but I charmed it away without a second's thought—and considered my shoe, which was irretrievably ruined. So I hardened the sole of my foot with *scelus sceleris* and went barefoot. No big deal.

(Query: why is there no known Form for fixing trivial everyday objects? Answer, I guess: we live such comfortable, over-provided-for lives that nobody's ever felt the need. Remind me to do something about it, when I have five minutes)

All this time, of course, it had never once occurred to me to wonder why, or who. Naturally. What need is there of speculation when you already know the answer?

My mother didn't raise me to be no watch officer; nevertheless, that's what I've become, over the years, for the not-very-good reason that I'm very good at it. A caution to those aspiring to join the Order; think very carefully before showing you have an aptitude for, but you have a proficiency in anything, you just don't know what it'll lead to. When I was young and newly graduated, my first field assignment was identifying and neutralising renegades—witchfinding, as we call it and you mustn't, because it's not respectful. I thought: if I do this job really well, I'll acquire kudos and make a name for myself. Indeed. I made a name for myself as someone who could safely be entrusted with a singularly rotten job that nobody wants to do. And I've been doing it ever since, the go-to man whenever there's an untrained natural on the loose.

(Gnatho is every bit as good at it as I am, but he's smart. He deliberately screwed up, to the point where senior men had to be sent out to rescue him and clear up the mess. It had no long-term effect on his career, and he's never had to do it since. Sulpicius couldn't trace an untrained natural if they were in the same bath together, so in his case the problem never arose.)

No witchfinding job is ever pleasant, and this one—I'd spent five hours in exquisite pain on the open moor, and I hadn't even got there yet.

I tried to make up time by walking faster, but I'm useless at hills, and the Mesoge is crawling with the horrible things, so it was dark as a bag by the time I got to Riens. I knew the way, of course. Riens is six miles from where I grew up.

Nobody who leaves the Mesoge and makes good in the big city ever goes back. You hear rich, successful merchants waxing eloquent at formal dinners about the beauties of the Old Country—the waterfalls of Scheria, the wide-open sky of the Bohec, watching the sun go down on Beloisa Bay—but the Mesoge men sit quiet and hope their flattened vowels don't give them away. I hadn't been back for fifteen years. Everywhere else changes in that sort of timespan. Not the Mesoge. Still the same crumbling dry-stone walls, dilapidated farmhouses, thistle- and briar-spoilt scrubland pasture, rutted roads, muddy verges, grey skies, thin scabby livestock and miserable people. A man is the product of the landscape he was born in, so they say, and I'm horribly aware that this is true. Trying to counteract the aspects of the Mesoge that are part and parcel of my very being has made me what I am, so I'm not ungrateful for my origins; they've made me hard-working, clean-living, honest, patient, tolerant, the polar opposite, the substance of which the Mesoge is the shadow. I just don't like going back there, that's all.

I remembered Riens as a typical Mesoge town; perched on a hilltop, so you have to struggle a mile uphill with every drop of water you use, which means everybody smells; thick red sandstone town walls, and a town gate that rotted away fifty years ago and which nobody can be bothered to replace; one long street, with the inn and the meeting-house on opposite sides in the middle. Mesoge men have lived for generations by stealing each others' sheep. Forty makes you an old man, and what my father mostly did was make arrowheads. Mesoge women are short and stocky, and you never see a pretty face; they've all gone east, to work in the entertainment sector. Those that remain are muscular, hard-working, forceful and short-tempered, like my mother.

The woman at the inn was like that. "Who the hell are you?" she said.

I explained that I was a traveller; I needed a bed for the night, and if at all possible, something to eat and maybe even a pint of beer, if that wouldn't put anybody out. She scowled at me and told me I could have the loft, for six groschen.

The loft in the Mesoge is where you store hay for the horses. The food is stockfish porridge—we're a hundred miles from the sea, but we live on dried fish, go figure—with, if you're unlucky, a mountain of fermented cabbage. The beer—

I peered into it. "Is this stuff safe to drink?"

She gave me a look. "We drink it."

"I think I'll pass, thanks."

There was a mattress in the loft. It can't have been more than thirty years old. I lay awake listening to the horses below, noisily digesting and stamping their feet. Home, I said to myself. What joy.

THE OBJECT OF my weary expedition was a boy, fifteen years old, the tanner's third son; it was like looking into a mirror, except he was skinny and at his age I was a little tub of lard. But I saw the same defensive aggression in his sneaky little eyes, fear mixed with guilt, spiced with consciousness of a yet-unfathomed superiority—he knew he was better than everybody else around him, but he wasn't sure why, or how it worked, or whether it would stunt his growth or make him go blind. That's the thing; you daren't ask anybody. No wonder so many of them, of us, go to the bad.

I said I'd see him alone, just the two of us. His father had a stone shed, where they kept the oak bark (rolled up like carpets, tied with string and stacked against the wall)

"Sit down," I told him. He squatted cross-legged on the floor. "You don't have to do that," I said.

He looked at me.

"You don't have to sit on the cold, wet floor," I said. "You can do this." I muttered *qualis artifex* and produced two milking-stools. "Can't you?"

He stared at me, but not because the trick had impressed him. "Don't know what you're talking about," he said.

"It's all right," I said. "You're not in trouble. It's not a crime, in itself." I grinned. "It's not a crime because it can't happen. The law takes the view—as we do—that there's no such thing as magic. If there's no such thing, it can't be against the law." I produced a table, with a teapot and two porcelain bowls. "Do you drink tea?"

"No."

"Try it, it's one of life's few pleasures."

He scowled at the bowl and made no movement. I poured myself some tea and blew on it to cool it down. "There is no magic," I told him. "Instead, there are a certain number of limited effects which a wise man, a scholar, can learn to do, if he knows how, and if he's born with the ability to concentrate, very, very hard. They aren't magic, because they're not—well, strange or inexplicable or weird. Give you an example. Have you ever watched the smith weld two rods together? Well, then. A man takes two bits of metal and does a trick involving fire and sparks flying about, and the two bits of metal are joined so perfectly you can't see where one ends and another begins. Or take an even weirder trick. It's the one where a woman pulls a living human being out from between her legs. Weird? I should say so."

He shook his head. "Women can't do magic," he said. "Everybody knows that."

A literal mind. Ah, well. "Men can't do it either, because it doesn't exist. Haven't you been listening? But a few men have the gift of concentrating very hard and doing certain processes, certain tricks, that achieve things that look weird and strange to people who don't know about these things. It's not magic, because we know exactly how it works and what's going on, just as we know what happens when your dad puts a dead cow's skin in a big stone trough, and it comes out all hard and smooth on one side."

He shrugged. "If you say so."

Hard going. Still, that's the Mesoge for you. We esteem it a virtue in youth to be unimpressed by anything or anyone, never to cooperate, never to show enthusiasm or interest. "You can do this stuff," I reminded him. "I know you can, because people have seen you doing it."

"Can't prove anything."

"Don't need to. I know. I can see into your mind."

That got to him. He went white as a sheet, and if the door hadn't been bolted on the outside (a simple precaution) he'd have been up and out of there like an arrow from a bow. "You can't."

I smiled at him. "I can see you looking at a flock of sheep, and three days later half of them are dead. I can see you getting a clip round the ear from an old man, who then falls and breaks his leg. I can see a burning hay-rick, sorry, no, make that three. Antisocial little devil, aren't you?"

The tears in his eyes were pure rage, and I softly mumbled *lorica*. But he didn't lash out, as I'd have done at his age, as I did during this very interview. He just shook his head, and muttered about proof. "I don't need proof," I said. "I've got a witness. You." I waited three heartbeats, then said, "And it's all right. I'm on your side. You're one of us."

His scowl said he didn't believe me. "All right," I said. "Watch closely. The little fat kid is me."

And I showed him. Simple little Form, *lux dardaniae,* very effective. One thing I didn't do quite right; one of the nasty little escapades I showed him was Gnatho, not me. Same difference, though.

He looked at me with something less than absolute hatred. "You're from round here."

I nodded. "Born and bred. You don't like it here, do you?"

"No."

"Me neither. That's why I left. You can too. In ten years, you can be me. Only without the pot belly and the double chin."

"Me?" he said. "Go to the City?"

And I knew I'd got him. "Watch," I said, and I showed him Perimadeia; the standard visitor's tour, the fountains and the palace and Victory Square and the Yarn Market at Goosefair. Then, while he was still reeling, I showed him the Studium—the impressive view, from the harbour, looking up the hill. "Where would you rather live," I said, "there or here? Your choice. No pressure."

He looked at me. "If I go there, can my mother and my sisters come and visit me?"

I frowned. "Sorry, no. We don't allow women, it's the rules."

He grinned. "Yes, please," he said. "I hate women."

GNATHO WAS SKINNY at that age. My first memory of him was a little skinny kid stealing apples from our one good eating-apple tree. They were my apples. I didn't want to share with an unknown stranger. So I smacked him with what I would later come to know as *stricto ense.*

It didn't work.

And then there was this huge invisible *thing* whirling towards me, so big it would've blotted out the sun if it hadn't been invisible, if you see what I mean. I didn't think; I warded it off, with a Form I would come to call *scutum veritatis*. I felt the collision; it literally made the ground shake under my feet.

We stared at each other.

I remember quite vividly the first time I looked in a mirror, though of course it wasn't a mirror, not in the Mesoge, it was a basin full of water, outside on a perfectly still day. I remember the disappointment. That plump, foolish-looking kid was *me*. And I remember how Gnatho, intently staring at me, lost his seat on the branch of the tree, and fell, and would almost certainly have broken his neck—

I handled it badly. I sort of grabbed at him—*adiutorem meum*, used cack-handedly by a ten-year-old, what do you expect?—and slammed him against the trunk of the tree on the way down. The rough bark scraped a big flap of skin off his cheek, and he has the scar still. Stupid fool didn't think to use *scutum*, he just panicked, he was so lucky I was there (only if I hadn't been, he wouldn't have fallen). But he thought I toppled him out of the tree on purpose and gave him the scar that disfigured him. I showed him my memory when we were eighteen, so he knows the truth. But I think he still blames me, in his heart of hearts, and he's still scared of me, in case I ever do it again.

THERE WERE ARRANGEMENTS. I had to go and see the boy's parents—long, tedious interview, with the parents scared, angry, shocked, right up until I introduced the subject of compensation for the boy's unpaid labour. The Order is embarrassingly rich. In the City, ten kreuzers a week will buy you lunch, if you aren't picky. In the Mesoge it's a fortune. I'm authorised to offer up to twenty, but it's not my money and I'm conscientious.

THE RETURN OF THE PIG

I WALK WHENEVER I can because I have no luck at all with carts and coaches. The horses don't like me; they're sensitive animals, and they perceive something about me that isn't quite right. I cause endless problems to any wheeled vehicle I ride on. If it's not the horses, it's a broken axle or a broken spoke, or the coach gets bogged down in a rut, or the driver falls off or has a seizure. I'm not alone; quite a few of us have travel jinxes of one sort or another, and it's better to be jinxed on land than on sea, like poor Father Incitatus. So, to get to the Mesoge, I take a boat from the City down the Asper as far as Stark and walk the rest of the way. Trouble is, rivers only flow in one direction. To get back from the Mesoge, I have to walk to Insuper, get a lumber barge to the coast and tack back up to the City on a grain ship. I get seasick and there's no known Form for that. Ain't that the way.

From Riens to Insuper is seventeen miles, down dale and up bloody hill. Six miles from Riens, the road goes through a small village; or you can take the old cart road up to the Tor, then wind your way down through the forestry, cross the Blackwater at Sens Ford and rejoin the main road a mile the other side of the village. Going that way adds another five miles or so and it's miserable, treacherous going, but it saves you having to pass through this small, typical Mesoge settlement.

Just my luck, though. I dragged all the way up Tor Drove, and slipped and slithered my way down the logging tracks, which were badly overgrown with briars where the logging crews had burnt off their brash, only to find that the Blackwater was up with the spring rain, the ford was washed out and there was no way over. Despair. I actually considered parting the waters or diverting the river; but there are rules about that sort of thing, and a man in the running for the chair of Perfect Logic doesn't want to go breaking too many rules if there's any chance of being found out; and since I was known to be in the neighbourhood...

So, back I went; up the logging trails and down the Drove, back to where I originally left the road, a journey made even more tedious by reflecting on the monstrously extended metaphor it represented. I reached the village (forgive me if I don't say its name) bright and early in the morning, having slept under a beech tree and been woken by the snuffling of wild pigs.

I so hoped it had changed, but it hadn't. The main street takes you right by the blacksmith's forge—that was all right, because when my father died, my mother sold it and moved back north to her family. Whoever had it now was a busy man; I could hear the chime of hammer on anvil two hundred yards away. My father never started work until three hours after sun-up. He said it was being considerate to the neighbours, all of whom he hated and feuded incessantly with. But the hinges on the gate still hadn't been fixed, and the chimney was still on the verge of falling down, maintained in place by nothing but force of habit—a potent entity in the Mesoge.

I had my hood pinched up round my face, just in case anybody recognised me. Needless to say, everybody I passed stopped what they were doing and stared at me. I knew nearly all of them, those that were over twenty.

Gnatho's family were colliers, charcoal-burners. In the Mesoge we're painfully aware of the subtlest gradations of social status, and colliers (who live outdoors, move from camp to camp in the woods, and deal with outsiders) are so low that even the likes of my lot were in a position to look down on them. But Gnatho's father inherited a farm. It was tight in to the village, with a paddock fronting onto the road, and there he built sheds to store charcoal, and a house. It hadn't changed one bit, but from its front door came four men, carrying a door on their shoulders. On the door was something covered in a curtain.

I stopped an old woman, let's not bother with her name. "Who died?" I asked.

She told me. Gnatho's father.

Gnatho isn't Gnatho's name, of course, any more than mine is mine. When you join the Order, you get a name-in-religion assigned to you. Gnatho's real name (like mine) is five syllables long and can't be transcribed into a civilised alphabet. The woman looked at me. "Do I know you?"

I shook my head. "When did that happen?"

"Been sick for some time. Know the family, do you?"

"I met his son once, in the City."

"Oh, him." She scowled at me. *Lorica* doesn't work on peasant scowls, so I hadn't bothered with it. "He still alive, then?"

"Last I heard."

"You sure I don't know you? You sound familiar."

"Positive."

Gnatho's father. A loud, violent man who beat his wife and daughters; a great drinker, angry because people treated him like dirt when he worked so much harder than they did. Permanently red-faced, from the charcoal fires and the booze, lame in one leg, a tall man, ashamed of his skinny, thieving, no-account son. He'd reached a ripe old age for the Mesoge. The little shrivelled woman walking next to the pallbearers had to be his poor oppressed wife, now a wealthy woman by local standards, and free at last of that pig. She was crying. Some people.

Some impulse led me to dig a gold half-angel out of my pocket and press it into her hand as she walked past me. She looked round and stared, but I'd discreetly made myself hard to see. She gazed at the coin in her hand, then tightened her palm around it like a vice.

I WAS OUT of the village and climbing the long hill on the other side a mere twenty minutes later, by my excellent Mezentine mechanical watch. There, I told myself, that wasn't so bad.

Once you've experienced the thing you've been dreading the most, you get a bit light-headed for a while, until some new aggravation comes along and reminds you that life isn't like that. In my case, the new aggravation was another flooded river, the Inso this time, which had washed away the bridge at Machaera and smashed the ferry-boat into kindling. The ferryman told me what I already knew; I had to go back three miles to where the road forks, then follow the southern leg down as far as Coniga, pick up the old Military Road which would take me, eventually, to the coast. There's a stage at Friest, he said helpfully, so you won't have to walk very far. Just as well, he added, it's a bloody long way else.

So help me, I actually considered the stage. But it wouldn't be fair on the other passengers, innocent country folk who'd never done me any harm. No; for some reason, the Mesoge didn't want to let me go—playing with its food, a bad habit my mother was always very strict about. One of the reasons we're so damnably backwards is the rotten communications with the outside world. A few heavy rainstorms and you're screwed, can't go anywhere, can't get back to where you came from.

So, reluctantly, I embarked on a walking tour of my past. I have to say, the scholar's gown is an excellent armour, a woollen version of *lorica*. Nobody hassles you, nobody wants to talk to you, they give you what you ask for and wait impatiently for you to finish up and leave. I bought a pair of boots in Assistenso, from a cobbler I knew when he was a young man. He looked about a hundred and six now. He recognised me but didn't say a word. Quite good boots, actually, though I had to *qualis artifex* them a bit to stop them squeaking all the damn time.

The *Temperance & Thrift* in Nauns is definitely a cut above the other inns in the Mesoge; God only knows why. The rooms are proper rooms, with actual wooden beds, the food is edible and (glory of glories), you can get proper black tea there. Nominally it's a brothel rather than an inn; but if you give the girl a nice smile and six stuivers, she goes away and you can have the room to yourself. I was sleeping peacefully for the first time in ages when some fool banged on the door and woke me up.

Was I the scholar? Yes, I admitted reluctantly, because the gown lying over the back of the chair was in plain sight. You're needed. They've got trouble in—well, I won't bother you with the name of the village. Lucky to have caught you. Just as well the bridge is out, or you'd have been long gone.

THEY'D SENT A cart for me, the fools. Needless to say, the horse went lame practically the moment I climbed aboard; so back we went to the *Temperance* for another one, and then the main shaft cracked, and we were ages cutting out a splint and patching it in. Quicker to have walked, I told him.

"I know you," the carter replied. "You're from round here."

There comes a time when you can fight no more. "That's right."

"You're his son. The collier's boy."

Most insults I can take in my stride, but some I can't. "Like hell," I snapped. I told him my name. "The old smith's son," I reminded him. He nodded. He never forgot a face, he told me.

Gnatho's father, in fact, was the problem. Not resting quietly in the grave is a Mesoge tradition, like morris dances and wassailing the apple trees. If you die with an unresolved grudge or a bad attitude generally, chances are you'll be back, either as your own putrifying and swollen corpse or some form of large, unpleasant vermin, a wolf, bear or pig.

"He's come back as a pig," I said. "Bet you."

The carter grinned. "You knew the old devil, then."

"Oh yes."

Revenant pests don't look like the natural variety. They're bigger, always jet-black, with red eyes. They glow slightly in the dark, and ordinary weapons don't bite on them, ordinary traps can't hold them and they seem to thrive on ordinary poisons. Gnatho's dad had taken to digging into the sides of houses—at night, while the family was asleep—undermining the walls and bringing the roof down. That wouldn't be hard in most Mesoge houses, which are three-parts fallen down from neglect anyway, but I could see where a glowing spectral hog rootling around in the footings wouldn't help matters.

I KNOW A little bit about revenants, because my grandfather was one. He was a bear, and he spent a busy nine months killing livestock and breaking hedges until a man in a grey gown came down from the City and sorted him out. I watched him do it, and that was when I knew what I wanted to be when I grew up.

Granddad died when I was six. I remember him as a big, cheerful man who always gave me an apple, but he'd killed two of our neighbours—self-defence, but in a small community, that really doesn't matter very much. The scholar sat up four nights in a row, caught him with a freezing Form (*in quo vincit*, presumably) and left him there till morning, when he came back with a dozen men, stakes, axes, big hammers, all the kit I tended to associate with mending fences. The only bit of Grandad that could move was his eyes, and he watched everything they did, right up to when they cut off his head. Of course, what I saw wasn't my dear grandfather, it was a huge black bear. It was only later that they told me.

I DON'T KNOW if embarrassment can kill a man. I could have put it to the test, but I got scared and dosed myself with *fons laetitiae*, which takes the edge off pretty much everything.

No chance, you see, of anonymity once I got back to the village. Old Mu the Dog—his actual name, insofar as I can transcribe it, is Mutahalliush—was mayor now; my last mental image of him was his face splashed with the stinking dark-brown juice that sweats off rotten lettuce, as he sat in the stocks for fathering a child on the miller's daughter, but clearly other people had shorter memories or were more forgiving than me. Shup the tanner was constable, Ati from Five Ash was sexton, and the new smith, a man I didn't know, was almoner and parish remembrancer. I gave them a cold, dazed look and told them to sit down.

I think it was just as bad for them. See it from their point of view. One of their own, a kid they'd smacked round the head with a stick on many occasions, was now a scholar, a wizard, able to kill with a frown or turn the turds on the midden to pure gold. We kept it formal, which was probably just as well.

The meeting told me nothing I didn't know already or couldn't guess or hadn't heard from the carter, but it gave me a chance to do the usual ground-rules speech and impress upon them the perils of not doing exactly as they were told. It was only when we'd been through all that and I stood up to let them know the meeting was over that Shup—my second cousin; we're all related—asked me if I knew how his nephew had got on. His nephew? And then the penny dropped. He meant Gnatho.

"He's doing very well," I told him.

"He's a scholar? Like you?"

"Very like me," I said. "He's never been back, then."

"We didn't know if he was alive or dead."

Or me, come to that. "I'll tell him about his father," I said. "He may want to—" I paused, realising what I'd just been about to say. Pay his respects at the graveside? Which one? A revenant's remains are chopped into four pieces and buried on the parish boundaries, at the four cardinal points. "He'll want to know." And that was a flat lie, but I have to confess I was looking forward to telling him. As he would have been, in my shoes.

GNATHO'S DAD WASN'T the sharpest knife in the drawer when he was alive. Dead, he seemed to have acquired some basic low cunning, though that might have been the pig rather than him. It took me three nights to catch him. He didn't come quietly, and God, was he ever strong. By the time I finally brought him down with *posui adiutorem* I was weak with exhaustion and shaking like a leaf.

Have I misled you with the word pig? Dismiss the mental image of a fat, pink porker snuffling up cabbage leaves in a sty. Wild pigs are big; they weigh half a ton, they're covered in sleek, wiry hair and they're all muscle. Real ones have the redeeming feature of shyness; they sit tight, and if you make enough noise walking around you'll never ever see one, unless you actually tread on its tail. If you do, it'll be the last thing you ever do see. The kind, brave noblemen who come out and kill the damn things for us will tell you that a forest pig is the most dangerous animal in Permia, more so than wolves or bears or bull elk. Real pigs are a sort of auburn colour, but Gnatho's dad was soot black, with the unmistakable red eyes.

Once you have your revenant down, you talk to him. I stood up, my legs wobbling under me, and approached as near as I dared, even with a double dose of *lorica*. "Hello," I said.

Only the eyes could move; the body was paralysed. They peered at me from under those disturbingly human lashes. "Don't I know you?"

Paralysed, remember? I was hearing his voice inside my head. "I'm the smith's boy."

"That's right, so you are. You went off to be a wizard in the City."

"I'm back."

He wanted to acknowledge me with a nod of the head, but found he couldn't. "What's going to happen to me now?"

"I think you know."

I sensed that he took it resolutely—not happy with the outcome, but realistic enough to accept it. "The pain," he said. "Will I feel it?"

This is a grey area, but I have no doubts about it myself. "I'm afraid so, yes," I said. I didn't add, it's your fault, for coming back. You don't score points off someone facing what he was about to go through. "You'll still be alive, so yes, you'll feel it."

"And after," he said. "Will I be dead?"

I hate having to tell them. "No," I said. "You can't die. You just won't be able to control your body any more. You'll still be there, but you won't be able to do anything."

I felt the wave of sheer terror, and it made me feel sick. To be honest with you, it's the worst thing I can think of—lying in the dark ground, unable to move, for ever. But there you go. It's not like you decide to be a revenant, and experienced professionals advise you as to the potential downside. It just happens to you. It's sheer bad luck. Also, of course, it runs in families, and thanks to a thousand years of inbreeding, the Mesoge is just one big family. I really, really hope it won't ever happen to me, but there's absolutely nothing I can do to prevent it.

"You could let me go," he said. "I'll move far away, somewhere there's no people. I won't hurt anybody ever again. I promise."

"I'm sorry," I said. "If my Order found out, it'd mean the noose."

"They'd never know."

Indeed; how could they? I would go back to the City, swear blind the pig was too strong for me, they'd send someone else, by which time Gnatho's dad would be long gone (though they always come back, they can't help it). And I'd lose my reputation as an infallible field agent, which would be marvellous. Everybody wins. And I sometimes can't help thinking about my granddad, still awake in the wet earth; or what it would feel like, if it's ever me.

"I'm sorry," I said. "It's my job."

We cut him up with a forester's cross-cut saw. If you aren't familiar with them, they're the big two-handed jobs. Two men sit on either side of the work, one pushes and one pulls. I took my turn, out of some perverse sense of duty, but I never was any good at keeping the rhythm.

I LEFT MY home village with mixed feelings. As I said before, once you've been through the experience you've been dreading for so long, you feel a certain euphoria; I've been back now, I won't ever have to do it again, there's a giant weight off my shoulders. But, as I walked up that horribly tiring long hill, I caught myself thinking: no matter how hard I try, this is where I started from, this is part of who I am. I think the revenant issue is what set me thinking that way. You see, revenancy is so very much a Mesoge thing. You get them in other places, but wherever it's been possible to trace ancestries, the revenant always has Mesoge blood in him, if you go back far enough. God help us, we're special. Alone of all races and nations, we're the only human beings on earth who can achieve a sort of immortality, albeit a singularly nasty one, born of spite and leading to endless pain. Reliable statistics are impossible, of course, but we figure it's something like one in five thousand. It could be me, one day; or Gnatho, or Quintillus, or Scaevola, learned doctors and professors of the pure, unblemished wisdom, raging in the dark, smashing railings and crushing windpipes. And, as I said, they always, we always come back, sooner or later. They, we can't help it.

Gnatho, a far more upbeat man than I'll ever be, used to have this idea of finding out *how* we did it, why it was just us, with a view to conquering death and making all men immortal. I believe he did quite a bit of preliminary research, until the funding ran out and he got a teaching post and started getting more involved in Order politics, which takes up a lot of a man's time and energy. He's probably still got his notes somewhere. Like me, he never throws anything away, and his office is a pigsty.

THE RIVER HAD calmed down by the time I got to Machaera, and the military had been out and rigged up a pontoon bridge; nice to see them doing something useful for a change. A relatively short walk and I'd be able to catch a boat and float my way home in relative comfort.

One thing I'd been looking forward to, a small fringe benefit of an otherwise tiresome mission. The road passes through Idens; a small and unremarkable town, but it happened to be the home of an old friend and correspondent of mine, who I hadn't seen for years: Genseric the alchemist.

He was in fifth year when I was a freshman, but for some reason we got on well together. About the time I graduated, he left the Studium to take up a minor Priorship in Estoleit; after that he drifted from post to post, came into some family money and more or less retired to a life of independent research and scholarship in his old home town. He inherited a rather fine manor house with a deer park and a lake. From time to time he wrote to me asking for a copy of some text, or could I check a reference for him; alchemy's not my thing, but it's never mattered much. Probably it helped that we were into different disciplines; no need to compete, no risk of one stealing the other's work. Genseric wasn't exactly respectable—he'd left the Studium, after all, and there were all sorts of rumours about him, involving women and unlawful offspring—but he was too good a scholar to ignore, and there was never any ill will on his side. From his letters I got the impression that he was proud to have been one of us but glad to be out of the glue-pot, as he called it, and in the real world. Ah, well. It takes all sorts.

As with the things you dread that turn out to be not so bad after all, so with the things you really look forward to, which turn out to disappoint. I'd been picturing in my mind the moment of meeting; broad grins on our faces, maybe a manly embrace, and we'd immediately start talking to each other at exactly the same point where we'd broken off the conversation when he left to catch his boat twenty years ago. It wasn't like that, of course. There was a moment of embarrassed silence, as both of us thought, hasn't he changed, and not in a good way (with the inevitable reflection; if he's got all middle-aged, have I too?); then an exaggerated broadening of the smile, followed by a stumbling greeting. Think of indentures, or those coins-cut-in-two that lovers give each other on parting. Leave it too long and the sundered halves don't quite fit together any more.

But never mind. After half an hour, we were able to talk to each other, albeit somewhat formally and with excessive pains to avoid any possible cause of disagreement. We had the advantage of both being scholars; we could talk shop, so we did, and it was more or less all right after that.

One thing I hadn't been prepared for was the luxury. Boyhood in the Mesoge, adult life at the Studium, field trips spent in village inns and the guest houses of other Orders; I'm just not used to linen sheets, cushions, napkins, glass drinking-vessels, rugs, wall-hangings, beeswax candles, white bread, porcelain tea-bowls, chairs with backs and arms, servants—particularly not the servants. There was a man who stood there all through dinner, just watching us eat. I think his job was to hover with a brass basin of hot water so we could wash our fingers between courses. I kept wanting to involve him in the conversation, so he wouldn't feel left out. I have no idea if he was capable of speech. The food was far too rich and spicy for my taste, and there was far too much of it, but I kept eating because I didn't want to give offence, and the more I ate, the more it kept coming, until eventually the penny dropped. As far as I could tell, this wasn't Genseric putting on a show. He lived like that all the damn time, thought nothing of it. I didn't say anything, naturally, but I was shocked.

Over dinner I told him about my recent adventures, and then he showed me his laboratory, of which I could tell he was very proud. I know the basics of alchemy, but Genseric's research is cutting-edge, and he soon lost me in technical details. The ultimate objective was the same, of course: the search for the reagent or catalyst that can change the fundamental nature of one thing into another. I don't believe this is actually possible, but I did my best to sound impressed and interested. He had shelves of pots and jars, two broad oak benches covered with glassware, a small furnace that resembled my father's forge in the way a prince's baby son resembles a sixteen-stone wrestler. He couldn't resist showing me a few tricks, including one which filled the room with purple smoke and made me cough till I could barely see. After that, I pleaded weariness after my long journey, and I was shown to this vast bedroom, with enough furniture in it to clutter up the whole of a large City house. The bed was the size of a small barn, with genuine tapestry hangings (the marriage of Wit and Wisdom, in the Mezentine style). I was just about to undress when some woman barged in with a basin of hot water. I don't think I want to be rich. I'd never get any peace.

I WOKE UP suddenly, feeling like a bull was standing on my chest. I could hardly breathe. It was dark, so I tried *lux in tenebris*. It didn't work.

Oh, I thought.

My fault, for not putting up wards before I closed my eyes. There's an old military proverb: the worst thing a general can ever say is, I never expected that. But here, in the house of my dear old friend—My fault.

I could just about speak. "Who's there?" I said.

"I'd like you to forgive me." Genseric's voice. "I don't expect you will, but I thought I'd ask, just in case. You always were a fair-minded man."

The illusion of pressure, I realised, wasn't so much the presence of some external force as an absence. For the first time in my life, it wasn't there—it, the talent, the power, the ability. *Virtus exercitus*, a nasty fifth-level Form, it suppresses the talent, puts it to sleep. For the first time, I realised what it felt like being normal. *Virtus* isn't used much because it hurts—not the victim, but the person using it. There are other Forms that have roughly the same effect. He'd chosen *virtus* deliberately, to show how sorry he was.

"This is about the chair of Logic," I said.

"I'm afraid so. You see, you're not my only friend at the Studium."

I needed to play for time. "The bear-trap."

"That was me, yes. Two cousins of my head gardener. It's a shame you had to kill them, but I understand. I have the contacts, you see, being an outsider."

You have to concentrate like mad to keep *virtus* going. It drains you. "You must like Gnatho very much."

"Actually, it's just simple intellectual greed." He sighed. "I needed access to a formula, but it's restricted. My friend has the necessary clearance. He got me the formula, but it came at a price. Normally I'd have worked round it, tried to figure it out from first principles, but that would take years, and I haven't got that long. Even with the formula I'll need at least ten years to complete my work, and you just don't know how long you've got, do you?" Then he laughed. "Sorry," he said. "Tactless of me, in the circumstances. Look, will you forgive me? It's not malice, you know. You're a scholar, you understand. The work must come first, mustn't it? And you know how important this could be, I just told you about it."

I hadn't been listening when he told me. It went straight over my head, like geese flying south for the winter. "You're saying you had no choice."

"I tried to get it through proper channels," he said. "But they refused. They said I couldn't have it because I wasn't a proper member of the Studium any more. But that's not right, is it? I may not live there any more, but I'm still one of us. Just because you go away, it doesn't change anything, does it?"

"You could have come back." They always do, sooner or later.

"Maybe. No, I couldn't. I'm ashamed to say, I like it too much here. It's comfortable. There's no stupid rules or politics, nobody to sneer at me or stab me in the back because they want my chair. I don't want to go back. I'm through with all that."

"The boy at Riens," I said. "Did you—?"

"Yes, that was me. I found him and notified the authorities. I had to get you to come out this way."

"You did more than that." I was guessing, but I had nothing to lose. "You found a natural, and you filled his head with spite and hate. I imagine you appeared to him in dreams. *Fulgens origo?*"

"Naturally. I knew they'd send you. You're the best at that sort of thing. If it had just been an unregistered natural, they could have sent anyone. To make sure it was you I had to turn him nasty. I'm sorry. I've caused a lot of trouble for a lot of people."

"But it's worth it, in the long run."

"Yes."

Pain, you see, is the distraction. As long as I could hurt him, in the conscience, where it really stings, I was still in the game. "It's not, you know. Your theory is invalid. There's a flaw. I spotted it when you were telling me about it. It's so obvious, even I can see it."

I didn't need Forms to tell me what he was thinking. "You're lying."

"Don't insult me," I said. "Not on a point of scholarship. I wouldn't do that."

Silence. Then he said, "No, you wouldn't. All right, then, what is it? Come on, you've got to tell me."

"Why? You're going to kill me."

"Not necessarily. Come on, for God's sake. What did you see?"

And at that precise moment, my fingertips connected with what they'd been blindly groping for; the bottle of aqua fortis I'd slipped into the pocket of my gown, earlier, when we were both blinded by the purple smoke. I flipped out the cork with my thumbnail, then thrust the bottle in what I devoutly hoped was the right direction.

Aqua fortis has no pity, it's incapable of it. They use it to etch steel. People who know about these things say it's the worst pain a man can suffer.

I'd meant it for Gnatho, of course; purely in self-defence, if he ambushed me and tried to hex me. Pain would be my only weapon in that case. I had no way of getting hold of the stuff at the Studium, where they're so damn fussy about restricted stores, but I knew my good friend Genseric would have some, and would be slapdash about security.

The pain hit him; he let go of *virtus*; I came back to life. The first thing I did was *lux in tenebris*, so I could see exactly what I'd done to him. It wasn't pretty. I saw the skin bubble on his face, pull apart to reveal the bone underneath, I watched the bone dissolve. You have to believe me when I say that I tried to save him, *mundus vergens*, but I just couldn't concentrate with that horrible sight in front of my eyes. Pain paralyses, and you can't think straight. It ate deep into his brain, I told him I forgave him, and then he died.

For the record: I think, no, I'm sure there was a flaw in his theory. It was a false precept, right at the beginning. He was a nice man and a good friend, mostly, but a poor scholar.

As soon as I got back to the Studium, I went to see Father Sulpicius. I told him everything that had happened, including Genseric's confession.

He looked at me. "Gnatho," he said.

I shook my head. "No," I said. "You."

He frowned. "Don't be silly," he said.

"It was you."

"Ridiculous. Look, I can prove it. I don't have clearance for restricted alchemical data. But Gnatho does."

I nodded. "That's right, he does. So you asked him to get the data for you. He was happy to oblige. After all, he's your friend."

"You're wrong."

"Genseric had to find the natural. You're hopeless at that sort of thing, Gnatho's very good at it. If you'd been able to, you'd have done it yourself. But you had to leave it to Genseric."

He took a deep breath. "You're wrong," he said. "But assuming you were right, what would you intend to do about it?"

I looked at him. "Absolutely nothing," I said. "No, I tell a lie. I'd withdraw my name for the chair. Just as you're going to do."

"And let Gnatho—"

Oh, the scorn in those words. He'd have hit me if he'd been able. He's always looked down on Gnatho and me, just because we're from the Mesoge.

"He's a fine scholar," I said. "Besides, I never wanted the stupid job anyway."

THE BOY FROM Riens duly turned up and was assigned to a house. He's settled in remarkably well, far better than I did. Mind you, I didn't have an influential senior member of Faculty looking out for me, like he has. He could go far, given encouragement. I hope he does, for the honour of the Old Country.

I'm glad I didn't get the chair. If I had, I wouldn't have had the time for a new line of research, which I have high hopes for. It concerns the use of strong acids for disposing of the mortal remains of revenants. Fire doesn't work, we know, because fire leaves ashes; but if you eat the substance away so there's absolutely nothing left—Well, we'll see.

He'll be back, my father used to say, like a pig to its muck. I gather he said it the day I left home. Well. We'll see about that, too.

The Thought That Counts

"...Wanted me to marry Logo the tanner. He's got a beautiful home, she said, and you soon get used to the smell. Mother, I said, I don't *want* to get used to the smell. I don't ever want to be the sort of person who doesn't notice the stink of sheep's brains. She just looked at me. That's when I knew I had to leave."

I decided I didn't like her mother. Priorities all wrong. Egging her on to marry defenceless tanners when she should have been teaching her not to talk to strange men in stagecoaches. Which raises the incidental question: am I a strange man? I guess, on balance, yes. Decide for yourself.

"So I went home, slung all the stuff I needed into a bag, and here I am, on my way to the big city. My name's Sinneva, by the way."

"Constantius," I lied. "Pleased to meet you."

Another lie, but she smiled. "Are you a priest?"

Two reasons why a man might be wearing ecclesiastical vestments in a coach on the way to Sempa Sacona. One, he's a priest. Or two, the lock on the vestment cupboard at the Blue Light monastery is so pathetic a blind man could open it with a sprig of damp heather. "Yes," I said. "Sort of."

"Are you going to Sempa?"

"Stopping off," I said. "On my way somewhere else."

"It'll be my first time in the big city," she said, "I'm looking forward to it so much. All my life I've wanted to go there. Is it really as wonderful as they say it is?"

"Depends on what you like," I said.

"I'm going to be an artist," she said. "Somewhere like Sempa, you can make a living as an artist. I do portraits. I'm not terribly good at it."

That would explain the bag full of little pottery jars nestling between her feet. I'd sort of looked at them sideways, when she first got on the coach. Worth money to somebody, but rather a specialised market. Besides, I'm through with all that sort of thing.

"Funny you should say that," I said. "I'm interested in paint."

"Painting."

"Paint," I said. "I dabble a bit in alchemy, and I reckon it might be possible to make synthetic blue. Instead of having to grind up ruinously expensive lapis lazulae in a pestle and mortar." She didn't say anything, so I went on; "There's definitely a demand for it. A genuine deep royal blue at a fraction of the price. A man could make a nice little bit of money that way."

"I've never used blue."

"Too expensive?"

She nodded. "That's why I started doing portraits, you don't have to have any sky."

"There you are, then," I said. "When I've perfected my synthetic blue, you can do portraits of people outdoors. You could corner the market."

She looked at me. Strange man, she was thinking. At this point, her mother's awful warning should have leapt into her mind and shut her up like a vault, but no such luck. "People like to be painted in their houses," she said, "surrounded by all their possessions. It's the convention. That way, you can see how rich and powerful they are, and what exquisite taste they have. Outdoors, they could be anybody."

"Ah," I said gravely. "I see."

"Not that I want to be constrained by conventions," she said, looking out of the window. "I want to paint what I really see. Does that make any sense to you?"

"As opposed to what other people see? Or what's actually there?"

I was starting to get on her nerves. Well; it had taken long enough. "What *I* see," she said. "Which may not be the same thing as what you see."

"Because I'm not particularly observant, and may have missed something."

"Because I see the world as it could be."

"Ah." I pulled a couple of walnuts out of my pocket and cracked them together in my palm. I have very strong hands. "In that case, maybe you should consider religious subjects. The spiritual dimension."

"Women aren't allowed to paint icons. You should know that, being a priest."

"Sort of a priest. And I didn't specify icons."

"If it's a portrait and religious, it's an icon. So I can't do those, it's illegal."

"I read somewhere," I said, quoting myself—well, I sometimes read my own books, when all else fails—"that the object of portraiture is to capture the soul of the sitter."

"That's an interesting way of putting it."

Thank you, I nearly said. "I reckon you'd have to know a lot about human nature. Do you?"

"Everybody does, don't they? Like fish know about water."

And still thirty miles to go until we reached Sempa. But you don't get to choose your travelling companions on the public coach. Next time, if there's any justice, I'll get a couple of rich tallow-chandlers who think they're good at playing cards for money.

ACTUALLY, I WAS telling the truth about blue paint. I came across the tantalising possibility a few years back, when I was making my living as a fraudulent alchemist, and I dream of the day when I can settle down and do the thing properly, in peace and quiet, not always having to jump out of windows in the middle of the night to avoid creditors, disillusioned investors or the Watch. It's a sad thing to say about yourself, but I'm not the most honest, upright citizen you're ever likely to meet—which Sinneva the would-be portrait painter should've noticed at first glance if she was in any way suited to her chosen profession. I won't tell you my name, because you'd recognise it immediately; and either you'd say, My God, it's *him*, or, Oh God, it's *him*, depending on the context in which you've heard of me. But you will have heard of me. Everybody has.

THE REASON I'D come to Sempa was to see the Polyglypton brothers. If you know Sempa, you'll know their stall; it's under the lime tree in the old Bird Market, and you've probably spent far more money there than you care to admit. They have their warehouse and scriptorium (rather a grand name for a long, draughty shed) out back of the stockyards, where the air is always heavy with the stench of blood. You get used to it, so they tell me, but I can't imagine how. As I walked there across the Victory Bridge I amused myself with the thought of Sinneva the aspiring artist; suppose she managed to land the job of her dreams, doing the illustrations for the extra-special-deluxe editions (no, not those ones, they don't let women work on those). She'd turn up for her first day at work, and the smell would hit her like a hammer—a tannery is roses and lavender compared to what the breeze wafts down from the slaughteryards—and someone would grin at her and say, it's all right, you get used to it. I stopped at the outer gate and splashed a fat blob of attar of violets onto the lapels of my coat. It helped, but not very much.

Sivia and Massimo Polyglypton receive visitors in their office, which is more a sort of hayloft over the warehouse; you climb up a ladder, for crying out loud. I'd never met them before. Sivia is tall and thin, Massimo looks like the sort of man they hire to throw undesirables out of brothels. They told me to sit down and offered me ginger tea.

"We liked it," Massimo said, "very much. But—"

"But?"

They looked at each other. "I mean, it's very clever," Sivia said. "Well argued and very well written. It's just—"

"What?"

Awkward pause. "I think," Massimo said, "the word we're looking for is, derivative."

Derivative. Good word, not one you'd expect to hear in a loft downwind of an abbatoir. "Derivative of what?"

Massimo pursed his lips. "You've read the *Metaphysics,* obviously."

The book he mentioned wasn't called that. I've changed the name. Why shouldn't I? I wrote the damn thing. "Well, yes."

"And *Reflections on the Abyss* and *Sunrise.*"

"Oh yes."

"That's what we're getting at," Sivia said apologetically. "Frankly, if He'd written this, we'd be all over it like ants on a dead donkey. Coming from you, though—"

"Someone nobody's ever heard of," Massimo added.

"It's a question of *authority,*" Sivia said. "Credibility. To get away with the sort of thing you're saying here, you need to be—well, someone like Him. You think: all this is very startling and original, but if He says it, obviously there must be something to it. No disrespect, but you don't carry that weight. You haven't earned that right to be listened to. It's not the same."

Annoying, because the Him they were talking about was, of course, me: universally respected as one of the greatest philosophers of my generation, but wanted in all the major jurisdictions for every crime in the book short of actual murder. "I see your point," I said. "So, you don't want it."

They looked at each other. "We didn't say that."

"Ah. So what are you saying?"

They said it, and then we haggled a bit, and the upshot was, I settled for thirty angels instead of the seventy-five we'd originally agreed. Annoying, because I needed the money, but thirty angels was twenty-nine angels ninety kreuzer more than I had in the whole world at that time (that's putting the value of one set of stolen ecclesiastical vestments at ten kreuzer) so I was, of course, pleased to accept. Not, I reflected as I scrambled back down that ridiculous ladder, that I had much to complain about. Writing the wretched thing had kept me mildly amused through the long, dreary months I'd spent holed up in a half-derelict sawmill in the hill country north of Copis City, waiting for the fuss to die down after one of my more misguided indiscretions; the parchment and ink had cost me maybe two kreuzer, so nobody could pretend I wasn't well ahead of the game. Even so. To be fined forty-five angels for not being me when I really am me is a bit hard. And since being me is such a wretched, troublesome business at the best of times, it sort of rubs salt into the wound, if you see what I mean.

BUT NEVER MIND. There I was in Sempa Secona, a place where there were no outstanding warrants for my arrest and no extradition treaties with either the Eastern or Western empire, with thirty gold angels in my pocket. For once in my life, I could walk down the street without looking for places to run to if I heard someone yell my name. That set me thinking; artificial blue paint. Well, a man has to have a dream. The fact that mine is so utterly prosaic is neither here nor there.

I hired a shed not far from the bone mills, for thirty kreuzer a week. One unfortunate by-product of alchemy is the smell (you get used to it, but...); my neighbours at the bone works would be in no position to get stroppy about a few noxious fumes, except on the grounds of breach of monopoly. I managed to buy the glassware ridiculously cheap from someone's gullible widow, with enough left over to keep me in stale bread and no-longer-perfectly-fresh salt fish for several months, by which time I was absolutely certain I'd have cracked the last few remaining problems. A life of honest endeavour; well, why not? Everyone ought to try it at least once before he dies.

I won't bore you with the results of my researches. Suffice it to say, I proved beyond a shadow of a doubt that making artificial blue paint using certain specific ingredients and a certain method, which I won't specify here, is absolutely impossible. As a scientist, I was pleased to have added to the sum of human knowledge. As a moral philosopher, I was able to conclude that living a pure and upright life doesn't of itself lead to happiness or even peace of mind. The day before the money finally ran out, I did come across a tantalising possibility which, one of these days, I really must get around to following up, since it might just be the missing ingredient that would make all the difference; but of course I was in no position to do anything about it at that time, so I sold the glassware for even less than I paid for it, and wandered into the centre of town, trying to figure out what to do with the rest of my life.

A number of rather unpleasant things have happened to me over the years in and around law courts, so I really can't tell you what possessed me to drift across Haymarket and down the Snailshell into the Forum of Justice. But I did, and sure enough, it being a week-day in Middle Term, the court was sitting. I guess the novelty of the situation—a court of law in session, and me not being the unwilling centre of attention—piqued my interest; anyhow, I sat down on an empty seat in the back row, next to couple of fat rich women eating apples, to watch the show. It was a fairly slow day, interlocutories in disputes over shipping manifests and bills of lading, and I was just about to leave when the magistrate banged his little hammer and four grim-looking gaolers led out, in chains, my annoying young friend from the coach: yes, her, the wannabe portrait artist.

Four gaolers; in my prime I only ever merited three, and I was pretty hot stuff, though I do say so myself. True, she was taller than average and no willow-wand, but four kettlehats, for crying out loud. What could she possibly have done? And, come to that, was it something so awful that the authorities might be interested in her known associates? I kept perfectly still and started paying attention.

It was a simple short-form arraignment, rather than the actual trial. The prisoner Sinneva was accused of treason, attempted murder and grievous bodily harm. She had entered a plea of Not Guilty, and the prosecutor was asking the magistrates to commit her for immediate trial.

The magistrate asked if the prisoner had a lawyer. The prosecutor didn't actually grin; none of the accredited public defenders were prepared to represent her. And therefore—

Remind me, when I've got five minutes, to have my legs cut off. They've come in useful over the years—running away, they're really good at that—but on this occasion they got me into serious trouble, and I can't risk them doing it again. They stood me up—I swear, I had nothing to do with it—and there I was, on my feet and listening in horror to my own voice, asking permission to approach the bench.

The magistrate looked at me, took in the ecclesiastical gown, and nodded. So, feeling incredibly bewildered and stupid, I waddled slowly down the main aisle until I was practically nose to nose with the magistrate, a small, red-faced man with thick, wavy white hair. I cleared my throat. "This woman," I said, "has no representation."

"That's right."

"On a capital charge."

He peered at me. "I don't know you," he said.

"I'm from out of town. Is this how you do things in Sempa?"

He sniggered. "No, not in the normal course of things. Are you a lawyer?"

"Yes," I said—truthfully, as it happens; at least, I have four degrees in civil and criminal law, though most of my experience has been on the other side of the fence, so to speak. “Constantius of Beloisa. I have diplomas from the Studium, the Imperial Institute in Mavortis, the Purple Chamber in Scona—”

“Mphm.” He was impressed. “You don’t want to get mixed up in this, trust me.”

I gave him a polite scowl. “I make formal application to defend this prisoner.”

“Don’t you want to know what she’s done?”

“Is alleged to have done. No, not particularly.”

A gentle sigh. “All right, Mister Out-of-Town, and on your own head be it. Duly accredited.” He looked at me. “Give your address to the clerk, you’ll be notified.”

I hesitated. “The fee,” I said.

“Ah.” He looked at me again, taking in the frayed cuffs of the robe, the sweatstains inside the collar. “Standard rates, one angel twenty a day. Want me to cross you off the docket?”

“It’s not about the money,” I said.

“Of course not. Dismissed.”

NATURALLY, I ASKED around. Information wasn’t hard to come by, it was the scandal of the month. This weird female had blown into town, nobody knew where she’d come from, and set up a stall in the market; your portrait painted, one angel. No takers, naturally; so she started doing portraits for free, and actually they were really rather good; you know how crazy fashions suddenly spring up out of nowhere, suddenly she was the new big thing. You had to have your portrait painted by the little peasant girl, or you were nobody. Soon she had a waiting list long as your arm. Naturally, the best people wanted to jump the queue, started offering her good money. She refused; one angel, no more, no less. Now an angel is a tidy sum in some contexts; you could buy the farm I was raised on for three angels, including the live and dead stock, the standing crops and my kid brother.

In Sempa, you could live elegantly on one angel for a month, or any-bloody-fashion for a year. But the high-class portrait artists, who were suddenly finding themselves with time on their hands ever since Sinneva showed up, routinely charged fifty angels for a cameo, three times that for a regular canvas. This curious reluctance on her part to make out like a bandit had been duly noted as significant, in the light of what followed.

The first case was Governor Scaevola, just back from three years in one of the northern provinces. There's a saying in revenue circles: the good shepherd shears his sheep, he doesn't skin them. Scaevola flayed his sheep alive, and was therefore nicely set up for life when he came home. He was one of her first high-class commissions; and three days after his portrait was delivered—he was delighted with it, by all accounts, and so was his wife—they found him in his study late one night, sitting in the dark, not moving, staring at the wall.

After that, Senator Juppito, the Friend of the Poor; the Lady Iphianassa, patroness of the arts and Sempra's leading society hostess; Genseric the banker, Mediobarzanes the playwright, Massimo Polyglypton the bookseller (oh dear, I thought, never mind), and half a dozen others—all the same, struck dumb and motionless, empty-eyed and living-dead, soon after the little peasant girl had painted their portraits.

Sempa is a rational, secular sort of place. They repealed their witchcraft laws about seventy years ago, and people only go to Temple to be seen in their new clothes. Be that as it may. There's only so much weird stuff people can take before they start jumping to conclusions. Poor little Sinneva was arrested and slung in jail, while they tried to figure out what to charge her with.

First, they had a go with administering a noxious substance, arguing that she must have poisoned their drinks. But she always painted her subjects at their houses—she didn't seem to have a studio or anything like that, and she lived in a nasty little garret over a fishmonger's, where presumably she was in the process of getting used to the smell when they took her away.

They examined her paints and solvents, but all they found was the usual stuff that every artist uses; besides, if it was something she was using that had done the damage, surely she'd have poisoned herself in the process. The debate moved up to the Senate, where Juppito's mob, the Optimates, tried to ram through a new witchcraft law, applicable retrospectively. But the Popular Tendency talked it out of time, simply because it was the Optimates who'd proposed it, and so nothing could be achieved that way. Meanwhile, the families of the victims were howling for something to be done, and the attorney general was up for re-election. He resolved to charge her with treason, attempted murder and GBH, on the strict understanding that anyone who defended her would never work in Sempa again, and trusted in Justice to run its ineluctable course.

As accredited counsel for the defence, I had the right to make certain investigations. So there I was, with two kettlehats making me nervous, climbing the stairs to Sinneva's rotten little lodgings and wishing, really wishing, I'd never got involved.

The kettlehats were along to make sure I didn't touch anything or interfere with evidence. They had a really quiet morning. It was a tiny little room under the eaves; bed, chair, second-best dress hanging behind the door, plain plank table with half a loaf of stale bread and a pitcher of badly gone-off milk, and a copy of *Human, All Too Human* open at the bit about the immortality of the soul (which nearly made me smile; I remember writing it, with a murderous hangover and the rain dripping through the roof), and that was it, nothing else whatsoever. Evidentially neutral: no hit list or subversive literature, correspondence with fellow conspirators, jars of poisonous chemicals; no evidence that the stupid girl had been spending her new-found wealth on anything nice, which is what any normal, innocent person in her circumstances would surely do. No money, come to that. Her known commissions must have netted her at least forty angels; the rent on the garret was three kreuzer a week—she was robbed, if you ask me—and bread and milk, ten kreuzers a month, tops. Where was the rest of it? In a bank? Or was she sending it home to her poor impoverished parents? Unlikely, I thought, given the terms on which she'd parted from them, but I wasn't going to tell the prosecutors that. Even so; I felt like I'd been dealt a piss-poor hand with which to defend the stupid child. Served me right, I suppose, for sticking my nose in.

It was what wasn't there, of course, that interested me. For that, I could see no alternative but to visit my client, something I really didn't want to do. Also, if the hypothesis I'd formed about five seconds after hearing the facts in the case was true, there was nothing she could tell me that would be any use to me in getting her neck out of the noose. No, the hell with that. I was going to have to wing it, make it up as I went along. So happens I'm good at that—very good indeed, which is how come I'm still alive and writing this. Actually, I told myself, I'd had so little experience with positive favourable evidence (because I've always been guilty as charged), probably this wouldn't be a good time to start trying to learn how to use it. Stick with what you know, is my motto.

I TOOK A deep breath. "Your honour," I said, "I've listened with great interest to the facts in this case, so ably presented by my learned friend. Imagine my surprise, therefore, when he stopped where he did. I was expecting so much more. I was waiting patiently for evidence—hard evidence—connecting my client in any way to the tragic events we've just had described to us. Surely, I said to myself, there must be something. But apparently not. My learned friend has just told you that he rests his case. Being a fair-minded man, I would like to give him one last chance to add to what he's just said. No? Sure? Very well. But please, don't say I didn't give you every opportunity.

"Let's consider the facts. My client, an innocent country girl, comes to this great city to fulfil her lifelong ambition. She is a naturally talented, I may say quite brilliant, artist; entirely self-taught, I might add, she's never had the benefit of any formal education—unless my learned friend would care to tell us about it, the schools she's studied at, the masters she's been apprenticed to. No? Are you absolutely sure? Very well. No formal education whatsoever. She grew up milking cows, churning butter, sweeping floors, and dreaming of a better life.

"After only a week or so in this uniquely cultured and appreciative city, her talents were recognised. Despite her disadvantages of class and gender, this plucky and determined young woman starts to make a name for herself. Clients besiege her door with commissions. My learned friend has tried to make her refusal to gouge her clientele for large sums of money into something sinister. I see it as evidence of the purity and integrity of her artistic nature. This poor innocent child, living only for her art, wasn't interested in money, or status, or any of the glittering distractions of the world. All she wanted to do was the one thing she'd always wanted to do. What, I ask you, could be more natural?

"And so she painted portraits, at least forty of them that we know about. And of these forty clients, a dozen have—most unfortunately—fallen ill. I feel sure that nobody has more sympathy for them and their families than my client. But what the prosecutor has signally failed to do—because it's impossible—is establish any faint thread of a connection between these misfortunes and my client. Unless and until he can do so, I honestly believe there's no case to answer.

"Consider the so-called victims. All of them are in late middle age or older. All of them—how can I put it delicately?—have enjoyed to the full the delights of the table and the wine cellar. All of them are men and women of great spirit and passion, with a tendency—a perfectly natural, indeed laudable tendency—to express themselves fully, to take matters to heart, to get excited and passionate about things they feel strongly about.

"In my hand, I have a copy of the standard work on diseases of the heart and brain, written by no less an authority than—" Well, modesty forbids. "In the passage in front of me, the distinguished author describes the causes, symptoms and effects of a stroke. I won't take up the court's time by reading it aloud, the matter is common knowledge. A stroke is an affliction of the brain, caused by an interruption of the blood supply. It leaves the victim paralysed, unable to speak or move. It is caused by excessive eating and drinking, combined with violent exertion of the body, mind or spirit. Consider what you know about the alleged victims in this case, all prominent members of society. They all ate and drank to excess, they all were involved in public life, in politics, government or the arts; they lived passionate, stressful lives. They were, in short, prime candidates for the terrible illness I've just told you about. That this scourge should have come upon them, cutting them down in their prime, depriving us of their talents and their usefulness to our society, is to be deeply regretted. For once, the word tragedy would scarcely be an overstatement. But to ascribe these disasters to my poor young client—on what grounds? I have heard none today, and once again, I call on my learned friend to enlighten me. Nothing more? Nothing at all? Well, then.

"Just in case you still aren't convinced, let me point out a few more relevant details. This comprehensive and universally respected book in my hand contains no mention of any poison, drug or artificial stimulant capable of deliberately causing a stroke. Leave aside the fact that no chemical apparatus was found in my client's possession; ask yourself this. Could this simple country girl have discovered or invented such a poison, on her own, uneducated, brought up among the cows and goats? I think not. As it happens, I know a little about alchemy. It would take a genius a lifetime of research to come up with such a complex toxin. My client is nineteen years old. Draw what conclusions you wish.

"As I've already mentioned—as the prosecutor himself admits—my client has painted at least forty portraits, almost certainly more. Twelve from forty leaves twenty-eight. If my learned friend's allegations have any substance at all, there should be at least twenty-eight other helpless victims in this city, sitting in chairs, staring helplessly at the wall. If so, we haven't heard about them, and they are therefore not admissible in evidence. In fact—I've made my own enquiries, since the prosecutor seems to have neglected to do so—all twenty-eight are in perfect health. Among them, please note, are senators, members of the aristocracy, leading figures in commerce, business and the arts. My learned friend made a perfunctory effort to connect the status of the alleged victims to their dreadful fate, as though my client had sought to strike down the flowers of our society. The fact is, all her customers came to her clamouring to be painted; she didn't choose them, they chose her. Twenty-eight rich, famous, influential, talented men and women were painted by my client and have suffered no ill-effects. Once again, the facts don't simply speak for themselves, they shout at the tops of their voices.

"Recently, the wise and distinguished Senate of this city ruled unambiguously that there is no such thing as witchcraft or sorcery. But witchcraft and sorcery, I put it to you, are precisely what my client is accused of; tacitly, because to say so openly would be to invite ridicule. Therefore, for consistency's sake, if for no other reason, I call on this rational, truth-loving court to dismiss these ridiculous charges and let my poor, long-suffering client go free. I rest my case."

God, I'm good, though I do say so myself. The magistrate shook his head, blinked a couple of times like a dazzled rabbit, and said the magic words, case dismissed. You could have heard a pin drop.

I left, quickly.

HAVING DONE WHAT I'd set out to do, I rushed off down West Street, through Absolution Square, short cut through the Shambles, up Pin Street. I'd known from the outset that the wretched girl had to have a studio somewhere, or where else did she keep her paints, her easel and her money? I'm good at ferreting out stuff like that, so it hadn't taken me long to discover where it was. I hadn't gone there, because—well, like I said, nothing helpful to my case to be learned there. Now that I'd won, however, I had no such compunction. I wanted, make that needed, to know.

Stupid cheap lock, I don't know why anyone bothers with them. Inside, I saw a chair, facing a shuttered window; two shelves lined with little pottery jars; two easels, on which rested two portraits of the same man, almost but not quite identical; a cheap earthenware plate; a pestle and a mortar; a tinderbox.

Oh God, I said to myself. Here we go again.

I THOUGHT: THIS time, I'm not involved. Nothing to do with me. True, I stuck my oar in, but even so, none of this is my responsibility, my job, my fault. I can just go a long way away and be free and clear. Above all, I owe no duty of care to the truth—me, of all people, perish the thought.

More to the point: if I interfere, what can I possibly achieve? Nothing.

I walked down to the Flawless Diamonds, where the stagecoaches leave for Mezentia and all points west. I had just enough money for the fare. The stage pulled in. Mezentia is lovely in the spring, when the cherry trees are in blossom. All aboard, they called out. It left without me.

Truth is, despite ferocious competition for the job, I am and always have been my own worst enemy.

LET ME TAKE you back a few years; I won't specify how many, because I don't suppose you'll believe me. I was a student at what was at that time the finest university in the world, though it's gone downhill a lot since then. I wasn't the smartest kid in my year, not by a mile. I did my best to make up for my shortcomings through diligence and determined effort. You have faith in stuff like that, when you're young.

I don't know when I first noticed her. She wasn't a student (no women at the university in my day) but she wasn't a local's daughter. She hung around in the square and the library forecourt, sketching in inks or charcoal; she wore a big straw hat which shaded out her face, and there never seemed to be anybody chaperoning her or keeping an eye on her, which was odd enough in itself. I can't say I remember any of my fellow students making any sort of play for her whatsoever, which was stranger still. It was almost as though she was invisible and only I could see her. Now there's a thought.

I have my faults, but chivvying unattached females isn't one of them. Besides, in those days I was desperately earnest, and I knew exactly what I was going to do with my life; graduate, join a respectable Order, teach, research, write papers, win a chair, tenured professor by the time I was thirty-five. It was all I'd ever wanted.

But things weren't going all that well. I was smart, but not quite smart enough. I could feel the boundaries of my abilities, and knew that what I wanted to achieve was just the other side of the rope. I could picture myself getting stuck somewhere in the middle, like a man stranded halfway up a mountain, unable to go farther up or turn back. I could see myself scraping a doctorate; then what? Fine if I had private means; I could spend the rest of my life floating around the university, taking twenty years to write a modest paper on some peripheral issue, adding a footnote to the great book of human knowledge. But I had a living to earn, and for that I would have to be good *enough,* not just quite good, and there were so many better men than me. So, in due course, the scholarship money would run out and then it'd be back on the coach, back home to the farm, or else a job as a clerk or a tutor to some rich man's loathsome son. It's a dreadful thing to be twenty-one and realise that you have no future after all.

Which may go some way to explain what I was doing on the bridge (not the famous one, the other one, about half a mile downstream), one foot on the parapet, staring down into the water. Whether I was thinking about jumping, or using the thought of jumping to force things back into perspective, I really don't know; anyway, I was too preoccupied to notice someone walk up behind me until I eventually took a step back and trod on someone's toe.

"It's quite all right," she said, grinning at me. "I'm just glad you decided not to."

I looked at her. "That obvious?"

She had the enormous hat pushed back on her head, so I could see her face. Not beautiful exactly, but striking. "You'd be amazed how many boys your age come and stand on this bridge, thinking what you were just thinking. Hardly any of them actually do it. What's the matter? Debts, exams or girl trouble?"

You know how easy, how fatally easy, it is to tell things to a stranger you wouldn't dream of telling anyone else. Also, unlike anyone I'd ever met in my entire life, she sounded interested. So I told her, the whole story, everything. She didn't interrupt, and when I finally ran dry, she smiled at me. "Is that all?" she said.

I pulled a face. "I know," I said, "it does all sound a bit stupid when you say it out loud. And of course there's millions of people in the world far worse off than me—"

"I didn't mean that," she said. "You have a real problem, a very serious one. I'd be suicidal too, in your shoes, if there wasn't a perfectly simple way out."

She'd lost me. "What?"

And then she'd linked her arm through mine, and we were walking side by side, down the broad steps to the towpath. "You come here a lot," she said.

"My lodgings are just down there," I said, pointing vaguely. Poor Town. Well, she'd probably guessed that from the deplorable state of my shoes, if she was even remotely observant. "I take the short cut through Long Meadow to the Schools." I stopped. She grinned.

"I've noticed you," she said. Curious way of putting it, I thought at the time. "You've got an interesting face."

Of course, she was an artist. "Interesting," I said. "That's not actually a compliment."

"It's a statement of fact."

"Ah," I said. "One of those."

When I left my room that morning, I hadn't decided what I was going to do with the day: either a short drop and a splash, or go to the library and read Psammetichus on essential transfiguration. What I hadn't anticipated, one little bit, was a stroll along the riverbank with a girl in a straw hat. "What perfectly simple way out?" I asked her.

"I'll tell you, if you're good," she said. "Later," she added. "Right, here we are. Now stand under that willow-tree over there and look thoughtful."

Out with the slate, the sheet of paper and the stick of charcoal. Ah, I thought.

"You're going to be Parthenius," she explained, "and the river's the Aurus, and somewhere over there out back of the charcoal sheds is presumably violet-crowned Olessa, though of course that won't be in the picture. No, keep still, you're no use to me if you keep moving about."

Keeping still isn't one of my strong points, as various law officers have discovered the hard way over the years. But I tried my best, and eventually she said, "All right, you can breathe now."

My left foot had gone to sleep. "Can I see?"

She turned the slate to her chest. "It's only a sketch."

"What on earth is the point of a picture if people can't look at it?"

"It's not terribly good," she said. "Now turn that way, and look melancholy. No, that's not melancholy, it's heartburn. That's better. Hold it exactly like that."

We ended up spending the rest of the day together, and the next day, and the day after that, but still she hadn't told me the perfectly simple way out. I tried reminding her tactfully, but she changed the subject. Besides, I'd sort of figured it out for myself by that point. The simple way out of my frustration and despair was to fall in love with a wonderful girl, which apparently I'd now done. Silly me for not having thought of it earlier.

"What would you like," she asked me, at some point, "most of all in the whole world?"

We were watching the swans on the river. Apparently they mate for life. "That's a good question," I said.

"Pretend I'm a goddess or a witch and I can grant wishes. Money?"

"Money isn't everything," I said. "No, what I'd like is to be clever."

She pulled her poor-baby face. "You are clever."

"I wish I was the cleverest, wisest man who ever lived."

"Mphm." She nodded. "You're sure you wouldn't rather have the money instead?"

"The wisest man who ever lived would never be short of money," I said. "But a lot of rich men are idiots."

"All right, then," she said, and threw a crust for the ducks.

"Can I ask you a personal question?"

She frowned at me. At that precise moment I was being Teudra dividing the upper and lower heavens, which is a confoundedly tricky pose to hold for more than ten minutes. "What?"

"It's a very personal question. You may not want to—"

"Keep still. What?"

I couldn't draw a deep breath without wobbling, so I just made myself say it. "Where does all the money come from?"

"Oh, that." What had she been expecting me to ask? "I've got a rich uncle in Permia. I'm all he's got, and he wants me to enjoy myself. What do you want to do most in the whole world, he said, and I told him, this. So here I am."

"Ah."

"Talking of which." She appeared to be peering past my ear, looking intently at something that wasn't there. Painters do that. "What do you want, most in the whole world?"

"Right now? To itch my nose."

"Tough. What else?"

"To stay here like this, with you, for ever." Well, it seemed the thing to say at the time.

"I see," she said clinically. "So as far as you're concerned, this is the perfect moment."

"Apart from the itch. Look, do you think I could just—?"

"No." She took a step back and looked at me, or at the god creating the firmament, through me his temporary proxy. "I once read that if there's a moment so perfect that it couldn't possibly be improved upon, it could never ever be any better than this in any respect whatsoever, then Time would stop still, everything would be trapped motionless like a fly in amber, and that would be the end of the world." She squidged the end of her brush between her fingers. "That's what made me want to paint."

"To bring about the end of the world? A bit antisocial."

"The perfect moment, captured for ever," she said. "A painter can do that. No more old age, no more death. In a painting, you can be for ever young, beautiful and happy. There would be no later, no decay, no decline, no consequences."

"I don't see a future in it."

She clicked her tongue to acknowledge the wordplay. "All right, relax, before you fall over. Take the weight off your feet, I'll make us some tea."

She made the most wonderful tea, full of obscure, delicate scents and flavours. I sat on a chair, massaging the calves of my legs. She perched in the window-seat, with the light behind her.

"And that's not all I can do," she went on. "I can make people what they want to be. I can make old women look young, poor men look rich, sad people look happy."

"Stupid into clever?"

"Piece of cake." She turned the easel slightly. "See for yourself."

She really was very good. Teudra, not only as the Creator, but in his aspect of bringer of wisdom, perfectly represented, a whole college of theologians couldn't have found fault with it. And yet it still looked just like me; weird.

"Anyway," she said, turning the easel back. "How are you getting on with Induiomarus?"

"Going through it like a knife through butter," I said cheerfully, and it was true. Ever since I'd met her, the standard of my work had improved dramatically; all my tutors had commented on it. Hence Induiomarus; we weren't supposed to get on to him until third year, but there I was, soaring through the notoriously obscure and elliptical *Shadow Analects* like an eagle. "Actually, I don't see what all the fuss is about."

"Is that right?"

I nodded. "He says everything in this really cryptic, mystical, up-himself way, but actually what he's saying is pretty obvious. And I think I've caught him out in a false premise."

"Ooh," she squeaked. She was alarmingly well-read. "Which bit?"

"Book seven, the clockmaker analogy. I don't think it works, because if the clock is found lying on the seashore—"

"How's it supposed to have got there? Yes, I wondered about that, too."

I gazed at her. Talk about your perfect moment. "I'm so glad I met you," I said.

She was excited. She'd got a commission to paint a portrait of the Professor of Alchemical Theory. I was stunned. As far as I was concerned, the man was a god. "How on earth did you manage that?" I asked.

"Through my uncle," she said. "He knows all sorts of people."

THE THOUGHT THAT COUNTS

"ALL THE BEST portrait artists do it," she explained. "Move, you're in my light."

She was sitting in her studio, with her back to the window. Before her were two easels, on which stood two almost but not quite exactly identical paintings of an old man with a bald head and whiskers. "You paint two pictures," she said, "precisely the same. But one of them will be perfect."

"The one on the left," I said.

"You see? It works. It's an old trick. I read about it in a book somewhere."

"Twice the work," I said.

"That's why the best artists get paid ridiculous sums of money."

I studied the painting for a moment. "I've never met him," I said. "But I feel like I've known him all my life."

"Euphronius says the job of the artist is to capture the soul of the sitter."

I smiled. "Well, you've done that all right," I said.

"I'll make us some tea."

THREE DAYS LATER, the professor suffered a devastating stroke. He was found in his study, surrounded by his books, mouth lolling open, eyes fixed on the wall. He never moved again.

"Just as well I got cash on delivery," she said. "For the painting."

That struck me as a bit insensitive. "At least his family will be able to remember him as he was," I said. "Thanks to you."

"When he was perfect." She smiled at me. "That's the point," she said.

She went to bed early. I sat up finishing an essay. As I sprinkled it with sand to blot the ink, I remembered that she'd left the lamp lit in her studio. That would never do; smoke from a guttering wick, with all that drying paint. I went in to put it out.

There was a distinct smell of burning; not just the lamp. I noticed a little brass stove, the sort elegant people use for making omelettes at the table. There was something in it, smouldering. I investigated. The charred ends of splintered limewood board, the stuff she used to paint on. I looked round and saw the two easels. On one of them was a finished portrait. I recognised it at once: my tutor, Lacasta, the most amazing likeness. The other easel was empty.

Three days later, Lacasta had a stroke.

(I ONLY FOUND out how she did it years later, in a digression in a book about witchcraft among the Permian nomads. To steal someone's soul, apparently, you paint a picture of the victim, burn it and grind the ashes up fine, into dust, which you seal in a small pottery jar. When you want to consume the soul, thereby adding its wisdom, force of character and other virtues to your own, you mix the dust with certain herbs and make an infusion; a bit like tea. All complete nonsense, of course, said the book I read, there's no such thing as sympathetic magic, and probably just as well.)

I WAS OUT of there like a shot, as you can imagine. I ran up the street in my nightshirt, hammered on the door of a good-natured friend, borrowed a change of clothes and two angels, and caught the night mail to Solitene. From there I wrote to my supervisor explaining that for urgent personal reasons I could no longer continue my studies at the university; however, I would be eternally grateful if he would write me a letter of recommendation to the faculty at the Golden Hook. The letter arrived by return, and it must have said something nice because the Dean of the Hook gave me a place on the spot. A year later I graduated top of the class, was awarded a fellowship, assistant professor eighteen months later, all the rest of it. Some bad stuff happened after that, but it's not relevant to this story.

She was in her studio when I got there. She looked different. She reminded me a lot of someone I used to know. "Hello, you," she said.

"You again," I said.

She smiled at me. "I've missed you," she said.

Behind her, the shelves were empty. On the floor, about a dozen little pottery jars, with their lids off. She had a little brass stove, on which sat a silver kettle. She'd just made a pot of tea.

"It wasn't a coincidence, was it?" I said. "You being on that coach."

"It was awfully sweet of you to defend me," she said. "Did you know it was me?"

"No."

"Fibber. Of course, they couldn't have hurt me. Nobody can hurt me, physically. Would you like some tea?"

"No, thank you."

"I made it for you."

I stood there rooted to the spot. "How did you find me?"

"Very easily," she said. "I only started looking recently. You see, I was very much in love with you back then, and when you ran away I was heartbroken, but then I met someone else and we were very happy together for a very long time. And then he ran away too, and I remembered you. Sure you don't want some? It's good for you."

I felt sick. "You ruined my life," I said.

"Rubbish." She had a nice smile. "I asked you what you wanted, and you said, to be the wisest, cleverest man who ever lived. And you said money wasn't everything, and you'd always be able to get some from somewhere. I gave you what you wanted, because I loved you."

I managed not to scream at her. "You made me a thief," I said. "A con man. Some days I wake up and even I can't remember which name I'm using."

"You can be anyone you want to be. That's another special gift."

I looked at her. "I don't think I've got anything more to say to you," I told her. "I don't ever want to see you again. Don't come near me. Just leave me alone."

She shrugged. "You don't mean that."

"Trust me."

A little sigh. "You won't know it's me, the next time, and the time after that."

"Yes," I said. "I will."

"You didn't in Blemya."

Oh God, I thought. But she'd died, surely. "Keep away from me," I said. "Do you understand?"

She didn't say a word, just carried on smiling like an angel. I reached the door.

"Cobalt," she said. "It's what you've been missing. For the blue paint. I love you," she said.

"See you in Hell," I said, and slammed the door.

KNOWING HER, I probably will. One day I'll be sitting there, burning quietly, up to my manacled ankles in molten sulphur, and there she'll be, smiling, holding a bunch of keys and a teabowl.

Draw your own conclusions about the doctrine of the perfect moment. For me, the world ended a long time ago.

Mightier Than the Sword

Translator's note

Although entirely lacking in literary merit, *Concerning The Monasteries* is a remarkable document in many ways. First and foremost, it is the oldest extant sustained piece of writing in the Robur language, so archaic in places as to be practically unintelligible, but fascinating nonetheless. Second, it was written at the time of the events it records (although see Baines, *AJA* 2007, 42-7 on the serious internal inconsistencies regarding chronology). Finally, it is a personal document rather than a formal chronicle, a unique example from such an early period. It therefore gives us an unparalleled opportunity to hear an authentic voice from the deep past—even if it is not, as Hansen (*CJ* 1987, 33ff) so ingeniously argues, the work of its apparent narrator, nevertheless it is *a* voice, from a world inexpressibly distant and remote from our own.

I have followed Pedretti's Cambridge text throughout, except where specifically noted. I am grateful to Dr John Lancaster of the University of Wisconsin–Madison for his interpretation of the notoriously corrupt final section, and his inspired suggestion of 'linen-press' for *ezaucho*.

The usual metaphor is a lighthouse: the monastery as a guttering flame devotedly tended, its small pale gleam resolutely defining the way through the tumultuous storm of barbarism until the Sun rises again—in the east, it goes without saying. They don't have metaphors for the monasteries in the north and the west, where such institutions aren't beautiful images but everyday facts—hard landlords, unreliable business partners, bad neighbours, slow payers. At one time, the cenobitic orders owned two-thirds of the land north of Dens Montis and west of Shevec; they owned the mills and the bridges, the mines, the tanneries, the lumber yards, the forges, the weirs, the moorings, the fishponds, the locks, the ferries, every damn thing you really need. True, they built most of them, nobody else had the money; because the monasteries had taken it all, in rents and tithes. At any rate, that's what they say in the north. I know, because I've been there.

And what do they spend it on, they say in the north, for crying out loud? The usual answer is perfectly true. They spend it on tending the guttering flame: on fifty thousand literate hands, endlessly writing, copying out; on paints and painters, music, sculpture, architecture; on wisdom, beauty, philosophy, mathematics, the glory of the Invincible Sun; on knowledge and truth. A small price to pay—don't you agree?—for everything valuable ever achieved by the human race, which only the Orders are left to preserve and maintain in the face of the approaching darkness.

And on other things, too. An insatiable need for vellum and parchment means vast herds and flocks; it also means veal and lamb until you're sick of the sight of it, and you long for a simple bowl of lentil soup.

And other things, too. The monasteries are where the emperors dump their awkward relatives, out of harm's way, out of sight, out of mind. That or slaughter them; a small price to pay for clemency.

MIGHTIER THAN THE SWORD

EVER SINCE THE emperor was taken ill, the palace staff have been reporting for their orders to the empress; five years now, and of course it's only temporary, until His Majesty is up and about again. In practice, this means that when you present yourself at the Lion Gate and bang timidly on the wicket, the kettlehats who peer at you through the little grill are Household Guard, not Companions. I'm all in favour of that. I can see the rationale behind the Companions being recruited exclusively from illiterate barbarians—loyal and answerable to the emperor alone, therefore outside and above politics, and so forth—but I still think it's nice to have gatekeepers who can understand Imperial. *I have an appointment with the deputy Chief Commissioner for Transpontine Waterways* isn't the easiest thing to get across in sign language.

On this occasion, of course, it wasn't a problem. If the empress sends for you, the herald gives you a dear little ivory spindle, inlaid with emeralds and garnets, which the gatekeeper takes away from you, and then you don't get any bother from anyone.

Some chamberlain in a blue gown with gold tassels relieved me of my helmet and sword and led me up about a million flights of stairs and down a million miles of corridor—I'd just got back from four months on campaign and reckoned I was in fairly good shape, but before long I was sweating and breathing heavily, while this little pot-bellied bald chap trotted happily along in front of me, sandals clip-clopping on the flagstones—until we arrived at the great bronze doors of the Purple, and suddenly I knew where I was. I hung back while he announced me—all the ranks and titles and general scrambled-egg, which I shall never ever learn to associate with my own name—and then I was in: alone in the Presence.

It's all a pose, of course, because everything to do with empire and authority always is, but I have to say, she does it rather well. When the empress grants you an audience, she receives you in the ludicrously named Small Inner Chamber—it's the size of Permia, but without the rivers—and you stand on one edge of this desert of polished marble while she sits on the other, by the twelve-foot-high window, so as to get the light for her needlework.

It is, let me tell you, the most politicised haberdashery in human history. The pose is: Empress of the Civilised World she may be, but at heart she's still just an ordinary hard-working housewife, diligent, thrifty, hard-headed, waste-not-want-not. So there she sits, in a gold and ivory chair, wearing a plain dress of worsted she spun herself, turning a shirt-collar or sides-to-middling a bedsheet. She's not just miming, it's genuine work, all the grooms in the imperial stable wear socks hand-knitted by Her Majesty; and as she sits there, counting her rows and biting off ends of thread, she's doing the budgets of six provinces in her head and calculating a new exchange rate for the hyperpyron against the Vesani thaler.

She didn't look up. "Oh," she said, "it's you."

I mumbled something about reporting as ordered. "Speak up," she snapped. I repeated it, shouting. She thinks it's appropriate for old women to be a bit deaf, though in fact she's got ears like a bat.

"I've been meaning to talk to you," she said, in a voice that made my heart sink. "I saw the reports from Supply. Eighteen thousand pairs of boots in the last six months, and nine hundred tons of chain-mail links. You're seventeen per cent overspent on this year's budget. Do I look like I'm made of money?"

"No, Aunt."

"Your father was just the same." She squinted, trying to thread a needle. "I told him till I was blue in the face, it's no earthly use you winning all those glorious victories if you haven't got the money to pay for garrisons and fortifications. You go out there, you kill a hundred thousand savages, then you've got to turn right round and come straight back again. And what does that achieve? Nothing at all, it just makes the savages hate us. Of course he never listened to me, and now look." She thrust the needle and cotton at me. I'm good at threading needles, I've had the practice. "You let the contractors rob you blind, that's what it is," she said. "You just don't think, that's your trouble. You imagine all I have to do is wave a magic wand and suddenly there'll be money. Well, it's not like that."

I cleared my throat. "Actually, Aunt, I don't do procurement of supplies, properly speaking I'm not even a soldier any more, I'm an imperial legate, which means—"

"Oh be quiet." She took back the needle and made a few stitches, neat and infinitesimally small. "I know what you are, I got you the job, remember, when your uncle wanted to send you to Scaurene. And now I've got another job for you, and let's hope you don't make a complete mess of it."

You could resent a remark like that. Let the record show that over the previous six months I'd negotiated a two-year truce with the Sashan, disposed of the crown prince of Ersevan and hammered out a horrendously fraught alliance with the Blemyans against the threat of the southern nomads. I don't expect any of that to be remembered, because it's all wars that never happened, mighty battles that never got fought, darkest hours of the empire that never had to be faced. But what the hell.

"Of course, Aunt," I said. "What can I do for you?"

"It's those wretched pirates." She made the dreaded Land and Sea Raiders sound like a butcher who persisted in overcharging for sausages. "They've attacked Cort Rosch and Cort Seul, burnt to the ground, nothing left. Disgraceful. It's got to stop. So I'm sending you. Pass me the small scissors."

I was too stunned to speak. I passed her the scissors.

ACTUALLY, SHE'S NOT a bad old stick. The strategic mention of Scaurene won't have escaped you; she'll never let me forget that, of course. If you're aware of my dreadful past history, you'll know that I was caught in bed with the Princess Royal, rest her soul, and His Majesty Ultor II, Emperor of the Known

World and brother of the Invincible Sun, was absolutely livid. He wanted to chop my bits off and send me off to a desert monastery, to reflect (his words) on what constitutes acceptable behaviour. But she saved me. She nagged him every morning over breakfast and went on and on at him during his afternoon nap, and just as he was about to fall asleep after a gruelling day's work she'd bring the subject up yet again; *he's only young, give the boy a chance to redeem himself, I owe it to the memory of my poor dear brother, who died saving your life,* over and over again. It's thanks to her I'm writing this, and not frisking my pillow every night for scorpions.

HAVING RECEIVED MY commission, I did what any responsible man does when he's posted to the frontier. I set my affairs in order.

The regular crowd doesn't dig in at the Diligence and Mercy until well after midnight, but I knew she'd be there. I pulled my hood round my face—silly thing to do, it marks you out to everyone in the place as Man Trying Not To Be Noticed, and everybody stares—and asked one of the serving women if she'd seen her.

She looked at me. "Haven't you heard?"

Most of the rest of the night I spent dashing frantically from one miserably depressing charitable institution to another; eventually, just when I'd given up hope, I found her in the Reform House. The bastards, they'd dumped her in the drunk-tank, with nothing but a filthy old blanket and a vague assurance that someone would be along at some point. She lifted her head and frowned at me. "Hello, you," she said.

I nearly broke up. Standing joke between us; her least favourite regular (he's about seven foot tall, absolutely no idea of the concept of personal space) always addresses her thus, and it makes her want to scream. "Hello," I said. "Taking the night off?"

The knife had gone in about an inch to the left of her navel. No way of telling how much blood she'd lost. "I think I might have annoyed him," she said. "How bad is it?"

She knows I know about these things, being a soldier. "It's not wonderful," I told her.

"The bleeding's stopped," she said. Her lips trembled as she spoke. "And it was a clean knife. Mine. You know, the silver-handled one."

She keeps it under her pillow. "We'll have you out of here," I promised her. "I'll get the sawbones from the Twenty-Third, you'll be fine. Just stay there, I'll be right back."

She said something as I ran out, but I didn't catch it. I sprinted up Cartgate, managed to find a chair—amazing luck—at the Chantry steps; the barracks, I told them, and showed them a five-thaler. They ran all the way, bless them.

By the time I'd rounded up the doctor (he was asleep in bed; had to give him a direct order) and the chairmen had run us all the way back to the Reform House—I wasn't expecting to find her alive. I remember praying under my breath all the way, my life for hers, as though I genuinely believed there was someone up there to pray to. I don't know. Maybe there is.

He's a miserable old bugger, that doctor, but once he sees his patient, nothing else matters. I'd dragged the chairmen in with me to be porters, and they carried her out like she was made of icing-sugar. "She can't go back to the barracks," the doctor told me. "It's against regulations."

I hadn't thought of that; and the doctor's a terror for the rules. You see, I don't actually have a house, or a home of any sort; I just camp out in various palaces. Stupid, really. And that was the first time I realised it.

I don't have a home but I do have money. "The Caecilia house on West Hill," I told the chairmen. "Know it?"

Stupid question; it's one of the principal landmarks north of the river. They found it just fine; weren't very happy when I told them to kick the door down, but another five-thaler changed all that. "You can't just barge in like that," the doctor said. I glared at him. The house is for sale, I pointed out. I've decided to buy it. First thing in the morning, I'll send someone round to the agents with a draft. Meanwhile, do your fucking job.

I stayed an hour or so, then I couldn't bear it any more; left him to it, told the chairmen (they'd hung around waiting without being asked; amazing how, when the world turns against you, there's so often some too-lowly-to-matter strangers who'll stick by you right to the end) to take me over to the Knights. I woke them up by kicking the door. The man who answered the door was about to call the watch when I told them I was there to buy the Caecilia house.

"It's three in the morning," the man said. "Can't it wait?"

"What's the asking price?"

He screwed his fingers into his eyes and ground the sleep out of them. "Six million," he said.

"Got some paper?"

I wrote out a draft, on the Golden Cross temple, and handed it to him. He stared at it, saw the name; his demeanour changed somewhat. Please come in, he said, sit down, make yourself comfortable. Would you care for some tea and honey cakes?

Thanks, I said, but I'm in a hurry. He blinked. The keys, he started to say. I told him, that's fine, I don't need any keys.

Funny, isn't it, how there are things—really big, huge, important things that shape and dominate your life—that you don't even know about until something like that happens. I hadn't realised that I had no home. I hadn't realised I loved her, more than anyone or anything in the world.

"It's all right, lads," I told the chairmen, "no need to run."

—Because I was in no hurry to get back to the Caecilia house (now my property, my home). It's better to travel hopefully than to arrive and be told something you don't want to hear. It seemed like it took no time at all to get back to West Hill. Just enough time to prepare my mind, as I've done on a number of occasions in my life. Well, you know what they say. Hope for the best, expect the worst.

So when the doctor scowled at me and said, "She'll be fine," I really wasn't expecting it. That unimaginable surge of relief, that lifts you off your feet.

"Really?" I said.

He gave me a look I deserved. "No, I'm just pretending. Yes, she'll be fine, eventually. Come on, you've seen wounds like that often enough." He frowned, suddenly remembering. "Didn't I stitch you up for something like that?" he said. "The Chloris campaign, about three years ago."

"So you did." I'd forgotten. Shows what sheer terror does to the brain. My guts had been hanging out over my belt. He stuffed them back in, like making sausages. So that was why I'd chosen him for this occasion. Honestly, I'd clean forgotten.

"Well, then. Complete rest and change the dressing twice a day. Can I go home now?"

At that moment I'd have given him anything—the empire, my head, whatever. "Thank you," I said.

"I ought to report this," he muttered at me. "I'm an army surgeon, not your personal bloody physician."

Actually, I think he did. I vaguely remember some talk of a court-martial, which my aunt had to put a stop to. But that was later, and who gives a damn? "Can I see her?"

He shrugged. "I imagine so," he said, "she's ill, not invisible. She's asleep now, don't wake her up. Your chair can take me home."

I gave each of the chairmen a gold tremiss. They stared at me and said how grateful they were. Them grateful to me, for stupid money. Ridiculous.

She woke up just after dawn. By that point, I'd located and hired a fancy society doctor and six nurses; amazing what you can get hold of in the wee small hours if you can pay for it. Something else I'd never realised before: in a desperate emergency, just how useful money can be. I see now why people prize it so highly.

"I've got to go away," I told her, "on business. Won't be too long. When I get back, I think we should get married."

She looked at me. "Are you completely mad?" she said.

"I don't think so. Why?"

Her face was as pale as milk. Inhuman, cross between an angel and a corpse. "One, they won't let you. Two, you don't want to marry me. Three, what on earth makes you think I want to marry you? Or anybody, come to that. Four—"

"You should rest now," I said. "We'll talk about it when I get home."

"Like hell we will. And don't walk away when I'm talking to you."

NOW, THEN. CONCERNING the Land and Sea Raiders. I guess we were so very scared of them because we had no idea who they were, where they came from, how many of them there were, what (beyond anything not nailed to the floor) they wanted. They showed up about a hundred and thirty years ago, during the reign of that old fire-eater Vindex II. Our first experience of them was seventy long, high-castled warships suddenly appearing off Vica Bay. The governor, a civilised man with several well-received volumes of theological essays to his name, sent a message to their leader inviting him to lunch. He came, and brought some friends; it was sixty years before Vica was rebuilt, by which time the harbour had silted up and all the channels had to be dredged out.

Next they manifested themselves as a long column of ox-carts trundling over the Horns. They looked like refugees; skeletal cows and horses, sad women and threadbare children plodding along behind the wagons. The prefect of Garania went out to meet them with relief supplies, food, tents, blankets. They cut his head off and stuck it on their standard, before marching on Beal Epoir and burning it to the ground. That, of course, was about the time when General Maxen was at the height of his incredible career.

He caught up with them a week later and hit them so hard that we were sure we'd never hear about them again.

Maxen lasted rather longer than most of our great generals; about six years, and then his head got nailed to the lintel of Traitors' Gate, along with all the others, so that when the Raiders came back there was nobody to deal with them. The next caravan of carts looked like it was here to stay and settle; they hung around for a couple of years, camped beside the ashes of Fort Narisso, dug wells and built sheep-pens and then suddenly disappeared, and where they went to nobody knows to this day. Then fifty years went by and not a sight or sound of them, and people started saying they must've been a myth or an allegory for the plague. And then the ships started appearing right across the northern seaboard, and we gradually came to realise that the ships and the carts were the same people.

Vindex's grandson Florian fought three great battles against them; one by land and two by sea. All three were victories, on a grand scale. After Mount Cortis, they counted the enemy dead by cutting a finger off each corpse, then weighing the filled baskets; half a ton of fingers. It was the Straits of Pallene that led to the growth of the shrimp fishery there, enough food to cause a population explosion. It made no difference at all. Two years later they were back: a hundred ships, a thousand carts. We got the impression that these people, whoever they were, grew like coppice-wood, the more you prune them, the stronger they grow back. Their resources of manpower and matériel were infinite, apparently; ours, of course, were not. It was Ultor's predecessor, Valens IV, who came up with the idea of defence-in-depth; forget trying to turn them back at the border, let them come and do their worst, then hit them on the way back. It didn't work then and it doesn't now, but you're not supposed to say that.

We knew nothing about them then, except that if you hit them just right they died, and we're not much the wiser now. Just goes to show; you can be really intimate with people (what's more intimate than killing?) and still not really know them.

I WAS ISSUED with a commission and letters patent, eight hundred Cassite archers, one million hyperpyra (in cash, bless her), a pair of fur-lined boots and a letter of introduction to Her Serenity the Abbess of Cort Doce, who happened to be my aunt's oldest and dearest friend. Thus furnished, I set out to save civilisation as we know it.

It was a bleachingly hot morning, and we were all in our Northern gear, because we wouldn't be needing southern-theatre kit where we were going, so we weren't issued with any. I don't know if you've had much to do with Cassites. They're splendid people, smart, resourceful, imaginative, artistic, individualistic, compassionate, articulate, absolutely useless soldiers. The one thing that marks them out from all the other nations of the empire is their exceptional sensitivity to temperature. In the hall of the prefect's lodgings at Corcina there's a remarkable gadget that tells you what the weather's going to be—there's a dial and a needle that points to wet, windy, sunny, hot, rain, thunderstorm and so forth. Obsolete and redundant, if there's a Cassite in town. You can tell precisely what the weather's going to be just by listening to two Cassites whining. Eight hundred Cassites boiling to death in thick woollen cloaks make a distinctive noise you can hear half a mile away, like roosting rooks or an approaching swarm of locusts.

I was fumbling with my helmet-straps when the message came: looking good, no sign of infection, she's sitting up and demanding to be let out, called you all sorts of rude names. I thanked the messenger and gave him a thaler.

NOBODY WALKS NORTH if they can help it. The roads are appalling. They used to be wonderful, of course, but that was a long time ago, since when generations of canny farmers have prised up the stone paving-slabs to build pigsties and dug out the rubble and scree for hardstanding. Harmodius II tried to do something about it. He decreed the death penalty for anyone found in possession of roadmaking materials. Since enforcing the law would've meant hanging every head of household from here to the coast, nobody was ever prosecuted. If you want to get anywhere, you go by boat.

Four stone-barges carried us down the Sanuse. At Boc Sanis we found wagons waiting for us, which came as a complete and very pleasant surprise. They'd been laid on by the Count of the Northern Shore, a thrice-removed cousin of mine I'd never met by the name of Trabea. He was a big man with a small head, one tiny chin and quite a few large ones, the sort of man you can't help liking and know you shouldn't trust. I'd amused myself on the boat-trip down the river by glancing through his accounts. A child could've seen what he'd been up to, so I took the view that he was confident enough about his position not to give a damn. None of my business anyway, except insofar as I needed to use him.

He filled me in on recent activity over a remarkably fine dinner at the prefecture at Boc. The pirates, he told me, had stepped up their activity over the last eighteen months. During that time they'd stormed three monasteries and seven priories. There had been no survivors. It was hard to tell what they'd stolen, since they'd been to great pains to burn everything.

"What about fittings?" I asked.

He looked at me. "What?"

"Iron fittings," I said. "Hinges, bolts, knockers, nails, all that sort of thing. Stuff that doesn't burn. Did they take them or leave them behind?"

"Oh, I see. No, they left all that."

I nodded. As I told you just now, pirates aren't a new phenomenon. Four centuries ago in the south, there was a wave of similar attacks, only they took everything; they sieved the ashes for roofing-nails. Turned out that what they were after was iron. Hyrcanus III found out where they lived and sent trading ships, iron for whatever they had a lot of and didn't want—which proved to be ebony, nutmeg, diamonds and lapis lazulae, which is why Hyrcanus is always depicted in portraits wearing a blue cloak. Why strangle a cat when you can drown it in cream?

"How about the people?" I said. "Did they kill them all, or take any?"

He shook his head. "They aren't slavers," he said. "They killed all the monks and nuns and didn't bother the villagers at all. But when we sifted the ashes we didn't find any blobs of melted gold or charred scraps of silk. They're here for the good stuff, I'm sure of it."

All information is useful, even when it confirms what you've already assumed. "There wouldn't be a letter waiting for me, would there?" I asked him.

He looked blank. "No. Should there be?"

Well, no. Civilian mail is carried on the stage, which takes for ever to cross the moors. "If something comes for me," I said, "be a pal and send it on, would you?"

He grinned. "Love-letters?"

"I doubt it. Probably the exact opposite."

THE LIFE CENOBITIC; from time to time it appeals to me, though never for very long.

March into a monastery and pick out ten monks. You'll find you have five religious zealots, two younger sons of good but impoverished families, two political exiles and a retired soldier. Now go next door and round up ten nuns. You'll have six younger daughters of good but impoverished families, three discarded wives and one religious zealot.

I'm talking, of course, about the ones who pray and copy out books. If you extend your sample to the brothers and sisters pastoral—the ones who shear the sheep, make the bread, dig the gardens and wash the bedlinen—you're likely to encounter a fairly homogeneous bunch, farmers and their wives and daughters who've defaulted on monastery mortgages or been sold up for unpaid tithes. It's a viable system, harsh but compassionate; the monastery taketh away and the monastery giveth. Everybody's poor, nobody starves, there's a doctor on hand when they're sick (show me a farmer who can afford a doctor and I'll show you a smuggler or a horse thief) and there's so much veal and lamb that everybody gets some, some of the time. Yes, it's a hard way to treat people. But life is hard, or so they tell me.

My first call was at Cort Malestan. To get there, you go up the coast road until you reach the Red River. It's called that because—well, it's red. The hills above Malestan are full of iron; that's why the monks went there, to dig it out and sell it. The Red River is really quite extraordinary. The water is poisonous. There are no fish, no plants grow in it, a few misguided willows trail their roots in it but they don't live long. It's crystal clear and blood red, if that makes any sense. Local legends say that Hell is under the mountain, and that the monks are there to keep the gates shut with their prayers, but even they can't do anything about the blood of the damned, which seeps out into every rill and stream. The monks have been there for centuries, and they've long since scarfed up all the loose ore lying on the surface or accessible from open pits. These days they drive long galleries into the mountainside. To break up the rock they stuff chambers full of charcoal and burn it till the rock glows red. Then someone opens a sluice on a diverted stream and water floods in; the rock shatters into chunks the size of your fist or your head, which the miners scrabble out into carts. You can see plumes of smoke and steam from miles away, gushing up through dozens of vents. It's not an attractive landscape. But the iron mine is an example of practical alchemy, they turn stone into gold through the application of sweat, and the wealth it produces pays for five hundred copying monks. The Malestan library houses something like eight thousand books, and they send copies of them all over the empire.

In charge of all this is my Aunt Thelegund. I say aunt; actually, she's one of my mother's father's nine half-sisters. I chose Malestan as my first call because of her. Before her appointment, she lived at Court—that is, before she took rather more interest in politics than was good for her, a classic weakness in our family—and I remembered her from my boyhood as a short, round, jolly old lady who didn't treat me as a child even though I was one. When she got sent to Malestan I wrote her a few letters. It was many years before I found out why she never wrote back—because conducting a secret correspondence with an exiled malignant would've landed me in no end of trouble; try explaining that to a nine-year-old. I was looking forward to seeing her again. So very, very few of my relatives are non-toxic, it'd be a shame to lose contact with one I could actually bear to be in the same room with.

I'd never actually been to a Northern monastery before, so I was expecting something along the lines of what we have back home. I was, therefore, mildly stunned to find that I was approaching, along a wide and beautifully maintained paved road, what appeared to be a castle. It was built on the only bit of flat for miles. Around it was a patchwork of cultivated land—wheat-stubbles at that time of year—out of which it rose like an artificial mountain, as though God had made a toy mountain for his kid to play with, a miniature version of the real thing looming over it on the skyline. Closer up, I admired the quality of the military architecture. Someone had read the right books, and angled the bastions to give enfilading fire from two sides on every conceivable line of approach. The double moat was a nice piece of work. I think it was based on the one at Ap' Escatoy. To fill it, they'd dug a spur off the river, so the moat was blood red and warranted poisonous to all living things; a garish but effective touch. Water for the monastery, I later found out, came from the only sweet-water well in the neighbourhood, which was safely enclosed by the walls.

If you're someone like me, you learn not to take offence easily. Offence, if you're the empress's nephew, is something that has to be taken seriously and avenged in blood; accordingly, I'm the easiest-going individual you're ever likely to meet. Spit in my face, I'll do everything I possibly can to interpret it as an accident, a joke, a quaint local custom or a back-handed expression of esteem. But being kept waiting annoys me. It's rude. I was, therefore, not in the best of moods after an hour kicking my heels in an anteroom, even though it was one of the most gorgeous and fascinating spaces I've ever been in. For a start, it was floor-to-ceiling with breathtaking frescoes. Heaven forfend that I should ever be mistaken for a man of culture, an aesthete. Those are fighting words at the court of the Emperor Ultor. But even I can recognise the composition, brushwork and light-and-shade effects of the immortal Laiso, the half-blind, cripple-handed divine madman who painted the sort of thing that normally only the gods can see. The whole of the north wall of that anteroom was one huge, heart-stopping Apotheosis. In the bottom left-hand corner cowered Men—pathetic little creatures, ploughmen, foresters, laundrywomen, milkmaids, bare-legged and crumple-faced, shielding their eyes from the radiance of the Invincible Sun as He presents Himself to the world, arms and legs spread wide, head uplifted, the heart of the glowing fire that seemed to fill the whole room—there was no stove or anything in there, but I felt warm just looking at the artwork. Appropriate décor for a room where you wait to see the Sun's temporal representative. But when the Sun's earthly brother is your uncle, with bunches of white hair like asparagus fronds growing out of his ears—well, the effect isn't quite the same.

Well, eventually she condescended to see me, and a monk in a long black robe escorted me up three flights of terrifyingly narrow, slippery-stepped spiral stairs to the Presence.

I don't know what it is about me, but everyone seems to imagine that I'm omniscient. They never tell me anything in advance. They assume I know. Just once, it'd be nice to walk into a difficult situation forearmed. A few terse words would do it—by the way, Aunt Thelegund's had a stroke—and then I'd know, and life wouldn't keep hitting me in the face like a carelessly-slammed door.

It didn't help that they'd dressed her up in all the gear. The abbess of Malestan wears the epitrachelion with lorus and zone, the dalmatic, with gold and pearl claves, open at the front with the omophorion draped across the shoulders, the great cope and the two-horned mitre; she holds the globe cruciger in her left hand and the labarum in her right. She was much smaller than I remembered, a tiny little thing, as though someone had put a baby down inside a heap of bejewelled laundry; her head lolled forward, so that the mitre looked like it was going to fall off any minute.

I don't hunt as much as I used to, I don't get the time. But any huntsman would recognise the look I saw in her eyes. You see it in the boar, when its back's been broken and it can't move, or the stag that's been run to exhaustion, or the bird that's been knocked down but isn't quite dead yet. It's the look that says, I'm through, finish me off, please.

The monk leaned close and whispered, "She can't talk but she can hear you." I nodded. If she could hear me, she could hear him, reminding her, though presumably it wasn't something she ever forgot. I cleared my throat. "Hello, Aunt," I said. She didn't move.

What the hell are you supposed to say? I never know. The monk stood behind me, respectfully hovering. I had absolutely no evidence to support it, but I got the strongest impression that he was enjoying the sight of her like that. Didn't take much imagination to figure out a hypothesis; she always was a bit hard on servants and subordinates, quite possibly he'd done something to annoy her and she'd had him for it—and then, one morning, like the wrath of God, this. You couldn't resist drawing inferences, could you? You'd take every chance you got to come up here and stand in the doorway where she could see you; possibly a few well-chosen words, when you could be sure there was nobody around to hear. In the circumstances of the contemplative life, I could imagine it was his greatest pleasure and satisfaction.

By one of those coincidences that get to you like a bit of grit in your eye, the sword I was wearing that day was the one she'd sent me for a graduation-day present. If I'd had a shred of humanity I'd have stuck it in her neck as quickly as possible, the way I'd have done without thinking for a buck or a pig. Instead I stood there grinning helplessly for a minute or so, then got out of there as fast as I could, nearly tripped on my cloak going down those horrible stairs.

WHICH BEGGED THE question; if she wasn't running Malestan, who was?

The answer, much to my surprise, turned out to be: nobody. What they'd done was split up the power, like turning a great forest oak into kindling. So long as everything in every department was done exactly the way it had always been done, they reckoned, they could get along just fine—until Her Grace was feeling better, they said, and could resume her duties; or until she died, and some other inconvenient princess was found to take her place.

WELL, I HAD a job to do there. I'm conscientious about my work, though nobody believes it.

I made a thorough inspection of the defences and found them to be admirable—the stonework sound and properly rendered, the woodwork newly tarred, all the chains and locks and hinges in order. I made a point of telling them, if half the cities in the east took as much care over maintenance, things wouldn't be in the state they were in. Then I asked about the garrison. They looked at me. What garrison?

Do you laugh, or cry, or just nod dumbly and change the subject? A magnificently appointed castle, but no defenders. Are there any weapons? I asked. They looked mildly shocked. Naturally, the copying brothers had no use for anything of the kind. What about the lay brothers? Embarrassed pause. No, we don't let them have anything like that. People of that sort, there's no knowing what they might do, especially when they've been drinking. I thanked them and rode away.

"ALL PERFECTLY TRUE," Count Trabea said. "But there's no reason to suppose the pirates know about it. All they can see is a bloody great big castle. Naturally, they assume the people in it are armed to the teeth."

It goes to show the depths I was sinking to; I'd come to regard Count Trabea as a friend, or at least someone I could talk to, someone who thought the same way and spoke my language. "That's a big assumption," I said. "Bearing in mind we know nothing at all about these pirates."

He shrugged. "They've left Malestan alone, haven't they? One thing I'm fairly sure of, they don't have any sources of local information. All they know is what they can see. And what they can see is a double moat and huge, newly-mended walls. I don't think you need worry unduly about Malestan."

"You're probably right," I said. "Oh, by the way, any letters come for me while I was away?"

He shook his head.

THE MONKS HAD given me a present, to thank me for advising them. It was about the size of a paving-stone, wrapped in a red silk cloth; no prizes for guessing, a book. Now I'm not a great reader, but a Malestan folio is a gift fit for a king. I waited till I was alone in my tent, and unwrapped it.

The cover was the sort of rich dark brown leather they make the very finest boots from; split calf, if I'm not mistaken, oak-tanned with eggs rather than brains, skived into three and worked for a whole day on the stretchers to get it beautifully supple. It was embossed with a falconry scene: four men and a fine lady in a wimple have launched a goshawk, which takes a heron in mid-air; below, the dogs peer hopefully upwards, in case they're needed to retrieve. I opened it. The title page was stunningly illuminated in gold, red, blue and green interlocking swirls and clusters, each colour bordered in black. Follow one line, then switch to another and the perspective shifts vertiginously, making your head swim; blue dives under red and over gold, branches out to enfilade and encircle green, explodes into a delta of tendrils, interlaced but never tangled, each one a clear narrative—but where each colour ends and where it begins is impossible to determine, until eventually it dawns on you that each thread isn't a line but a loop, perpetually circulating, like blood or the circuit of the stars. In the centre of all this was a miniature of the Invincible Sun *orans*, palms uplifted and facing, His head encircled in a glowing gold halo, His eyes dark, compassionate, disturbing; at the corner of the left eye, a single unexplained teardrop. I went to turn the page, but I didn't want to break the eye contact; I sat quite still, looking at Him as He looked into me, until my heart was perfectly empty. Then I closed the book and wrapped it up in its sheet.

I forget what the book was: the *Sermons of Perceptuus* or something like that.

CORT DOCE WAS next. I handed over my letter of introduction.

I could see why Abbess Svangerd and my aunt had always got on so well; also why they'd chosen to live so far apart. Two somewhat forthright women who value a friendship too much to risk damaging it by close proximity; don't have two flints rattling around in a small box if you don't want sparks.

You could tell Svangerd had been a raging beauty once, just as she wasn't one now. Old age had parched her, where it had swollen my aunt; she had bones you could've shaved with. Even now she was tall, probably an inch taller than me and I'm six foot; I couldn't judge properly because she stayed sitting all the time I was with her. She wore a plain black gown with a single thin line of silver thread at the neck and cuffs; somehow she made it look almost wickedly elegant. She nodded at me to sit down on a rickety little stool with three spindly legs. It took my weight with a few creaks of protest. Then she read the letter.

Svangerd and my aunt were from the same village, somewhere up in the north-eastern mountains—I don't know where, and nobody wants to find out. They both lost their families to the plague when they were kids; nothing left for them in the village, so they walked down the mountain to the nearest city, looking for work. Is that the right word? I guess it is; work is what you do to make a living. If your work happens to be someone else's pleasure, it's still work, isn't it? Anyway, they both turned out to be extremely good at it. Word quickly spread, and they graduated from the provinces to the big city, from a high-class cathouse in the Goosefair to their own exclusive establishment on Temple Hill. Reliable accounts of that era in their lives are hard to come by, since nearly all their regular clients either died or received a sudden, urgent vocation to the monastic life, not long after my aunt married General Ultor, as he then was. When Ultor was called to the Purple, Svangerd announced that she was quitting the business and wanted a monastery, preferably a big, rich one, a long way from Town. It was a graceful thing to do (and it's always better to volunteer than be dragged away by the hair), and they've maintained their friendship ever since.

She lifted her head and looked at me. "She says you're here about the pirates," she said, as though I was the man come to fix the weathervane. "Well? Have you got a strategy?"

"Not yet," I said. "I don't know enough about the situation."

A good answer, apparently. She nodded. "I can help you," she said. She picked up a brass tube and handed it to me. "That's everything I've been able to find out about them," she said. "It's not very much, but it'll give you somewhere to start. Kremild says you're quite bright."

Stunned isn't the word. "Does she?"

A faint smile. "Reading between the lines," she said. "But you know what she wrote, surely." I looked blank. She frowned. "You read the letter, didn't you?"

"No," I said. "It was sealed. And anyway, I don't—"

"My God." She raised both eyebrows. "Before you leave," she said, "I'll teach you how to lift a seal so that nobody will ever know." She looked at me for a moment, as though I was something brought back by travellers from a distant land. "A word of advice, if I may presume. If a superior gives you a letter to be delivered unopened, *always* open it. One time in a hundred it'll say something like *the bearer of this letter is to be put to death immediately.*" She picked up a little brass bottle, showed it to me and put it away in the handsome walrus-ivory box on the table. "Won't be needing that now," she said. "So is that all you are? A good soldier?"

"I'm not a soldier," I said. That fleeting glance of a small brass bottle—it was like when you inadvertently look straight at the sun, and when you look away, there's a big raw red patch in the middle of your vision. "I'm an imperial legate."

She grinned at me. "I knew your father," she said. "He was much younger than Kremild and me, of course. When the plague killed his parents, the neighbours took him in. A boy, you see, he'd be useful on the farm. We sent for him as soon as we could, and Kremild got him a commission in the Guards. You're a lot like him. Solid. I expect you'll be the next emperor."

I stared at her. "I sincerely hope not," I said.

She laughed. "I believe you," she said. "Now, I've given orders for your men to be quartered on the lay brethren. They won't like that, but they'll just have to put up with it. You can use the library, obviously. I have good couriers, they can be in Town in three days. Naturally, you'll use this as your headquarters."

"Actually—"

"Splendid. Don't trust Count Trabea any further than you can kick him. I don't know what enemies you may have at home, but he'll definitely be out to get you. Poison, almost certainly, but not in your food, he's smarter than that. If you get a cut or a scratch, don't have a local doctor see to it. And don't sleep in a tent with a charcoal stove. It's amazing the number of people who've asphyxiated in their sleep since Trabea took office."

I was feeling a bit dizzy. "Why would Trabea—?"

"Because he hasn't been doing his job properly, or you wouldn't be here. And it's not a difficult job, and Trabea's a very competent man, so you have to ask yourself, why has he failed?" She smiled at me. "I'm forgetting my manners," she said. "Would you like something to drink?"

"No thank you."

She laughed again; silvery, like a young girl. "It's all right," she said, "you can trust me, Kremild's told me to look after you. It's everybody else you should be terrified of. Have some wine, it'll put colour in your cheeks. We make a passable white, even this far north. It's quite dry but with a rather pleasant flowery aftertaste."

"Convenient."

"Oh, don't be silly." She gave me a stern look. "Now, then. Getting rid of these wretched pirates is important," she said, "so I'll expect you to put some effort into it. Clearly Kremild thinks so too, or she wouldn't have sent you." She studied me for a moment, the way I've seen butchers look at carcases. "I imagine you think the monasteries are just irrelevant monks and inconvenient royal women. You're wrong. Actually, they're the only justification I've ever managed to come up with for the empire. Did your aunt ever tell you how the plague came to our village? There was an outbreak among some auxiliary cavalry just arrived from Sembrotia. As soon as the symptoms were confirmed, the governor had them driven out of the city, with no food or water. They went looking for something to eat; they found us. We didn't know about plague, of course, what the symptoms are or anything like that. We took them in and tried to look after them." She shrugged. "It wasn't anybody's fault. But it takes an empire to hire nomads in Sembrotia and bring them all the way to the western mountains. That's what empires do, they bring people together, make connections." She opened the ivory box and put away a small penknife and a stick of sealing wax. "They make it possible to build great libraries, places like this, that endure. The same plague that killed my village wiped out all the monks at Cort Valence. They all died, but the books remained intact. One of the first things I did when I came to this house was send two dozen carts and have them brought here, where they're safe. In the end, you see, books are all that matter. How did Saloninus put it, the past speaking to the future? It's what survives, you see. When those carts arrived from Valence, I found all three books of Licinius' *Eternal Crown*. The third book's been lost for centuries, and it's the only record of the Seventh Dynasty. Just a few sheets of parchment, that's all, but in it is all that's left of four hundred years of people's lives. And there was Pacatian's *Mechanics*, and four completely unknown dialogues of Constans. That's what we are here, we're beachcombers finding little scraps and fragments of wrecks on the beach. It's only scraps, but it's *everything*." She shrugged. "And the pirates will just burn it all, if we let them. Do you understand what I'm saying?"

"I think so," I said awkwardly. "And yes, obviously—"

"This is no good." She stood up, a little stiffly. "I'll have to show you. Follow me."

I'll say this for her, she was quicker up and down those stairs than I was. We went all the way down, then across a courtyard and a stable yard, through a doorway and down a very long stair until we reached a big oak door. She took a lantern down off the wall. On the other side of the room there was nothing; just an empty cellar, that's all.

"Over here," she said.

She held up the lantern, and I looked into its pool of light. "It's a wall," I said.

"There's half a million people in this room. Look closely."

I looked, and I believe I could just make out some marks on the wall. "What's that?"

"Writing," she said. "Very old writing."

"Ah. What does it say?"

"I have no idea." She'd been holding the lantern at arm's length; tiring. She lowered it, and its light was confined to a square yard of floor. "That's the point. That bit of wall is all that's left of the building that was here before we came. We don't know how old it is, or who built it, or what the writing says. That's the point. Calyx's *Chronicles* give us the history of this region for the past thousand years, but he doesn't say anything about anybody living here. Whoever *they* were, they've gone for ever, as though they'd never existed. That's all that's left of them, those letters on a stone slab, and we can't read them." She raised the lantern again. "Do you understand now?"

I nodded. I don't like dark rooms underground, and I wanted to get out of there. "Yes," I said. Actually, I'd have agreed with anything for a chance to get back into the open air. Half a million people in one room; she'd made her point. From where I was standing—maybe it's a morbid dread of ending up in a cell for the rest of my life, *cell* being an ambiguous term; such a fear being understandable, given our family history—it felt more like half a million prisoners, yearning to be free.

YOU'RE SAFE IN a prison. They bring you your food, regular as clockwork. Most cells are a bit damp, but nothing compared to the sort of houses most people in the north-west have to live in. And there are armed guards on every door, so your chances of being cut down by hordes of vicious marauders are practically nil.

I remember visiting my father in one of those places. The poor fool said he was happy. He lay on his back, arms behind his head; this is the life, he said. I can lie around all day, read when I feel like it, do a bit of exercise, and I don't have to do any work—work being ruling and governing, issuing orders, deciding destinies, signing death warrants. And no visitors (he grinned at me when he said it); no visitors is absolute fucking bliss, after all those years with my family. Finally, he said, after a lifetime in the conflict business, I can get some peace.

The ambiguity of the word *cell*; keep an eye on it.

BEFORE I SET off for Sambic, she sent for me. There was a letter on her desk. One of my most useful survival skills is the ability to read upside down. The letter was from my aunt; I recognised the handwriting before Svangerd could cover it up.

"She's worried about you," she said.

"Really?" The surprise was genuine. My aunt's always given me the impression that she believes me to be immortal, invulnerable and immune to all known diseases; or else why would she keep sending me to the wars?

"She thinks you're on the verge of making a most unsuitable marriage."

Oh. "She turned me down," I said.

"I know." Svangerd looked at me, just briefly. "She's fine, by the way. Not your aunt. Whatsername. What in God's name possessed you to spend six million on a house for a prostitute who refuses to marry you?"

I grinned feebly. "It was the middle of the night."

When you're as smart as Svangerd, I guess you get out of practice hearing things you can't understand. She scowled. "What?"

"She was very badly injured and I needed to find some place where the doctor could treat her. I don't have a house of my own, and I couldn't think of anywhere. Then I remembered the

Caecilia house was for sale, which meant it'd be furnished but empty. She needed to be treated straight away. So I told them to take her there. We kicked the door down to get in."

She sighed. "Yes, all right," she said. "But *buying* the place—"

I shrugged. "It was simpler that way."

She gazed at me for an uncomfortably long time, as though she was doing complicated mental arithmetic. "Your aunt thinks you should have nothing more to do with this female," she said. "I'm not sure I agree."

I didn't know what to say, so I made a sort of grunting noise. Bad habit of mine.

"Your aunt," she went on, "maintains that if you marry a tart, it'll look like a declaration of intent to try for the throne."

I opened my mouth and closed it again.

"Think about it. Ultor married your aunt, and three years later he was crowned. By following in his footsteps, so to speak, you're making a loud, clear statement. You're saying, I don't give a damn what people think, because quite soon I'll be emperor and I'll do what I like. Your aunt believes you don't yet have enough of a power base for that sort of gesture. I have to say, I beg to differ. I think that by biding your time, keeping out of the cut and thrust of politics and doing dull but worthy things out on the frontiers, you've lined yourself up as the obvious compromise candidate, for when the Optimates and the Populists tear each other to pieces. Also, marrying this woman will be seen as you deliberately putting yourself out of the running for the throne; so, of course, people will say, here's a man who isn't hell-bent on the Purple, if we make him emperor he'll be sensible and moderate, because that's how their minds work." She nodded. "Svangerd won't listen to a word I say, naturally, we've known each other far too long. But my advice is, go ahead. It's a gamble, but what isn't?"

"I love her," I said.

For a long time she didn't say anything, just considered me, in the abstract. "Have a safe trip," she said.

MIGHTIER THAN THE SWORD

WHILE I WAS on the road from Cort Doce to Cort Sambic, the pirates attacked. They appeared out of nowhere—our lookout station on the headland at Petrobol saw nothing—and burned Cort Amic to the ground. By the time I got there, all that was left was ash.

There's a large, quite prosperous village at the foot of Amic Hill. The monks had a sawmill there, and a tannery, and a substantial clay pit, with a brickworks and a pottery. The first thing they knew about any attack was a bright light on the hilltop, sunrise in the middle of the night. Being sensible people, they ran into the woods and didn't come out until their scouts promised them it was safe: about an hour before I turned up. No help from them, then.

I set my Cassites to picking through the ashes for bones. Skulls, I told them, were the thing to look for, since a human being has only one head, and I needed to know if the entire complement was accounted for. I came up short; there were a hundred and sixteen praying monks, ninety-seven nuns and a hundred and forty-two lay brethren, but all we could find was two hundred and seventy-six skulls. I could live with the discrepancy. A good hot fire, such as you get from burning dry wood or dry paper, will consume bone completely. It all depended on where in the building they were. Of the two-hundred-seventy-six, fifty-three skulls showed evidence of crushing, cutting or piercing. We also recovered forty-seven arm and leg bones that showed blade-marks. Inconclusive, but the impression I got was of monks and nuns cut down in a general fox-in-the-henhouse panic, rather than the more systematic approach I'd been postulating—the entire congregation herded into the temple or the chapter house, say, and then burnt alive. I didn't get a chance to make the sort of detailed analysis I'd been hoping for, because it came on to rain and turned the ash to black mud. But we sifted trial areas with sieves, and came up with bone and metal fragments and charred timbers we could identify as heavy furniture. The metal was almost all iron. There was something about the ash I couldn't quite understand, but as I said, the rain came and put a stop to my speculations.

I WAS TEMPTED to head back to Cort Doce and correlate what I'd found with the report Svangerd had compiled for me, but my schedule said Cort Sambic was next, so that was where we went. Needless to say, when we got there we found them in a pretty desperate state. Sambic was even better fortified than Cort Doce, and when we got there, all the monks were on the wall, praying brethren as well as lay; as soon as we came in sight they started making the most appalling racket, banging on tin buckets and saucepan-lids, as though we were rooks on the spring wheat. They didn't want to open the gate, even when I walked up alone and bare-headed, with my warrant in my hand. They didn't believe me. I could've waylaid a genuine imperial legate, cut his throat and stolen his credentials. I think they'd have shot arrows at me if I'd hung about any longer. So we pitched our tents in the Foregate, and I sent a rider back to Doce; could Svangerd please spare a couple of irreproachably genuine monks to vouch for me? They came the next day—amazingly fast—in a beautiful low-sprung chaise drawn by four thoroughbred Hill Aelians (you wouldn't find better horses in the Hippodrome back home), and after a rather embarrassing yelling-at-the-tops-of-our-voices conference under the guard tower, we were acknowledged as authentic government agents and allowed in through the door.

The abbot of Cort Sambic was a complete surprise.

"Stachel?" I didn't mean to shout. "What're you doing here? Aren't you dead?"

He gave me a stone-face, dignified look. "It's a grey area," he said. "Come in and have a beer."

Once I'd seen Stachel, Sambic made sense. It wasn't just a fortress, it was *the perfect* fortress, as described by Vitalian in *The*

Mirror of Warlike Virtues. Very recently, within the last ten years, someone had miraculously found the money and the labour and the time and the energy to follow Vitalian's blueprint down to the letter—triple walls, staggered gateways, huge fat dirt bastions to soak up artillery bombardments, projecting galleries to frustrate scaling ladders, the whole nine yards, with some wild-eyed enthusiast directing the work with his thumb stuck between the pages of the book to mark the place. Guess who gave Stachel a copy of Vitalian, as a birthday present, because he couldn't afford to buy one for himself?

"It's a grey area," he said, snapping his fingers to summon attendants, "because when a man joins the holy monks, he's deemed to undergo death of the earthly body and rebirth as a new spiritual entity, which is why he takes a new name and has nothing more to do with his disreputable friends from the old days. No, don't sit on that one, it's pretty but it won't take your weight."

I sat on a stool. "You're dead," I repeated. "They cut off your head, for crying out loud. I went and saw it on the Northgate."

He shrugged. "You're confusing me with someone else," he said. "Mind you, I seem to remember there was this cooper's apprentice in Lonazep who looked a bit like me, or would've done if someone had smashed his face in with a hammer and pulled out all his teeth. Maybe it was his head you saw. I wouldn't be a bit surprised if he came to a bad end. Anyway," he added, with a huge grin, "how the devil are you? What's she like?"

So that was how they'd managed it. I'd wondered, at the time. His parents had been so cool and stoical; our son has been found guilty of conspiring against the emperor, we're not sorry he's been executed, we're glad the plot was detected in time. Still, a monastery. I'd have thought Stachel would've preferred the axe. Though I don't imagine they gave him the choice.

"What's who like?"

"This girl," he said. "The tart you bought a six-million-tremiss house for. What can she do that's worth that sort of money?"

When I knew him Stachel couldn't afford his own copy of Vitalian, but he had quite a few books, the sort with pictures in. He'd always been of an academic turn of mind. He used to talk about collating all the available source material, adding in the results of his own extensive researches and compiling the definitive work on the subject—sort of an equivalent to Vitalian's *Mirror*, but with full-page coloured illustrations. I wouldn't last five minutes inside his head.

"I have no idea what you're talking about," I said. "Are you really an abbot? I can't believe it."

Two tall men in elegant grey gowns brought us honey cakes and sweet fortified wine in tiny silver beakers. "Screw you, then," he said, knocking his wine back in one. I knew better than to try. "I started off as a simple novice, no name, no past or antecedents. I got this far by sheer unadulterated merit, because I happen to be an outstanding scholar. And a damned good administrator, come to that."

I tried one of the biscuits. Excellent. "You're very young to be wearing the silly hat," I said.

He nodded. "Second youngest in history, discounting the political appointments," he said. "If you gave a stuff about spiritual matters you'd have come across my five-volume commentaries on Sechimer and my proposed revision of the minor catechism. As it is—"

A light glowed in my head. "Oh, you're *the* Honestus," I said. "Sorry, I didn't make the connection. Anyway, I'd assumed he was someone a hundred years ago."

He looked up. "So you've read them?"

I pulled a face. "The commentaries, sorry, no," I said. "The catechism, yes, of course."

"What do you think?"

There was an eagerness in his voice I remembered so well; drunken adolescent discussions of the Nature of the Soul in noisy bars, surrounded by bad company. "I'm not sure," I said.

"Oh."

"You put your case too well. Any argument so elegantly and persuasively presented makes me suspicious."

He hated me for a second and a half, then shrugged. "I let myself get carried away," he said. "It's like decorating a chapel. Why just have carvings and mosaics when you can have frescoes and gilded mouldings as well? And the result's not the splendour of God, it's bad taste."

Later, when I'd retired to bed with a slightly thick head, I reflected on Stachel and me. When he was arrested, I did everything I possibly could, used all my connections and influence; deaf ears, coupled with grim warnings about choosing my friends more carefully. I couldn't understand why I couldn't save him, being who I was, until it dawned on me that I was nobody special, after all; that there were ever so many things the empress's nephew couldn't do, and the only result of trying was getting myself in trouble. That realisation had a big effect on me, and I vowed to learn the lesson; humility, realism, think about what you're doing, how it'll impact on you and other people. But of course it wasn't like that. Execute the empress's nephew's best friend? Of course not. Instead, we cut off the head of some poor innocent apprentice and crush it in a mortar till it can be mistaken for him, and then we send the friend to a distant monastery and make sure he does well (though Stachel didn't seem to have guessed that bit; he's bright, but he has a high opinion of himself). And they didn't tell me at the time because I'm a known blabbermouth, and afterwards it must have slipped their minds, the way things do. It's a bit like finding out, late in life, that the Invincible Sun made the sky blue because He knew it's your favourite colour.

I also considered the fact that Stachel got in all that trouble because he was part of a conspiracy to murder my uncle and aunt, and quite possibly me as well, for tidiness's sake, and at the time that thought never entered my head. Was he still a red-hot republican? You think you know people.

Actually, I remember the cooper's boy. He was no good anyhow and no great loss. Even so.

"TRABEA IS AN arsehole," Stachel told me, as I got ready to leave after a much longer stay than I'd anticipated. "You really want to watch him. He's corrupt and greedy and lazy and treacherous, and as soon as you get home you want to get him recalled and strung up."

I nodded. "You don't like him much."

Stachel frowned. "Actually I do," he said. "He can be very charming, and occasionally very thoughtful, and efficient, so long as what you want fits in with one of his personal agendas. And he makes me laugh, which is a special blessing. But a lot of bad people are very likeable, and a lot of good people are boring and dead miserable."

"I'll watch out for him," I said.

Stachel nodded, satisfied that I'd taken the point. "They say he's got a Scherian doctor who knows every single poisonous substance in the world," he said. "Snake venoms, mushrooms, berries, seeds, special kinds of mould you sprinkle on cheese, the lot. If you get sick, for pity's sake don't let him near you."

He poured himself a drink, offered me one, which I refused. "What can you tell me about Cort Auzon?"

He shook his head. "No more than you'll have read already in your briefing notes. It used to be a great house with a fantastic library, but it fell on hard times about fifty years ago, nobody knows why, and now they haven't got two coppers to rub together." He scratched his ear. "I sent a man over there, year before last, offered to help them out by buying some of their books. He came back with a shipload, literally—one of those barges they use for hauling bulk timber, and it was riding dangerously low in the water. Complete mixture of junk and treasure, they must have just pulled books off the shelves at random. That's how the fifth eclogue of Ausonius came to light, when we all thought it had been lost five hundred years ago, and three brand new Terpaio comedies." He smiled. "Don't worry, I've got my boys copying them for you right now, soon as they're done I'll send them on. The abbot's a man called Gensomer, but I don't know a thing about him."

Halfway from Sambic to Auzon—by land—is the *Hope of Redemption*, a big old inn that used to be an imperial staging post, when we still ran a regular mail beyond the mountains. I expected it to be quiet—actually I expected it to be derelict, with no roof and thistles growing up through the kitchen floor—but in the event I had to wave my warrant around before I got a room, and that meant turning out a prosperous merchant, his wife, son and three daughters. The Cassites pitched their tents in some poor devil's hay meadow (we're not supposed to pay compensation because of setting precedents, but I do) and I sent a military tribune, in full armour and regimentals, to terrify the kitchen staff into heating me some water for a bath.

"You're busy," I said to the landlord.

"No more so than usual."

I asked him about that. Apparently, over the last few years, a brisk trade had started up between our north coast and the Fleyja Islands, which are silly little bits of rock out in the deep, stormy sea. I didn't know anybody lived there, but apparently they do, and they have amber, beaver pelts for making felt for hats, freshwater pearls, hops and huge quantities of small, smooth-shelled walnuts, no good for eating but just right for making oil. In return we trade them wheat, wool, salt and copper. Amazing, the things that go on that we don't know about. Apparently it's worth it for some of the great merchant companies from the City to send stuff up here, in spite of the cost and the risk. You'd have thought some of them might have seen fit to mention all this to the government, but I can see why they haven't; we'd start levying taxes, and maybe send a fleet to conquer the islands, and once government barges in, the days of easy profits and quick returns are over and done with. I gather the Fleyja people use their own boats, which are stupid little things, no more than faggots of twigs tied together with rope and decked over. Hundreds of them drown every year, but that doesn't stop them coming.

The bath was an enormous terracotta thing, like the clay coffins of Blemya, where they bury their dead sitting up. The water was warm, and there was a china sprinkler for sand and a Mezentine jar of rose-scented oil, and a bronze scraper in the shape of a leaping dolphin.

I'd just got out, and was drying myself off in a sort of warm, cosy daze, when one of my tribunes banged on the door. "You'd better see this," he shouted. He sounded rattled, and it takes a lot to do that to a Guards officer.

I threw on my tunic and cloak and stumbled out onto the balcony. Below in the courtyard, I saw something that turned my knees to water; an imperial courier's chaise, with six heavy lancers for an escort.

They haven't built one of those chaises for fifty years, but no need, they made them to last. They look so frail and delicate, you can't believe they'd stand up to five minutes over the ruts and potholes, but they go like the wind, drawn by four of the best horses you'll ever see anywhere. I've ridden in one about a dozen times, and the springs are so good you can put a glass of wine down on the floor and it won't spill a drop. Even so; an imperial courier is the last thing a general on campaign wants to see, because it's a surer bet than the emperor's horse in the Hippodrome that out of it will climb an imperial legate, bringing you a summons, in purple ink with the Dragon seal; return to the City immediately to answer charges. I was there when the chaise came for my father—don't worry, son, he told me, this is just some stupid misunderstanding, I'll be back again before you know it. I wanted to go with him but he wouldn't let me.

I remember thinking a lot of things, between the driver jumping down and unfolding the steps and the door opening. One of them was, *it's not fair, I haven't done anything,* which shows how naïve I was, even then. Also selective with my memories. Everyone who's carried the imperial warrant's done something, at one time or another, and I'm definitely no exception. And I remember thinking, *it's all right, Aunt won't let anything happen to me,* followed by *what if it's her who sent the coach?* And then the door opened, and the last person in the world I expected to see got out.

I leaned over the balcony and shouted; "What the hell are you doing here? And what do you mean by giving me the fright of my life?"

She was terribly pale, and she was leaning on a stick. "Pleased to see you too. Didn't you get my letter?"

Nothing, especially the mail, travels as fast as the couriers; but maybe she didn't know that. "What are you doing here?" I repeated; and then, "How are you?"

"Still alive," she said. "Now find me somewhere I can lie down, before I fall over."

YOU'VE GOT TO hand it to her. "I made your man Mnesarchus break into your desk and steal your signet ring," she told me calmly. "And then I made him forge me a travel warrant, and then we went to the courier's office and they gave me this coach. And the six bull-eaters, which I confess I wasn't expecting. Still, they look pretty in their shiny trousers."

As simple as that. I made a vow to send Mnesarchus to the slate quarries, and a moment later another one to bring him back and give him a nice farm somewhere. "I'm going to be in so much trouble," I said.

She grinned. "Really."

"You bet. Misuse of the imperial courier, forgery of the Imperial Seal—"

"It was your ring."

"Yes, but I'm not supposed to have it, am I? And I'm most definitely not supposed to use it to transport my tart *du jour* halfway across the empire. My aunt is going to skin me alive."

She thought about that. "I doubt it," she said. "It shows style, and a total disregard for the rules and conventional opinion. People like that sort of thing in an emperor. He broke the rules to be with the woman he loves."

"I'm not the emperor. I will never be the emperor. That pinhead Scaurus is going to be the next emperor." I stopped and gave her the nastiest look I could summon up. It made her giggle. "Is that why—?"

"Don't be stupid," she said, and I believed her. "But your aunt won't be cross, though she'll probably write you a rude letter. She wants you to start acting the part."

I was suddenly furious. "How the hell can you say that? You don't know her, you've never met her."

She sighed. I could see how tired she was. "You talk about her enough. I probably know her better than most people. Definitely better than you do. And she'll be fine about it. She's got much more important things to worry about, believe me."

I was still trying to be angry, but it was getting harder and harder. "I asked you a question," I said. "Why are you here? You must be mad, thirty hours in a coach with your belly full of needlework."

She smiled at me. I love her so much. "It was you asked me a question," she said. "Well, you made it into an order, but you know I never do what you tell me to."

I couldn't speak. She waited, then went on, "Well, I thought about it a lot, and I decided that probably this—" she pointed "—was a hint that I ought to retire, and that begs the question, what do I do now? And most of us in the trade try and sucker some poor fool into marriage. And I thought, I know a poor fool who'll do. So here I am."

"Yes?"

"Yes."

Strange how you react sometimes. Several times I'd tried to imagine the moment when she said she'd marry me, and always, in my imagination, I whooped with joy and ran through the streets yelling at the top of my voice. Wasn't like that. I just stood there, still as a rock, while the completely changed and utterly transformed glorious new world enveloped me. "Good," I said. "And now my aunt really is going to kill me."

She changed instantly to a serious face. "I don't think so," she said. "You're following precedent, the best possible precedent in the world, from her point of view. Of course, you're going to have to change your name."

Turned over two—no, make that three—pages at once. "You what?"

"To Ultor. Then you'll be Ultor the Third. Continuity," she said. "At the moment, it's what the empire needs more than anything else. But no, your aunt will be fine. You don't seriously believe I'd be here if I didn't think so."

"Yes, but—"

"This is something you need to do. Politically," she added quickly. "Politics is all gestures, and you don't have a clue when it comes to gestures. But this is a good one, which is why I've agreed. Politically—"

"Will you shut the fuck up about politics," I said, and kissed her.

A moment later she yelped with pain and I let go. "What did the doctor say?" I asked.

She hesitated, just a little. "No permanent damage," she said. "An inch to the left, I'd have been dead. I think they always say that."

I've heard it myself a few times. "You shouldn't have come," I said. "What if you'd burst the stitches? It was a ridiculous risk to take."

She gave me her you're-impossible look. "It was a gesture, stupid," she said. Then that serious look again. "Are you happy?"

"Yes," I said. "For the first time in my life, there'll be someone I know is on my side. You have no idea what that means."

She nodded gravely. "No matter what," she said. "And don't worry about your aunt. When she looks at me, it'll be like looking in a mirror. And no woman can resist doing that."

I HAD TO send the chaise back, but we had a stroke of luck. One of the merchants at the inn agreed to sell us his luxury coach—for a ludicrous sum of money, and only after I'd threatened to requisition it. It wasn't as sleekly efficient as the government chaise, but speed was no longer of the essence, and it was damnably comfortable.

"I won't be able to go in it, naturally," I said mournfully.

"No?"

"Of course not. I've got to ride at the head of the damn column, it's expected of me."

"Poor baby." She pulled a wonderfully soft-looking rug over her knees and plumped up the cushions. "And will you have to eat barley porridge and drink horse-piss, just like the men?"

"Not the horse-piss. That's only in the desert."

She raised her eyebrows. "They packed me a hamper at the inn," she said. "There's smoked lamb sausage with truffles."

"I don't love you any more."

She smiled. "Gestures," she said. "See? You can do them if you want to. Look, I'll sneak you out some goat's cheese with chives. Your favourite. Nobody will know."

I shook my head. "Can't risk it," I said. "Anyway, it's no big deal. I've been eating Beloisa porridge since I was fifteen, and sleeping in ditches."

She sighed. "Spoiled rotten, that's what you are. All you rich kids are the same."

I THOUGHT ABOUT what she'd said as we rode on to Auzon, and it didn't take me long to realise she was right, as usual. I went back through all the marriages in the various imperial families for the last few generations, as far back as I could remember, which isn't very far, and there haven't been many of them, because of all the civil wars and usurpations and such. Fact; in the last two hundred years there have been thirty-six emperors, of whom nine died in their beds (and three of them were probably poisoned). Of the thirty-six, only ten were born in the purple and only six of them lived long enough to marry. Of those six, five married commoners; the rationale being that whereas the petty kings of lesser nations have to choose their queens for politics and diplomacy, the Emperor of the Robur is so incredibly far above any other mortal that nobody could possibly be his equal, and no other nation could conceivably aspire to a marriage alliance; so, logically, the emperor is free (almost uniquely among humanity) to marry for love. It's the only argument in favour of having the rotten job I've ever come across, and presumably that's why emperors and crown princes are so often the heroes of soppy romances. Anyway, the same principle applies to sons, nephews and first cousins of the Dragon Signet—put it another way, if tradition was to be observed and the prestige of the purple maintained, I really had no choice but to marry out of the gutter. My duty, in fact. Oh well. Guess I have no alternative but to comply. I still wasn't looking forward to telling my aunt, though. She's a bit like that. If you brought her the severed head of the Great King of the Sashan, she'd moan at you for dripping blood on the carpet.

It's probably the soldier in me; once I've identified an objective, I want to crack on and achieve it—get there first with the most, Sechimer's lightning strike across the frozen river at Three Bridges, all the great cavalry commanders you've ever read about. So I'd made up my mind that we'd get married at Auzon, with the abbot officiating and presumably my Cassite archers as bridesmaids. It didn't quite work out like that. When we got to Auzon, Auzon wasn't there.

Rather a melodramatic way to record a horribly sober fact. By way of background, if by some chance you aren't reading this with the map on the desk beside you, the monastery at Auzon is—was—barely half a mile from the sea. The monks, at one time great traders and seafarers, built a harbour in a superb natural location; necessary, because that stretch of the coast is murder, with sudden squalls, hidden rocks and that ghastly white wall of mist that comes down out of nowhere and cuts visibility to the point where you can't see your hand at arm's length, half an hour after a clear blue sky. Of course, you'd have to be mad to use that mist deliberately, to mask your arrival from the watch towers on Carason Point and Alsingey. But that, it turned out, was precisely what they'd done, or so the handful of survivors from the village told us. Apparently there's these tiny skerries about ten miles out, where ships piloted by suicidal lunatics could lie up until the fog rolled in. Mist means no wind, so they must have rowed across, ten miles completely blind and somehow avoiding the Devil's Teeth and that vicious riptide. Then say five hours to reduce the monastery to rubble and ash, and back out to sea again before the fog thinned.

Speaking as a military man, I despise fighting against lunatics. I've done it once or twice, and it sets your teeth on edge. You can't predict what they'll do, you don't share the same frame of reference regarding the definitions of victory, defeat, surrender or acceptable losses; if they lose, you find yourself staring at a battlefield piled obscenely high with their smashed, slashed bodies, and if they win, they'll probably burn you alive in a wicker cage. Really, they shouldn't be allowed to make war. It's bad enough as it is without all that sort of thing.

This time, as well as slaughtering the monks they'd butchered nearly all the villagers as well, and burnt the farms and barns. Call me a sissy, but I don't hold with all that. Also, it made dreadful problems for us, since we'd been relying on the monastery and the village for provisions for the Cassites and, most of all, fodder for the horses. The best we could do was hobble them and turn them off to graze on what they could pick out from the heather and the gorse. That's no way to treat good livestock if you want them to give of their best.

"Aren't you going to bury them?" she asked me.

"No point," I said. "Burnt bones aren't a health risk, and the rain'll wash the ashes away in a day or so. It's unburnt bodies that cause the plague."

"Yes, but—" She shrugged. "You can't leave people's skulls and bones just lying around. It's not decent."

"No," I said, "it's horrible. But if we stay here and collect them all up and dig a big hole, we won't have enough food to get back to Sambic, let alone press on to Cort Varon. It'll have to go on the big list of things to be done later by someone else."

She frowned. "Do you have to make a lot of decisions like that? I suppose you must do."

"All the time," I said. "And each one is truly bad. All that can be said for them is that the alternatives are even worse."

But she'd made me think, and I compromised. I sent the Cassites back to Sambic, under the command of my senior tribune, and I made her go with them. The other eight tribunes, the six lancers of her escort and I stayed there until we'd picked up all the skulls—the hell with arms and legs—dug a big hole and buried them. By then it had started to rain. I recited something or other from the Long Catechism, and then we wriggled into our oilskins and made a dash for it. I had ash on my hands all the way back to Sambic. It ran in the rain and turned into little black muddy rivers, all down my trousers.

DECISIONS; AH, DECISIONS. I signed my first death warrant the day before my sixteenth birthday. The poor bastard I condemned was guilty of cowardice in the face of the enemy. Imagine it.

You know what a Sashan phalanx looks like, a thousand men wide and fifty deep, but all you see as they come towards you is those terrible long spears, like a forest sideways—a forest that was planted by some optimist who lost interest and never got around to thinning the saplings, so the trees are far too close together, so they shoot straight up to get to the light. Actually, it's not the sight that gets to you, it's the sound, fifty thousand hobnailed boots hitting the deck at *exactly* the same moment, and the ground really does shake, it goes in through the soles of your feet like a tapeworm and strangles your heart. For two seconds you can't think of anything at all; the third second, all you can think about is how you're going to run away with all these people blocking your path. I signed the warrant six hours after the captain of my personal guard grabbed hold of my horse's bridle to stop me hauling right round and bolting like a rabbit. I felt so utterly ashamed, for nearly running and for killing a man who did what I tried to do. My tears splodged the ink. They had to copy it out again, and I had to sign it again. Then I was sick, all over the tribune's shiny boots.

It gets easier with time, but not because you develop into a better person.

On the successful completion of my first campaign, Uncle had me made a Companion and awarded me the headless spear, which is the highest honour a soldier can receive. Looking back on it, eighteen years later, I recognise that, yes, I fought a damn good war. I broke a Sashan phalanx with intelligent use of terrain, light infantry and field artillery. I followed up well but resisted the temptation to pursue too closely, which so often leads to last-minute disaster. I had two old steelnecks to advise me, but the overall strategy and the detailed battlefield tactics were my own (well, taken from the *Art of War,* volume six, chapter three; but their man must've read the same books). We stopped an invasion of the eastern mountains dead in its tracks, and as a result were able to negotiate a peace that lasted for five years, which was the record until quite recently. I was sixteen, for crying out loud, and what I remember most vividly was pissing my trousers. My uncle was thirty-three—my age now—before he got his first command, and he lost three battles and eight thousand men. I think I coped all right. I shouldn't have had to.

I know that I beat the Sashan because their general was an idiot. They had an idiot for a general because they execute all the good ones, in case they try and seize the throne. My uncle was a good general. He seized the throne, burned down half the City and slaughtered his predecessor's family like sheep. What can you do?

STACHEL WAS APPALLED when I told him what had happened. The library, he kept saying, my God, the library. When eventually he pulled himself together, I got him to give me his very best maps of the north coast, the old ones that bothered to show all the islands. Also, I said, I needed him to perform a wedding.

He stared at me. "You must be out of your tiny mind," he said.

"It's an emotion often compared to madness, but only in poetry. Come on, you're a priest. It's what priests do."

"Not on your life," he said, and he actually backed away a couple of steps. "You they'll exile. They'll kill me. That's what happens to witnesses."

"It'll be fine," I told him. "I'm just following precedent. Politically—"

"I've already been in one condemned cell," he said. "Two in one lifetime is too many. Look, we were friends once. Don't spoil it."

I balled my fist so he could see the signet ring. Actually it was the fake, which I wear because I'm scared I'll lose the real one. "I'm giving you a direct order," I said.

"Go fuck yourself," said my friend.

WELL; A PRIEST is a priest is a priest, and even the most weasel-faced administrator from the Clerk of the Works' office is pervaded by and marinated in the Holy Spirit, provided he's passed the relevant exams. After six refusals I found an ordained minister who was prepared to marry us, in return for a cash sum and a sinecure on the eastern frontier. The job took six minutes, and as soon as we were done, the Holy Father jumped on a cavalry horse, slung clinking saddlebags over the pommel of his saddle and thundered out of the main gate in a cloud of dust. If he yelled a blessing over his shoulder as he left, it was drowned by the thunder of hooves on the planks of the drawbridge.

For medical reasons we postponed the traditional wedding-night activities; instead, I sat up into the small hours reading reports that had just reached me from Cort Acuila, where the six-hundred-year-old monastery had been burnt to ashes by raiders who rode down out of the morning mist on small, stocky ponies.

"FORTUITOUSLY," COUNT TRABEA said, "we had a routine patrol out that way. They picked them up the day before and followed them in, so they were able to see what happened."

The Count had rushed to my side, which was nice of him. He'd brought five hundred local militia; also, rather more usefully, two dozen very competent clerks and a big folder of maps. "Fine," I said. "It didn't occur to your men to intervene?"

"There were twelve of them," he said. Well, fair enough.

After the massacre, the raiders had loaded their plunder onto pack-horses. I questioned the patrol myself; what did the raiders take? They were very sorry, but they didn't dare get close enough to see. Whatever it was, the raiders put it in sacks, which they appeared to have brought with them. Heavy sacks or big bulky ones? Just sacks, the patrol leader said. We were six hundred yards away. All right, how many sacks on each horse? Two on some, four on others. Anyway, after that they trailed the raiders across the moor. They made straight for the coast, to a little cove much used by the local smuggling community, where five ships were waiting for them. They turned the ponies loose before they sailed away, and the patrol caught some of them and looked for brands, but there weren't any. So they brought a few back with them, and one of the locals, a bit of a trader when he wasn't mending pots and pans, reckoned he'd seen ponies like them in the Fleyja Islands, which he'd visited once when he was a boy. Nobody else had ever seen anything like them. The local horseflesh is squat and stocky but taller at the shoulder and with a much bigger head.

"So these pirates come from the Fleyja islands," I said. "Does that sound likely to you?"

Trabea thought before answering. "I'd be very surprised," he said. "Of course, I've never been there, and I don't know a lot about them, nobody does. But the impression I've formed over the years is that they're just a bunch of small-time crofters, dead keen to trade with us, because we seem to want all manner of garbage they've got no use for, like beaver-skins and amber, and picking up trash off the beach and trapping vermin is a much easier way of getting food than growing it yourself."

"Stealing's even easier," I said.

He shrugged. "Maybe. And maybe we come across as soft, leaving all those valuable things lying around with just men in dresses to guard them. But they're not stealing food, they're stealing gold and silver and works of art. As far as we know, the only people they trade with is us."

I remembered something I'd seen: affluent City merchants roughing it at the *Hope of Redemption*. Now one of the defining characteristics of the empire is that it's very big; also, it contains a good number of rich, cultured men who value fine art and beautiful objects rather more than conventional morality. Would a wealthy banker in, say, Procopia worry too much about the provenance of a magnificent Mannerist icon, if he was offered it at the right price? And who would ever recognise a specific piece from the other side of the world, with enough certainty to identify it as stolen property? And plain gold and silver can be melted down into bullion, which tells no tales.

"I've got some orders for you," I said.

"Gosh," Count Trabea said politely. "Just bear with me while I get something to write on."

An immediate embargo on ships from the Fleyja Islands. Spot checks on the goods of merchants. A full investigation to ascertain whether items stolen from the monasteries were turning up on the market anywhere inside the empire. "And when you've done that—"

"Hold on a minute," Trabea said. "No disrespect, but how many officers do you think I've got? For a start, I'm going to need ships. I've got three customs sloops and a ceremonial barge."

I wrote him a chit. "Twelve warships," I said. "That'll have to do."

He stared at me. "I think we ought to be able to manage with that," he said quietly. "How about soldiers?"

Not quite so easy. The twelve galleys weren't a problem, since I happened to have twelve galleys at my disposal at that particular moment. They'd been assigned to me for sabre-rattling purposes in my negotiations with the Sashan, and I'd sort of neglected to give them back. Soldiers are different. For entirely sound historical reasons, individual commanders don't get to keep soldiers once they've finished with them. If I wanted more than fifty men, I'd have to write to my aunt and say Please nicely. "I'll see what I can do," I said. "Meanwhile, though, I suggest you improvise. You've got a hell of a lot of non-military manpower—roadmenders, clerks, grooms, all those men on your payroll that feature so prominently in your accounts. Give them a spear and a shield each and tell them to look warlike. They're not going to have to fight anyone, so who'll know the difference?"

I WROTE TO my aunt; to my great surprise, she promised me a thousand regular steelnecks, due back from the Mesoge any day now. I was stunned. Steelnecks are gold dust, and not entrusted to just anyone; they have a nasty habit of choosing who'll be the next emperor, even when there isn't an immediate vacancy. At least that answered one question I hadn't dared ask. She couldn't have heard about my wedding. If she'd done so, steelnecks would have been sent, but not for me to command. As it was, as and when one of those fast chaises showed up to take me home, a thousand regular heavy infantry would give me the option of not going, if I really didn't want to.

Interesting times.

SHE INSISTED ON coming with me to Cort Maerus. I told her I was deeply touched but it was a tough journey and she really wasn't well enough yet. Patiently she explained that it'd be much easier to murder her if I wasn't there, should anyone wish to do so. I had one of those moments where your guts turn to water, and said yes, of course she was coming. In fact, I wasn't going to let her out of my sight.

Cort Maerus is a long way north. Snow lies on the mountains all year round, though you can grow grapes and figs in the valley; the monks used to have extensive orchards and vineyards a hundred years ago. Now they're just nettles and briar entanglements, and nobody seems to know why. Sheep graze where barley once grew, and every half-mile or so you come across ruined cottages and farmsteads, and nobody could even be bothered to steal the stone. I read everything I could find (there isn't very much) and asked everyone who might know, but there's no memory of any raiders or invasion, no plague, no specific disaster. Once there were a lot of people in those parts, making a good living, and now there are very few, quietly starving. My own theory, for which I have no real evidence, is that their well-earned prosperity was their downfall. Sturdy, well-fed peasants are proverbially the best recruits for the heavy infantry, and we've had ever so many wars in the last two hundred years. I think all those strong, self-reliant farmers' sons went off to war and didn't come back, and without them the place just died. If so, does it say something about the nature of the beast called empire? The idea is that empire protects the towns and villages and little farms from the enemy, and in order to do so recruits soldiers, so that the towns and villages and little farms won't be laid waste, and grass won't grow in abandoned streets and good productive land won't be smothered in weeds and briars. But if the act of protection brings about the destruction it was designed to prevent—well. I'm not a trained philosopher, so I'm not qualified to comment.

Unlike most of its sister houses, Cort Maerus isn't built on a hilltop. It squats comfortably in a valley, where the rainwater comes tumbling down the mountains in a broad river and splays out in a dozen useful little rivers across the flat valley floor. My abiding memory of it is a hundred subtly different shades of green; from the pale green of new shoots of bracken, which grows so well where there's been extensive burning, to the dark, waxy green of well-established ash and willow, quick and efficient colonists of abandoned pasture. There was a narrow road between head-high tangles of briar and dead brushwood, out of which spindly trees shot up gasping for daylight. One of my tribunes, a keen sportsman, had brought along his beautiful new Aelian bow, hoping to pot a few deer, or at the very least the odd rabbit. He never got the chance. We saw any amount of little twittery birds but nothing living at ground level. No animal bigger than a mouse could live in that horrible tangled mess.

The abbot of Cort Maerus was a big, jolly man, who was overjoyed to see us, because he rarely set eyes on anyone he hadn't known for twenty years. He wasn't quite so cheerful when we explained that we hadn't brought much food with us, imagining that he'd be able to feed us; eight hundred archers, seventy general staff, my wife and me. He recovered well from the shock.

One of the principal duties of the monasteries, he said, was to provide hospitality for hungry travellers, and if that meant that he and his monks would have to tighten their belts a bit that winter, the pleasure of our company would be more than sufficient recompense. In any case, they had plenty of dried beans, and the villagers could be prevailed upon to spare oats for our horses, and a little bacon goes a long way in a nourishing soup. Also, if we hadn't tried the local speciality—nettle soup with tiny bits of diced sausage—we had a real treat in store.

There were forty monks at Maerus, all over fifty. Mostly they worked in the ten-acre walled garden, of which the abbot was enormously proud—fresh cabbage all year round, and heavy crops of roots, which store so well for the hungry months. He showed me a great long gallery above the main dormitory, crammed to the rafters with shelf upon shelf of dull, waxy-skinned apples; he thought it was once the scriptorium, where they used to copy out books, but he couldn't be sure. The old library had been gutted and was now a splendidly dry wood store; a place this size took a lot of heating and it could be bitter in winter, but his people were hard workers and skilled foresters; they coppiced the willow-brakes and the overgrown hazel, and made trips up the mountain with a big old cart to fell the huge pines and firs that grew on the side-of-a-house slopes. Good honest work, he told me, is the closest way of achieving communion with the Creator of All Things, the universal gardener who grew us all from seed. He had short, dirty fingernails and forearms like a blacksmith, and it made me feel tired just listening to him.

"I heard about that," he said, when I mentioned the raiders. He made it sound like interesting gossip from a faraway country of which we know little. "But I can't imagine they'll want to come here. We don't have any gold or silver, we sold all that stuff years ago."

We were sitting in the main chamber of the abbot's lodgings. It was bitter cold, so we sat practically nose to nose on either side of a small brass brazier. It had been there a long time, because its smoke had blackened a wide patch of the ceiling, blotting out the Invincible Sun *orans,* flanked by grubby cherubim with tar-smudged halos. It was too dark to see the rest of the mosaic—I'm woefully ignorant about art, but my guess is, it's early Figurative, probably complete under all the soot and congealed fat from the tallow candles, because the damp didn't seem to have penetrated that far. "Anyway," he said, "if they come, we'll be ready. We've got a plan worked out. There are shepherds' huts up on the mountain, we can gather our tools and supplies for a month at the drop of a hat, and nobody can get into this valley without us seeing them. As you probably noticed, there's only one path through the furze."

I stooped, and shot out a hand instinctively to stop him. "What are you doing?"

He looked at me blankly, then understood. He'd lifted the lid of a big wooden chest and taken out a book. He'd been about to put it on the brazier. "Would you like it?" he asked.

I couldn't read the lettering on the spine, it was too faded. "Thank you," I said, and took it from him. He opened the box, took out another one and threw it on the stove. I didn't try and stop him.

"Nobody reads them any more," he explained. "And books aren't the way to salvation, we realised that a long time ago. Waste not, want not, that's our philosophy here."

The book had thick wooden covers, which burned long after the paper had flared away. It produced a surprising amount of heat. You've got to be practical, the abbot told me gravely. The book I'd rescued turned out to be Frontinus' commentary on Annius, of which there are tens of thousands of copies in every major city in the empire. I've never read it; not my sort of thing.

We didn't stay long at Maerus. They were very pleasant to us, but we didn't want to be a burden. On, instead, to Cort Neva, three days' trudge inland, though mostly downhill, thank God.

I was very glad I'd brought my wife with me, because otherwise the abbess of Neva would have been a problem. I recognised her straight away; hard not to. Seven years earlier, she'd caused havoc at Court. Rumour has it my aunt tried to have her poisoned; if that's true and she failed, it's a striking tribute to Abbess Honoria's intelligence and resourcefulness, because when my aunt wants something done, it generally happens. I could see why my aunt would have wanted rid of her. Intelligent, beautiful, aristocratic young widows with money and ambition are about as welcome at Court as locusts in a vineyard. She's a distant cousin, apparently. I wouldn't have been her food taster for all the gold in Blemya.

Seven years in the frosty north had tightened the skin of her face, and the backs of her hands were a dead giveaway, but she'd still have been a force to be reckoned with if I hadn't had the woman I loved by my side more or less constantly. *Tell me everything that's been happening at Court,* were practically her first words to me, and I don't think she meant hemlines or whether hair was off the shoulder this season, though that was what I told her about. She pretended to be frightfully interested, and I promised to send her a couple of bolts of Priene silk, as soon as there was room on a courier's coach.

"We're terribly worried about these raids," she said, inviting the big, strong man to take care of her. In fact, she'd taken the precaution of hiring seventy Vesani mercenaries, practically as good as steelnecks and much cheaper to maintain. She could afford to, since she'd just sold a Ctesippus altarpiece for two million hyperpyra, to an anonymous buyer from the east. Seventy good men could hold those walls against a thousand regulars. She'd quartered them in the stables, which she'd had made over into a big, comfortable barracks. She still had two Ctesippus icons and a Frontinus triptych of the Ascension, for which she was considering a number of serious offers. As good as a cellarful of arrows and catapult bolts, she told me with a grin, and I agreed with her. You couldn't sell a Ctesippus without a provenance, even in the remote east. But a legitimate one would man your walls and fill your armoury for ten years. She always was smart, that one.

If she was mildly surprised when I asked to see the library, she recovered well, though she summoned the librarian to give the actual commentary. The library building was spotlessly clean, no dust on any of the surfaces and the slate floor gleaming. It had all the standard works in uniform modern bindings, every book numbered and in its proper place at all times, the chains drooping like ripe beans off the vine. There was no one else in there when we went round. I suspect casual readers weren't encouraged. They'd have made the place look untidy. Sister Librarian was obviously very proud of her charges. I saw pots of lanolin, for greasing the spines so they wouldn't dry out and crack. That would make the book sticky and awkward to hold, but I got the impression that wasn't much of a problem.

"It's a tremendous privilege to be here, of course," Abbess Honoria told me, for the fifth time, "and I'm enormously proud to head up such an important institution. I don't miss the old days at all, and it's wonderful to be doing His work in this sublimely peaceful place." On the other hand, she didn't say, and didn't have to. I've only ever seen that sort of hunger in the eyes of neglected dogs: *rescue me, please, before I wither away and die.* A wicked thought crossed my mind; if I wrote my aunt and told her I'd married Honoria, she'd be so relieved when she found out the truth that she'd strew our marriage bed with flowers. But I could be wrong, and the food in the north tastes so strong, you wouldn't notice an out-of-the-ordinary flavour until it was too late, and I was a married man now, with responsibilities.

Cort Bealfoir was my idea of how a monastery should be. The buildings were small and very old, with a high wall and a strong gatehouse. Inside there was one long dormitory with a refectory over it and a functional reredorter out back; the rest of the site consisted of a magnificent Archaic chapel, a beautifully decorated chapter house and a huge library/scriptorium, with floor-to-ceiling glazed east-facing windows. Sixty brothers worked there, nearly all of them copying books, under the less-than-rigorous command of Abbot Gennasius, author of the famous *Twelve Questions*.

I'd read his book when I was fourteen and had no idea he was still alive. I wanted to ask him about it, but he fended me off politely with answers polished smooth from decades of use, and we talked about the raids instead. Faced with the terrifying unknown, he'd fought back with the full armoury of scholarship; he'd collated every reference in the Early Fathers to swarms of unidentified savages, and was able to prove to me conclusively that this lot weren't any of them. He'd had copies made of every *Art of War* and *Soldier's Mirror* in the catalogue, ready to be sent to anyone who needed them; I was presented with bound copies, and was too embarrassed to mention that I'd got them all already. He also had chapter and verse ready to justify the use of deadly weapons by contemplative monks in defence of their books and lives. He didn't have any deadly weapons to go with them and I promised him fifty longbows and twenty suits of armour of an obsolete pattern, which I'd noticed in Trabea's inventory. He was as pleased as a cat with two tails, and promised to drill his monks as rigorously as a steelneck sergeant. I'd have loved to have seen that, but I never got the chance. I imagine he'd have used the *Institutions* of Florian rather than the *Manual of Military Practice,* which is later and prone to textual corruption, due to an uncertain manuscript tradition.

From Bealfoir to Cort Erys, down the horrible North Road, which needs a lot of money spending on it before it could count as a goat-track, let alone an artery of empire. Talking of goats: plenty of wild ones in the combes and valleys, and the Cassites were good shots, so we had plenty to eat, if you like goat, which I can't say I do. So we took our time—four days to Erys, and I blame myself. If we'd taken just a few hours longer, I hate to think what the result would have been.

The noise was the first sign of trouble. It was a perfectly still day, and sound travels in the mountains when there's no wind. At first we thought it was a foundry or an arms factory, except there aren't any in the north any more, but monks can be very enterprising, maybe they'd built a steel mill or a mine. It was definitely a clashing, thumping noise, and when we got closer we could hear yelling as well. At that point we knew exactly what we were listening to; once heard, never forgotten, believe me.

It's one of the weird things about this world and human life generally. Two miles from a full-scale battle, where men are being hacked to pieces with sharp tools, you'll see sheep grazing and rooks lining up on the branches of trees overhanging the ripening corn, as if they were the subject of the picture and the confused human events nearby are merely a minor detail in a corner of the background. I've never run away from a battle in my life—too scared to, if the truth were known—but suppose you did, and when you stopped to catch your breath, all around you there's ordinary everyday life, the sun shining, the river flowing. You'd have to stop and ask yourself, which is real, this or the hideous unnatural mess going on where I just came from? It has to be one or the other, it can't be both; because if the two can co-exist, separated only by a little bit of geography, why would anyone in his right mind be down there when he could be up here?

I HAVE MANY sterling qualities. Moving silently and avoiding observation aren't two of them. I sent scouts, who reported that a large body of men, at last fifteen hundred, were attacking the monastery with ladders and a battering-ram. I got that helpless feeling that always hits me when I know I've got to fight. I'm not sure how to describe it, because there's nothing else like it. I'm terrified, I know it's all going to end very badly, but I have no doubt in my mind whatsoever about what I'm going to do. It's like I'm looking down a tube or a tunnel at the future, a point in time when I've done it all and I'm watching the result, almost like I'm suddenly living my life backwards. I know that I've got to lead with a weakened centre to draw them in, while looping round the left flank to take them by surprise when they burst through, because I've already seen it happen. It doesn't always work, of course. Sometimes it goes spectacularly wrong, and then I'm back to making it up as I go along, a skill at which I do not excel.

The situation in a nutshell. Cort Erys: a modest foundation, on top of a steep hill, a wall all round it, with one gate, protected by a three-storey gatehouse. The bad people—ant-sized, but occasionally flashing in the sun, suggesting at least some armour—seemed to have given up on the ladders and were concentrating their efforts on the gate. The regular thumping noise we'd heard a mile away was the ram. The monks were doing something to annoy them; twinkles in the air told me the raiders were shooting arrows at them to keep their heads down, but clearly with indifferent success. The scouts' estimate of fifteen hundred struck me as being on the conservative side. I had eight hundred archers, and to reach the enemy I'd have to descend a steep slope and cross four hundred yards of open ground. The Cassite bow is a marvellous thing, capable of shooting two hundred yards at maximum elevation, but how many shots would they get before the enemy reached us and swept us away? That was assuming the Cassites hung around long enough to be reached, a big and unwarranted assumption. Conclusion: this was a fight I couldn't expect to win.

A wise man once said: the best way to fight is not to fight. It sounds really profound (most statements that scrape the paint of nonsense tend to, I find) but there's a germ of wisdom in it. My job was to find a way of not fighting that would achieve the objective. Luckily, practically everything has been done before at some stage, and I've read an awful lot of books.

Only a lunatic would divide a small army into two and attack the enemy at the extreme edges of his formation, particularly with inferior numbers. To do so would be to invite his opponent to envelop his two wings and wipe them out to the last man. The emperor doesn't give command of his armies to lunatics; they must know that, even in the Fleyja Islands, or wherever these people were from. Thus it would be logical to assume that the two detachments of lightly-armed archers advancing on the raiders were simply an advance guard, skirmishers; and the apparent tactical error was part of some typically fiendish imperial stratagem, which would inevitably lead to the total annihilation of the enemy.

The raiders weren't born yesterday. Long before the first archers were in range, they dumped their ram and drew back, in no particular order; when the archers kept on coming, they turned on their heels and ran. That was exactly what happened at Sanga Cuona, and isn't it nice when history repeats itself?

Well, almost. My fault, I guess, for not having paid more attention to the map. If I had, I'd have known that the vector of their probable flight was directly into a dense wood, just over the skyline. Now put yourself in the raiders' position. An imperial army takes you by surprise. Wisely you withdraw, only to find you're being shepherded into that classic killing ground, the dark forest, in which you can bet your life the crackerjack imperial general has previously stationed a huge detachment of his dreaded heavy infantry. What can you do? You shy away like a startled animal, double back on your tracks and run like hell for the rapidly narrowing gap between you and the advancing Imperials. If you're lucky, you might just make it; and if you almost get there in time but not quite, desperation leaves you no alternative but to try and punch your way through.

I remember yelling "Get out of the way!", just before one of the bastards ran into me and knocked me spinning. I don't know if he hit me with his shield or I was simply in its way; the iron rim smacked into my eye-socket and I felt the rivets drag across my eyeball.

I had, and still have, a very fine helmet, with a broad steel brim. I wasn't wearing it, of course. Commanders don't, when they're leading from the front. The men have to be able to see it's you, out there being recklessly brave.

I was still on my feet when some other bastard stabbed me, in passing, like an afterthought. The swordpoint skidded off my expensive breastplate and down into my thigh. I was still on my feet. Someone else cannoned into me and sent me down. With my working eye I saw a boot, complete with hobnails—one was missing; top left, from memory—bearing down and blotting out the light. Turning my head away was sheer instinct. The boot and its owner's weight landed on my ear, and for a moment I thought my head was going to burst. Then I was out of things for a bit.

What happened next, so I'm told, is that the tribune Bagoas (who never liked me much) threw himself in front of me and took the spear that should've finished me off. He fell across me—it was his blood, not mine, that I woke up soaked to the skin with, though I didn't know that at the time—and immediately the standard-bearer Leuxis took his place; he cut down four of five of the bastards before they did for him, and by then Teutomer and Gontharius, two of the coach-escort steelnecks, had hacked their way across and stood over me chopping and stabbing like maniacs until the danger was past. They got badly cut up for their pains. Teutomer lost his left hand, and they cut off Gontharius' chin and a slice of his jaw. I can't begin to find words for how I feel about that. I'm sorry, but I can't imagine doing that for anyone, let alone someone I barely know.

I CAME ROUND in the monastery, with a little old man leaning over me dabbing at my face with a tuft of bog cotton. I knocked his hand away (because the last man I'd seen had been trying to kill me) and he tutted and tried again. I grabbed his wrist. He took the cotton from his trapped hand with his free hand and went on dabbing. The effort was too much for me and I went back to sleep.

When I came round again I was alone. Above me was a gorgeous fresco of the punishment of the damned, and for a moment I wondered if I'd died and was in real trouble. There was something really big and sharp and painful in my left eye, a grain of sand or something like that, and I couldn't see through it because some fool had trussed it up with bandages. My cheekbones ached, right down into my chest. Past experience identified the other pain as a cracked rib. Here we go again.

Then a thought occurred to me, and I started to panic. I tried to get up, but some fool had taped me to the bed with bandages. I tried yelling, but my voice came out as a little froglike croak, so I drummed my feet up and down like a little kid; it sounded very odd, and I realised I was stone deaf in one ear. But it must've worked, because the door opened and she came in, and there was no need to panic any more.

"You're all right," I said (and it sounded very far away). "I was worried."

She knelt down beside me. "I'm fine," she said. "You're not."

Another of those moments. "How bad?"

"They don't know yet," she said. "They may have saved the eye, or they may not."

She was sitting on my left side, which was fortuitous, since I couldn't seem to hear with my right ear, the one that got trodden on. Then—oh.

"The deafness will be permanent, apparently," she said. "Actually, you were very lucky. An inch to the right—"

I couldn't help myself. I burst out laughing.

THEY SORT OF saved the eye, more or less. I can't see much through it, just blurry shapes, and bright light gives me a splitting headache. Actually, I really ought to have died. The crushed ear went bad and the fever set in, and I was a real mess for four days. The little old tutting man pulled me through, apparently; turns out he was the best doctor in the north, with fifty years of experience, all of which he needed to keep me from quietly drifting away. So many people went to so much trouble over me. I can't understand it, but I'm grateful.

As soon as the news reached him, Count Trabea sent his personal physician to look after me. He arrived while I was still out of my head with the fever. My wife and newly-promoted tribune Scaeva intercepted him, told him I was out of danger and sleeping peacefully, and entertained him with fortified wine and honey cakes while Brother Cellarer and Brother Herbalist went through his medicine-chest, opening and sniffing all the bottles and feeding samples of anything they didn't like to a dozen or so caged rats. Disappointingly, the rats came through completely unscathed, and the good brothers couldn't find anything they could possibly take exception to. In due course, Trabea's quack examined me, concurred with everything the little old man had done and told me how lucky I'd been to have such an outstanding doctor when I needed one most. Scaeva was all for planting some poison on him, chopping his head off and having Trabea arrested for conspiracy. I like Scaeva and I'm glad he's done so well for himself, but sometimes he gets a bit carried away.

AT LAST WE had some dead bodies to look at. They were a bit ripe by the time I was well enough to see them, swollen and purple and no use for anything, but the general consensus was that they weren't the Fleyja people, who are short and dark, not tall and fair. Captain Eleocarta of the Cassites reckoned they could be Elorians or Cure Doce, while tribune Segimer fancied they might be Aram Chantat from way beyond the eastern frontier, or possibly no Vei or Rosinholet. Their clothes were crude homespun linen dyed with blueberry juice and their swords and spearheads were the most amazing pattern-welded work, the sort of thing only a handful of smiths in the whole empire know how to do. They caught one live one, but he died of gangrene two days later without saying anything helpful. No amulets, charms or identifiable religious talismans, no rings, earrings or personal items of any kind. Oh, and they were wearing stout, well-made boots. Well, yes, I already knew that.

ERYS, HOWEVER, HAD been saved, so that was all right. And I'm glad about that, because it's a beautiful house; one of the small ones, but with fantastic artwork and a complete set of early Grotesque communion plate, and the best collection of early Robur history and drama anywhere.

The abbot had, he told me, been there practically his whole life; he joined as an eight-year-old novice and turned down four other abbots' mitres and an eastern see because he couldn't imagine working anywhere else. He was a short, chubby man with a broad face and not many teeth; his speciality, he admitted rather nervously, was the dual procession of the Holy Spirit, which I've never understood and still don't, though he did his best to explain it to me. When not contemplating the awful complexity of the Divine, he ran a cheerful, efficient house that copied more texts per head than anywhere in the north apart from Cort Doce and actually paid its lay brothers for their labours in real money. Anyone in the five surrounding villages could use the mill and the shearing-pens for free, or have their horses shod at the monks' forge at cost, or load their surplus goods on the monks' ship, which made one trip a month down the coast to Aubad. When the raiders came, they'd kept them at bay for two hours by pouring boiling water on their heads—just as well they had ten huge coppers for brewing—and pushing the ladders off the walls with hayforks and winnowing-fans. They braced the gate against the ram with benches from the chapel and beams from the stonemason's crane. Smart people, who didn't lose their heads in a crisis.

"THIS IS NO good," she told me, sitting at my bedside. "First I'm all cut up and then you are."

The same thought had occurred to me. One of the five grounds for annulment is non-consummation. And beforehand doesn't count; I'd checked. "Sorry," I said. "Put it on the big list of things to do later."

She told me that the scouts had tracked the enemy's retreat back to the coast, where they'd been met by six large ships; they were well out to sea by the time our people got there, so no idea where they were from. Meanwhile, Trabea had taken delivery of his new warships and sent them to cruise off the Fleyja islands; if the raiders showed up there, the fleet would be ready to intercept them.

Stachel came up from Sambic in a rickety old cart, which was all he could lay his hands on at short notice. "God, you're in a state," he said to me. "You want to go easy on that sort of thing. If you're not careful you'll ruin your health."

"Noted," I told him. "Actually, it was supposed to be a bloodless victory. I've always wanted one of those."

"Showing off," he said scornfully. "Serves you right for trying to be clever."

I told him about Trabea's doctor. He seemed surprised. "I still wouldn't trust that creep as far as I could sneeze him," he said. "You must be mad, letting him get his hands on warships." He sat down on the end of my bed, took an apple from his sleeve and bit into it noisily. "Want to know what I think? I wouldn't be a bit surprised if Trabea turned out to be behind all this. Think about it. Everything seems to suggest these pirates or raiders or whatever you want to call them are people we've never encountered before. So you tell me, how do they know where the monasteries are?"

"There's such things as books," I pointed out. "And the monasteries aren't exactly a state secret."

"Yes, but they seem to know their way around the country pretty damn well. Don't tell me they've got detailed maps as well. *We* haven't got detailed maps. You know how I found this place? Followed the map until I was halfway up the wrong mountain, backtracked to the nearest village, had to ask a dozen people before I found one who'd even heard of it. But they know the best way in, the best way out, how to steer through the rocks and shoals, what time of day the fog comes down. Which means," he said, "somebody's telling them."

"Then it can't be one of us," I said. "As you just pointed out, we don't know these things."

He gave me a sour look; don't be flippant. "Trabea's been here a long time," he said. "He's in charge of the taxes and the census. He's got surveyors and mapmakers, plus access to all the best libraries. Also he's got connections in the City to get rid of the stuff. Think about it. The value's in the artwork, not the bullion. If you just melt it all down into ingots, it's not exactly a significant return on the sort of money you'd have to have invested."

Interesting point, but I wasn't immediately convinced. "Not if it's being organised by one of us," I conceded. "But if they're savages from across the sea, who knows how much our stuff's worth where they come from?"

He gave me his patient look. "I think we just established it's not savages," he said, "because of the degree of local knowledge. Which I take to be proven fact," he added. "Look, this isn't like the City, where there's foreigners everywhere you look, or the east. If you were planning something like this out there, sure, you'd send a couple of your people over here to spy out the land, nobody would pay them any mind, they'd assume they were just sightseers. Round here, anybody like that would stick out a mile. Therefore, whoever they are and wherever they come from, it's one of us who's organising it all and, presumably, reaping the rewards. Now ask yourself, who has access to that kind of local knowledge?"

STACHEL WAS STILL there when the news came in. Cort Maerus, sacked and burned, no survivors, no witnesses; they'd killed the lay brothers and the villagers as well.

"Maerus," she said, "I get confused. Which one was that? Was that the toffee-nosed tart with the bottle hair? If so—"

I shook my head. "Maerus was where they grew all their own food and the roads were clogged with brambles," I said. "I can't make it out. What did they have worth stealing?"

She shrugged. "Maybe they didn't tell you about it. Maybe it was something they didn't know they had."

I pulled a face. "But Trabea did, right? You've been talking to Stachel."

"Actually, Stachel's been talking to me. I think Trabea's far and away your best suspect. I know his sort, believe me."

"Maybe. Or maybe you're both wrong, and it really is just savages, and they don't know what's there until they're inside. This time they were unlucky, you win some, you lose some."

"Oh come on," she said. "Remember what a hard time we had finding the place? It's in a valley, you can't see it from the sea. You'd have to know precisely where to look."

The road ahead of us lay under a natural arch of trees, cut perfectly half-round by the tops of passing wagons. A fine place for an ambush; but the four steelnecks had been through before us and pronounced it safe. We were heading up the long, steep escarpment to Cort Igant, the northernmost of the northern monasteries, a mere twenty miles from the Permian border. The trees were holm-oaks, short and twisted, slow-growing, thriving on steep slopes where carts can't go, no good for planking and miserable to split for firewood, so nobody came to chop them down; you can survive by being contrary and useless. But the road was regularly used, the trees proved that, and someone came along from time to time and filled the ruts and the potholes with gravel from the riverbed, a very long way away, and nobody I'd spoken to seemed to know who. I don't like it when people do essential public works for free, without being asked. It means they're up to something.

Cort Igant practically jumped out at us from among the trees; we turned a corner and there it was, blocking our way like a bandit. The road led straight up to a massive grey gate, which I later learned was three cross-plies of oak. It turned out that there was a back gate and the road carried on out of it, as straight and broad as ever. So; everything that moved along the road went in one gate and out the other. I began to see daylight.

The abbot met us at the gate; he was very friendly, a solemn-looking man just under medium height, with a close-cropped grey beard and neat, short hair. It was an honour to receive such a distinguished guest, and all that sort of thing. He was the first abbot I'd met with inkstains on his fingers, rather out of keeping with the smart, well-groomed rest of him. You can't help getting inky if you do a lot of writing. The foul stuff gets sucked up into the pen and oozes through the thin wall, and next thing you know you're smudging the paper.

"Igant is a relatively recent foundation," he told me, "which means it's only been here four hundred years. In monastic terms, that means the paint's barely dry. But we've been quite fortunate with donors and patrons, and of course we have the revenue from the tolls."

Odd to find an abbot who admits to being well-off. Mostly they plead desperate poverty, so they won't be asked to contribute to one of those strictly voluntary loans my aunt is so fond of. I didn't ask if his people saw to the road-mending. Strictly the business in hand.

"We've heard all about it, of course. Maerus too, such a tragedy. A great house in its day, though I gather it had fallen on hard times. Do you have any idea who these people are?"

No, I didn't say, but maybe you do. "Our best lead at the moment is the Fleyja Islands," I told him. "Only we don't know a great deal about them."

"I think I can help you there," he said quickly. "Our choirmaster was a sailor on a trading ship before he left the world. I believe he went there once."

We walked through the cloister, with a charming garden in the centre. I asked to see the library. The abbot didn't actually express surprise. "Of course," he said, as though I'd just asked him for an elephant. "This way. We have a decent collection, and of course we're adding to it all the time."

And decent enough it was; a smaller building than I'd become used to. The shelves were golden rather than dark brown, and the spines of the books were splendidly uniform, like a regiment of steelnecks on parade; all recent copies, or older books rebound. "Any treasures?" I asked.

"Ah." He smiled. "There is one we're rather proud of."

He showed me a Greater Missal. It was the size of an infantry shield, covered in thin gold sheet studded with gemstones and pearls; possibly the most vulgar thing I've ever seen in my life. "A gift from a generous patron," he said, "who wished to remain anonymous." He turned the pages, and I wanted to shield my bad eye from the glare of the gold leaf. The vellum was milk-white. And that was when the notion that had been struggling up between the paving-slabs of my largely unsatisfactory brain finally burst into flower. "Of course," I said aloud.

"Excuse me?"

"Of course you must respect your donor's wishes," I said. I lifted a couple of links of the chain. It reminded me of the stuff they use for big, savage guard dogs. Perhaps that's what scripture is, though (big, noisy, bites you if you're bad) in which case the precaution is justified.

We toured the defences, which were quite admirable. "I have sixty armed lay-brothers on call at all times," the abbot told me, "we take these things seriously. After all, we're a rich house, and we live in a violent world."

"I don't think you've got very much to worry about," I reassured him.

"He's a smuggler," she said.

I nodded. "Of course he is. And he launders the proceeds by turning them into ghastly works of religious art, and if that's not blasphemy, I don't know what is." I sat down on the bed. I really wanted to rub my bad eye, but I'd been given awful warnings not to. My cracked rib made me whimper. "My guess is that at some stage there'll be a raid and all the gold and silver garbage will be stolen, the abbot and his people will, by some miracle, be away from the house at the time, and they'll retire out east somewhere and divide up the proceeds. Or maybe I'm doing them an injustice and this is their way of glorifying the house of God, I really don't know. In any case, they're a red herring."

I hadn't said what she expected me to say. "Hardly," she said. "Obviously, this is how Trabea gets the stuff out of the empire. Up into Permia, then down the Long River, then overland with the silk caravans to Beloisa and all points east."

"Oh," I said. "Trabea again."

"Of course. And more to the point, that's where the ponies come from, and possibly the men as well."

I shook my head. "Permians are dark and brown-eyed."

"Permians are, yes, but there's any God's amount of savages up beyond them we know nothing about, except that they're dirt poor and love to fight. That's where your blue-eyed giants come from, bet you anything you like."

"In any case," I said, "this house has nothing to fear from the raiders, so we don't need to stay here any longer. Pass me that map, would you? I seem to remember there's a river we can follow all the way back to the Doce valley."

"Aren't you going to do anything? He's a smuggler."

I sighed. "Not my problem," I said. "Law enforcement and revenues are Trabea's business. Besides, they've been nice to us, I don't see why we should be nasty to them."

MIGHTIER THAN THE SWORD

My uncle once said—in public—that I'm too stupid to be allowed out without a keeper. My aunt treats me like an idiot, but she's the same with everyone who's not as smart as she is, into which category falls the rest of the human race and several gods. At the University my tutors said I had a reasonably good mind buried under a coal seam of aristocratic inertia (rather a splendid phrase, don't you think?) but I was always the one who had to have things explained to him by his kind friends after the lecture. In the army, intelligence is like ginger hair; some people have it, some don't, and it really doesn't matter. I have other stirling qualities to compensate. I work hard when there's absolutely no alternative, I bother about details, I try and find the best in people while expecting them to do their worst. And I'm loyal, I will say that for myself.

And I'm lucky. Fool's luck if you like. I get away with things. Fate intervenes to rescue me from the consequences of my ill-judged actions. And I'm lucky with the people around me. For some reason, I seem to attract the most wonderful people, like filings to a magnet—clever, brave, kind, patient, forgiving, resourceful; my wife, of course, and various tribunes and captains who've served with me over the years and won my battles for me and taken spears and arrows that were meant for me. That never ceases to amaze me. Apart from her, I couldn't see myself doing that for anyone.

But I can read, and anyone who reads the right book has an ally, an advisor who's far more clever than he is and can tell him what to do. I have a box of books that goes with me everywhere: my cabinet, terrible pun intended. Various *Arts of War* and practical guides to geology, meteorology, agriculture, economics, sensible stuff; if in doubt, look it up—it's a good, solid box so I can sit on it as well, or stand on it to make speeches, and it stopped a dozen arrows when our camp was attacked at Trigentum. I take the utilitarian view, in other words, probably because I've always been acutely conscious of needing all the help I can get. Accordingly, I'm damned if I'm going to let the accumulated wisdom of the past perish from the face of the earth, whether through damp or fire or being used as arsewipe. And, since I'm not nearly bright enough to know which books are solid gold and which are expendable garbage, I have no alternative but to try and protect them all.

Is that a fault in me? Have I got it wrong? Could I do a lot of harm along the way? A wise man once said that ninety-five parts out of a hundred of all the evil in the world stems from good intentions, and the older I get, the more I believe him. But that could never apply to me, could it, because I *know* my intentions are good—

The first man I killed with a pen died for doing what I'd have done if someone hadn't stopped me. The question is: should I have spared him, or confessed and handed myself in?

THERE WAS A road to Cort Doce, but we never even got to start. Bright and early in the morning, that sight a general dreads most of all—an imperial chaise, with outriders.

"She's heard about you," I said. "I'm dead."

"Pull yourself together, for crying out loud," my wife advised me. "Cut their throats, dump the bodies in the woods and say they never got here."

Sound advice, I guess, but I didn't take it. I put on my brave face and went to meet the legate. Turned out I knew him slightly; a sour-faced old boy with a sharp edge to his tongue, staunch ally of my uncle in the House. He handed me a plain brass tube and said, "I'm sorry."

That turned my throat dry. I fumbled with the tube, trying to poke out the rolled-up letter. He took it back and did it for me. I'm useless a lot of the time.

The usual greetings; then—

I have to inform you that your uncle died this morning after a long and painful illness, which he did not bear well.

I have tried to keep this news restricted, but I am well aware that I will not succeed. Our enemies have sources very close to the Signet, and will probably get the news before you do.

For this reason, you cannot return to the City at this time. Proceed to gather whatever forces you can. I have reason to believe that the enemy army is in the north, and it is logical to assume that they will seek to dispose of you, as heir apparent, before marching on the City. Defend yourself as best you can. I regret to say that I have no soldiers to send you on whose loyalty I would be prepared to rely. The commanders of the Sixth, Eighth and Fourteenth Armies are waiting to see what happens; presumably, if you are killed, they will proceed to fight it out among themselves. It is essential for the wellbeing of the Empire that this should not happen, and I therefore urge you to stay alive if at all possible.

Given the resources at your disposal it would be unrealistic to expect you to bring the opposition to battle with any chance of success. I have written to the Great King of the Sashan asking him for troops; at times like these, when our friends are useless or hostile, our best hope lies with our enemy. In theory, the treaty obliges him to send help. In practice, I hope he will prefer the devil he knows, although obviously it will cost us dear in the east. If he refuses, frankly I have no idea which way to turn. It is all most frustrating; if we could field ten thousand men, the problem would be solved, and we pay the wages of a standing army twenty times that size.

Although it is entirely up to you, I strongly urge you to send your wife back to the City with Commissioner Clarus; she will be safe here, at least in the short term, and as the situation deteriorates I am confident I can make arrangements for her to obtain asylum in Scheria or Scona. It goes without saying that I thoroughly disapprove of the match, but at this time it is the least of our problems.

I trust that it is unnecessary for me to tell you how proud I have always been of you, as was your uncle. If you survive this, I feel sure you will make a fine emperor. I hope very much to see you again.

Your loving aunt,

Eudoxia Honoria Augusta

—and directly under that, the Seal, which I've always thought looks more like a horse than a dragon, but what do I know?

I stared at the letter for a bit. Then I said; "What enemy?"

"The republicans, of course," the legate said. "Didn't you know?"

I WISH PEOPLE would tell me things, instead of assuming I'm omniscient.

The republican movement has always been there, as long as we've had an empire. Get rid of the emperors, give power back to the people—quite; except the people never had any power at any stage in our history, which was probably just as well. In this context, *the people* means the two dozen ancient aristocratic families who own half the land in the empire, the six dozen rich men who hold the mortgages on that land, the priesthood and, of course, the army. They governed the Robur for a thousand years before Florian staged his coup, and because of or in spite of their best efforts we somehow conquered the world. All in self-defence, of course. You'd be amazed how many people we've had to defend ourselves against over the years.

Republicans rebelled against Marianus and nearly won; they gave Detterich a run for his money, and we had to call in the Vesani, which cost us the Delta. It was republicans who assassinated Pacatian and Thrasianus, thereby doing the world an enormous favour, and we're all told to believe that they started the Great Fire. Their heads have decorated arches and gateways for as long as I can remember. I'd never taken them seriously.

"We don't know anything for certain," the legate told me, "but our best intelligence says that they have between four and seven thousand mercenaries standing by on the Permian border—not Permians, probably some new kind of savages we haven't come across yet. Obviously you're their primary target, and then they'll head for the City; at which point it'll be a race to see which general reaches them first and annihilates them. Whoever wins the race will get the City, and then we can look forward to twenty years of civil war, while the Sashan pick off the eastern provinces."

I shook my head. "They must be mad."

He didn't disagree. "It seems they genuinely believe the City will rise in their favour, and the other cities will follow suit. Quite possibly they're right, except that the army would never let them reach the City." He paused, choosing his words carefully. "The empress believes you're safest if you gather whatever men you can lay your hands on and hole up somewhere, but I'd venture to disagree. If you want my advice, get a ship and head for the Great King's court. The empress is right about one thing, the Sashan are our only hope, and they know you, they know they can do business with you. It's not much of a hope but it's all we've got."

My wife wanted to stay with me but I nagged her into going back with the legate; mostly because I agreed with my aunt, she'd be safer in Town, but also because if she stayed she'd advise me, and I'd take her advice, because she's probably the smartest person I know. And I knew what that advice would be, and it wasn't what I intended to do.

Trabea could move like lightning when he wanted to. By a sublime stroke of good luck he'd just taken delivery of the thousand steelnecks my aunt had agreed to send him, and they would be the backbone of our army. Add to them my seven-hundred-seventy-five remaining Cassites and fifteen hundred local militia, neither useful nor ornamental— And the stupid thing was, I reckoned I knew where I could get a thousand ferocious and highly effective warriors just for the asking, except that I couldn't possibly ask. I did consider it, very seriously. But there are some things I won't be complicit in, even for the empire.

When I told Trabea that I was planning to fight, he went white as a sheet and told me I was mad. But I calmed him down by threatening to cut his head off for embezzlement, and once we'd got that sorted out he proved to be efficient and useful. "It'll be two to one or thereabouts," I told him, pretending to be casual about it, "which is better odds than my uncle had at Boc Gresc, and for all we know, these savages of theirs might turn out to be useless, so—"

He stared at me. "We know they aren't," he said. "Well, don't we?"

I shook my head. "You're assuming the raiders are the mercenaries," I said.

"Well, of course they are. It stands to reason."

"I disagree," I told him, in my subject-closed voice. "Of course they may turn out to be fire-eaters, or they may turn out to be woolly lambs, we just don't know. All we can do is make damn sure we're ready for them."

Trying to train militia will break your heart, so we didn't bother. Instead, I made a deal with them. Stay where you're put and don't move until you're told to go somewhere else; that's all. Put like that it doesn't sound much, but in fact it's everything—don't run away, even though Death comes charging towards you. I couldn't promise to do it, but they did.

Steelnecks are extraordinary creatures. For them, life is a series of competitions, the Lathrian Games three-sixty-five days a year. They train like lunatics because every month there's a prize for everything—the archery medal, the javelin medal, the laurel wreath for long-distance running in full armour, at company, battalion and regimental level, team and individual. Ten medals automatically gets you promotion, fifteen means double pay, twenty is double pension. On campaign there are endurance awards, and on the actual battlefield there's a long list of prizes and honours, from the Silver Buckle to the Headless Spear. After ten years in the service, gongs and braid are all you're capable of caring about, the honour of the corps and who's where in the league table. What or who you're fighting for, or whether you'll still be alive in the morning, doesn't enter into it. They're even worse than athletes, and without them that guttering flame I talked about earlier would've been snuffed out centuries ago.

Steelneck tribunes are a different kettle of fish altogether. I think I understand a little bit about them, because I used to be one. You take a spoiled rich kid, age about thirteen. You make him live in conditions they'd jib at down the quarries, you send him on twenty-mile marches in full kit and when he gets back, you make him learn Cirra's *Elegiacs* by heart and recite them in front of the whole class; you teach him to be fluent in four living languages and three dead ones, make him learn philosophy like it was weapons drill and weapons drill like it was philosophy; you don't feed him properly, so he's forced to steal food and thereby learn stealth and deception, but if he's caught he's tied to a gate and flogged; when he's sixteen you give him powers of life and death over a hundred steelnecks and send him off to war. Then, if he's one of the few who lives to reach fifty, you enrol him in the House and let him shape the future of the empire. It's a completely ridiculous system, and seems to work quite well.

I've lived with these people most of my adult life, I admire them and some of them I actually like, but I'm not one of them. Not sure I'm one of anybody else, come to that. If I felt at home anywhere it was probably the University—sometimes I wake up and, in that dreamy half-awake-half-asleep interval before you really come to, I'm convinced I'm still a student, with lectures in the morning and the library all afternoon. I was only there for a year, before I had to rejoin my regiment, and to tell you the truth I was always out of my depth, though mostly people were very kind.

SEEK OUT THE enemy and destroy him; quite. I was asking myself how on earth I was going to find the enemy, in a country with seven roads and thousands of forests, combes and valleys, but I needn't have worried. They came to us.

IT TAKES SEVEN years for an apple tree to mature and bear fruit. Roughly seven years earlier, someone—monks, presumably, nobody else would've had the capital—had planted out sixty acres of gently sloping hillside in cider-apple trees. Whoever it was knew their business. They'd clear-felled a rectangular tongue into one of those ancient holm-oak forests, so the plantation would be sheltered on three sides and still get plenty of sun; the slope faced west, so it would catch the frost in winter, and frost is essential for setting the fruit. I imagine it must have been monks, and they read about orchard-building in a book; stored wisdom put into useful practice, which is the point of the exercise.

We ruined all that. I drew up my militia halfway down the slope in two long, sparse lines, stretching from the woods on the left to the edge of the steelneck phalanx, five ranks of one-hundred-eighty, hard up against the woods on the right. That left a hundred steelnecks as a reserve and my personal bodyguard. The Cassites—

What I really hated about the plan was the way everything depended on the Cassites. If the enemy believed the message I'd allowed them to intercept, saying that the Cassites had deserted *en bloc*, they'd look to outflank me by going through the woods. If they didn't believe it, they'd assume that I had my archers hidden in the woods, and launch a frontal assault on my paper-thin militia. All I knew for sure about the enemy was that they'd been seen riding in column two days earlier; whether they were cavalry or infantry who preferred not to walk remained to be seen. I had a backup plan, of course, but I didn't like it much.

The mist cleared early that morning, which was a bit of a blow; we'd have the sun in our eyes until noon, and you'd be surprised what a difference that can make on a sunshiny day, which was what that day turned out to be.

Trabea was commanding the steelnecks, so we said our awkward goodbyes quite early. "For what it's worth," I told him, "if by some miracle we win this, I want you to know the slate'll be clean, as far as you and I are concerned. You can keep the money you've been creaming off the poll tax and the harbour dues, and anything else I don't know about, and I'll give you a province out east, where you can really fill your boots."

He laughed. "Thanks, but no thanks," he said. "I've made my pile. That was the idea all along, do ten years in the sticks, then retire somewhere warm and live like a civilised human being. My trouble is, I'm lazy. Fleecing Aelia would be too much like hard work."

I shrugged. "The offer stands," I said. "Good luck. And thanks for standing by me."

"I never really had a choice," he said, and I never saw him again.

Tribune Tarsena made me put my armour on, even though it hurt. "You're mad," he said. "You shouldn't be on the field at all, the state you're in."

"I lead from the front," I told him. "You know that. I wish I didn't have to, but I do." He lifted the helmet off the table. I shook my head.

"You've got to wear it," Tarsena said. "The doctor says—"

"Don't nag, you're worse than my wife."

"The doctor says—"

I backed away, putting the table between him and me. Utterly ludicrous. "If I wear the helmet," I said, "I'll get a splitting headache. If I get a headache, I won't be able to think. If I can't think, we're all going to die. I'll wear the stupid breastplate, and that's it."

"And the greaves."

"Definitely not the greaves. I can't run worth spit with those things on."

He gave me that look. "Honestly," he said, "you're like a little kid."

I scowled at him. "Remember who you're talking to. Like a little kid, *sir.*"

We compromised. I wore the breastplate and the left greave, because you lead with your left leg, and I was excused the helmet. Of course the first thing I did when his back was turned was pull off the greave and hide it under some blankets. Bloody fool I'd look, hobbling around with one greave.

I'd chosen tribune Rabanus to be my chief of staff. That's a fancy way of describing the man who stands next to me so I can have someone to think aloud to; a general who talks to himself doesn't inspire confidence. "Out of interest," I asked him, as the sun caught the enemy spearpoints in the valley below, "what's your real name?"

"Sir?"

"Rabanus isn't a Mesoge name. What do they call you back home?"

He grinned. "I'm Hrafn son of Sighvat son of Thiudrek from Gjaudarsond in Laxeydardal."

"Fine," I said. "I'll call you Rabanus." I peered into the sun. "I can't see a damn thing."

He shaded his eyes with his hand. "They've stopped. They're dismounting."

"Nuts," I said. I'd chosen the field chiefly on the assumption they were cavalry. "What's their order like?"

"Slovenly," said the twenty-year steelneck. "They're just milling about, like a crowd at the races."

"First good news I've heard all day."

That must've puzzled him, but he didn't comment. Good news, because I'd been doing my reading. If, as seemed likely, they were from one of the tribes in the far north, it was a reasonable bet that their society was structured round the clan—big chief, his immediate household, then the off-relations and poor relations. In a setup like that, the whole point of war isn't capturing territory or securing lines of communication. You fight to prove how good you are, how many heads you can cut off, with the chief watching; and you can't do that if you're stuck at the back waiting your turn. So they charge; it's a race to see who can get to the killing-ground first, and only the bravest men in the world can withstand a charge like that. Good news? I must've been out of my mind.

I hate the standing-about-waiting stage, but on this occasion it didn't last long. The brown blur in the valley surged forward and started to swarm up the hill toward us. It wasn't long before we could hear them, and I'm ashamed to say the yelling and the howling got to me. I felt that old familiar tugging sensation, the urge to run—I'd have done it if it hadn't been for Rabanus, still as a statue, relaxed, breathing deeply. I started to edge away; he caught hold of my elbow, low down so nobody could see. He didn't say a word. I'd have given a thousand hyperpyra for my helmet and five hundred each for my greaves; better still, a solid iron box with ten padlocks to hide in until it was safe to come out.

"Look," Rabanus said. I was watching the steelnecks. I glanced down the valley, and saw that the brown surge was veering left, to avoid the phalanx and hit the militia. Which was what I'd have done; smash through the weak part of the line, then swing round and take the regulars in flank and rear.

"We're on," I said quietly. "Ah well. Here we go."

The militia had sworn me a solemn oath to stand their ground, no matter what. When the enemy were two hundred yards away, they turned and ran like deer; one moment they were there, the next they weren't, and who can blame them? The only thing that held them up was the trench I'd had dug during the night—sorry, did I forget to mention that?—in which stood my Cassite archers; but it wasn't very wide and most of them were able to jump clean over it, and the rest of them sank to the ground in terror and lay there when the Cassites stood up and started shooting.

It's a cliché to talk about men in a battle falling like grass under the scythe, but I can't think of a better image. The front runners stop in their tracks and drop in a heap; the ones behind stumble over them and pile up as they change from a moving to a stationary target; they fall in windrows, like cut, raked hay, the interval between the rows being the time it takes an archer to take an arrow from his quiver, nock and draw. It's a horrible sight, because those are human beings in those heaps and stacks, living and not-quite-dead buried under the corpses, bleeding to death or buried alive and suffocating. You want the wind to be in the other direction, because it carries away the noise. But it can't last for ever. Sooner or later, the men farther back figure out what's happening and have the common sense to swerve out of the way. The swarm veers round the tangled mess; the archers adjust their aim and a new windrow forms, but it's a dozen or so yards closer to where they're standing, which means they don't have quite enough time to nock and draw. Most of them realise this; they drop their bows and scramble up out of the ditch, just as the enemy reach them. A few moments later, half of them are dead; the other half are running, and so aren't aware of the solid wall of steelneck shields slamming into the savages' right flank; it's only when they can't run any farther and have to stop that they realise there's nobody chasing them, because the phalanx has rolled right over the enemy like a cartwheel over a stray cat.

Steelnecks are pleasant enough people most of the time, but they do like killing, when they get the chance. We shouldn't really encourage them, but we do.

The idea had been that, at the crucial moment when the savages overwhelmed the archers' position, I would charge at the head of my hundred picked men, to give the phalanx time to reform and deploy. In the event, they got there before we did, probably because I'd promised ten tremisses a man and the Bronze Crown to whichever unit contacted the enemy first. It was a cheap incentive, because of the hundred men of D company, only seventeen survived. I don't have any figures for the enemy dead, because we didn't bother counting. We heaved bodies into the ditch until it was full, and left the rest for the crows.

Trabea was killed, leading D company from the front. Tribune Tarsena was killed when we got in the way of a bunch of terrified savages trying to escape the slaughter; he shoved me aside and let them crash into him, and they trod him into the dirt. Tribune Rabanus was luckier; he only lost two fingers, when he parried a sword-cut aimed at my head with his hand, because his shield had been hacked away. I can't remember if I hurt anyone, on purpose or accidentally; it was all over very quickly, and then those of us who were left just stood there for a while, like we'd just woken up and were wondering what the hell was going on.

We still have no idea who those people were, or where they came from. They were tall, with high cheek-bones and long black hair in braids. They went barefoot, and fastened their cloaks with bronze pins shaped like grasshoppers. That's all I know about them, and I couldn't care less.

As soon as he saw what had happened, the enemy commander jumped on his horse and rode away. We caught up with him the next evening, in a hayloft. He scrambled out when the soldiers started jabbing the hay with their spears, jumped through the loft door and broke his leg.

They dumped him in a cart and brought him to me. He stank of his own piss. He started to plead. He was pathetic.

"Sorry," I told him. "Not this time." Then I looked past him to the tribune, who nodded, took a long step forward and cut off his head.

So died my good friend Stachel, who used to help me with my Logic essays, and the blood from his neck spurted all over my sleeve, and I had to change my shirt. He died for what he'd always believed in, a better world free from tyranny and oppression, and we buried him in a dunghill. I feel sure he'd have done the same for me.

I QUITE LIKE a lot of the old traditions, but not the one where soldiers on the battlefield acclaim the new emperor by raising him on a shield. I was scared stiff I'd fall off and hurt myself and look a fool. Rabanus suggested gluing the soles of my boots to the shield. I think he was joking, but it's hard to tell.

When I reached the City, there were declarations of undying loyalty from thirteen of the fifteen regional commanders-in-chief waiting for me. The other two arrived the next morning, because the courier from the east takes that much longer. I found it really hard to accept. I never wanted to be emperor, and I'd always assumed it'd land on my cousin Scaurus, except that he inexplicably fell out of a high window ten minutes before my uncle died. I'd always thought my aunt liked him much more than me. I don't know, maybe she did. After that, she never once mentioned his name to her dying day, and neither did I.

When I was five yards from the Lion Gate, it opened—not just the wicket, the whole twelve-foot-high embossed bronze monstrosity, and the kettlehats stepped back smartly and presented arms, instead of peering in my face to see if my beard was stuck on with gum.

"IT'S NOT SO bad," my aunt said, after a careful examination and a long pause. "And you were never a thing of beauty at the best of times."

"That's all right, then," I said.

"Can you see anything at all on that side?"

"Light, colours, vague shapes. Lucky it's not my master eye, or I'd have to learn archery all over again."

She'd actually stood up when I walked into the room. I'd been horrified. She was head to foot in red homespun, which threw me until I remembered that red was the proper colour for mourning where she came from. Sorry, where we came from. A very long way away. "He was a good man, in his way," she said. "He had a chip on his shoulder all his life, about who he was and what he used to be. He was one of those men whose faults make them strong. I won't miss his temper, but I'll say this for him, sooner or later he always listened."

We sat still and quiet for a moment. Then I said, "Why me?"

She didn't smile. "Not for your personal magnetism and giant brain," she said, "that's for sure." She gave me the exasperated look: sit up straight, can't you, don't slouch. "Continuity," she said. "Stability."

"Because I'm family."

She shrugged. "Thousands of unsuitable men inherit valuable property every day for that very reason," she said. "Also, the pool of candidates is restricted; you or one of the generals. If it's one of them, we get a civil war."

"Out of interest," I said, "why haven't we got a civil war? Why have they all rolled over and accepted it? I can't make it out."

She handed me the needle and thread; I licked the end and twisted it into a point so it'd slip through the eye. Long practice. "I think, because none of them want to be emperor badly enough to go through all that again. Your uncle chose them, remember."

"You chose them."

"I gave him the benefit of my opinion. And he chose well. They're none of them military geniuses, God knows, but that's all right, who are we going to have to fight?"

"Let me see. Oh yes, the Sashan."

"Who choose their generals in exactly the same way; not the brightest, not the best, because that only makes trouble." She concentrated on her stitches for a moment. "Will you lead the army yourself?"

"What do you think?"

"Probably you should. You have a knack of being liked by the men, and so long as the army's behind you, you're relatively safe. Besides, it'll give you something to do. Men should have jobs. It keeps them focused. A man of leisure starts thinking about things, and that leads to trouble."

Ah well, I thought; no peace for the wicked. "But not right away," I said. "I think the treaty will hold for a while yet. I think I'll send a new ambassador. Tellecho's been out there too long, and he's never liked them much."

"What you should do," she said, "except that now you can't, is marry the Great King's sister."

I made an unintended noise. "I don't think so," I said. "She's eleven."

"Your son would have ruled the world. Still," she added, snipping the thread with a tiny pair of gold scissors, "I know it's no use trying to convince you of anything once your mind's made up."

News to me. "He may yet," I said. "You never know."

She put down the fabric and looked straight at me. "You won't ever have a son," she said, "or a daughter. Not unless you marry again."

I couldn't understand what she was saying for a moment. Then I remembered. *What did the doctor say?* I'd asked her, and she'd hesitated just for a fraction of a second. An inch to the left—

"How many people know?" I asked.

She nodded her approval; it was the right question. "By now," she said, "probably everybody. The generals certainly, and the Great King, and the Vesani senate." She frowned. "She should have told you before she married you."

"It'd have made no difference."

That got me a look. "Well, there you are, then. No point telling the news to a deaf man." Then she put her hand on mine and actually smiled. "I like her," she said, "she reminds me of my friend Svangerd. You know, you met her, the abbess of Cort Doce. How is she, by the way?"

My heart turned to stone. "Actually," I said, "I wanted to talk to you about her."

She was still smiling. "I miss her, you know. Obviously she had to be out of the way while your uncle was alive, but now, I'm thinking of letting her come back. I do so miss having someone my own age to talk to."

Some things you just have to do. "I'm sorry, Aunt," I said. "I don't think that's going to be possible."

She stared at me as though I'd hit her. "What did you say?"

I wanted to run away, and there was no tribune to stop me. But; "I'm sorry," I said, "but Abbess Svangerd is under arrest. I issued the warrant before I came south."

"What on earth are you talking about?"

Deep breath. There are times when I loathe the sound of my own voice. "Abbess Svangerd is directly responsible for the destruction of the monasteries and the deaths of thousands of people. She's behind the whole thing. She hired the raiders and told them what to do."

"You're mad."

I shook my head. "She wanted the books," I said. "She couldn't bear the thought of all the rare, unique books in the other monasteries being at risk, with people who didn't care about them and weren't looking after them properly. She wanted them all safe at Doce, where she could protect them. I imagine she tried asking nicely first, but when she couldn't get what she wanted that way, she took matters into her own hands. I really am sorry. I know she was your friend."

She was staring at me. "You've got no proof."

"Actually, by now I probably do. I sent a couple of tribunes to Doce with orders to search the place. They know what to look for, the books where only one copy exists, that used to be in the other houses. I've also got the Permian traders who made the contacts with the savages. Quite by chance, we caught a couple of their business partners while we were rounding up Stachel's general staff, and they gave us the names. But that's just the icing on the cake, the books are all the proof we need. And I imagine she'll confess. She didn't strike me as the type who wriggles on the hook." Then a door opened in my mind, and a crack of light gleamed through. "You knew."

She looked at me. "It didn't take a genius to figure it out."

"But you sent me to investigate."

"I wanted you out of the way." Her voice was strained but level. "I knew your uncle didn't have long. If you'd been at Court, they'd have killed you. You were safe in the north."

"It never occurred to you that I'd figure it out."

"No. You're smarter than I gave you credit for." She picked up her sewing, put it down again. "What made you realise it was her?"

"Things she said, and the way she said them. And I knew it had to be the books the raiders were after, because paper leaves a distinctive kind of ash, and there wasn't any like that. And there was nothing worth having at Cort Maerus except books, and they went there anyway. Once I knew it was books, it had to be her or Stachel, nobody else cared enough. And it wasn't Stachel, because he wanted something else. So it had to be her."

I'd never seen her look like that before. She looked old, and frightened. A few days before, she could have had me killed just by nodding.

"Let her go," she said, "for my sake. Please."

My poor friend Stachel, who pleaded with me, his trousers soaked with piss. "I can't do that," I said. "I'm sorry."

THE STEELNECK TRIBUNES found the books in a disused cistern. There was a reference to it in an old book, but the entrance had been cleverly bricked up and disguised, you'd never have known it was there if you didn't know exactly where to look. But I'd copied it out for them, and they went straight to it. The cistern was a huge space; filled right up with books, so she'd have had to find more storage if she'd carried on. The rarities were in her bedroom, in a cedar linen-press, with a newly fitted padlock.

I sent her a bottle of poison, but she didn't use it. She told her maids that she knew my aunt would save her. When the time came, they had to drag her to the block and hold her down, a little old lady, my aunt's age. She died pleading, cut off in mid sentence.

I have this habit of killing people for doing what I want to do. One of my first official acts as emperor was to found three imperial libraries, in the City, at Lonazep and at Beloisa. I appointed a commission of the world's best scholars to catalogue every library in the empire, to find out precisely what we've got, and get copies made so that there's one copy of everything in each of the three. It's been ten years and nobody seems to be in any great hurry, except when I shout and make a fuss. The one in the City will be called the Ultor Library, in honour of my uncle, who didn't learn to read till he was twenty-three and never willingly opened a book in his life.

Among those who pleaded for Svangerd's life was my wife. If I spared Svangerd for her sake, she said, my aunt would love her for it and we'd have no more aggravation out of her. Politically—

I told my wife, who knew she could never have children but didn't tell me, that my aunt would love her just as much for trying.

Ten years. In eighteen months, it'll be the longest reign in two centuries, and yet it feels like I've barely started. I can't say I've done anything in particular. We beat the Sashan, I suppose; nine battles, of which eight were victories and one was a horrendous defeat, and now the border's more or less where it's always been, and there's a treaty. I still lead from the front, because I've got to, and General Rabanus is always right beside me, to grab my arm and stop me running. I have good people around me and they run the empire as well as it's reasonable to expect.

My aunt has been abbess of Cort Doce for five years now. I don't think she likes it there, but I bet she runs a tight ship. I send her blankets and nice things to eat, but I simply can't find the time to visit.

YOU'RE READING THIS, so it must have survived; been kept, and copied out, and copies made from the copies. It must have a home on a shelf in a library somewhere—possibly one of my three, or maybe they were all burned to the ground years ago; you'll know about that, and I won't, I'm delighted to say. This book has no right to survive on its merits, just as I had no right to survive on mine. We made it this far because my aunt's husband, an illiterate savage called Ultor, won a civil war, in which a lot of innocent people died and a great many beautiful and irreplaceable things were lost. As my aunt said, I represent continuity. All I have done and can do is tend the guttering flame; and if that flame sets the house on fire and burns down the City and the whole world, I guess that'll be my fault too.

All Love Excelling

Love God and do as you will
St Augustine

Today I'm supposed to be at the dedication ceremony for my father's statue in the Basilica. There's a seat reserved for me in the front row, wedged in between the Prince Regent and the Minister of the Interior. After the show there's going to be a procession through the streets to the palace, where the Prince will make me a Knight Companion of the Order of the Teardrop, the highest honour he can bestow. I won't be there. I've sent a note saying I've got food poisoning or the flu or something. Instead, I'm sitting down and writing this. I see no alternative.

To make matters worse, yesterday I had a visitor. I try not to see people if I can help it, but she insisted; she started yelling and sobbing, and the porter hates scenes so he caved in and let her come up. I opened my door and she burst in, tears rolling down her cheeks, and fell at my feet.

I'd never seen her before in my life; somewhere between thirty-five and sixty, grey hair in a tight bun, face eroded by experience like the carvings over the front door of the cathedral.

She was wearing one of those gowns they hand out at the Refuge; my father designed them himself. "Please get up," I said, but she took no notice. She had a cloth bag, from which she produced a small jug, a basin and a tiny bottle of cheap scented oil. My heart sank. Here we go again, I thought. She was going to wash my feet, if it was the last thing she did, and I knew there was nothing I could do to stop her.

It happened to my father all the time. You have to let them, he told me, it means so much to them. My brothers and I used to make jokes about it, among ourselves. We pretended we could hear squelching noises whenever my father approached. We speculated on the possibility of his feet eventually becoming webbed, on account of spending so much time in water. Then, as we got older, our feet started getting washed too. The first time it happened to me was when I was at school. This mad-looking female slipped past the doorkeeper and made a beeline straight at me, when I was sitting under the cherry tree in the middle of the Old Quad, surrounded by the clique of really cool friends I'd gradually and with infinite effort managed to acquire, like the speck of grit in the core of a pearl. They laughed—I was the colour of beetroot—and then they stopped laughing, as the mad woman unbuckled my sandal and gripped my left foot in her horny hand while pouring the water into the basin with her right. It wasn't funny any more, it was uncomfortable and indecent, and they couldn't tell who should be ashamed, them or me. That was the end of my brief membership of the cool gang. After that, I was either a saint or a leper or both, and nobody wanted to talk to me in case it was catching.

The same thing happened to my brothers, of course, to the point where we all had to be taken out of school and taught at home. I remember the carriage coming to fetch me. It shouldn't have driven right into the Quad, but nobody had told the coachman that. The coach was a gift from the Prince to my father, so it had the royal livery painted on the doors. It stopped right in the middle of the yard, next to that bloody tree, and I had to walk a hundred yards from the dormitory, with every kid and every teacher watching me in dead silence. These things shouldn't matter, but they do.

The day before I was taken home, my father preached to a hundred thousand people under the arches of the Aqueduct of Hilarion. Then he healed the sick, about a thousand of them, and handed out food and clothing to the poor. They say that when the supplies ran out—there'd been the usual balls-up at the warehouse, or one of the hauliers was double-booked and didn't send enough wagons—my father told his people to gather up all the empty jars and barrels and put them back on the carts, and suddenly they found they were full again, and everybody in the crowd took home as much food as they could carry, and there was still a whole lot left over, which had to go back to the depot. I don't doubt it for a moment. That sort of thing happened all the time when I was a kid, and we got used to it.

Let me state for the record that I've never healed the sick, or parted the sea, or turned sand into flour or quelled so much as a light shower. Occasionally I've dropped a coin in somebody's hat—pure instinctive reflex, I try to tell myself, a perfectly normal human reaction to the sight of suffering and nothing to get concerned about, but afterwards I feel really bad about it. I tell myself that nothing is inevitable, my own conduct has always been entirely above reproach, there's nothing anywhere in writing, everybody makes his own bargain and besides, it's all over now and I survived. The more I say it, the less I believe it, so please don't ask me to say it again.

YOU CAN DO all right for yourself in the scented oil business these days, ever since my father started his ministry. Traditionally it was a high-end trade, concentrating on small quantities of best quality product selling for silly money. Now it's all about bulk and how tight you can shave your margins. If you care to do the math—how many feet can be washed per gallon of significantly diluted oil, how many gallons in an industry-standard jar (fifty-four, if you're interested), how many jars can you cram on board one of the big purpose-built freighters (1,008)—it's big business, no doubt about it, a substantial contribution to the economy, a substantial drain on the reserves of hard currency.

My father came from a long line of priests. His father's family had been village pastors in the Mesoge for nine generations, in a region where the ministry is just another trade, and father follows son because that's just how it is. Back then, of course, priests weren't supposed to marry, but either the memo about that never percolated through to the Mesoge or else it was filed in an old flower-pot along with all the rest of the Government laws and forgotten about.

But my grandfather was different. As soon as this became impossible to ignore, the local squire got up a subscription to pay for him to go to the seminary, and in due course he passed out top of his year and was ordained by St Gelasius himself. Immediately thereafter he was appointed Reader in doctrine and doxology at the Studium and started writing his magnum opus, *Types of Ethical Theory,* which was to occupy him for the rest of his life. He also set about getting himself a wife. Having first demolished the theological foundations of clerical celibacy in one short, devastating paper, he made a list of suitable families (wealthy but not aristocratic, pious and doctrinally above reproach) and made enquiries about their daughters. One family fitted the bill exactly. The only drawback was that their daughter was nine years old, and my grandfather was twenty-seven. Typically, he turned this setback into an opportunity, and devoted a considerable portion of his valuable time to educating his prospective bride so that, in nine years' time, she would be perfectly prepared to carry out her duties as his wife. It also gave him time to get the ban on clerical marriage overturned, and for people to get used to the idea of married priests—my grandfather hated to be conspicuous.

That was to prove unfortunate, because there never was a more conspicuous son than my father. He started off acceptably enough: a distinguished five years at the Studium, though he only came third out of five hundred in his year; a good deaconate in a high-class City parish, followed swiftly by a curacy, followed by a sideways move to a chaplaincy at the palace which led to other preferments—He was doing all the right things, and it seemed as inevitable as night following day that he'd be a dean by age thirty, precentor at thirty-five, and then either a City monastery or a provincial see, leading ultimately to one of the five patriarchal chairs and a chance at the Big Red Hat five years or so before he died. His life, like my grandmother's, seemed to have been built and furnished for him, right down to the doorknobs and the scatter-cushions, and all he had to do was accept it gracefully and be properly grateful.

My father heard the call in the same year that I was born. I was the youngest of six; three elder brothers, then two sisters, then me. My father was forty-two years old, principal of the Imperial Seminary, chancellor of the Wardrobe and *ex officio* dean of the palace, all three of them key stepping-stones on the traditional alternative path to a diocese; probably Aelia, because it was currently occupied by a ninety-year-old, but possibly Mezentia—the incumbent, a mere boy of sixty-eight, had a weak heart and could pop off at any moment... Forty-two was rather young, of course, but Convocation had been making noises for some time about appointing younger men to the higher offices, so the timing was exactly right.

Everybody knows what happened that night: the road to Ap' Escatoy, the blinding light, the voice that no one else could hear, the three days hovering between life and death, the reawakening, the early miracles. My eldest brother was a freshman at the Studium when it happened, and for him it meant a summons to the rector's office. There's been an accident, he was told, your father's still alive and the doctors are hopeful, but it might be a good idea if you went there straight away, just in case. My other brothers were still at home with my mother and sisters. They followed on in a carriage paid for by the Seminary, and by the time they got there, everything had changed. The forty days that shook the world had already begun, although of course they weren't to know that. My younger sister told me once that after my mother had seen him, she came out with her face as white as a sheet, and told them all that Daddy had had a bad accident and they must all be very patient and understanding with him, because he wasn't at all well. It might seem that he was acting very oddly, but they mustn't worry, because that was just the illness and he'd get better soon.

I OWN A box, which I've never opened. It's the most gorgeous thing you ever saw. It's also worth a lot of money, which is a nuisance. I managed to get an exemption from the Revenue on the grounds of exceptional religious and cultural importance, so I don't have to pay tax on it, but there's always the lurking dread that someone'll break in and steal it, and quite possibly smash my head in while he's at it. After all, everybody knows I've got it, as the only surviving heir, and I can't afford armed guards or expensive Mezentine locks or grills on the windows. For two pins I'd give it to the nation and let them have the worry and the expense, except for the danger, albeit infinitesimally small, that someone might take it into his head to open it and look at what's inside; and that, of course, would never do. Inside the box is the original contract, or at least my father's copy of it. I really ought to put the wretched thing on the fire, except I'm not sure it would burn.

I'M FINDING THIS hard to write. I meant it to be a sort of vicarious confession, the one my father should've made but obviously never did. Instead, it wants to be—I don't actually know at this point. A narrative of my father's ministry, even if it's scrupulously accurate and I leave out anything that's not attested to by a wagonload of reliable witnesses, would just be another gospel, and there's plenty of them already. A personal history, what it was like being a small kid when your dad was out every day curing lepers, raising the dead, jumping off temple roofs and floating gently to earth supported by the arms and wings of invisible angels—The fact is, I witnessed none of his major stunts. My brothers saw a few, and my younger sister claimed she'd seen the walking-stick turn into a snake when he bashed it against the cathedral door, but I suspect she only said that because she hated being left out. My elder sister was occasionally allowed to change the bandages on his hands and feet, and said the stigmata were real wounds; brownish scabs of dried blood overlying the raw unhealed flesh beneath, and the skin swollen and raw round the edges, and it was all real because one time she got blood on the cuffs of her best party frock, and her mother sent her to bed without any supper. I asked her more than once if she thought he'd inflicted those wounds on himself, and she said no, absolutely not. After you'd made a hole like that in one hand, there was no way you could use it to hold a spike to impale the other hand. But I was too young to remember anything like that, even if my mother had been mad enough to risk the crush in the streets, let alone take a babe in arms along with her. So I'll leave all that stuff out, since there's nothing new or useful I can add to what's already been written, and stick to what I actually saw and heard. Therefore this record will be much more about my brothers and sisters and mother than my father. To be honest, I hardly knew him at all when I was growing up, and after that—Well.

I WAS ONLY six when my eldest brother died. He'd been helping out at the fever hospital, feeding and washing the patients who were too weak to help themselves, carrying sacks of charcoal from the store to the boiler room, chopping onions and garlic in the kitchen, making himself useful. He caught the fever. It wasn't supposed to be particularly dangerous to young people. Rather than take up bed space there, he came home, and my mother made him chicken soup. By the early hours of the morning, it was pretty clear he wasn't going to make it. My father knelt beside him as he died. They prayed together, and then a look of great joy came over my brother's face. Look, he said, trying to point at something on the opposite wall, and then he died.

I hardly knew him. He'd been away most of my life, at the Studium (he was the valedictorian in his year) and then at the Golden Horn, where he did his novitiate while researching his thesis on the Dual Procession of the Divine Essence. My father told me later that Martial's death was the worst thing that ever happened. He'd been relying on him to continue the mission; it was logical and inevitable, because Martial was a far better man than he could ever be: wiser, more perceptive, a much better theologian, with a mind strong enough to hold the truth of the message without crumpling or bursting; truly compassionate, completely untroubled by doubt, totally committed to the mission. In fact, until he closed his eyes for him, my father was convinced that Martial was the Messiah and he himself was simply there to lay the foundations and announce his coming. According to my sister Ancyra, after Martial died he shut himself up in his study for nine days, with the door bolted on the inside and the shutters closed. My mother was scared out of her wits. She was afraid he'd caught the fever from Martial and had died in there; my brother Eudo says he saw her on the eighth day, down on her hands and knees, sniffing at the crack under the door for any hint of putrefaction. She'd more or less made up her mind to send for men with prybars and big hammers when the door opened and my father came out, looking like death warmed up but (this detail is vouched for by my sister Volutis, who wouldn't have made it up) smelling perfectly fresh and with no trace of stubble on his chin, even after nine days with no razor. He'd been mistaken, he announced. Martial hadn't been the promised redeemer after all, so that meant he himself must be. According to my mother he sounded surprised and confused when he said it, stating a fact that he found hard to believe yet knew to be true. The next day, after burying Martial in an unmarked grave in the fever cemetery, he performed the miracle of the parting of Lake Abro, walking dryshod across the lake bed from Dremans to Beal Regard with the water heaped up on either side of him like dark green snowdrifts. I didn't see that, of course. I was in bed, sick with the measles.

I asked him once; why didn't you cure Martial, the way you cured all those hundreds and thousands of other people who were sick with the fever? And you raised four people, or was it five, from the dead; why not your own son? He looked at me like he didn't understand the question, and then we talked about something else.

THIS ISN'T GETTING us anywhere. You know all about Martial, just like you know all about my father, or you think you do. I haven't told you anything you can't read about somewhere else. I feel like I'm wasting my time, and yours.

So I think we'll have to go back to the point immediately after the forty days, when for a while it seemed as though the power had left him. He'd tried to cure the man with the withered hand, and it hadn't worked. Then the mysterious sword appeared, driven up to its hilt into the marble of the high altar in the Golden Horn chapel, and he'd tried to pull it out and failed. At the time, my mother told me, he didn't seem unduly concerned. The power had come upon him, he said, and for a while he'd had it and used it joyfully, and then it left him; blessed be the name of the Lord. It was God's way of demonstrating that His was the kingdom, the power and the glory; that He could bestow it on whoever He chose, and then take it away again just as easily, which was surely the point of the exercise. Otherwise, people might start worshipping the agent instead of the principal, the monkey rather than the organ-grinder. He was secretly relieved, he told my mother, that it was all over and he could go back to being himself again. It had been wonderful, of course, but he couldn't have kept going like that, any more than a candle can give light indefinitely. He was, after all, only human.

Years later I asked him about that too. No, he told me, the relief was absolutely genuine. The truth of the matter was, all through the forty days he'd been scared stiff. He had no idea what was happening to him, or exactly what the power was, or what he was supposed to do with it. It hadn't come, he told me, with a book of instructions, or sealed orders, or a manifesto or a mission statement. It just turned up, like opening your door one morning to find a newly born baby in a basket on the doorstep. So he'd done what he thought was right. He'd helped people and cured people and saved people, and while he was doing it he gave a sort of commentary, explaining why being kind to those less fortunate than yourself is a good thing and probably what we were put on earth to do. But all through the experience he was tortured with doubt and worry; was that all he was supposed to be doing, or should he be doing more? Should he use the power to change the way society worked? Should he be driving the emperor from his throne, slaughtering the provincial aristocracy and proclaiming the Kingdom of Heaven on Earth? Should he be leading the true believers against the infidels and the heretics? If so, could he blast their armies with thunderbolts the way a storm flattens a field of standing corn? He had no idea if he could unless he tried, but he couldn't bring himself to, or he was too busy and never got round to it. Afterwards, he couldn't help wondering if the power had been taken away from him because he'd done the wrong things with it, or not done the right things, or frittered it away in trivial acts of compassion when he should have been tearing down all the works of human hands and rebuilding with the hands of God. Was he like the peasant in the fairy story, who meets an angel who promises to grant him three wishes; so he asks for a slice of cheese, and then he asks for a pint of beer, and then he asks for another slice of cheese.

Anyway, that's the moment I've chosen as the fulcrum, the turning-point, whatever you care to call it. A line could've been drawn there. Something extraordinary had happened and obviously it was bound to have far-reaching consequences, but that was the point at which it could've been contained—a story with a beginning, a middle and an end, if you like, or an outbreak that ran its course and then died away, leaving dead bodies stacked like cordwood but no further reported cases. And here, it goes without saying, I'm unable to cite my sources or quote my eye-witnesses, because the only evidence I can offer is private conversations between my father and myself, many years later; and maybe he wasn't telling the truth, or maybe he told me what he believed was true but it wasn't, or maybe I dreamed the whole thing after eating Scona cheese last thing at night, and the dream was so vivid I can't distinguish it from reality. There may be valid corroborative evidence in that exquisite wooden box I told you about, but it can stay there as far as I'm concerned. Actually, it's years since I last saw the key to the box, and for all I know I don't have it any more.

Let's go back to where we're still on relatively solid ground. After the forty days, my father appeared to have lost the power, and to begin with he accepted that and was ready and willing to move on. He could look back at thousands of lives saved or improved, a genuine and lasting revival of faith, a sea change in attitudes. It was over, it had been glorious while it lasted, but he was better now.

But other people didn't see it that way. The hopelessly and chronically sick still hung about outside the main gate, or shouldered their way past the porter and camped out on the sacrosanct grass of New Quad, demanding (no other word for it) to be healed and made whole. It wasn't fair, they said. A few days ago, he'd have healed them, so why not now? It was a lottery, sheer chance. If they'd turned up a week ago, everything would've been fine, but it hadn't been possible or convenient for them to come last week. But they were here now, and the rules hadn't changed. They were the deserving sick and the deserving poor, and they knew their rights. Or had the whole thing been a put-up job, a stunt, a cruel hoax? Come to think of it, had anybody actually witnessed all these so-called miracles, and if so, where were the sworn affidavits? And even if there were witnesses, wasn't it far more likely that arrangements had been made, money had changed hands and it was all a fraud; and nobody could actually put their finger on how exactly my father was making a fortune out of all this, or show a single scrap of evidence that he was, but that didn't mean he wasn't; it was only a matter of time before the whole sordid affair was dragged out into the light, and then there'd be trouble, you could bet your life on it. The revelations, when they came, whatever they proved to be, would shake the established church to its foundations and lead to massive upheavals at every level of society—

"That's people for you," one of my father's colleagues told him. "I really don't see why you bother with them." Wise words, which my father of course ignored. All he could see was that everything he'd achieved during the forty days was in danger of slipping away, being spoiled, turning from gold to shit by some sort of horrible reverse alchemy, and instead of things being better because of what he'd done, they'd be worse.

So, according to the authorised version, he shut himself up in his study and prayed for three days and three nights, and his prayers were heard and the power came back. Whether that counted as a miracle is an interesting point, hotly debated by academics; Lusinans confidently lists it as my father's forty-third miracle in his *General Catalogue*, which is of course an approved document and therefore (theoretically) orthodox doctrine, but both Renthinus and Prosper of Schanz—risking anathema, so they must be pretty sure of their facts—classify it as an epiphany rather than a miracle. Not that it matters particularly. If it's a miracle, the officiating priest wears a red stole on the anniversary feast-day, if it's an epiphany, he wears blue instead. If you're smart and you don't want to commit yourself, you can always opt for purple.

My sister Volutis once told me that while Dad was in his study praying for the return of his powers, she happened to be passing the locked and bolted door, and she reckoned she heard voices. Note the plural: voices, not voice. One voice; no big deal. My father often prayed aloud when he was on his own, and when he had a big speech or address coming up, he liked to rehearse beforehand—he had a slight stammer, and running through what he was going to say a few times helped a lot. But Volutis definitely said voices, implying that he was talking to somebody; somebody, moreover, who was actually there and talked back. Then it must've been God, I told her, obviously. No, she said, she didn't think so, or else if God sounded like that, she was going to have to revise some of her most deeply-held preconceptions. So what did this other person sound like, I asked her: man or woman, old or young, received pronunciation or regional accent—? She frowned and said she wasn't sure. I pointed out that the categories I'd mentioned were hardly grey areas, but she repeated, she didn't really know, and we left it at that, because she'd decided that I didn't believe her, which entitled her to take offence.

When you look at it closely and dispassionately, the second wave or tranche of miracles was significantly different from the first. For a start, the miracles he performed during the forty days were much more varied. The second wave was almost exclusively healing the sick and feeding the poor, but the first lot, the stuff he did during the forty days, was half useful and constructive things, half—well, stunts, really. Walking on water, walking through fire, jumping off tall buildings, turning walking-sticks into snakes and rivers into torrents of wine or blood—quite rightly, the received interpretation is that these were done to announce that he was here and he'd arrived, to grab people's attention and make them listen to what he had to say. And yes, obviously that was legitimate, something that had to be done. Rescue a kid from a burning building and you save one life. Walk through a curtain of fire without a single hair being singed, with five hundred people watching, and you save five hundred souls straight off and fifty thousand shortly afterwards, once word's had a chance to get about.

The qualitative difference between the first and second waves is, therefore, easily explained, which is probably why the commentators have by and large seen no need to look into it in greater depth. Those of us who were there, so to speak, at ground zero probably had no better idea than anyone else of what the true significance really was. Growing up with a father who went to work every day healing the sick—There were doctors' sons at my school, and their fathers were in more or less the same line of work, so what of it? Also, when I started at school my brother Eudo was still there, a sixth-former and unusually tall and strong for his age, so either witty remarks about our father didn't happen or we didn't get to hear them. Really it was only when the foot-washing thing (see above) started to get out of hand that Dad's profession or vocation began to impact in any serious way on our everyday lives. That and Martial's death, of course, but at that point there was absolutely no reason to connect the two in any way.

When Martial died, we all assumed that Ardorus would take his place as deputy-in-chief and heir apparent. Certainly that was what my father thought. Up to that point, Ardorus had been a rather colourless individual. I don't mean that he was bland or lacking in character or boring or anything like that. It was more that he hadn't decided yet what or who he was going to be. My sister Volutis put it rather well. Imagine, she said, a pint of water, flowing in a river. You could scoop it up and pour it into a wineglass, in which case it would be a sort of inverted bell shape; or you could pour it out into a dish, in which case it would be shallow and flat; or a jug, in which case it would end up squat and nearly spherical. That was Ardorus, while Martial was still alive. It was as though he was waiting to see what Martial would turn into, so that he could be something quite different. Once Martial died, however, he couldn't just be his reflection in a distorting mirror; he had to make up his mind and choose. Dad assumed he'd choose to be a replacement Martial. Ardorus had other ideas.

There was no hint of rebellion in his choice, no defiance or spite. That would've been just another form of reflection, equal but opposite; shaped and influenced by his father just as much as Martial had been, just in a different vector. Instead, Ardorus chose to be respectful and loving but *different*. He didn't reject what his father stood for. He ignored it, as though it wasn't there and none of it had happened. It was a bit like international diplomacy, where countries refuse to recognise regimes they don't approve of, even though it's patently obvious that there they are, big as life and twice as ugly. Ardorus didn't recognise that there was anything unusual or odd about how my father made his living; he was a priest and an academic, which was fine and perfectly normal, admirable too, in its own way, but Ardorus wasn't going to follow in those particular footsteps, thanks all the same. So when he turned sixteen he joined the palace secretariat as a junior clerk, with a view to being Controller of the Wardrobe by the time he was thirty.

My father found his choice baffling, like a paragraph in a language he didn't know. He was angry and hurt, but it never occurred to him to give Ardorus a hard time about his choice. There were no arguments or scenes. Instead, my father pretended he didn't know what Ardorus did in the daytime and didn't ask. When my brother came home at night, conversation in our house changed completely. We couldn't talk about religion or doctrine or ethics or any of the things my father lived for, and we couldn't discuss current affairs or the government or politics, because Ardorus quickly became as completely absorbed in his work as Dad was in his. Books and art and music were out, because to my father, all that side of things only existed as an adjunct to faith. That just left everyday domestic trivia, in which none of us ever had the slightest interest. So we talked about anchovy sauce and the ants' nest under the step in the pantry and what was causing the damp patch under the scullery window and the ridiculous price they were asking for silver polish these days. It was actually rather interesting to observe the seven finest minds of their generation concentrating their ferocious powers of analysis and problem-solving on what to do about a loose slate on the roof or a missing slipper—and since there was an unspoken but unbreakable law against arguing or disagreement of any sort at the dinner table, all of those extraordinary summit conferences were unrelentingly positive and constructive, the challenge being to agree with everything everybody said, however idiotic, and incorporate it in your own proposed scheme of action… One side-effect was that we had the most orderly and best-maintained house in the City, apart from one particular grumble in the plumbing, which we never managed to get to the bottom of. Ardorus always swore blind that it was the Holy Ghost, curled up fast asleep in the water-pipes and snoring, and the reason why we couldn't fix the noise was because the Holy Ghost is by definition ineffable and can only be perceived by faith, so the only way to make it go away was to believe in it implicitly. My father loved that idea. He always said that the worst possible blasphemy was to assume that God can't take a joke.

My elder sister Ancyra was the musical one in our family. She played the harp, the flute and the violin, and she wrote the tunes to most of my father's hymns and canticles. Women weren't supposed to be able to do that sort of thing in those days; it was my sister who proved they could. My father made a point of telling everybody that his daughter wrote his tunes for him, which meant nobody could ignore the fact that all that beautiful music, which nobody could help adoring, had been composed by a girl... A few blowhards insisted she could only do it because the Spirit of the Lord was upon her, but it wasn't long before other women started daring to admit that they could write music too, and now we've got Pamphile and Symothis and Hildegard, and all thanks to my sister and my dad.

Ancyra and my mother didn't always see eye to eye. If you were to ask me what they fell out about, I'd be hard put to it to tell you, since it seemed to me that they thought very much alike about nearly everything. Often it was a case of not being able to take Yes for an answer. When they'd contrived to get in a really monumental huff with each other, they'd take the dispute to my father for arbitration, and he'd point out that there was no quarrel, because both of them were saying the same thing in the same way, and there was no difference between them whatsoever—Whereupon they'd both get furiously angry with him for not understanding, and their common cause against him reconciled their argument immediately, and they were once again one soul shared by two bodies. The only person Ancyra ever had genuine differences of opinion with was my brother Eudo, but I can't ever remember a cross word between them. They agreed to disagree, to the point where the miasma of sweetness and light that surrounded them was practically toxic.

I was fifteen when Ancyra died. She'd gone out to the Window—if you don't know the City, it's that point where Florian the Great cut a pass in the mountains for the road to go through, and you look down on the City from above, spread out before you like a banquet. It was a favourite place for well-bred young ladies to sit and sketch on fine summer mornings, when the light was from the east, and that morning was as fine as any other, but Ancyra caught a chill, which turned into a fever, and she died. She was twenty-five.

She was a plain girl—nobody in our family's good-looking except my father and me—squat and chunky, with a round face like my mother's. Everybody loved her. She had plenty of offers, in spite of the fact that she was my father's daughter (would you want the Messiah as your father-in-law?) but she simply couldn't be bothered; she had ever so many friends, all girls of her own age, and men didn't interest her in the least. She died halfway through composing her second symphony. The first movement is complete—you know that, because you'll have heard it. She'd sketched out the second movement but hadn't started the scoring and orchestration. Symothis begged my father to be allowed to complete it, but he wouldn't let her. In fact, he burned the manuscript, because she'd asked him to, just before she died.

Ancyra's death hit us all much harder than Martial's. There was something about Martial that made sense; too good for this world, maybe. People said that it was the price my father had to pay for the gift of ministry, and at times I think we almost believed it. Besides—Martial was a wonderful person, genuinely good and kind and everybody loved him, but after he was gone the world somehow managed to continue. We weren't all suddenly conscious of a hole, big enough to blot out the sun, where he used to be. Not so with Ancyra. It was as though a colour had been removed from the spectrum—blue, say—and every shade of blue and purple and all the other colours that have a bit of blue in them suddenly weren't there any more. Instead there were outlines, waiting to be filled in, but there was nothing to fill them in with apart from rapidly dwindling memories and the inescapable knowledge that something was missing.

About a month after Ancyra died, I remember my mother and father having a blazing row. I was upstairs, and the yelling was so loud I didn't dare come out of my room, but Eudo was in the study and Volutis was sitting outside in the garden, and they both reckoned they heard enough to get the gist of it.

By way of context; this would've been shortly after my father cured the thirty-six lepers and immediately before he healed the stonemason who fell off a roof and broke his neck. That means he'd just recently preached the Sermon at the Fountainhead and the parable of the five foolish courtiers, but probably not the prophecy of the rebuilding of the Temple—the truth is, I lose track of when all these things were supposed to have happened, and the forests of scholarly commentaries don't help at all. When Frontinus and Egenhard assure me in black and white with illuminated capitals that the prophecy was delivered on the same day as the cleansing of the poisoned well, I really don't want to contradict them on the basis of my own fallible memory, even though I was actually there—I think. I'm not cut out to be a witness. When stupendous things happen, I have a knack of thinking about something else or looking the other way; and then I turn round and ask someone, *What's going on?* and they tell me…

Eudo reckoned my mother started the argument, and that sounds right. My father didn't start quarrels. He created the circumstances whereby quarrels happened but never actually spoke the first angry word; a bit like a canny general who gets there first, digs in, cuts all the bridges and clears the brushwood away from the road to give a clear field of fire, then waits to be attacked. Volutis on the other hand was adamant that my father was the one who lost his temper, and she backed up her claim by stating that she heard his side of the opening salvoes and not hers because he was shouting and she was talking quite normally. That's a convincing bit of circumstantial detail, so I leave it to you to decide for yourself.

Anyway: my mother was saying that Ancyra's death was all my father's fault. He was shocked and appalled, which I think is fair enough, because that's not the sort of thing you say, even if it's true; but according to Eudo (Volutis' version was subtly different at this point) he didn't deny it. He just kept on and on, saying it was necessary and it was God's will and those who die in the Faith are better off than the living—now that bit definitely rings true, because he said that sort of thing all the time, though whether he said it on that particular occasion is another matter, I suppose. But it's plausible enough, because it's just the sort of thing that would've made my mother really angry, enough to have a stand-up slanging match with my father and not care who heard it, which under normal circumstances she'd never have dreamt of doing.

In Eudo's version she offered nothing to support her statement; she just said *it was all your fault,* and left it at that. Volutis, on the other hand, reckoned she said something, or he said something, about some kind of bargain. I couldn't get her to be more specific, because she was pretty emotional when she told me, and by that point it was only possible to keep her lucid for so long, and then she'd be off on one of her wild hysterical sleigh-rides where she'd say more or less anything... Her testimony wasn't exactly blue-chip at the best of times, and this definitely wasn't one of them. But any scholar will tell you that you can't always discount something just because it comes from an unreliable source. It could be completely made up, or it could be the wrong end of the stick; in which case, it's the scholar's job to use the wrong end to extrapolate what the right end could have been. Accordingly, I'm inclined to believe that the word bargain, or a synonym or words to that effect, was actually used by one or both of them on that occasion.

YOU'VE UNDOUBTEDLY HEARD the story of the celebrated headless chicken of Ana Strouthoe; you know, the one that lived for three years after its head was cut off, and never failed to lay at least one egg a day. I think the first reference to it is in one of the pastoral letters of St Auxentian, where he mentions it in passing as something his reader is bound to be familiar with so he doesn't bother going into details. Then it crops up in Ermanaric's third missionary journey, and then you get the full-blown account in Corbo's Life of Ducatian, where the chicken is the property of the Duke of Neryotis, and St Gossa miraculously finds the missing head under her pillow and puts it back on the chicken.

It'd be going too far to say that after Ancyra died my father was that headless chicken. If it had an effect on his ministry, it was to urge him on to greater efforts; in which case, you'd have to amend the story so that before its head was cut off the chicken laid one egg a day, and after its decapitation it always laid two. The headless part, however, is more or less apt. Not long after Ancyra died, Ardorus moved out and started renting a house in the Rookeries, ostensibly so as to be nearer to his place of work, and Eudo graduated from the Studium and went to live in Old Town (he didn't bother trying to find a pretext, he just went). That left my father, my mother, Volutis and me, and I was at home all day because I couldn't go to school any more on account of the foot-washing and so on and so forth.

It was a curious set-up to say the least. Previously our house had been like a barrel filled with cats and dogs, with the lid shut tight. Now someone had removed the cats, leaving only the dogs. It was quieter, that was for sure, but the noise most noticeable by its absence was laughter. One thing nobody appreciates is that my father had a sense of humour. It was rather a blunt instrument—he was a bludgeon in a cupboard full of rapiers—and sometimes it took him a while to get the point, and sometimes he never got it at all. But we all made jokes, pretty much all the time when we weren't deep in pits of black depression. We spoke comedy like a language—a bit like Aelian, which is the only language (so they say) where it's possible to express certain philosophical concepts in words. A lot of what we had to say to each other could only be communicated, or safely communicated, in joke form. Once Ancyra died and my surviving brothers moved out, the atmosphere changed completely. To continue with the image, we were now a bunch of people all trying to talk to each other in a language we just about understood but weren't really fluent in.

That was about the time—I'm sorry my grasp of chronology is so vague. Because my father's life has been so closely examined and minutely documented—people make their livings doing that sort of thing, which is extraordinary, when you think about it—I really ought to be able to be more precise. If I want to know what he was doing at a certain time on a certain day, I don't have to rely on my rapidly failing memory, I can look it up in a book, a choice of books; I can read ten learned papers on the subject, all of them explaining in patient detail why the other nine are wrong. The authors of these papers are, of course, an unmitigated pest. It got to the point (about five years ago) where they took to camping out under my window, and I had to have bolts fitted on the inside of my door. The nuisance has abated somewhat, ever since I poured a kettleful of boiling water over the heads of six Fellows of the Imperial College of Theology who were trying to climb the drainpipe, but even now, if I want to go down into the town to buy a pair of shoelaces, I have to leave the house via the cellars and scramble up the coal chute.

Regrettably—and I hope the scholars read this—the more I try to form my memories into a coherent narrative, the more jumbled they get. Accordingly I try not to, in the hope that eventually the muddy water will settle down and clear and I'll be able to see the past again. Not that I want to particularly, but I guess it's a sort of duty.

So: that was about the time when Eudo made his terrible decision. He didn't tell any of us about it, not even Ardorus. He simply turned up one day—we hadn't seen him for weeks—and announced that he'd seen the light and converted to the Left Hand, and if we wanted to watch him being ordained as a priest of the Eternal Flame we were welcome to come along to the Fire Temple in Northgate at noon the day after tomorrow, though if we chose not to he'd quite understand. Then he turned on his heel and stalked out of the house, and none of us except me ever set eyes on him again.

We all reacted in our different ways. My father locked himself in his study, and we could hear him quite plainly, sobbing like a child and praying for his son's immortal soul, now irrevocably damned for all eternity. Volutis turned on my mother, as if it was all her fault, and said, "How could he be so bloody *selfish?*" My mother, who'd gone as white as a sheet, immediately started defending her son and his right to choose with all the ferocity at her command (and that was a lot of ferocity)… My first thought was how on earth I was going to break the news to Ardorus. It'd be my job, I knew that without having to be told, and he'd be livid—the scandal of it, his own brother turning heathen on him, just when he had the Secretaryship of the Standing Committee on Drains and Aqueducts practically sewn up; it had to be deliberate sabotage, there was no other possible explanation, and what had he ever done to deserve such vicious, reckless hatred?

After that, nobody was talking to Eudo except me, and nobody was talking to me because I was talking to Eudo, and Eudo didn't want to talk to me because nothing anybody could possibly say would induce him to change his mind—

"I don't want to change your stupid mind," I pointed out. "I couldn't give a flying fuck about your mind, or your soul, for that matter. As far as I'm concerned, if you've joined the Fire-Botherers, they have my sympathy, and that's that. I just thought, you're still my brother, and maybe you might want to talk about it."

He looked at me. "Talk about what?"

Fine. That was Eudo. "You do realise," I said, "your mother and your sister are tearing each other to shreds about this. Mother hates what you've done every bit as much as Volutis does, but she'd die before she hears a word against you, so you can't hear yourself think for those two yelling and Dad sobbing and the dog barking its head off—"

"What do you think?" he asked me.

"About what?"

He rolled his eyes. "My decision," he said. "Do you think I've done the right thing in following my conscience?"

I opened my mouth and shut it again. "I don't think anything," I said. "All I'm concerned about is the torrent of shit you've unleashed on our family."

"Mphm." He nodded vaguely. Clearly I was only concerned with trivia, not the real issue, and therefore I was of no further interest to him.

It was only to be expected that the apostasy of the prophet's son would sent hundreds of people flocking to the Fire Temple, just so they could have a good laugh. What nobody had anticipated was that Eudo would turn out to be such an outstanding preacher. When I heard what people were saying I couldn't resist, even though I knew what it'd do to the family if they ever found out; I borrowed the gardener's oldest coat and the stable-boy's hat, and went and stood at the back, where there was barely room to breathe because of all the fanatical new converts. I have to say, I never knew Eudo had it in him. I knew he was smart, very clever indeed, because he was one of us and we're all so fucking brilliant. I took all that for granted, naturally. But he wasn't just clever, he was magnificent. I was rooted to the spot (I seem to recall there was a blacksmith in heavy work boots standing on my toe) and for a while I forgot he was my brother and that I'd known him all my life, and that my father was the Messiah, with all those miracles to prove it. For two pins I'd have converted there and then, and had my head shaved and put my name down for circumcision and applied to join a Lodge, if I hadn't known for a fact at the back of my mind that it was all dogshit and the eternal Flame was just a few logs and a quick fumble with a tinderbox.

My sister Volutis, on the other hand, never went near the Fire Temple or a hundred yards this side of Northgate. She was convinced that Eudo had been possessed by a demon, as an act of spite against my father, and it was now his duty to cast the demon out and restore his son to health. I don't think my mother ever really believed in demons, even though Dad had evicted scores of them in front of irreproachably reliable witnesses, but she pounced on Volutis' theory as an eminently honourable compromise, which would allow face to be saved and everything eventually to drift back to normal. So she started nagging Dad about it, the moment he emerged from his study. She told him that I agreed with her and my sister (which I didn't) and it was utterly ridiculous for him to go around saving perfect strangers when his own flesh and blood was being polluted by the Common Enemy of Man.

The Prince Regent once described my mother as the cleverest woman in the empire, and for once he wasn't far wrong. When my father heard his call and started his ministry she quietly put away the book she'd been writing ever since she was a teenager—a history of music in the West, from Florian to the present day, I've read what there is of it and it's brilliant—and devoted herself to being the helpmeet of the prophet. That was far more important, she said, and it wasn't a duty, it was a privilege and a joy. She believed it, too. She could believe anything, if it helped her family. She absolutely believed that my father was the Promised One, sent by God to redeem His people from their sins and spread His word to the nations. But God was all very well, but compared to her family He couldn't reasonably expect to be a priority, now could He? That wouldn't be right, and He obviously understood that, otherwise He wouldn't be Him.

My father said he wasn't going to talk about it. My mother insisted. He left the room. She followed. It was a big house, but the supply of rooms wasn't infinite. After one complete circuit, Volutis joined the procession; then me, trying to get them all to be reasonable, which was actually the worst possible thing I could've done… And so we trailed round and round the house, three of us all talking at once, one of us deadly silent; under any other circumstances we'd all have realised how ridiculous it all was and collapsed laughing, in a heap, like puppies sleeping. But being ridiculous had turned into just another tribulation, and we ignored it. I think that when you reach that stage as a family, there's nothing left to do but bury the dead and euthanise the survivors. But I was only sixteen, so it wasn't up to me.

IT WAS EUDO who solved our problem for us, by dying. One of my father's fanatical disciples stabbed him to death on the steps of the Fire Temple. There were riots for three days. Eighteen thousand dead, the whole Northgate district burnt to the ground, the handful of surviving fire-worshippers rounded up and marched off to the coast for deportation to the Sashan Empire.

My father tried to stop it, of course, but the Prince wouldn't listen. So he went and stood on the Fire Temple steps, right where Eudo died, and commanded the soldiers to turn back; they stopped dead in their tracks, because they were all true believers, and the fire-worshippers started pelting them with roof-tiles and slabs of pavement, and thirty-odd soldiers were killed, and that was that. They brought my father home on a door with a huge gash on his head and two broken ribs, which mended overnight, and the next day he preached the Sermon of Blood, ending with the words, *Forgive them, Father, for they know not what they do,* and everybody was truly sorry but of course it was too late by then.

Ardorus was furiously angry with the lot of us. It was intolerable, he said. He'd worked really hard, he'd applied every last scrap of body, mind and soul, and finally the chairmanship of the Standing Committee on Graves & Monuments was practically within his grasp—and then this had to happen. The directors of the department took a dim view of men whose fathers and brothers caused riots. The best he could hope for now was an assistant governorship in one of the maritime provinces, and that would mean leaving the City, and once your back was turned in this game you might as well not exist. Our tomfoolery had condemned him to a pathetic existence in some backwater, border feuds and famine relief and incessant bargaining with foreigners and savages—It simply wasn't worth the candle. He was resigning from the Service and coming home, and if we didn't like that, we had nobody to blame but ourselves.

My mother was bitterly ashamed of herself. She'd caught herself thinking that if Eudo's death meant that Ardorus was coming home, maybe it wasn't so bad after all... She must be some kind of monster to think like that, she told me; what kind of mother loves one of her children more than the others? I don't think the news registered with my father at all. As for Volutis, I don't think any of us understood what was going through her mind any more. There are some places where nobody can follow.

"Of course he's the bloody Messiah," I remember Ardorus telling me once, when I was trying to make sense of things. "Nobody with half a brain could doubt that for a moment. But that's beside the point. What about us? We didn't ask to be involved. We're not the ones who'll get all the statues and icons, not that I'd want any of that rubbish, thank you ever so fucking much."

"But if he's the Messiah," I said—I was just eighteen—"surely that matters, doesn't it? And surely, like Mother says, it's a privilege—"

"You clown," Ardorus said. Then he forgave me and went on, "Yes, if it's God's will that our entire lives should be turned to shit because He's chosen our dad to be His rotten prophet, I guess that's fine and we've just got to put up with it, like plagues and wars and evil and all the other stuff that's not supposed to matter. But there's putting up with it and there's liking it, and I can do one but not the other. It's not fair, that's what it boils down to, and if there's one thing I can't be doing with, it's unfairness."

"I'm worried," I told him, "about Volutis."

He glared at me. "And that's another thing," he said. "Obviously, she's been possessed by a devil, that's obvious, plain as the nose on your face. Just like Mother said happened to Eudo, except this time it happens to be true. And does Dad do a blind thing about it? Of course not. And you know why? It's because it says in scripture somewhere, *he saved others, his own he could not save,* and he's more interested in fulfilling some stupid prophecy than casting a demon out of his own daughter. That's so monumentally selfish, I don't see how I can possibly ever forgive him for it."

That made me uncomfortable, because the same point had occurred to me. My father could exorcise demons with a flick of his finger or a twitch of his eyebrows; he didn't even need to be there, he could do it remotely. He could cure sickness too, and raise the dead, but Martial had died, and Ancyra and Eudo, and now Volutis was spending more and more time in her room with the door bolted on the inside; and the cut on my mother's face hadn't been an accident, no matter what she said. I sincerely didn't believe the prophecy had anything to do with his refusal to help his own children, but if that wasn't the reason, what in God's name could it be?

If it wasn't for the fact that I've seen devils being cast out, I don't think I'd believe in them. It's an unforgettable sight. The first one I saw (it was the woman with the cleft palate, if you're interested; Lenseric 44 or Euthus & Ioannis 67A, depending on which system you use) crawled out through the old woman's nose. It was as big as my hand, and to this day I can't understand why the skin and bone didn't burst as it forced its way through the nostril. But when you think what happens at childbirth, I guess it's not so improbable after all.

But devils are hard to believe in because they're *unnecessary*... By which I mean you don't need devils to account for what happens to some people, like my sister. She's in all the standard references as a demonic possession, but I have my doubts. I think being my father's daughter was quite enough on its own.

Your eyebrow just shot up. Come off it, you're saying, you're your father's son and you didn't try and cut your mother's throat with a bit of broken jug, or set fire to the linen chest, or appear one morning in Victory Square stark naked and covered in self-inflicted gashes. True; but I've always been what my brother Ardorus used to call a stolid sort of a swine, meaning that I don't feel or think particularly deeply. I let things skate off me, like a razor off glass. But Volutis was much smarter than me, and infinitely more sensitive. She had my mother's mind and my father's heart; and with blessings like those, who needs demons?

She also had one other thing that I conspicuously lack, namely the ability to love properly. And she loved her parents and her siblings, the way I never could, so when they started dying, she started haemorrhaging inside…

It wasn't long before people started to talk. Mostly they just repeated that bloody scripture, *he saved others* &c. It was the price my father had to pay, they said. It was somehow right and proper that he cured tens of thousands of sick people but let his sons die and his daughter go mad. If anything, it reinforced his sanctity, and if he'd relented and gone all soft and saved them, it would in some way have been a betrayal, a corrupt act, the sort of thing you'd expect from a politician.

Peachy for Dad; not so wonderful for us. Obviously, that's a gross distortion. What it did to my father, I can't begin to imagine; the loss, the natural pain, and on top of that knowing that somehow it was his fault—My mother bore it all in crushed silence, but Ardorus wouldn't leave it alone. Every day, when Dad came home, worn out from healing and preaching, Ardorus would be there waiting for him, having spent most of the morning (he was a late riser) and all the afternoon honing and polishing the cutting remarks he was going to make that evening. All our family had a real way with words but Ardorus was far and away the best of us; I've got three trunks full of his writings and when I die they'll be published, and then you'll all be able to see what I'm talking about. All these remarkable gifts Ardorus used to crucify my father, from the moment he walked through the door until Ardorus finally gave up and went to bed. My father was a sensitive man, maybe not to the same extent Volutis was but not far off, and those daily sluicings-down with refined acid must have stripped him down to the bone.

ARDORUS STAYED AT home for three years, and then he was offered the secretaryship of the diocesan Treasury Committee, which he accepted so fast he was practically a blur. The job is a well-paid sinecure and a house goes with it, right in the middle of town. Ardorus was a very clever man, but he never figured out that my mother arranged for him to get the job, to get him out of our house and away from my father. Sending away her own son was possibly the bravest and most selfless thing she ever did, and none of us realised it at the time.

Shortly after that, Volutis took a turn for the worse. Somehow she got hold of a bit of metal—I think it was a shelf-bracket—which she sharpened by patiently rubbing it against the brick surround of the fireplace in her room until it had an edge like a razor. She carved up the nurse who looked after her, then my mother, then me. The nurse wasn't too badly hurt, apart from a faceful of scars that meant she had to wear a veil for the rest of her life. I lost most of my nose and part of my left ear. My mother wasn't so lucky. Volutis wanted to hurt the nurse and me, but she'd decided the time had come to kill my mother. She sliced off her lips, then cut through her jugular vein. It was relatively quick, which was a blessing.

Ardorus made the necessary arrangements. It wasn't hard to find an institution prepared to take in the Saviour's daughter, no matter how afflicted; in fact, there was practically a bidding war between the leading convents, which the Poor Sisters of Charity eventually won, and I gather it was worth millions to them in endowments over the next five years, so that was all right. She had a room of her own at the top of one of the highest towers in the City, and as soon as they put her in there and turned the key she was happier than she'd ever been in her life. She had comfortable furniture and books, and although she wasn't allowed sharp things like pens, the Sisters used to take dictation, so she was able to write to her heart's content, and that was what she'd always wanted to do. None of it made any sense, of course, but the Sisters didn't seem to mind. They all loved Volutis, and when she died they were genuinely heartbroken. The only thing that upset her was any mention of my father; if anyone said his name, she was immediately as bad as ever, gashed skin and broken teeth and bones. When she was in that state, she used to say that my father was the devil, not just an assistant or an acting deputy-in-chief but the One and Only, and was it any wonder if she took after her father? The next day she'd be right as rain, placid and smiling, looking out of her tiny window at the flower-gardens below. I try to tell myself that at least she had five years of peace. I'm no great shakes at lying, especially to myself.

Once my injuries had healed up I left home. Someone in authority got me a commission to paint the ceiling of the Hilarion Chapel—did I mention I'm a painter?—and since it was clearly going to be a long job, it made sense for me to live on site... As it so happens I'm a very good painter, though I take no pleasure in the fact whatsoever; the thought of where the talent comes from worries me, and I'd far rather have been a clerk, or worked in a sawmill. Anyway, I spent the next nine years mostly on my back, on top of a scaffolding tower, with paint and turpentine dripping on my face, painting—well, you know what I was doing as well as I do: the five crucial moments in my father's ministry, starting with the road to Ap' Escatoy and culminating in the Transfiguration on the Mountaintop. The sixth panel I was told to leave blank; it was reserved for my father ascending bodily to Heaven in a fiery chariot, or whatever. Yes, that's who I am, *that* painter. Hadn't you guessed?

Naturally they wanted me to do it, because who better to record the Saviour's career than the Saviour's own son? I told them, I wasn't there, I didn't witness any of it, I'd have to get it out of books, same as anyone else. They looked at me like they didn't really believe me, and then we changed the subject and talked about money. I asked for twice what the job was worth, and they didn't bat an eyelid.

ARDORUS USED TO say that he could distinctly remember every time in his life when he'd broken into a run. There were six of them, he said, and he had no plans for a seventh. He was exaggerating, but not by much. I've always enjoyed exercise and physical activity, and so did Eudo and Volutis. Ardorus could never see the point. Any farmer's son could walk farther, run faster, skate more nimbly and lift heavier weights than we could. Why waste energy and spirit on doing something at which you know you'll never be the best, or even in the top one hundred? For fun, we used to tell him. You call that fun, he used to say, and there the matter would rest, until the next time.

In spite of which, Ardorus was always ridiculously healthy. He didn't get fat because he didn't really enjoy food, it was just something you needed, and the quicker it was done and out of the way, the sooner you could get on with something useful. He got plenty of exercise traipsing up and down stairs and endless corridors at the palace or the consistory. He showed me round once, and after the tour was over he was fresh as a daisy and I, the self-proclaimed athlete, was ready to drop. He was the sort of person who never gets a cold, presumably because it would involve time off work and he was far too busy for that. When he quit the Service in a huff and hung around at home for three years, spending all his time thinking up spiteful things to say to my father, he didn't put on weight or lose his wind, and once he was safely dug in at the diocesan treasury, where there are lots and lots of stairs and lots and lots and lots of miles of corridor, he was soon back in peak condition. It was, he told me once, the ideal environment for a human being—warm, dry, well-ventilated, no heavy lifting or any of the grinding hard activity that ruins your back and wrecks your knees. No wonder, he said, that churchmen, academics and civil servants live to be old men. That sort of lifestyle is what the human body was designed for, when you thought about it.

After Volutis died, he changed slightly. I don't think many people noticed, because in order to see it you had to know him well, and there were only two people who did, and he refused to have anything to do with my father. He tolerated me for old times' sake and force of habit, and because when he was talking to me he didn't have to be brilliant and charming and wonderful. Instead I got a certain percentage of what he was actually thinking. A human being can only bottle up so much without poisoning himself. Sooner or later it's got to go somewhere. Poor Volutis got rid of the excess by means of violent acts. Ardorus didn't, probably because it would've involved energetic physical activity, so instead he talked to me.

He was terrified, he said, of ending up like his sister. He lay awake most nights, scared stiff, endlessly analysing everything he'd thought, said and done the previous day, looking for the telltale signs that the final disintegration was about to begin. He was pretty sure, he said, that he wasn't being possessed by a demon, since he hadn't noticed any diminution of his intelligence, and demons sap that first; they make you stupid, and then they eat you from the inside out. But he was, he assured me, still the cleverest man in the City… So it wasn't that (which sort of begged the question as far as Volutis was concerned, but the cleverest man in the City didn't address that issue), in which case it had to be some kind of curse or malediction, since my sister had had it and he was going the same way, and of course our father—

"What do you mean?" I said.

He gave me a blank stare, then rolled his eyes. "Oh, come on," he said.

"I don't understand. Dad's not crazy."

He sighed. "You always were an unobservant little toad," he said. "Of course he is. Nuttier than squirrelshit. Think about it, for pity's sake. One day out of the blue he starts hearing voices in his head—"

"That was God."

"He starts hearing voices in his head," Ardorus repeated, "and his behaviour suddenly changes. He believes he's the Saviour. He goes around preaching—"

"And healing the sick and casting out demons," I said. "Really. It works. Ask all those people who aren't sick any more."

Ardorus gave me a gentle smile. "You're so stupid it's really rather endearing. It's all hysteria. There are books about it, though of course you've never read them. If people truly believe, they can heal themselves of the most frightful illnesses, it's a scientific fact. No, Dad's a fraud. Not a deliberate one, because he truly believes. And he truly believes because he's off his rocker."

Made no sense. "But you think he's genuine," I said. "Else why did you keep on and on at him about not healing Volutis and not bringing Eudo back to life?"

He sighed. "I used to believe," he said. "And then I realised, because it's so blindingly obvious. He didn't heal them because he *couldn't*. And if he couldn't, he can't have any powers. Not real ones, only the hyperactive imaginations of hopelessly suggestible fools. I should've figured that out ages ago, except I was so angry it blurred my judgement."

Words come dangerously easily to our family, but on that occasion I had absolutely no idea what to say to him. But he was my brother and clearly in pain, so I had to do something. "Look," I said, "even if you're right and there's something wrong with him, and Volutis wasn't possessed like you always reckoned she was, it still doesn't follow that you—"

"Don't rabbit on about something you know nothing about, there's a good lad. In Echmen there are proper doctors who study illness scientifically. I've read their books. Madness isn't demons, it's a disease, like gout or dropsy. And some diseases you catch, and some you inherit. Diseases of the mind are often hereditary. The only reason they didn't show up in Martial and Ancyra and Eudo is that they died too young. But he's got it, so I've got it and presumably you as well. Something to look forward to, in your case. We're both of us going to end up in some tower somewhere, dictating gibberish to a bunch of patient monks. And you ask me why I've been feeling depressed lately. There's your answer."

I couldn't bear to look at him any longer, so I stared out of the window. He had rooms in the west wing of what used to be the old chapter house about six hundred years ago, and his window overlooks the cloister garden, probably the most beautiful view in the City. "I think you're wrong," I said.

"Of course you do. It's because you're not very bright. But if you care to give it some serious thought, I imagine you'll get there in the end. Slow and steady does it, like a salt freighter."

I KEPT CLEAR of Ardorus for about six months after that. Obviously I thought very hard about what he'd said, to the point where I almost managed to convince myself. I read the books he'd mentioned, and they seemed to make a lot of sense. Meanwhile I was painting the Adoration. It amuses me when people say it's the most searingly spiritual work of art in the whole wide world, the one that comes closest to capturing the essence of God. While I was painting it, I'd more or less decided that God didn't exist and religion was just a cruel hoax perpetrated by bad people who wanted to make money. But in the end I couldn't quite manage it. The logical arguments were all very well, but deep down inside me they had no effect whatsoever. I knew that God was real, and that my father was His Messiah. It wasn't a happy thought. Quite the reverse.

I was up on my scaffolding one day, trying to clean a brush one-handed by wiping it on my shirt-front, when someone very close to me called my name. It was a very tall scaffolding and (since I'd built it myself) rickety and rather dangerous. I'd put up a sign at the bottom of the ladder, *do not climb if you value your life*. Visitors were therefore a rare phenomenon.

It was the archdeacon. He was seventy years old and a martyr to lumbago. Why would he want to climb a dangerous ladder?

"Your brother is sick," he told me. "They think you ought to go straight away."

Go where, I nearly asked. Then I scuttled down the ladder as fast as I could go, but not, as it turned out, fast enough. It was his heart, they told me, and up to a point they were quite right. Your heart is likely to give way if you drink an eighth of a pint of foxglove essence. I found the empty bottle on the floor next to the bath in which he died. I knew what it was because it was written on the label.

ENOUGH IS ENOUGH. I went to see my father.

Some monk let me in. My father was in his private chapel, praying. It was the strictest rule of the house; when Dad was in the chapel, nobody was allowed to interrupt him for any reason whatsoever. I pushed the door open so hard it slammed against the wall, and the doorknob knocked out a small chunk of plaster.

He was kneeling in front of the small, bare altar. As I walked in, I thought I saw something small and fast-moving scuttle out from under the hem of his monk's habit and vanish behind the altar. If I saw it, which I can't confirm, it was about the size of a large rat and moved at a rat's speed, but it wasn't a rat. Most likely it was just a trick of the light.

"You heard," I said.

He looked at me. I hadn't seen him in quite some time. He hadn't changed at all. "Yes," he said.

"That just leaves me."

I watched the colour drain from his face. I'd never seen him afraid before.

"I'm sorry," he said. "I don't understand what you mean."

Which proved, to my satisfaction at least, that he knew exactly what I meant. "Me next," I said. "And then what are you going to do? You'll have run out."

"Get out," he said.

"No," I said.

He raised his hand, and it suddenly occurred to me that I'd chosen to pick a fight with someone who could call down lightning and part seas. But it didn't matter. He couldn't kill me, because in the eyes of God suicide is a crime.

"Go on," I said. "I dare you."

The hand drooped back to his side, like a faithful dog harshly spoken to. "How did you know?" he asked.

There are no chairs in my father's private chapel, so I leaned my back against the wall and slid down onto the floor. "I don't," I said. "I guessed. But I'm right, aren't I?"

Maybe I'd known him all my life and never really seen him before; as though there had always been a veil over his face, or my eyes were watery and running. "I don't know, do I? What conclusion have you jumped to? Tell me, and I'll tell you if you're right."

"No," I said. "You first."

Just for a moment, there had been a flicker of someone I recognised from long ago. It vanished very quickly. "Fine," he said. "It started on the road to Ap' Escatoy."

THE REVELATION HAD been real enough, he told me: the flash of light, the unmistakeable and unavoidable call to do God's work, the sudden terrifying access of miraculous powers. He hadn't asked for them. They'd been issued to him, like a soldier gets issued with the latest model of deadly weapon, and when the war's over, he has to give it back.

"Or rather," he said, "it was taken from me. I woke up one morning, and I knew it was all gone. The job was done, He'd finished with me, it was over. As simple as that."

And as brutal. Now let Thy servant depart in peace, quickly and by the tradesmen's entrance, not the front door. No explanation and no word of thanks. Unnecessary.

"That must have been very upsetting," I said.

That made him laugh out loud, and me turn bright red. "You could say that," he said. "Oh, I understood. I understood perfectly. Enough had been done, there wasn't any need for any more. He's very"—pause to choose the right word—"very economical, when it comes to things out of the ordinary. I can see why, of course. When He does something like that, it's unavoidable interventions, not conjuring tricks. What it takes and no more."

"I can see that," I said. "Sort of."

"But that left me," he said. "If I'd dropped dead the moment He'd finished using me, that would've been fine. But there was no need for me to die, so I didn't. I was like a soldier demobbed from the war. In theory, I should go back to being a bricklayer or a footman or whatever it was I used to do. But some people can't. I guess I was one of them."

He was silent for a long time. "So what did you do?" I asked.

"I prayed," he replied. "I prayed for hours and days and weeks, but there was nobody there, I was just talking to myself. He'd given orders that I wasn't to be admitted any more, and that was that."

"So you started praying to—"

"Someone else." He closed his eyes for a moment when he said that, but his face didn't change. "Do you know, I never really believed in—in all that. There seemed to be no need for an Evil One, in a red cloak and cloven hooves. I always assumed that evil was the absence of God, just as darkness is what happens when something obscures the light." He shrugged. "It just shows how wrong you can be."

"You prayed to—"

"Yes." His face was as white as chalk. Volutis looked like that when they laid her out for burial. "I had no trouble at all getting His attention. Actually, He's quite charming when you get to know Him."

I stared at my father for quite a while, until he remembered I was there and he hadn't finished talking to me. "I asked Him," he said, "for my powers back. I made it absolutely plain from the outset that I intended to use them exclusively for God's work; healing the sick, feeding the poor, preaching the word of God to those who dwell in darkness. That was fine, apparently, it wouldn't be a problem. But in return—"

"Go on."

It took him a great deal of effort. "I was given a certain specified quantity of power," he said. "When it was all used up, I would die and my soul would be forfeit, and I would spend the rest of eternity in unimaginable torment." He breathed out slowly. "I agreed," he said.

"How could you—?"

"You have no idea what it was like," he snapped. "For forty days I was the link between God and Man. I felt—" He searched for a word, realised there wasn't one and gave up. "And I knew I'd do anything, anything at all, to have that back again. It was a small price to pay, for doing God's work."

Nothing I could have said at that moment could possibly have been of any value whatever. I waited and he continued.

"I came to the end of my allotment," he said. "He came to me and told me. My time was up and I had to go with Him, unless—"

"Go on."

"Unless I gave him Martial in my place. I had no choice. I was doing God's work. The look in the eyes of the people I healed—"

"And Martial wouldn't have minded. Did you ask him first?"

"No. He might have refused. I'm sure he wouldn't have, but I couldn't take the risk."

"Then Ancyra. And Eudo, and Mother, and Volutis, and Ardorus."

"Yes."

"And then me."

"Yes."

My mouth was dry and I felt cold all over. "Can I refuse?"

He looked at me, pleading. "It's God's work," he said. "What could possibly be more important than that?"

"Fuck you," I said.

YOU KNOW THE rest. On what's now Ascension Day, he preached to a huge crowd in the big meadow beside the river, cured sixty blind men—they were shipping them in from abroad now, since Dad had used up all the blind and sick in the home provinces—cast out five quite spectacular demons into a flock of starlings, which promptly flew into the river and drowned themselves… Then he went home, went into his study and bolted the door from the inside. That was nothing unusual, it just meant he didn't want the servants to disturb him while he was praying. Four days later, he still hadn't come out, and his housekeeper sent for a carpenter.

There was only one small window in my father's study, and when they broke in, it was shuttered and bolted. The room was empty, apart from a ridiculous number of books.

When they told me that my father had ascended into Heaven, my first feeling was overwhelming relief. I didn't want to die, and I certainly didn't want to spend eternity in unbearable torment. Nobody actually knows what that means, but I saw Volutis before they took her to the convent, so I can hazard a guess. Some time later I made a real effort to feel some sympathy for him, but I was kidding myself.

So there I was, the sole surviving issue of the Saviour. The Prince Regent granted me a state pension, a specially convened ecumenical council declared me a minor saint and ex-officio honorary precentor of the Golden Arrow monastery—the monastery was razed to the ground when the Sashan invaded Rumeli and all the monks were slaughtered, but the endowment naturally remained, invested in gilt-edged securities, and all that money's got to go somewhere; I give three-quarters of it to the poor, which leaves me enough to buy my own fleet of warships, if I ever wanted to. Actually, I live very quietly on what I make as a painter, and all the money from the pension and the precentorship is piling up grotesquely in an account with the Knights of Equity. I really ought to give it to something charitable, but I can't bring myself to do it somehow. It would be like giving money to Him—the other Him, my late father's associate. Somehow in my mind, good and evil have got so thoroughly mixed up and confused that I don't trust either of them as far as I can spit. So I made a will leaving the whole ghastly lot to the Prince Regent. Maybe he can buy himself a nice war with it. I really don't care.

I paint religious subjects exclusively, because nobody wants me to do anything else. The other day, I tried to paint a vase of flowers. It came out horrible, and I scraped all the paint off the board and tried again. No better. Then I resumed work on my latest commission, which is the sixth panel of the Hilarion Chapel roof. It's turning out to be the supreme artistic achievement of the human race. You can imagine how I feel about that.

Many Mansions

"So you can raise the dead." She yawned. "How clever."

With women (in my limited experience), ninety-nine times out of a hundred it's the way they say it. They're so much better at nuances than we are. It's what they don't say, what they imply by voice or gesture, that's so infuriatingly eloquent.

"Not that I ever would," I replied, "goes without saying. Absolutely forbidden."

She smiled and said nothing. The smile was a case in point. *You aren't impressing me,* it said, and God knows, I had no reason to want to impress her, but I did want, very badly, and I was trying too hard and making a real hash of it. All that, conveyed in one constriction of the facial muscles. Makes you wonder why they talk all the damn time when their silences are so eloquent.

"You don't believe me," I said. "Ah, well."

"I didn't say that." The smile changed shape slightly. "I'm sure you can do all these wonderful things, if your superiors let you. But they don't, so really, what's the point?"

In my line of work I visit the Mesoge quite often, and I frequently stop overnight in inns. After I've washed my face in the freezing cold water provided absolutely free of charge and eaten the inevitable house mutton and lentil stew, I take a book and sit by the fire in the common room. I only do this because the common-room fire is actually warm, as opposed to the feeble glow you get in your bedchamber, and there's enough light to read by without giving yourself a headache. I don't do it for the company. I'm an educated, refined man, a scholar. I reserve my conversation for the select few who can understand and appreciate it. I most certainly don't chat up women in taprooms.

"Indeed," I said. "But it's like a soldier. He's trained to kill people with extreme efficiency. But he only does it when his commanding officer tells him to. It's the same with me and—"

"Magic?"

She only used the word to rile me. Everybody knows, we don't do magic. The members of my order are not wizards. We're scholars, scientists, natural and metaphysical philosophers. True, we can do things the uneducated can't; a blacksmith or a carpenter can say exactly the same thing. A blacksmith can take two metal rods and join them so you can't see where one ends and the other begins; but that's not magic, it's welding. No; some things, some apparently extraordinary and miraculous things, can be done, if you know the trick. Others can't, no matter how many books you've read. That's what we tell people, and in many respects it's true.

"I'm sorry," she said, "I only said it to tease you. And you're quite right. If people went about doing things just because they can, there'd be mayhem." She smiled again, in a totally different way. "It's been so nice talking to you. Goodnight."

And she stood up and walked out of the room, leaving me feeling like a hunter who's stalked a deer for two hundred yards, only to tread on a twig just outside bowshot. But I hadn't started it. I was sitting by the fire reading Saloninus on conditional uncertainty. She was the one who sat down opposite and said, That looks interesting, not many people read Saloninus these days. And she wasn't even particularly pretty or particularly young. And anyway, I don't do any of that sort of thing, we're not allowed, as everybody knows perfectly well. My guess was, she did it because she could. Understandable and very antisocial, as she'd no doubt have been the first to agree.

MANY MANSIONS

I HATE THE Mesoge. Heavy winter rain had turned the roads to mud, and the cart got bogged down. I asked the carter, how far to Rysart? Two miles, he told me.

"Fine," I said. "I'll walk."

He looked at me. "You paid all the way to Rysart."

I hauled out the sack I carry my stuff in. About thirty pounds, dead weight. "No problem," I said. "Fresh air and exercise."

"I got to go on to Rysart anyway. I got stuff to deliver."

In the back of the cart lay a shovel, two iron crowbars, wedges, sacking; all the paraphernalia needed for getting the cart unstuck. A two-hour job, in the dark, the mud and the rain. Needless to say, I could have got the cart out of the rut and back on the road in five seconds; *tollens aequor,* a second-level Form you learn in first year. But I'm not allowed.

"Drop in at the inn when you get there," I said. "I'll buy you a beer."

I started to walk. The mud sucked at my boots, the rain trickled off my hood into my eyes, and the weight of the sack made my fingers ache. I trudged fifty yards, which I guessed was enough to be out of sight, in weather like that, at night. Then I muttered a few simple words under my breath. The sack suddenly weighed about six ounces. The soles of my boots floated on the surface of the mud. The rain flew down at me but somehow missed. A light that only I could see illuminated the road, all the way down the valley. I wasn't allowed, of course, but who was there to see?

I WAS THERE because I have a field-officer rating. I wanted it about as much as I wanted a sixth toe on my left foot, but you have to get your field ticket before you can be made up to seventh grade, and I'm deplorably ambitious. I'm also a theorist, not a man of action: naturally contemplative, at home in the study, the cloister, the library, the chapter house. Outdoors, in the wet mud, on my way to deal with problems in the real world, is not where I belong. But they send me because I get the job done—an early mistake on my part. On my first field assignment, I was under the impression that a splendidly successful outcome would win me merit and commendation. Silly me. What it got me was a reputation for being able to do this sort of thing. What I should've done was make a total hash of it, and they'd never have sent me again, and I'd be an abbot by now.

("You understand these people," Father Prior said to me, after he'd broken the bad news about this job. "You talk their language. You're one of them." I didn't hit him because it's not allowed. Perfectly true, of course. I was born and raised on a farm, in the horrible primitive Mesoge. I left it to get away from backbreaking work and stupid people. So, what happens? They keep sending me back there.)

How can I begin to describe Rysart in the rain and the pitch dark? Yet another nasty little Mesoge village; the smell told me everything I needed to know before the first silhouetted barn loomed up out of the darkness. I knew the inn would be opposite the meeting house, which would be at the north end of the one broad street. There's no reason why it always should be, but it always is. It's the way it's always been done, you see. Lots of alwayses in the Mesoge.

The inn door was shut, but there were cracks of light under it. I tried the handle, but the bolts were shot. I banged on it and waited for a very long time, during which rain fell on me. I'd cancelled *fulvens dissimilis* as soon as the smell hit me, just in case, so I was getting wet.

"What the hell do you want?"

I smiled. "A bed for the night, please. You're expecting me."

She looked like I'd insulted her, but she opened the door anyway. The smell of dogs and wet wool made me catch my breath. I grew up with it, but when you're used to a smell, you don't notice it, until you've been away for a while, and then it hits you like a fist. It's not actually an unpleasant smell, but it said home to me, and I left home a long time ago.

The room was the sort of thing you'd confidently store logs in without worrying too much about mould. The lentil and mutton stew came with a mountain of fermented cabbage. The water had that taste. The fire in the common-room had burnt down to embers. "In the morning," I said, "I want to see the Father and the mayor, and probably the reeve and the constable."

She stared at me, as though I'd asked her to bring me her son's head in a cream of asparagus sauce. But my tone of voice was just right. She nodded, and got away from me as quickly as she could.

I WAKE UP at sunrise, even when I don't have a window. It's a farm-boy thing, and I get teased about it all the time.

Even so; by the time I'd washed and had a good scratch, they were all waiting for me in the taproom, sitting in dead silence: six extremely worried men, the answer to whose prayers I was. They looked at each other as I walked in. I guess they'd had a vote and elected the Father to be the spokesman; fair enough. Did you ever meet a country priest who didn't love the sound of his own voice?

"Are you—?"

I nodded. Spare him the embarrassment. "My name is Father Bohenna, and I'm from the Studium," I said. "Now, I know the basic facts, but I'll need you to fill me in on specifics. Then I can decide whether our intervention is called for, and if so, what the procedures will be, where your jurisdiction ends and ours begins, and so on and so forth. If we could start with some names."

They introduced themselves. I'm hopeless with names. Unless I write them down, they're in one ear and out the other. There are men I've known and worked with for fifteen years, but I have no idea what they're called; they told me once, and you can't keep asking, you make yourself look ridiculous. But I never forget a face, or a voice, or a body odour. So, the names washed over me like the spring floods, but I made a mental note. The tall, thin, crafty-looking man, around fifty-five, bushy white hair, was the mayor. The two round-faced bruisers with the red cheeks—brothers—were the reeves.

The little rat-faced man was the constable; I knew his sort, looks like the wind would blow him off his feet, but he draws the strongest bow in the village and God help you if you pick a fight with him. The seven-foot fair-haired idiot was somebody's son, there to open doors for his father and sit still when not in use. A competent body of men. I've dealt with far worse.

The Father took a deep breath. "It all began," he said—

Obviously, you hear some crazy stories in this job. Some of them you can safely discount. It depends on who tells them, and how they tell them. The thing in this case was that the Father couldn't ever possibly have had an imaginative thought in his entire life. He wasn't the sort. If you told him you were having a whale of a time, he'd look round the room for a whale.

It all started, he said, when two of the village girls began having fits. Nothing unusual in that, or at least not in the Mesoge. My sister was singularly prone to them; temper tantrums, floods of tears, right up till she realised that prospective husbands don't really like that sort of thing, at which point she calmed down remarkably until the ring was safely on her finger. But these weren't the usual sort of fits.

There's something profoundly unsettling about hearing wild, spooky stories told by an utterly prosaic man. He described what the girls claimed they'd seen.

One night—you're reading this, so you can read, so I don't suppose you're familiar with daily life in the Mesoge, so I'd better explain. Our houses have two rooms, one for the family and one for the livestock. The family room is square, with a hearth in the middle. We never quite got around to inventing the chimney, so we pitch our roofs high, to give the smoke somewhere to flock up and hover. We sleep on straw or feather mattresses in a square around the hearth. Rich folk with pretensions curtain off the back end for the man of the house and his wife—we did in our family; I can picture the curtain to this day, it was heavy felted wool painted to look like tapestry, the Ascension, and to the day I die the Invincible Sun will always have that crude, slightly half-witted face, like he's just been woken up in the middle of the night. Children sleep in a heap, like puppies, on the opposite side from their parents, with the elderly, the poor relations, the dog and the hired help making up the other two sides of the square. None of this should matter; the idea is that you should come in from work so tired out from your honest labours that as soon as you've bolted down your food you go straight to sleep. In practice: yes, we get on each others' nerves like you wouldn't believe, which is probably why the murder rate has always been so high in the Mesoge.

Anyway. One night these two girls (fifteen and fourteen) started screaming in their sleep. It took a lot to wake them up, and once they were awake they were lashing out, biting and scratching. Their father laid into them with a broom handle to quiet them down. When they were coherent again, they said that a tall, well-dressed woman in a white lace cap had knelt down beside them and stuck them repeatedly with a brooch-pin.

Don't be so bloody stupid, said their father, or words to that effect; but it happened again the next night, and the night after that, and then in broad daylight. Their mother went to see the Father, much to her husband's annoyance. The Father found himself in a difficult position. He was and always had been a convinced sceptic. He didn't believe in witchcraft, but he looked in his book—like most Mesoge priests, he only had one—and sure enough, the facts as related were a classic case of bewitchment, and he had no alternative but to treat it as such. He told the parents that their girls were bewitched, then sat down with his head in his hands and tried to figure out what he was supposed to do about it.

Now, so far, the only people who knew about all this were the family and the Father; but shortly after that, three girls in another family on the other side of the parish started doing exactly the same thing. They too were terrorised by an elegant woman in a white lace cap, though sometimes she came as a tall black-and-white nanny-goat, and sometimes she had a goshawk on her wrist. When the Father went to see them, the eldest girl started to tell her story, then broke off and tried to bite off her own tongue; she did quite a lot of damage before her mother got her jaws apart and stuffed her mouth with rags. And then a man in the village jumped out of a tree and broke his back; he lived long enough to say that a fine lady in a white bonnet had scooped him up off the ground, carried him to the top of the tree and pushed him off. A rich farmer in the valley lost ninety sheep to some sort of scouring sickness he'd never seen before. Six hayricks caught fire in the space of a week. A man came home from market to find a huge black bear waiting for him on his doorstep, in a district where the bears are brown and never come into the villages. It scratched up the side of his face pretty badly—the scars were plainly visible—he hit it with his stick and it vanished into thin air.

By this point, the Father's scepticism was wearing pretty thin. He called in the mayor, who sent for the reeves and the constable, who convened an assembly of heads of families in the meeting house. Needless to say, the meeting just made things worse. Everybody had strong views about the identity of the witch, and no two people had the same candidate in mind. When at last the Father could make himself heard, he told them there was only one thing they could do. And now, here I was, and what did I intend to do, and how soon could I start?

By this point, apparently, the witch was definitely getting above herself. She no longer operated at night—presumably she needed her sleep like everyone else, and she appeared to be operating on a massively overcrowded schedule, so who can blame her? On average there were between six and ten attacks a day, affecting roughly half the families in the village. Although the witch appeared only as herself or the black and white goat, there was no recognisable description, because as soon as anyone tried to describe her they bit their own tongue or bashed their head against a wall. She was visible on her own terms, generally only to the person she was afflicting, but very occasionally to three or four bystanders as well. The Father and the other elders tried to meet a few times to discuss a plan of action, but they gave up when she took to sitting down with them, on a chair that hadn't been there before she arrived but which stayed there after she left. In fact, the same chair I was sitting in right now—

I STOOD UP quickly, then slowly sat down again.

"So you've seen her."

The Father nodded. "But please, don't ask me to describe her."

I nodded. "No need," I said.

He frowned, then all the colour drained from his face. "You can see inside my—?"

"Yes. But don't worry. I'm an expert, and anything else I might happen to see I'm really not interested in." He didn't seem reassured, but I couldn't help that. I mumbled *aspergo devictos* under my breath and looked straight at the side of his head and through it. "Thank you," I said. "All over."

The look on his face: rather the witch than me, any time. "You saw her?"

"Clearly."

The constable said; "She's standing behind you, right now."

Nobody moved, especially me. "Is she now," I said.

No reply. The constable's mouth was open, but he didn't seem able to speak. The others were looking down, at the ground, as though they were afraid of catching something really nasty through their eyes. Slowly I reached for my tea-bowl and drank what was left in it. Then I stood up and turned round.

Something lashed out at me. *Scutum fidei* and *lorica* will stop practically anything, but I felt the smack. Like a man in armour; the arrow or the javelin is turned and doesn't pierce, but even so you get a hell of a thump. Instinctively—no, I'm ashamed to say impulsively, with no proper control at all—I hit back with *stricto ense* or *benevolentia* or something of the sort, like you do in second year when you're just starting on the military Forms; suddenly I'd regressed twenty years and forgotten everything I'd ever learned about fighting. It must have worked, though. I distinctly heard a scream, and then there was nothing there, except a bloodstain on the rushes.

I felt a complete fool. But the constable said, "Did you kill her?" in a tiny voice.

"No," I said.

"But you beat her."

I was still feeling disgusted with myself, and I really didn't want to talk or deal with the public. I sat down again, carefully not looking at any of them. My hands were shaking. "Thank you for coming, gentlemen," I said. "You can leave it to me now. This shouldn't take long."

"You can—?"

"Yes. Now, I think it would be advisable for everyone to stay in their houses for the rest of the day, if that's at all possible. There's no immediate danger, but it's best to be on the safe side."

That got rid of them, and I sat for a while perfectly still, thinking; what the hell was all that about? A stripe hard enough to put a dent in *scutum* and *lorica*, and a twenty-year professional panicking, overriding a lifetime of training and conditioning to swipe wildly with thunderbolts. I wasn't afraid—there's no power on earth, literally, that scares me any more, because I know I can beat them all—but I was bewildered and unnerved and unsettled, and I had to think to remember things that are usually part of the furniture of my mind: the Rooms, the Wards, the precepts of engagement. I felt like I was heading for a duel with a sword in one hand and a fencing textbook in the other.

Still. The hell with it. I could outfight tenured professors when I was fourteen years old. I despise fighting, of course. That's why I'm so good at it. I just want it done with and out of the way.

SOMEONE ASKED ME why there aren't any women at the Studium. I said, the same reason there aren't any fish. She gave me a foul look and changed the subject, but it's a valid answer.

There are things men can do and women can't (and vice versa, goes without saying) and what we do is one of them. To put it crudely, they don't have the parts. We don't actually know what the parts are—we've picked over God knows how many brains, looking for a particular blob of mush or twist of gristle, all to no effect. I don't suppose we'll ever find it until we get a chance to dissect one of the very, very few women (we figure something like one in two million) who's got it, and that's not likely to happen any time soon.

No great loss, is how we see it. What we do, the power we have, is of very limited practical value. We're theorists, pure scientists; we aren't actually very much use to anybody, and where we could make ourselves useful—wiping out armies, destroying cities, sinking whole continents under the sea, bringing the dead back to life—we don't allow ourselves to, for obvious reasons. Stripped of all pretences, euphemisms, justifications and obfuscations, the main reason we do magic is because we can. Generally speaking, though, either it's useless or it mustn't be used. Now, why would women, who are so much more sensible and practical than us, want to bother with something so pointless?

Witches are, of course, the exception. It's a sad fact that, out of the tiny number of women who are born with the talent and figure out how to use it, ninety-nine out of a hundred go on to make insufferable nuisances of themselves, hurting, persecuting, terrorising the district with acts of petty spite.

My learned colleagues say that this is because in everyday life, women are powerless and marginalised; they have no way of striking back against a society that subordinates and belittles them. Thus, when one-in-two-million suddenly finds herself powerful, her first instinct is to settle scores. Personally I dispute this. Anyone who says women are powerless never met my mother. What they really mean is, *upper-class* women are powerless and marginalised—which is entirely true; and of course, that's the only sort of women my colleagues have ever had dealings with. But most witches are your basic peasant stock, simply because so are most people. There's no higher incidence of witchcraft in the gentry, and so the oppressed-and-victimised theory doesn't convince me. Myself, I figure that anyone, man or woman, who has the talent but isn't identified and whisked off to the Studium at age ten to be taught polite behaviour would naturally use such powers to bully and torment others because that's human nature for you. Let any man pick up a stick and he'll use it to hit someone else, unless the other man's got a stick too. And nothing will ever change that, believe you me.

My colleagues and I, however, are civilised, educated men. We know what to do in practically every eventuality. Which is why we have nothing whatsoever to be afraid of.

FINDING HER WAS no problem. *Insignia verborum*: you learn it in third year because it's nominally a restricted Form, God only knows why, it's harmless enough. It lights up a glowing trail, like a phosphorous snail. A tiny drop of blood, or a hair or a nail-clipping, is all you need. I picked up one of the bloodstained rushes, and I was off.

It was raining again, and when I opened the door I could see the trail winding away over the hills and far away. I considered requisitioning a horse, but I hate riding, my back gives me hell for days afterwards. You're not supposed to use Forms just to keep from getting wet and muddy, but who was there to see or care, and if they did, so what? It's the Mesoge. Nothing that happens there matters worth a damn. I fortified myself discreetly and set off on my long trudge.

It was well after sunset when the trail petered out, and by then I'd walked farther than I had since I joined the Studium. Forms can give you strength but they can't stop your feet aching. But anyhow, I found myself on the wrong side of a gate set in a thick hedge; the quality live here, it said. Gates don't hinder me much, locked or unlocked. On the other side, I saw a short drive leading to a large square black shape. I tweaked the view a bit with *lux in tenebris* and made out one of those fortified manor houses that you get in the Mesoge: half farmhouse, half castle, our legacy from the Troubles three centuries ago. Curious, I thought. No reason to assume my witch was the lady of the house. Probably between fifteen and twenty women would live in a house that size, most of whom would be working for a living. My witch could just as easily be a scullerymaid or a cook.

But she wasn't. I looked for her—standing in the pitch dark, with rain dripping off my hood—with *victrix causa*, and saw her in the great hall. She was sitting on a stool by the fire, sewing a cushion. A few feet away, her husband was serving the loops on a new bowstring. He was about fifty, a fine-looking man with a neatly trimmed grey beard and broad shoulders. Two sons played chess on a low table; twins, most likely, around twenty. A greyhound slept on a bearskin rug. Your ideal picture of the country gentry at home, a beatific vision of aspiration for yeomen farmers and uppity merchants. Awkward. I had a problem.

I was, of course, entirely within my rights to burst in, seize her by force and blast anybody who tried to stop me. I was perfectly capable of all that. I had the power, the strength and the authority. But you don't do stuff like that just because you can. It's insensitive and uncivilised, and we aren't thugs or bullies. I was going to have to wait until they'd all gone to bed. I went and stood under a tree, from where I could watch the windows.

The bedroom would be on the first floor of the big round tower; it always is. After an eternity, a faint light flared in the narrow window. I muttered *victrix causa*, and peeped in.

Country squires in the Mesoge are old-fashioned, and they don't throw out good furniture just because it's two hundred and fifty years old. The bed, therefore, was a huge thing, size of a small shed, with heavy tapestry drapes. I'm no voyeur; I cut the Form and gave them plenty of time to undress, get into bed and blow out the candle. The window went dark. I gave them another eternity to fall asleep, then squelched in my sodden boots up the drive to the front door.

Any fool can draw bolts with *summa fides*, but it takes real skill to do it quietly. There'd be servants and dogs sleeping in the hall, and anybody I woke up would have to be put back to sleep with *benevolentia* or some other unpleasantness. But I'm really very good at all the sneaking-about side of things. I'd have made a good thief or assassin; now there's something to be proud of. I climbed the stairs without a sound. The bedroom door had old-fashioned leather hinges, and the floor was spread with rugs. Perfect.

She was fast asleep, her head on one side, her hair loose. When we met at the inn, she'd had it done up in those horrible spirals, like wicker mats; it suited her much better *au naturel*. She was still neither particularly pretty nor particularly young, but a part of me envied the silver-haired gentleman lying with his back to her. Still; if there's one thing I hate, it's being made a fool of.

I slipped into her mind, exactly the way she'd do it. I kept my scholar's robe, because that's what people see when they look at me; not the prematurely bald head or the weak chin or the silly little snub nose. I wanted to be sure she recognised me.

You can't take anything into someone's dream; you have to use what you find there. In her dream, on the bedside table lay a fine old silver and amber brooch, heirloom quality—my guess is, a real brooch she'd always hankered after but never managed to acquire. I picked it up and unfolded the pin. In her dream, she was fast asleep. I stuck the pin through the lid of her closed eye, then pulled it out.

She opened her eyes. One she couldn't see through, the other stared at me. "Hello," I said.

In her dream, she yelled. I shook my head. "Nobody can hear you," I said. "We need to talk. You'll find me at the inn." Then I stuck the pin in her other eye, and got out fast.

She hadn't moved, though her eyes were tightly screwed up. Her husband was still fast asleep, so I guess she was a restless sleeper at the best of times. I blew her a kiss and went back down the stairs. I think a servant opened one eye and saw me as I thumbed the latch of the front door. So what?

I SLEPT WELL that night. Genuine Mesoge sleep; healthy exhaustion after a hard day of useful, profitable work.

Some fool woke me up while it was still dark outside. Just as well for him I have perfect control; there are horror stories of servants at the Studium being blasted into cinders after waking up senior faculty members who weren't morning people. There's a lady to see you, said whoever it was. Note the choice of noun. He sounded deeply impressed.

I'm afraid of nothing, but I'm still capable of embarrassment. How do you start a conversation with a witch you recently blinded in her sleep, who also happens to be the local bigwig's wife? As I pulled my hose on I decided I'd better be cruel and heartless, though I know full well I'm not very good at it. Probably she'd see through it straight away. As I stuffed my feet into my boots, which were ice-cold and clammy with last night's rain, I thought; the hell with it, I'll just be myself. Not a part I've ever been happy playing, but it's less of a drain on my limited imaginative faculties.

She was sitting on the chair she'd conjured up and then not known how to dissolve. I don't think she meant anything by it, probably she didn't recognise it. A spiteful man would've vanished it with her still sat in it, but I'm not like that. I had no idea how to address her, so I settled on 'Madam', which is usually correct in the country.

She looked at me. Her eyes were bloodshot. Also, she had a cut on her cheek, just starting to scab over. I hadn't noticed it the night before, so presumably she was lying on it. I did that, I thought guiltily, lashing out like a schoolboy. She was wearing a white lace cap and a heavy wool cloak, fastened at the shoulder with a simple silver starburst brooch.

I cleared my throat. "The cap," I said. "Indiscreet."

She shook her head. "I wear it all the time, so naturally nobody sees it any more. I assume you've told them."

I was shocked. "No, of course not. I think we ought to find somewhere a bit more private."

That made her grin. "Are you suggesting I go up to your room? I don't think so."

"Allow me."

So, I wanted to impress her; of course I did, from the first moment I saw her, in the inn. So what? A show of power would terrify her, let her know she was dealing with someone infinitely stronger than herself; it would serve a useful purpose, and therefore was allowed.

I touched her shoulder with the tip of my finger, and took her to the third Room.

IT'S JUST OCCURRED to me that you may not know about Rooms. You're not supposed to. Rooms are classified top secret, not to be mentioned or hinted at in front of unqualified personnel. I could get in big trouble if I were to tell you anything at all about Rooms. Basically, it's like this.

Imagine you're in a big house, or a palace, or a government building. There are lots of rooms in it, but for some reason I can't begin to imagine, you've lived your entire life in just one of them. The concept of a door is so weird and unnatural to you that either you dismiss it as some crazy fantasy or else it terrifies you—anathema, abomination, other words beginning with A to convey pious disgust.

At the beginning of second year, the class tutor shows you how to make a door. It's the most extraordinary thing that ever happens to you, and you remember it for the rest of your life. After that, your sense of wonder gets work-hardened, miracles make you yawn, inconceivable wonders are just another day at the office. But your first door is always with you. It's the moment when the world changed for ever.

In theory (and if I do manage to get tenure, it's the area of theory I intend to devote the rest of my life to) there's an infinite number of Rooms, linked by an infinite network of doors, stairways and passages. In theory, you could get so good at this shit that instead of going to the Rooms, you could just sit there and all the Rooms would come to you. In practice, there are seven Rooms, and if you're really brave and incredibly skilful and outrageously lucky, you might get to visit six of them by choice before you end up in the seventh very much against your will. In everyday life, you use three. I chose the third Room on this occasion because it's always been my favourite. If there's anywhere in the world this Mesoge farm boy is at home, it's the third Room. When I'm there, I'm in control.

Normally, wherever and whoever you are, you aren't in control. You may think you are, but you're not. If you're the Great King of the Sashan, brother of the Sun and bridegroom of the Moon, and you happen to let your favourite crystal goblet slip through your fingers, it'll fall on the marble floor and smash into a thousand pieces, and if you cut yourself on one of the pieces and get blood poisoning, you'll die. But when I'm in the third Room, if I drop something it needs my permission to fall. Don't get the idea that it's like that for everyone in the third Room, by the way. I know a tenured professor of applied metaphysics who wouldn't go in there if you paid him, because there are monsters under the bed. I know how he feels. You wouldn't get me in the fifth Room if the rest of the world was on fire; yet my friend the professor goes there to relax and hide from his married sister when she calls for a visit.

I'm a bit of an old fusspot when it comes to décor. I know what I like. My rooms in the west cloister of the Old Building are small, cold and damp so I can't really be bothered with them, but I've fixed up the third Room exactly how I like it. The walls are panelled oak, sort of a dark honey colour, with genuine late Mannerist tapestries depicting scenes from *Chloris and Sorabel.* On the floor I've got a rattan mat, because I love the smell and the way it cushions your feet. The ceiling is plaster mouldings with the details—birds nesting among the acanthus leaves, that sort of thing—picked out in gold leaf, because what is life without a few restrained splashes of vulgarity? The furniture is dark oak, almost black; two carved chairs, a table, a bookcase which only occupies half a wall but which somehow manages to hold all the books I ever want to read; three brass lamps, my grandfather's sword on the wall just above my head, nice and handy if ever I need it; a footstool. And the nice thing is, I can go there for a whole afternoon and when I get back, I've only just left.

"What the hell?" I said.

I don't usually swear in front of women, especially upper-class ones. I stared at her. She smiled.

It was the third Room, because I'd brought us here, up the second staircase, across the dark landing. I'd opened the door, my thumb on the old-fashioned wooden latch. More to the point, I was in front of her. It's different when someone gets into a Room ahead of you, or you go in and it's already occupied. I'm always very careful about that, believe me. But no, I'd opened the door and walked in, and then she followed me. "What have you done?" I said.

She pushed past me and sat down. There was only one chair. I had to make do with a low three-legged stool by the fire. She picked up her embroidery and carried on where she'd left off the night before. The boarhound lifted its head and growled at me.

"You can't bring dogs into the third Room," I objected.

"Can't you?"

"It's against the rules."

"Then the rules are silly," she said, licking the end of her silk before threading her needle. "You wanted to talk to me about something."

I stood up. This wasn't right. I headed for the door, which wasn't there.

FATHER ANTHEMIUS TAUGHT me how to make a door. The shameful fact is, I was a slow beginner. All the other kids could do it, I couldn't. Not for want of trying; but it's one of those things where effort is useless bordering on counter-productive; like falling asleep, the more you try, the less you succeed. It's easy, they all told me, you just think of a door and there it is. So I thought of a door, and there one wasn't. All right, they said, try this. Think of a door, but you can only see it out of the corner of your eye. Didn't work. So they explained to me about peripheral vision, and how you can see things without looking straight at them. Made no difference. I was ashamed and desperate. If I couldn't make a door, I couldn't learn anything else, they'd have to send me home, back to a two-room shack in the Mesoge. I wasn't having that. In all other respects I was well in advance of the rest of my year and I'd already sneaked a look at the basic military Forms in the textbook. I reckoned *ruans in defectum* standing in front of a mirror would do the trick nicely, and there wouldn't be enough of a body left to be worth shipping home.

Enter Father Anthemius. He retired from the teaching staff the year before I arrived and nobody was sorry to see him go. He was a miserable old bastard who hated kids, and he'd only got into teaching because he couldn't make the field grades, which was all he'd ever wanted to do. His students had hated him, partly because he was hypercritical, judgemental and mean, partly because of his habit of farting loudly during tutorials; the smell, they told me, had to be experienced to be believed. He found me in a corner of the cloister, crying my eyes out. He looked at me.

"You're pathetic," he said.

I looked up at him. "I know," I said.

He sighed. A stupid little kid bawling like a girl because he couldn't do the simplest thing in the syllabus. "You're trying too hard," he said.

"I know."

"No bloody good you knowing if you keep on doing it." He slapped my mind with *eget regimine* and I squealed, which made him even angrier. "You're disgusting," he said. "The sooner they throw you out and you go back to mucking out pigs, the better for all of us. They shouldn't let you people in here in the first place. You're no good for anything."

I think he was trying to provoke me. He could see I knew some military forms, and if I lashed out with one of them he'd be justified in blasting me till I glowed. He filled my head with bees and locusts so I couldn't think, then started up again with *eget regimine.* I don't know if you're familiar with it; they call it the teacher's friend, because it hurts like hell but leaves no marks or traces whatsoever. I tried to get up and run, but he'd locked me down with something or other that made me feel like the whole building was pressing down on me. I could hardly breathe. He was grinning at me, and I felt him inserting something into my mind; memories, false ones, about having fits when I was a baby. Clever; he'd crush me until a blood vessel burst and I had a stroke, and when they looked inside my head they'd find memories of similar attacks going right back through my life. I wasn't sure why he hated me as much as he did, but there was no doubt in my mind at all. Something about me was so objectionable that I couldn't be allowed to continue, and he was going to see to it that I didn't. I felt his hand pass through my skull, feeling for the vein he was going to pinch shut. Out of the corner of my eye I caught a glimpse of a door. I jumped to my feet, wrenched it open, tumbled through, slammed it shut and collapsed.

"See?" said a voice. "Nothing to it, really."

I looked up. Father Anthemius was sitting in a carved oak chair, with his feet up on a footstool. "This," he said, "is the third Room. Most kids your age wouldn't make it this far, but you're precocious."

I turned my head and looked at what I was leaning against; a massive oak door, studded with nails, like you see in castles. The nails are clenched over to hold the plies of wood together. You lay six plies with the direction of the grain alternating at right angles. A door made that way is practically unbreakable, even with a battering ram.

"You came here because it's safe," he said. "Once that door's shut, nothing can get in unless you want it to. Nobody taught you that, you figured it out all by yourself."

"I made a door?"

He laughed. "I certainly didn't, so you must have, mustn't you? I told you it was easy."

I lashed out at him with *ruat caelum*. He swatted it aside. "Too slow," he said. "Do it again."

"I'm sorry," I said. "I don't know what I was—"

"Do it again."

Nobody taught me *ruat caelum*. I do it better than anyone else in the world. I'd been practising it for years on birds, flies, anything really small and fast, before I found out it was called that. To do it right you have to focus on a pinprick. I narrowed everything right down and let him have it. But he wasn't there.

I stared. Had I hit him so hard he'd completely disintegrated? But then a door opened in the wall and he stepped through. "Which proves my point," he said, sitting down and putting his feet up. "Rooms are everything. Doesn't matter that you're faster than anyone else I've ever seen. All I have to do is go next door and you can't touch me."

I felt as though a tap had been opened and my soul drained out of it. "I'm sorry," I said. "I got mad."

"Of course you did," he said. "You were angry with me, instead of yourself. And before that you were afraid of me, instead of afraid of failing. You could be good at this. But you won't ever be unless you stop feeling sorry for yourself all the damn time." He stood up. "Like I said, you're pathetic. If I hadn't taken pity on you, you could've gone on trying the rest of your life and never got there. Lucky for you I'm such a sweetheart." He stood up. "Till we meet again," he said. Then he walked through the door he'd made and closed it behind him, and I was sitting alone on a stone bench on the cloister. I never saw him again; he died that afternoon. I didn't find out he died until a week later. Apparently he was born at Spire Cross in the Mesoge, just a few miles downhill from where I used to live. Small world.

ANYWAY, THE POINT is, ever since then I've been really good at doors. I can make one in a flash and my doors go to places my esteemed colleagues would never dream of being able to reach. It's the one thing I'm supremely good at. Hopeless at many things, good at doors, that's me.

I tried to make a door. Nothing happened.

She yawned. "You can try again if you like. Won't do you any good. This is my place. I'm in control here."

I fixed my eyes on her so she was the centre of my field of vision. At the edge there should be, had to be, a door. There wasn't.

"You're pathetic," she said. "Did you know that?"

"Actually, yes," I said. "Let me out of here right now, or I'll kill you."

She smiled. "I wouldn't," she said. "I'm sure you could, you're so much bigger and stronger and more aggressive than me, but then you'd be stuck in here for ever and ever, since you can't make doors. Of course you wouldn't be entirely on your own, you'd have the dog for company. But he farts. It can be pretty unbearable in a confined space, believe me."

That draining feeling I told you about. Only the second time in my life I'd experienced it, but once endured, never forgotten. "Fine," I said. "You win."

She clapped her hands together in girlish glee. "Do I really? How nice." I felt a searing pain in the backs of my knees, as though someone had cut the tendons. Then I slumped forward, kneeling before her. I couldn't feel my feet at all. "Now then," she said. "The thing is, I don't know how to do the next bit, never having been to college. But that doesn't matter, because you do." She smiled. "Much better really," she said. "Why should I give up years and years of my life sitting in draughty libraries learning stupid old theory when all I actually need to do is open up your head, and there it all is, ready for me to use?"

My head was splitting; now there's a coincidence. "It doesn't work like that," I said.

"Doesn't it?" She reached out and picked up a book, the only one in the room. She opened it, and I screamed. It was as though she'd pulled the two halves of my skull apart, like opening a clam. "What a pity. No, you're wrong, here it all is." She ran a finger down the page. "Chapter six, how to steal someone's mind." She turned a few pages. "Doesn't look too hard. Shall we have a go?"

I slashed at her with *stricto ense*. She parried with the cover of the book. I yelled and clamped my hand round the gash in my cheek. Blood was gushing between my fingers.

"Let's see," she said, turning a page. "It's all pretty straightforward by the look of it. Stands to reason, really. If it was hard, you couldn't do it."

Desperately I tried to remember about Room theory, but I couldn't. "I feel a bit guilty," she said, as I felt my mind emptying. "Playing all those nasty pranks on my neighbours. They're stupid and dull as chicken broth but there's no real malice in them. But it was worth it, to get you down here. I knew it was the only way. I'd never be able to go to your stupid college or read your stupid books, so all this wonderful talent I've been given would just go to waste, and where's the sense in that? But then I thought, what's a book? It's the inside of someone's head put down on paper so anyone can see it and it'll never, ever die. Do you know I can't read? Women don't, not even delicately nurtured ones like me, it's not ladylike. So it's just as well I've got a wise, clever man like you to do it for me."

"Please," I said. "Don't."

She looked at me over the top of the book. "You're pathetic," she said, and carried on reading.

I tried *ruat caelum*, which I've known since I was thirteen years old. I couldn't remember it. I tried to think of a Form, any bloody Form. They'd all gone. She looked up and folded down the corner of a page. The pain made me howl like a dog, and the boarhound lifted its head off its paws and growled again. "Don't set him off," she said, "or he'll start barking."

And he farts, I know, you told me. I could feel slices of myself falling away like apple-peel in spirals, things that were a part of me before I was truly myself. Meanwhile she read, calm and steady, and each time she turned the page I screamed, and she took no notice.

"I don't know what you're making all that fuss about," she said. "Anyone would think I was skinning you alive. It's only knowledge, after all. When I'm done I shall turn you loose, and then you can live the rest of your life the way I'm supposed to live mine. I think that's only fair, don't you?"

I didn't have the strength to argue, or the words or the wit to argue with, or even enough understanding to know if she was right or wrong. The only argument left was strength; she was strong and I was weak, so presumably everything she was doing to me was just fine and exactly how it ought to be. I can live with that, I remember thinking, it's so simple even I can understand it, and if it pleases her to spare my life and let me crawl away, I'll be grateful and worship her for her goodness and loving kindness.

She knew what I was thinking, of course. "You're pathetic," she said. "But I guess you know that."

"I'd sort of gathered."

That made her laugh. "You're just a book, see?" She held up the book. She had it upside down. "All those clever men spent years copying things into you, and now I've copied them out again. Actually, not copied." She grinned. "A real book must be a wonderful thing. It can be read over and over again and it's not diminished. You're not a book after all, you're just a barn."

"Make your mind up," I said. It cost me the last of my strength. One last wisecrack and now I'd be stupid for ever. Ah, well. Everything was, no doubt, all for the best.

"I ought to thank you," she said. It was one of those books that has clasps, and a hasp for a tiny lock. "But screw that. The hawk doesn't thank the sparrow, because it's rude to talk with your mouth full. All right, you can go now. I don't need you any more."

A door opened and swung wide. She wasn't looking at me. She had her nose in the book. I tried to stand up but my legs were numb, so I started to crawl toward the door, pulling myself along with my elbows.

The boarhound lifted its head again and made that ominous grinding noise. What the hell, I thought. I pulled myself a few inches closer to the door, and the boarhound sprang up and leapt at me—over me—

I turned my head in time to see her on the ground, the huge dog standing over her, worrying at her neck locked between its jaws. It used its shoulders and back to rip her throat out; a quick, spasmodic movement, a snatch. It's rude to snatch, my mother used to tell me. Now I could see why.

The dog lifted its head and swallowed, two big gulps, all gone. She'd stopped moving. The dog sat up straight and farted.

It was really bad, enough to make your eyes water. When they cleared and I could see again, Father Anthemius was sitting in a chair. The room was different. There was a big, broad table covered in clutter—rolls of paper, books, empty cups, chunks of mouldy stale bread, rat droppings—and a fireplace. The fire was lit. That room was always too hot, I remembered people telling me. What with the heat and the godawful smell, how was anybody expected to learn anything?

He was reading a book. He closed it, looked at me and tossed it into the fire. The pain, which was worse than anything I'd ever felt before, lasted as long as it took the book to burn. He reached over with the poker and pounded the dove-grey ashes into dust, then looked at me.

"Well?" he said.

I nodded. It was all back again, everything she'd taken from me. I felt as though I'd had a big brush, like the sort sweeps use to clean chimneys, shoved down my throat and pushed really hard until it came out through my arse. "I saved your life," he said. "Again. You're pathetic. But you know that."

"Yes."

"Even so," said Father Anthemius, "I suppose I owe you a certain degree of gratitude. Don't you think?"

I nodded. "You were dying," I said.

"I was," said Father Anthemius.

"You knew you didn't have long. It made you angry."

"Very angry. If there's one form of vandalism I can't stand, it's burning books."

I reckoned I could afford one wan smile. "Quite," I said. "You'd spent your entire life writing all that learning and wisdom into a book, and the moment you write the last word, it's snatched away from you and thrown into the fire. Where's the sense in that?"

He nodded. "I don't mind cruelty," he said, "but I can't abide waste."

"So," I went on, "you considered room theory. It's always been your best thing. Whenever there's any danger, you just duck into another room. You showed me that, when I got angry."

"Fancy you remembering."

"You saw me," I went on. "And you saw that I was—"

"Defective," said Father Anthemius. "Or would you prefer inadequate?"

"Defective, thank you. You saw I wasn't capable of making a door. I could do Forms and other stuff, but I was missing the ability to make a door, which meant I could never progress any further, or qualify, or be a practitioner. Which meant they'd throw me out of the Studium and I'd have to go back to the Mesoge and spend the rest of my life ploughing and herding pigs."

"Actual useful work." He grinned. "Perish the thought," he said.

"So you pretended to teach me how to make a door," I said. "But that's not what you did. You got me scared out of my wits so I wouldn't see what you were doing—"

"Like a fly," he said, "laying its eggs in a wound. A dreadful thing for a man of my distinction, but what choice did I have?"

"You turned my head—me—into a Room," I said. "Your body died, but you weren't in it. You were—"

"Plenty of space in there," he said, "which you weren't ever going to use. Admit it, I've been as quiet as a little mouse. You never even knew I was there. And thanks to me, you became a great wise scholar, which you never ought to have done."

The maggots of wisdom, I thought, gnawing away at me and building nests of scholarship in the holes they'd made.

"Without me," said Father Anthemius, "you were pathetic. You were as weak and useless as a woman. Actually," he added, "I take that back. I was tempted, you realise. She was so strong, more natural untrained ability than I've ever seen in one human being in my entire life. I could have slipped into her mind and she'd never have known I was there, and I'd have had access to more strength, more sheer *ability* than I'd ever thought was possible." He shook his head. "But she was still a woman," he said.

"Even with me to guide her, nobody would ever have taken her seriously. And then what? She'd have ended up making war on the whole world, like she did on the people in her silly little village, out of frustration and sheer spite. I hate waste," he said. "I would've been wasted on her. So I decided to stay with you, even though you're pathetic."

But very good at Forms nonetheless. I formed *stricto ense* in my mind and aimed it at him. He smiled at me. "Sure," he said. "Go ahead. You kill me, I die, you'll never be able to make another door as long as you live. Well, get on with it. I'm waiting."

He's still waiting, and that was a long time ago.

I met the mayor and the constable on my way out of the village. All done, I told them.

"You found out who it was?"

I nodded.

"Who was it?"

I took a deep breath. "Tell you what," I said. "Give it a week, then ask around. Whoever hasn't been seen for a week, that's who it was. All right?"

They wanted to ask me questions, buy me a drink, hold a parade, give me money, put up a statue, make speeches, rename the village after me, all that sort of thing. Go away, I told them. I just want to get out of the horrible Mesoge. I think I offended them. So what?

I can raise the dead. Not that I ever would, it goes without saying, because it's absolutely forbidden. Actually, I always assumed that was a convenient cop-out on the part of the profession—yes, we *could* do it, of course we could, we can do anything. But we don't, because it's illegal and unethical, so you'll never know if we're telling the truth or not. Big deal.

But yes, I can do it. Crazy, really. I can call back the dead, take those ashes and that dust and turn them back into pages. I can unburn books, but I can't make a simple door. A bit pathetic, really, but there you go.

And it was the Mesoge, for God's sake. There was nobody to see me do it, and if someone did see, nobody would ever believe them, because all country people are superstitious idiots, everybody knows that. A woman would stand more chance of being taken seriously by my esteemed colleagues at the Studium. So why not?

I won't tell you the Form, not that it really matters. What matters is standing in the narrow passage off which opens the door to the seventh Room. I'd been there before, but this time I was all too painfully aware that he was there with me. I couldn't see him, but the lingering stench of dog fart was unmistakable. Never mind. I knocked on the door. "Come in," she said.

She was sitting in front of the fire, embroidering something. "Oh," she said. "It's you."

I stood in the doorway. Believe it or not, I was in no tearing hurry to go fully inside the seventh Room. You're all right if you have one foot firmly planted in the passageway, or so they tell me. How they would know that I have no idea.

"Don't give me that look," I said. "I didn't kill you."

"No, your dog did. Big difference."

I grinned. "Actually, I think it's a moot point whose dog was whose, if you see what I mean. You go through life thinking you're the owner and it's the dog, and then you realise, who's actually walking who?"

She gazed at me. "You're an idiot," she said.

"I suppose I must be," I replied. "All that time and I never realised. How about you?"

"Oh, I always knew, right from the start. I knew I was better than everybody else in the whole world, but they wouldn't let me be myself."

"So you took to sticking pins in people. To show them how much better you were."

She shrugged. "Not through choice. If I'd been allowed to use my gifts and realise my true potential, it'd have been thunderbolts, not pins."

"What did they ever do to deserve it?"

"What did you ever do to deserve what you've got and I could never have?" She put down her needlework and took in the room with a wide, circling gesture. "I spent my whole life stuck in this place," she said. "And now I'm dead and look where I end up."

The Mesoge, I thought. It's where you go when you die, if you've been really bad. Or you're born there; same difference. The Mesoge is where I belong.

I left her to her vengeful wallowing, which I regarded as pathetic, and went back to the third Room, but I couldn't stay there for more than a minute, because of the smell.

My Beautiful Life

I've done some truly appalling things in my life. I'm bitterly ashamed of them now. Saying I did them all for the best—and saying, those things weren't my idea, other people made me do them, is just as bad; admitting that I'm a spineless coward as well as morally bankrupt. I'm a mess, and no good nohow.

I can say all that and get away with it; you can't. Don't even think about it. If you were to repeat what I've just told you word for word, let alone paraphrase it or add a few rhetorical flourishes of your own, they'd have you up for high treason and stretch your neck. Speaking ill of me is slandering the Crown, therefore by implication the empire, therefore by implication the eight million people who live in it. Quite probably, Bemba—that's the poor devil I'm dictating this to—is guilty of a capital crime just because he's writing down what I told him to—though of course, if he'd refused, that would've been treason too.

It's treason because the Law assumes that anything nasty or bad about the emperor can't possibly be true; which says an awful lot about the Law and laws in general, if you ask me. I'd write it all out myself and avoid the risk of yet another innocent man going to the gallows for my sake, only I never learned to write, and it's far too late now.

Once upon a time—

Bemba's shaking his head at me; you can't start a history, even an unofficial one, with *Once upon a time.* Screw him—sorry, Bemba, I didn't mean that. But *Once upon a time* it's going to have to be, because that's the only way I know to start a story, never having had any education to speak of. You can fiddle with it later if you like.

Once upon a time, there were three brothers.

Where was I?

I've really had enough of the pain. It's always there. You think you've got used to it, up to a point, and then it suddenly flares up and reduces you to a snivelling heap. For crying out loud, says the little voice inside me, pull yourself together, try and preserve the little dignity you've got left, there are people watching you. And besides, adds the little voice, perfectly correctly, you brought all this on yourself, it's all your own fault, like everything else. And whatever you do, don't you dare ask for sympathy.

Fine. But it's a real pest, because it snaps my train of thought like a carrot and I can't concentrate worth a damn, and when I get one of the bad attacks it wipes my mind clean, so I can barely remember who I am. No bad thing, in a way.

All right, let's start again. This is the story of my life, which is shortly going to end, and about time too. I guess you could call it a confession. There's a difference of opinion among the leading theologians on this point. Some of them say you can confess your sins silently, without actually moving your lips, while others maintain that in order to be valid, a confession must be made out loud, *to* someone, or it doesn't count. A third school maintains that that someone has to be a priest, but I have my doubts about that, mostly because priests get paid for hearing confessions. My brother Nico, when he was High Precentor, charged four hundred thousand solidi just for *Bless me, father, for I have sinned,* and if you wanted to give him chapter and verse it was extra, fifty thousand solidi per hundred words. I remember saying to him, Nico, you can't charge that much, nobody's going to pay that when a friar'll give you absolution for a solidus fifty. He laughed at me. He was right, too. He got so much business that towards the end, he was actually turning people away.

My brother Nico was a bad man, perhaps the most evil human being I've ever met. He loved me more than anyone or anything in the world. I miss him.

ONCE UPON A time there were three brothers.

The empire functions on the basis that heredity is everything. Eldest sons inherit from eldest sons. All of us inherit the fruits of the wisdom and valour of our ancestors, who by definition were a hundred times better and smarter than we could ever hope to be. We live in enlightened comfort because our forefathers conquered the world and then made sense of it; we in turn are entitled to enjoy our legacy, because we are the end product of five thousand years of thoughtful, selective breeeding, we're the distilled essence of our ancestors, which must mean we're pretty damn near perfect—none of our doing, of course, it's just a fact. We are what we were bred to be.

But the three brothers weren't born inside the empire, nor were they citizens. Their mother was beautiful, charming and friendly for a living, and if she knew who their fathers were, she neglected to mention it. There's a remote possibility that one of them was a nobleman in disguise, a prince of the Blood Royal, or maybe even the Invincible Sun Himself, in mortal guise, like in the fairy tales. It'd be nice if that was true, because then the fact that one of the three brothers became emperor wouldn't be a glaring insult to everything we believe in, but I'm inclined to doubt it.

The three brothers lived with their mother in a wattle-and-daub hut in a village in the mountains. They didn't have any land of their own, not even a scrap of garden to grow cabbages in, so life was something of a struggle when they were growing up. By the time the eldest boy was twelve, their mother was still charming and friendly but no longer beautiful enough to be worth money, so she made her sons sit down one evening and talked to them seriously. Because we're so poor, she said, one of you three will have to be sold. I love you all very much, so I can't possibly decide, you'll have to sort it out among yourselves.

The middle and younger brothers burst into tears, but the eldest brother didn't hesitate. Don't worry, he said, I'll go. I'm the oldest, it's my duty.

The other two agreed. They were very upset, because they loved their brother, and he was big and strong, and protected them from the other kids, and stole things for them to eat when they were hungry. But they didn't want to be sold, so apart from crying a lot they raised no objections.

If you wanted to be sold, you had to go to the fair at Kalenda Maia. Buyers came to the fair from all over, Scheria and the Vesani republic as well as the empire. A week before it was time to leave for the fair, the eldest brother went out early and didn't come back. The other two were very sad; they figured he'd changed his mind and made a run for it. They didn't blame him—it was exactly what they'd have done if they'd been chosen—but it meant one of them would have to be sold instead, which they didn't fancy at all. They would have tossed a coin for it, but they didn't have a coin. They asked their mother to choose, but she'd recently been paid for her friendliness with a small barrel of brandy and wasn't up to making decisions.

I know, I said. Let's get the Invincible Sun to choose for us.

My brother Edax didn't believe in the Invincible Sun. At least, he didn't deny that He exists—he was a peasant, his mind simply couldn't conceive of something like that, we're alone in the universe and there's nobody up there at all, just clouds—but he figured that Heaven didn't give a shit about us. He said as much, so I picked up a rock and hit him. It's very important to nip blasphemy in the bud. You bloody fool, he said, look what you've done. It'll heal up, I assured him (and I was right, up to a point, but the scar makes people wince when they see it, even now) and don't you dare talk like that ever again. He looked at me, then grinned. It'll have to be you now, he said. Who's going to pay good money for a kid with only one eye?

He was exaggerating, of course, but the point was a valid one. I couldn't argue, and he started to laugh. I wanted to hit him again, but I was too scared by what I'd already done. So I patched him up as best I could with plantain boiled in water and a needle and thread. He whined like hell. I didn't do a very good job, because he kept wriggling and flinching.

The next evening, the day before the fair, Nico came back. He was white as a sheet and his clothes were brown with dried blood. Where the hell have you been, we asked him.

He explained. He'd been told that eunuchs fetch twice as much as whole kids at Kalenda fair, and he figured, if he was going to be sold, why not get the best possible price? So he went to see the stockman at the next-door farm, who told him he was crazy and chased him away. So, being Nico, he sat down under a tree somewhere quiet and thought about it, figured out what to do, from first principles. Then he sharpened his knife—call it a knife; it was three inches of broken blade he'd found in a hedge when he was six—and lit a small fire, and threw a couple of biggish stones on it to heat up. Then he cut off his dick, as far up the shaft as he could manage.

He said he hadn't imagined there'd be that much blood. It gushed out like water from a split pipe, he told me later, and for a moment he was really scared. The idea was to cauterise the cut with one of the hot stones, but he tried to pick the stone out of the fire using two sticks and it kept slipping out again, and by this time there was blood everywhere and he could feel himself draining away, a bit like being drunk, a bit like feeling very, very sleepy; so he grabbed the stone out of the red embers, but he couldn't hold it, and it fell out of his hand, and then he passed out.

He came round in a sort of swamp, where the blood had soaked away into the leaf-mould, like a pig's wallow. He was so weak he could scarcely breathe. But he looked up and saw the sun was a lot farther round that it had been, so time was getting on... And then it occurred to him that maybe he'd been out for a long time, maybe a whole day, maybe more, and for all he knew, he'd missed Kalenda fair, and one of us had had to be sold instead. So he got up and walked back to our village.

When our mother heard what he'd done, she burst out screaming and sobbing and wouldn't snap out of it, so she was no use for anything. Edax and I stuffed Nico full of stale cheese and dried apple, which was all there was in the house, and he said he was feeling much better, which I don't think was strictly true, and then it was time to set off for Kalenda.

I think I said Nico was strong. Years later, I asked a famous doctor and he said that Nico should've died, it was a miracle he survived—and then he paused, because miracle usually means the Invincible Sun intervening to some good purpose, and this was Nico we were talking about. It was extraordinary, the doctor went on, that Nico had survived at all, after losing a ridiculous amount of blood, not to mention the risk of infection, and lockjaw from the rusty knife. And then walking twelve miles up the mountain to Kalenda, it was—and then words failed him. Monstrous, I suggested. And he thought about it for a moment, and nodded. Monstrous, he said, quite.

We got to Kalenda somehow, and the fair was just about to start. You want to get to a buying fair early, before the dealers have spent all their money. We hauled Nico up to the first stall we got to, and they looked at him. Five shillings, they said.

Then Nico explained; he'd been cut, so the price was twelve and six. Let's have a look, then, said the dealer, and Nico pulled up his tunic, and the dealer laughed. Sorry, son, he said, that doesn't count.

To be a proper eunuch, he explained, you had to cut the balls off. That's what gives the eunuch his calm, docile, pleasant disposition, which is what people pay good money for. Simply docking the cock was no good; if anything, it reduced the price, since you couldn't breed from a docked man. Then he asked; who was the clown who did this? And Nico said, I did it myself. The dealer stared at him. Four shillings, he said. Take it or leave it.

We left it. Then we went round all the other dealers, but none of them were interested. He's a big, strong lad, they said, but obviously either very stupid or not quite right in the head; four bob, and that's being generous.

By this point we were feeling very sad. I was practically in tears, because obviously we couldn't go home empty-handed, and three or four of the dealers had looked at me quite hard, and one had offered six bob for me. Edax was sulking at Nico for being stupid, and Nico had started bleeding again, though it was just a trickle running down his leg, like a little boy taken short. Mother's going to be so mad at us, Edax kept saying. And I knew I ought to say, it's all right, I'll go instead, but I couldn't, I was too scared and too selfish, so I started snivelling, and Nico had to tell both of us to shut up.

Then, the very last stall we came to, there was an old man with a bald head and another, very short, with a huge mane of flowing white hair, very fine, like a girl's. By this point Nico was so tired he could barely speak, so I had to do the talking. I explained, and the bald man said the usual, let's have a look, then; and I tugged up Nico's hem. The bald man and the man with the silky hair looked at the mess, frowning slightly. How much do you want for him, they asked.

Twelve and six, I said. The two old men looked at each other, and the bald man whispered something in the other man's ear. Then he looked at me and said, the most we can give you is fourteen shillings.

I nearly said, No, twelve, but Edax poked me in the ribs. All right, I said. And that's how we sold my brother. Simple as that.

THIS QUESTION OF belief.

Nico believed—and Edax too, but who cares what he thinks?—that the Invincible Sun exists, but He can only be bothered with important events and important people, which is why Nico felt justified in charging so much more for an absolution. Sure, he said, you can get one for a buck fifty, but if it comes from some red-nosed village Brother, it won't work, it's useless. But if the High Precentor intercedes for you personally, He will actually hear and take note, and your sins will be forgiven and your soul will be washed clean; and what else could you buy for four hundred thousand that could possibly be worth that much money?

(Bear in mind that Nico never had a day's theological training in his life. He got to be High Precentor because the job comes bundled up with being Count of the Stables. It was useful, Nico told me, because of benefit of clergy. He used to go to Temple regularly when he was precentor, mostly so he could get on with some work during the anthems.)

I disagree. I believe that He watches us all, taking careful note of everything we say and everything we do, and that sooner or later He rewards us and punishes us according to our deserts. That's not a comfortable thought. Actually, it's wrong to say I believe. I *know*. Belief implies there's some doubt or uncertainty about the matter. I know. Trust me.

SOME YEARS LATER, Nico had the silky-haired man hunted down (the bald man was already dead), and before he had him crucified, he asked him; why did you buy me, and why did you pay so much? To which the man replied that he and his partner did a lot of business with the imperial civil service, who were crying out for eunuchs—there was a shortage, would you believe, on account of peace with the Erbafresc, which meant no more prisoners of war—and wouldn't care particularly about the balls so long as they could fill their quota. And why did you pay more than we asked? Well, the man said, you all looked so sad and bedraggled, we felt sorry for you. Didn't do him any good, of course. At that point, Nico was anxious to get rid of all the witnesses to his earlier life, and the crucifixion—well, he had this mean streak. Always there, under the surface. Just the way he was, or the way the Invincible Sun made him.

Also, Nico found out about the beautiful silky fine hair; apparently, if you have the cut before your voice breaks, you'll never go bald and your hair will be beautiful. The dealer had been done when he was six years old, and never gave it a moment's thought.

But I'm getting ahead of myself. Nico was sold to the Commissioners of the Secretariat, who trained him as a clerk. He took to it wonderfully well. He learned his letters and figuring in no time flat, so diligent, so eager to learn, so eager to please. He always did have a tidy mind, and he always was smart. In no time flat, he was absolutely indispensible in Supply; knew where everything was, remembered everyone's names, knew which forms had to be used for which requisitions, pretty soon he was running the place, while his superiors took long lunches. They were mad as cats when he was poached by the Household, but of course, nobody says no to the Household; and so Nico left the provinces and came to the City. Wasn't long before everyone was saying what a splendid Clerk of the Works he'd make, except you have to be a free man to be Clerk. It's a rotten job, of course, though terribly important and grand, because every crumbling wall, loose roof tile and project overdue or over budget is your fault, which was why they were all happy for Nico to get it. But when Nico was Clerk, there weren't any crumbling walls or loose tiles, and every job was finished on time, under budget.

Now, the whole idea of eunuchs in the Service is, they don't get distracted like normal men do. They don't chase around after women and nobody wants to be their friend, so what else is there but work? But Nico was the extreme, prodigious, monstrous; he started work well before Prime and didn't stop till after

Compline, he slept on a bench in his office and ate his bread and cheese at his desk, washed down with water in a pottery cup. Usually the Clerk is loathed and hated by everyone who comes into contact with him, by the very nature of his job—if he wants to get something done, he's got to yell at the man who's supposed to be doing it, and if he doesn't he gets yelled at by the man who's waiting to get on with the rest of the project. But somehow Nico managed to keep everybody sweet and happy, weaving the men and their schedules and difficulties together like withies into a basket—he always could bend people, either by sweetness or force, but at this time he was all honey and smiles, a little bit extra squeezed out of the budget for a bonus here, a job for an unemployable idiot nephew there—like the jugglers who balance spinning plates on top of sticks on the tips of their noses, all done with little imperceptible wriggles and flexings of muscles, but from a distance all you see is a man standing still and relaxed, with a happy smile on his face, while a beautiful, ordered firmament circles serenely around him.

EDAX AND I didn't know about any of that, of course. All we knew was, those two old men put a collar on our big brother and led him away, and we took fourteen shillings back to our mother, and three weeks later she died.

It wasn't long before we wished our big brother was in Hell. Where we lived—don't get me wrong, we worshipped the Invincible Sun same as everybody else does except the heathens, but let's say we didn't get many theologians and professors of divinity in those parts; most of what we believed in we'd made up ourselves, or vaguely remembered some missionary telling our great-great-grandfathers. And one of the things we vaguely remembered was the Book of Abominations; all those long lists of things you mustn't eat and mustn't touch. You'll remember, of course, that men with missing or deformed sexual organs are right up there with shellfish and yellow-spotted mushrooms—but of course, nobody takes any of that stuff seriously any more, not since the Erbafresc came up with langoustines in mushroom and white wine sauce. But we did. Just the sort of thing we loved to hear; because it was a reason, an explanation. Every time the crops failed or the plague came round or the free companies stole our sheep or the imperial army marched off a whole village in wooden collars, we knew exactly what had gone wrong, some selfish bastard had been eating raw fish or buggering chickens, and we were all being punished for it. It made sense, which it simply wouldn't do without the abominations and the tribulation and the wrath of God. So, when word got around about what Nico had done (himself, with a rusty knife, for *money*) and then our mother had died, call that a coincidence because I don't—let's just say Edax and I weren't popular. Everyone knows that an abominator's family are just as filthy as he is himself. Properly speaking they should have boarded us up in our house and set fire to it, except my mother had cousins down in the valley, and they'd have been morally obliged to make a row about it, even though they'd disowned her.

Letting us live was one thing. Giving either of us a job was something quite other. We had the house; we didn't own it, of course, but nobody else would have dreamed of living there, so the owner left us alone. That was all. There wasn't enough ground out back to grow a row of carrots. Neither of us had a trade, and if we'd been the finest blacksmiths or wheelwrights in the country, nobody would have wanted anything we made. We were useless. I had—well, my advantage, even then, but Edax was a scrawny, evil-looking little runt, looking just the way you'd expect an abomination to look. We had no money, and even if we'd had plenty, nobody would've sold us a sack of mouldy oats. We were a problem that would solve itself, given time, and not much time, at that.

(My advantage. I was a tall, thin, skinny kid, but around the time we lost Nico, I started filling out. People say that—for a while—I was the best-looking man in the empire. I don't believe that, not for one moment. But I was handsome, or pretty, or somewhere between the two. Not that I knew it. We didn't have mirrors where I come from, and how often do you stop and gaze into a bucket of water?)

I remember Edax looking at me, the day we realised there was nothing left to eat in the house, and I looked at him back; and then he said, Fine, if we're evil and damned already, why not? Not usually given to saying clever or perceptive things, my kid brother, but—well, it made me feel a whole lot better about the idea. So we waited till it was dark, and walked out over the back paddock, through the orchard, out onto the lane, up the hill, through the hunting gate, short cut across the four-acres to our nearest neighbour's barn. Nothing was locked or barred, needless to say, so we simply helped ourselves. Then we went home, stopping to rest a few times along the way because of the weight of what we were carrying, and gorged ourselves silly on barley porridge, roots and store apples. And we waited. I think we both expected the neighbours to come crashing in through the door with dungforks and a noose; but morning came, and then afternoon and evening. They can't have noticed yet, we said to each other, how often do people check their barns to see if the stuff's still all there? Days passed, nobody came by. We finished up the last of what we'd stolen, so we went back for some more.

To find new two-inch-board shutters on the windows and a new door, all fastened with padlocks, the Mezentine pattern with a key that looks like a comb. So they knew we'd been there. Somehow, I think that was what disturbed me most. We were so unclean, they couldn't bring themselves to lynch us for fear of defilement. We smashed a shutter with a big rock and climbed in over the splintered panels.

A week passed; no retribution. But the next time we went there, it was empty, cleaned out. So we trudged on over the other side of the ridge and robbed the priest's tithe barn.

Front and centre with a nice little snippet of theology, exactly the sort of thing you need to know when considering a career in theft. All mortal things, according to the Book of Abominations, are susceptible to defilement, a condition so unspeakable that you put up with crippling loss rather than lay hands on an unclean thief. But the Invincible Sun can't be defiled, any more than you can spoil the sea by pissing in it. And a priest, even a poxy little village Brother, is His agent and minister, by virtue of the principle of apostolic association, therefore undefilable; and the same goes for his duly appointed agents and ministers, their dungforks, their nooses and everything else appertaining to them, under a general licence of devolved absolution. They came for us just before dawn the next day, kicked us awake, smacked us around a bit, snapped collars on our necks and marched us, barefoot and stumbling, down to the village, where we saw two ropes waiting for us on the low branch of the hanging tree.

They'd stuck wads of sheep's wool in our mouths, so all Edax could so was mumble and bleat; I didn't bother. We'd done wrong, we'd been caught, and it wasn't as though I'd enjoyed being alive very much, so what the hell. If they'd taken the wad out of my mouth I'd have felt constrained to tell them Edax was completely innocent, I'd done all the thieving on my own; but they didn't, so I never got the chance to redeem myself by penitent sacrifice, probably just as well. They hauled us under the tree, and a couple of men I knew by sight, old friends of my mother's as it happens, came up holding milking stools, and I had a pretty good idea what they were for.

Edax was sobbing his heart out, and that bothered me. I can't say I ever liked him much, there's not really anything about him that anyone could possibly like, but he's my brother. So I prayed; Father in Heaven, please. Now there are learned men who'll tell you a prayer won't work unless it's said aloud, and I had a face full of wool at the time. I can only assume He has a discretion to make exceptions, because just then the Brother came out of his house. He had a scarf wrapped round his face, so only the tip of his nose was sticking out, and he made a special point of not looking at us; we couldn't be hanged today, he told them, because it was the old moon before Ascension.

Dead silence. Then someone piped up and said, No, you're wrong there, old moon's not till tonight; and there was a bit of a discussion, until the Brother pointed out that in orthodox doctrine, old moon starts at noon, not sunset—a certain amount of grumbling about that, but you can't really tell a priest he's wrong about theology, not unless you're a priest yourself. So then one of the parish wardens, trying hard to keep his temper, said, All right, but what are we supposed to do with them in the meantime? I'm not having them at my place, that's for sure. Apparently theology didn't have an answer to that, and nobody was in any hurry to volunteer, and there was a long silence, until the priest sighed and said he had a woodshed out back, but someone would have to put a lock on it.

I've often thought about that. I prayed; and my prayers were answered. But how, exactly? The schedule of festivals and holidays is set out in Scripture, written down about a thousand years ago. The phases of the Moon were, presumably, ordained way back at the moment of Creation, when He set the stars and heavenly bodies in motion. Is it possible that, ten thousand years ago, when He had all sorts of important concerns and difficult calculations on His mind, He spared a moment to factor in the requirement for noon of the old moon of that particular month of that particular year… I find that hard to believe. But even so, I believe it. I believe that from the very Beginning, He so ordered the cosmos and the gearing of the celestial machine to accommodate Edax and me, at that precise moment the most worthless, least valuable articles of livestock in the whole of His illimitable estates. I have to believe it, since the fact is there and irrefutable. I prayed, and we were spared the noose. It happened.

Try all you can, wriggle as much as you like, you can't get round it. It's a fact.

No, you fool, you're saying, it's a coincidence. And I forgive you, because I've preached my fatuous little sermon before giving you the other fact: namely that just after midnight, when Edax and I were lying on an excruciatingly uncomfortable pile of big logs in the Brother's woodshed, there was an earthquake.

We do get earthquakes in those parts; about once every ninety years, as far as anyone can make out, and there'd been one eighteen months earlier, bad enough to shake the half-ripe pears off the trees, misery for the farmers but a source of great joy to their pigs. This earthquake was different. I remember Edax squealing and suddenly shutting up—a huge round of green oak bounced and hit him a glancing blow on the head as it sailed past me and smashed the woodshed door into splinters. Then the shaking stopped, and we sat there, looking at stars through the open doorway.

But not, you can bet your life, for very long. Edax is scrawny, but back then he was fast, and I have long legs. We went sprawling a few times, either aftershocks or we tripped over things, but we picked ourselves up and kept going, didn't stop until the sun rose; at which point it occurred to both of us without the need for words that we didn't want to be seen, so we dived in under a briar hedge and lay there gasping, until I realised (it hit me like a hammer) exactly what had happened, and Edax started whining about being hungry.

THIS MAY COME as a surprise, but nobody seems to know you're an abomination just by looking at you. We made it to Chastel, fifty miles barefoot, walking all night and hiding up during the day, at which point we sort of gave up; either they were looking for us or they weren't, we'd find out quickly enough, but we couldn't go on like that. Turned out they weren't looking for us.

In fact, nobody gave a damn about us. And nobody wanted to give us work, either.

So Edax and I had a discussion. We tried stealing, I told him, and it very nearly got us hanged. Yes, he said, because we were careless, also it was in the village, where everybody knows everybody and everything. In a city—I suppose I should have explained to him, about praying and being delivered; sort of an implied condition that you don't do it again. But I couldn't bring myself to tell him about that and have him laugh in my face, so I had no valid argument to oppose him with, and as he pointed out, stealing is a two-man job if you want to get away with it, one of you steals, the other keeps a look out. If I abandoned him and he was forced to work alone and got caught, his blood would be on my hands.

But we weren't caught. Not for a long time.

NICO WASN'T CLERK of the Works for very long. There was one of those power-struggles in the civil service, the sort where you get two incredibly powerful and influential ministers who can't stand the sight of each other. To give you an idea; a man I used to know told me about one time when he was out hunting, bow and stable, and he came across two stags fighting. Normally you can't get within a hundred yards, he told me, but these two idiots were so preoccupied with smashing each other to bits that he was able to walk right up close, twenty yards, and shoot them both with consecutive arrows. I don't know if the hunting story is true, but that's exactly how it happens in the civil service. The two mighty stags were so busy clashing horns and gouging each others' flanks, they didn't notice the real enemy until it was all over, and they were sitting in mail coaches on their way to deputy assistant postmasterships in the Perioeca.

Now the man who won the power struggle was a shrewd judge of character and a marvellous operator in the confined spaces of the Chancery corridors; he wasn't quite so hot on which form to use for which application, and when the quarterly appropriations were due in by. Just as well he'd noticed my brother Nico. Stick with me, he'd whispered in his ear, and I'll see you right; and Nico left the Clerk's office and moved into the offices of the Count of the Stables.

Goes without saying, the Count of the Stables doesn't have anything to do with hay, oats or fresh straw. Once upon a time; but that was many years ago. The story goes that Tryphon IV, realising that the nest of vipers who ran the Treasury were out to get him, set up a parallel underground treasury routed through the royal stables, and put the chief groom in charge of the whole thing because he was the only man in the City he could trust. And the chief groom did such a good job that within two years the budget deficit was just a memory and the soldiers were paid on time and twelve billion in taxes that had sort of trickled away into the pockets of the Treasury bosses found its way back into the Exchequer; whereupon the chief groom had Tryphon quietly stabbed and in due course assumed the purple under the name of Basiliscus II. Nice story; quite possibly true. Anyhow, the Count of the Stables does a great many things, but none of them with a pitchfork.

Nor, if you want to borrow a horse, is the Stables a good place to look for one. It's a huge building out back of the Red Palace, with a hundred and sixteen windows and just the one door. Getting round inside it is a nightmare until you've been there a year; and don't bother asking anyone the way, because they'll lie to you. The theory being, if you need to ask, you must be new; and novelty is a terrible sin in the Stables. If you're new, chances are you're either a spy for the Exchequer or a pushy young cut-throat after somebody's job.

Nico, of course, was both. On his first day, some old clerk took him for a long walk, the long way round so as to confuse him, and showed him his office, then walked away and left him to it. But Nico was ready. He'd been counting under his breath all the way;

thirty paces, turn left, twenty-six paces, up the stairs, seventeen paces, turn right, and so on. Not many men would have bothered, but Nico was smart, he knew how much it mattered. So, the first thing he did when he was alone in his new lair was to pull a wax tablet out of his sleeve (there was no paper or pen in the office, needless to say) and wrote it all down before he forgot it. For the first three weeks he had to follow the same roundabout route, but at least he didn't get hopelessly lost; and every night he made additions and corrections to the map he was making of the place, the only one in existence; there'd never been one before and Nico made damned sure there never was one again. By the end of his fifth week, he knew the geography of that building better than the men who'd been there twenty years, and he always reckoned that was the key to his later success. Just knowing where everything and everybody was, and who you'd have to go past on your way to talk to so-and-so, and who'd be able to overhear whose conversations—

For his first year in the Stables, Nico was the perfect henchman. The great man whose coat-tails had carried him there relied on him for everything, and he was never disappointed. Also, though he'd said nothing to anyone, the great man's key enemies in the department started retiring early, transferring to rubbish jobs in the provinces or dying. A marvellous run of good luck, he thought for a while, and then he realised that nobody's that lucky, and he must have a guardian angel he didn't know about; and by the time he'd figured out who the guardian angel was, it was too late. Nico didn't say a word; he didn't have to. All he did was leave a dossier on the great man's desk—copy statements, excerpts from the record, letters, memoranda, no big deal on their own but taken together, proof positive that the great man had been systematically blackmailing and murdering his colleagues until there was nobody left standing.

I didn't do it, he protested. It wasn't me.

No, Nico told him, it was me. But nobody's going to believe you didn't tell me to.

So the great man retired—honourably, they made him permanent secretary to the governor of the Snake Islands, and within a year he was dead from malaria—and Nico became the new Count of the Stables, on his predecessor's vehement recommendation. The first thing he did, so he told me later, was to burn the map. He didn't need it any more, and (as witness the forty-seven high officers of state who Nico's predecessor had murdered without even knowing it) it was too dangerous to exist.

Stealing for a living is like falling off a roof. For a while, you sail along, exhilarated by the slipstream, free as a bird and twice as fast through the air, and then you hit something and it's suddenly no good at all.

There was this goldsmith in Roches. We'd taken it in turns to watch his shop from the street, and as far as we could tell there was nothing to worry about; no dog, the old man lived there on his own, no family, no living relatives apart from a cousin two hundred miles away. The door was four plies of oak laid cross-grain, but there was a side window with a shutter fastened with an old-fashioned fist-and-elbow padlock, and Edax reckoned he could deal with that, no problem. He was right, too, for once. He picked it in about two minutes, his hobnailed boots on my poor shoulders, and then we were inside. And we were quite right, there wasn't a dog—we'd have known if there was, because we'd have heard it bark, and seen someone taking it for walks. We were right about everything, as it turned out, apart from one thing.

And here's a bit of very good advice. If you've got something valuable and you don't want it stolen, don't bother with a dog; get a goose. It costs practically nothing to feed, you can keep it shut up in a cage all day, and doesn't it ever make a racket if something disturbs it in the middle of the night. A goose, for crying out loud.

First thing we knew about it was this horrible noise, and something dimly white in the moonlit room, thrashing about.

First a sort of blaring noise, like someone blowing through a cow's horn, and then hissing, like a bad play in the theatre, and the thump of the bloody thing's wings against the bars of the cage. Fact is, we were so scared we didn't stop to think; what's that, oh, it's only a goose. We scrambled for the window. I got there first but Edax elbowed me out of the way, hauled himself through, jumped and broke his ankle. A moment later I landed on top of him, and he howled so loud it set all the dogs in the street barking. I scrambled up; he just lay there. Come *on*, I yelled; I can't move, he said. I grabbed his arm, and he howled even louder. It hurts, he said. So I let go his arm, which I'd contrived to break when I landed on him. Don't leave me, he said. So I got my arms under his shoulders and started to lug him down the street, and then the watch arrived.

The watch commander sympathised, I could see that, but he explained; it wasn't up to him, his hands were tied. Theoretically, he had a budget for medical care for suspects in custody, but the fact was, money was tight, the surgeons in Roches were a bunch of thieves and bandits, and there really wasn't any point spending money fixing up my brother's arm and leg when we were both going to be hanged in two days' time, sure as eggs. Think about the next poor devil who occupies this cell, he told me. He'll come in here with a broken leg or busted ribs, and who knows, he could be innocent as a new-born babe, and all the money for fixing up injured criminals had been wasted on a dead man, or as good as. I thanked him, told him I could see his point, and asked nicely for four sticks and some old rag. He grinned, came back with a length of batten he'd fished out of the firewood, and two military-issue scarves. I'm no doctor, but I'd seen a leg set a couple of times. Edax squealed like a pig while I was hauling him about trying to fit the two ends of the breaks together, and it nearly broke my heart. You clown, he told me with tears in his eyes, you're doing it all wrong. Probably, I told him, but you heard the man, it really doesn't matter. And then he called me a whole bunch of names, all of which I deserved, until I managed to get the splints tied down tight.

They had us up in front of the judge the next morning. I did the talking, what little there was of it; names and where we were from, while Edax clung to my arm and sobbed. And it occurred to me to think that I hadn't really made the best use of my life so far, so maybe it was just as well I'd be relieved of the responsibility. It's like the parable, the one about the rich man who goes away leaving his steward in charge of the vineyard, and when he comes back it's choked with weeds and all the crops have rotted. And then the judge yawned and said, death by hanging, and that was that.

It's hard to pray when you're squashed up in a cell the size of a chicken coop with someone bawling his eyes out. In prayer, you're looking to forget your earthly body and join in metaphysical union with the Eternal, and it spoils the mood if you can't hear yourself think, and someone keeps prodding you in the ribs with his splinted leg. I did my best. Lord, I said, I have no right to call on You. I had my chance and I wasted it. I'm weak and worthless and I can't see any point in going on, but my brother here must love his life or he wouldn't be making that dreadful noise at the thought of losing it. If You could see your way to getting him out of this, it would be more than either of us could ever possibly deserve, but to You all things are possible, and maybe You can find a use for him some day, who knows?

And then I guess I must have fallen asleep, because I distinctly remember the dream I had. I was sitting on a golden throne, and next to me was Edax; we were both wearing the lorus, divitision and greater dalmatic and the triple crown and pendetilia—I knew that's what they were, though of course I'd never seen them in my life—and I held the sceptre and globus cruciger, and across my knees was a beautiful sword; and someone said to me; this is why. And I remember thinking, what could that possibly mean?

In the morning, they came to get us. But there were three of them: the watch captain, an old man with a leather satchel and a short, small man with hedgehog-bristle hair who obviously scared the other two to death. He didn't say anything. The watch captain said: terribly sorry, this whole thing's been a dreadful mistake, you're free to go, and this is the surgeon, would you please let him have a look and see if there's anything he can do? He was sweating, I remember, great fat drops of sweat rolling down his forehead, down the bridge of his nose. And the surgeon, the old man with the satchel, was furious; what stupid bloody fool set this leg, he said angrily, and I said, actually, that was me; and he went all quiet and gave Edax's ankle a little twist which made him yell; a little click, and then he bound it up nice and tight with proper splints and proper new linen bandages. Then they had two soldiers help Edax out of the cell, up the stairs and out into the daylight, where there was a coach waiting; the mail, no less, fastest thing without wings in the world, with cushioned seats and rugs to put over our knees, and a wicker basket with fresh bread, cheese, dried sausage and a bottle of wine.

And I thought: that's twice I've prayed, and twice it's worked.

We were two days in the coach—the mail doesn't stop, except to change horses—and we hardly said a word to each other, mostly because when we were half an hour out of Roches I told Edax to for God's sake stop whining, and he sulked a lot after that. Gave me a chance to think. Where were we going? No idea. But even if Edax hadn't been all busted up, we couldn't have jumped off the mail and survived, and when we stopped to change horses—at some point I think I must have tried the latch on the coach door, and it was bolted on the outside. And then I thought: well, my prayers have been answered, and this is the form the answer takes. Presumably I'm just too stupid to understand.

Then the coach slowed down, and we were in a big city, much bigger than Chastel or Roches, the way a bull's bigger than a day-old calf. So we slowed down, and I saw Edax try the door-latch. Don't be stupid, I told him, you can't run and I can't carry you, and he looked daggers at me and hugged his broken arm.

And then we went under a low arch into a little yard, and the coach stopped, and someone jumped down and shot the bolts on the doors and opened them, and I stepped out; and there, standing right in front of me, was Nico, except he was wearing a long black gown like a priest. And he grabbed me and crushed all the breath out of me. You idiot, he said, you complete arsehole.

HE'D BEEN SEARCHING for us, he told us later, for two years, ever since he'd got himself well enough established in the Service to be able to look after us and provide for us; but we would insist on moving about and making ourselves hard to find—we were both officially dead, for one thing, except he'd chosen not to believe that (faith; my brother had faith the way a soldier keeps the sword he brought back from the war, even though his side lost and the country's now occupied by the enemy). So he'd paid the best portrait painter in the City to paint miniatures of us both, on little ivory cards—a hell of a job, because he could only remember us the way we'd been when we were still just kids; he kept making the artist stop and scrape off what he'd done and try again. And then he sent his man Gigax (the little man with the hedgehog hair) all round the country with the miniatures in his pocket, have you seen these men? And eventually he found someone in a bar who said yes, but you'll have to be quick, they're getting hanged in the morning.

But all that, Nico said, was over now. We were here, and we were safe, and nothing bad was ever going to happen to any of us ever again. And he told us all about his amazing rise to power, how incredibly successful he'd been; it was all for you, he said, it was all so we could be together again, as a family, and safe. After all, he said, what could possibly be more important than that?

HE HAD THE best doctors in the City in to look at Edax, but they shook their heads and said the damage was already done, there was nothing they could do; he'd be lame for the rest of his life, and his right hand would never close properly. That made Nico very sad, but he told me it wasn't my fault, not really, given the circumstances.

I told him about how I'd prayed, and how my prayers had been answered. But Nico just laughed. Don't be stupid, he said. There is no Invincible Sun, didn't anyone ever tell you that? There's just a big white thing in the sky that makes you go blind if you stare at it, and there's Edax and you and me, and that's it. Nothing and nobody else matters, just us.

But Nico, I said, I prayed—twice—and both times my prayers were answered. You idiot, he said. Think about that just a moment. If He exists and He wanted to save you, then surely the sensible time to do it would've been *before* you were right on the point of being killed, rather than leaving it to the very last minute. Better still, he'd have had you find a five-shilling piece in the street, so you wouldn't have had to go thieving. But no, He waits till the noose is practically round your neck, and then He intervenes. If I had a clerk who arranged things as badly as that, I'd fire him tomorrow. Tell you what, Nico said, if your Invincible Sun ever needs a job, tell Him not to bother applying to the Service. He'd never make the grade.

NICO HAD ROOMS, a room, in the attic of the Stables, though he more or less lived in his office. For us he bought a house on the Savatina, with an acre of garden, and a dozen servants to look after us. Are you crazy, I asked him. He grinned. He could afford it, he said. He could afford it out of a week's pay, and still have change to buy a warship. Then he said; Look at me, what do you see?

I told him, I didn't understand the question.

What you're looking at, little brother, he said, is the second most powerful man in the empire. And in case you're wondering, no, not the emperor, he's number three. There's me and there's Cratylus, the Guardian of the Orphans, and between you and me, I'm planning to do something about that.

You've lost me, I said. Nico, what the hell is going on?

SO HE EXPLAINED.

Let me take you back, he said, to when the old emperor died. Basiliscus V, greatest emperor we've ever had; on the throne for fifty-seven years, found the empire in ruins, left it bigger and richer and stronger than it's ever been. He really was a great man, Nico said (and when Nico says something good about someone, without any excepts or apart froms, you'd better believe it) but there was one thing he didn't do which made everything else a complete waste of time. He never had a son.

Daughters, yes; two of them. But no son. Not for want of trying. Basiliscus never failed in anything because of not trying. Twice a day, morning and evening, whenever he wasn't away at the wars, and according to the palace guards you could hear him trying out in the courtyard; but all the empress ever came out with was two daughters, until at last she'd had enough and withdrew to a convent. By which point Basiliscus was an old man, but he was halfway through getting the marriage annulled so he could remarry when he died himself, of lockjaw, and that was that. Because he assumed he'd live for ever, and because he didn't want his daughters to marry until he'd produced a son, the princesses were both old maids by then. The elder, Apollonia, had gone off to the convent when she was nineteen and had been there ever since; which left the other one.

Now even I'd heard of her. The Princess Bia; Bia Carbonopsina, meaning coal-black eyes, the most beautiful woman in the world. Yes, Nico said, that's her. But that was twenty years earlier. Twenty years, and she's still there, still a princess wrapped in swansdown and ermine, only not quite so pretty as she once was. Never mind; the obvious answer was, Princess Bia had to marry and produce an heir, and then we'd be back on track and everything will be fine.

True, we all said, it's cutting it a bit fine. Princess Bia is, as a matter of cold genealogical fact, forty-five years old; but stranger things have happened, and the alternative is civil war, so let's give it a shot and see what happens. The princess herself was all for it, of course. All her life, all forty-five years of it, she'd been led to believe that one day she'd marry a handsome prince and live happily ever after, and as time went on, her patience was wearing thin. Didn't help, of course, being a princess and blood royal. Other girls, other women, can usually find ways of amusing themselves, so long as they're discreet and nothing disastrous happens, but not her, because of the unthinkable dynastic consequences. So she lived in what was essentially a prison, and the only men she ever saw were, well, (Nico said), men like himself. Most of the time she spent brewing perfumes; she was really good at it, good enough to earn her own living, and bottles of her choicest concoctions were sent as marks of special favour to queens and empresses right across the world. She, however, never left the North Tower, and she wasn't happy about that at all.

So, when they broke the bad news that she was going to have to marry and breed to save the world from drowning in a sea of blood, she was only too happy to comply. As to who the lucky man was going to be, she had very strong opinions on that. Years ago she'd fallen in love with a handsome senator. She hadn't seen him for a while, but no matter. There had been a slight delay, but never mind about that, either. One day my prince will come, and here he finally was.

Vestinus Apsimar had been every woman's dream when he was twenty-seven and Bia was fourteen; he was still solidly handsome at fifty-eight, so long as he stuck his chin out and his stomach in. He'd been married, very happily, for thirty years, but off went his wife to the convent, along with their three daughters, and Apsimar had a haircut and a shave, splashed his face all over with rosewater, and went to the palace to be married to his princess.

What he found when she lifted the veil was a tall, thin woman with big, dark eyes, and I don't suppose he felt like he'd been ill-used or cheated. She wasn't exactly hideous, and he was to be the new emperor, and the one duty expected of him was something he'd been doing all his adult life, with boundless enthusiasm and a fair degree of skill.

Well, said Nico, that was eleven years ago. For the first six years, Apsimar went about his one duty with all the diligence and sense of civic duty that you'd expect from a son of one of the oldest families in the empire; after that, I guess, he came to the conclusion that there really wasn't any point to it; and besides, he told himself, the empire didn't need another emperor, because it had him, and he was doing a fine job; and as for an heir, there was always his nephew. So back went Princess Bia to her tower and her alembics—didn't go quietly, so they tell me, and she may be thin but she's wiry, but they got her there in the end—and Apsimar set about being the best emperor in history. Apsimar the Great was what he was aiming at, though he'd probably settle for Apsimar the Strong, or Apsimar the Wise would do at a pinch. And there he still is, and there she still is, and everything would be fine, except—

Except what? I asked him. And he looked at me.

Apsimar, said Nico, lowering his voice even though we were alone, is a pinhead. An idiot. Far worse than that, he's a pinheaded idiot who thinks he's great and strong and wise.

Now, that needn't be a problem, Nico went on. Half of our greatest emperors—Florian III, Cleophon, Artax II—have been pinheads, or drunks, or crazy as jaybirds, but it didn't matter because they took no interest in the job and were happy for the Service to deal with everything for them. Not so with Apsimar. He interferes. First thing he did was have Ninus arrested, tonsured and sent to a monastery. Who's Ninus? Before your time,

I suppose. They used to call him Ninus the Weasel. He was a loathsome little man who ran the empire for Basiliscus when he was away at the wars, and he did it very well, very well indeed. But Apsimar got rid of him the moment the lorus landed round his neck, and that's how come I got promoted from Count of the Stables to Chancellor, because Cratylus, who was Chancellor before me, got kicked upstairs to Guardian of the Orphans. And when I tell you Apsimar and Cratylus deserve each other—

Actually, that's not quite fair. Cratylus is smart. But for the last thirty years he's been systematically robbing the Treasury on an industrial scale—you take a ride on the mail from the City to Trabasc, and all the land you'll ride over belongs to him, through one dummy corporation or another—and he knows for a fact that if he ever loses his grip on power, his head will be decorating a pike in the Square. So, whatever Apsimar tells him to do, he does it, no matter how crassly idiotic it might be, because his only chance of staying alive is to be second-in-command to an easily led clown. Now if I was him, I'd look back and ask myself, if that's the outcome, was it all worth it? Still, it wouldn't do if we were all the same.

How bad? Oh boy. Second thing Apsimar did, he cancelled the protection money to the Robur.

Yes, really. That's what I mean. Even Basiliscus, who never lost a battle, made sure the savages got their money, twenty million in gold, first day of spring every year. There's just too many of them, he used to say, and if we were to fight them instead of buying them off, first, we'd lose, second, it'd cost a hundred and fifty million a year to keep an army on the frontier which stands any chance of keeping them in check. So, what does Apsimar do? He cancels the tribute and uses the money to endow a school of philosophy. Apsimar the Wise. Idiot.

And then Nico sighed, and said; That's why it's so important that we're together, where I can look after you. Trust me, everything's about to go to hell, it won't be long before nowhere and nobody's safe, not unless they're really in tight, where they can pull the walls in round them like a blanket and snuggle down till it's all over. It's not just the wars. The Treasury's empty, there's fifty thousand men out of work in the City alone, rents are so high the farmers can't pay the taxes to keep the army in the field, there's honest men selling their kids, honest men who can't sell their kids because nobody can afford to buy them—from here you'd never believe it, but out at the edges it's all coming apart, and everyone still thinks it's like it was when the old emperor was alive; and it looks that way, because we keep up appearances as though our lives depend on it, but it isn't.

And then he grinned at me and grabbed me by the shoulders. But we'll be all right, he said, you and Edax and me. I've got it covered. I know what I'm doing.

I DON'T LIKE talking about myself, for obvious reasons. I've felt that way all my life. It's always seemed so unreasonable, if you see what I'm trying to say, like a bad joke or a prank.

Doesn't he take after his mother? they used to say when I was a little kid. Then, later: when he grows up he'll be a real heartbreaker (like that's a good thing). Then, later: who's a pretty boy, then? as the other kids threw stones at me, because they were jealous, and I was my mother's son.

Sometimes I ask myself: did my mother pray, when I was born? Did she say, Lord, make him handsome, the best-looking man in the world? And were her prayers answered, or did I just turn out that way because of chance?

The stupid thing is, Edax and I look quite alike—not Nico: big and dark, with a broad face, though he got our mother's eyes. But Edax and I have got the same nose and chin, the same forehead. But he turned out small and scraggy, and I'm tall. And for some reason, the things that look good on me make him look sly and evil. You can't go by appearances, obviously, though people do.

Nico said, and I agreed with him, that the best thing we could do with Edax was keep him indoors, with lots of nice things to play with, so he wouldn't be tempted to make trouble for anyone. What about me, I asked him, is there anything I can do to help? Funny you should mention that, Nico said.

(LATER, I ASKED him how it had been. What do you mean? he said. Oh, that. Well, I can't say it's bothered me particularly, what you've never had you don't miss, and I'm glad to have done without the distractions. It's like an archery match. You shoot the arrow, but it's got a hundred yards to fly, and the wind's blowing on it all that way. You allow so much when you let fly, but even so, it's much better to shoot on a still day. Me, I've never had so much as a slight breeze between me and where I needed to go.

But what about a family, I said, and kids? And he laughed. I've got you two, he said.)

SO NICO GOT me a job as an equerry. To this day—and I have a hundred of them at my command, day and night, lucky me—I have no very clear idea of what an equerry actually does. What I mostly seemed to do was stand about, something I'm not bad at, though I do say so myself. First I stood about in the anteroom outside the Purple, which is the throne-room. Then I stood about inside the Purple, near the doors, at the back. Then I graduated to about halfway up, where I was occasionally called upon to fetch things, or laugh at someone's joke. I must have done that very well indeed, because before I knew it I was standing about at the far end, from where you can actually see the throne, if you're tall and you stand on tiptoe and peek over people's shoulders. And the man sitting on it.

From where I was standing, he didn't look so bad. He was a big man, with a fine head of snow-white hair, a firm chin, piercing blue eyes, broad shoulders, and he sat there with dignity, talking in a low, pleasant voice; and what he said seemed to make sense, except I didn't know the context. Anyway, he seemed to be doing a fine job; just like me, I guess. And he seemed to spend most of his time listening, which always makes a man seem wise; philosophers and scholars and theologians, I couldn't follow most of what they said but he could, or he looked like he understood every word, and every now and then he'd nod gravely. Apsimar the Wise, which would do, at a pinch.

One day, when I got off work, some clerk came up to me and told me my brother wanted to see me in his office. So off we went, up a mountain of stairs and down again, along corridors, down tunnels, up towers, until I had absolutely no idea where I was, though my feet told me I must have walked at least two miles. And then he suddenly stopped, in front of a plain dark oak door looking exactly the same as the thousand-odd plain dark oak doors we'd walked past; no name or number on it, goes without saying. In there, the clerk told me. I knocked and waited, and I heard Nico telling me to come in.

I'd never been in that part of the palace before, and I was under the impression that Nico's room was in the Stables—

That's right, he said, that's exactly where we are. And he explained that there were corridors that ran through the attics and the cellars, all the way from the palace to the Stables—about two miles, he told me—which meant that government clerks could come and go from one department to another without ever seeing the sun, or being seen. I'd have thought you'd have a bigger place than this, I told him, and he looked at me. What for? he said. I couldn't think of an answer to that.

Anyhow, he told me, good news, you've been promoted. Why? I asked him, and I don't think it was the question he was expecting. I haven't done anything clever, I explained, I just stand there. He nodded. Very well too, so I gather, he said, and so they've promoted you. From tomorrow, you're going to be chief equerry to Her Majesty the Empress.

Why? I asked him.

Nico didn't lose his temper, the same way poor men generally don't drop gold coins in the street. She asked for you, he said, by name. But she's never seen me, I said. He scowled. Well, he said, someone obviously has, because she's asked for you. And it's a big promotion and double the money, and you should be bloody grateful instead of standing there saying why, like a corncrake.

I didn't say anything. Nico sighed. All right, he said. This is just a theory, and I may be completely wrong, but her previous equerry, who had to quit the post on account of being indicted for treason—

You're kidding, I said.

Treason, Nico repeated. Anyhow, he was seventy-two and bald and only had three teeth. I fancy Her Majesty would like something a bit prettier to look at.

I'm not sure I like the sound of that, I said.

Nico wasn't happy. Who gives a damn what you like or don't like? he said. You've got your orders. Do you want to make trouble for me?

THIS MAY TAKE some explaining, and it's not something I'm comfortable talking about, but here goes. At that point in my life—well, think about it. Use your imagination. Back home in the village, everybody reckoned we were the plague, and you don't get to meet girls that way. Then we were thieves, in Chastel and Roches, doing our level best to be completely invisible. Also, to be absolutely honest with you, it wasn't something I was, well, all that interested in. I think to a certain extent it was about Nico, what he'd done to himself; and what my mother had been, and what people thought about her because of that. All in all, that stuff only made people unhappy and led to a lot of trouble.

Edax didn't think so; but he's always looked quite a lot like a rat, so what he got in that line he mostly had to pay for, and generally speaking we couldn't afford it.

So—what Nico said, what you've never had you don't miss. Also I was awkward about how I looked, guilty even, as though I'd been given more than my fair share—and it wasn't something I could hide, it was like a rich man's kid sent to work down at the docks, kitted out in twenty-thaler shoes and a silk shirt. I felt ridiculous, a walking contradiction; because it says in Scripture, the beautiful is good and the good is beautiful. Anyway, you get the general idea.

With an attitude like that, you won't be surprised to learn that I hadn't had very much to do with women generally, apart from my mother, who doesn't count. They scared me; partly the way men scared me, because I was afraid they were going to throw stones at me or hit me with a stick, partly because I was worried they might like what they saw and want it. I'm not excusing any of this, incidentally, I'm not asking you to forgive me or say that I was right, or anything other than a mess. I've always had a thing about not being touched. It makes me feel sick.

THE EMPRESS BIA lived in the North Tower, everybody knew that. You can see the North Tower from practically anywhere in the City, because it's so very tall. People liked that. They felt safe because the old emperor's daughter was watching over them, they said.

It takes a very long time to walk up all those stairs. It's one of those horrible spiral staircases, with nothing to hold on to, and if you meet someone coming up when you're coming down, both of you are screwed. By the time you get to the top, your knees have turned to jelly and you get splints in your shins enough to make you burst into tears.

Her Majesty's apartment was the whole of the top floor. It was huge. There were no walls dividing it up; there in the far distance was the imperial bed, hung round with curtains, and all the rest of it was a tumultuous sea of cushions, with benches, like in a carpenter's shop, all round the walls. All the benches were crowded out with bottles and jars and iron stands fitted with clamps, and there were these little charcoal stoves under tripods, with pans and glass jars bubbling away. The place stank of roses and violets and honeysuckle, and there was a thick bank of fog about two feet thick directly under the ceiling.

There was no door at the top of the stairs, so I just walked in and there I was. And there she was, bending over the bench, looking at me over her shoulder. Who the hell are you? she said.

I explained. She looked at me. Well, don't just stand there, she said. Come over here and make yourself useful.

Things never seem to turn out the way I expect them to. I never imagined I'd ever be useful. I never thought I'd learn the perfume trade. I never thought I'd fall in love with an old woman, or an empress. Come to that, I never expected my prayers would be answered, ever.

She taught me the perfume trade, which was the first useful thing I'd ever learned in my life. You make perfume by crushing, infusing, distilling and compounding. It involves a lot of hard, repetitive work, grinding stuff in a mortar, and a lot of standing around holding things steady over a flame, and an awful lot of washing out bottles. I enjoyed it. The empress said I was good at it, which pleased me a lot. She talked to me—mostly things like hold this, do that, no, you're doing that all wrong, but sometimes explaining why this added to this was so much more than just the sum of its parts, and why that essence added to that oil worked, and that added to that didn't. It was as though she'd known me all her life, and we were just two people working together.

And she was beautiful. Her hair was dyed—she told me the ingredients and how to mix them, and why she used this rather than that—and there were crow's feet round her eyes and the backs of her hands were all veins, but she was the most beautiful woman I'd ever stood close to. Her arms were long, a bit skinny, with muscles like a man's, but she shaved off all the hair (I'd heard of that but never seen it before). She had about two dozen porcelain jars full of stuff she put on her face and arms, and the edges of her eyes were traced round with a sort of blue pencil.

NICO SENT FOR me. By now I was used to long walks and long staircases. You're looking good, Nico said. How's it going?

I told him I was happy and doing well. He looked at me as though I was talking a foreign language. How's it going, he repeated. Come on, don't be all shy, I'm your brother.

I just told you, I said.

He looked at me like I was simple. The old woman, he said. Has she jumped you yet?

SHE'D TOLD ME about her life; not a single, sustained narrative, just little scraps here and there, which I'd stuck together like the bits of a broken pot. When she was a girl, she was given to understand that she was sitting on a golden throne on top of a very high mountain, and all the world was at her feet, and that was exactly how it should be. One day, they told her, her prince would come; but not just any prince, oh no. Actually, her prince wouldn't be a prince. For her to marry into the ruling house of another nation would be to imply that that nation was equal in stature with the empire, which was utterly ridiculous. So, her prince would be an imperial subject, but that was all right; and he'd be a member of one of the twenty or so great and honourable families, but no problem there. And she wouldn't be able to marry until His Imperial Majesty Daddy had given her a baby brother; well, that was all right too, because Daddy was trying really, really hard on that score, and what Daddy set his mind to do, Daddy did.

(She saw him, she said, on average twice a month—when he wasn't away at the wars, which was actually most of the time.

Nurse and a small army of handmaidens would take her through the corridors, under all the mosaic ceilings and past all the gilded murals, to a little room with plain whitewashed walls, where Daddy went to sit when he wasn't on duty. She remembered him as a short man with a mostly bald head burnt brown by the sun, looking up at her from a jumble of papers, which he'd be staring at through a thick circle of glass on a golden stick. He'd look at her as though he'd never seen anything like her in his life, then smile, and ask her some questions about things he obviously wasn't interested in, and then she could go. She was a bit scared of him but she quite liked him, because he looked so funny.)

But there was no baby brother. So she waited, spending the time improving her already perfect self. She learned all the languages that ever there were, read all the books, studied music (stringed instruments, because blowing into a tube isn't ladylike). She was taught how to glide rather than walk, the exactly ideal way of sitting, back and neck straight, chin at precisely ninety degrees to the horizontal, checked from time to time with a set square. She learned to be witty without being insufferable, and how to be bored to death without showing it.

The longer she had to wait, the more lessons she had time for, therefore the more perfect she got. And she knew she was the most beautiful woman in the world, because everyone told her so, and she believed them because her father was Daddy, brother of the Invincible Sun, so it was just common sense, really. And she waited, growing steadily more perfect, like a stalactite built up by drips; and still no baby brother, and time was getting on. There's plenty of time, her maids and tutors told her; but they were starting to sound worried when they said it, and maybe (it occurred to her for the first time) perfection isn't something you can hold on to for ever. True, with every day that passed she was getting more fascinating and brilliant, but now her maids were taking longer and longer to do her face, and there were all these creams and ointments for her skin, and then she noticed her first grey hair, and then a few more.

Now she'd started looking at boys around the age when girls do that sort of thing; but she knew who she was, and it wouldn't do to burn the poor creatures up with her unattainable radiance, now would it? One of her tutors had a serious talk with her when she was fifteen. Think of the empire, he said, and there'll be plenty of time for all that later. And day followed day, and every day was pretty much the same. She was content to drift, she said, because she had faith. She had faith in God, and Daddy was God's brother, it said so on the backs of the coins.

And then she stopped looking in mirrors, and took up perfume-making instead. It came, she said, as a complete revelation to her. Something she could do, and do well. I knew how she must have felt, I told her, and she looked at me.

Then Daddy died, and suddenly everything was different. She was the princess again, and everything depended on her. She could come down out of the Tower now, if she wanted. She could do anything she chose. She could marry that nice boy she'd noticed, a few years back.

She'd been looking forward to it, she told me, for twenty years, and when it happened, it was horrible. Partly the disappointment. She'd imagined what it must feel like, over and over again; like it feels when you use your finger, she reasoned, only so much better. Instead, she told me, she panicked, and started yelling; keep your voice down, he'd hissed at her, they'll think you're being murdered. So, back to square one. But she remembered that she was Daddy's daughter, and you keep trying, and you never give up, no matter what. And then, she told me, suddenly it was wonderful, and she loved her handsome husband, and she couldn't stop thinking about it, every minute, every day. True, it didn't seem to be having the desired effect. But that only made him try harder—like Daddy, presumably—and she didn't mind that at all.

And then, one morning, she woke up to find maids and equerries packing her clothes and pots and hairbrushes into big wicker baskets. What's going on? she asked, and they told her she was being moved, back to the North Tower. She was furious about that, but it turned out that there was nothing she could do—which came as a bit of a surprise, since she'd been under the impression that she was the emperor's daughter and niece of the Invincible Sun, but apparently not.

Since then—Do what you like, he'd written to her, (written, mind you; maybe all those stairs were too much for him, at his age) so long as you don't make trouble and don't leave the Tower. So she lit her little stoves and sent out for herbs and oils, and she created the post of principal equerry to the empress. Five or six of them had come and gone, and nobody seemed to care what a barren old woman got up to at the top of a tower, and she realised she simply wasn't interested any more. So she got rid of the handsome young men and appointed an old one who knew a bit about alchemy. But he didn't have much conversation and his eyes were bad so he started knocking over bottles, and then there was me.

You arranged it, I said. You fixed it because you wanted her to—

Well, yes, Nico said, surprised by my stupidity, of course I did. Catnip to a cat.

Why? I asked him.

You keep asking me that, said my brother. It's obvious, isn't it? You're going to be the next emperor.

So I went to the empress and told her everything.

Not sure what I expected to happen. Most likely, she'd send for the guards and have me and my brothers executed. Or she'd look at me like I was something she'd walked in on the sole of her shoe. Or she'd start crying, or yelling. She looked at me. Why not? she said.

It would be relatively easy, she told me. She'd been giving it serious thought, on and off, for some time, and she knew how it could be done. The problem had always been finding someone to help her.

Last time she'd seen the emperor, he was pretty fit and hearty for a man of his age. But old men have weak hearts, everyone knows that; and old men don't listen to their doctors, who tell them to take it easy, not eat this, lay off on that. The emperor liked to take a morning swim in the big indoor pool, heated by underground hypocausts, he'd had built in the south wing. He'd splash up and down, revelling in the freedom from his steadily increasing weight. And generally he was alone, with guards no closer than the doors outside.

She showed me how to brew foxglove flowers to extract the medicinal essence. Useful, she said, because it stimulates the heart if it should happen to stop; a lifesaver. But you know what they say about too much of a good thing.

When I told Nico I'd do it, he laughed. Of course you will, he told me, you're a good boy, and it's the only way we can be absolutely safe. I'm not doing it for you, I told him. Don't talk stupid, he said, of course you are. He didn't believe me. I don't know why.

There was a lot of planning involved; Nico saw to it, of course. The problem, he said, was who we could trust. He had people who'd do anything he told them without a moment's thought, but he didn't trust them further than he could spit. Which left the three of us. And Edax—we looked at each other and decided, no. All right then, Nico said, it's you and me. And everybody in the palace knows me, so you'll have to do quite a bit of the actual running about.

First, he had me reassigned back to the emperor. That wasn't hard for people to believe, since people said Her Majesty used up her pretty young men quite fast (people say a lot of things, don't they?). After I'd been there a few days, the Cupbearer General had a terrible accident. A loose tile fell on his head, and he died. There was a vacancy for a new cupbearer. I got it.

Nico, I said to him, what the hell did you have to go and do that for? He told me it really was an accident; the tile was meant to break his collar bone, but the man I used was a fool, it's so hard to get good help these days. I believed him, or I chose to believe him. Next time, I said, for crying out loud hire someone competent. There won't be a next time, he said. We're nearly there now, home and dry.

(ON ONE CONDITION, she'd said.)

I looked at her. What?

She looked at me back, then did one of those oh-for-crying-out-loud sighs that women seem to specialise in. All right, fine, she said. In years to come, how do you think the history books will describe us?

That wasn't something I wanted to think about. Murderers, I said. Traitors. The most evil man and woman who ever lived.

She shook her head. They'll say, the empress and her lover. But you aren't, are you? Not yet.

Like I said, I have this problem with physical contact. I like you a lot, I said, more than any woman I've ever known. More than any man, come to that, outside of my family. But—

It's the deal, she said. Either we're in this together, or we aren't.

(By that point, it was too late to back out. Nico had told me that, when I'd asked him, the day before, if we couldn't just forget about the whole thing. We can't, he said. Why not? You and your damned questions, he said. Because I've started Cratylus on a course of slow poison—I couldn't use a quick one, he's got a food taster—and when he dies, not if, when, all hell is going to break loose. And if by then you're not the emperor, we're all three of us dead. Capisce?)

We're in this together, I said, I promise you.

Well then, she said.

When all else fails, be honest with the people you love. And I did love her, at that moment, under those circumstances, on that anvil. I've never done it before, I said.

You're kidding, she said; and then, Oh well. Late starters, both of us. But you'll soon catch up.

It was awkward, the first time. She told me what I had to do, and I remember saying, Are you sure? And she gave me a look that would've killed slugs. Yes, she said. Actually, the first few times were a mess. But after that; after that, I fell head over heels in love with her. Still am, to this day.

THE FOXGLOVE POWDER was in a little bottle, which she gave me. I took it down to the Stables and showed it to Nico. He unstoppered it and gave it a sniff. That's the good stuff, he said. She really made it herself?

I nodded.

She's a clever lady, Nico said. Then he pulled a ring off his finger. It was a big, broad ring with a fat stone. I hadn't seen him wearing it before. He didn't do jewellery, or any of that stuff. Watch carefully, he said, and did something I couldn't see, and the stone popped out and hinged back. Plenty of space in there for six grains, he said, which is all it'll take.

He made me put the ring on, and practice flipping the tiny catch till I could do it without looking down. Then he filled it with powder and snapped it shut. Be careful, he said. That's nasty stuff you've got there.

Are you sure that'll be enough? I asked.

Trust me, he said. I'm your brother.

It had to be done, Nico had told me, because the Guardian had been out to get him for a long time, ever since he'd risen to Count of the Stables. Why? Because the Guardian was afraid of him, the same way the rabbit is afraid of the fox, and so he'd resolved to kill him or disgrace him, preferably both—that's how the Service works, Nico told me, predators and prey. He'll destroy me unless I destroy him first. And if I go, so will you, and Edax. And all of this has been about you, right from the start. And then he got impatient with me. Come on, he said, it's the last step, and then we'll be safe. We've come so far, ever such a long way from the village, and if we stop now we're all dead men. He looked at me. Is that what you want? Nico said. Do you want to see me and Edax flayed alive in the Square and our heads on pikes? No, sorry, you won't see that, because your head'll be up there too. Is that really what you want?

It was his heart, the doctors said, though the immediate cause of death was drowning. He'd been found floating face down in his private pool, the one I told you about. There was nothing anyone could have done. It was his own fault, the doctors told her privately. He ate too much of the wrong sort of food, never took any exercise, it was simply a matter of time. He could have gone at any moment over the last two years.

I was waiting at the foot of the North Tower stairs when she came down. We both knew exactly what had to be done. Nico had made me repeat it, over and over again till I knew it by heart; I'd told her and she didn't need any of it repeated. We were to go directly to the Purple Chamber, not stopping, not saying a word to anybody. There would be a company of guards waiting for us outside the Tower, in the little quad; if anyone tried to stop us, their orders were to use their swords, flats for choice but edges if needs be. But that shouldn't happen, because Nico had called a meeting in the Ivory Chapter, to announce the death of the

Guardian of the Orphans. So we ought to have the place to ourselves, he said, and he was right.

We got to the Purple, and there was the abbot of the Studium, with the precentor and a half-dozen other priests I didn't recognise. First we were married, and then she sat me down on the throne and put the crown on my head and the lorus round my shoulders. Then she sat down beside me, with her own crown and lorus; I got the sceptre and globus cruciger, and the Sword of State across my knees, while she got the labarum and the golden acacia. And that, Nico had assured us, was all we had to do. Just leave the rest to him.

So we sat and waited, and the distinguished clergymen stood about, because there didn't seem to be any chairs for them. Sweat was running down my face in streams, but she just sat there with a sort of faraway look in her eyes; and I remember thinking: in my dream it was Edax instead of her, but of course I didn't know her back then. And otherwise, it's pretty much the same. This is why, the dream said. After about ten minutes of just sitting, she carefully put down the labarum (still looking straight ahead, not at me) and took the globe off me and put it down somewhere, and took my hand and gave it a little squeeze.

Then the doors flew open, and I remember feeling the sort of sharp stitch in my guts that you tend to get when you've eaten too much fried food. And all these men came in; men in black robes, and soldiers in armour. I looked for Nico but I couldn't see him. Oh well, I thought, and I'd have prayed, only there wasn't time.

Then a side door I hadn't realised was there opened, and in came Nico. He was wearing this ridiculous cloth-of-gold thing that trailed along the ground after him, and there were a dozen steelnecks in full parade armour behind him. And I noticed that they had weapons, and the ones who'd come in earlier didn't. In fact they weren't proper soldiers, just generals and admirals in uniform. And Nico turned to face us, and bowed deeply, and all the people I didn't know followed suit, and that was that, basically.

NICO HAD STITCHED it all together quite beautifully. He'd framed the Guardian by transferring about a million acres of government land into his name, using a whole load of shell corporations and stuff like that; his death was presented to the imperial court as suicide. Found in his cold dead hand was a letter (Nico had a wonderful forger; he had him killed afterwards, just to be safe, but he said it was a dreadful waste) confessing that he'd embezzled public property and been found out by the Count of the Stables—Nico—and fear of arrest and execution had driven him to murder the emperor and empress, using a decoction of foxglove, and seize the throne. But the empress had eluded his clutches, thanks to the interference of her equerry, and he knew the game was up, so he'd taken the easy way out, and may the Invincible Sun have mercy, etcetera.

My part in it all (according to Nico's version, which became the official version, which is by definition the definitive truth) was rather dashing and romantic. I'd grappled with the assassins sent by the Guardian and hurled them from the top of the Tower into the moat below—that was a nice touch, wasn't it?—whereupon the empress, in an access of magnanimous gratitude, had married me on the spot. Now, there could be absolutely no doubt that she was the old emperor's daughter—the only one available for secular duty, her elder sister being a Bride of the Sun—and therefore by indisputable right the empress. And there was no doubt whatsoever that she'd married me, because here were eight of the leading churchmen in the empire to bear witness. And the empress's husband was the emperor. So simple, even a child could get it. After all, the idiot Apsimar had only been emperor because he was married to Princess Bia, and now he was dead, and she had a new husband. Well, then.

It's because it was done quickly, Nico told me later, and because I pinned everything on the Guardian (Nico was Guardian now, needless to say) and it made people feel like there'd been an attempted coup that failed, rather than an attempted coup that succeeded. Also, the people love her, because of her dad, and they reckon she's been hard done by, and in their minds she's still twenty-one and pretty as a picture, and all the stuff about me fighting off the assassins and her marrying me out of sheer gratitude was pure fairytale and so they loved it. And it doesn't hurt that there's absolutely nobody else, not unless we want a civil war.

THIS IS WHY, said the dream. And you've probably noticed, I have a habit of asking, Why? Used to drive Nico mad; it doesn't matter a flying fuck why, he'd yell at me, just do as you're told; and I did, because he was my big brother and he loved me. *Why?* isn't something you say to those who are bigger and stronger than you are, and who have your destiny in their hands, and who love you without limit or reserve.

Like that story in Scripture—my favourite—where He sends all sorts of affliction down on His most faithful and loving servant, and the servant asks, why? And He says, For reasons you couldn't possibly begin to understand. Where were you when I laid the foundations of the Earth? He says, and what the hell do you know about anything?

Which is a good answer, sure enough, except it's always niggled away at me, like a bit of crab meat stuck between my teeth. And so I keep my speculations to myself, except He can read my mind.

But He'd been good enough to explain, though, hadn't He? This is why; clear as daylight, except it was in a dream. But I don't ever remember my dreams when I wake up, and I remembered that one. This is why. And I'd started it, by praying to Him, twice, and twice He'd answered me, and rescued me out of the hands of my enemies. True, there's Nico's point. But all that goes to prove is that He made the messes that He later got me out of. Why? Why indeed? And what the hell do I know about anything?

This is why. He put me on the imperial throne—me, the last person in the world to expect or deserve it—and therefore He had to have a reason. I wasn't entirely sure I understood, but that didn't matter. I'm too stupid to understand, I accept that. I don't understand trigonometry either, but I have absolutely no doubt that it's valid and true. I believed. I trusted. I had no choice but to believe and trust, because it was as plain as the nose on my face.

He'd put me there; not, obviously, as an end in itself, but as a beginning. I was there to do a job. For that job, he'd chosen me, just as Nico chose me to be Apsimar's cupbearer. So, what was it about me that made me the right man for the job? Think about that.

I had no ambition to be emperor. The pleasures of the flesh, for want of a better word, had never meant much to me (what you've never had, you don't miss). Most of all, I knew that He existed and had put me there to do the job that He wanted. As far as any mortal man could be, I was empty of any kind of selfish thought or motive—

Well, not quite. But I'd have to be.

I loved my wife, and I loved my brother. And both of them were murderers, traitors, regicides. Me too, of course. But He hadn't chosen them to be his instrument.

It won't come to that, I thought. And then I dropped to my knees and clasped my hands together so tight my fingers hurt, and I prayed: don't make it come to that.

BIA AND I stayed in the throne room for the rest of the day, mostly because we couldn't be sure it was safe anywhere else. Then Nico came back and told us to go to bed. Fortunately she remembered the way.

The royal bedchamber was smaller than I'd expected; very plain, almost dingy. It used to be Daddy's room, she explained, and when Apsimar wanted to change it she'd thrown a dozen fits, and he'd given in to stop her making a scene.

When he'd banished her back to her tower he'd moved to the apartments in the Pearl Cloister, with his mistress du jour. He couldn't fuck properly in the old emperor's room, he used to say, he always felt like the old devil was in there, looking down on him and scowling.

She sat down on the bed and took her shoes off. They'd been killing her all day, she said. I found a chair—there were two in the room—and sat down opposite. What now? I said.

I don't know, she answered. I guess it's all up to that clever brother of yours.

I took a deep breath. I want to be a good emperor, I said.

She looked at me as if I was mad. Is that right?

Yes, I said. Nico says Apsimar was a bad emperor. He says he's ruined the economy and wasted huge amounts of money, and the farmers can't afford to pay their taxes, and there are thousands of people starving in the City because of the corn monopolies, and the Robur are going to attack because he stopped paying the tribute. He says unless something's done, the empire will fall.

She shrugged. I don't know much about politics, she said. But I think people always say that sort of thing. And sometimes it's true and sometimes it isn't. And you never know which it is at the time, because everything always looks the same. At least, it does in the palace.

Nico should know, I said. And he told me things are very bad.

She didn't look particularly interested. You be a good emperor, then, she said, if that's what you'd like.

I'm serious, I said. She gave me one of her looks. You clown, she said. It's not up to you. You're just—and she stopped. What? I asked her. Never mind, she said. Look, why don't you just leave everything to your brother? He's a smart man, anyone can see that. He wouldn't have got where he is today if he wasn't the smartest man in the empire.

Then Nico came in, without knocking, and sat down on the bed, right next to her. That went off all right, he said, you both did very well. Now, listen carefully, I haven't got much time.

And he told us what we had to do, which wasn't very much; show yourselves in the throne room immediately after Matins, stay there till noon, then ride in an open carriage to the White Shell temple for Low Mass, then down to the Arsenal to bless the new flagship of the fleet, then back to the throne room for afternoon petitions; here's what you have to do about those—and he gave Bia a piece of paper. He can't read, he told her, but that's all right, just give him a nudge, once for yes, twice for no. Then there's a reception for the Mysian ambassador, which is basically just sitting still and looking royal, then dinner and the rest of the day's your own.

YOU'VE GOT TO get rid of her, Nico said.

I'd avoided being alone with him, but he knew the palace routine. He knew, for example, that Her Majesty took a bath, in asses' milk and honey, at a certain time every other day, and I couldn't very well follow her in there, because she didn't like me watching while she was patched up and maintained, which took a long time and a large staff.

No, I said. I love her.

He had that look on his face. No, he said, you don't. And besides, it's ruining everything.

I don't understand, I told him.

He sighed. You look ridiculous, he said. A young man, not much more than a boy, and an old woman, holding hands, in public. People are starting to make jokes about it.

I didn't understand. You told me she was really popular. You said the people love her.

Yes, but they hadn't seen her for years. Now they can see she's got old. They're making all sorts of dirty cracks about the two of you, and it's really bad for morale. Also, it's obvious she's far too old to have a kid, which sets people thinking. She's got to go.

I felt cold all over. No, I said.

Don't be stupid, he said. You can't divorce her, obviously, and while she's alive you can't marry and have a legitimate heir. Tell you what, he went on, as though he was doing me a tremendous favour, we'll pretend she's dead, and that'll be just as good. We can have a grand state funeral, mother of her country and all that, and then she can stay up in her tower, you can marry and breed and we'll be safe. A stable, guaranteed succession is the only way to ensure stability, everyone knows that. You needn't kill her if that'd upset you, but she's got to go.

I THOUGHT ABOUT how I was going to do it for a long time. I'd never done anything like it before—Nico had always seen to everything like that—and if I got it wrong there'd be hell to pay. But I was a complete novice, a virgin. Not a clue.

So I got into the habit of an hour or so alone in the evenings, between dinner and bed. I told Nico I was having a course of massage, which made him smirk, and I told Bia I was learning to read, which she approved of. And I found myself a clerk.

I came across him quite by chance. I'd got lost—something that happened painfully often in that place—and I wandered into some office or other, where there were half a dozen clerks on tall stools, copying things out. One of them, I noticed, was a brown man; not a common sight. I only noticed him because he looked different. All the other clerks in the Service are indistinguishable.

You, I said. Come with me.

He looked worried. I'm not supposed to leave my desk, he said. I'm the emperor, I told him. Do as you're told.

So I had a quiet time, a place to go (I found a little room everyone seemed to have forgotten about and nobody ever used) and a clerk. I told him, go to the library and get me a book about government.

He gave me a terrified look.

Get me, I said, a book about how you run an empire. There's got to be one. Bring it here and read it to me.

He must've thought I was mad, but away he went, and some time later he came back with a big book, which turned out to be *Institutions of the Imperial Court*, written a hundred years ago by the old emperor's grandfather. That sounded promising. Read it to me, I told him.

I lasted about five minutes, then stopped him. That's no good, I said.

Majesty?

That's all useless, I said, it's ceremonial and protocol, and who has precedence at levees and lyings in state. Skip all that.

So he flipped though the pages, most of the book, until there was only about a finger's breadth left. Then he started reading again; and it was the good stuff. Sources of revenue, organisation of the provincial governments, chains of command in the military, the structure and function of the civil service. He read for about an hour, and then there wasn't any more to read.

You're Robur, aren't you? I asked him

He looked nervous. I used to be, Majesty, but I'm a citizen now. I love the empire.

What's your name? I asked him.

Gemellus Constantianus, he said. I shook my head. Your real name, I said. What your mother called you.

I'd asked him something personal and embarrassing, which he was ashamed about. My Robur name, he said, was Heaven Thunders The Truth.

I raised my eyebrows. That's a name?

Where I came from, Your Majesty.

I can't call you that, I said. All right, say it in Robur.

So he said something, and I only caught the first bit of it, because it was just noises. Would it be all right, I said, if I call you Bemba, for short?

As Your Majesty pleases, he said.

Bemba was a short man, he just about came up to my shoulder; about fifty years old, bald as an egg, only a faint trace of an accent; he'd been sold to the Service thirty-six years ago, after he was stolen from his family by traders, and the City was his home now, and the Service was his life. And now, having read me the book, he knew as much about running the empire as I did, and probably more. Well, you've got to start somewhere.

Why haven't you got rid of her yet? Nico kept asking me. I'm scared, I told him. What if it goes wrong? You're useless, he said, I'll do it. Just leave everything to me. You won't hurt her, I asked him, will you? And he looked at me as if I'd just wet myself. No, of course not, he said. You're my brother. Would I ever do anything that'd upset you?

THANKS TO BEMBA and the book I was beginning to understand who ran the empire. The emperor, obviously; except the empire is huge, so one man can't do all that, even if he's God's brother, so naturally he delegates; and over the years, everything had been delegated. Most of everything was done by the Service, which was run by two senior officials, the Guardian of the Orphans and the Count of the Stables. The Count was in charge of three of the five departments, but the Guardian had the two that mattered: War and the Treasury. Now, of course, Nico was both the Count and the Guardian, which meant he had everything.

But not quite. The army had its own traditions. For centuries, it had chosen its leaders from six families, who between them owned about a quarter of the land in the empire, and naturally enough they hated the Service and the Service loathed them. Money to pay the troops came from the Treasury via the War Office, which was how the Service kept the army commanders under control; also, it was a long-standing rule that no military units were to be stationed within two hundred miles of the City (apart from the palace guard, which was under the command of the Count of the Stables) and any general who came within that distance without first resigning his command was automatically a traitor and sentenced to death.

The old emperor had spent more time with the army than in the City, and he'd been a good commander. Apsimar didn't like soldiers and was scared stiff of the generals; also, he wanted money for the university he'd founded, and it pained him to think of the soldiers getting paid for just sitting around, so he'd dissolved two of the eight field armies, the two which happened to be commanded by the Stilian brothers, members of the oldest and proudest of the six army families. With no soldiers to lead, he figured, they couldn't be a threat to anyone, now could they?

Bemba wrote a letter to Stilian Zautzes, asking him to come to the City as soon as he possibly could, and sealed it with my private seal, which Nico had carelessly left lying about in a locked desk (I owed Bemba a dukedom for that; if they'd caught him, he'd have been crucified). Now, chances were, Stilian would think it was a trap, and a pretty crude one at that. But he had reason to feel safe in the City, even if it was. The palace guard, about eight thousand strong, was recruited from the very best men in the field armies; it was a sort of pension for fifteen years plus of exemplary service. And Stilian's army had been the best in the empire (before Apsimar dissolved it), so half the men in the guard were his veterans, and they worshipped him. The letter hadn't gone into detail—too risky; we only dared send it because Bemba found out there was one other Robur clerk, just one, in the domestic Service, and he was in the Postmaster's office, and could get away and deliver it without anyone taking much notice—but Bemba had chosen his words well, with the lines artfully spaced for reading between. So Stilian came; and Bemba let him in at the back door of the kitchen and brought him to see me.

He didn't like me, not one bit, I could tell. I was too pretty, for one thing, and my clothes stank of Bia's perfumes, and he didn't approve of an old woman's gigolo being emperor, even though he'd thought Apsimar was the devil incarnate. I rather liked Stilian. He was short and stocky, grey-haired and grey-eyed, and he had that accent that only army officers have, which I must admit I quite like. Anyway, I told him what I had in mind and what I wanted him to do. He looked at me as if I was mad. Can't be done, he said. And if they catch us, they'll cut my head off. I felt like I was about to piss down my leg I was so scared, but I looked straight at him. If we don't do it now, I said, we won't get another chance. You do want what's best for the empire, don't you?

You're either mad or very stupid, he said. What's that got to do with anything? I asked.

I WASN'T THERE to see it, of course. I was in our bedroom when it happened, in the middle of the night, which is always the best time for anything like that. But Bemba went along, to be my witness and to carry the Great Seal in case anyone needed to see it.

Later, Stilian told me the story. He'd had no trouble finding the men. He'd chosen a dozen of his old NCOs, men who'd served under him in the old emperor's time; he told them to meet him in the quad next to the South Cloister at the start of Prime, and sure enough, there they were. They made their way quickly and quietly through the corridors, with Bemba leading the way, until they reached Nico's room. The door wasn't even locked. He was sitting up in bed reading official papers. They didn't give him time to say a word, according to Stilian. They stuffed his mouth with rags, tied his hands and hustled him out of there in his nightshirt and bare feet.

They didn't have far to go; about a hundred yards to the kitchen gate, where Bemba had let Stilian in, and then a quarter of a mile through empty streets to the Golden Shell temple. One of the canons there owed Stilian's cousin a large sum of money, so there was no trouble; doors unlocked, everything they needed laid out ready for them. They tied Nico to a prebendary stall, shaved his head so he'd be acceptable as a monk, and put his eyes out. It's an old-established tradition, so they tell me, in the imperial court; it effectively gets rid of someone as a potential threat without actually killing them, which is why it's referred to as the Divine Clemency of the Emperor. I wish they hadn't told me that.

From there, he was taken by boat down the South Canal to the harbour, where Stilian had arranged passage (you can see why he was such a good general) for Nico and three guards to the Blue Rock monastery on the island of Olethria. In case you haven't heard of it, it's a rock in the middle of the sea—sailors know how to find it, apparently, but it's not on any maps.

SHE STARED AT me when I told her. What the hell did you do that for, she said.

I told her. She went white as a sheet. He wanted me to have you killed, I told her, so I could marry someone else and have kids, for the succession.

I want him dead, she said. Right now.

He's my brother, I told her. And he did it all for me, and Edax. Then I realised. She hadn't known Nico was my brother. She'd figured out that we knew each other, that Nico had arranged for me to be assigned to her because I was good-looking, but that was as far as she'd got; and I assumed she knew, and besides, I never really talked much about myself. It doesn't matter, I told her. He had to go anyway, for the empire.

She scowled at me. What are you talking about? she said.

For the empire, I said. He'd never have let me put anything right. He wasn't interested in that sort of thing. He only cared about getting power and holding on to it—so we'd be all right, him and me and our kid brother Edax. He'd have told me not to be so bloody stupid, and leave everything to him, and keep out of things that don't concern me. And when he got rid of the old Guardian, he took all that embezzled land for himself, and I know he'd never have given it back, and we'll need that money. He'd have said it was for just-in-case; in case anything went wrong and we had to clear out in a hurry and go somewhere else. He's very careful, my brother, he always expects the worst.

(Except he hadn't; not the very worst. But nobody's perfect.)

She looked at me as though I was a stranger. Well, she said, it's done now. And nobody liked him anyway.

I APPOINTED GENERAL Stilian as the new Guardian. It had never been done before, having a soldier in charge of the War Office, not to mention everything else. I had no idea whether I could trust him or not, and I was well aware he didn't like me, but I didn't see that I had any choice. I didn't know anyone else.

And I made Bemba the new Count. I figured, he has no friends, nobody's ever wanted him on their side, nobody's spoken to him unless they absolutely had to, but he knows his way round the Service; he'll be on my side, because he'll know that if anything happens to me, he'll be dead within the hour. That's how you make sure of loyalty. Love and trust don't work, I've found.

First thing I had them do was make a list of everything that was wrong with the empire. It sounds stupid, doesn't it? but I thought, we might as well start at the beginning.

It was worse than I thought; worse, I think, than anyone had realised, even Nico, who was so smart. To start with, all the money had gone. When the old emperor died, we'd had a surplus of something like twelve billion; now we owed something like seven billion to the banks and the merchant venturers, and we didn't dare default because it'd start a panic and everything would go to hell. We couldn't raise taxes, because taxes were too high already. The way it works is, the Treasury fixes on an amount for each province and charges it to the districts, who pass the assessments on to the landowners, who pass it on to the tenants, with a little bit extra added for luck at each stage. Things were so bad that farmers were simply packing up and leaving, without any clear idea of where they were going, and large parts of the eastern and southern provinces—where all the grain for the City comes from—were just empty houses and fields full of briars and nettles. A fair number of them ended up in the City, where they thought they might find work, but taxes were high there, too, and workshops and factories were going out of business every day. The price of grain in the City had doubled over the last six months, and rather too often there simply wasn't any grain to buy, not at any price, because the corn-chandlers were in debt to the merchant-venturers, who had a habit of sequestering the grain barges before they reached the City harbour and sending them off to Scheria or Messagene, where prices (because of the strength of the Scherian angel and the Messagene thaler against the imperial solidus) were higher.

None of which bothered General Stilian particularly, since his family estates were in the north, and the City could burn to the ground for all he cared. What really upset him was the fact that the peasant farmers and smallholders whose sons had supplied the army with recruits for a thousand years were being driven off the land by the thousand, when the rich City aristocrats called in their mortgages, so they could take the land and work it with slave labour. That and Apsimar's dissolution of three regiments meant that the army had shrunk to a third of what it had been in the old emperor's time. But we're at peace, who is there left to fight? Apsimar had said to him, with that winning smile of his, and hadn't waited for an answer.

Besides, Stilian told me, even if you really feel the need to make things better for people, as you put it, you can't, the Service won't let you. I said that the old emperor hadn't allowed the Service to interfere; that made him roar with laughter. The Service is three times bigger than it was in his day, he told me;

and I had Bemba look into it, and he was right. Also, its budget was four times what it had been in Basiliscus' day, and ninety per cent of that went on wages, although the pay of the junior grades, three-quarters of the total staff, who do the actual work, had fallen by fifteen per cent.

I've never done an honest day's work in my life, so I don't know how it feels. But I can use my imagination. I picture myself walking up from the house to the barn just when the sun rises. I can see myself walking the oxen into the yoke, linking up the plough, driving the team to the field, leaning on the plough-handles to dig the share into the earth as the oxen lurch forward. I can see myself stopping at the end of each furrow to wipe the sweat off my face and look back at what I've done and what I've still got to do. It'll never happen, of course, but I can imagine it.

The field I had to plough in real life was a bit more daunting; and I didn't know how to go about it, or where to start. My plough-oxen, God forgive me for calling them that, were an ill-matched pair. One of them despised me, and the other one was scared stiff of more or less everything; and one was a blue-blood military aristocrat, with a better pedigree than God, and the other one had been born in a Robur caravan and weaned on broth boiled down from the bones of his father's enemies—did I mention the Robur are cannibals? But there; I don't suppose either of them ever thought they'd be serving an emperor whose mother was a village whore. Things don't ever seem to turn out the way we thought they would, but here we all still are. For now, anyway.

I asked Stilian to have a word with the bankers. He scowled at me, but I think the idea appealed to him; his family had lost about a hundred thousand acres to the banks over the last fifty years. He came back and told me that they'd agreed to accept forty nummi on the solidus, with payments spread out over fifty years, at two per cent (we'd been paying five). I have no idea what he said to them, which is probably just as well.

Bemba wrote me a report on the Service. It was very long, carefully copied out on new parchment and rolled up in a gold tube. I pointed out that I couldn't read it, so he read it to me. We put our heads together and decided what to do. The next day, Stilian's guards arrested all twelve heads of department on charges of embezzlement, peculation, dereliction of duty and fraud; the charges would be dropped, Bemba told them, if they cut their departmental budgets by a half and got rid of a third of their staff. Since the penalty for embezzlement in public office is crucifixion, they agreed to see what they could do.

It took a lot of work, ingenuity and imagination to unravel the paper trail Nico had left to cover his ownership of the public land he'd taken over from his predecessor. When we finally got to the bottom of it, we were stunned. A million acres, and none of your rubbish; prime arable in the most fertile districts of the home provinces. We parcelled it up, ten acres a man for a hundred thousand homeless farmers—freehold, I insisted on that, though Stilian called me all the names under the Sun and even Bemba frowned and asked me if I was sure that was a good idea. But it had to be freehold; no rent, no debt. The proviso was, the land couldn't be sold or mortgaged for fifty years. That was for Stilian, and he eventually got the point. A new generation of soldiers for the empire.

Bemba did a bit of digging, and found out that the merchant venturers who held the debt on the corn chandlers' barges had neglected to pay any tax for the last eight years; they'd paid about a quarter of what they owed to Nico's predecessor, and their tax demands somehow got lost in the paperwork. I set Stilian on them—he was starting to enjoy bullying civilians, and I like people to be happy in their work—and we got possession of the barges, which meant we could guarantee supply. We also managed to bring the price down twelve per cent, by cutting costs; not nearly as much as I'd have liked, but at least it was a start. In the medium term, corn would be cheaper, once the newly installed smallholders started producing and selling. I had Bemba set up a cooperative to buy their grain and sell it to the chandlers at an honest price, though how long that'll last remains to be seen.

Apsimar had commissioned a whole lot of building work—temples, his precious university and a whole new palace (we've already got four palaces in the City). I cancelled all that, but the contractors didn't lose out. Instead, I set them to work renovating the walls—they hadn't been looked at since the old emperor was a boy, and large parts of them were a mess—and paving the City streets, which are so bad in places, you can drown in the wheel-ruts if it's been raining heavily. Ridiculous extravagance, Stilian called it, but it made work for about twelve thousand City men who hadn't had any work for a long time, and I paid for it by selling the books from Apsimar's university, or at least suggesting to the bankers that they might care to take them in lieu of cash for their next instalment of interest. I didn't have to make Stilian go along and make the request, I just had Bemba mention his name. They remembered him very well.

I HAD A private chapel on the top of the East Tower. It used to be a lookout post for the beacon system, before the mail was set up. It was small and circular, whitewashed walls, with an icon of the Transfiguration—at least until I found out how much that was worth; then I had it sold and made do with just the wall.

I went there every day to pray. Lord, I said, I have sinned. I murdered the emperor. I let my brother murder other people—I don't know how many, dozens maybe. I can't think of anything worse than what I've done. And You rewarded me with the empire, and a chance of making life better for Your people, and—I wasn't quite sure what the word meant, but I used it anyway; happiness. Does this mean I'm forgiven?

The thing is, I had no idea. I'd had a dream, once, under difficult circumstances; this is why. And I'd been shown myself, sitting on the throne (but with Edax next to me; that part of it I couldn't figure out), so I'd assumed that He meant me to become emperor, so I could do what was pleasing in His sight—and I'd assumed that feeding the poor and putting the empire to rights must be pleasing in His sight, though maybe I'd been jumping to conclusions. But in order to do that, I'd murdered a man, and I'd stood by while Nico murdered probably dozens more; and there was treason and adultery and all those other bad things, and surely that couldn't be His will?

Where was I when He laid the foundations of the Earth? Good question.

So I prayed; Lord, if I'm doing the right thing and what I'm doing is pleasing in Your sight, send me a sign. Something so clear, even an idiot like me can understand it.

I REMEMBER THAT day very clearly. It was the day the news reached the City that the Robur had sacked Charnac.

I ASKED BEMBA about the Robur. Were they really cannibals? Well, yes and no. Most of the time they lived on milk, cheese, butter and yoghurt, along with whatever wild fruit they came across as they lumbered in their enormous wagons across the north-eastern plains. But when they fought anyone, assuming they won, they ate the bodies of men they'd killed, and what they didn't eat fresh they salted down, like bacon. And were they really as merciless as people made out? Yes and no, Bemba said. Among themselves they prized justice, honour and mercy; but none of that applied to people who weren't Robur, therefore by definition inferior and not really human. What did they want?

I asked him. To be left alone in peace, mostly; except that when they felt their honour had been insulted, it was their highest duty to avenge it. For instance; they didn't care a damn about gold, silver, silks, ivory, all the things we set so much store by in the empire. To them, it was all just so much junk that took up space in the wagons that could be used for something useful; when the emperor sent them gold coins, they buried them, with a pile of stones to mark the spot. No risk of them getting stolen, because who in their right mind would want them?

But when a Robur king dies, he's buried with all the prizes he's won in his lifetime; and Robur kings tend to die at frequent intervals, because they're a competitive people. Now the king had just died, but the emperor had stopped sending gold, so there was nothing to bury him with, and this was the most appalling dishonour. No good sending tribute now, because the damage had been done. Honour would only be satisfied if they took it by force.

Just how much force exactly, I asked, before honour was satisfied? Bemba thought about that and said he didn't know precisely; as much as it took until they felt better, was about as close as he could get. Also, he said, his people had been cooped up in their grazing lands for many years, ever since the emperors started paying tribute, which meant the Robur could no longer honourably raid the empire. A whole generation had grown up without the chance to establish their status by fighting, and to the Robur that sort of thing was desperately important. The most likely thing was that they'd set their heart on burning the City itself. Could they do that? I asked him. Oh yes, he said.

So I asked General Stilian, who told me that the old emperor had never fought the Robur, but his grandfather had; four battles, three of which he lost, the fourth one drawn, and that was when the tribute started. What made them so special he didn't honestly know. The Robur don't have horses; their wagons are drawn by oxen, and they fight on foot, but they're superb archers with the most marvellous composite cane bows; also, they're very big and strong and brave, and they don't seem to care about getting killed. If only it was possible to hire them as mercenaries, he'd have done so like a shot. But they don't use money, and they think fighting for hire is the most disgusting thing a man can do.

I asked him: do we stand a chance against them? He thought for a very long time, and said: yes, because we've got very good cavalry. But it'd mean bringing up the main cavalry forces from the south and the west, as well as the northern heavy infantry; we only really stand a chance if we hit them in overwhelming force, and like I've been telling you all this time, the army is dangerously under strength.

Never mind about that, I told him. Overwhelming force it is. He shrugged. I can do that, he said, but I'll need money. I'll see about that, I said, not having the faintest idea where it was going to come from. And I'll want my brothers and my uncle Tzimisces as my battalion commanders. Fine, I said. And then he couldn't think of anything else to ask for on the spur of the moment, and I left him to his plan of campaign.

THE NEXT DAY I received a delegation from the Supreme Conclave. It was led by the abbot of the Studium, and the heads of all the City temples were with him. It was imperative, they told me, that I should put away the empress at once. Otherwise, they would have no choice but to close all the temples and pronounce sentence of excommunication on the entire City.

I asked them as respectfully as I could if they'd all gone raving mad. The City takes its religion seriously; excommunication, particularly with the Robur on the warpath, would mean panic, riots, the guards being called in to stop the riots, at least one horrendous massacre—they knew all that, they assured me, but it had to be done. The law was quite clear. They had no choice.

There's always a choice, I told them, and what's this all about anyway? They looked at me, very gravely. There was evidence, they said, that the empress had murdered her husband, the late emperor. As such she was an abomination in His sight, and unless she was removed and confined, He would punish the empire. Indeed, it could hardly be a coincidence that His scourge had already been set in motion, a point their priests would be sure to make from every pulpit in the City unless I took immediate action.

I can't do that, I said, she's my wife. I love her.

Maybe I was mumbling or something; they didn't seem to have heard me. At once, they said. In fact, we would prefer it if you issued the order in our presence, right now.

You've got it all wrong, I told them. It wasn't her who killed the old man, it was me.

They looked at me as if I was stupid or something. You are the emperor, they said, the emperor can do no wrong. It would be a legal impossibility for you to be guilty of murder. But someone clearly is; and since there are only two parties involved, it has to be her.

Besides, said the archimandrite of the Crooked Horn, lowering his voice just a little, she's lived in that tower most of her life, she's used to it by now. And you're a young man, and the empire needs an heir. And you're quite popular in the City right now, what with all the reforms, you needn't worry on that score. We've got just the formula for annulling the marriage, and then you'll be free.

I didn't answer him. I can't do it, I said.

You must, they said. It's God's will.

SHE DIDN'T GO quietly. I made sure I wasn't anywhere I could hear, but I gather there was a terrible scene. That evening, the abbot of the Studium made an official announcement at evening prayers. There were no riots, but only because Stilian had posted guards on all the street corners. I sent for the abbot and told him, but he shook his head. It's too late now, he said, the annulment has gone through, and besides, you can't go back on your word. If you do, we'll excommunicate you, and that would mean civil war.

Bemba told me that any support I'd had in the City was gone. I was the cunning, contriving usurper who'd seduced the old emperor's daughter, then had her locked up the moment she stopped being useful. They'd never forgive me for that.

I went to my chapel and prayed. Lord, I said, I think I understand. I did what was unpleasing in your sight, and you punished me; first my brother, now my wife. But you sent me a dream, after I'd prayed to you; this is why, you told me. I've tried to do what I thought you wanted. I expect I got that wrong. I get everything wrong, according to Nico.

So what I'd like you to do, if it's perfectly all right, is to punish me, not the City or the Empire. If you punish me, with death or disgrace or anything You like, I'll know I was wrong all along and I'll go quietly, and I won't ask you for anything ever again. But please, if it's all my fault, don't hurt anyone else because of it.

ON THAT UNDERSTANDING, I sealed Stilian's formal commission for the Robur campaign.

He'd taken me at my word and put together the biggest land army ever fielded in the empire outside of a civil war. He'd brought up the Second and the Fourth from the south, mostly comprising light and heavy cavalry, and the First from the west, with its eight battalions of heavy infantry. I'd found him some money by appealing to the better nature of the abbot of the Studium, who issued a bull for a tithe of all ecclesiastical property in the City. I was stunned by how much that came to, but never mind; that particular gift horse had golden teeth.

We had a big service for Stilian in the Studium chapel, and another in the Offertory, and then off he went. That night I repeated my prayer, just in case He hadn't heard me.

It would be all right, Bemba told me. If there was one thing on earth his people were terrified of, it was men on horses. In the past, when they'd fought us, they'd stuck to the mountains, where cavalry can't go. But now they were down in the plains, with nowhere to hide. Besides, Stilian was a fine general. He'd learned his trade under the old emperor.

Next morning I woke up and found both my ankles had swollen. They were as thick as my calves, and when I pressed them with my thumb, I left a thumb-sized hollow. So I sent for the doctors, who said it was nothing to worry about, and they'd be back the next day. The morning after that, the swelling was up to my thighs. You've got dropsy, the doctors said.

Ah, I thought. So that's all right.

In the weeks that followed, I drew great strength and satisfaction from my sickness. I don't know if you're familiar with dropsy; you swell up like a wineskin, your skin goes purple, your joints ache horribly all the time and no matter what you do, you can't get comfortable. I couldn't get to my chapel at the top of the tower—I couldn't leave my chair without three men to help me—but I prayed nonetheless. Thank you, I said.

I knew it had to be the answer to my prayers, because it was just the right illness for me to have. All those good looks, all that prettiness, gone. Instead I turned into this ludicrous bloated monster, like an animal that's been dead for a week. My skin was sort of glazed, like ham cured with honey, and it took me all my time and effort just to breathe. Thank you, I said to Him. That's a sign even I can understand.

The doctors made me drink things and rubbed stuff into my skin, all of which made the pain worse but did nothing about the swelling. After a bit I thanked them and told them to go away. The last thing I wanted was for them to cure me, at least not until Stilian was back home with his army intact.

And the news was good. Stilian had encountered a Robur raiding party, five thousand strong, heading for Beal Defour. He surrounded them with horse-archers and drove them like sheep onto the spearpoints of the 5th lancers. Only a handful of the enemy survived, and his own losses were trivial.

The swelling moved into my neck, and then my head, making my eyes blurry. I sent for the doctors. That's perfectly normal, they said. Nothing to worry about, then, I said. Not quite, they told me. It's perfectly normal for your vision to blur when you're as seriously ill as you are. Look on the bright side, though; your heart will probably give way before you go blind.

Thank you, I said, and I thought about poor Nico. The Divine Clemency of the Emperor, only in reverse. But divine clemency was what I'd prayed for, and if my prayers were granted I could ask for no more.

THEY WOKE ME up to tell me the news. Stilian and his entire army were dead.

I tried to get up, but there weren't enough people to help me. I fell on the floor, which was agony. They fetched a doctor, who said I wasn't to move for at least an hour on any account. So I received the messenger flat on my back, and hardly able to think straight for the pain.

The messenger was one Aelian Boutzes, a colonel in the Lancers. He'd been sent off to reconnoitre, but he got lost, and by the time he found his way back it was all over. He had no idea what had happened, but there was our camp, swarming with Robur, and dead men everywhere, very few of them Robur. He pulled out quick sharp and galloped off to find the survivors. It was a flat plain. He didn't find any.

He spent the rest of the day avoiding Robur scouts, and the night trying to figure out what to do. Just before dawn he rode back, and saw the remains of the biggest harvest festival the Robur had celebrated for a very long time. Then he headed straight back to the City. It was just possible, he said, that a few hundred of Stilian's men had made it, but he doubted it very much. If there'd been any significant number of survivors, in that terrain he'd have seen them. And so, of course, would the Robur. No, he said, it was far more likely that he and his men were the only survivors. In which case, he added, there was nothing apart from a bit of geography between the Robur and the City.

It wasn't easy for me to talk right then. Drawing breath was like drawing water from a very deep well. But I asked him; so who's the most senior officer in the army right now?

He looked at me, very sad. That would probably be me, he said.

WELL, HE EXPLAINED later, strictly speaking that wasn't true. But he was from the six families himself (younger son, junior branch, but he obviously knew what he was talking about) and he could pretty well guarantee that as soon as the news of the disaster reached the remaining field armies—the ones Stilian hadn't marched off to their deaths—their commanders would immediately withdraw to their home provinces with an view to defending them in depth, and let the City burn, if so be it. As far as the six families were concerned, the army was the empire and the empire was the army, and wherever there was an army in being, that was the capital city and all the provinces. The City was just some place where money went to and never came back from, and idiotic parasites dictated bloody stupid orders to an army of eunuchs, more often than not sending brave men to their deaths. Let it burn, in other words. Who gives a damn?

But there's a quarter of a million people here, I told him. He shrugged. Omelettes and eggs, he said. That's how my cousins will see it, anyhow, he added quickly. As of now, there's no army. And no officers.

Except you, I said.

He gave me a please-don't-do-this look. I'm only a colonel, he said. And besides, like I just told you—

There's the palace guard, I said. That's eight thousand men.

Last we heard, said Aelian, as gently as he could, there were a hundred and sixty thousand Robur. And Stilian was right. The only way you can beat them is overwhelming force.

I nodded. So if I asked you to lead the palace guard against them, you'd refuse.

I can't refuse, he said, not a direct order. But do you know what the Robur do to their prisoners?

Eat them, I said, yes, I know.

He shook his head. Not the high-ranking ones, he said, not the kings and princes and generals. What they do is, they get a round wooden post, about eight feet long, two or two and a half inches diameter, and they put a nice sharp point on it. They ram the pointy end about eighteen inches up your arse, then they plant the other end two feet in the ground. It's reckoned to be the most painful way a man can die, and it usually takes about six to eight hours. And it's no good your friends rescuing you, because by then the damage is done, all that happens is you live another twelve hours or so in unimaginable pain. I'll go if you tell me to, he went on, but on balance I'd rather not.

Later, I asked Bemba if it was true. He nodded. But they only do that to their worse enemies, he said; sorcerors and traitors and anyone who brings dishonour on the king. Like we have? I asked. Yes, he said.

THAT WAS ALL I could manage that day. While I was trying to get some sleep, Edax came to see me.

I hadn't set eyes on him since they made me emperor. In fact, I seemed to remember giving explicit orders. Keep him the hell away from me, I think I might have said. But there he was, looking pale and thin but otherwise more or less normal. You're ill, he said.

So they tell me, I said.

He nodded and sat down on my bed. Are you going to die?

I don't know, I told him. The doctors say, sooner or later all this bulk will collapse my heart. Or I may suddenly get better.

He frowned. You look terrible, he said. Look, if you die, does that mean I'm emperor?

No, I said.

I think it does, he said. You don't have any kids, and I'm your only relative. Well, there's Nico, but he's blind and he's got no cock, and the law says that means you can't be emperor. I've got a cock, he said. I'm qualified.

Have him poisoned, they'd told me, or put away somewhere, a nice quiet island or a monastery on a mountaintop, the ones where they raise and lower visitors in a basket. I was shocked. He's my brother, I told them.

I'm emperor, I told him, because I married the old emperor's daughter.

Fine, he said, I'll do that. But I don't think it's necessary, strictly speaking. I think, soon as you die, it just sort of happens. Look, why don't you get that clerk of yours to look it up? Never hurts to be prepared. You know, in case the worst happens.

Listen to me, I said. I'm sorry. About what happened with Nico. I had no choice.

He shrugged. Water under the bridge, he said. You're the boss now, that's what matters. But if anything were to happen to you, I think I ought to know where I stand. Continuity, he said. It's essential for the well-being of the empire.

To everything there is a purpose, Scripture says, and everything is useful under the Sun. Except for my brother Edax. I'll ask Bemba to look into it, I said. And I did.

No, he told me, there's not a great deal you can do, unless you want him killed or blinded. Actually, he's quite right. He would be the lawful heir.

Me on the imperial throne, with Edax by my side. This is why. I never knew He had a sense of humour.

I SENT FOR Colonel Aelian. I want you to take command of the City guard, I told him, while I'm away.

He looked at me. You're going somewhere, he said.

Bemba will be City Prefect, I said, but most likely everyone will give him a hard time, because of who he is, so I want you to look after him. You'll do that for me, won't you?

He didn't like the idea of nursemaiding a Robur eunuch, but he'd already refused one direct order. Of course, he said. Where are you going?

Thank you, I said. You've set my mind at rest.

Stilian had been the colonel-in-chief of the Guards, and he didn't have a second-in-command. Or rather he had eight, each leading a battalion of a thousand men. I sent for them. We're going north, I told them.

There was an awkward silence. Excuse me, Your Majesty, one of them said eventually, but the Guards never leave the City.

Talking hurt me and tired me out. The duty of the Guards, I said, is to guard the person of the emperor. Yes? They nodded. And the emperor is going north, I told them. So you're coming too.

Another long silence. May I ask where we're going?

To fight the Robur, I said.

They looked at each other. They weren't born-and-bred sons of the six families. They were working soldiers who'd spent their lives in the army and gradually worked their way up, from junior subalterns to majors. Bloody stupid orders that got you killed were their natural predator, like foxes are with rabbits. Didn't mean they had to like it. Do I understand, one of them said, that Your Majesty will be leading the army in person?

I was getting tired of the conversation. Unless one of you wants to do it.

No volunteers. Does Your Majesty have any military experience?

I sighed. No, I said. But while I've been lying here, my clerk has read me a couple of good books about strategy, and if I don't shame you into going, you won't go. Or if you do, you'll find an excuse to stop somewhere and wait till the Robur have sacked the City and gone back home. Which is fair enough, you've got a duty to your men. But your duty to me comes first. Doesn't it?

I could see what was going through their heads. There's nobody here but us, we could hold a pillow over his face and then tell everyone his heart gave out. Nico would have done it like a shot. Doesn't it? I repeated. They nodded. But with respect, Your Majesty, one of them said, you must be out of your mind.

THEY FILLED A cart with goose feathers. It was bearable, most of the time.

Even so, I didn't enjoy the journey north. The Great Military Road, which the old emperor's great-grandfather built to be the main artery of the empire, hadn't had any money spent on it for about forty years, there being no money to spend, and the farmers had taken to robbing the paving slabs to build walls and barns. I must do something about it, I thought, and then it occurred to me that, one way or another, I wouldn't be around long enough. That bothered me. You spend your life thinking, it's all right, I'll do something about this or that later, when I've got five minutes, I'll put it all right. Then suddenly you're like a man setting out on a long journey, and just as the ship casts off, he remembers all the things he forgot to pack.

I'd left Bemba behind to mind the store, but he'd found me a countryman and colleague of his, the only other Robur in the Service. His name was Sidoco (actually his name was Buffalo With A Split Horn, but life's too short) and he was a year or so older than me, a big, strong man. Bemba had made him swear by his honour to defend me to the death, which made me feel uncomfortable. Look, I said, if it comes to anything like that, run like hell. But he shook his head and explained that if he did that, his spirit would be cursed and he'd probably be reborn as a cockroach, and he despised cockroaches.

The Robur, Sidoco told me, live in huge wagons, with wheels taller than a man. These wagons are the only homes they have, or want; so when they go to war, their wives and children and sheep and goats and cows all go with them, and when the men are fighting, they form the wagons in a circle with the livestock in the middle. The wagons are so massively built, they're as good as a city wall, and a few good archers can defend them against an army. They despise settled people, he said, and the only reason they hadn't invaded the empire long ago was that we didn't have anything they wanted. Wealth to them means women, children and livestock; they're polygamous, and treat anyone's children as their own, because they need the manpower. So, when a man kills his enemy, he takes his family as his own, and everybody seems quite happy about the arrangement. They don't eat meat, apart from their dead enemies; they reckon rearing living things for slaughter is barbaric. Who'd take something as graceful as an antelope or a partridge, they say, and turn it into shit? One of the reasons they fight so well is, they aren't really afraid of death. They believe in reincarnation, and the purpose of life is to live and die well, to earn merit, to be born into a better status next time round. So they don't understand about ambition. Your position in society isn't something you earn for yourself—at least you do, but not in this lifetime—and trying to improve on what you've been allotted is the most appalling blasphemy, and all it'll get you is a short, horrible life as a beetle next turn of the wheel. I have to admit, I liked the sound of the Robur. A lot of what they thought and how they went about things made a certain degree of sense, and it irked me that I was duty bound to wipe them off the face of the earth. Still, not much chance of that.

The eight battalion commanders asked me what my plan of campaign was. I told them I didn't have one, but I was open to suggestions.

AT LEAST IT was over relatively quickly. At this point, the Robur had split into two roughly equal parties, about eighty thousand fighting men in each. One party had gone east, to sack Macestre. The other struck south, with a view to clearing up the string of big towns along the north bank of the Redwater before rejoining their friends for the main assault on the City. It was the southern party that found us, as we struggled through the mountain passes at Cans Juifrez.

The Robur realised that they had us exactly where they wanted us. If they waited for us to come down into the plain, there was a risk—small, but you never know—that our cavalry might work some miracle and carve them up. In the mountains, our cavalry were useless. A large part of tactical genius is taking advantage of the critical moment. An hour after the news of our arrival reached the wagons, eighty thousand Robur warriors were running—literally running—up the mountainside to catch us before we could slip away.

When they got there, they could see the way our minds had been working. We were waiting for them in a superb defensive position, a canyon with steep sides, only one narrow way in, and there we'd deployed the finest heavy infantry in the world, drawn up in phalanx. It was, they conceded, the best anyone could have done, in our position, given our pathetically small numbers. And yes, it'd be difficult, and their losses would be heavy, but they outnumbered us ten to one. And true, the imperial heavy infantryman wears the best armour skill and money can provide, but the Robur archers are the best in the world, and their bows are very strong.

They shot at us. We knelt behind our shields, and the arrows mostly didn't penetrate. They charged. We drove them back. Shooting and kneeling, charging and repulsing; it was a long day, and come nightfall, very little to show for it. But during the evening, Robur scouts came in and said they'd found a narrow track that led round the back of the canyon. If the army split into two, and half of them went round the back way, when the Sun rose they'd be able to take us in front and rear, and that would be that.

So that's what they did; and the Guards fought like heroes, to the very last man, and then it was all over. And then the Robur, carefully counting the dead, for obvious reasons, made a disturbing discovery. There were only a thousand dead Guards. But the scouts had seen eight thousand men marching into the other end of the canyon.

Dear God, it shouldn't have worked. The battalion commanders told me it wouldn't, that I was a fool and I'd get them all killed. I said, yes, it's a stupid idea, so please, give me a better one. And they couldn't, so we did it my way, and it worked.

One thousand men—volunteers, God forgive me—stayed to defend the pass, while the other seven thousand slipped out down the funny little goat track, crept past the Robur and dashed like lunatics to get to the wagons before the Robur figured they'd been had. We made it, and in good time, even though we were hindered by having to lug me along on a stretcher. Eliminating the sentries on the wagons was an awkward moment, a point at which the whole thing could have gone horribly wrong, but the Guards are good at that sort of thing, and we managed it. In half an hour, in the dark, we got control of the wagons, and when the Sun rose, we had all the women and kids rounded up and roped together. And now, one of the battalion commanders said to me, we can negotiate.

I shook my head. No, I said.

But that's crazy, he said. We've got them by the balls. The Robur love their kids. We can get out of this alive, if we play our cards right.

No, I told him. All right, let's suppose we strike a deal and they honour it, which they won't, because it's no sin to break a promise to the likes of us. Let's suppose we do a deal, and they go away. And next year, they come back. Sorry, I told him, but we've got to do it properly. He closed his eyes and counted to ten, and stalked away to organise the defence.

We let the scouts get up nice and close, so they could see we had the women and children up close to the wagons. That way, if the best archers in the world shot at us with their wonderful cane bows, they'd be shooting their own families. So instead they charged us with their spears and scimitars, and we shot them with our second-best archers and second-best bows as they came. They charged six times, and then they faltered, because suddenly there were so very few of them left; and then I gave the order to mount up, and our cavalry burst out of there and slaughtered them, until they were all dead.

I say we. All I did was lie there, in my feathers, listening to the horrors and not knowing what was going on. Then something happened—later they told me a Robur managed to scramble onto a wagon, he got shot and fell on me. Anyway, it hurt like hell and I passed out, and when I came round I couldn't see.

The Divine Clemency of the Emperor, I believe they call it.

WE SPARED ONE man, just one; and we sent him to tell the other Robur army to come and collect their widows and orphans, and not to come bothering us again.

(And that was the good part; because wealth to the Robur is women and children and livestock, and suddenly the survivors were twice as rich as they had been; so they went home perfectly satisfied, and with honour. I imagine they'll be back in thirty years or so, once a new generation has grown up, but that's a problem for another day. The war is never over.)

The doctors told me my sight would return, could well return, might possibly return, until I told them to leave me alone. The bump I got in the battle did me no good at all, and then it rained and I got soaked to the skin, which more or less finished me. The ride back to the City was no fun at all. They tell me my heart stopped once, and Sidoco jumped on me and punched me and got it going again; and I had a stroke, and various other unpleasant things. None of which I minded, but I couldn't make anyone else see that. Not that it mattered, at that.

What I wanted was for them to put me on a ship to the island where I'd sent Nico, so he could tell me what he thought of me before I died, but the doctors wouldn't allow it; and besides, I can't imagine I'd have lasted as far as the island, and politically it was important that I die in the City. Talking of which: Edax will almost certainly be emperor. The soldiers kept telling me to have him killed while there was still time, all the way from the Redwater to the City, and I knew they were giving me good advice, but I couldn't make myself do it, he's my brother; this is why. When I die, in the City, he'll be there to take the crown off the bed and stick it on his head, and then he'll be safe for a little while, until people get sick to death of him, which probably won't be very long. I hope not, anyway; the less time he's in charge, the less harm he'll be able to do. What happens after he's gone, I simply can't imagine. Those are other prayers, for someone else to make. I can't do everything myself; and what little I've done, I've done badly.

But—that's why I've told Bemba to write on the top of his scroll, *My Beautiful Life*. All my life I've done terrible, bad things. I've stolen, I've murdered, I've betrayed. I had my wife locked up in a tower, and I blinded my brother. Sometimes I ask why; and the answer stays the same. Where was I when He laid the foundations of the earth? This is why. I know I've been given the answer, and I know I've never managed to understand it. But that's my fault. And then I was given the sign, a sign so clear, even a fool like me could see it. And it was the last thing I ever saw, which pleases me. Anything else after that would've been a dreadful anticlimax.

Beauty is in the eye of the beholder; if thine eye offends thee, pluck it out. It's been a beautiful life, one way and another.

Stronger

Blessed are the meek, for they shall inherit the Earth—
Matthew 5,5

"How much to write a letter?" I asked him.

He gave me a business smile. "That depends," he said.

"On what?"

"On whether it's a fairly ordinary, straightforward sort of thing, where I can use one of my standard precedents, or if I've got to make it all up out of my head. If all I've got to do is copy it out and fill in the blanks, four obols. If I've got to be creative, six to nine."

"Right," I said. "Well, it's a letter to the parents of the girl I love with all my heart and soul, telling them how I've just watched their daughter being dragged away screaming by soldiers and loaded on a ship to be taken as a sacrifice to the Black Island and eaten by a monster."

He looked at me. "That'll be one drachma."

Every morning, ever since I was a small kid, I wake up, turn my head just a little and look out through the window. I see the light blue sky and the dark blue sea and the promontory, with the temple a blaze of white, and the white gold of the sand, and the red and white sails of ships. I see warmth and beauty and the joy of life. And then I remember and think, Oh.

You can't see the Black Island from Castletown because the promontory is in the way, but it's easily the most visible thing in the city. You can see it everywhere, in everything: in the frayed hems of worn-out clothes and the split seams of boots, in the bald heads and hunger rashes and sunken eyes of starving children, in the bull's-head insignia of the guards on every street corner. Lately I see it all the time, in my mirror.

He owns a *mirror*, you're saying to yourself; a rich bastard. Well, quite. One death and I'd be the richest bastard in Castletown. But that death would be my father, so I'm in no hurry. And yes, my father is a rich man. He owns a ship, two fishing smacks, seven farms, six orchards, two vineyards, a lime kiln, a copper mine, a foundry, a wheelwright's shop, an olive press, half a ton of bronze ingots and the only mountain on the island, which just happens to be covered in valuable timber. So yes, I have a mirror while there are people out there who don't have enough to eat. But the mirror belonged to my mother, so it's not going anywhere. One of my earliest memories was watching her holding it while she combed her hair. So I keep the stupid mirror, because I look at the back of it and I see her. Then I turn it round and see myself, and in my eyes a reflection of the Black Island.

My father and I don't work all those ships, farms, orchards, workshops and forests on our own. We employ about a hundred men and women and we pay good wages. I have nothing to feel guilty about.

THE LAST THING she said to me was, I won't have to go, will I? Promise me.

"I promise," I said. "It's all fine. We've fixed the ballot."

She breathed out, as though she'd been holding her breath for ever. "How?" she asked. "I didn't think that was possible."

We were sitting under the crooked fig tree, looking out over the bay as the fishing boats came back in. "Don't worry," I said. "It's all arranged. Lexias is this year's ballot commissioner. He works for us at the mill, and he's got a family, and debts. He guarantees he can fix it."

She smiled. All her life, she'd been terrified that one day it would be her turn. "You have no idea," she said, "how good that feels."

I hate the fact that I'm stupid. Lexias worked for us, but Philopoemen bought up the mortgages on his seven acres of scrub and gravel; Philopoemen has three daughters and two sons. If Philopoemen foreclosed, he could take Lexias' wife and kids as part payment for the mortgage and sell them to the Sherden, and Lexias would never see them again. I like Philopoemen, he's a good, kind man with a sense of humour, but when you're scared out of your head you do things that normally you wouldn't countenance. Like extortion, or rigging the ballot, like I tried to do.

Afterwards, I went to see Lexias. I happened to have an axe-handle with me. He made no effort to defend himself. I wanted to keep hitting him till there was nothing left I could recognise, but when he just knelt there, not even shielding his head with his arms, I sort of ran out of enthusiasm. He kept saying how sorry he was. If he'd tried to argue the toss, I'd have smashed his head in. As it was, what was I supposed to do, for crying out loud? So I gave him three drachmas and came home.

"Could've been worse," my father said. "Could've been you."

That, of course, is what's wrong with love. My father loves me as much as I loved her, so I couldn't even put a rope round my neck or open a vein. I shot a hare once, and the arrow passed through its hind quarter and stuck in a tree stump, pinning the hare down until I could get to it and break its neck. Love is the arrow that pins us down so we can't escape.

History lesson. Once upon a time we were just us. Our great-great-great-you-name-it grandparents came here, found the island empty and got stuck in. After a while, they found they could make a living, and a little bit over. It's not a bad place. There's a river and seventeen wells, so water is rarely a problem. Apart from the mountain, whose slopes are covered in useful trees, the land is good for growing things; barley down on the flat, vines and olives in the hills, provided you don't mind half-killing yourself piling up rocks to build terraces. Quite good soil in the river valley. The copper mine—call it a mine, it's a bare patch on the north side of the mountain, like a scab you keep picking at so it never heals. But you can scrabble about for a day and fill six bushel baskets with ore, for which the Sherden will give you six drachmas. My great-grandfather built the lime kiln, and ever since we've been able to put a bit of heart back into the land. Most of what we don't need for ourselves we sell to the Sherden, who rip us off savagely, but my father's ships make four trips a year to Long Island, where they give us four times what the Sherden pay. Left to ourselves—

But we weren't.

Once upon a time, they were just them. But monstrous creatures from the north, crook-backed savages who shot from the saddle and ate babies, drove them from their homes until they reached the sea and had nowhere else to go. So they built ships, and eventually after many cruel wanderings they reached the Black Isle. It's a fertile country, they say, deep-soiled, well-watered. Left to themselves they'd have been happy there. But they didn't get vacant possession. *He* was there before them, before everyone, left over from some earlier phase of existence, overlooked when the rest of the world was made safe for mortal men. They say he's nine feet tall with the body of a man and the head of a bull, unimaginably strong, perpetually hungry. He ate the whole complement and crew of the first of their ships. They shot arrows and threw spears at him, but he barely noticed. Only when he'd quite finished cracking the bones for the marrow did he turn his head and look at the rest of them. The calculating expression on his face they put down to mental arithmetic.

So they made a deal. He would leave them to themselves, provided they fed him. At first they gave him their own men, women and children, but that obviously wasn't sustainable. So they built more ships, sailed out into the open waters of the Friendly Sea and started taking islands. To begin with they'd appear out of the darkness just before dawn and snatch five or a dozen from the houses nearest the harbour, but that was too uncertain. Why hunt when you can farm? So they made a deal.

First, because from now on they'd be too busy patrolling and guarding and keeping law and order to do their own farming, they took a sixth of every kind of produce. They didn't just grab a percentage out of the air, they sat down and figured it out, with the aid of surveys, statistics, demographic theory and differential calculus—oh, they're a very advanced people, as they keep on reminding us; they were calculating the recurrence of comets and predicting eclipses when we were still chipping axes out of flint. They used this superior knowledge to work out exactly what we needed to keep ourselves fed and tolerably healthy, and took the rest. Naturally you'd want your livestock in prime condition. Their revenue collection directorate has a motto: the good shepherd shears his sheep, he doesn't skin them.

The other form of revenue was also calculated to a nicety, based on birth rates, infant mortality levels, labour requirements, the average useful working life of the average useful worker. They settled on twelve young men and twelve young women, once a year; the surplus. Remove the surplus, they told us, and you get stability. Stability brings security, security brings content. Do as you're told and pay your taxes and leave everything else to us, and you'll be happy as fleas on a dog.

Not an idle promise. The good shepherd doesn't just shear. He clips feet, dags the caked shit off tails, wards off predators and rotates grazing, because they are the sheep of his pasture, his to shear, his to kill and eat. So they gave us laws, which somehow we'd never needed before, and institutions, mostly to do with gathering census information and quantifying produce levels. They taught us how to improve crop yields and breed better strains of livestock, how to stop so many of our children dying in infancy, how to dam streams and dig irrigation channels. They stopped us killing each other in pointless ancestral feuds, because it was such a shocking waste. They even taught a handful of us to read, write, compile records and conduct an entirely fair, democratic and incorruptible ballot. We owe them so much.

Some of us did deals with them and were granted licences and limited authority over our neighbours. My great-grandfather was one of them, which is why our family is so rich. We say that we look out for our own, do our best to soften the wolf's bite; that you can't fight them, but you can work with them to make everybody's lives just that tiny bit less shitty. We say that, and people believe us. Just because everybody believes something, it doesn't always follow that it's true.

A WHOLE DRACHMA for one lousy letter. Just because it's us, people think they can take the piss.

He wrote it out on a nice square slab of clay, four inches by two, using a reed cut into a chisel point. Then it went in the kiln along with the rest of the day's correspondence—tax returns, a couple of probate inventories, the garrison commander's weekly report, three bills of sale and a charterparty. A day to bake, a day to cool off and there it was. He read it back to me. A bit impersonal, I thought, but I don't suppose I could've done any better myself. Then I gave it to one of the farm boys to deliver. I paid him two obols. I'm generous, sprinkling silver like rain wherever I go.

You sent them a letter, my father didn't say because I didn't tell him, how much did that cost? Followed by; a drachma two, for crying out loud, do you think we're made of money? Couldn't you just have walked over there and told them yourself?

No, I couldn't. One drachma two obols well spent.

So I went to see Anaxandron at the foundry. He was in a mood because he was short-handed, having just sent his son to the Black Island. I offered to work the bellows for him but he just looked at me.

"I need something made," I said.

"What?"

"A sword."

He rolled his eyes. "You know better than that."

"I won't tell the bulls if you don't."

"What do you want it for?"

"Trimming my fingernails, what do you think?"

He'd never made a sword before, understandably enough; but if you can make a sickle or a billhook, you can make a sword, the principle's the same. I stood over him while he whittled the pattern. No, I kept saying, that's a tad too long, and I want more of a curve there. What the hell do you know about swords? he asked. Nothing, I said, truthfully.

I watched him press the pattern into the two halves of the sandbox and left him cutting runners and ingates. Burn the pattern when you're done, I told him, I won't be wanting another one.

The bulls aren't too bad, or so they tell you. They're just people doing a job, like you and me.

I knew one of them to talk to. He was round at our place one time getting my father's sealprint on a warrant (my father's a civilian magistrate) and he stopped for a drink, and then dinner. I was polite and friendly to him, because it costs nothing and doesn't leave a visible mark. So when I called round at the station house he gave me a big friendly grin and poured me a drink. I recognised the mark on the jar; one of ours, and he hadn't paid for it. Sorry to hear about your girl, he said.

He was watching me the way a dog watches a stranger. It happened to me once. I was over the other side of the island and two huge dogs ran out at me, barking their heads off. I froze. So did they. They growled but didn't move. If I'd so much as twitched they'd have ripped my throat out, but so long as I kept perfectly still, nothing could happen and I was completely safe. Odryas the bull was watching me for the first move. I shrugged.

"The hell with it," I said. "Plenty more fish in the sea."

"You don't mean that," he said.

They don't send them overseas unless they're at least moderately smart. "No, but it's not the end of the world," I said. "We learn to live with stuff like that. You'd understand, if you were one of us."

He laughed. "Glad I'm not, in that case. The day I learn to live with something like that, kill me, I don't deserve to live." He watched for a reaction. "You're a smart kid, Lysidemus. You're like your old man. We can do business with someone like you."

"Thank you," I said. "Talking of doing business."

While I outlined my proposition, he was watching me like a hawk. But as well as being third in command of the garrison and a big wheel in military intelligence, he was also the trade attaché. Bulls sent here have to do a lot of different jobs, because it's really difficult to get anyone even slightly more intelligent than a trowel to take a posting like this at all. "Sure," he said when I'd finished, "why the hell not? Assuming the price is right, of course."

I mentioned some figures. He barely haggled at all.

Either you go to the Black Island against your will, kicking and screaming, or you don't go at all. It's not somewhere you can just decide to visit, even if you own a ship that'll take you there. Only authorised visitors clutching a clay slab sealed by a proper officer are allowed to land, and since there's only one place you can land a ship, there's no chance of sneaking ashore unobserved. If you jumped overboard and tried to swim, you'd be drowned by the currents or smashed up on the rocks; if by some miracle you survived, you'd die trying to scale the unscalable cliffs. I asked the scribe about forging a landing permit. As soon as he figured out what I was asking, he started to hum very loudly, so he wouldn't be able to hear any more of what I was saying. Besides, why would anyone in his right mind *want* to go there?

But, as Odryas the bull told me to my face, I'm a smart kid. People can't go there; it's different for things. Slaves of the monster they may be, but the bulls aren't averse to making money, and a good way to do that is to buy something dirt cheap on one island in their dominion and sell it for an extortionate price on another. The only problem with that is that if the goods go direct from Island A to Island B, central government might easily miss out on customs, tariffs, purchase and sales taxes; also, things might get bought and sold and commodities moved around from place to place without them knowing about it, which might tend to screw up their economic models and distort their projections. So, if you want to take a hundred jars of pickled walnuts from Aeschros to sell in Callirhoe, the shipment can't just hop the three miles of clear, calm water across the straits. It's got to go island-hopping from Aeschros to Deisidaemon to Pandateria to Seleuthoe to the Black Island, where it's registered, invoiced, weighed, measured, ticketed, given a number and stuck in a bonded warehouse for a month before setting off for the longer anticlockwise leg of its journey, only this time sailing into the prevailing winds. It's not an ideal way to do business but it ensures that the revenue gets its rightful two obols in the drachma. More to the point, it means that jar of pickled walnuts can go where a man can't.

Pickles, then, have all the luck. Even so. Who in his right mind—?

"SINCE WHEN," MY father asked me, "have we been in the lumber business?"

"There's money in it," I said.

"That doesn't answer my question."

Sixty-four cedar logs, thirty feet long, three feet diameter, in a neat stack outside our door. I'd neglected to mention that they were coming. Simpler that way. If I'd asked him first he'd have said no. "Since that bull Odryas called me in and told me to do it," I said.

My father knows me too well. "Told you."

I shrugged. "I may have mentioned that I was looking around for a sideline of my own. You know, to take my mind off things."

We hadn't talked about the things I might want to take my mind off. Even a hint of the subject was enough to drive him off, like when you clap your hands and a whole flock of rooks rises up screaming at you out of the spring barley. "Still," he said. "Lumber."

"The bulls are crazy for it," I said. "For construction."

He looked at me. "It's a thing about lumber," he said, "it grows on trees. What makes you think it could possibly be worth anyone's while to shift these great big heavy logs all the way from here to—?"

"Not just logs," I said. "Cedar logs."

He paused, as though he'd just put his foot in something. "They've got cedar on Aeschros," he said. "And Pandateria."

"Not as good as what we've got," I said.

"How would you know that?"

"The bull told me," I said. "It's something to do with growing higher up the mountain. You get a straighter grain or something like that."

One of the many things my father and I have in common is complete ignorance about the technical aspects of forestry. "That figures," he said, trying manfully to look as though he knew what he was talking about. "And there's enough in it to make it worth our while?"

"Using our ship and crew, yes," I said.

"You want to use the ship."

It's been a bone of contention between us for ages. He had the wretched thing built so he could haul grain and lumber from one side of the island to another without having to cart it overland. It was, he freely admitted, a good idea at the time. It cost him more than he thought it would, considerably more than he could afford. My mother, rest her soul, gave him a really hard time about it, every chance she got.

"Yes, the ship," I said. "That's where we've got the edge. It's a slim margin, but if we can get a foot in the door, we can undercut the competition and start getting big orders. The bigger the scale in this business, the more money you make." He was about to say something, so I went on quickly; "There's thousands of good trees on the mountain just sitting there, no use to anybody. And we've got a ship, which just sits there most of the year doing nothing, and people. We could make a lot of money."

He looked at me as though I'd suggested we start breeding peacocks so we could have the feathers. Why would we want to make more money, he didn't ask, we've got plenty already. He was reassessing me in the light of new and unexpected evidence, and his conclusions surprised him. "I guess we could," he said. "It's a risk, though. You pull people off other work to do this, suppose it doesn't work out? We lose what we've put into it and what we would've made from the other stuff that didn't get done."

I told him, "It's about cold, hard numbers. If the arithmetic works out, you do it. If it doesn't, you don't. Tell you what, Dad, if you want to get ahead in the bulls' world, you've got to start thinking like them."

He looked at me as though I'd just pissed on his shoes. "There's an element of truth in that," he said, and walked away.

HESYCHIUS, MY OLDEST and best friend, came to see me. "What the hell do you think you're playing at?" he asked me.

I picked myself up off the ground and wiped blood from the corner of my mouth. "You hit me," I said.

He did it again. This time I was expecting it and managed to stay upright. He's not a violent man. "You bastard," he yelled at me. "I don't know what's got into you. You never used to be like this."

"For crying out loud," I mumbled, "get a grip and stop hitting me."

They say that a bow at full draw is nine-tenths broken. He was at full draw. The slightest move on my part, or the wrong words, and he'd flatten me. He's a tad shorter than I am but much stronger. "When they told me I couldn't believe it. You, of all people."

"Don't you think you're overreacting a bit?"

The wrong words, definitely. I tried to block with my forearm but all I parried was the feint. It hurt and I couldn't breathe. This time I landed on my arse, which wasn't so bad. "No," he said. "Get up."

"Not likely."

He took three or four deep breaths, and I watched the will to murder seep out of him, like wine from a cracked skin. "You really are a sorry piece of shit, Lysidemus," he said. "I ought to smash your face in."

"You just did."

Normally he laughs at my jokes. Mind you, it wasn't all that funny. "You could try explaining," he said.

I got up. He didn't knock me down again. I sat down on a log and explained.

His family are tenants of ours. What I'd done that had annoyed him so much was take them away from the haymaking, which has to be done when the weather's right or there's no point bothering, and order them up the mountain to brash and haul timber. Properly speaking he should have been up there with them, but I didn't feel like rebuking him just then. He'd assumed that I'd done it because I was brown-nosing the bulls, or simply to make money. I was disappointed. I thought he knew me better than that.

"Think," I said. "What's the special thing about trees?"

"You what?"

"Trees," I said. "What makes them different from everything else that gets carried on a ship?"

You can see the thoughts crossing his mind through the windows of his eyes. When I can't sleep, I imagine Hesychius thinking. Other people count sheep; same principle. "They're heavy."

"By volume, copper's five times the weight. Try again."

"I don't know, do I? They're—" He frowned. "Long?"

I touched the tip of my nose with my forefinger, then pointed at him. "They're long," I said. "Why is this significant?"

"I'm going to kick your head in in a minute."

"It's significant," I said, "because the bulls desperately want good cedar in lengths suitable for building, but they can't carry them on their ships. They're galleys, designed for war."

"So they pay more?"

I shook my head. "So they've got to go where they're going via the Black Island, but they can't go on a bull ship. They've got to go on one of our ships. Crewed by our people." I paused. He hadn't got it. "One of whom will be me."

He looked at me as though after all these years I'd suddenly turned out to be somebody else. "You want to go to the—"

"Yes."

"Why?"

"Three fucking guesses."

I'd shocked him. "You're out of your mind," he said. "Does your father know?"

"Good God, no," I said. "It'd kill him."

All the anger melted out of him. "You're a lunatic," he said. "What do you think you could possibly achieve?"

"Remains to be seen," I said. "And don't you breathe a word of this to anybody, all right?"

He nodded wretchedly. "Everyone's saying you've sold out to the bulls. They reckon all you're interested in is money."

"Good," I said. "It's really good they think that."

"They hate you."

"Doesn't matter."

"Don't talk stupid. You've got to live with these people."

I grinned at him. "Chance would be a fine thing."

He breathed in deep, then out through his nose. That means; I want to tell you how stupid you're being, but you wouldn't listen. Some people are harder to read than one of the scribe's clay bricks. Hesychius is practically a map. "I suppose you want me to come with you."

"Absolutely not. What harm did you ever do to me?"

The look on his face was a sight to see; as though I was drowning, and he'd just let my fingers slip through his hand. "You can't fight the bulls," he said. "You know that."

"Absolutely," I said. "That's why I'm not even going to try."

BECAUSE, YOU SEE, I figured it out for myself. Actually it came to me in a flash, a blinding moment of pure insight. There is no monster.

That's not strictly true. There are lots of monsters, thousands of them. But human, just like you and me, and mortal, and capable of being reasoned with.

Think about it. Supposedly we've been sending our annual tribute for hundreds of years. Now, then: either this monster is mortal, in which case he must've died years ago, because nothing lives that long except oak trees; or else he's a god, and gods don't need food. Think about it some more. The stories say he'd been there on the Black Island long before the bulls arrived, and when they got there it was uninhabited, apart from him. Therefore, no people for him to eat, for a long time. He hadn't starved to death, but there was no food. Think about it some more. The bulls rule five islands. We're one of the bigger ones, with a larger human surplus. Let's assume for the sake of argument that each island sends an average of twenty victims. That's a hundred bodies. The monster is supposed to be nine feet tall and incredibly strong; therefore it follows that he needs to eat a lot more food than you or I do. My grandfather told me about a king on the mainland who kept a lion as a pet, and it ate a whole ox every day. He'd have the appetite of two lions. A hundred human bodies to last him a whole year; he'd starve. So, either he's a god and doesn't need food or he isn't real. And if he's a god he doesn't exist, because gods don't. Trust me on this. I prayed every day, every long, sleepless night, for them to let her go, but they didn't. Therefore, there aren't any. Logic.

So: no monster, lots of monsters. And the twenty-four victims rounded up and herded onto ships every year don't go to the Black Island to be eaten, they go there to work, because the bulls don't work, they're too busy being soldiers and overseers and revenue officers. They tell us they're dead so we won't go over there and free them, and to terrify us, but it isn't true. So she must still be alive, on the Black Island, existing there as property. And the thing about property is, you can buy it, even if you have to pay silly money.

Everybody cheats. For us, it's more than simply a business practice, it's the only form of cultural expression the bulls have left us with. And we take it seriously. It used to be that we only cheated the bulls, but now we cheat each other, to keep in practice, to perfect the art.

Take the drachma. Everybody knows that a drachma is the weight of a handful of barley grains. You owe someone a drachma, you get your bag of chop silver, your scales and a jar of barley. A level handful of grain goes in one pan, and you drop bits of silver into the other pan until they balance. It's absolutely fair and everyone knows where they stand.

When my father and I do business, one of us buys, the other one sells. I have small hands, like a girl. He has hands like shovels. He sells, I buy. Over the course of a year's trading, it makes a substantial difference; enough to pay two men's wages, so cheating isn't just an art form, it provides employment.

The bulls drink wine, not beer, so they don't know about malting. If you soak your grains so that they're just about to sprout, then roast them enough to kill them, they weigh just a little bit more. Furthermore, all barley isn't the same. We grow one variety down on the flat and another on the upland terraces. The upland variety has very slightly smaller, lighter grains. The bulls don't know this. When they came round in my grandfather's time, teaching us how to farm more efficiently and maximise our taxable yields, they gave, sorry, sold us Black Island seed corn, which derives from a mainland variety and was much better than what we used to have. They assume that all the barley we grow is that variety. It was my father who figured out that the old strain might have its uses, and searched till he found an old boy up in the back country who still grew the garbage variety. He's smart, though maybe not as smart as me.

Everyone cheats, even when it isn't really worth the effort. If you ask him nicely, Anaxandron at the foundry will melt down your silver, mix in an unnoticeably small proportion of copper, cast the resulting alloy into ingots and draw it down into wire. You have to pay him for his time and trouble, of course. I generally give him half a jar of honey for making me two pounds of slightly polluted silver wire out of thirty ounces of good stuff.

Half a jar of honey for a morning's work is daylight robbery and I'd be losing on the deal if I didn't get the honey more or less for free from one of our tenants, in exchange for letting him draw water from a well that I didn't dig and which would be no use to me if he didn't use it. Besides, you can water honey down a bit, if you're careful not to overdo it. And when we weigh the wire, we use my scales.

Everyone cheats. I tried to fix the ballot, but Philopoemen got in ahead of me. He cheated me before I could cheat him. Both of us tried to cheat the bulls, but that doesn't count.

I MAY HAVE overdone the loading a little bit, because by the time we had the lumber on board and secured so it wouldn't move about, the ship was a smidgeon too low in the water for comfort. Not to worry. We weren't going far and it's plain sailing to the Black Island.

The crew were all men I'd sailed with before, but there was something slightly different in their manner, as if they were ready, willing and anxious to forgive me just as soon as I apologised, though what for wasn't at all clear. Maybe it was because the ship was full to bursting, so no room for personal stuff, and traditionally everyone brings along a few jars of this and that to sell on his own account—that was how my great-great-grandfather got started, incidentally, trading top-quality almonds from half a dozen spindly trees in his father's back yard, until he earned enough to buy his own ship. Or maybe it was simply that nobody likes going anywhere near the Black Island, understandably enough. Anyway, it was a quiet trip, with nobody in the mood for talking. I didn't mind that particularly, though usually I like to chat. I had things on my mind.

Obviously none of us had ever been to the Black Island before, so we had no idea how to get into the harbour without ripping out our keel on some hidden peril we didn't know was there. They'd thought of that, naturally. If you're the hub of a major shipping enterprise, obviously you get ships coming in all the time who don't know the waters. So there were plenty of nice, clear seamarks—buoys, flags, piles driven into the seabed and posts on the harbour wall to line up with. The main hazard wasn't rocks, shoals or reefs, it was keeping clear of other ships. When you think what a ship represents, in terms of materials, manpower, time, skill and expense, it was amazing to see so many of them all together in one place; dozens of them, merchantmen and galleys, just lying about as if they didn't matter. "Do you reckon it's like this all the time?" one of the men said, with a look on his face like he'd accidentally gatecrashed the wedding of two gods. I knew how he felt. Not just the ships, but all the stuff they must be carrying, all that cargo, all that wealth of material goods, all that money.

Odryas the bull had given me a lump of baked clay the size and colour of a flattened turd, pecked all over with little wedge-marks, which was supposed to make everything all right with the harbour authorities. To my utter amazement, it did. The harbourmaster—actually I think it must've been the deputy harbourmaster's acting deputy assistant, in a busy place like that—glanced at it, nodded and told us to stay there, someone would be along in a minute. We stared at him. Here we were, perfect strangers from another island, he didn't know our names or whose sons we were, but everything was fine because everything about us that anybody needed to know was somehow contained in a few squiggles poked in a wet tile. Extraordinary. And yet people live like that, apparently, all the time.

We hung about, not daring to get off the ship. Time passed. To begin with we were too busy drinking in the sights and the sounds to worry about anything. Then we began to wonder if they'd forgotten about us, or whether there was something we didn't know about that we were supposed to have done and we were holding everyone up and making a nuisance of ourselves. Maybe, someone suggested, we ought to go and ask someone.

That was generally considered to be a good idea, but the definition of *we* in this context was something of a sticking point. In the event, *we* turned out to mean me. Probably a dialect usage from the remote hill country.

Feeling like I was walking on hot embers I clambered off the ship onto the quay and looked round for someone to ask. At home, no problem. At home there's only a limited number of bulls and you know them all by sight and they know you. I tried my best, but the first half-dozen I approached didn't seem to be able to see me. The seventh stopped, mostly because if he hadn't he'd have walked right into me. "What?" he said.

"We're new here," I said. "what do we do?"

He looked over my shoulder at our ship. "You been checked in?"

"I don't know. We brought a tablet from home and a man looked at it and told us to wait."

"Then wait."

He walked away. Nice to have cleared that up. I went back to the ship. "We're to wait," I told them. "Someone'll be along directly."

Eventually, someone was. He looked at the ship, then at the flattened turd, then at us. "You're in the wrong place," he told us. "You want Dock Four. This is Dock Three. Dock Four is over there."

He pointed at something a long way away, on the other side of the quay. "Sorry," I said. "We didn't know."

He sighed. "Your best bet," he said, "is to go back out the way you came in, then follow the north-east lane as far as the seventh quarter-post and come in backwards on an angle of forty-five degrees. Got that?"

"No."

He rolled his eyes. "Then you're just going to have to sit there," he said, and walked away.

I watched him go, speechless. Then one of the men prodded me in the back and I remembered I was in charge and ran after him. "I'm very sorry," I said, "but we're new to all this. Do you think you could possibly explain?"

He looked at me as though I was all the troubles he'd ever known sewn up in a sack. "Fine," he said. "You stay there, we'll come to you. It'll be quicker in the long run."

We stayed there. It got dark. We were hungry, but all we had left was a few bits of stale crust and a few dried figs. "We could just leave," Pythias the helmsman said. "They wouldn't give a shit."

"We can't do that," someone else said. "They know we're here. We can't leave without a departure permit. A bull told me that, back home."

"Fine," Pythias said. "What's a departure permit?"

The man shrugged. "I don't know, do I? One of those baked brick things."

"We've got one of them. Let's go."

"Doesn't work like that," I explained. "It's got to have the right squiggles on it. Our brick's only got coming-in squiggles, not going-out. Let's all just hold our water and see what happens, shall we? These people must know what they're doing, it's their job."

Sure enough. Shortly before first light, when we'd all finally managed to drop off to sleep, a gang of bulls turned up with huge carts and a crane and told us to wake up. They hadn't got all day, they explained, and where was our bill of lading?

The bill of lading turned out to be the other side of the clay turd, and told them everything they needed to know about everything. All we had to do was manhandle the logs so they could get the chains round them and hoist them onto the carts. While we were doing that, I had a good look at the men working the crane. They weren't bulls. You can tell, quite easily. Bulls are tall and lean, apart from the short, fat ones, and these men were sort of square and stocky. Also they did what they were told without answering back. I've never worked with anyone who hasn't known a better way of doing the job. It's practically a point of honour.

They got the lumber onto the carts in no time flat, and the chief bull handed me a small clay tile with squiggles on it. Take this to the paymaster, he said, and then you can get your clearance and go home. Thank you, I said, and where would I find the paymaster? He looked at me as though I'd asked him what the big shiny white thing in the sky was, and pointed in the direction of a row of brick buildings half a mile away. Then he yelled at the carters, and the carts rumbled away, taking our valuable lumber with them.

"You stay here," I told the men. "I won't be long."

They scowled at me. I grinned at them, as though I had the faintest idea of what was going to happen next, and set off toward the brick buildings.

If I'd had the sense to bring the scribe with me, always assuming he'd have been prepared to come, it wouldn't have been so bad. He could've read what was written up over the doors of all the buildings, and we'd have found the paymaster without too much trouble. Instead I spent most of the morning standing around waiting for other people to finish their conversations before being told I was in the wrong place and I wanted to go over there. When eventually I found the paymaster, he glanced at my bit of tile and told me it was no good.

"Oh," I said. "Why not?"

"Needs countersealing. You want the merchants' association."

"Of course I do. Where—?"

"Over there."

Actually, the merchants' association was exactly what I wanted, though I hadn't realised it. At the merchants' association, once they realised I was the man with all the sensibly priced three-foot cedar, they were delighted to meet me. Sit down, they said. Have a drink while we get your chit sealed.

Gradually, as I talked to them, I came to realise that not all bulls are the same. The ones we get at home are one sort, but these were different; easy-going, friendly, only too happy to know you if they thought there was a chance of making some money.

They explained to me, very kindly and patiently, where I'd gone so disastrously wrong. I'd allowed Odryas to talk me into selling my valuable lumber to his friends in Consortium A, when what I should have done was sell it to Consortium B, who would treat me with respect and pay me very slightly more. Alternatively—and only because they liked me so much and felt guilty because I'd been treated so badly—Consortium B and I could get together and form Consortium C; in which case I wouldn't actually get paid for my logs, but I'd be entitled to a full share of profits at some point further down the line, once Consortium K had sold them to Consortium L. I said I'd like to think about it. Of course, they said, and in the meantime, have another drink.

"All this money," I said. We were drinking wine. We make a lot of wine at home but we drink beer and sell the wine. The bulls mix it, three parts water to one part wine. I could drink that all day and hardly notice, so I had to pretend. "All this money," I repeated, "what's it *for*?"

They grinned at me. "You can buy stuff with it," one of them said.

"Stuff," I said scornfully.

"Stuff is good," another one said.

"Nah," I told him. "Takes up space and you've got to dust it. Who needs stuff? I don't. All stuff is shit."

One of them looked at me severely, to let me know that words of wisdom were on their way. "Stuff," he said, "is what marks us out from them. We've got stuff, they haven't. That's what stuff's for. It's for having."

"Bullshit," said another one. "What you want is nice things. Pretty things, none of your rubbish. Why does everything in life have to be horrible? Why can't you have something nice for a change, if you can afford it?"

Another bull said; "Sure. Nice things, not shit. And we've got it and you haven't. No offence," he added graciously. "That's the point, isn't it? Stuff is how you know who's better than everybody else. Stuff is how you keep score."

I was concerned they'd drink themselves incoherent before I could ask my questions. I'd been working towards my goal slowly and carefully, patiently stalking it through the long grass. But with the bulls in that state there didn't seem to be much point. "What happens to the slaves from the islands?" I asked.

"You what?"

"All the young kids who get brought here," I said. "Back home, they tell us they get fed to a monster and eaten, but that's all shit. Bullshit," I couldn't resist adding, but it was lost on them. "So what happens to them really? They're sold as slaves, right? Only I'd really like to buy one, with all this money I'm going to be making. Expense no object," I added. "Top dollar."

They were all looking at me, as though I'd exposed myself. "You what?" one of them said again.

"The kids from the islands," I repeated. "That's what you do, right? You make them into slaves. You turn people into stuff. Fine. That's fine by me." I held up my hands, palms outwards. "We all do it, it's cool, you've got to do it or nothing ever gets done. I've learned that, since I've been dealing with you gentlemen. It's progress, it's what builds cities, it's what makes you better than us. That's great. That's the stuff I really want to buy. Why are you looking at me like that?"

"Are you out of your mind?" one of the bulls said. "You can't *own* people. That's sick."

I wasn't having that. "Oh come on," I said. "You do it all the time. Look what you do to us."

He stared at me, then laughed. "You're nuts," he said. "Listen, my stupid provincial young friend, you've got us all wrong. Sure, we don't treat you like we treat our own, of course not. We're better than you, go figure. So we push you around a bit, we rip you off right, left and centre, of course we do, that's natural. That's the point of being strong. So we cheat. Everybody cheats. Cheating's as natural as the air we breathe, and the fact we can do it gives us the right. But *owning* a *person*? That's horrible. If we did that, it wouldn't make us better than you. It'd make us worse."

"They do it in Assur," one of the others pointed out. "On the mainland."

"Yeah, well," he said angrily, "that proves my point, doesn't it? They're animals over there. Anybody who could think that sort of thing is all right, got to be something wrong with them." He looked at me. He was upset. "Look," he said, "you want to sell us your fucking logs or not? If not, piss off. I don't think I like you any more."

I wasn't really interested in whether he liked me or not. "Answer my question and I'll *give* you the stupid logs," I said. "What do you do with the kids from the islands? Where do they go? What happens to them?"

For a very long two seconds nobody spoke. Then one of them said; "They go to the citadel."

"And?"

"They go to him. He eats them."

"This man is starting to annoy me," said the bull who didn't like me. "I say the hell with him. Some cheap lumber is too fucking expensive."

"Free lumber," I corrected him. "You can have the whole cargo for free, if you'll just tell me the truth. What really happens to the kids from the islands? Who buys them? Where do they end up? Who do they work for?"

They looked at each other. Then they threw me out.

ALL THAT TROUBLE and unpleasantness, just to obtain one word. But it was worth it. The word was *citadel*. Cheap at twice the price.

Back outside in the bright sun, I lifted my head and looked around. I could see a ridiculous number of buildings, some stone, some brick, some with flat roofs, some with arched roofs sheathed in copper, would you believe. But there was one building that stood out from all the rest, because it was bigger and taller and it was built on top of a hill. The sort of building, in fact, for which the word *citadel* was invented.

I went back to the ship to get something. "Well?" they asked me.

"Deal's off," I said. "Go home."

"You what?"

"Take the ship," I said, "and go home. It's all been a waste of time. You can dump the cargo in the sea if you want, it's dangerous, the ship's riding far too low. If you hit a squall on the way home you'll go straight to the bottom. Fuck it."

They were staring at me. "What about you?"

I was wrapping cloth round my leg. "I'm not coming."

"You what?"

"I'm staying," I said. "There's something I want to do. You go."

"Don't be stupid," they told me. "How are you going to get home?"

"I'm staying," I said. "I like it here."

WHEN I WAS a kid, my father told me about a pet notion of his. He called it the dominion of the weak. I don't understand, I told him. Well, of course you don't, he said, you're just a kid. But it goes something like this.

I'm stronger than your mother, he said, so if I wanted to, I could beat her up real good. And sometimes I really feel like doing that, like when she nags me or goes on and on about how much money I spent on that stupid ship. But I don't, he went on, because I'm stronger than she is, so she can't fight back. And your mother is stronger than you are. She could pick you up by the ankles and bash your head against the wall. And you make her so mad sometimes. But she doesn't, because she's stronger. And if I wanted to, I could burn down old Chares' house and push him off his land and take it for myself, because he's old and he's got a gammy leg, he couldn't stand up to me and six of the hired men. I could do with that ground of his, it's right between my top pasture and the river. But I don't, my father said, because I'm stronger.

I don't follow, I said. It's not about who's stronger. You don't do that stuff because it wouldn't be right.

He smiled at me. You're just a kid, he said. What does right mean?

I didn't understand. Right and wrong, my father said, what do they mean? Tell me.

So I tried to tell him. Wrong is the stuff we aren't supposed to do, I said, because it's not right. Like beating up on people who can't fight back, or taking stuff that isn't ours.

Fine, he said. Why is it wrong?

I knew the answer but I couldn't find words. Because it isn't fair, I told him. You can't go around beating up on people just because you can, because who made you the boss of them? I drivelled on like that for a bit, and then he stopped me. It's because you're strong and they're weak, he told me. That's why you mustn't do it. You mustn't hit girls or take what doesn't belong to you, because you're strong and they're weak. Is that right or isn't it? I guess so, I said.

Well then, said my father, let's try something else. Give me your best shot.

So I hit him, right in the pit of the stomach, as hard as I could. He laughed. You see, he said, it's fine if you hit me, because you're weak. Do you understand now?

I shook my head. I was being particularly dumb that day. It's the dominion of the weak, my father said. Try thinking about it. If you can hit me but I'm not allowed to hit you, who's the boss? Or take me and your ma. Or me and old Chares. He drives his sheep over onto our pasture every spring, soon as the new grass comes, and what do we do about it? We shoo them back and don't say anything, because he's just a poor crippled old man. So he takes advantage and we do nothing. It's like when we cheat the bulls. Who's the boss, him or me?

That made no sense. My father was the richest man on the island and Chares was nobody. It's the dominion of the weak, he repeated. Right and wrong, that's all it is. It's how the weak are the boss of the strong, and it's not fair, and there's absolutely nothing you or I can do about it.

On that day I decided I couldn't make sense of what he'd told me because I was seven years old. Then, as I grew up and became aware of the bulls and the way they cast their shadow over everything, I decided that my father was just plain wrong. It's all about strength. The weak are nothing, so all you can do in this life is try and make yourself a little bit stronger, to shift the balance a fraction in your favour, as regards the balance of who tramples on you and who you trample on. The phrase stayed with me though, perhaps because *dominion* is how the bulls describe their operation in the islands. Meanwhile old Chares, frail and shaking, gradually shifted the boundary stones, a few yards every spring. We did nothing about it, because he was just an old man in poor health, and when he died, he had seven acres more land than his father had left him, and we spent a lot of money buying it back from his nephew. It's like the war between the ants and the elephant. The elephant started by trampling a million ants, but the other fifty million scurried away into cracks in the ground where he couldn't get at them. Then, at night, when the elephant was asleep, the ants crept in through his ear and ate his brain. My father would say that the ants won because they were small and weak. I prefer to think that they cheated.

A KIND STRANGER saw me hobbling up the street. "What happened to you?" he said.

"My own stupid fault," I told him. "I fell out of a tree and tore my knee."

He didn't laugh. "Nasty things, knee injuries."

"I've got it strapped up well," I assured him. "Just makes walking a bit difficult."

He hesitated for a split second, then gave me his walking stick. The handle was carved in the shape of a leaping dolphin. I thanked him. As soon as he was out of sight, I threw it away.

I'd anticipated that getting inside the citadel would be a major problem, quite possibly insuperable. Not so. There were two sentries at the gate, sleepy-looking bulls who snapped awake when they heard the sandal of my dragged foot on the cobbles. "Excuse me," I said.

"What?"

"Can you tell me how to find the captain of the guard? Only I've got something for him."

"What?"

I showed them the clay turd. It was too dark for them to read it, even if they could read. "He bought some stuff from us," I said. "He needs to take this to the bonded warehouse, and then they'll hand it over."

One of the sentries peered at me. "Give it here," he said. "I'll see he gets it."

I put on a scared look; who am I afraid of more, my master or this soldier? "Sorry," I said, "but my boss said only to give it to him, in person. I don't know why, that's just what I was told."

My luck was in. The sentries grinned at each other. "Figures," one of them said. He leaned forward a little and lowered his voice. "He's a fucking twister, he is. Mind he gives you a receipt."

"What's a receipt?"

They laughed and stood aside. Through there, they said, first left, second right, up two flights, first left, straight on, you can't miss it. And what happened to your leg? Ah. They can be nasty, torn ligaments. Try plantain mixed with goose fat, or a hot stone wrapped in a bit of linen.

As soon as I was out of sight of the gate I stopped, slid down the wall into a crouch and closed my eyes. In my mind was the view of the citadel I'd been studying all afternoon until it got too dark to see. I'd been trying to figure it out, this stone and brick puzzle; how would you build something like that if you wanted to house a monster? Or a king? Gradually, the purpose grew into the shape; a secure container inside a bubble of security. Or, taken in reverse; high walls, guardhouses and the keep itself, a series of concentric circles so as to leave no one weak point. For the centre to be equidistant from all directions of hazard, the perimeter must be a circle. Therefore, if you have a circle, the thing secured must be in the—

I was standing in front of a door. It was pitch dark, apart from a moonbeam slanting in through an arrowslit, but I've always had good night vision. I could see that the door was massive, strong and old; ten feet high, five feet wide, and four bolts as thick as my forearm. Bolts on the outside.

Not a king, then.

I thought about the story. I tried to remember who I'd heard it from; was it my father or my mother or my nurse or one of the other kids or one of the hired hands? No idea. It had been a part of me all my life, like my hands and my feet, or a scar from an injury when you were very small. He was there before the bulls, wasn't he? That was how I'd always known it. The bulls came here in their long, low ships and thought they'd found the promised land, and then suddenly, in the night, they found out they weren't the first here, or the strongest. In which case, surely, *he* was the boss of them. In which case, surely, the bolts would be on the—

They were stiff, and they made a horrible screeching noise as I pulled them back. So much for sneaking about quietly. Unless the guard were deaf or dead they must've heard it, and so must whatever lived behind the door. I tried spitting on them and it helped a little bit, but too little and too late. The third bolt drew two thirds of the way back and then stuck solid. I bashed on the handle with the heel of my hand until I realised I was making a real mess of something I might need quite soon, so I tried kicking it instead. I think I broke my toe. Then I got wise. I drew the top bolt out all the way and used it as a hammer. It sounded twice as loud as Anaxandron at the foundry making horseshoes, but apparently nobody was interested. It worked. The fourth bolt came out easy as anything. Presumably it had been watching what I'd done to its brother and was terrified.

So there I was. The door would open if I pushed it. I knelt down and unwrapped the cloth from around my leg. The sword Anaxandron had so reluctantly made for me dropped into my hand, like a dog bringing you its lead in its mouth. I closed my hand around the grip. We'd had a long discussion about the shape and profile of the grip, Anaxandron and me. He said, you want a crossguard so your hand won't slide forward, and something similar on the back end. I said, that'll screw up the balance, balance is important. Neither of us knew the first thing about swords. In the moonlight it glowed the colour of honey, my last and best possession. I put my foot against the bottom of the door and pressed down. The door swung open, just a little.

Light came streaming out; golden light. I froze where I was waiting for roaring and the onset of a monster. Maybe the room was empty after all. If I was a monster, would I crouch behind the door to gain a tactical advantage? I put the fingertips of my left hand against the door and flexed my fingers. The gap was now wide enough to let me through, just about.

It was the most amazingly beautiful room. On the walls, paintings; white background, with terracotta-red figures of men, slightly more than life-size, carrying dishes and trays of fruit. The floor was black and white tiles. The ceiling was so high up I couldn't see it; it sort of folded in on itself in a blaze of gold leaf, and I guessed I must be looking at the underside of a dome. There was a bed, made of what could only be ivory, and a table and a chair made of some sort of black wood I'd never seen or heard of before. In the chair, which was huge, sat a man with his back to me. He was huge too, and his head wasn't human. He was looking into a mirror.

Ah, you're saying to yourself, he's got a mirror. Clearly a rich bastard.

Some mirror. The back was ivory and from the way the face seemed to shine in the lamplight, I figured it had to be gold. He was looking into the mirror, so what he saw was himself, and in the background, me.

He put the mirror down on the table, no great hurry, then slowly stood up and turned to face me. A very tall man, very broad, and instead of a man's head, he had the head of a bull. Around his wrists were gold bracelets, and chains on his ankles, tethering him to the wall.

I took a step forward. The room was round, with his table and chair in the exact centre. Propped against the wall was a big sack. It was full of bones. I guess, just because you're a monster doesn't mean you're untidy. The room smelt faintly of roses. The bulls pay good money for dried roses, for distilling into perfume. You can pack the bottom of the jar with cabbage leaves and they never seem to notice.

I wondered if he could speak, but I decided I wasn't interested. Even if he could, what would he and I possibly have to say to each other? It was nine paces from the door to the centre of the room. He stood there, not moving, and I couldn't understand the expression on his face, because it wasn't human.

I hadn't killed a man before, but I've killed plenty of animals. When I was a kid it bothered me, but when you get older you realise it's just something that's got to be done. When you kill a large animal, like a big old sow or a bullock, it makes it much easier if you stun it first, with a pollaxe or something like that. I only had the sword, so I figured quick and neat was the way to go. Normally you'd cut the big vein in the neck, but he was so tall I couldn't reach and I didn't fancy trying to do it standing on the chair. So I stuck the sword into the pit of his stomach. It went in quite easily. Anaxandron and I had been a bit concerned that the blade would just bend instead of going in. Anaxandron wanted to stiffen it with a central rib, but I didn't want the extra weight. It turned out that Anaxandron was fussing about nothing, as usual.

He dropped to his knees and I took a quick step back, to keep away from the tips of his horns. He gave a great sigh and toppled over onto his side, and that was the end of him. I waited to see if he'd twitch or jerk about, but apparently not. I couldn't get the sword out. The way he'd fallen meant that the blade was clinched in the wound by the full weight of his upper body. Shucks.

I sat down on the chair. My head was splitting and I felt sick, first-time-on-a-boat sick only worse. It was as if someone's hands were deep inside my stomach, swapping things over and moving things around. I was trying to think—I had a lot to think about—but thoughts slipped away, like when you take live fish out of a net. I had those floating things in front of my eyes, the ones that you can see even with your eyes shut. If this is what murder does to you, I said to myself, I'm surprised people bother with it, because it's no fun at all.

I started shivering. Something fell on the floor with a clatter. It was the clay turd. I must have shaken it loose from inside my shirt, where I'd stuffed it for safekeeping. I stared at it, because there was something very odd about it. It took me a moment to figure out what it was. I could read it.

Not that it was particularly interesting; it said, forty-eight logs, cedar, two obols per board foot, sixty-two drachmas two obols payable. I looked at it again and couldn't understand how I hadn't been able to read it before. It was perfectly clear, if a trifle mundane. Just business, that's all. The floating things had cleared away. I glanced down at the dead body. It was changing; it had changed. Not a bull's head, not any more. It took me a moment before I realised that I recognised her—my own, my darling, the light of my life, my reason for living, the whole object of the exercise. I reached for the mirror. In it, I saw the monster, the one I'd just killed.

Ah, I thought. I asked for that.

I TRIED BANGING on the door but nobody came. Someone had shot the bolts while my attention was elsewhere. I found a small jar of oil to top the lamp up with. Then I ate the dead man. It's an acquired taste.

I guess they spy on me through a gap in the wall somewhere, though I've looked everywhere and I can't find one. When I'm asleep they come in and dust, fill the lamp, sweep the floor, empty the bone sack. Sometimes they leave a block of wet clay, an unexpected kindness, and if I write something they take it away, bake it and bring it back. I tried writing *help, please let me out* but they didn't take that one, or the letter to my father. I tried kicking the door down. I broke another toe. The next night they put the chain on my ankle and now I can't get that far.

Sometimes I feel angry, sad, frightened, disappointed, even cheated, but mostly I just feel hungry. I'd never known what it feels like to be hungry all the time. You can't think about anything else, no matter how you try.

Where I went wrong (it seems so obvious now) was assuming there was no monster; that a monster was *unnecessary*, therefore superfluous, therefore there wasn't one—just good old human nature, grafting its bull's head onto everyday human flesh and blood. No monster, just people, and people can be reasoned with, bargained with, exploited, bullied; cheated, let's not forget cheated, because everybody cheats. I was right about that, of course, but what I hadn't taken into account was the true nature of the bull, and how smoothly it grows on your shoulders when you're least expecting it. Some smartarse once said that anyone who fights monsters is at risk of becoming a monster himself; likewise that staring into a mirror is dangerous because after a while the mirror starts staring into you. Actually, I think he said "abyss" rather than "mirror" but in practice it's the same thing. As previously noted, you have to be a rich bastard in order to own a mirror. By the very process of being able to acquire one, you turn it into something no sane man would want to gaze into, for fear of seeing the bull. The magic that changed my body was just melodrama, Infinity rubbing my nose in it. I think I started to grow the horns the moment I let the means enchant me away from the end. Now look at me; king of the bulls, the strongest of the strong, fixed to a wall by the strongest of all possible chains.

Even so, I reckon that my father was partly right. Not completely right, because of course he didn't understand, not being able to see the whole picture, as I can now; like a drawing of a ship by a man who's never seen the sea, and here I am, adrift in it. I still maintain that everybody cheats; the boss, the monster, the hero, the victim, the man in the street and the starving beggar at his door. By the same token, everybody gets cheated, and I think that's only fair.

Portrait of the Artist

He was sweating. "What've you got for me?" he said.

I smiled at him. "One archduke," I said, quickly glancing round to make sure no one could hear. "Four marquises, two first cousins of an earl, six wealthy silk merchants, a field marshal, an admiral, a brevet major of dragoons and a small brown dog."

He picked up the bag, as though he could tell if I was lying just by the weight. It clinked softly. "What's with the dog?" he said.

"I felt like it."

He was a tall man, about forty, bald patch like a monk's tonsure, big nose. Ugly but interesting face. Expensive, sombre clothes in shades of dark brown and dove grey. I'd have enjoyed painting him, for several reasons. Sorry, private joke. "Two hundred gulden."

"Very funny."

He was staring at the bag, like he could see through the cloth. For all I know, he could. But that sort of thing doesn't impress me any more. "Aristocrats," he said disdainfully. "Soldiers. All I ever get from you is blue-bloods. What I need is intellectuals."

"Some of them are quite bright."

"Fox-hunters," he said, with a faint curl of the upper lip. Bet he practised it in the mirror.

"Well-educated," I pointed out. "Finest education money can buy."

"What I want," he said, glaring at me, "is philosophers. Scientists. Poets."

I was hungry. I'd skipped breakfast again. "Poets and philosophers can't afford to have their portraits painted," I told him. "And you don't pay me enough for doing freebies."

"Right. So that explains the dog?"

"Like I told you. I felt like it." I waggled the bag under his nose. He winced.

"Three hundred," he said. "Don't shake it around like that, for crying out loud."

The urge to draw him was overpowering. Just a quick charcoal sketch, on the tablecloth? But he'd see me. "Besides," I pointed out, "you're forgetting or being wilfully blind to the tradition of the noble dilettante. The archduke's one of the leading authorities on the later dialogues of Saloninus."

He tried not to show it, but I could see the frisson of lust slide over him. "The archduke—"

I grinned. "No names," I said. "No names, no indictable complicity. But yes, him. And one of the silk merchants is a notable alchemist."

He looked up sharply. "Porphyrius?"

I clicked my tongue. "I said, no names."

"You killed Porphyrius."

Silly me. It hadn't occurred to me that they might be friends. "Of course not. Go round and call on him this minute. He's perfectly healthy."

"You know what I mean," he growled. "Still—"

That old academic curiosity, it wins out every time. I saw where my mistake could now be useful. "Five hundred and fifty gulden," I said.

"For pity's sake, woman. I haven't got that sort of—"

"Fine," I said. "I'll take my merchandise elsewhere."

Got him. The thought of someone else, one of his rivals, getting his friend—Really, I should've asked for the round six hundred. Six-fifty, even. "This is the very last time," he said, "that I do business with you."

I relaxed. "We'll see," I said, and beckoned the waiter. "Let's celebrate the deal," I said. "A bottle of the '46 and a plate of honey cakes, please."

The waiter withdrew, visibly shaken. "You're buying," I said.

"No, I'm not."

"Yes you are. A lady never pays."

ALAS, NOT TRUE. Five hundred and fifty gulden sounds like an absolute fortune, probably because it is. But—The nearest comparison is a heavy fall of snow. You wake up and the whole world is buried in white. You could fill a million carts and barely touch the surface. Noon and bright sunlight, all gone, as though it had never been. By the time I got home, having made various business calls, I was left with thirty-seven gulden seventy-five. Still a huge amount of money, by one of my sets of standards; enough to buy a farm, or a half-share in a small merchant ship. But not enough. Never enough.

"I DON'T NEED you here all the time," I told him.

"Oh." He looked disconcerted; disappointed, even. "I thought—"

"It's not how I work." Understatement of the century. "How I go about it is, I make a series of sketches from life, charcoal mostly, some pen and ink, and then I do the actual painting from them."

"That's unusual, isn't it?"

I smiled. "Very," I said. "But it means a busy man like you doesn't have to spend hours of his valuable time sitting perfectly still in a chair."

He shrugged. The light fell across his face like a birthmark. "Actually," he said, "I was looking forward to it. I don't get many chances to sit perfectly still and stare into space."

My hand was starting to shake as I adjusted my grip on the charcoal. It usually does. I like to pretend it's guilt, the last vestiges of decent feeling. But I have a nasty suspicion it's the excitement of the—kill? Oh, let's not mince words. "Up to you," I said. "If you'd like to come here and sit, please, feel free. I can always work in the other room."

"Surely it's south-facing." He frowned. "Don't you need the light?"

"I paint by the inner light," I said. I tried to make it sound like I was being facetious.

THE POINT IS, I'm an exceptionally good artist. If there's a tragedy here, that's it. The things I could've done, the work I could've produced, if only—

But.

I'd have been perfectly happy staying at home in the country and painting cows, and waterfalls, and meadows of spring flowers, and happy, contented country people cheerfully going about their appointed tasks. Mid-morning, after a leisurely breakfast (with my husband, before he set off for hunting or inspecting the spring wheat or meeting the tenants, whatever the hell it is that men of my class do all day), my maids would pack my paints and easel onto the dog cart, and the coachman would drive me to some idyllic spot; I'd paint for an hour or so, until it was time to get back to supervise lunch. And people would compliment me on my work; it really is very good, they'd say, every bit as good as the professionals. And I would be, would have been, perfectly happy.

Didn't work out like that. Ah, well; no use moping after what you could never have had, even if it was always so close, all through my childhood—I always felt that if I tried I could reach out with my arm and with just a little bit more effort I could pull it down off the tree and have it. I grew out of that, in due course.

It made me sullen and sharp-tongued, qualities that didn't actually help the issue very much.

Or I could, in spite of being plain and just a bit too poor, have grabbed life by the scruff of the neck, forced the world to acknowledge me; the finest artist of her age, just look at—(insert here a list of the masterpieces I could have painted, would have painted if things had turned out just a little bit different; the thickness of a sheet of paper is all that divides me from those unattained possibilities). It all comes down to such tiny differences; if I was one inch taller, then by standing on tiptoe and really, really straining, I could reach the apple on the branch. But when you lack it, one inch, half-inch, quarter-inch is the same as a mile. Depends where you're standing. In my line of work, we call it *perspective*.

So I do this instead. A quarter of an inch is all it takes to separate heaven from hell.

My clients don't negotiate with me direct, face to face. They send people. The Patriarch Sighvat sent an archdeacon. I think he was nervous at the prospect of having to spend time alone with, you know, a woman. One look at me and he relaxed visibly.

"His Grace will wish to be seen three-quarter face," he said. "He will of course wear the divitision and formal dalmatic."

"Naturally."

He peered at me down far more nose than any contingency could ever justify. "You know what a dalmatic is?"

I smiled. "It's a wide, long-sleeved tunic with a broad strip of embroidery down the front," I said. "A formal dalmatic is blood red, knee-length. I have a book," I explained. "With pictures."

Eventually he had no choice but to address the question of money. "His Grace feels that a fee of fifty gulden will be satisfactory."

I tried to look sad. "That's a shame," I said. "I would've liked to paint His Grace. He has interesting bone structure."

There was a moment of dead silence. I kept perfectly still, smiling sweetly.

"Fifty-five."

"Am I right in thinking," I asked, "that His Grace has written a series of exegetical commentaries on Carchedonius' *Metaphysics*?"

He didn't know. Look at faces all day, you learn to read them. "His Grace is a preeminent scholar."

Translates as; always got his head stuck in a book. My mother said the same about me. "Seventy gulden."

"Sixty-five."

"It'll be an honour to paint His Grace. When will it be convenient for him to sit for me?"

Well, I'd been specifically asked for intellectuals, so I could afford to be beaten out of five gulden.

"His Grace feels it would be more appropriate for you to call on him."

It's the light, I explained. It's technical. He didn't like it, but he was even less keen on jeopardising the mission. "His Grace will be pleased to sit for you at noon tomorrow."

I shook my head. Noon light very bad. Early morning much better. He agreed, reluctantly. I specified one hour after sunrise; just because I could, I guess. (Another thing my mother used to say: *don't play with your food.*)

He stood up to go, paused to admire the icon on my wall. "Is that—?"

"Genuine?" I did my silvery laugh. "Sadly, no. It's a copy. I painted it."

"Remarkable."

"Thank you."

Actually, it's genuine, cost me a fortune. My one indulgence. "His Grace would be pleased to buy it," he said.

Would he, now? "I'm afraid it's not for sale."

"His Grace would be prepared to offer forty gulden."

I winced. I paid ten. Still. "It's not for sale," I repeated. "It wouldn't be right, selling a copy. Besides, I did it for my own devotional use, as an act of penance. Taking money for it would undo all the good work, don't you think?"

"His Grace would grant you absolution."

Sorry, but I don't take absolution from strange men. "Let me think about it," I said.

He pulled a grumpy face. "As you wish. Peace be upon you."

"Thank you," I said politely. Always say thank you, even for presents you didn't want.

THIS MATTER OF a quarter-inch, and the difference it makes.

I refer you to Saloninus, *On Beauty*, chapter twenty-six, paragraph four. You'll recall that Saloninus proves, mathematically and by examples drawn from great art, that the divide between beautiful and ugly is almost exactly a quarter of an inch—fifteen sixty-fourths of an inch, to be precise. Take the most beautiful nose you can think of, and shorten it, or lengthen it, one quarter-inch. Result; ugliness. Same goes for lips, chins, distance between eyes, all the geometrical relationships that make up the human face. Seven thirty-seconds longer or shorter you can get away with, but fifteen sixty-fourths is the killer. It's an absolute rule, infallible, inflexible.

It's also true. I proved it once. I did a series of self-portraits—possibly the best work, the second-best work I've ever done, certainly the most lifelike—and when they were finished, I moved the various features about, to scale, in proportion. A quarter of an inch here and there made me into a goddess.

Well, I exaggerate slightly. Nice-looking, anyhow; nice enough-looking to get a husband, have my choice of two or three. Cross-reference with a mirror, measure carefully with calipers. Saloninus was right. A quarter-inch separates butt-ugly from beauty, what I am from what I should have been, hell from heaven. I soaked a rag in turpentine and wiped my face off the panels, leaving a neck, hair and a gap in between. Now that's what I call a portrait.

To paint the Patriarch Sighvat I made myself a brush.

To make a brush fit to paint the Vice-Regent of the Earth, brother of the Invincible Sun with, first of all you need a woodcock. You probably know more about birds than I do; apparently a woodcock is a little fluttery thing, lives by pecking worms out of the mud with its ridiculously long beak. Anyway, they're notoriously hard to catch, which makes them expensive. Also, they don't live around here—don't ask me why; we have worms, we have mud, but apparently not the right sort—so they have to be fetched down from the north at vast expense, packed in crates of ice. People eat them, so I'm told; rich people, naturally. Takes three of the little buggers to make a snack. Tastes like chicken. Why bother?

But the pin feathers of a woodcock make the very best paintbrushes. They're tiny, about as long as a fingernail, and you have to know what to look for. You find them on the outside of the crook of the wing—where the index finger would be, if a wing was a hand. Be very careful pulling them out; use tweezers and extreme care, or you'll crumple them up and they'll be useless. I have a tiny little pair of silver tweezers, which I use for this purpose only.

Consider the feather. Consider the various categories of its usefulness. The Invincible Sun designed them to make possible the unimaginable miracle of flight, something a bird can do and we brilliant, resourceful, educated humans can't. So we kill the stupid, magically gifted birds and pull out their amazing feathers, stuff pillows with them, fletch arrows, or throw them away. The birds, you see, have a talent, an ability that supercedes anything we can do in godlike proportion—them up there, us down here, utterly divided and distinct from each other; except that birds are too thick to figure out that the white sticky stuff daubed all over the branches is birdlime, and all the divine grace and engineering of their wings won't save them once they touch their claws to it. I assume the Invincible Sun intended it to be that way. Otherwise, why did He equip the woodcock with a feather that makes the best possible paintbrush?

My father was an idiot. He once told me, in all seriousness, that he was without question the most intelligent man I would ever meet in my entire life. On one level, I'm sure he was right. He was a scholar by inclination and training. What he didn't know about history, literature and art wasn't worth knowing. He was so smart, he was able to throw up a thriving law practice in his early forties and retire to his library and his study. He was clever enough to predict the Scherian war five years before anyone else, shrewd enough to invest the family fortune in shipyards (having foreseen that the war would be mostly at sea), wise enough to sell out of shipbuilding six months before war was declared and the shipyards were appropriated by the Crown; smart and clever and shrewd and wise enough to reinvest the substantial profit he made, along with the original capital, in the Neumis goldfields, literally weeks before the gold price shot up tenfold overnight. His only mistake, if you can call it that, was assuming the Cure Hardy would ally with us, rather than the Scherians. That was unfortunate, because as soon as the Cure Hardy joined up with Scheria, they occupied the goldfields and our investment was wiped out in a fingersnap. To be fair to him, it was a pretty close-run thing—most of the tribespeople wanted to join us, but the tribal chiefs liked the Scherians' gifts slightly more than ours. So very little in it, you see; a quarter of an inch, maybe, certainly no more.

Pity and despise the poor bird, who can fly (on wings of paper, soaring above the heads of pedestrian, mundane humans), but who's too dumb to suspect the white-smeared branch may not be all it seems. All right; idiot may be a trifle harsh. Unfortunate and foolish; is that better? But the division between getting it right and getting it wrong—fifteen sixty-fourths, give or take—might as well be the width of the Eastern Sea, when the bailiff's men come to take your furniture away. And his books; they took all his books, loaded them on a cart and wheeled it round to a dealer, who glanced at them, pointed out that there wasn't much call for that sort of thing, and gave them ninety trachy for the lot.

I was the one who found him, hanging in the coach house. Thanks, Dad.

I MAKE NO excuses for what I do. On that day, my thirteenth birthday, I learnt an essential lesson about the value of money. Money, I suddenly realised (sort of a revelation, but without angels and sunbeams) is life; absence of money brings death. And we—my mother, my brothers and I—had no money at all. What to do?

DO YOU KNOW the City at all? Maybe you don't. Back then, my studio was at the junction of Goosefair and Foregate, right at the top of the South Hill, highest and most expensive district south of the River. Also the only place in Town where you can get decent light more than five hours a day; everywhere else, the buildings are so close together that everyone is in everyone else's shade. The rent on that place was unbelievable, but my clients liked it because it was walking distance from home—not that they walked; they arrived in chairs and carriages. I was up two flights of stairs (they moaned about that) for the same reason that I lived on top of the hill. The very best light. And nobody could see in through the window. I also had the floor below and the cellar, but that wasn't common knowledge.

The Patriarch turned out to be rather a nice old man. He'd have been quite distinguished-looking, if it wasn't for the way his nose ended in a distinct knob. He had a full head of snow-white hair, fine and rather lifeless, which for some reason he saw fit to part down the middle. The trimmed moustache and tiny chin-tuft beard were the pinnacle of style fifty years ago (study portraiture and you get a working knowledge of men's fashions through the ages absolutely free). Pale blue eyes, but not watery-pale. His lips were thin and moist. Rumour had it that he kept six mistresses, including a mother-daughter pair; but you know what? Half the time, I think Rumour makes stuff up.

Anyway, I was perfectly safe. Like Senoebis; six hundred years of peace, because the Senoebites have nothing anybody could possibly want to take away from them. "This portrait," I said. "Where's it going to hang?"

He did something with his mouth that expressed mild embarrassment extremely well. "In the chapter house at the Silver Wing," he said. "They insisted. One doesn't want to cause offence by refusing too often."

I paused for a moment and pictured the place in my mind. Bare golden stone, high vaulted roof, sidelit, the glass mostly red and blue. "Would you mind standing up for just a moment?"

He raised an eyebrow and stood up. I rotated his chair forty degrees north-east. "Ah," he said, "the light."

"I paint by the inner light," I told him. "But sometimes it needs a little prompting."

That got me a little smile; I squiggled it down in coarse charcoal sweeps before it got away. Naturally I wouldn't paint him smiling, but it helps to understand the mechanism of the face, if that makes any sense; where the various bits go to when they move. "I'm going to sketch you from lots of different angles," I said. "Otherwise you'll come out looking all flat. Please just carry on looking straight ahead, and try and pretend I'm not here."

"I was very taken with your portrait of the Marchioness Svangerd," he said to the wall, as I snuck round the side of him like an outflanking army.

"Thank you," I said. "Though I have to say, I don't think it was terribly like her, somehow."

"I think that was why I liked it."

Ecclesiastical wit. I was honoured. I looked round to see if there was a clerk hovering in the shadows to write it all down. "I do try not to improve people," I said.

"Ah. Pity. So many people could do with improvement."

"True. But I prefer to bring out the best of what's actually there."

"Indeed. Which aspect of me will you be focussing on?"

"Your compassion."

"Oh." Bewilderment, probably, rather than disappointment. "Oh well, carry on."

Most painters establish proportions by variants on the rule-of-thumb principle—you've seen them hold a brush upright at arm's length and squint at it. What they're thinking is; his head's from the tip of the bristles to the top of the ferrule. Then, once you've got the head, you can go by the rules—from the collar-bone to the ankles is eight heads, and so on. I pretend to do all that, because it's expected, but really I work entirely by eye. I guess perspectives and proportions just come intuitively to me; like there are people who can add up columns of figures at a glance, or catch a ball with their eyes shut. It's another way of saying: I know what's right without having to think. And what's wrong, naturally.

Most of what I do is wrong. I don't think about it.

It helps if you make conversation. "Can I ask your professional opinion?"

Again I'd surprised him. "I wouldn't have thought you'd be interested."

"My father was a scholar," I said. Men find that an acceptable explanation.

"What did you want to—?"

"Ah, right," I said. I confined his forehead, nose and jaw inside a rather cavalier sweep of the charcoal. "What do you make of the doctrine of the dual procession of the Divine Aura?"

Naughty of me, I guess, to lead with something like that. "The dual procession—?"

"Only," I went on, "it seems a bit over-complicated, to a layman like me. To say that the Aura proceeds simultaneously and equally from the Body Spiritual *and* the Body Material; how would you reconcile that with the economy principle and Saloninus' Razor?"

He blinked. "Well," he said.

I waited. I filled in the time outlining the bags under his eyes.

"It may seem complicated on a simplistic level," he said eventually. "Considered ontologically, it's in fact a sublime example of the overarching unity of Form. What I mean by that is—"

"I see," I said. "But in that case, what about the implications for the material transmigration of the soul? I'm assuming you're going to tell me that the Aura transubstantiates in the same way as the soul transmigrates, through grace into essence, from essence into affirmation."

"Yes."

"I'm with you so far," I said. "I think. But in that case, surely you're implying that the soul is capable of reduction into physical form."

I had an idea I was beginning to annoy him. "I don't think so."

"Well, it follows, doesn't it? If the Aura can proceed *from* the physical, then so can the soul. And, by the same token, it can also proceed *to* the physical." I did my silvery laugh again. "Which means in theory you could, I don't know, distil it in an alembic and bottle it. Which is—"

"Not possible," he said firmly.

"No, of course not. Though I gather there's a sort of fringe group of alchemists—"

"HERETICS," HE SAID. "Heretics and blasphemers. I do hope you haven't been filling your mind with that sort of nonsense."

"Of course not," I said primly. "It's impossible, like you said. All I was wondering was, *why* is it impossible? It's just me being stupid, I know, but I can't seem to grasp the theory."

"Read Pacatian," he snapped. "It's all in there, everything you need to know."

"Pacatian." I did a dumbshow of making a note of the name on the back of my hand in charcoal. Let the record show, however, that I first read Pacatian when I was nine, and a dozen times since then, and he's about as convincing as a one-sided coin. "Thank you," I said. "You've set my mind at rest." Which, poor devil, he had.

MY BROTHERS, LET it be said, are nothing like my father, or my mother, or me. They've got energy, drive, a sort of restless vitality that's practically irresistible—rest a kettle on their heads, my mother used to say, it'll boil before you can count to ten. Add to that charm, looks and a moderate amount of brains; look out, world, here they come.

My father's death and our complete and utter ruin did slow them down just a little. They were away at the time, at the University. Bohemund was in his final year, Amalric in his third, Juifrez had only been there three months when the news reached them. Naturally, they came straight back, riding through the night (completely unnecessary; a man who's dead today will almost certainly still be dead tomorrow, and the next day, worse luck; I guess they were so fired up with tormented energy, it was either some dramatic feat of endurance or spontaneous combustion) and practically their first words were: it's all right, Mum, don't worry, sis, we'll get it all back, and more, you'll see. It, you'll have observed, not him. They're wired, but not stupid. They know the dead don't return, and that if anything is to be done, it must be with the living. They were determined to do something. They always are.

Among the few assets remaining to us was a tiny patch of barren rock up in the Crowfoot Mountains. We still owned it because nobody was prepared to buy it, or even give my father fifty gulden on it as security. Understandable. Mondelice (the Delectable Mountain; cartographers' humour) sits on the flat Crow plains like a scab on smooth skin, with the Redwater curling round it like a cat's tail. Generations of my mother's family have been unable to sell it. They call it the Redwater because the river runs red; there's some sort of poisonous salt in the rocks, which the snowmelt dissolves and washes down off the mountain. There are no fish in the Redwater, no grass grows on its banks. There are a few spindly willows; they last about ten years and then die. You can't graze livestock anywhere near there; sheep just die, even goats. It's two days across the plains in a cart to the nearest town, so quarrying would be prohibitively expensive. Besides, the rock is crumbly red sandstone, not much good, and there's dozens of better sites much closer to civilisation, with better access and drinking water that doesn't kill you. Also, bear in mind that we owned the mountain, not the plain, and there's no public road; to get there, you cross about seven different owners' land. Add to all that the fact that it's searingly hot in summer and lethally cold in winter. Did I say tiny, by the way? Actually, it's twice the size of the City, and you can see it from miles away. Anyway, we had that, and the town house, and a back-sun vineyard in the Mesoge, and that was it.

My brothers called Mother and me into Father's study. On the desk was a big sheaf of old parchment. The title deeds, they said, to Mondelice.

Mother pulled a sad face. "Put them away," she said. "You know as well as I do. It's useless."

Bohemund did his big smile. "Agreed," he said. "But did you ever stop and ask yourself: *why* is it useless?"

Mother's lived with Mondelice all her life. She grew up with her father moaning about it. He included it in her dowry as a joke. "Well," she said, icy patient, "it's poisonous."

"Mphm. *Why* is it poisonous?"

When Bohemund dies, they'll carve *why?* on his headstone. "Because it is," Mother said. "There's something nasty in the rocks. You know that."

But all three of them were grinning. "Iron," Bohemund said.

"You what?"

"That's what turns the river red," Amalric said. He had one finger inserted in between the pages of a book. He flipped it open, spun it round and pointed. "It's rust. Got to be. Look, it says, in Sulpicius' *Minerals*. There's a river in Aelia, just like the Redwater. Right next to the biggest iron ore mine in the world."

Mother frowned. "What's he talking about?"

"Don't you get it?" Bohemund was starting to fizz. "We're rich."

"Iron," Amalric said. "You know how much the price of iron's gone up since the war? Two hundred per cent. Since we lost Scheria, every scrap of iron we use has to come on a ship to Lonazep and then overland in a cart two hundred miles just to reach the border."

"And here we are," put in Juifrez, "most likely sitting on the biggest deposit of iron in the world. A whole mountain made of the stuff. No wonder it kills all the fish."

For some reason I've never understood, Mother listened to Juifrez. The other two she was more or less immune to, had been since they were toddlers, but she had some weird notion Juifrez is smart. "That can't be right," she said. "My father—"

"He thought it was just a heap of toxic rock," Amalric said. "It's understandable. We've all been taught that for generations; Mondelice is useless, don't even think about it."

"Maybe," I put in, "for a good reason."

Nobody heard me. "It can't hurt to find out," Juifrez said. "I mean, if we're wrong, we're wrong. And if we're right—"

So off they went to Mondelice. Forget the word *went*, it's hopelessly inadequate. They wore out six horses galloping to Mondelice up the Great North Road, no nonsense about stopping to sleep or eat. My father always reckoned his sons moved at the speed of narrative; they could cover a thousand miles in the space of *some time later they arrived at their destination*. Distance is meaningless to people like that. And, almost before anyone had noticed they'd gone, they were back. It's iron, they yelled (stumbling in through the door, riding-coats caked in dust and mud, faces ash-white with exhaustion). It's iron all right. We brought back samples. Look!

So that was it. In the nick of time, my brothers had found the treasure that had been there right under our noses all along; curtain, applause, house lights, all bow. But there was one small problem.

One of the reasons my work is so expensive (though the clients don't know this, of course) is that I do everything twice. One canvas, one exact copy. When they're both finished, I stand back and look at them—because no exact copy is ever *exact*—and decide which one's best; qualify that, which one's most lifelike. That one I keep. The other one goes to the client.

The Patriarch was delighted; he sent a clerk to tell me so. I even got a bonus, which I confess I hadn't been expecting, and which made me feel bad. I consoled myself by thinking of the tenant farmers in the Mesoge whose rents make it possible for the Patriarchs to have their portraits painted by the likes of me.

The other copy, the one I kept, I hung in my cellar. I was incredibly lucky there. Of course, everybody knows how the City was rebuilt after the Fire, a quarter of a mile to the east of the old site; and how, when they were digging the foundations, they literally fell into the ruins of a much, much older city, so old that nobody knows who the builders were or what became of them. Slightly less well known is the extent to which the forgotten ancients were cleverer and more advanced than us—for example, they had a huge network of underground cisterns and sewers (just think of it; all the yucky stuff was flushed away down tunnels into an underground river, instead of being slung out the window into the street) One tiny portion of that network lies directly under the building where I live, and I have the use of it, for an extra ninety trachy a week. My gallery.

You'd never think it had once been a watercourse. It's bone dry, with a high vaulted roof supported by a dozen fluted granite columns, crowned with Archaic capitals. I went to a great deal of trouble to get the lighting right. I installed forty-seven large oil lamps and six chandeliers—you can adjust the height by an ingenious system of ratchets and pulleys, which I designed myself. Excuse me for boasting, but it really is the finest art display in the world (I'm talking about the room, not its contents) I've got fifty yards of wall space. I'm rapidly running out of room. Soon I'll have to have a gallery built round the walls, and a staircase, to give me a second floor.

In the middle of the floor, I have this drawing-table. It's lit by a dozen lamps backed with mirrors, to close in the light. That's where I do my best work.

I had my specialist instruments made by a clockmaker. I didn't tell him what they were for, and he didn't ask. I gave him the drawings, which were so detailed as to be entirely unambiguous, and told him they were a present for my father. He looked at me and suggested a price. I didn't argue.

Among the things he made me was a magnifying glass. It's a wonderful thing. Basically, take an inch-thick circle of clear glass, grind the edges thin, leaving the centre thick. I read about it in a book. The writer said such a thing ought to be theoretically possible, though he never tried to make one himself. The clockmaker told me it was the most amazing thing he'd ever come across in all his life. I ought to—correction, *we* ought to go into business making the things, we'd be rich, it was the sort of opportunity that only comes along once in a lifetime. I smiled at him. You've got ever such an interesting face, I told him; would you mind terribly much if I did your portrait? For free, naturally. He jumped at the chance, and now he's seventeenth from the doorway on the right as you come in.

With my wonderful glass, I can read the calibrations on the unbelievably precise calipers the clockmaker made for me. He had to use the glass to engrave them. To the naked eye, they're invisible. Precision, it goes without saying, is the very essence of what I do. Seven thirty-seconds, remember? Only, with my wonderful instruments, I can be ever so more precise than that. I work in ten-thousands of an inch, to a margin of error of plus or minus two ten-thousandths.

I measured up the Patriarch, reducing the intervals between the features of his face to absolute numbers. For measuring the angles, I had the clockmaker make me a protractor. It's two sheets of thin glass with single threads of spider's web silk sandwiched between them. If you know of anything thinner, please let me know. It's the crudest instrument in the box, and one of these days I'll make a mistake with it, and God only knows what'll happen.

Once you've got the numbers, the rest is just melodrama. I find it tedious and rather distasteful. I'm a scientist and an artist, after all, not a witch. Still, it works.

I'm as jumpy as a cat when I'm working. The slightest noise, and—

"I'm so sorry," he said. "I didn't mean to startle you."

Luckily I'd just managed to grab hold of the tiny bottle before it tipped over. "Who the hell are you?"

"I knocked," he said, "and called out, but I guess you didn't hear me."

I scowled at him, trying my best to look furious rather than terrified. Just as well I've got the face for it. "So you barged in anyway. All right, what do you want?"

"Just a minute or two of your time."

Not everyone in this town who dresses like a priest is one, so he could have been a lawyer or one of the high-up administrative grades, except people like that don't make house calls. "You're collecting for something."

Little smile. "No," he said. Then he told me my name (which, as it happens, I already knew) and asked if I was the famous society artist.

"You want your portrait painted."

"No." Shake of the head. "No, I don't think that would be a good idea."

I looked at him. He was making me very nervous. "Oh come on," I said. "You're not that bad."

He had very pale blue eyes, and a snub nose; about my age, maybe a year younger. And I've seen and made the best of enough receding hairlines to know that in his case, the tonsure had been no great loss. Yes, of course I judge by appearances, they're my job. On which basis I made up my mind about him on one second flat, exactly the same way people make their minds up about me.

"Nice of you to say so," he said, "though even little white lies are still a sin. But that wasn't what I meant."

"Perhaps you'd better leave."

"Perhaps." He nodded. "I'm small and weedy and I don't know the first thing about fighting or anything like that, and we're underground, so nobody's likely to see or hear anything. And you're right, who would miss me? I didn't tell anybody where I was going."

Mind-reading is of course impossible, even for a fully-trained adept of the Studium, or at least that's what they tell us. "I don't know what you're talking about."

He didn't react to that at all. "Do you mind if I sit down?"

"Yes."

"Fair enough. You painted all of these?"

"Yes."

He nodded. "In case you were wondering," he said, "I can't prove a damn thing. Certainly not enough to make charges stick in a court of law. Actually," he added with a grin, "I don't think there is a law that covers what you do, and nobody's going to be passing one in a hurry, everybody would think he was mad. I mean, it's not murder, or grievous bodily harm, or administering a noxious substance with intent. I've got to hand it to you, you're clean as a whistle."

"Who are you?"

He smiled awkwardly. "Eustatius," he said. "At least, that's my name in religion. I'm from Scheria originally, so you probably couldn't pronounce what my mother used to call me. I'm a junior deacon of the Studium, currently assigned to field duty."

"Good for you," I said. "And what exactly am I supposed to have done?"

He sighed. "Oh, don't make me say it," he said, "it sounds so silly. And, like I just said, I can't prove it. Sure, I can point out that in the last year, forty-six people, rich and famous and influential people, who've had their portraits painted by you have suffered catastrophic strokes, leaving them paralysed and catatonic. But you would then point out, equally truthfully, that sixty-seven equally rich, famous and influential people have also been painted by you and are as fit as fiddles. And then you'd challenge me to tell the jury exactly how you're supposed to have done these dreadful things, and I'd just shrug and admit I don't have a clue, beyond basic philosophical and theological theory." He was looking past me, at the bookshelf; Pacatian, and Saloninus' *Existence and Reality*. I winced. A bit like hanging the murder weapon on your wall, mounted on a little plaque. "In case you're wondering," he went on—he seemed to like that phrase—"I'm a duly ordained priest."

"Good for you. So what?"

"Duly authorised," he said, "to hear confessions, and bound not to repeat them. Not even if ordered to do so by a court. Not even if they torture me. And if I did, it wouldn't be admissible in evidence."

I looked him straight in the eye. Long practice. "Sorry," I said. "I'm not religious."

"Me neither. I'm a scientist. And I'm curious. And I can't prove anything, but sometimes there are circumstances where my order feels obliged to take action that isn't strictly in accordance with due process, and to be brutally frank, you don't have any relatives or friends who could make trouble for us if we did. And as the field officer assigned to your case—" He gave me a sort of dying-lamb look. "Tell me how you do it, that's all I want to know. And then I'll go back to my superiors and tell them the whole thing's just a string of coincidences and you're just a harmless working girl. Please?"

THERE WAS ONE small problem; namely, in order to gouge unlimited wealth out of Mondelice, we needed a little bit of working capital—a few measly thousands, fleabites, the sort of sum we could make in a couple of hours once we were up and running and in full production. Or, if you cared to look at it from a slightly different perspective, a vast fortune; roughly the same as it would cost to buy a cattle ranch, or build and equip three warships, or a small aqueduct.

At this point, opinions started to differ, like a beam of wood splintering. Mother said, let's just sell it for what we can get, now that we can prove it's worth something. Bohemund said, don't be stupid, we still owe God knows how much, they only leave us alone because they know we're broke; if anybody thought we had anything worth having, all he'd have to do would be buy up our debts for a trachy on the gulden and then he could take it from us for practically nothing. Juifrez said, fine, in that case, we'll borrow the money. Using what as security, said Bohemund; you can't have been listening, because the moment we tell anyone we've got something, they'll be on us like wolves.

"Fine," I said. "We'll just have to raise it some other way. Work for it, something like that."

They all looked at me. "Sweetheart," my mother said, "if we could earn that sort of money, we wouldn't need Mondelice. We wouldn't need *anything*. But we can't." She turned back to Juifrez. "Surely we can find someone who'll give us something for it. Just enough to clear the mortgages off the vineyard, and then we could sell this house and move to the country."

"I know a way to make money," I said.

"Will somebody put a cloth over her or something?" Amalric said. "She's starting to get on my nerves."

So I moved out. Nobody was happy about this, me included. My mother pointed out that a young single girl living on her own was either a whore or begging to be treated like one, and quite apart from anything else, the shame and dishonour I would bring on my family—We haven't spoken since.

I found out what to do from my father's research notes. He had a whole shelf of notebooks, tastefully bound in mellow brown calf, which nobody had ever read. I missed him so much. His handwriting was very distinctive—at first sight it looked classically neat and elegant, but when you tried to read it, you could barely make it out—and even if I couldn't understand what it was about, at least it was a little part of him, my father still present in the world in some form. Like a portrait, I guess, which is why people want the damn things; you can still see his face, even though he's dead.

Dad always had to know best, and he loved picking fights with dead scholars. In the seventh volume of his collected notes and observations, he really tore into Modestus of Apamene (who lived six hundred years ago) because Modestus believed that it might be possible—purely theoretically—to reduce a man's soul into material form, on the same principle as the dual procession of the Divine Aura as outlined in Pacatian and developed by Saloninus in the third book of the *Republic*. Dad wasn't impressed by any of that. It can't be done, he reckoned; and to prove it, he scrawled page after page after page of complex mathematical calculations (so that's what he used to get up to, locked away in his study, with my brothers and me forbidden to make the slightest sound, on pain of death) leading to the triumphant conclusion that Modestus was a fool and a rogue. What he proposed doing about that, he didn't say, but digging up his bones and flinging them into the sea would probably have been a good starting-off point.

Except that Dad got his sums wrong. It was only a tiny little slip, and if I wasn't unnaturally good at figures (a secret I've kept to myself all my life, since nobody likes a smartass, particularly if she's a girl) I'd never have picked up on it. But there it was, a very small difference between what he thought was true and the truth.

So I did the sums again, having made the very slight adjustment, and you know what?

I HAVE THIS wonderful memory for faces. If I meet someone just once, I can close my eyes and there's the face, just so.

"That's blackmail," I said.

He shrugged. "It's scholarship," he said. "A man's all-consuming need to know the truth, to add to the sum of human knowledge. Of course, the idea is, once you've learned something, you're supposed to share it with other people, like they said I had to share my toys with my sisters when I was a kid. But I never liked doing that. I just want to know, for myself."

"My father was like that," I said.

"Well, there you go. You can understand. And I promise, I won't tell anyone, ever. Or," he added, turning his face to stone, "I can have you burned as a witch. Your choice."

So I told him. He didn't believe me, of course. So I pulled out my notebooks and showed him the pages and pages and pages of scrawled mathematical calculations, which he obviously didn't understand. But he had faith. "All right," he said. "How do you *actually* do it?"

So I told him. After a bit he asked for a pen and some paper. No, I said, no notes. You never know whose hands notes might fall into. He sighed, but he'd come so close, so very close, within a quarter-inch of getting what he wanted, and having me killed wouldn't make up for that, not one bit. He gave in. I like it when people are reasonable.

When he'd gone, I made a few sketches, while the memory was fresh in my mind.

My brothers decided they'd do it all themselves.

Nothing to it, really. Just hack galleries into the side of the mountain, drag out the ore, crush it, smelt it, stack the ingots, carry them down the mountain, load them on a cart, job done. They were strong as bears and proud as lions. They could do anything.

Actually, they really were as strong as bears, and utterly determined, and my God, they stuck at it. They had pick-axes and rakes and big wicker baskets; they'd traded their fine Permian horses for a dozen good oxen, guaranteed salted, which promptly caught the fever and died, so everything that went up or down the mountain went on their backs. The people who told me about it later said the locals thought they were mad. For one thing there was no water, apart from the red, poisonous stuff. As you know, a gallon of water weighs ten pounds. The nearest clean spring was a mile and a half away. But they'd made their minds up; wealth beyond their wildest dreams was there for the taking, and all that separated them from it was a little hard work and a little inconvenience. A matter of perspective, you see; compared to the rewards, the expenditure of effort was trivial. So they stuck at it, for three months, until a gallery caved in and broke Amalric's back.

THAT WEEK, I got three new commissions; also my first ever cancellation.

"Why's he changed his mind?" I asked the clerk. His Grace had decided that it would be inappropriate. I asked what that meant, exactly, and got no answer.

Well; you can get so far and no further. I sat down and did some figuring. The cost of setting up a viable iron ore mine on Mondelice, doing everything properly, which is the only way—I'd found out all about it; read Auxellus on mining operations, talked to surveyors, contractors, gangmasters, hauliers, commodities merchants, compared prices on everything from shovel handles to flat-bottomed barges—was nine thousand, eight hundred gulden. So far, forgetting about the three new commissions, I'd earned nine thousand, four hundred. Almost there; so very, very close.

I sat and looked at the figures. Four hundred gulden. A trivial sum, or just slightly more than a stonemason in the slate quarries would be likely to earn in his lifetime. So I went back through my costings, to see if I could shave a little off here and there, like the industrious gentlemen who make their living clipping tiny little bits of silver off the edges of coins. But I'd done too good a job. Everything was pared right down to the bone.

Well, I thought. It's begun. First the intellectually curious monk from the Studium, who by some weird coincidence had a massive stroke forty-eight hours after he visited me. Nothing could be proved, of course, but as he'd pointed out, the fine and upstanding scholars of the Studium don't need evidence. And if I had an unfortunate accident (these old houses are firetraps, everyone knows that) who would miss me? But a Brother of the greatest house of learning in the world is a different matter entirely; if he's not in his stall in Chapter, questions are asked. My first cancellation; word starting to spread, you don't want anything to do with her, bad things happen to her customers.

Presumably the fine and upstanding scholars had been keeping a lid on the rumour while they conducted their scientifically organised investigations, waiting for enough instances, a sufficient ratio, to satisfy their particular version of the burden of proof. Quite possibly they'd sent poor Brother Eustatius along to see what would happen to him, like a canary in a coal mine. All in all, this would be a good time to run; don't stop to gather your five most treasured possessions, or even put on your hat. Just go.

Four hundred gulden short. I thought of Amalric, my brother—apparently he still knew what was going on and could understand what was said to him, but the only part of him that moved was his eyes; his eyes could still follow you round the room, like a tricksy portrait. The nine thousand four hundred was safely invested with the Knights, along with my will; if anything happens to me, anything at all... Four hundred stupid gulden. That's two more portraits and two more sales to my unpleasant friend, and was it really likely that I'd be around that long? To do one more, quite possibly. Two, though; no. The Studium is many things, but nobody can accuse them of inefficiency.

I consulted my diary. An appointment early in the morning, to paint a portrait of Her Grace the Countess—a fascinating woman, by all accounts; born in an obscure little village in the mountains, joined the Opera at age fifteen, married to the Count at eighteen, widowed at twenty-three; mistress of kings, prelates and philosophers, the most celebrated and notorious patron of the arts in the empire, officially still the fourth loveliest woman in the City; and it was a rush job, she needed the portrait as a birthday present for some hapless satellite or other, and she'd promised cash on delivery, and her word was as good as money in the bank. Seventy gulden from her, a hundred and thirty from my friend, who'd rather have all his teeth pulled with rusty pliers than miss out on a collector's piece like that. Still two hundred short. So close, but not enough.

A family of five could live quite happily—luxuriously—on capital of nine thousand six hundred gulden. And, if Mondelice hadn't turned out to be one huge iron nugget, we'd have been perfectly content to do just that (only, if there had been no Mondelice, I would never have gone into business or earned so much as a bent trachy) But if I simply went home and handed them a draft on the Knights, I knew perfectly well what they'd do. They'd charge ahead, spend the lot, cut just one or two little corners that couldn't possibly matter; they'd be bankrupt within the year, or crushed to death under a collapsed roof, and this time everything would be gone. So close you could practically touch it, but not close enough.

I PAINTED THE Countess, and she took away the finished result while the paint was still wet. She paid cash, and a thirty gulden tip—ridiculously generous, but she could afford it and she was overjoyed with my work, proving that she was a woman of taste, because it was the best, second best, painting I've ever done. That's me exactly, she said, several times; it's like you've opened up my heart and looked inside. And thanks to you, I'll be me for ever and ever, long after this flesh is dead and gone. I could see what she was getting at; a year or so later, and she wouldn't be her any more. There would be slight changes, little differences, and she'd go from being the fourth loveliest woman in the City (with certificates to prove it) to a sad, hideous monster, a hermit crab in a brilliant pearl shell, a peasant family squatting in a ruined palace. You caught me just in time, she told me. Well.

Thirty gulden. Thirty gulden is a hell of a lot of money, but not enough, so she might as well not have bothered. And if she'd had thirty gulden when she was fifteen, she'd never have left the mountain village. She'd have stayed there, and married a carter or a farrier, and lived happily ever after. Or at any rate a damn sight longer.

I went to see my friend. I had a proposition for him.

"YOU'VE NEVER TOLD me," I said. "What do you do with them all?"

He gave me a horrified look. "You don't need to know that."

"Actually," I said.

"You don't need to know."

I opened my portfolio and showed him a charcoal sketch of the Countess. He went white as a sheet. "Yes," I said.

"Her—"

"Yes."

Actually, the way he managed to pull himself together was quite admirable. "We were lovers once," he said. "Did you know that?"

"No. I need two hundred for her."

"I haven't got two hundred." He wailed it at me, as if I'd got him stretched on a rack. I believed him. "How much have you got?"

"A hundred and five. That's all. That's me wiped out."

Yes, but I had the extra thirty, so that was all right. But no, it wasn't. I needed more. "When you say wiped out—"

He was breathing fast and shallow. "There's a few things I can sell," he said. "A farm in the Mesoge, a half-share in a ship, some family silver."

"Good," I said, "because you'll need the money. But first, you've got to tell me. What do you do with them?"

He explained. I'd broken him, I think, because it all came out in a rush. My guess is, he was relieved to be able to tell someone. He was, he told me, an alchemist. Like his father before him, he'd devoted his entire life to the search for immortality. Quite early on, he'd proved, mathematically, that eternal preservation of the physical is impossible, can't be done (pages and pages and pages of calculations, no doubt); so he'd concentrated his researches on the doctrine of the dual procession of the Holy Aura—

"Oh," I said. "That."

Yes, that; and he was convinced that it was possible to reduce the very essence of a man's intellect, character and memories into substantial form, something tangible, something—

"Something you can keep in a bottle."

He gave me a look of pure loathing. "Yes," he said. "Something you can keep in a bottle, for ever. True immortality. I know it can be done, and I'm so very close—"

I looked at him. "Sure it can be done," I said. "Tell you what. Give me four hundred gulden and I'll tell you how. It's not that difficult. If a woman can do it, it can't be."

He shook his head, like a bull bothered by flies. "I don't need to know that," he said. "And I couldn't do it, not to a living person, it'd be worse than murder."

"So you pay me to—"

"Yes." Hard to tell who he hated most, me or himself. "Because, you see, they don't keep." He stopped. I thought he was going to be sick. "Like apples, you know. If you don't store them right, they go bad. But it's not difficult, storing apples, so long as you know how. And I will," he added savagely. "It's just a matter of practice and experiment. I'm nearly there. It can only be something very slight."

"Thank you," I said. And then I told him my proposition.

I thought he was going to faint.

He accepted.

Ask any artist and they'll tell you. The biggest test, the greatest achievement, is the successful self-portrait. I set up my easel (for the last time) and looked for the light. I paint by the inner light, but the other stuff helps too.

When he told me about the storage problems, the going bad, he wasn't telling me anything I didn't already know. And money is useful—it's everything—but I didn't get started in this business just for money.

And I'm an artist, and I'm good at it. I set up my mirror; back to the window, mirror towards it, so that the light was reflected onto my face. I laid out the basic lines in ochre, then built up in colour, shadows first, then the light. It's a cliché, isn't it, about not being able to look at yourself in the mirror when you're ashamed of something. Now I'm more ashamed of what I've done than anyone else alive, but for me, looking in the mirror was the only way out, the only way I could put it right. Actually, that's garbage. Skewed perspective. Hardly surprising. Live with someone like me for twenty-six years, of course you'll end up seeing all twisted.

There's a moment when it stops being just lines and shapes and it becomes a face; like a house, when people move in. I took a step back and looked at her, me, on the canvas. Hello, I said.

The reason I started in the business was, I missed my father, so very, very much. I closed my eyes and saw his face, exactly, fresh, perfect in every detail. So I painted him; over and over and over again, that's why I learned, that's how I learned, and each painting was better than the last until finally I got it just right, the best, really the best work I've ever done. My father in his habit as he lived; that's a quotation, isn't it? Anyhow, it was him, looking back at me. And I remembered, Modestus of Apamene, the fool and rogue who'd been right all along; and I thought, I can do it. I can bring him back.

And I did. I painted him, and I did the sums, and I reduced him, his intellect, character and memories, his very essence, and I put him in a bottle, for ever and ever. But my friend is right. Unless you store them right, they don't keep. They go bad. And I really don't want to talk about that.

My friend will pay four hundred gulden into my account with the Knights, and in exchange I'll give him this self-portrait, of the most remarkable mind and soul he'll ever encounter, he agrees with me on that, together with the formula, the pages and pages and pages of maths. He's agreed to give me time to write this, which I've now done. He thinks he's figured out what he was doing wrong with the storage; it was just a little thing, he says, a tiny adjustment. I hope he's right.

Prosper's Demon

> After many unhappy experiments in the direction of an ideal Republic, it was found that what may be described as Despotism tempered by Dynamite provides the most satisfactory description of ruler...
>
> —W. S. Gilbert

I woke to find her lying next to me, quite dead, with her throat torn out. The pillow was shiny and sodden with blood, like low-lying pasture after a week of heavy rain. The taste in my mouth was familiar, revolting, and unmistakable. I spat into my cupped hand: bright red. Oh, for crying out loud, I thought. Here we go again.

I crawled out of bed and tried to get my sleepy brain working. Some people are galvanised into decisive action by a crisis. I get all fogged up, like a cart stuck in soft ground; the wheels turn and turn, but no traction.

Blood *spreads*; you can't seem to confine it, no matter how you try. So I took a leaf out of the First Emperor's book and built a huge circumvallatory wall, out of fabric—sheets, curtains, the hangings off the walls, all my shirts except the one I was wearing (which was ruined, too, of course)—practically every fiber in the house. By gradually closing this cloth embankment in around the bed, I managed to keep the blood from getting on the walls and the doors, where it'd be sure to leave an indelible mark. Trust me, I know all about blood; every time a sheet or a curtain got soaked through, I wrapped it in something else and shifted it to the upper layer of the heap. The body itself went on the very top, like a beacon on a mountain peak. Luckily the floor was marble, about the only substance on earth blood doesn't soak into permanently. I wrapped the body up in a beautiful and rather expensive Aelian rug I'd bought only a week earlier, then tied it tight with string.

To get the whole horrible mess out of the door, I used a modification of the travois principle: a heavy-duty coir mat, which I happened to have by me for some reason or other, with two holes stabbed in two corners to pass a rope through. It slid along quite nicely across the smooth marble floor and left only a few rusty brown streaks, which were no bother at all to wipe up afterwards. Out the side door, then just a matter of lifting the ghastly bale of ruined textiles and the rolled-up rug into my eight-hundred-gulden fancy chaise (served me right for indulging myself; I make a lot of money, and I'm always broke), harnessing up the horse, and off we went. There's a worked-out quarry two miles or so from where I was living at the time. Sheer sides, deep, and the bottom is grown over with briars and withies and rubbish. I got the horse out of the shafts, put my shoulder to the back wheel, and sent my lovely expensive chaise tumbling over the edge. It disappeared into the tangle like a stone sinking in a pond. Job done.

On the ride home, I looked down at my hands, and I thought: it's a bit much. If you can't trust your own hands, what can you trust? Except I can't, not after the last time, or the time before that. One of Them had crept inside me while I was asleep and taken control of my hands away from me, used them to murder a young woman, practically a stranger, whose only crime was a little commercialised affection. In this jurisdiction, the worst you get for that is a two-thaler fine and a morning in the stocks (and that's excessive, if you ask me). Instead, a savage and violent death, at my hands. My hands, you bastard. I'll have you for that.

My fault, for thinking I could get away with even a cash-down travesty of ordinary human feeling; my fault for involving a civilian. I thought about that and looked at my short, stubby fingers, used against me like a club snatched from a watchman's belt by a violent drunk. Not my fault, I decided. Never mine. Always His.

I HAVE AN idea you aren't going to like me very much.

That may prove to be the only thing we'll have in common, so let's make the most of it. I do terrible things. I do them to my enemies, to my own side, to myself. In the process, I save a large number of strangers (on average, between five and ten a week) from the worst thing that can happen to a human being. I'd like to say I do it because I'm one of the good guys, but if I did that, you'd see right through me. And then you'd quote scripture at me: Render to no one evil for evil.

Really? Even if they're the enemy? Even if They're not human?

You decide. Not sure I can be bothered with it anymore.

I HAVE ONE thing in common with the emperor: I was born into a certain line of work, without the faintest possibility of choice. A blacksmith's son might just possibly decide to run away and enlist or join a troupe of traveling actors or pick cotton or beg on street corners. Not me. Like the heir apparent, I can't just melt away into the crowd. I'd be recognised, found out, forced back to my honors and obligations. And as for not doing the work I was born to do: inconceivable. Might as well say, it's entirely up to me whether I breathe or not.

It's a commonplace in the trade that ours is a lonely existence; perfectly true. The first thing you do, on discovering that you have the gift (the word gift here used in its technical sense, meaning the ability, as opposed to something anyone in his right mind might conceivably want to be given), is to run away from home, severing all ties with your previous life. This is, it goes without saying, absolutely essential. When I left home, I stole my father's gold signet ring, all my mother's jewelry, and my sister's silk shawl, which she loved more than anything else in the world. I had to. As a family we were comfortable but hardly well-off, and I needed small, portable items that could be turned into money quickly and without fuss. With the proceeds I booked a passage on a lumber barge. Didn't bother asking where it was going. The point being: they can go anywhere on land, but They can't cross salt water. Small mercies.

Actually, now I think about it, I have something else in common with His Serenity. I have absolute authority. Lucky, lucky me.

I KNEW HE couldn't have gone far. They can't; They get hungry as soon as They leave a human host, and hunger makes Them weak. He wouldn't be hard to find, and after pulling off a prank like that, He'd be relatively quiet and peaceful for a day or so. So I went home, had a good wash, brushed my teeth thoroughly (first with soot, then with myrrh and peppermint); packed up my remaining possessions and loaded them into the donkey cart—it was only then that it occurred to me that I could have sacrificed the donkey cart instead of the chaise and it'd have done just as well. His fault, of course. All His fault.

I'm used to moving on at short notice. Plenty of practice, over the years, and I'm uniquely adapted to a life without roots and connections, although wherever I go, I know exactly whom I'm going to meet, sooner or later. Objectively speaking, needless to say, it's a wonderful thing that there are so few of Them—otherwise, the human race would be over and done with, finished. But for me, it means I have to deal with the same old faces (so to speak) over and over and over again, until They're sick of me and

I'm sick of Them. And believe me, I'm sick to death of Them, especially when They pull stunts like that.

My luck was in. The first small town I came to, it was market day. I sold the donkey cart, the donkey, and all my worldly goods at not too unbearable a loss, leaving me with sixteen gulden forty-seven, plus the value of one bloodstained shirt, one coarse brown ecclesiastical gown, and a pair of army boots. When you think what I charge for even a run-of-the-mill, in-and-out-in -five-minutes, everyday kind of job, it'd reduce some men to floods of tears, but fortunately I'm not really bothered. Money, things have never really mattered to me very much. Incredibly difficult come, easy go—so what? It's a bit like being the biggest landowner on an island dominated by an active volcano. You know it's always just a matter of time.

When I arrive in a new place, I try really hard not to notice Them, but it's impossible. I can't help it, like a dog in a field of sheep. Actually, make that a dog in an alleyful of cats, and it's not a bad analogy. It's the same unthinking, instinctive, bred-in-the-bone antipathy, and They don't like me much either. I catch sight of Them in the farthest corner of my peripheral vision, and I can't help it; I point, people tell me, like a hunting dog.

Note peripheral vision. They know when I'm coming, and They freeze, dead still, not a flicker. Sure, I know They're in the neighbourhood, I can smell Them. I can track Them down by smell alone if I have to, though it very rarely comes to that, obviously. But when I walk down the street, the most I ever see is that tiny flicker of movement right on the extreme edge. And that's all I need.

But the hell with it. It's all about being professional, and not being on duty. Poets don't write hexameters on their day off, whores don't make love, soldiers don't kill people; I can't help noticing, but I'm under no obligation to do anything about it, particularly when I'm not getting paid. Not unless—

I heard a woman scream. Reluctantly, I turned my head. A man was lying on the ground, his back arched, his heels dragging furrows in the mud. His face was just starting to turn blue, and the crotch of his trousers was sodden wet. A dozen or so people were forming a loose ring around him, backing away. He made that unmistakable noise. It's not an actual shout or yell; it's purely mechanical, the muscles in spasm forcing air out of the lungs through a tightly constricted throat. Another unique sound: the sharp dry-stick crack of a bone, broken by the monstrous contraction of its own muscles and sinews.

Hence, I guess, the dog-and-cat reaction. Possibly it's just that I find it offensive when one of Them dares do Its stuff when I'm there, as though I'm nobody, don't count for anything, chopped liver. I prefer to put it down to compassion, and an undying hostility toward the Common Enemy of Man. But I would say that, wouldn't I?

Five long strides brought me up close enough. I looked in through the sides of the poor devil's head and caught Its eye. It stared back at me; always the same expression, like a bad boy in your apple tree with half of one of your apples in his mouth.

You again, It said.

Me, I replied.

That's the thing about our line of work. Some monk with far too little to do once calculated it exactly, using the very finest scriptural materials; there are 72,936 of Them. Sounds a lot, except that's *all*. That's to cover, or service, or garrison—choose your inadequate and inappropriate verb—the entire human race, all fifteen *million* of us. And, of course, They have Their territories, as all predators do; like my fellow practitioners; like me. And, of course, They can't be killed or die—They just get moved on, like the poor—so, of course, I keep meeting Them, over and over and over again. And moving Them on. I have, after all, the authority.

It looked so sad and wistful. *Give me a break*, It said.

Out, I said.

I just got here.

Tough.

Five minutes, all right? Just give me five minutes and then I'll be on my way.

Out, I said.

I have the authority. Out, I say, and out They have to go. They go because They know that if They don't, I can haul Them out, I can reach in, inside, grab hold of Them by—God only knows what, let's just say They aren't put together quite the same as you and me—and drag Them out of there. When I do that, it hurts, rather a lot to judge by Their reaction, though for all I know They may have really low pain thresholds, or They may just make a lot of fuss about the littlest thing, like pigs.

But—you have to be careful. I can pull Them out; a bit like when you've got toothache so bad, you go to the blacksmith. And if he's a gentle, sensible man, he'll get a firm grip on it with his tongs and just turn his wrist, this way then that, then one quick, strong, controlled flick and it's all done and no bother. Or he could break your jaw, and still leave splinters of crushed tooth in there.

Makes you shudder just to think of it. Well, that's mouths. These things live in minds. So, as I said, you have to be careful.

Give me five minutes, It said.

At which point, you have to make a decision. You consider the amount of damage It's already done—in this case, a broken leg, because I'd heard it break, and almost certainly a rib or two, high chance of internal bleeding, the little bastards never can resist *playing*—and then you weigh the harm It'll do if you leave It in there a moment longer, against the havoc It could cause if you have to yank It out. Factor against all that the pain and trauma It'll feel being extracted, of which It's so very, very scared; and then you ask yourself, is It really so tired and hungry that It'll risk being manhandled, or is It simply trying it on, the way They all do, 999 times in 1,000?

Which is why, in actual appalling fact, it's a good thing that we have our territories and They have Theirs and we all get to know each other so terribly, terribly well—

No, I said. *Count of three. One—*

Not going.

Two.

The man—I think he was some sort of merchant, by his clothes and the fact I didn't know him—sprang to his feet. No, he was lifted to his feet, for the split second in question he was actually standing on his broken leg, it folded and he collapsed, and by the time he hit the ground it was all over, nobody in there who shouldn't be, no longer any business or interest of mine. I looked away and walked on.

And there's the thing. Anybody who happened to be watching me and not the motionless twisted wreck of a human being on the ground would have seen a man in a shabby priest's robe stop, gawp, and then pass on by—callous, unfeeling bastard, he'd say to himself; and who am I to contradict? I'd done my professional duty, and there my involvement ended. Sometimes I wonder if it's more that I hate Them than that I love my fellow humans. But nobody pays me to think that, so I don't do it often.

Scripture, about which I'm vaguely skeptical, tells us that when the Invincible Sun rose for the very first time, He drew up out of the marshes and swamps that covered the face of the Earth all the noxious, foul damps and vapors in which our universal Mother had been quietly marinating since the beginning of time. These vapors were promptly carried away on the breeze, and according to the highly respected authority I quoted just now, there are 72,936 of Them.

People ask me, I really wish they wouldn't, but they do: What do They look like? To which I give various replies, all untrue. Fact is, I don't know. When I ask the same annoying question of my professional peers, on the rare occasion that I meet one and we're on speaking terms, I get an answer, and I try and give an honest answer in return. To one practitioner They look like horrible insects; to another, ghastly, unnatural fish or rats, or disgusting birds, or shrunken, desiccated children. To me They look like shellfish. And all that proves is, beauty isn't the only mote in the beholder's eye.

More interesting is when you ask one of Them what we look like. But I digress.

Seventy-two thousand nine hundred thirty-six, of which one hundred nine operate in my jurisdiction, which extends from the Charyabda Mountains to the Friendly Sea, mercifully excluding the cities of Bomyra, Euxis, and Bine Seauton. Within that area, which comprises three temporal nation-states, at least two of which are at war with at least two of the others at any given time, I'm licensed by His Holiness to expel demons for money. To prove my bona fides, I have a certificate with illuminated capitals and a lead seal, which at least one in a thousand people can read, and a gold ring with a white stone given to me by the Metropolitan Cardinal. Correction, I have a piss-poor imitation of same, a pebble set in brass, which I had made for me when I lost the original. Thus my credentials, and it's a funny thing. People never seem to ask to see them before I operate; only afterwards, when they're called upon to pay the bill.

Mostly, though, I don't bother, just as the dog doesn't look round for someone to recompense him for chasing the cat. Why should they believe it was me; and even if they did, what can I do to them if they don't pay? Put the bloody thing back where I found It? Actually, I have made the empty threat before now, and it works like a charm, but you can't always rely on people being deplorably ignorant.

So, having saved the merchant's soul and sanity and probably his life, too, I passed by on the other side, with nothing to show for it but the splitting headache They always give me afterwards. I went up the street to Haymarket, and looked in at the Harmony & Grace.

"Oh," they said. "You again."

Inhospitable but fair enough: last time there had been an unfortunate incident, and the time before that, though not of my making. But they respect the gown and they know what the stupid brass ring stands for, and there's always the lurking fear at the back of their minds: better not to piss off this loathsome and troublesome man, just in case we need him one day. Which is why nobody is ever pleased to see me, and why I never have to buy my own drinks.

I told them I'd be staying for a while. How long, they asked sadly, is a while? I smiled and said I didn't know. Would that be a problem? No, they told me, no problem at all.

You have to learn to think like Them, they told me when I was just starting out in the business; only, don't get too good at it. They say that to all the students, and none of us really understand what it means at the time.

In and out of each other's heads, like neighbours in a small, friendly village, which is exactly what we aren't. Or, to put it another way, it doesn't do to get too familiar.

But it didn't take me long to figure out what He—

Excuse me, I have a lot of trouble with pronouns. The proper singular form for one of Them is, of course, It. We neither know nor care whether They are divided into genders as we are, nor, as far as I can tell, do They. But rules were made to be broken, at least as far as I'm concerned, and this one particular, unique, individual specimen was definitely, in my mind, a He. I don't know why; I suspect it has more to do with me than—well, Him. For some reason I need Him to be male in order to deal with Him. That's one of the many dangers I was warned about. Precisely because everybody sees Them differently, the risk is always of creating Them in your own image.

So, indulge me: Him. It didn't take me long to figure out what He was up to, or why He'd gone to all the trouble of attacking me. All I needed, therefore, was a copy of the *Court Circular* and a fast horse.

PROSPER'S DEMON

I TOLD YOU that you wouldn't like me.

I understand. It shows proper feeling. If you said to me: There's this man who is so callous and brutal that he doesn't give a damn about his fellow human beings, wouldn't shed a tear over the death of an innocent; would you care to meet this person, shake hands with him, maybe invite him into your home and have dinner with him? You're kidding, right.

That hypothetical piece of shit is, of course, me. All my life—

MANY OF THE great civilised nations have a foundation myth in which their national hero was abandoned on a hillside at birth and brought up by wolves, or bears or hyenas or whatever your local gregarious predator happens to be. To all intents and purposes I was brought up by Them. What the hell do you expect?

I feel guilty because I don't feel guilty. Sure, I could defend myself, if I wanted to. I could describe to you what it's like having one of Them inside your head. It hurts, like nothing else, all the time. It makes you do things, the sort of things you'll never forgive yourself for, even though you know it's not you doing them. You'd kill yourself to be rid of the pain and the shame and the dread of what you're going to do next, only It won't let you. It's torture and rape and all the worst things that can possibly happen, and it's not just suffering it but doing it to others, friends, lovers, children. It lays eggs of sheer horror deep inside you, and you can feel them hatching, growing, their burgeoning new life trapping your nerves against the bone.

I can tell you about that, and case histories of lives ruined, and lives saved when I intervene. But I'm not going to defend myself. I'm too far down the road for that. The victims aren't what motivates me, not anymore. Or not the only thing.

All I can do, am prepared to do, is ask you to consider two things: my motives and the effect of my actions. The effect of my actions is to save my brothers and sisters from the worst possible thing that can happen to anyone, and only I, and a handful of others like me, can do this. My motivations are my own business, my privilege and my intolerable burden.

THE WEDDING OF Grand Duke Sigiswald of Essen to the Princess Hildigunn, daughter of the Elector Frohvat of Risenem, was rather a low-key affair. There were ten thousand guests at the wedding breakfast, and all the fountains in Essen ran with sweet white wine, but that was about it. No triumphal procession, gladiatorial displays, mock sea battles, or mass sacrifice of prisoners of war on the Temple steps; no nationwide amnesty or emancipation of slaves; and only a modest donative, five gold kreutzer a man, to the soldiers in the army. Times, whispered the underlying message, are hard, money is tight, and your Duke and his lovely bride are setting an example.

The message was received loud and clear and went down well with the taxpayers, so that was all right. But the Princess insisted on one small indulgence. Unless she could be accompanied into the wilderness (her words, not mine) by her faithful tutor and confidant, Prosper of Schanz, she wasn't going, and her father and six years of eggshell-brittle diplomacy could go to hell.

No, it wasn't like that at all. Prosper was sixty if he was a day, and it took four strong men to prize him out of his chair and load him onto a specially reinforced chaise every time Her Highness felt like a spot of intellectual conversation. His salary at the time was sixty thousand kreutzer a year, and he insisted on a fifty per cent raise to compensate him for leaving Risenem and going to live among the woad-painted savages (he'd said something similar when the Elector headhunted him from Fal-hoel), so he was rather more than a trivial whim. Ninety thousand would pay the

Sixth Legion for a month, or fit out twelve warships. You'd have to have a heart of stone, though, if you didn't reckon Prosper of Schanz to be a bargain at three times the price. The finest painter and sculptor of his age, even though he very rarely finished anything; the most learned scholar, though everything he'd ever published fit neatly into one small, handy pocket edition; the most exquisite and refined musician; the most outstanding natural philosopher and engineer. By all accounts, Hildigunn had a tin ear, didn't like any painting that wasn't blue, and had to sign her name through a stencil, but she knew a class act when she saw one, and always had to have the best. So Prosper came to Essen, with all his books, machines, tin boxes full to bursting with notebooks and diaries, mechanical and philosophical paraphernalia, clogging up the mountain roads for a week. They say he spent his first month in residence watching a sheep's head decaying on a mounting block in the stable yard. He wanted to see for himself exactly how the process of deliquescence and entropy worked, in real time, second by second. So he had a comfortable chair brought down from the royal apartments on the sixth floor, and a footstool, a handy writing table, and a good supply of nice things to drink and snack on, and sat there, night and day (with a brazier to keep him warm and a huge silk umbrella to keep him dry), just watching. Whether the result was any special insight into the natures of change and mortality, I couldn't say, but you have to admit, the man's a class act, by any standards.

When the news broke that Sigiswald and Hildigunn had fulfilled their royal function and a tiny Elector was on the way, Prosper declared that this would be the ideal opportunity for him to put into practice a project that had been growing like a stalactite in the back of his godlike mind for absolutely ages: nothing less than the handcrafting of the ultimate superior human being—an enterprise, he modestly said, worthy of himself, at last. Since he was the greatest living authority on obstetric medicine, Prosper announced that he would deliver the child himself. As soon as it was born, he would personally supervise every aspect of its upbringing, nurture, and education. He would mould the child in his own image, teach it everything he knew, with a view to giving the world its first true top-notch very-best-quality philosopher-king, who would in turn solve every problem, make the world into an earthly paradise, and serve as a fitting monument to the greatest man who ever lived.

Now, conceding that Prosper was at least forty per cent full of the stuff that makes roses grow, that still left quite a lot of sheer unparalleled genius. The royal parents, no doubt reflecting on their own childhoods and education and figuring that anything had to be better than that, announced that they were delighted to give the great man carte blanche.

They nailed up a new copy of the *Court Circular* on the front door of the Temple in Jasca on the first day of the month. The lead story was Hildigunn's due date. It gave me precisely six days to cover the two hundred miles of rutted roads and broken-down bridges to Essen, a miracle that I somehow managed to accomplish.

I WAS IN a foul mood when I reached the palace gate. I bounced up to the sentry and told him I needed to see the duty officer. He looked at me, weighing my derelict boots against the priest's gown, and decided I was too difficult for him. That got me inside the lodge, where I hung around for most of the morning until the duty officer was available. Being an officer, he could read, so I showed him my certificate. It worried him. It's supposed to.

"How can I help you, Father?" he said.

"I need to see the palace chaplain." I told him. "Now."

I could see the poor man's brain grinding to a halt, as though I'd stuck an iron bar through the spokes. The chaplain, needless to say, wasn't part of his chain of command and he had no idea how to get in touch with him. Lucky for him, he had me to do his thinking for him. "You'll need to get a pass from the

Prefect." I told him, "to take me inside so I can explain to the deputy chamberlain why I need to see the chaplain. He'll take it from there."

Joy unbounded for the duty officer, who whisked me up seven flights of winding narrow stone stairs to the Prefecture, where I spent far too long hanging about while my pass was written up. Then a sad-looking clerk led me down the stairs I'd just come up and up an even longer staircase to the chamberlain's office, where I showed my certificate to somebody's poor relation's younger son, who went white as a sheet and told me to follow him. Nine flights of winding narrow stone stairs up to the Chaplaincy, where the junior deputy chaplain asked me what I wanted.

"I want to see the chaplain."

"That's not possible right now."

"Yes," I told him. "Actually, it is."

So we went to see the chaplain, who scowled at my certificate as if it were a turd floating in his soup, and shut the door so nobody could hear us. "What?" he said.

"I need to see the Duchess," I told him.

"Nobody sees the Duchess."

Bless him, he was having a bad day, I could tell. He had twelve large-scale services to plan out, for at least three of which there was no clearly established precedent, which meant he was going to have to wing it, liturgically speaking, and hope nobody present would be sufficiently erudite to find him out. On top of that, me: a fully authorised representative of a branch of the Ministry that is always bad news at any time; at a time like this—

I'd have liked to help him out, but I couldn't afford to indulge myself. I sat there and stared at him, a bit like the Sun, which you're not supposed to look directly at.

"Why?" he said.

"Three guesses."

"You're not making any sense," he said. "Are you trying to tell me that a member of the royal household is—?"

"Not yet."

"But that's absurd." he said. "It's impossible to predict when and where—"

"No," I told him, "it isn't."

People really don't like looking at me if they can possibly avoid it. There's something about me that makes me objectionable to have in their field of vision. The company I keep, presumably.

"I can't just admit you to the royal birth chamber," he said. "Not without very good reason and documentary evidence to corroborate—"

He tailed off. I was the worst thing that had ever happened to him in his entire life, and he'd done nothing whatever to deserve me. "All right," he said, "if you insist. But I'll be making a written memorandum that I'm doing this under protest."

Which was probably the most aggressive thing he'd ever said, and he watched it bounce off me like gravel off a breastplate. "When you're quite ready," I said.

"Follow me."

HOW FAR BACK can you remember? When you were a toddler? Before you could walk? Before you could speak, just possibly? I can trump that. I can remember before I was born. Being unborn, and not alone.

It was in there with me, you see; the first one I ever met. They're not stupid. They know where They're safe. If They can get inside a child before it's born, They know They've got security of tenure for at least ten years, maybe as many as twelve, because of the unspeakable level of collateral damage that would be involved in digging Them out. Works both ways, mind; leaving an infant hurts Them just as much as it hurts the host, so if They choose to enter an unborn child, They're stuck there until the child matures, and the pickings are slim. It's *boring,* living in something so small and crude and stupid, so They take that option only when They're hurt and need somewhere to hole up and recover, or when They've had a really rough ride at the hands of me and my lot. In my case, It had just been evicted, with rather more force than absolutely necessary, from Its previous home. It was smashed up and raw, a real mess, and It had just enough strength to crawl inside my mother before It passed out and collapsed; and then It encountered me.

I remember It very clearly. It was a voice I could understand, outside me but very close. *Let me in,* It said. *Please,* It said.

I can remember what it was like, thinking without words, knowing nothing—nothing at all. But It wanted to come inside me, and I didn't want It to. I pushed It away. It tried to push back, but It couldn't. *Go away,* I told It.

Oh, for crying out loud, It said. *You're one of Them.*

I didn't understand, of course, but I didn't like it, not one little bit. I pushed It away. I could feel myself hurting It. It was the first thing I ever came across that was weaker than me, that I could prevail over, that I could hurt. It wasn't bothering me anymore, but I could bother It, if I wanted to. I wanted to. Good game. I pushed harder.

Stop that, It said. *You're hurting me.*

Go away, I told It, but I didn't mean it. I wanted It to stay and be played with. Rough games, the sort small children enjoy.

I'm stuck, It said, *I can't get out. Stop pushing.*

Memories are tricky; there's what you remember, and what you think you remember, the editions and redactions of memory, the corrections and amendations and blundered readings and the whole *apparatus criticus* of the conscious mind trying to make bread out of soup. The way I remember it, I bashed Its head against something until It screamed, then I tried strangling It, then I broke Its arms and legs, and then I bashed It some more. All impossible, I now realise, since They don't have arms, legs, heads, so whatever I did to It could only have been equivalents. But whatever I did, I hurt It, and it was fun.

I have no way of knowing, of course, how long we were cooped up in there together. My best guess, based on what my mother told me (about recurring nightmares she'd had, that sort of thing), is something between three and four months; but, what the hell, time is subjective, especially between us and Them. We were in there together for a long time, and then I was born and It was able to crawl out and escape, at desperate cost to Itself, but better than staying in there with me. By all accounts, I was a fairly ordinary baby after that, though inclined to be willful.

So, WE WENT to see the Duchess. But we couldn't; not even the chaplain. Master Prosper was in there, they told us, with the royal midwife, two nurses, and Master Prosper's authorised biographer (he had two of them working twelve-hour shifts), and nobody could go in until it was all over, not even the Duke. Especially the Duke. I showed them my certificate. They went all thoughtful—it's a really good certificate—but apparently the penalty for disobeying Master Prosper's slightest whim was death by garrotting, so clearly nothing could be done.

They parked the chaplain and me in a small anteroom, empty except for one straight-backed ivory chair. I sat in it.

"Can you really predict what—?"

I nodded. "In this instance, yes."

"But I thought—"

I turned and looked at him, my full professional look. Someone once explained to me why it's so terrifying. He told me: just for a moment, you get the impression that you can see some of the things those eyes have seen, like a sort of trick mirror. I hope he was exaggerating.

"Sorry," he said.

"That's all right." He'd made me feel guilty. "In this instance, I'm pretty sure."

"Would you care to—?"

I shrugged. "Why the hell not?" I said. And I told him; about waking up next to the dead girl. He went a funny sort of grey color. "It made you do that?"

"While I was asleep." I said. "I know it was Him."

"How can you—?"

"Not the first time," I said. "Not by a long chalk. And the last time this one did something like that—no, I tell a lie, time before that—I was out of action for months, dodging the dead girl's family and the law and all that sort of thing. During which time He was free to get up to all sorts of mischief without having to look over His shoulder every five minutes in case I was sneaking up on Him. So I thought: if I were Him, what would I be up to, that would justify pulling a prank like that? Bearing in mind what I'm going to do to him when I do catch up with him. Which won't be pretty, believe me." I smiled. I don't think it was a happy smile. "And then I glanced through the *Court Circular*, and the question kind of answered itself."

Years ago, I came across a man lying in the road. He'd been run over by one of those gigantic carts they use for shipping oak trees down from the forest to the ship-yards, and his back was broken. He was still alive but completely paralyzed, and he had much the same look on his face as my unfortunate friend the chaplain had after I'd explained the position to him. "You think—?"

"Yes," I said. "I think, because I think like He does."

"Dear God."

I grinned. "Oh, we're quite alike in many ways," I said. "In fact, there's only two differences between us that really matter. One, I'm stronger than He is. Much, much stronger."

For some reason, this didn't seem to set the chaplain's mind at rest. Rather the reverse.

"The other," I went on, "is that one day I'll die, but not Him. They can't die. He can hurt—trust me, I know, He can suffer more pain than you could possibly imagine—but He can't die. It's a sort of equilibrium," I explained. "Two very different things but nonetheless equivalent."

I'd lost him; not that it signified. "But if you're right," he said, "if that *thing* has got inside—"

Through the closed door we heard that unmistakable sound, a newborn baby's first scream. The chaplain shuddered as though he'd just been stabbed, by his mother.

"Surely there must be something I can do?"

I shook my head. "Not a lot, no."

"But—" Poor sod. Windows of understanding were opening in his mind, but through them poured something that wasn't really light. "Master Prosper—"

I nodded. "He's smart," I said. "Not Master Prosper. Him. He'll have known all about that, you can bet your life."

"The experiment. The philosopher-king. There must be *something*—"

I breathed out slowly, as though I'd just put down a very heavy weight. "Master Prosper," I told him, "doesn't believe in demonic possession. He thinks it's just superstition. In his view, the Invincible Sun is a ball of burning gas floating an incomprehensible distance over our heads, and demons are how we account for the symptoms and effects of various disorders and diseases, entirely mechanical in origin, curable with herbs and therapies. I've read his book, and the case he makes out for it is overwhelming. Did you know, he reckons we weren't created on the sixth day? Instead we're the descendants of those furry things from Permia who live in treetops. I was entirely convinced, until I remembered it isn't actually true. Anyhow, we haven't got a hope in hell of persuading Master Prosper to let me in there, and right now, his word is law. Which is just as well," I added, "because the only possible thing I could do to make things a bit better and avoid the disasters that must inevitably follow would be to kill the baby"

He stared at me, opened his mouth, closed it again. I think people hate me the most when they realise I'm right.

"Which I'd do," I went on, "easy as breathing, because I'd have to. But it wouldn't make me very popular with the Duke, and like I mentioned just now, I'm mortal. And while I can't feel nearly so much pain as He can, I can still feel rather a lot. Hence just as well. For me, anyhow."

I felt sorry for the chaplain, and I'm not the most sympathetic person you'll ever meet. So, yes, I felt guilty. I don't cause the problem, but I'm definitely part of it. Between fifty-five and sixty per cent, I'd say.

"What should we do?" he asked me.

I made a show of thinking about that. "You," I said, "are going to arrange for a transfer, to a post a very, very long way away from here. It may mean less money and less status, but believe me, it'll be worth it."

He stared at me with those dead fish eyes, then nodded. "You?"

"I don't know." I said. "But I'll think of something."

THINK OF SOMETHING. Think like Him. What would He do? I didn't have a happy childhood. My parents were prosperous, good people and loved me very much, but I was a miserable, spiteful child, given to picking fights with kids who were bigger and stronger than me, and getting beaten bloody by them. They asked me: Why do you do it, it makes no sense, you know you can't beat us, we're bigger than you are? Why don't you pick on someone your own size—or, better still, someone smaller?

I couldn't tell them they'd completely missed the point, obviously. So I carried on baiting them, and they carried on beating me up and feeling sorry for me, and if it ever occurred to me to wonder why I needed to do these stupid things, I simply assumed that it was just one more of the many simple and obvious things that I didn't know yet, but would in the fullness of time. Meanwhile, I just *knew*, without being able to explain or show my working. After all, you don't ask *why* the square on the hypotenuse is equal to the sum of the squares on the other two sides. It just is.

Then one day one of the bigger boys got sick. His friends went to see him and came away horrified. Half the time, they said, he was yelling and screaming and thrashing about, and the rest of the time he just sat there, as if he were dead or something.

It was a while before I could visit him, because he'd beaten me up so badly I was confined to bed; but when I felt strong enough I sneaked out of our house and sneaked into his. I wanted to see him suffering, because he'd hurt me.

I crawled in through a window. His parents had strapped him down tight on a stretcher, for his own good, because they loved him. I stood over him. His eyes were tight shut. I said his name. He opened his eyes and looked at me.

"Oh, for crying out loud," He said. "You again."

For a moment I was confused; then I realised. I realised that I could see Him. Him, the enemy inside my enemy: the cat, the prey. Of course, I knew a tiny bit about it, demonic possession—the tiny bit that everyone knows, of which ninety per cent is garbage. "I can see you," I said.

It, no, He grinned at me. *Small world.*

I could hear Him inside my head. "You shouldn't be in there," I said aloud. "Is it you hurting my friend?"

Not your friend. He smashed your face in. He really did you over. The enemy of my enemy is my friend, right?

"That's like saying the cat's cat is a dog. You shouldn't be in there."

Poor devil, He must have thought it's just a kid, I'll risk it. *So what? What are you going to do about it?*

I showed him. And, being very young and clumsy and inexperienced and uneducated, and not knowing my own strength—well. Fortunately, nobody could ever prove that I'd been in that room; and even if they could have, they'd have had a devil of a job explaining how a nine-year-old child could have done that much damage, even when the victim was strapped to a board.

THEY CALCULATE (PROBABLY the same bunch of scholarly know-it-alls who came up with the figure 72,936) that in a botched extraction, whatever the host feels, the demon feels it ten times as much. Based on my experience, I'd say that's roughly accurate. But they don't die, and we do. As I said: equilibrium.

What would He do? Well, I knew the answer to that. He wouldn't bother.

It's a lie to say They're incapable of compassion, because self-pity is still pity, and they're red-hot on that. But put Themselves out to rescue someone else, an individual, a country, a whole region? Forget it. But suppose They *had* to; a direct order from whatever passes among Them as a hierarchy, authority, chain of command? No idea if They've got one, but for the sake of argument.

I had one ally, but useless and busy packing his books and vestments for a long sea voyage. I needed another ally, but all I had to choose from was enemies. So? Story of my life.

When you're making something, you don't choose the tools you use because you like them, because they're your particular friends. You choose the ones that will be most useful. Well, then. That's what He'd do.

MODESTY, SAID MASTER Prosper (speaking slowly, so his duty biographer could take dictation) is simply saying about yourself what other people think about you, and therefore preventing them from saying it out loud. It's certainly a shortcoming of which Master Prosper was entirely innocent. And what he loved above all other things was being right.

Not merely having people acknowledge that he's right; because they might be wrong, more than likely in fact, because everyone else is so dumb. No, it doesn't satisfy him unless he believes it himself. So, in order to get Master Prosper to like me, I had to give him an opportunity to prove that he was right and I was wrong, deluded, an idiot. Easy peasy.

My friend the chaplain had left me with a letter of introduction addressed to the chamberlain asking if he'd be so kind as to introduce a certain favourite cousin of his to Master Prosper. Said cousin had long been a fanatical admirer of the great man's work, et cetera, and if it was remotely possible that the Master might be induced to spare him a few moments of his inexpressibly precious time—

My guess is that the chaplain had something really good—not just the standard palace dirt but something so rank, you'd need gloves and a mask just to think about it—on the chamberlain, because the very next day I got my papers—full pass, permission to enter the royal apartments at will, all manner of rich and wonderful things, together with a note from Master Prosper's deputy assistant junior secretary stating that the most brilliant man who ever lived would be pleased to receive me in such and such a room at such and such a time. Friends in high places, I said to myself. Sometimes I'm so stupid, I'm amazed I manage to breathe.

I WAS PREPARED for a fat man in the same way that someone who has grown up on the shores of a five-acre inland lake is prepared for the sea. There was a *lot* of Master Prosper. Quite how much of it was necessary, I wouldn't care to say; maybe sixty per cent, which was roughly the ratio of genius to bullshit that made up his mental and spiritual being, so probably about that.

Sixty per cent of Master Prosper would have been a tall, handsome, imposing man, with a perfectly bald head of prodigious size, and a high, pleasant voice, and hands like a girl. You could tell he was an artist by the way he'd had the room composed, right down to moving the windows (I could see the new plaster) so that he'd be perfectly lit, sitting in his marvelous gold and ebony throne—his own work, and uncharacteristically actually almost finished—to receive disciples and worshippers in the late morning and early evening. It was a big room, forty feet square, and apart from the great man and the great man's chair, all it contained was a low, three-legged stool. I could see why. Anything more would have been clutter.

The chamberlain had told me, whatever you do, look him straight in the eye; he can't be doing with toadies and flatterers, only sincere admirers. And what an eye it was: small, clear, bright blue, and singular, its twin having been lost to an exploding flask during some exceptionally important chemical experiment. In its place was a ball of clear glass, transparent and slightly magnifying. I could see how that would be an asset in the course of abstruse philosophical debate. Catch sight of it when you aren't absolutely prepared, and your mind goes instantly blank.

(Mine did. Tell you why later.)

He smiled at me. People don't usually do that. "You wanted to talk to me."

I nodded. "I want to ask you something."

"Ask away."

"What do you believe," I said, "is the greatest force for good in the whole world?"

He thought about it for nearly a whole half heartbeat. "Art," he said.

"Really?"

"Yes."

Well, I thought, that didn't take long. "Could you possibly explain why you think that?"

He nodded graciously. "Because art," he said, "is beauty, and beauty is the essence of goodness made visible or audible. When you look at a beautiful statue or listen to beautiful music, you are looking at and listening to beauty, which is goodness itself, a force no human can withstand for very long. Therefore, by creating beauty, the artist opens doors and windows in the human mind through which goodness can come flooding in. What we call evil is simply darkness, the absence of light. Light dispels darkness; goodness dispels evil. Beauty dispels evil. Therefore art is the greatest force for good in the whole world."

I nodded. Then I said, "Excuse me, but that's bullshit."

He grinned at me. "Yes," he said. "And no. What I just told you is essentially true, but only under ideal conditions. And conditions are so very rarely ideal?"

"For example?"

"If you see light through a glass or a raindrop, the light can be distorted. There's a saying, beauty is in the eye of the beholder. Actually, that's wrong. Beauty is absolute, but the eye of the beholder"—he closed his good eye, leaving the glass monstrosity staring straight at me—"is capable of weakening or corrupting it. If you pass light through a raindrop, you break it up into its component parts. If you pass beauty through the eye of an imperfect beholder, you may get nothing; just canvas daubed with oil, or a piece of stone, or the noise made by blowing down a tube with holes in it. Also," he added, "the art may not be particularly good art."

"Ah," I said.

"To counter which," he went on, "we must train the eye, so that the beholder beholds correctly. And we must make good art. When we've done that, art can be the greatest force for good in the world."

"Excuse me." I said. "I said *is*, not *can be*."

He laughed. "But you used the superlative, *greatest*. There are other forces for good, and very strong some of them may be, but you asked for the greatest, and I answered the question you asked. I was also generous enough to point out certain conditions and qualifications, which I needn't have done, strictly speaking."

"I see," I said. "And so you create art to make the world better."

Tiny nod. "And for money." he said, and paused; and when I didn't laugh, continued, "but mostly to open windows in dark places. Such as this."

"You have a project in hand?"

Bigger nod. "The Duke has commissioned me." he said, "to cast for him a great bronze statue to be set up in the parade grounds out there beyond the palace. I have agreed. I shall cast a statue of a colossal bronze horse. It will be my lesser masterpiece."

"Ah yes," I said. "After the child."

I'd said the right thing. "Art is the greatest force for good, but only under the right conditions. Second greatest is the creation of a truly wise and good king. Under the conditions prevailing, the second best is more likely to have more effect more quickly. Once the land is ruled by a truly wise and good king, the conditions necessary for the greatest force to be effective will be established." That was all right, then.

"Thank you," I said.

"I've answered your question?"

"Perfectly. Now I know."

"Knowledge is everything."

"Thank you. I'll go now"

It took me all my strength and determination to back out of the room. As I left, pausing on the threshold to wipe sweat out of my eyes, I glanced at the great man's face. He was white as a sheet.

Let me inside your head for a moment. You're thinking: something is wrong here. That was supposed to be a true record of a debate between—well, yes, some nonentity on the one hand, but on the other, the greatest genius who ever lived. So, either the record is accurate and Prosper of Schanz was just an egotistical fat man, or the narrative is in error, and (come to think of it) we have only this clown's word that he ever met Prosper—

There is, of course, a perfectly reasonable explanation. You try holding two conversations simultaneously, and see how you like it.

It came as a shock, now I think of it, to meet a new face after so many years in the business. When I say *face*—

I don't know you, I said.

She—I'll come back to that in a minute—She looked at me as though I was unimportant but mildly interesting. *I don't suppose you do,* she said.

Of course, I said, *I wouldn't. You're from Schanz, presumably.*

A smile, faintly patronizing but so what? *Falhoel, actually. But well outside your territory. Where I'm originally from, you really don't want to know.*

Of course, I said, and realised I'd repeated myself. *He lived in Falhoel for a while.*

Published Principles of Mathematics *there. And that's where I picked him up.*

And that's why he hasn't published since?

She sort of twinkled at me; smart, She didn't need to say, I like a boy with spirit. *I picked him up before he wrote* Principles.

Ah.

Why *She*? To which I can only say, you had to be there. She looked like—well, maybe they all look like that in Falhoel; in which case, I definitely got a raw deal when the territories were apportioned. I doubt it, though. And why on earth should I be surprised? We—humans—aren't all the same. Some of us look and talk and act like gods and goddesses; some of us look and talk and act like pigs. Just that on my patch, I'd only ever encountered pigs. But so what? That's no more than the difference between Downtown and Old Town, after all.

Now, then, She said. *You're not going to be difficult, are you?*

I thought about it. *I have a duty.*

She yawned. *Yes, of course you do. And if you insist, I'll leave.*

And take half his brains with you?

More than half. She twinkled again. Say about sixty per cent. *And wouldn't that be a loss to the human race?*

Prosper of Schanz, the greatest, et cetera. *Yes,* I said.

Well, then. Or you could leave me in peace. It's not like I'm doing anyone any harm, after all.

I thought about that too. *You must be,* I said. *You have a duty.*

Oh, well, in the very long term, obviously, yes. Her voice was like honey: the sweet-scented honey, where the bees suck on lavender. *There's a grand design, in which he plays a part. But it's very big. It's so big you have to stand a long way back to see it. Close up, what harm am I doing? Quite the reverse, actually.*

I had to ask. *Everything he's ever done, everything he's achieved. That was all—?*

Oh, not everything. Just the best bits. At a rough guess, I'd say sixty per cent.

Not just the paintings and the sculptures (though I had it on the very best authority that art is the greatest force for good in the world). The science, the medicine, the engineering; so little of which he'd so far published—

And which would all be lost, She broke in, *if I had to pack my bags and go. But if I stay—*

He'll start finishing things.

That made Her giggle. *You could put it like that, yes. No promises, mind. But why not?*

I frowned. *Why should you? What about your duty?*

Tut-tut. Silly me. I think Saloninus puts it so well—

And oftentimes, to bring us to our harm,
The instruments of darkness tell us truths

—which, She went on, *is only the half of it. It's so easy to think in black and white all the time, either I win or you do. But it's so much easier and better if we both win. One of us more than the other, maybe, but both of us, definitely. Can't you see the sense in that? No, I don't suppose you can.*

I felt hurt. *Sure,* I said. *Like a joint venture. We get something out of it, so do you. No, come to think of it, I can't imagine that. You and us, collaborating—*

Sigh. *Oh, why not? Just think. Open your mind, just for once. Imagine a man, a single man who contributes more to his species than anyone else, ever. The whole world made bright and glorious by his genius, his ideas—*

Which you put in his head.

Not entirely. Sixty per cent. Well, maybe sixty-five. Yes, She said, *and what's wrong with that, for pity's sake? Like that saying you have: his money's as good as yours. The ideas are pure gold. Well, aren't they?*

Principles of Mathematics. And *Madonna of the Oak Trees.* And the Ninth Symphony. And why should the angels have all the best tunes? *There's got to be something in it for you,* I said.

Twinkle. *Of course there is. But, like I told you, it's the big picture. So big, it probably won't even start working out and coming good in your lifetime. So—not your problem, not your fault. Or would you rather be remembered as the man who murdered Prosper of Schanz?*

I'd always hated all of Them, on sight, instinctively. But not all of Them are alike. The same level of difference as between, say, me and Master Prosper.

This whole thing, I said, *was your idea.*

By "this whole thing," you mean—

The philosopher-king. The perfect society.

Oh, that. No, that wasn't me. That's the grand design. Well, a part of it.

Sixty per—?

Much smaller. Say five. That's one of the good things about not having to die, you can plan for the long term. On the other hand, you do have to be accountable for your mistakes. You've got to face the music, you can't just cheerfully die before you're found out.

*Your grand de*sign, I said. *I could stop it.*

She thought about it. *Stop it,* She said, *probably not. Derail it, divert it, make it take some other shape entirely—well, maybe you could and maybe you couldn't. But don't quote me on that.*

Your grand design.

Yes. But, stop and think, will you?

What on earth could there possibly be to think about?

At which point I heard myself talking to someone. "I've answered your question?"

"Perfectly. Now I know."

"Knowledge is everything."

—and I knew the audience was over. She couldn't get rid of me, but Prosper could. It all comes down to who's stronger, after all.

Knowledge is everything? Bullshit. Besides, it's not what you know—

Their grand design. Think about it, as They would.

They can think long-term much more easily than we can. So, long-term, what would be the worst damage They could do with the ingredients currently under Their control?

The trouble is, you can't always think like Them, just as you can't walk up a wall like a spider, even though you have legs too. Different sort of legs. So, if it were me, designing the grand design—

Easy peasy. Here's a child with all the advantages—monarch of all he surveys, which is always a good place to start from, and also educated by the great man himself, the greatest man ever, who's taught him *everything he knows*. And no secret has been made of this; everyone knows that this kid is destined to be the Superman, the ultimate human being. Absolute power, backed up by absolute and universal goodwill. Just think what the instruments of darkness could do with that.

Just think; not as we think, we mortals, we mayflies. Instead, think as *They* think, aiming for a bigger, better result a hundred years from now, five hundred years, a thousand years, five thousand. And in the meantime, five thousand years of meantime, while their grand design is working itself out… Cities will rise and fall, civilizations. Dust and grass and sand will cover all of us, all our achievements, apart from those of Master Prosper, whose work will survive in translations of translations of translations, while our bones and stones will lie forgotten in the wet earth, unless the plow turns them up, and scholars will puzzle themselves to death trying to decipher our work. And still the grand design won't be complete, the hammer won't have fallen, the snare won't have tightened round the ankle of poor stupid mayfly humanity; so that, when it does, who the hell will there be to connect cause to effect?

But I could stop it. And the price we'd all have to pay would be the life and work of Prosper of Schanz. I ask you, what would you do?

WHAT WOULD *HE* do?

(All my life, I've met so many people, but for me there's only ever one *Him*.) Why would I ask myself a question like that? I'd known Him all my life, so I knew (among other things) that He wasn't exactly bright, certainly not a towering genius like Master Prosper. But I knew Him so well I knew His finer qualities.

Oh, They have them, for sure. It's a bizarre but widespread myth that only heroes have good qualities, and the only qualities heroes have are good; villains are, by definition, all bad. Bullshit.

Think about it. Think of the qualities it takes to be a successful or even a competent criminal. You need courage to climb into a stranger's house, the floor plan of which you don't know, fully aware that the householder is almost certainly well provided with weapons, large dogs, strong and active servants—would *you* want to do that?—and for what? A sackful of small, portable artworks, for which you'll probably get ten groschen on the kreutzer. To which add a calm, deliberate mind, resourcefulness, a steady hand, a delicate touch, the ability to work quickly and methodically. And that's just your scum-of-the-earth, back-alley burglar. Take the truly dreadful, evil men of history, slaughterers of nations in the name of some twisted ideal. Of necessity you must allow them to have had faith (which moves mountains, and without which mere works are in vain) and Hope, Loyalty, and Self-Sacrifice in the Name of the Cause, and practically every other noble and glorious characteristic you can possibly think of, except for the small matter of being in the right...

(Which—the older I get, the more convinced I am—is just fashion anyhow, like the brims on hats or the trimming of ladies' sleeves. And if you don't believe me, just think how much morality has changed—in your lifetime—and then read a little history and ask yourself: Do you really, honestly think these changes will be *permanent*?)

So, He has finer qualities. He knows, instinctively, what's worth suffering pain for, and what isn't. He knows when to leave quickly and gracefully, and when to stick around and be torn out by the roots. In judging whether the game is worth the candle, He knows the price of candles better than anyone else I ever met.

It's not something you tell people about, obviously. Not your parents, not your friends, not your dear old uncle or your favourite aunt: *I can see the devil in people. I can see the devil in you.* And, when you're just a kid, you don't know the rules, what's expected, what is and isn't done, and there's nobody to ask, and you're scared. But you keep on seeing the cat, out of the corner of your eye, and it becomes unbearable not to bark, chase, bite.

Maybe I was different; maybe I'm just a thoroughly bad person, with loads of bad, wicked qualities, such as wanting to bark and liking to bite. Whatever. I managed to keep myself on the leash until I met Him again, in the eyes of my enemy, and that was it, all my self-possession used up. From then on, I was out of control. If I saw one of Them, I went for the throat, and that was that.

We had to move; several times; a lot. Sometimes it was because of all the desperate people crowding round our door, begging, imploring—heal me, make my son better, please cure my mother, she's going to die—and nothing I could do, because it wasn't Them, it was consumption or fever or all the thousands of things that tear you up and kill you that aren't Them. And sometimes it was because It wouldn't go quietly, or reckoned I was only a kid and could be messed with, and you can guess by now how that ended.

Word gets around. They—the other *they*, the good guys—tracked me down and took me away, and taught me to be a better dog; faster, neater, slicker, deadlier. They told me: in all our years of doing this, we've never found one quite like you. Quite a few of them said that to me, but none of them cared to explain exactly what they meant by it.

Ours is a small, select order. We don't have hierarchies, endowments, liturgies, orthodoxies, prebendaries, cathedrals. We aren't exactly popular or fashionable. Kings don't give us vast estates, people don't leave us money in their wills, we don't have handsome vestments or valuable silverware; just authority. But what we lack in wealth and the younger sons of the nobility we make up for in efficiency. And we do have respect. Nothing clears a crowded street faster than one of us.

We don't have a hierarchy, but we can't help having the occasional dog who's even bigger, faster, nastier than the other big, fast, nasty dogs. Nobody wants to be like that—another thing we don't have is ambition, that'd be like pushing and shoving to get to the front of the queue for the gallows—but it happens. It happened to me, and I owe it all to—

You again.

I smiled. *Me.*

I was younger then, of course. Twenty-three, and four years a qualified professional. Cocky as hell and enjoying myself.

Look, He said. *This is stupid. You can't keep picking on me like this. It's unreasonable.*

(Curious thing: as I grew older, more articulate, better educated, so did He. First few times we met, He talked in grunts. But when I started reading books and going to lectures, He started using long words and complex syntax. Would you care to speculate about how that happened? I can't be bothered.)

Fuck unreasonable, I said. *Get out. Now.*

Also, I couldn't help noticing, He was getting smarter. More sophisticated, let's say. Impossible, because He was thousands or millions of years old when I was born, so it wasn't as though we were growing up together. But definitely more cunning. *Sure,* He said. *If you really want me to.*

The host this time was, believe it or not, the public executioner for the south-eastern district of Elagaba Province. He'd been acting funny, people said, for a long time. One day he'd be happy as birds in springtime, whistling, smiling, taking his hat off to ladies in the street. Next day, you'd find him sitting in the dark somewhere, head in hands, crying his eyes out. And the effect on his work—it's quite a skilled business, they told me, there's far more to it than people realise. You need to be able to figure out the length of drop based on the individual's height and weight. You need to judge angles and the precise degree of power to sever the spinal cord. Otherwise, you get people's heads coming off when they're hanged, and not coming off when they're beheaded, and that sort of thing reflects on the community as a whole.

You can pull me out, if you really want to, He said. *You know you can.*

I looked a little bit closer, and got that shivery feeling. Sophisticated; He must have been in there quite some time before it started to show, because He'd sort of expanded into all the tendrils and nerve endings, like grass growing up through netting. Sure, I could pull Him out, but—

You've been busy, I said.

I'll be straight with you, He said. *I've had a rough time of it the last few years. Every time I've got anything settled, one of you bastards comes and moves me on, and every one of you was rough. There's such a thing as proportionate use of force, you know. Or wasn't that on the syllabus where you were?*

I was away sick that day.

What I need, He said reproachfully, *is somewhere I can rest up, just for a bit, long enough to get myself back together, in one piece.*

What you need, I said, *is to get out of there right now.*

Oh, come on, He said. *Be reasonable, for once in your life. I'm not doing any real harm in here. All right, sometimes he's dead miserable, but sometimes he's really happy. It's not like he's biting people or bashing his head against walls.*

I grinned. *You're interfering with his duties.*

Yes, sure. People aren't getting killed on time, and what an appalling state of affairs that must be. You do realise, most of the people he'd have killed, but for me, are completely innocent.

Most?

He sort of shrugged. *Roughly sixty per cent. That's innocent lives prolonged, because of me. That's a good thing, surely? Anyway, here's the deal: you go away and come back in six months, and I promise faithfully, I'll undo all my clever little knots and unpick my stitches and I'll go quiet as a lamb, and not a mark on him. Or you can force me out now, and what's left of his brain will leak out of his ears like honey. Up to you.*

I shook my head. *You're bluffing,* I told Him. *You're playing me for an idiot. I know you. If I leave you in there, you'll just intertwine your way deeper and deeper inside.*

No, I promise. Word of honor.

Have you any idea, I told Him, *how much I could hurt you, getting you out of there by force?*

He took a moment to answer. *Actually, yes.*

And are you asking me to believe that you'd risk that, just to play games with me?

There was a sort of artful gleam about Him, though He tried to hide it. *It's not about how much it hurts me, surely,* He said. *It's how much it hurts* him.

I smiled at Him. *Can't let the likes of you get away with anything,* I said. *Bad precedent. Rule One, we don't negotiate with the instruments of darkness. If the host is injured, that's very regrettable, but it's entirely your fault, not ours.*

I told you, He said, and for all I know, His distress was genuine; for all I care. *Word of honor, I said, didn't I? We can't break our word, you know that. Don't you? Didn't they teach you that at wizard school?*

They taught me Rule One, I said. *No negotiating. Besides, you think you've been really clever, but you're stupid. I can have you out of there with a flick of the wrist, and hardly any damage to speak of. To him,* I added. *Not to you.*

Sorry, I didn't quite catch that. Which of us did you say was bluffing?

I don't appreciate being spoken to like that, not by one of Them, not by Him. Besides, I honestly believed I could do it, without too much friendly harm. We all make honest mistakes sometimes, even the best of us.

Just as well that nobody really likes public executioners, even though they do a necessary job that nobody else is prepared to do.

And word gets about. It must have been a colossal, titanic struggle, people said (even among my own order, who should know better; should have known me better), or it wouldn't have made such a godawful mess of a battlefield. And anyone capable of winning a battle that did so much damage must be—well. *A real piece of work,* I think was the term they used. Meant kindly, I'm sure.

SHE SENT FOR me.

For Her, of course, I wouldn't have gone. For Master Prosper, I had no choice. I could have refused, theoretically; in which case, a range of options, from being thrown out of the Duchy to being dragged into the palace by my heels. I gather schoolmasters have a saying when they're about to thrash some poor kid within an inch of his life: this will hurt me more than it hurts you. Bullshit.

Master Prosper received me in the Alabaster Room, which he'd taken over and converted into a drawing office, studio, and workshop. The end wall had been whitewashed—covering a thousand-year-old fresco of the *Ascension of the Invincible Sun*—and on it, the great man had sketched out in charcoal, actual size, the seven components of the great bronze horse. He was standing on a ladder with the charcoal in his hand, motionless, when I was shown in. He turned his head and smiled at me.

"We were talking," he said, "about the power of art to do good."

"I remember."

"This"—he waggled the stick of charcoal—"will be my masterpiece. What do you think?"

When all else fails, tell the truth. "Magnificent," I said.

He backed down the ladder, feeling for the rungs with his toes. "As a work of art," he said, "and as a piece of engineering. Nothing—nothing—on this scale has ever been attempted before."

"Is that right?"

He laughed. "Take my word for it," he said, "as an engineer."

The Alabaster Room is where they used to hold state banquets and receptions for really important ambassadors. The end wall is vast. It was only just big enough. "I suppose it won't be easy," I said, "casting something that big."

"You could say that." He sat down, waved to me to do the same. "One hundred and forty tons of bronze." He smiled at me once more. "If I tried to cast it in one piece, the sheer weight of the liquid metal would burst the mould, unless I made a mould the size of a mountain, which in turn would crush the wax core inside it as it was built up. But if I make it in pieces, how do I put the pieces together? And consider this: molten metal cools from the outside, while the inside remains hot, and as it cools it shrinks. With an ordinary statue, say life-size, it hardly matters, but on a scale like this, the force of the contraction will shatter the casting. There's a reason—many reasons—why nobody has ever made a statue this big before. Quite simply, it can't be done."

He paused. I think I was supposed to say something, but I didn't.

"The statue," he said, "will be my present to the young Prince. It will be unveiled on the day of his baptism, two months from now."

"That doesn't leave you very much—"

"Can't be done." He grinned at me. "Simply bringing about the golden age isn't enough. People have to be convinced, or they won't believe. They need miracles. My job is to provide them. Simple as that."

I nodded blankly. "Was there something?" I said.

"What?"

"You sent for me."

He gave me a mild frown. "You were interested," he said. "In beauty and the power of art."

He had a point there. I'd forgotten. "Naturally," I said. "But you're a very busy man. I didn't imagine you could spare the time to talk to someone like me. Not unless there was something I could do for you."

He paused again, looking at me as though deciding how best to cut me into sections, for ease of remanufacture (in his image, presumably). "You didn't come here to ask me a facile, pointless question, of no possible relevance to yourself."

"No."

"I know who you are. I know what you do. You know I don't believe in any of it."

I dipped my head slightly in acknowledgment. One must be polite.

"Do you suspect that I...?"

He didn't finish the sentence. Big surprise. The one thing everybody knows about Master Prosper, he never finishes anything. Why should he? Completions are for assistants and apprentices; genius needs only to make the incredible, inspired start.

"It did cross my mind," I said.

He looked at me. Or at least, part of him did. At a rough guess, say forty per cent. "And?" he said.

"Excuse me?"

It hit me like a fist in the mouth. Forty per cent of him was very scared indeed. "You wouldn't have come here, gone to all this trouble, if you didn't have reason to believe— Well?"

"I'm sorry," I said. "I don't understand. You're a skeptic. You think it's all garbage."

"Am I or am I not?"

I counted to three under my breath, and said, "No." He closed his eyes, just for a moment. Then he leaned back in his imperial chair and he wept.

And while he was preoccupied, I looked past him. *I know you're in there,* I said.

No answer.

Was that entirely necessary? I asked.

Playing games. So I reached in—taking very great care that the cuff of my sleeve didn't brush against anything, like the curator of the imperial porcelain, or the imperial scorpion collection—and prodded very gently. She bit me.

That's rude, She said.

What was all that in aid of?

Twinkle. *He's smart,* She said. *He's been thinking. It's gradually starting to dawn on him that he couldn't have done all that clever stuff on his own. Of course, if it hadn't been for me, he'd never have been smart enough to get that far, but that's the thanks you get for helping. So, anyway, you've just set his mind at rest. Thank you.*

If I'd told him the truth—

She sighed. *I'd have had to kill him and then I'd have had the whole tedious job to do all over again, with someone else. Setting the grand design back a hundred years, and depriving humanity of its homegrown god. Not to mention the bronze horse, which is going to be gorgeous, trust me. Though I don't suppose you like art.*

Not much, no.

Barbarian. She sighed. *I'm going to let him make his horse,* She said. *In fact, I'm going to encourage him, and tell him how to do it. Not because it's part of the grand design, or at least it's only a tiny peripheral part, and something far more mundane would do just as well. Simply for the joy of it. You know—a thing of beauty and a joy for ever. Something I can point to, a thousand years from now, and say,* I did that. *Just because it's beautiful.*

I was sick and tired of the sight of Her. *It can't be done,* I told Her. *Not without magic, at any rate.*

No such thing as magic. You should know that, better than anyone.

Delighted to hear it. In that case, it can't be done. He knows why. Ask him.

He's a smart boy. She sounded like a proud mother. *He'll think of something.*

THERE'S SMART, AND there's smart *enough*.

I went away and did some reading in the Temple library; starting (of course) with *Principles of Mathematics* and moving onward and outward—Numerian, Otkel the Stammerer,

Saloninus on the properties of materials, Carnifex's *Mirror of Various Arts*. They confirmed what I already vaguely knew and what Master Prosper himself had told me. Couldn't be done.

There are limits, said the consensus of a thousand years of learning and research. They may seem arbitrary—they are arbitrary—but there are limits to what you can do with wax and clay and molten bronze. Even if you were a giant, twenty feet tall, strong enough to pick up small islands one-handed, there would still be limits. These limits were thoroughly tested by Aimo of Boll, seven hundred years ago; he was commissioned by the emperor to make the biggest possible bronze statue of his eldest son, who had just died of venereal disease at the age of twenty. Expense no object; the full resources of the empire at his beck and whim. So Aimo started with the biggest statue he thought he could get away with, and that worked just fine; then he made one five per cent bigger, and that was fine; the next one five per cent bigger still, and so on. As he progressed, he figured out a series of the most amazingly ingenious fixes, work-arounds, and cheats to cope with various insuperable problems as they arose, learning whole bookfuls of valuable, undreamed-of new stuff about breaking strains and shearing forces and sectional densities and tensile strengths with each successful augmentation, until eventually he reached the point when there were no more fixes, work-arounds, or cheats (like a man on a rock in the middle of the sea, finding he's run out of higher ground to retreat to) and declared, for all time: this is as far as you can go, and no further. And then he set to with his logarithmic tables and his abacus and figured out the ratios and wrote them down; and when I read them, I understood why Master Prosper had arrived at the dimensions of his Great Horse. Aimo's maxima, plus five per cent.

He was too busy to see me, so I wrote him a letter. I said: *If you make your Great Horse five per cent smaller, it'll still be a very big*

horse indeed, and it'll be possible. I didn't expect a reply but I got one. A single word: *Exactly.* And a postscript: *Come and see me, any time you like.*

Valid point. For a man like Prosper of Schanz, if something's possible, why bother doing it?

Fine. But, for reasons of my own—

Why have you suddenly decided to help me? She said.

I shrugged. *You convinced me. Well, he convinced me. Both of you together. You're right, of course.*

Are we?

I nodded. I think so. It's a matter of perspective.

Perspective.

Ask him about it, he's an artist. It's about what's close, what's a very long way away, and all the stuff in between. Also the old saying about birds in hands and bushes.

I'm not sure I follow.

That's because you're not very good at taking yes for an answer. All right. Granted, I told Her, *that your grand design is undoubtedly something very nasty and bad, eventually, in the long term. But you're immortal and I'm not, so if I stop you now, you'll just wait till I'm dead and start all over again, so really, what's the point in me interfering?*

She gave me the look I deserved. *Immortal, yes. Also, not born yesterday.*

I'm not saying I'm happy about it, I told Her. *Or reconciled to it, even. But I've just read a very interesting book about what is and isn't possible. And stopping you isn't possible. Making life difficult, yes. Stopping, no.*

She didn't say anything. I blundered on, like a blind man on a cliff edge. *I can't see a thousand years into the future,* I told Her, *so I can't see the nasty, evil outcome. What I can see is Master Prosper's horse, which is going to be amazingly beautiful. And thousands and millions of people who haven't even been born yet will look at that horse and hear about how it was made, even though it was impossible, and maybe it'll give them that little extra bit of strength and hope they need to persevere with scrambling up this shit heap we call life. And—I don't know, I really can't imagine what you've got up your sleeve that's so incredibly bad and horrible that Prosper's horse wouldn't have been worth it. From our perspective, I mean.*

Twinkle. *I do believe you've actually been listening to what I've been telling you,* She said.

Don't sound so surprised. After all, we're the same in so many things, it's our differences that matter. The only real difference is duration. And, given that difference, why can't we both win? Since our definitions of what constitutes victory—

Ah! She purred like a cat. *Exactly.*

Short-term and long-term, I said. *Who says a thousand years of enlightened peace isn't worth the inevitable smash that comes after it? We both win.*

Also, She said, *you can't stop me. You already admitted it.*

There is that. And you've never actually won anything. Have you?

She didn't answer that. Sore point.

Like the famous general in the Revolutionary War, I went on tactlessly. *Fought twenty-seven battles, got beaten twenty-seven times. But he won the war. Every time we catch up with you, we stop you and throw you out, and it hurts, and you're back to square one. Guess what,* I said. *I'm not unique. After I'm dead, there'll be another one like me, just as powerful. But he won't be prepared to break Rule One.*

Rule One.

Never negotiate with the enemy.

Oh, that's Rule One. No, I see what you mean. And you would?

Rules are made to be broken, I said. *If it's the right thing to do.*

I'd given Her a lot to think about, and Master Prosper was starting to wake up from his after-dinner snooze. *So,* She said, *you want to help me.*

Yes, I said. *I suppose I do.*

A sort of collaboration. Twinkle twinkle. *No offense,* She said, *but how can you help, exactly? He's a genius. You're—*

Yes, I said. *But there's something that's holding you back that I don't have.*

Really? What?

I gave Her my very, very best grin. *Scruples.*

So I WENT to a foundry, where they showed me how you cast things in bronze.

You start with a slab of beeswax, which looks like stale cheese and smells like honey. You carve the wax, and you warm up bits till they're soft and mould them like clay, and squidge them on until you've got what you want, only made of wax instead of bronze. Then you pack the right sort of fine-grained clay all around the wax and fire it in a kiln to make it hard, like brick; this melts out the wax, and you're left with a hollow mould.

Then you get molten wax and you dribble it into the mould and swirl it round, until the sides of the mould are covered in a thick layer of wax. Then you break the mould—very, very carefully; and guess what, you've now got more or less what you started off with (a wax statue), only it's hollow. This is important, because all bronze statues are hollow, to save expensive metal and horribly inconvenient weight. You fill your hollow wax with a sort of soup made of plaster mixed with fine sand, which sets hard; that's called the core. It's brittle, so when the statue's finished, you can smash it into lumps and powder with a thin metal rod and get it out again. To keep the core from shifting during the casting process, you drive little nails through the wax into the plaster.

Next, you warm up some extra wax and roll it out like pastry into thin rods, which you stick at strategic points to your waxwork. These will be the channels, through which the hot metal will flow in and the displaced air will be pushed out. (That's very important; otherwise, you get air pockets and bubbles, which are disastrous.)

Next, you get a whole lot of *exactly* the right kind of clay and you pack it round the waxwork and very *carefully* round the wax channels, packing it very thick indeed, and then you put it in a kiln and fire it, melting out the wax, leaving you with a hollow brick mould with an inner plaster core pinned to the mould with nails. The gap between the mould and the core is where you pour the bronze, and that'll be your sculpture. Melt a load of scrap bronze in a crucible, being very careful not to let the sweat from your face fall in the melt (water and hot metal, very bad; a small explosion, and your eyes full of white-hot shrapnel); grip the crucible in a pair of long tongs and slowly and carefully pour the bronze into the upside-down mould. Go away for twelve hours, come back, smash the mould, and there's your statue, plus strange-looking ivy growing up it (that's the bronze-filled channels, called runners or sprues), which you cut off with a hacksaw and smooth off with a file. Then a quick rubdown with sharp sand, and you're done.

That's a small statue, something you can lift with one hand; a paperweight. Now imagine doing it with a mould the size of a house.

Master Prosper had mentioned some of the problems—the sheer weight of the metal being too much for the mould, differential cooling. There were others. Shoring up the mould internally, with beams like house rafters, so it wouldn't pull apart under its own weight before it set. Or how about balance? The horse would, of course, be rearing on its hind legs, front legs pawing the air. The weight of the front end would be far more than the back legs could bear; they'd either bend or snap like carrots, unless you had an ugly great, big prop to support the front, off-the-ground end. And how do you lift up, swirl round, and upend a brick as big as the White Feather Temple?

I REMEMBER ONE time when I woke up and found myself surrounded by men I didn't know. Two of them had axes, and one had a sledgehammer. They looked terrified. "Don't try anything," one of them said.

"What's going on?" I said. "Who are you? I don't understand!"

They were looking at my hands. I looked at my hands. "Don't try anything." one of them said. A different one, I think.

They tied my hands behind my back, real tight, then tied my feet together with a rope just shorter than my stride, as people do with horses. Don't try anything, they told me, and led me across the street to the Brother's house.

"Ecclesiastical jurisdiction," the Brother explained, looking slightly past rather than at me. "Technically you have benefit of clergy, so civil authority can't try you."

"What did I do?"

My hands were behind my back, but I'd seen what they looked like. I couldn't remember anything; my memory was soft and raw, like the socket where a tooth's been pulled out. But I guessed I'd done something more than cut myself shaving.

He didn't answer in words. Instead he pulled a sheet off something lying on the table—a girl, about twelve; most of her, anyway. I recognised her. I'd evicted an old acquaintance from her brother three days earlier.

"I plead benefit of clergy," I said.

The Brother gave me a sad look. "I'm a clergyman," he said. "I have jurisdiction."

"Not over my order."

Which was, of course, completely untrue, but did he know that? Turned out he didn't.

"You'll have to write to Headquarters at the White Feather Temple," I told him. "They'll send down a duly accredited arbitrator. It'll take about a month?"

That why-does-it-have-to-be-me look—I know it so well. The town council held a brief discussion, which the charcoal merchant lost. He had a cellar, with only one door and no window, only a hatch with bolts on the outside and a padlock. He wasn't happy about it, but what can you do?

One of my colleagues turned up six weeks later. I have no idea what he said to the Brother, but I was back outside in the light before his horse had finished its nosebag. "You clown," my colleague said, once we were out of town.

"You don't understand," I told him. "There was nothing I could've done. It got inside me while I was asleep. The first thing I knew about it was when they showed me the body."

He didn't answer. At the crossroads, he took the left fork, indicating with his hand that I should take the right.

Four months later, I caught up with my old acquaintance.

You should be dead, He said.

I pulled Him out, but not before I'd given Him a few experiences to remember me by. *We'll meet again,* I told Him, *and by then I'll have thought of something even better. Lots of better things. I'm looking forward to it,* I told him quite truthfully.

It was self-defense, he mumbled when eventually I let him go. *You're always so vicious, I can't stand it anymore. So I tried to get rid of you. And whose fault was that?*

Yours, I told Him. *For existing.*

You haven't heard the last of this.

Almost certainly not.

He's persistent but not imaginative. I'm remorseless and my imagination is prodigious. And so it goes, on and on.

THE YOUNG PRINCE, Master Prosper told me, was coming along very nicely. Very clever, very clever indeed. A prodigy.

Master Prosper had taken a liking to me. Whenever he had a spare moment, he liked to walk with me in the cloister. Before the first Duke overthrew the old Republic, the palace had been a monastery. At the center was half an acre of herb gardens, with cloisters running round three sides. Partly, he said, he enjoyed my company; it wasn't often that he had a chance to talk to someone whose mind was so little cluttered with education or accepted opinions—

("You mean I'm stupid."

"Good heavens, no. Just ignorant.")

Partly, he confessed, he wanted to have me near him, because he was scared. Not that he believed in that sort of thing. (He had a sort of intellectual integrity, I'll give him that.) He had proved beyond any reasonable doubt that gods and devils were simply myth and superstition, but deep in his unruly peasant heart ("My father was a village apothecary and my mother was a goatherd's daughter. Can you imagine?") he believed... And belief, like love and sleep, is something you can't do anything about. You can't make it come if you want it, and you can't make it go if you don't.

"It's stupid of me." he told me, in a low voice, "but I'm worried. I don't feel *right*, somehow. Recently I feel as though something is trying to peer inside me. Yes, I know. Me, of all people. But having you close to me reassures me. So, indulge an old fool."

"I've been thinking about what you said the other day," I said, a few days later. She was glaring at me but I ignored Her. "This anxious feeling you've been getting."

He laughed. "Oh, that's all right. Superstition. Just my inner goatherd getting above himself."

Many a true word. "Humor me." I said. "I happen to be a professional. Tell me, this feeling. When did you first notice it?"

He frowned. "I don't really know."

"Might it have been," I said, "shortly after the Prince was born?"

He stopped dead and stared at me. He wasn't the only one. She was yelling at me, but I tuned Her out.

"I think it might have been." he said. "You don't think—?"

"I try not to theorise without data," I said. "You taught me that."

"But the Prince. A newborn child—"

I shrugged. "Particularly vulnerable," I said. "And incredibly tempting, under the circumstances, if you consider the implications."

He sat down on a window ledge. "But that would be terrible. The worst disaster imaginable."

"Yes."

He looked up at me, the way people do. "If it's true—"

"I could tell you at a glance if it is or not."

"Would there be—? Could you do anything?"

I gave him the customers' smile. "Like I said. I'm a professional."

"But very young children—I understand the dangers are considerable."

"Yes," I said. "But I'm the best there is."

He thought, for a very long time. She was howling and screaming and threatening to stop his pulse or give him a massive stroke. It was fun, watching Her lose Her cool like that. "All you need to do is see the Prince, and you can tell, one way or the other?"

"I need to be ten feet away or closer," I lied, "to be absolutely sure."

"That can be arranged."

"If it'll set your mind at rest," I said. I can be so thoughtful and considerate. "It'll only take a minute."

Me again, I said.

Poor soul, He was terrified. *Keep that bastard the hell away from me!* He yelled. I'm not used to Them addressing me in the third person. Then I realised. He was talking to Her.

She didn't seem unduly concerned. *Is that him? The one you told me about, who keeps picking on you?*

That's him, all right. You said—

Did she promise? I asked him. *To protect you from the horrible monster?*

Yes.

After all these years, you still don't know me very well. I grinned at him. *You're safe,* I said. *I can't get you out without hurting the Prince.*

You don't care. You don't give a damn. You never did.

Oh, come on, I said. *You know me better than that.*

I know you. A world of pain and resentment in three little words. *I get it, you're trying to kid—what did you call it,* Her? Pause, while the implications sank in. *You're sick, you know that?*

Why should I bother trying to deceive one of you?

You're capable of anything.

Bless the child, I said, so She could hear me—neat trick, by the way, which to the best of my knowledge none of my order has ever attempted, let alone succeeded. *He doesn't like me. Trying to get me into trouble by pretending I've done bad things. She knows better than that.*

Don't use that word. It's disgusting.

She knows I wouldn't try and pull you out of the Prince, because of the risk. The baby and the bathwater, as the saying goes. I paused, letting him have a nice long soak in my personality. *My job's to save people, not to rip them apart. No, I'm just paying my respects to an old friend, that's all.*

Can't you get him killed or something? he yelled past me, at Her. O*r arrested or banished or something? He's evil. He's a lunatic.*

I sighed. *She's been keeping you out of the loop,* I said. *Didn't She tell you? We're all on the same side now.*

I turned my head, so I couldn't see either of them. "Well?" said Master Prosper.

Smile. "Clean as a whistle," I said. "Nothing in there except the future Duke of Essen."

ACTUALLY. LITTLE WHITE lie there.

Which might explain the violence of His reaction on seeing me; also various other incidents in our relationship. Because it's true, we don't intervene when the damage we'd do to the host outweighs the damage caused by the infestation. Defeating the object of the exercise. Whose side, it could reasonably be asked, are we on, anyhow?

But—well. I'm—I was going to say, only human. On reflection, you may disagree.

It was still His fault, for bearing grudges. I grant you, I was a bit excessive, after that first time He tried to fit me up and kill me. I may have overstepped the line just a bit, with regard to the purely voluntary code of conduct we have in these matters. But what He did after that was—

Did I mention I have a sister? And my sister had a baby.

GENIUS IS A word you hear far too often these days, like *hero* or *tragedy*. Properly speaking, following the criteria officially approved by the Studium's standing committee on nomenclature, there have been only two geniuses so far in the whole of history: Saloninus (of course) and Prosper of Schanz.

Saloninus I know nothing about, except that a lot of scholars now believe he never existed. But Master Prosper, arrogant pinhead and grandson of a goatherd, is a genius, or the word simply has no meaning. To hell with whether or not the Great Horse would eventually get cast in bronze; the sketches alone, scrawled onto a painted-over masterpiece of early Mannerist fresco with a stick of charcoal, were among the most sublime expressions of the human spirit I've ever come across. Now, whether the credit for that goes to him or to Her...or maybe to both of them. There's a school of scholarly opinion that maintains (on what grounds, I have no idea) that They are incapable of creating anything. They can't die; neither can they impart life, either literally or metaphorically. If that's true, then the divine creations of Master Prosper must be, for want of a better word, a collaboration, just as man and woman are both needed to collaborate on a child. The alternative is that all that remarkable stuff was dreamed up and put into practice by that clown, on his own, unassisted—which, having met the man and spent a lot of time with him, I solemnly declare to be unthinkable.

A collaboration, between us and Them—enough to turn your stomach just thinking about it. But maybe that's what it takes to come up with something so unspeakably, unthinkably—impossibly—wonderful as the sketches for the great bronze horse, or the violin concerto, or that extraordinary contraption of birchwood laths, feathers, and string that—if he ever gets around to building it—will turn a human being into a bird.

And if so, would it be too high a price to pay?

Speaking of impossible—I was there when he solved most of the major insurmountable difficulties in the casting process. We were sitting in the cloister garden, on either side of a section of broken column, which served us as a table for our drinks and nibbles. He liked talking to me, he said, forgetting he'd already told me that; or rather, thinking aloud at me. I made him feel safe, and his mind could come out of its shell and soar, instead of cowering.

The weight of the molten metal bursting the mould was nothing, he told me. Simply do the casting in a deep pit, and let the walls of the pit support the sides of the mould. The balance problem? Obvious, really. Fit massive steel rods inside the hind legs of the horse, reaching from hoof to fetlock in one direction and the same length in the other; cut a screw thread on the lower section; the projecting ends of the pins pass through the marble plinth and are secured with washers the size of well-covers and gigantic nuts; thus the statue is bolted solid to the plinth, the ankles are reinforced so they won't snap or bend, and the length of the plinth supplies the balance. As for the problem of moving around these colossal weights: he'd happened to cast an eye over the inventory of the royal arsenal and noticed that somewhere, in a deep, dark shed, the Duke had forty-six trebuchets, mothballed in his father's time, when cannon first came in. Now, what is a trebuchet but an enormous crane, fitted with a substantial counterweight, and perfectly serviceable mechanisms for raising and lowering both counterweight and beam without undue effort through the proper application of mechanical advantage? A few simple modifications, and that would be that.

What about the differential cooling? I asked him. He smiled. He'd given that a lot of thought, he said, and then it suddenly came to him, out of the blue, like (his own simile) being shat on by a seagull. Into the plaster core, insert a network of coiled copper pipes, through which cold water can be continually circulated during the actual pouring of the metal, thereby making sure that the outside and the inside of the bronze cools at approximately the same rate.

Genius, I said. He tried to look modest. Well. Nobody, not even Master Prosper, can be expected to succeed at everything.

Which just leaves, I said, the coating of the inside of the initial mould with wax. Which, unless you can think of a way of picking the mould up and swirling it around—

He scowled at me, and She smirked. *He's a clever boy,* She whispered. *He'll think of something.*

SCRUPLES. YOU MAY remember, I volunteered my lack of such as my contribution to the partnership.

It all depends on how badly you want something; in this case, the success of the project. A few years ago, it was revenge, or (a bit less melodramatically) to get my own back on Him for trying to have me killed. As I said, I may have overreacted slightly. That was His excuse, the next time I met Him, inside the head of my sister's three-month-old daughter.

It's the only place where I know I'll be safe, He said.

You may also recall that when one of Them gets inside an infant, it's horribly dangerous to the host to evict it before the child reaches a certain age, usually two or three years before the onset of puberty. *I give you my word,* He said, *I'll bide here nice and quiet, nobody will know I'm here, I won't hurt her, I'll just curl up in a ball and go to sleep, like a squirrel.*

I was too angry to say anything. I'd warned Him, over and over again: leave my family alone. Play your nasty games with me, if you have to; but if you do anything to them, anything at all, then so help me— And He'd taken no notice. Making a big show of being terrified, but really just laughing at me.

When you're being trained, they give you various no-win scenarios, to see how you react. One of them is a very strong demon firmly dug in to a very weak, vulnerable host. Getting It out would kill the host, no question about it. So what do you do? Leave It in there, to torture and agonise a fellow human being, for as long as the malevolent intruder can keep the physical body alive, purely and simply for the purpose of suffering torment? You have to use your own judgment, they tell you. No good can come of the situation. You have to choose the lesser evil. And if you listen to your scruples, the bleatings of conscience and its misguided appeals to the basic standards of our common humanity, you could well allow a greater evil because you shrink from getting your hands red with a lesser one.

I learned that lesson well. Ten out of ten, alpha double plus, and a commendation.

Afterwards, my sister said it wasn't my fault. I'd done all I could—somehow she'd got the impression that I was a medical doctor—and I wasn't to blame myself.

And I didn't. I don't. I blame Him.

The horse had to succeed. It would mean so much. It would mean everything.

We live in a miserable world, where the best we can honestly hope for is that one empty, meaningless day will follow another without things getting actively worse. A great man once said that the beating of the heart and the action of the lungs are a useful prevarication, keeping all options open. It's a good line (though it doesn't scan properly, in the original), but it presupposes that at least some of the options are good. I'm not convinced. Maybe it's because I've spent so much of my life around immortals (creatures, by definition, of pure evil); the way I see it, when you've got only seventy-odd years maximum, and half of those are going to be spent gradually sliding downhill into arthritis and senility, how the hell can you expect to achieve anything worthwhile?

Unless you happen to be a genius, like Master Prosper. The idea that there are men like that, capable of fiddling around with paper, pens, paints, bits of rock, and using that rubbish to create things so wonderful that even a soul-dead idiot like me has to stop and take his hat off and stare in wonder—it makes you doubt your etched-in-the-bone pessimism, just a little, just for a moment. Only Master Prosper never finishes anything; whereupon we can all say that that proves our point. He gets good ideas, but life is too short.

To put it another way, more concise and less whinging: only two things live for ever, the instruments of darkness and works of genius. Which, I now had disturbingly good reason to believe, might not be such separate categories as I'd once thought. Collaborations.

(Good word. Two artists collaborate on a masterpiece. Traitors collaborate with the enemy.)

Therefore, the horse *had* to succeed, to show that the impossible could be done, and that occasionally, works of genius do get finished. But how—how, in God's name—do you apply a three-inch coating of wax to the inside of a mould for a colossal statue of a prancing horse?

Differential cooling, Master Prosper suggested. Molten wax cools faster against the edges than in the middle. So, fill the mould with liquid wax, and pump it out again.

We tried it, on a one-tenth scale model. Disaster. The wax cooled and went solid inside the hoses of the pump; and with hot wax, you only get so much time. Result: a quarter of the way down, the ample coating on the sides of the mould turned into a solid block. Solid block meant no core, no core meant no water-cooling, meant the whole thing would crumble into bits as soon as the clay was chipped off. Can't be done. Some things are possible; others aren't. Simple as that.

How about, Master Prosper suggested, cutting a hole in the top of the mould and reaching inside with a paintbrush on a very, very long handle? We tried that on the small model. It forty per cent worked, which is to say it sixty per cent failed. There were too many bits where a straight long handle simply wouldn't reach, and hot wax runny enough to apply with a paintbrush won't stick properly to the sides. You'd have to get a man inside, I pointed out, and have him knead half-soft wax into the cracks and crevices with his thumb. And, of course, you couldn't get a man in there. Not enough room.

Stupid, isn't it? You solve half a dozen insuperable difficulties, so why can't you solve just one more? Because some things are possible, and some aren't. Simple as that.

BUT THE HORSE had to succeed. So I made an excuse, and went hunting.

As luck would have it, the first one I ran into was an old sparring partner; we must have run into each other a dozen times over the years. It knew me very well.

Fine, It said as It saw me scowling in at It through some poor devil's eyes. *I give up. I'll go quietly.*

No, you won't, I said. *I've got a job for you.*

You what?

You're going to do something for me, I said. *Or I'll hurt you so badly you'll remember the pain every day for the rest of your everlasting life.*

Two pale eyes gazed at me. If I'd been capable of pity, I'd have felt it. *You're serious, aren't you?*

About the job, yes. And the pain.

Completely stunned. Tens of thousands of years of existence, you think you've heard it all, but apparently not. *You want me to help you?*

I nodded. *Collaboration,* I told It. *It's the next big thing.*

I'd already suggested it, minus one salient detail, to Master Prosper, but he hadn't been interested. Yes, he said, a five-year-old child (a particularly small, skinny one) might just fit inside; but first, where would you find a kid who'd go in there without fainting or dying of fright; and even if you found one, you couldn't possibly trust a kid to do the sort of careful, thorough, skillful job we'd need him to do. Forget it, he said. It's a nice thought, but impractical.

So I went away, and then I came back, leading by the hand a five-year-old girl. She was mine; I'd paid good money for her, in a back alley in Poor Town where you can buy *anything.*

Master Prosper was horrified. "You did what?"

"For the project," I said. "For the horse."

He struggled with himself; and while he was doing it, She was demanding to know what I thought I was playing at. But I wasn't talking to Her.

"It'll be fine," I said. "Think about it. If I hadn't bought her, she'd have led a nasty, brutish, short life in Poor Town and probably be dead at thirty. Instead, she does a quick, simple job for us—not pleasant, but not exactly torture either—and the Duke settles money on her, she grows up well-fed and educated and marries an army officer. We're actually doing her a favour."

He gave me an agonised look. "What makes you think," he said, "she'll go in there? Or do a proper job?"

"Leave that to me."

"But that's—"

"Don't ask."

"What do you mean, don't—?"

"Don't ask."

He went white as a sheet.

Master Prosper's authorised biographers (two of them: one or the other on duty round the clock, day and night) had been part of the royal marriage settlement, to be paid for, naturally, by the Duke. Accordingly they were, strictly speaking, public employees, and therefore had to be accredited members of the Notaries' Guild, whose members take a solemn oath to tell the truth.

But not necessarily the whole truth. For one thing, there simply isn't room, in a book that anyone could ever be expected to lift, let alone read; not for every last detail. Some things, no matter how true, get left out, inevitably. So the account of the casting of the Great Horse lists some of the insuperable problems that the great man overcame and the measures taken to overcome them, but not all. Space does not permit, and so forth.

I see what you meant about scruples, She said to me. We were back on speaking terms, just about.

You were the one who convinced me of the merits of this collaboration idea, I told Her.

Absolutely, She said. *Even so.*

As well as notaries, the biographers are also fully paid-up associates of the College of Authors, so their description of the casting of the Great Horse is much, much better than anything I could come up with. Look it up, enjoy, be suitably inspired. It's an amazing story of obstacles overcome, dreams made real, abstract perfection trapped in a blob of metal like a fly in amber, and if they hadn't done it justice, they'd have deserved to have their legs broken. After all, the making of that story was expensive, even though the end result absolutely justified the means.

I can't describe what it looked like, when the cranes winched it out of the pit—still unfettled and unpolished, gritty and dull from the mould, with the sprues still branching out of it, as though it had been stored all winter and started to sprout. Even so, it was, quite literally, staggering. I turned to Master Prosper and said, "The best thing ever," and I meant it too.

He—they—looked at me. Couldn't say anything, because it wasn't something any of us would talk about, ever, to anyone. But words weren't necessary. We all understood.

ANYWAY, IT ROSE up out of the pit, and was mounted on rollers and hauled into the enormous shed they'd built to house it while it was cleaned up and polished, ahead of the grand unveiling ceremony, in the presence of the royal family, the great man himself, and the entire ruling nobility of the nation. The day before the ceremony, my old friend the chaplain came back from his far-distant posting to bless the statue. I met him outside the shed; it was just starting to get dark. There were four or five heavily laden carts outside, and a small bunch of carters.

I DIDN'T ATTEND the actual unveiling ceremony, which was just as well.

The account in the official biography makes thrilling reading, especially the bit when, at high noon precisely, the Great Horse exploded like a cannon shell, blowing out a crater a quarter of an acre across and raining fragments of bronze shrapnel over half the city. The entire royal family was killed instantly, along with Prosper of Schanz and the flower of all Essen.

To this day, nobody knows who was responsible for filling the inside of the horse with gunpowder, though naturally the finger of suspicion points at the leaders of the Republican faction, who immediately took control of the Duchy and continue in power to this day. Nor—not that it matters, unless you have a morbid taste for technical trivia—has anyone ever been able to explain how the bomb was set off, since a burning fuse would have been painfully obvious, with all the security attending such an event.

Actually, I can explain that. After we sawed a hole in the top of the horse's head and poured in the powder, thirty-five barrels of the stuff, I replaced the horse's enamel eyes with glass ones, which I'd had specially made, following a design in Prosper's *Principles of Mathematics*: the section on burning glasses. I knew where the horse would be at precisely noon, and also the sun. The rest was simple optics. Soldering the top of the head back on was a ticklish business, with all that powder in there, but we got away with it.

The Great Horse was very beautiful indeed. The mythical version of it, which will survive in people's imaginations until there are no more humans left on earth, will be many, many times lovelier, and its effect infinitely more powerful and inspiring. Moral: you can blow up a statue, and its creator, but you can't kill goodness and beauty. Which is another way of saying that the greatest force for good in this world is, of course, Art, especially Art filled with high explosives. I think Master Prosper would have liked that.

(You see, I could have dragged Him out of the Prince, which would have killed the Prince, but then the Duke would've had me hanged, and She'd have got away free. Or I could have thrown Her out of Master Prosper, and She'd have killed Prosper on the way out—the gallows for me, and the Prince would've grown up with my old friend lodged inside him. One but not both—if it hadn't been for Prosper's wonderful horse.)

I met Him again, not long after. He told me He'd lodged an official complaint about me with the proper authorities. Bloody cheek, which I've since given Him reason to regret.

And the grand design goes on, presumably, in some form or other, world without end, amen. But not on my watch.

The Best Man Wins

He was in my light. I didn't look up. "What do you want?" I said.

"Excuse me, but are you the swordsmith?"

There are certain times when you have to concentrate. This was one of them. "Yes. Go away and come back later."

"I haven't told you what I—"

"Go away and come back later."

He went away. I finished what I was doing. He came back later. In the interim, I did the third fold.

FORGE WELDING IS a horrible procedure and I hate doing it. In fact, I hate doing all the many stages that go to creating the finished object; some of them are agonisingly difficult, some are exhausting, some of them are very, very boring; a lot of them are all three, it's your perfect microcosm of human endeavour. What I love is the feeling you get when you've done them, and they've come out right. Nothing in the whole wide world beats that.

The third fold is—well, it's the stage in making a sword-blade when you fold the material for the third time. The first fold is just a lot of thin rods, some iron, some steel, twisted together and then heated white and forged into a single strip of thick ribbon. Then you twist, fold, and do it again. Then you twist, fold and do it again. The third time is usually the easiest; the material's had most of the rubbish beaten out of it, the flux usually stays put and the work seems to flow that bit more readily under the hammer. It's still a horrible job. It seems to take for ever, and you can wreck everything you've done so far with one split second of carelessness; if you burn it or let it get too cold, or if a bit of scale or slag gets hammered in. You need to listen as well as look—for that unique hissing noise that tells you that the material is just starting to spoil but isn't actually ruined yet; that's the only moment at which one strip of steel will flow into another and form a single piece—so you can't chat while you're doing it. Since I spend most of my working day forge welding, I have this reputation for unsociability. Not that I mind. I'd be unsociable if I was a ploughman.

He came back when I was shovelling charcoal. I can talk and shovel at the same time, so that was all right.

He was young, I'd say about twenty-three or four; a tall bastard (all tall people are bastards; I'm five feet two) with curly blond hair like a wet fleece, a flat face, washed-out blue eyes and a rather girly mouth. I took against him at first sight, because I don't like tall, pretty men. I put a lot of stock in first impressions. My first impressions are nearly always wrong. "What do you want?" I said.

"I'd like to buy a sword, please."

I didn't like his voice much, either. In that crucial first five seconds or so, voices are even more important to me than looks. Perfectly reasonable, if you ask me. Some princes look like rat-catchers, some rat-catchers look like princes, though the teeth usually give people away. But you can tell precisely where a man comes from and how well-off his parents were after a couple of words: hard data, genuine facts. The boy was quality; minor nobility, which covers everything from over-ambitious farmers to the younger brothers of dukes. You can tell immediately by the vowel sounds. They set my teeth on edge like bits of grit in bread. I don't like the nobility much. Most of my customers are nobility, and most of the people I meet are customers.

"Of course you do," I said, straightening my back and laying the shovel down on the edge of the forge. "What do you want it for?"

He looked at me as though I'd just leered at his sister. "Well, for fighting with."

I nodded. "Off to the wars, are you?"

"At some stage, probably, yes."

"I wouldn't if I were you," I said, and I made a point of looking him up and down, thoroughly and deliberately. "It's a horrible life, and it's dangerous. I'd stay home, if I were you. Make yourself useful."

I like to see how they take it. Call it my craftsman's instinct. To give you an example: one of the things you do to test a really good sword is make it come compass—you fix the tang in a vice, then you bend it right round in a circle, until the point touches the shoulders; let it go, and it should spring back absolutely straight. Most perfectly good swords won't take that sort of abuse; it's an ordeal you reserve for the very best. It's a horrible, cruel thing to do to a lovely artefact, and it's the only sure way to prove its temper.

Talking of temper; he stared at me, then shrugged. "I'm sorry," he said. "You're busy. I'll try somewhere else."

I laughed. "Let me see to this fire and I'll be right with you."

THE FIRE RULES my life, like a mother and her baby. It has to be fed, or it goes out. It has to be watered—splashed round the edge of the bed with a ladle—or it'll burn the bed of the forge. It has to be pumped after every heat, so I do all its breathing for it, and you can't turn your back on it for two minutes. From the moment when I light it in the morning, an hour before sunrise, until the point where I leave it to starve itself to death overnight, it's constantly in my mind, like something at the edge of your vision, or a crime on your conscience; you're not always looking at it, but you're always watching it. Given half a chance, it'll betray you. Sometimes I think I'm married to the damn thing.

Indeed. I never had time for a wife. I've had offers; not from women, but from their fathers and brothers—he must be worth a bob or two, they say to themselves, and our Doria's not getting any younger. But a man with a forge fire can't fit a wife into his daily routine. I bake my bread in its embers, toast my cheese over it, warm a kettle of water twice a day to wash in, dry my shirts next to it. Some nights, when I'm too worn out to struggle the ten yards to my bed, I sit on the floor with my back to it and go to sleep, and wake up in the morning with a cricked neck and a headache. The reason we don't quarrel all the time is that it can't speak. It doesn't need to.

The fire and I have lived sociably together for twenty years, ever since I came back from the wars. Twenty years. In some jurisdictions, you get less for murder.

"THE TERM SWORD," I said, wiping dust and embers off the table with my sleeve, "can mean a lot of different things. I need you to be more specific. Sit down."

He perched gingerly on the bench. I poured cider into two wooden bowls and put one down in front of him. There was dust floating on the top; there always is. Everything in my life comes with a frosting of dark grey gritty dust, courtesy of the fire. Bless him, he did his best to pretend it wasn't there and took a little sip, like a girl.

"There's your short riding-sword," I said, "and your thirty-inch arming sword, your sword-and-shield sword, which is either a constant flattened diamond section, what the army calls a Type Fifteen, or else with a half-length fuller, your Type Fourteen; there's your tuck, your falchion, your messer, side-sword or hanger; there's your longsword, great sword, hand-and-a-half, Type Eighteen, true bastard, your great sword of war and your proper two-hander, though that's a highly specialised tool, so you won't be wanting one of them. And those are just the main headings. Which is why I asked you: what do you want it for?"

He looked at me, then deliberately drank a swallow of my horrible dusty cider. "For fighting with," he said. "Sorry, I don't know very much about it."

"Have you got any money?"

He nodded, put his hand up inside his shirt and pulled out a little linen bag. It was dirty with sweat. He opened it, and five gold coins spilled onto my table.

There are almost as many types of coin as there are types of sword. These were besants; ninety-two parts fine, guaranteed by the emperor. I picked one up. The artwork on a besant is horrible, crude and ugly. That's because the design's stayed the same for six hundred years, copied over and over again by ignorant and illiterate die-cutters; it stays the same because it's trusted. They copy the lettering, but they don't know their letters, so you just get shapes. It's a good general rule, in fact; the prettier the coin, the less gold it contains; the uglier, conversely, the better. I knew a forger once. They caught him and hanged him because his work was too fine.

I put my cup on top of one coin, then pushed the other four back at him. "All right?"

He shrugged. "I want the very best."

"It'd be wasted on you."

"Even so."

"Fine. The very best is what you'll get. After all, once you're dead, it'll move on, sooner or later it'll end up with someone who'll be able to use it." I grinned at him. "Most likely your enemy."

He smiled. "You mean I'll reward him for killing me."

"The labourer is worthy of his hire," I replied. "Right, since you haven't got a clue what you want, I'll have to decide for you. For your gold besant you'll get a longsword. Do you know what that—?"

"No. Sorry."

I scratched my ear. "Blade three feet long," I said, "two and a half inches wide at the hilt, tapering straight to a needle point. The handle as long as your forearm, from the inside of your elbow to the tip of your middle finger. Weight absolutely no more than three pounds, and it'll feel a good deal lighter than that because I'll balance it perfectly. It'll be a stabber more than a cutter, because it's the point that wins fights, not the edge. I strongly recommend a fuller—you don't know what a fuller is, do you?"

"No."

"Well, you're getting one anyway. Will that do you?"

He sort of gazed at me, as if I was the Moon. "I want the best sword ever made," he said. "I can pay more if necessary."

The best sword ever made. The silly thing was, I could do it. If I could be bothered. Or I could make him the usual and tell him it was the best sword ever made, and how could he possibly ever know? There are maybe ten men in the world qualified to judge. Me and nine others.

On the other hand, I love my craft. Here was a young fool saying: indulge yourself, at my expense. And the work, of course, the sword itself, would still be alive in a thousand years' time, venerated and revered, with my name on the hilt. The best ever made; and if I didn't do it, someone else would, and it wouldn't be my name on it.

I thought for a moment, then leant forward, put my fingertips on two more of his coins, and dragged them towards me, like a ploughshare through clay. "All right?"

He shrugged. "You know about these things."

I nodded. "In fact," I said, and took a fourth coin. He didn't move. It was as though he wasn't interested. "That's just for the plain sword," I said. "I don't do polishing, engraving, carving, chiselling or inlay. I don't set jewels in hilts, because they chafe your hands raw and fall out. I don't even make scabbards. You can have it tarted up later if you want, but that's up to you."

"The plain sword will do me just fine," he said.

WHICH PUZZLED ME.

I have a lot of experience with the nobility. This one—his voice was exactly right, so I could vouch for him, as though I'd known him all my life. The clothes were plain, good quality, old but well looked after; a nice pair of boots, though I'd have said they were a size too big, so maybe inherited. Five besants is a vast, stunning amount of money, but I got the impression it was all he had.

"Let me guess," I said. "Your father died, and your elder brother got the house and the land. Your portion was five gold bits. You accept that that's how it's got to be, but you're bitter. You think: I'll blow the lot on the best sword ever made, and go off and carve myself out a fortune, like Robert the Fox or Boamund. Something like that?"

A very slight nod. "Something like that."

"Fine," I said. "A certain category of people and their money are easily parted. If you live long enough to get some sense beaten into you, you'll get rather more than four gold bits for the sword, and then you can buy a nice farm."

He smiled. "That's all right, then."

I like people who take no notice when I'm rude to them.

"CAN I WATCH?" he asked.

That's a question that could get you in real trouble, depending on context. Like the man and woman you've just thought of, my answer is usually No. "If you like," I said. "Yes, why not? You can be a witness."

He frowned. "That's an odd choice of word."

"Like a prophet in scripture," I said. "When He turns water into wine or raises the dead or recites the Law out of a burning tree. There has to be someone on hand to see, or what's the good in it?"

(I remembered saying that, later.)

Now he nodded. "A miracle."

"Along those lines. But a miracle is something you didn't expect to happen."

OFF TO THE wars. We talk about 'the wars' as though it's a place; leave Perimadeia on the north road till you reach a crossroads, bear left, take the next right, just past the old ruined mill, you can't miss it. At the very least, a country, with its own language, customs, distinctive national dress and regional delicacies. But in theory, every war is different, as individual and unique as a human being; each war has parents that influence it, but grows up to follow its own nature and beget its own offspring. But we talk about people *en masse*—the Aelians, the Mezentines, the Rosinholet—as though a million disparate entities can be combined into one, the way I twist and hammer a faggot of iron rods into a single ribbon. And when you look at them, the wars are like that; like a crowd of people. When you're standing among them, they're all different. Step back three hundred yards, and all you see is one shape: an army, say, advancing toward you. We call that shape 'the enemy'; it's the dragon we have to kill in order to prevail and be heroes. By the time it reaches us, it's delaminated into individuals, into one man at a time, rushing at us waving a spear, out to do us harm, absolutely terrified, just as we are.

We say 'the wars', but here's a secret. There is only one war. It's never over. It flows, like the metal at white heat under the hammer, and joins up with the last war and the next war, to form one continuous ribbon. My father went to the wars, I went to the wars, my son will go to the wars, and his son after him, and it'll be the same place. Like going to Boc Bohec. My father went there, before they pulled down the White Temple and when Foregate was still open fields. I went there, and Foregate was a marketplace. When my son goes there, they'll have built houses on Foregate; but the place will still be Boc Bohec, and the war will still be the war. Same place, same language and local customs, slightly altered by the prevailing fashions in valour and misery, which come around and go around. In my time at the wars, hilts were curved and pommels were round or teardrop. These days, I do mostly straight cross hilts and scent-bottle pommels, which were all the rage a hundred years ago. There are fashions in everything. The tides go in and out, but the sea is always the sea.

My wars were in Ultramar, which isn't a place-name, it's just Aelian for "across the sea". Ultramar, which was what we were fighting for, wasn't a piece of land, a geographical entity. It was an idea: the Kingdom of God on Earth. You won't find it on a map—not now, that's for sure; we lost, and all the places we used to know are called something else now, in another language, which we could never be bothered to learn. We weren't there for the idea, of course, although it was probably a good one at the time. We were there to rob ourselves a fortune and go home princes.

Some places aren't marked on maps, and everybody knows how to find them. Just follow the others and you're there.

"THERE'S NOT A lot to see at this stage," I told him. "You might want to go away for a while."

"That's all right." He sat down on the spare anvil and bit into one of my apples, which I hadn't given him. "What are you doing with all that junk? I thought you were going to start on the sword."

I told myself: he's paying a lot of money, probably everything he's got in the world; he's entitled to be stupid, if he wants to. "This," I told him, "isn't junk. It's your sword."

He peered over my shoulder. "No, it's not. It's a load of old horseshoes and some clapped-out files."

"It is now, yes. You just watch."

I don't know what it is about old horseshoes; nobody does. Most people reckon it's the constant bashing down on the stony ground, though that's just not true. But horseshoes make the best swords. I heated them just over cherry-red, flipped them onto the anvil and belted them with the big hammer, flattening and drawing down; bits of rust and scale shot across the shop, it's a messy job and it's got to be done quickly, before the iron cools to grey. By the time I'd finished with them, they were long, squarish rods, about a quarter-inch thick. I put them on one side, then did the same for the files. They're steel, the stuff that you can harden; the horseshoes are iron, which stays soft. It's the mix, the weave of hard and soft that makes a good blade.

"What are they supposed to be, then? Skewers?"

I'd forgotten he was there. Patient, I'll say that for him. "I'll be at this for hours yet," I told him. "Why don't you go away and come back in the morning? Nothing interesting to see till then."

He yawned. "I've got nowhere in particular to go," he said. "I'm not bothering you, am I?"

"No," I lied.

"I still don't see what those bits of stick have got to do with my sword."

What the hell. I could use a rest. It's a bad idea to work when you're tired, you make mistakes. I tipped a scuttle of charcoal onto the fire, damped it down and sat on the swedge-block. "Where do you think steel comes from?"

He scratched his head. "Permia?"

Not such an ignorant answer. In Permia there are deposits of natural steel. You crush the iron ore and smelt it, and genuine hardening steel oozes out, all ready to use. But it's literally worth its weight in gold, and since we're at war with Permia, it's hard to get hold of. Besides, I find it's too brittle, unless you temper it exactly right. "Steel," I told him, "is iron that's been forged out over and over again in a charcoal fire. Nobody has the faintest idea how it works, but it does. It takes two strong men a whole day to make enough steel for one small file."

He shrugged. "It's expensive. So what?"

"And it's too hard," I told him. "Drop it on the floor, it'll shatter like glass. So you temper it, so it'll bend and then spring back straight. But it's sulky stuff; good for chisels and files, not so good for swords and scythe-blades, which want a bit of bounce in them. So we weave it together with iron, which is soft and forgiving. Iron and steel cancel out each other's faults, and you get what you want."

He looked at me. "Weave together."

I nodded. "Watch."

You take your five rods and lay them side by side, touching; steel, iron, steel, iron, steel. You wire them tightly together, like building a raft. You lay them in the fire, edge downwards, not flat; when they're white hot and starting to hiss like a snake, you pull them out and hammer them. If you've got it right, you get showers of white sparks, and you can actually see the metal weld together—it's a sort of black shadow under the glowing white surface, flowing like a liquid. What *it* is, I don't know, and not being inclined to mysticism I prefer not to speculate.

Then you heat the flat plate you've just made to yellow, grip one end in the vice and twist your plate into a rope, which you then forge flat; heat and twist and flatten, five times isn't too many. If you've done it right, you have a straight, flat bar, inch wide, quarter-inch thick, with no trace of a seam or laminations; one solid thing from five. Then you heat it up and draw it out, fold it and weld it again. Now can you see why I talk about weaving? There is no more iron or steel, no power on earth will ever separate them again. But the steel is still hard and the iron is still yielding, and that's what makes the finished blade come compass in the vice, if you're prepared to take the risk.

I lose track of time when I'm forge-welding. I stop when it's done, and not before; and then I realise how tired and wet with sweat and thirsty I am, and how many hot zits and cinders have burnt their way through my clothes and blistered my skin. The joy isn't in the doing but the having-done.

You weld in the near-dark, so you can see what's going on in the heart of the fire and the hot metal. I looked to where I know the doorway is, but it was all pitch dark, outside the orange ring of firelight. It's just as well I have no neighbours, or they'd get no sleep.

He was asleep, though, in spite of all the noise. I nudged his foot and he sat up straight. "Did I miss something?"

"Yes."

"Oh."

"But that's all right," I said. "We've barely started yet."

LOGIC DICTATES THAT I had a life before I went to Ultramar. I must have had; I was nineteen when I went there, twenty-six when I came back. Before I went there, I seem to recall a big comfortable house in a valley, and dogs and hawks and horses and a father and two elder brothers. They may all still be there, for all I know. I've never been back.

Seven years in Ultramar. Most of us didn't make it past the first six months. A very few, the file-hard, unkillable sort, survived as long as three years, by which point you could almost see the marks where the wind and rain had worn them down to bedrock, or the riverbeds and salt stalactites on their cheeks; they were old, old men, the three-year boys, and not one of them over twenty-five.

I did three years and immediately signed on for another three; then another three after that, of which I served one. Then

I was sent home, in disgrace. Nobody ever gets sent home from Ultramar, which is where the judge sends you if you've murdered someone and hanging is too good for you. They need every man they can get, and they use them up at a stupid rate, like a farmer with his winter fodder in a very bad year. They say that the enemy collects our bones from the battlefields and grinds them down for bonemeal, which is how come they have such excellent wheat harvests. The usual punishment for really unforgivable crimes in Ultramar is a tour of duty at the front; you have to prove genuine extenuating circumstances and show deep remorse to get the noose instead. Me, though, they sent home, in disgrace, because nobody could bear the sight of me a moment longer. And, to be fair, I can't say I blame them.

I DON'T SLEEP much. The people in the village say it's because I have nightmares, but really I simply don't find the time. Once you've started welding, you don't stop. Once you've welded the core, you want to get on and do the edges, and then you want to weld the edges to the core, and then the job's done and there's some new pest nagging you to start the next one. I tend to sleep when I'm tired, which is roughly every four days.

In case your heart is bleeding for me, when the job's done and I get paid, I throw the money in an old barrel I brought back from the wars. I think originally it contained arrowheads. Anyway, I have no idea how much is in there, but it's about half full. I do all right.

Like I told you, I lose track of time when I'm working. Also, I forget about things, such as people. I clean forgot about the boy for a whole day, but when I remembered him he was still there, perched on the spare anvil, his face black with dust and soot. He'd tied a bit of rag over his nose and mouth, which was fine by me since it stopped him talking.

"Haven't you got anything better to do?" I asked.

"No, not really." He yawned and stretched. "I think I'm starting to get the hang of this. Basically, it's the idea that a lot of strands woven together are stronger than just one. Like the body politic."

"Have you had anything to eat recently? Since you stole my apple?"

He shook his head. "Not hungry."

"Have you got any money for food?"

He smiled. "I've got a whole gold besant. I could buy a farm."

"Not around here."

"Yes, well, it's prime arable land. Where I come from, you could buy a whole valley."

I sighed. "There's bread and cheese indoors," I said, "and a side of bacon."

At least that got rid of him for a bit, and I closed up the fold and decided I needed a rest. I'd been staring at white-hot metal for rather too long, and I could barely see past all the pretty shining colours.

He came back with half a loaf and all my cheese. "Have some," he said, like he owned the place.

I don't talk with my mouth full, it's rude, so I waited till I'd finished. "So where are you from, then?"

"Fin Mohec. Heard of it?"

"It's a fair-sized town."

"Ten miles north of Fin, to be exact."

"I knew a man from Fin once."

"In Ultramar?"

I frowned. "Who told you that?"

"Someone in the village."

I nodded. "Nice part of the world, the Mohec valley."

"If you're a sheep, maybe. And we weren't in the valley, we were up on the moor. It's all heather and granite outcrops."

I've been there. "So," I said, "you left home to seek your fortune."

"Hardly." He spat something out, probably a hard bit of bacon rind. You can break your teeth on that stuff. "I'd go back like a shot if there was anything left for me there. Where were you in Ultramar, precisely?"

"Oh, all over the place," I said. "So, if you like the Mohec so much, why did you leave?"

"To come here. To see you. To buy a sword." A decidedly forced grin. "Why else?"

"What do you need a sword for in the Mohec hills?"

"I'm not going to use it there."

The words had come out in a rush, like beer spilt when some fool jostles your arm in the taproom. He took a deep breath, then went on, "At least, I don't imagine I will."

"Really."

He nodded. "I'm going to use it to kill the man who murdered my father, and I don't think he lives round here."

I GOT INTO this business by accident. That is, I got off the boat from Ultramar, and fifty yards from the dock was a forge. I had one thaler and five copper stuivers in my pocket, the clothes I'd worn under my armour for the last two years, and a sword worth twenty gold angels that I'd never sell, under any circumstances. I walked over to the forge and offered to give the smith the thaler if he taught me his trade.

"Get lost," he said.

People don't talk to me like that. So I spent the thaler on a third-hand anvil, a selection of unsuitable hammers, a rasp, a leg-vice and a bucket, and I lugged that damned anvil around with me—three hundredweight—until I found a half-derelict shed out back of a tannery. I offered the tanner three stuivers for rent, bought a stuiver's worth of rusty files and two barley loaves, and taught myself the trade, with the intention of putting the other smith out of business within a year.

In the event it took me six months. I grant you, I knew a little bit more about the trade than the foregoing implies; I'd sat in the smithy at home on cold mornings and watched our man there, and I pick things up quickly. Also, you learned to do all sorts of things in Ultramar, particularly skills pertaining to repairing or improvising equipment, most of which we got from the enemy, with holes in it. When I decided to specialise, it was a toss-up whether I was going to be a swordsmith or an armourer. Literally; I flipped a coin for it. I lost the toss, and here I am.

DID I MENTION that I have my own water-wheel? I built it myself and I'm ridiculously proud of it. I based it on one I saw (saw, inspected, then set fire to) in Ultramar. It's overshot, with a twelve-foot throw, and it runs off a stream that comes tumbling and bouncing down the hill and over a sheer cliff where the hill-side's fallen away. It powers my grindstone and my trip hammer, the only trip hammer north of the Vossin, also built by me. I'm a clever bugger.

You can't forge weld with a trip hammer; you need to be able to see what you're doing, and feel the metal flowing into itself. At least, I can't. I'm not perfect. But it's ideal for working the finished material down into shape, takes all the effort out of it, though by God you have to concentrate. A light touch is what you need. The hammer head weighs half a ton. I've had so much practice I can use it to break the shell on a boiled egg.

I also made spring-swedges, for putting in fullers and profiling the edges of the blade. You can call it cheating if you like; I prefer to call it precision and perfection. Thanks to the trip-hammer and the swedges I get straight, even, flat, incrementally distal-tapered sword blades that don't curl up like corkscrews when you harden and quench them; because every blow of the hammer is exactly the same strength as the previous one, and the swedges allow no scope for human error, such as you inevitably get trying to judge it all by eye.

If I were inclined to believe in gods, I think I'd probably worship the trip-hammer, even though I made it myself. Reasons: first, it's so much stronger than I am, or any man living, and tireless, and those are essential qualities for a god. It sounds like a god; it drowns out everything, and you can't hear yourself think. Second, it's a creator. It shapes things, turns strips and bars of raw material into recognisable objects with a use and a life of their own. Third, and most significant, it rains down blows, tirelessly, overwhelmingly, it strikes twice in the time it takes my heart to beat once. It's a smiter, and that's what gods do, isn't it? They hammer and hammer and keep on hammering, till either you're swaged into shape or you're a bloody pulp.

"Is that it?" he said. I could tell he wasn't impressed.

"It's not finished. It has to be ground first."

My grindstone is as tall as I am, a flat round sandstone cheese. The river turns it, which is just as well, because I couldn't. You have to be very careful, with the most delicate touch. It eats metal, and heats it too, so if your concentration wanders for a split second, you've drawn the temper and the sword will bend like a strip of lead. But I'm a real artist with a grindstone. I wrap a scarf three times round my nose and mouth, to keep the dust from choking me, and wear thick gloves, because if you touch the stone when it's running full-tilt, it'll take your skin off down to the bone before you can flinch away. When you're grinding, you're the eye of a storm of white and gold sparks. They burn your skin and set your shirt on fire, but you can't let little things like that distract you.

Everything I do takes total concentration. Probably that's why I do this job.

I DON'T DO fancy finishes. I say, if you want a mirror, buy a mirror. But my blades take and keep an edge you can shave with, and they come compass.

"Is this strictly necessary?" he asked, as I clamped the tang in the vice.

"No," I said, and reached for the wrench.

"Only, if you break it, you'll have to start again from scratch, and I want to get on."

"The best ever made," I reminded him, and he gave me a grudging nod.

For that job I use a scroll monkey. It's a sort of massive fork you use for bending scrollwork, if that's your idea of a useful and productive life. It takes every last drop of my strength (and I'm no weakling), all to perform a test that might well wreck the thing that's been my life and soul for the last ten days and nights, which the customer barely appreciates and which makes me feel sick to my stomach. But it has to be done. You bend the blade until the tip touches the jaw of the vice, then you gently let it go back. Out it comes from the vice, and you lay it on the perfectly straight, flat bed of the anvil. You get down on your knees, looking for a tiny hair of light between the edge of the blade and the anvil. If you see it, the blade goes in the scrap.

"Here," I said, "come and look for yourself."

He got down beside me. "What am I looking for, exactly?"

"Nothing. It isn't there. That's the point."

"Can I get up now, please?"

Perfectly straight; so straight that not even light can squeeze through the gap. I hate all the steps on the way to perfection, the effort and the noise and the heat and the dust, but when you get there, you're glad to be alive.

I slid the hilt, grip and pommel down over the tang, fixed the blade in the vice and peened the end of the tang into a neat little button. Then I took the sword out of the vice and offered it to him, hilt first. "All done," I said.

"Finished?"

"Finished. All yours."

I remember one kid I made a sword for, an earl's son, seven feet tall and strong as a bull. I handed him his finished sword; he took a good grip on the hilt, then swung it round his head and brought it down full power on the horn of the anvil. It bit a chunk out, then bounced back a foot in the air, the edge undamaged. So I punched him halfway across the room. You clown, I said, look what you've done to my anvil. When he got up, he was in tears. But I forgave him, years later. There's a thrill when you hold a good sword for the first time. It sort of tugs at your hands, like a dog wanting to be taken for a walk. You want to swish it about and hit things with it. At the very least, you do a few cuts and wards, on the pretext of checking the balance and the handling.

He just took it from me, as though I'd given him a shopping list. "Thanks," he said.

"My pleasure," I replied. "Well, goodbye. You can go now," I added, when he didn't move. "I'm busy."

"There was something else," he said.

I'd already turned my back on him. "What?"

"I don't know how to fence."

He was born, he told me, in a haybarn on the moor overlooking his father's house, at noon on Midsummer's Day. His mother, who should have known better, had insisted on riding out in the dog-cart with her maid to take lunch to the hawking-party. Her pains came on, and there wasn't time to get back to the house, but the barn was there and full of clean hay, with a stream nearby. His father, riding home with his hawk on his wrist, saw her from the track, lying in the hay with the baby on her lap. He'd had a good day, he told her. They'd got four pigeons and a heron.

His father hadn't wanted to go to Ultramar; but he held of the duke and the duke was going, so he didn't really have any choice.

In the event, the duke died of camp fever a week after they landed. The boy's father lasted nine months; then he got himself killed, by his best friend, in a pointless brawl in a tavern. He was twenty-two when he died. "The same age," said the boy, "as I am now."

"That's a sad story," I told him. "And a very stupid one. Mind you, all stories from Ultramar are stupid, if you ask me."

He scowled at me. "Maybe there's too much stupidity in the world," he said. "Maybe I want to do something about it."

I nodded. "You could diminish the quantity considerably by dying, I grant you. But maybe it's too high a price to pay."

His eyes were cold and bright. "The man who killed my father is still alive," he said. "He's settled and prosperous, happy, he's got everything he could possibly want. He came through the nightmare of Ultramar, and now the world makes sense to him again, and he's a useful and productive member of society, admired and respected by his peers and his betters."

"So you're going to cut his throat."

He shook his head. "Not likely," he said. "That would be murder. No, I'm going to fight him sword to sword. I'm going to beat him, and prove myself the better man. Then I'll kill him."

I was tactfully silent for a moment. Then I said; "And you know absolutely nothing about swordfighting."

"No. My father should've taught me, it's what fathers do. But he died when I was two years old. I don't know the first thing about it."

"And you're going to challenge an old soldier, and you're going to prove yourself the better man. I see."

He was looking me straight in the eye. I always feel uncomfortable when people do that, even though I spend my life gazing at white-hot metal. "I asked about you," he said. "They reckon you were a great fencer."

I sighed. "Who told you that?"

"Were you?"

"*Were* implies a state of affairs that no longer prevails," I said. "Who told you about me?"

He shrugged. "Friends of my father. You were a legend in Ultramar, apparently. Everybody'd heard of you."

"The defining characteristic of a legend is that it isn't true," I said. "I can fight, a bit. What's that got to do with anything?"

"You're going to teach me."

I remember one time in Ultramar, we were smashing up this village. We did a lot of that. They called it *chevauchée,* but that's just chivalry talk for burning barns and stamping on chickens. It's supposed to break the enemy's will to fight. Curiously enough, it has exactly the opposite effect. Anyway, I was in this farmyard. I had a torch in my hand, and I was going to set fire to a hayrick, like you do. And there was this dog. It was a stupid little thing, the sort you keep to catch rats, little more than a rat itself; and it jumped out at me, barking its head off, and it sank its teeth into my leg, and it simply would not let go, and I couldn't get at it to stab it with my knife, not without stabbing myself in the process. I dropped the torch and danced round the farmyard, trying to squash it against walls, but it didn't seem to make any odds. It was the most ridiculous little thing, and in the end it beat me. I staggered out into the lane, and it let go, dropped off and sprinted back into the yard. My sergeant had to light the rick with a fire-arrow, and I never lived it down.

I looked at him. I recognised the look in his silly pink face. "Is that right?" I said.

"Yes. I need the best sword and the best teacher. I'll pay you. You can have the fifth coin."

A gold besant. Actually, the proper name is *hyperpyron,* meaning 'extra fine'. The enemy took so many of them off us in Ultramar that they adopted them in place of their own currency. That's war for you; the enemy turn into you, and you turn into them, like the iron and steel rods under the hammer. The only besants you see over here are ones that got brought back, but they're current everywhere. "I'm not interested in money," I said.

"I know. Neither am I. But if you pay a man to do a job and he takes your money, he's obliged."

"I'm a lousy teacher," I told him.

"That's all right, I'm a hopeless student. We'll get on like a barn on fire."

If ever I get a dog, it'll be one of those rat-like terriers. Maybe I just warm to aggressive creatures, I don't know. "You can take your coin and stick it where the sun doesn't shine," I told him. "You overpaid me for the sword. We'll call it change."

THE SWORD ISN'T a very good weapon. Most forms of armour are proof against it, including a properly-padded jerkin, it's too long to be handy in a scrum and too light and flimsy for serious bashing. In a pitched battle, give me a spear or an axe any time; in fact, nine times out of ten you'd be better off with everyday farm tools—staffhooks, beanhooks, muckforks, provided they're made of good material and properly tempered. Better still, give me a bow and someone in armour to hide behind. The fighting man's best view of a battlefield is down an arrow, from under a pikeman's armpit. For self-defence on the road, I favour the quarterstaff; in the street or indoors, where space to move is at a premium, the knife you cut your bread and peel your apples with is as good as anything. You're used to it, for one thing, and you know where it is on your belt without having to look.

About the only thing a sword is really good for is sword-fighting—which in practice means duelling, which is idiotic and against the law, or fencing, which is playing at fighting, good fun and nobody gets hurt, but not really my idea of entertainment—and showing off. Which is why, needless to say, we all went to Ultramar with swords on our hips. Some of us had beautiful new swords, the more fortunate ones had really old swords, family heirlooms, worth a thousand acres of good farmland, with buildings, stock and tenants. The thing is—don't say I told you so—the old ones aren't necessarily the best. There was even less good steel about two hundred years ago than there is now, and men were stronger then, so old swords are heavier, harder to use, broader and with rounded points for cutting, not thrusting. Not that it mattered. Most of those young swashbucklers died of the poisoned shits before the desert sun had had a chance to fade the clothes they arrived in, and their swords were sold to pay their mess bills. You could pick up some real bargains back then, in Ultramar.

"I DON'T KNOW how to teach," I said, "I've never ever done it. So I'm going to teach you the way my father taught me, because it's the only way I know. Is that all right?"

He didn't notice me picking up the rake. "Fine," he said. So I pulled the head off the rake—it was always loose—and hit him with the handle.

I remember my first lesson so well. The main difference was, my father used a broom. First, he poked me in the stomach, hard, with one end. As I doubled up, gasping for breath, he hit my kneecap, so I fell over. Then he put the end of the broom-handle on my throat and applied controlled pressure.

I could only just breathe. "You didn't get out of the way," he explained.

I was five when I had my first lesson, and easier to teach to the ground than a full-grown man. I had to tread on the inside of his knee to get him to drop. When eventually he got his breath back, I saw he was crying; actually in tears. "You didn't get out of the way," I explained.

He looked up and me and wiped his nose with the back of his hand. "I see," he said.

"You won't make that mistake again," I told him. "From now on, whenever a fellow human being is close enough to hit you, you're going to assume that he's going to hit you. You'll keep your distance, or you'll be ready to avoid at a split second's notice. Got that?"

"I think so."

"No exceptions," I said. "Not any, ever. Your brother, your best friend, your wife, your six-year-old daughter, it makes no odds. Otherwise you'll never be a fighter."

He stared at me for a moment, and I guessed he'd understood. It was like that moment in the old play, where the Devil offers the scholar the contract, and the scholar signs it.

"Get up."

I hit him again when he was halfway to his feet. It was just a light tap on the collarbone: just enough to hurt like hell without breaking anything.

"This is all for my own good, I take it."

"Oh, yes. This is the most important lesson you'll ever learn."

We spent the next four hours on footwork: the traces, which is backwards and forwards, and the traverses, which is side to side. Each time I hit him, I laid it on a bit harder. He got there eventually.

MY FATHER WASN'T a bad man. He loved his family dearly, with all his heart; nothing meant more to him. But he had a slight, let's say, kink in his nature—like the cold spot or the inclusion you sometimes get in a weld, where the metal wasn't quite hot enough, or a bit of grit or crap gets beaten into the joint. He liked hurting people; it gave him a thrill. Only people, not animals. He was a fine stockman and a humane and conscientious hunter, but he dearly loved to hit people and make them squeal.

I can understand that, partly because I'm the same, though to a lesser degree, and I control it better. Maybe it's always been there in the blood, or maybe it was a souvenir from Ultramar; both, probably. I rationalise it in forge welding terms. You can heat the metal white-hot, but you can't just lay one bit on top of the other and expect them to weld. You've got to hit them to make the join. Carefully, judiciously, not too hard and not too soft. Just enough to make the metal cry, and weep sparks. I hate it when they burst into tears, though. It makes me despise them, and I have to take pains to control my temper. Anyway, you can see why I like to stay out of people's way. I know what's wrong with me; and knowing your own flaws is the beginning of wisdom. I'm sort of a reverse fencer. I stay well out of distance, partly so that people can't hit me, mostly so I can't hit them.

ONCE YOU'VE LEARNED footwork, the rest is relatively easy. I taught him the eight cuts and the seven wards (I stick to seven; the other four are just elaborations). He picked them up quickly, now that he understood the essence—*don't let him hurt you*, followed by *make him safe*.

"The best way to make a man safe," I told him, "is to hurt him. Pain will stop him in his tracks. Killing doesn't always do it. You can stab a man and he'll be past all hope, but he can still hurt you very badly before he drops to the ground. But if you paralyse him with pain, he's no longer a threat. You can then despatch him, or let him go, at your pleasure."

I demonstrated; I flicked past his guard and prodded him in the stomach with my rake-handle; a lethal thrust, but he was still on his feet. Then I cracked him on the knee, and he dropped. "Killing's irrelevant," I told him. "Pain wins fights. That's unless you've absolutely set your heart on cleaving him to the navel, and that's just melodrama, which will get you killed. In a battle, hurt him and move on to the next threat. In a duel, win and be merciful. Fewer legal problems that way."

I was rather enjoying being a teacher, as you've probably gathered. I was passing on valuable knowledge and skill, which is in itself rewarding, I was showing off and I was hitting an annoying sprig of the nobility for his own good. What's not to like?

You learn best when you're exhausted, desperate and in pain. Ultramar taught me that. I kept him at it from dawn till dusk, and then we lit the lamp and did theory. I taught him the line and the circle. Instinctively you want to fight up and down a line, forward to attack, backwards to defend; parry, then lunge, then parry. All wrong. Idiotic. Instead, you should fight in a circle, stepping sideways, so you avoid him and can hit him at the same time. Never just defend; always counterattack. Every handstroke you make should be a killing stroke, or a stopping stroke. And for every movement of the hand, a movement of the foot—there, I've just taught you the whole secret and mystery of swordsmanship, and I never had to hit you once.

"Most fights," I told him, giving him a chance to wipe the blood out of his eyes before we moved on, "in which at least one party is competent, last one to four seconds. Anything more than that is a fitting subject for epic poetry." Judging that he wasn't ready yet, I shot a quick *mandiritto* at the side of his head. He stepped back and left out of the way without thinking, and my heart rejoiced inside me, as I sidestepped his riposte in straight time and closed the door with the Third Ward. So far he hadn't hit me once, which was a little disappointing; but he'd come close four times, in six hours. Very promising indeed. He just lacked the killer instinct.

"The Fifth Ward," I went on, and he lunged. I almost didn't read it, because he'd disguised the Boar's Tooth as the Iron Gate; all I could do was trace back very fast and smack the stick out of his hands. Then I whacked him, for interrupting me when I was talking. He very nearly got out of the way, but I wanted to hit him, so he couldn't.

He had to pick himself up off the ground after that. I took a long step back, to signal a truce. "I think it's time for a progress report," I said. "At the moment, you're very good indeed. Not the best in the world, but more than capable of beating ninety-nine men in a hundred. Would you like to stop there, and save yourself further pain and humiliation?"

He got up slowly and dabbed at his cut eye. "I want to be the best," he said. "If that's all right."

I shrugged. "I don't think you ever can be," I told him. "In order to be the best, you have to lose so much. It's just not worth it. Being the best will make you into a monster. Stick with just plain good, you'll be so much happier."

He was a pitiful sight, all cuts and bruises. But still, under all the blood and discoloured tissue, a hopeful, pretty boy. "I think I'd like to carry on just a bit longer, if you don't mind."

"Please yourself," I said, and let him pick up his stick.

Actually, he reminded me a lot of myself at his age.

I was a brash, irritating boy when I went to Ultramar. I'd known all along that I wasn't going to get the land, having elder brothers in good health. Probably I'd always resented that. I think I'd have made a good farmer. I was always the one who wasn't afraid of hard work, who saw the need to get things done—not tomorrow, or when we've got five minutes, or when it stops raining, but now, right now; before the roof-tree breaks and the barn falls down, before the fence-posts snap off and the sheep get out into the marsh, before the oats spoil on the stalk, before the meat goes off in the heat; now while there's still time, before it's too late. Instead, I saw the place gradually falling to pieces—and decline and decay are so peacefully gradual; grass takes so long to grow up through the cobbles, it's imperceptible, therefore not threatening. But my father and my brothers didn't share my view. I was keen to get away from them. I wanted to take a sword and slice myself a fat chunk of the world off the bone. There's good land in Ultramar, they told me, all it needs is a bit of hard work and it could be the best in the world.

The very best; that's a concept that's danced ahead of me, just out of reach, all my life. Now, of course, I am the very best, at one small corner of one specific craft. I'm stuck, wedged in by my own preeminence, like a rafter lying across your leg in a burning house.

But never mind; I went to Ultramar aiming to be a farmer. When I got there, I found what was left after seventy years of continual reciprocal chevauchées. I recognised it at once. It was what was going to happen to my father's land back home, but in macrocosm. All the barns fallen, all the fences broken down, all the crops spoilt, briars and nettles neck-high in all the good pastures; the effects of peace and idleness accelerated and forced (like you force early crops, under straw) by the merely instrumental action of the wars. Cut myself off a slice of *that*, I said to myself; why the hell would I want to bother? So I started hurting people instead.

And the thing is, if you do it in war, they praise you for it. Strange, but true.

In war, there's so much scope, you can afford to be selective. You can afford to limit yourself to hurting the enemy, of whom there are plenty to go round, and twice as many again once you've finished what's on your plate. I survived in Ultramar because I was having the time of my life, for a while.

Odd thing about farmers; they love their land and their stock and their buildings, fences, trees, but give them the chance to wreck someone else's land, kill their stock, burn their buildings, smash their fences, maim their trees, and after a brief show of reluctance they go to it with a will. I think it's just basic revenge; take that, agriculture, that'll learn you. Volunteers for a chevauchée? My hand was up before I had time to think.

And then I did something bad, and I had to come home. I cried when they pronounced sentence. I despise men who cry. They told me, I was to be spared the noose in recognition of my years of valiant and honourable service. I don't think so. I think they were just being very, very spiteful.

THERE CAME A moment, very sudden and unexpected, when it was over, and I'd succeeded. I went to smack him—a feint high followed by a cut low—and he simply wasn't there to be hit; and then my ear stung horribly, and while I was confused and distracted by the pain, he dug me in the pit of the stomach with his broom-handle.

He wasn't like me. He took a long step back and let me recover. "I'm sorry," he said.

It took me quite a while to get back enough breath to say, "No, don't apologise, whatever you do." Then I squared up into First. "Again."

"Really?"

"Don't be so bloody stupid. Again."

I let him come at me, because attacking is so much harder. I read him like a book, swung easily into a traverse and the devastating *volte*, my speciality; and he cracked me on the elbow as I floundered past him, then prodded me in the small of the back, just before I overbalanced and fell over.

He helped me up. "I think I'm starting to get the hang of this," he said.

I went for him. I wanted to beat him, more than I've ever wanted anything. I couldn't get anywhere near him, and he kept hitting me, gently, just to make a point. After a dozen or so passes, I dropped to my knees. All my strength had drained out of me, as though one of his gentle prods had punctured right to my heart. "I give up," I said. "You win."

He was looking down at me with a sort of confused frown. "I don't follow."

"You've beaten me," I said. "You're now the better man."

"Really?"

"What do you want, a bloody certificate? Yes."

He nodded slowly. "Which makes you the best ever teacher," he said. "Thank you."

I threw away the rake-handle. "You're welcome," I said. "Now go away. We're finished with each other."

He was still looking at me. "So am I really the best swordsman in the world?"

I laughed. "I don't know about that," I said, "but you're better than me. That makes you very good indeed. I hope you're satisfied, because as far as I'm concerned, this has been a pretty pointless exercise."

"No," he said, and his tone of voice made me look at him. "This was all for a purpose, remember."

Actually, I'd forgotten, briefly. "Oh yes," I said, "it's so you can kill the man who murdered your father." I shook my head. "You still want to do that."

"Oh, yes."

I sighed. "I'd hoped I might have smacked some sense into you," I said. "Come on, you must've learned something. Think about it. What's that possibly going to achieve?"

"It'll make me feel better," he said.

"Right. I don't think so. I've killed God knows how many people, all of them the enemy, and believe me, it never makes you feel better. It just hardens you, like forging the edges."

He grinned. "And hard is brittle, yes, I know. The extended metaphor hasn't been lost on me, I assure you."

It didn't hurt quite so much by then, and I was breathing almost normally. "Well," I said, "I guess it's something you've got to get out of your system, and then you can get on with your life. You carry on, and good luck to you."

He smiled at me, awkwardly. "So I have your blessing, then?"

"That's a bloody stupid way of putting it, but if you want to, then yes. My blessing go with you, my son. There, is that what you wanted?"

He laughed. "As a father you have been to me, for a little while." It was a quotation from somewhere, though I can't place it. "You think I can beat him?"

"I don't see why not."

"Neither do I," he said. "It's always easier the second time."

Now I'm not particularly slow on the uptake, not usually. Burt I admit, it took me a moment. And in that moment, he said, "You never asked my name."

"Well?"

"My name is Aimeric de Peguilhan," he said. "My father was Bernhart de Peguilhan. You murdered him in a brawl, in Ultramar. You smashed his skull with a stone bottle, when his back was turned." He dropped the broom-handle. "Wait there," he said, "I'll fetch the swords and be right back."

I'M TELLING THIS story, so you know what happened.

He had the best sword ever made, and I'd taught him everything I ever knew, and he ended up better than me; he was always better than me, just like his father. Nearly everybody's better than me, in most respects. One way in which he excelled me was, he lacked the killer instinct.

But he made a pretty fight of it, I'll give him that. I wish I could have watched that fight, instead of being in it; there never was better entertainment, and all wasted, because there was nobody to see. Naturally you lose all track of time, but my best educated guess is, we fought for at least five minutes, which is an eternity, and never a hair's breadth of difference between us. It was like fighting your own shadow, or your reflection in the mirror. I read his mind, he read mine. To continue the tedious extended metaphor, it was forge welding at its finest. Well, I look back on it in those terms, the same way I look back on all my best completed work, with pleasure once it's over, but hating every minute of it while I'm actually doing it.

When I wake up in the middle of the night in a muck sweat, I tell myself I won because he trod on a stone and turned his ankle, and the tiny atom of advantage was enough. But it's not true. I'm ashamed to say I beat him fair and square, through stamina and the simple desire to win; killer instinct. I made a little window of opportunity by feigning an error. He believed me, and was deceived. It was only a tiny opportunity, no scope for choice; I had a fraction of a second when his throat was exposed and I could reach it with a scratch-cut with the point, what we call a *stramazone*. I cut his throat, then jumped back to keep from getting splashed all over. Then I buried him in the midden, along with the pig-bones and the household shit.

HE SHOULD HAVE won. Of course he should. He was basically a good kid, and had he lived he'd probably have been all right, more or less; no worse than my father, at any rate, and definitely a damn sight better than me. I like to tell myself, he died so quickly he never knew he'd lost.

But on the day, I proved myself the better man, which is what swordfighting is all about. It's a simple, infallible test, and he failed and I passed. The best man always wins; because the definition of *best* is, *still alive at the end*. Feel at liberty to disagree, but you'll be wrong. I hate it, but it's the only definition that makes any sense at all.

Every morning I cough up black soot and grey mud, the gift of the fire and the grindstone. Smiths don't live long. The harder you work, the better you get, the more poisonous muck you breathe in. My preeminence will be the death of me, some day.

I sold his sword to the Duke of Scona for, I forget how much; it was a stupid amount of money, at any rate, but the Duke said he wanted the very best, and he got what he paid for. My barrel of gold is now nearly full, incidentally. I don't know what I'll do when the level reaches the top. Something idiotic, probably.

I may have all the other faults in the world, but at least I'm honest. You have to grant me that.

Habitat

Deserts grow. Woe betide him who harbours deserts.
—(Nietzsche, Also Sprach Zarathustra)

He looked at me.

I looked back at him, trying to think of something to say. Go to hell isn't something you say to a prince, not when you've been obliged by protocol to leave your sword at the porter's lodge, and the royal grooms have control of your horse. I might just get away with No, but then again, I might not. Yes was out of the question.

"I'm sorry," I said, "I'm a bit deaf in one ear. Could you just say that again?"

He sighed. "I want you," he said slowly, as if to a foreigner, "to catch me a dragon. A live one. You can do that, can't you?"

Well, I'd bought my time. Paid through the nose for it. "Probably not," I said.

Not what he'd been expecting to hear. "Why not?"

I KNOW A lot of people who complain, quite justifiably, that one small failure has ruined their lives. In my case, one success completely screwed up mine. No good saying I was just a kid at the time, I didn't know what I was getting myself into, if I'd known I'd have run a mile; too late for that now. It's on my record, I'm branded with it for life (so probably not for very long, given the nature of that brand). I have HERO burned into the skin of my face, too deep for rouge, too tall for the shadow of a wide-brimmed hat.

I was nineteen, youngest of three sons of an impoverished knight. What that meant in practice was that we had a damp, leaky hall decorated with rusty inherited armour, and we looked after our own sheep. Correction: Juifrez and I looked after the sheep, because Raimbaut was the eldest, therefore the heir designate, therefore too grand to get his hands dirty with anything useful. He spent all his time bashing a wooden pole with a wooden sword and learning heraldry, while we clipped shitty wool off the arses of the pregnant ewes. I can't tell you who got the worst of it; they were both miserable ways of spending a day, but at least ours put food on the table.

We had two hundred and six sheep; and then one day we had two hundred and two. The other four had vanished. Juifrez and I went looking for them, and found a few bones and straggles of wool. That made no sense. A wolf leaves a big red mess, rustlers leave nothing at all. We split up. I wandered around for an hour or so and saw nothing at all. Then I went back to where I'd told Juifrez to wait for me. He wasn't there.

I hate that feeling when panic sets in. I felt it rather too often in Outremer, but never quite so badly as I did then. Juifrez was a year older than me, but somehow he was always my kid brother; I was smarter, more sensible, it had always been understood it was my job to look after him. Let's split up, I'd said. I could picture myself telling my father that. It wasn't a comfortable thought.

I tried to find a trail, footprints—I was good at that sort of thing—but I couldn't find any, and that made me burst into tears. I started running, just to cover the ground quicker, and it was only when I stopped that I realised I'd run myself out of breath and could hardly breathe for the cramps. I'd been yelling his name for God knows how long, and my throat was raw. I put my back to a tree, to keep myself from falling over, and slid to the ground. I'd had enough. I was beaten.

I was sitting there with my head in my hands when I felt something splash on the top of my head. It was light enough to be a raindrop, but rain generally comes thicker than a drop at a time. I put my hand on my head, then looked at the fingertip. Red. I looked up, and saw Juifrez, hanging by his heels from a high branch, with his head twisted round a full half-turn.

And I heard a voice, in my mind. *Go away*, it said.

I was in no state to be bothered with voices. A moment or so frozen stiff, unable to move; then I was scrabbling at the trunk of the tree, trying to climb it, but there was nothing to get a grip on. *Go away*, repeated the voice in my head, but that made no sense, and there was my brother, my elder-kid brother, hanging just out of reach like the biggest, fattest plum always does. *I warned you*, said the voice, and something shifted, right up in the canopy.

At first I took it for a pig, except pigs don't climb trees, and they aren't that big, or that colour. A great big blue-gold pig, with tiny eyes with human eyelashes. Then it raised its crest, a collar of flat spikes, like flag-iris leaves as long as your arm, and stuck out its ridiculously long neck, thick as your waist. At which point I realised what it was. You've got to be joking, I thought, because of course they don't exist.

Which hardly mattered. This thing, whatever it was (didn't matter what it was) had killed my brother, twisted his neck like a chicken and hung him up in a tree, like you'd do with vermin, stoats and weasels and rats, to scare away their nasty little relatives—The hell with that, I thought.

I believe anger is a gift from God. I bent my knees and jumped, but I still couldn't get a handhold, and all I did was rip my fingernails.

Suit yourself, idiot said the voice in my head, and the thing, let's call it what it was even though it sounds ridiculous just saying the word, the dragon slid down the tree straight at me, jaws open, so I could see inside. The roof of its mouth was pink, and its fangs, tusks, I don't know the technical term, were the pale buttermilk colour of mature ivory, except one of them was split at the point.

I was unarmed, and according to our old Bestiary, dragons' fangs are deadly poison. Which is why I believe anger is a gift from God. It allows you to confront the risks and say to yourself, be that as it may.

I'm neither brave nor clever, but over the years I've noticed that an overpowering desire to kill someone or something brings out the best in me. I let it come on, watching it—anger makes me calm, sometimes—until it was right on top of me, jaws wide open. At which point I stuck my right arm in its mouth, grabbed its tongue as close as I could to its roots, and planted my elbow against the floor of its lower jaw.

It tried to close its jaws, but it couldn't. My forearm was propping its mouth open, and the force of its jaws drove my fist and elbow into its soft palates, anchoring them. I kept my arm straight; I knew that if I didn't, my wrist would break and that would be that. I noticed, almost dispassionately, that the lower jaw fangs were half an inch from digging into my upper arm.

It tried to pull away, found that it was ripping its own tongue out, and gave up in a hurry. Then it paused, just for a moment, trying to figure out what to do. Fortuitously, it took me precisely a moment to stick my thumb in its eye, as hard as I possibly could.

I broke my thumb, of course, but that was the least of my concerns. The dragon yanked its head back sharply, so sharply its tongue came away in my hand.

I learned a useful lesson that day, one which served me well in later life, when I managed to get myself into real trouble (as opposed to minor inconvenience, like fighting a dragon bare-handed). I pass it on to you in the hope that you may find it as useful as I did, and always have done. If you're fighting an enemy who's much bigger and stronger than you are, don't try and kill him. Just cause him as much pain as you possibly can. There'll be a split second when it hurts so much that for all his strength he just can't think straight; and in that split second you can (for example) stoop and pick up a big stone and smash his head in.

Later we found out that I'd been incredibly lucky. A dragon's skull is far too thick to be crushed by anything less than a direct hit from a trebuchet—except for a little spot, no bigger than the palm of your hand, right on the very top, where the two main plates of its skull form a weak seam.

When things go badly wrong, I've always found, there abide these three; terror, dumb luck and anger. But the greatest of these is anger.

"WHY NOT?" HE said.

What a question. "Because it's too difficult," I said. "It's difficult and dangerous, and I don't want to get killed."

He gave me a hurt look, as though I'd just refused to marry him. "You're too scared," he said.

"Yes."

He nodded. "Yesterday I bought up all the mortgages on your land," he said. "If I foreclose, can you find two thousand angels within fourteen days?"

"No," I said.

"Will you do this perfectly straightforward little job for me?"

"Yes," I said.

TWO THOUSAND ANGELS is a lot of money. It's about half what our estate is worth; two angels an acre. It's roughly what it costs to fit out two knights and send them to fight in Outremer.

When my brother Raimbaut was twenty-four, my lord the Duke decided to follow the call of his conscience and his heart and join the soldiers of God fighting the heathens in Outremer. It was a noble, beautiful thing to do, or so people said. And of course he called up his tenants and his subinfeudees to go with him, since one man on his own can't achieve very much in a war, even if he's a peer of the realm whose ancestors were dukes in the Cascenais when the king's ancestors were still chasing goats up mountains. My father was too old to go, so Raimbaut went instead.

Have you ever stopped to think how much all that stuff costs? Item, one mailshirt. Item, one pair of ankle-length mail chausses. Item, one coat of plates. Item, one helmet, with nasal. Items, one gambeson, one aketon, two gauntlets; one warhorse, one palfrey, two pack-horses, three amblers for his squire and his two men at arms. One sword, two lances, one shield, and so on, and so on. Total, eight hundred and thirty-six angels. Add to that travelling expenses, and living expenses—

Only he didn't. He died of dystentery three weeks after he got there. The army was in full retreat at the time, so they had to dump his body, and all his expensive kit; presumably the enemy got the kit and sold it to the Tedesci brothers, who buy all their plunder and sell it back to the Defenders of the Faith at the Foregate fair at Aescra. But not to worry, the Duke's marshals told him, plenty more where he came from. The obligation was still due, and my father still had a son. So that was all right.

Two thousand angels, which my father raised by pledging his land to the Aechmalota twins, at three per cent interest, to send Raimbaut and me to Outremer. You know what they say, about a fool and his money.

But if I succeeded, on the other hand, His Majesty would give me the mortgage deeds, and a thousand angels cash. A thousand angels is a lot of money.

First, find a dragon. Not as easy as it sounds. The species isn't native to our part of the world; it's too cold, and a good crisp winter will achieve more in the way of pest control than a hundred knights, with or without enchanted swords. The only specimens to be encountered north of the Middle Sea are the handful brought back by noble lords returning from Outremer as souvenirs or gifts for the man who has everything.

It is more blessed, Scripture tells us, to give than to receive; and although I have my doubts about that as a general rule, it surely applies when the gift is a dragon. For a start, you've got to build a special house for it to live in, with very thick stone walls and underfloor heating, and you've got to feed it a ruinous amount of fresh meat every day; and if, God forbid, the wretched thing ever gives you the slip and gets loose on your neighbours' land, you've got to go and deal with it, or find some poor fool who'll deal with it for you. Unless, of course, you're lucky enough to live next-door-but-three to a young idiot who'll rip its tongue out and smash its head in free of charge, just to settle a score, but that almost never happens. Who'd be stupid enough to do it?

I said just now that dragons can't survive the northern winter, and that's almost true. Out of the few that escape, a very few of them can. Usually they find a deep cave to insulate themselves against the frost and the bitter wind and hibernate until spring. Caves that deep are few and far between, and in those places where there are such caves, generally speaking there aren't enough sheep and cattle for the dragon to feed up on, to build its fat reserves to see it through until spring comes along.

In fact, the only place north of the Saëve where you might reasonably expect to find one is where the moors meet the mountain foothills, near the small market town of Loucy. It's a godforsaken place. The Blood River—so called because it runs red with rust, from the iron ore deposits at Weal Jehan; the water's poisonous down as far as Boc Loucy, and nothing grows on its banks for a hundred yards on either side—bisects a deep, windswept valley, half of which (roughly two thousand acres) just about grows oats and barley, while the other half is forested with small, twisted holm oaks, no use for anything except firewood. There are four tiny villages north of the town, surrounding the small, dilapidated manor house where the de Loucys have lived for about three hundred years, and where I grew up.

We reckoned the dragons escaped from the grange at Emm, the furthest outpost of my lord the Duke's estate at Chastelbest, though of course we couldn't prove it. Shortly after my lord's father came back from Outremer, they built an enormous barn in a deep combe between the ridge on which the house stands and the forest (which extends over the Hog's Back and joins up with the Loucy woods at Moyenchamber). They were three years building it, and they had masons and tradesmen in from the city, sixty miles away—odd, don't you think, just to build an ordinary barn?—but nobody ever heard of straw or pease or hay being carted there. But flocks of sheep were driven down there from the top pastures, and herds of pigs came up from the home cottages; and nobody ever saw them come out again. Proving nothing, of course. But the first dragon showed up in Loucy woods about five years after the barn was built. I was nineteen at the time.

Not so very long after that, the barn burned to the ground in a great fire, which spread to Hog's Back Wood, over the top and down into our woods, though no great harm done, since they're all useless, as I told you just now; about nine hundred acres lost on our side, which is all tangled briars and withies now. The grange people never rebuilt the barn, and over the years the tenants have helped themselves to the stones for making and mending walls, so there's nothing to see there these days except a long rectangle of foxgloves and gorse.

Anyway, if I wanted to find a dragon, that's where I'd look; just as, if I wanted to look for death, I'd throw a rope over a tree or eat yellowcap mushrooms.

HABITAT

I WAS IN Outremer for five years.

Doesn't sound all that long. My lord the Duke's eldest son has just got back from seven years at the University, where I gather he distinguished himself by reading several books and being seen at a number of lectures, modestly attired in a black silk scholar's gown trimmed with sable. That's two years away from home longer than me, and more or less the same distance, and yet you'd hardly know to look at him that he's been away at all.

Five years in Outremer, however, is a very long time. Half of the new arrivals—my brother Raimbaut, for instance—die within the first three months. Those who don't tend to last anything between six and eighteen months; two years makes you a veteran, someone to be pointed out and stared at. After three years they send you home.

I was there for five years; and while I was there I met an interesting man. He wasn't one of us. He served the emperor, on whose behalf we were supposed to be fighting the war, though it was no secret that the emperor reckoned we were worse than the heathens, and did ten times as much damage to his long-suffering people. This man told me that before he was conscripted, he'd worked for a master who caught wild animals for the Hippodrome games in the Golden City—lions, bears, elephants, that sort of thing—

(In case you aren't familiar with the high culture of the Cradle of Civilisation, once a month all the citizens of the City crowd into a huge enclosure to watch the fighting: men against wild animals, animals against animals, men against men. Now I find this odd, since the empire has been at war against the heathen for six hundred years, doing quite badly most of the time; every family loses at least one man every generation, and the City itself has been besieged twelve times, so you'd think they'd have seen quite enough fighting and killing for free, without paying a silver sixpence for a seat at the back, probably behind a pillar or a woman with a tall hat. Apparently not.)

Oh, and dragons, of course, he told me. We caught half a dozen dragons. Then he stopped and grinned at me. You think I'm shitting you, he said. I bet you don't think dragons even exist.

Oddly enough, I said, I do.

He looked at me. Well, they do, he said, and we had to catch them, alive, undamaged. Bet you can't guess how we did it.

I'm more interested in lions, I told him. Tell me how you used to catch lions.

Same way as we caught dragons, basically, he said. What you do is—

He was a good man, though he took some getting used to, and what he didn't know about dragons—Somehow he never quite grasped that it wasn't a subject I was comfortable talking about. But he was a wonderful horseman, and he taught me how to shoot a hundred-pound-draw shortbow from the saddle, and how to set a broken arm, and cure mountain fever. I have no idea what happened to him. His squadron was cut off by an outflanking wing that came out of nowhere. A day or so later I went back and picked over the bodies, but I didn't find his there. Proving nothing.

A THOUSAND ANGELS. A lot of money.

I met an alchemist once, and he explained the theory to me. All things corrupt, he told me, all things decay and fall apart and go to waste and ruin, except for gold. You can leave it out in the rain or bury it in the damp earth for a hundred years, and it'll come out looking just as shiny and clean as when it went in. There are only two things, he said to me, that survive and pass through the taints and decays and corruptions of this world unscathed and unchanged: God and gold. And one of them is all around us every day, in everything and comprised in and comprising everything, and the other one is very rare, and has to be crushed and sweated out of a rock or sifted, tiny speck by tiny speck, from the stinking silt of a riverbed. Guess which one people value the most. Go on, guess.

And (he went on) neither of them can be reduced to an essential form, since they're both perfect already; but both of them have the virtue of rejuvenating, of restoring and perfecting. Both of them, in fact, can work miracles.

I told him I wasn't sure about that. I'll show you, he said, and he led me through the bazaar to an archway in a wall, and through the arch into a courtyard with a door, and he rang a little brass bell. Someone opened the door for us, and beyond it I saw a walled garden, rows of lavender and sage and marjoram, apple trees espaliered on wires, and in the centre a fountain. Ten years ago, he told me, this was a tanner's yard, and you could smell the slurry and the rotting brains halfway across town. Then I bought it, and I spent a thousand nomismata making it like this, but it was worth it. Gold transforms, he said, gold purifies. Gold can turn a cesspit into a paradise.

I like a pretty garden as much as the next man, but if I had a thousand angels I knew what I'd do with it. First I'd hire all the casual labour I could get, and I'd clear and plough up all the land in Loucy that's gone to rack and ruin since my grandfather's time, and I'd rebuild all the fallen-down barns and walls, have all the hedges laid so the stock couldn't get out and stray onto my lord's land, never to return. I'd plant out a vineyard on Conegar, clear the weeds and the cow-parsley out of the millrace and get the mill working again, get the fish-traps and weirs on the river fixed up, order new ploughs and harrows, maybe even go to Chastelbest abbey fair and buy a really good pedigree bull—They'll tell you in the Schools that alchemy is abstruse and difficult to understand, but I think it's pretty clear and simple, once you understand the basic principles.

I'll need money, I'd told him, for expenses. He'd looked offended and sad, and told the chancellor to give me a writ for fifteen angels. What I'd actually asked for was fifty, but the prince is slightly deaf in one ear.

Still, fifteen angels is a lot of money. I took the writ down to the chancellery and they counted fifteen coins into my hand and made me sign a receipt.

I'VE KNOWN THE blacksmith at Loucy all my life. When I was a boy, I used to hang around the forge watching him, trying not to get under his feet. If I'd been Raimbaut, that wouldn't have been allowed, but a third son has more latitude in precise gradations of status, especially when his father isn't entirely sure when he'll be in a position to pay the blacksmith's bill. It'd be an exaggeration to say that he ever liked me much. I was a small boy who sat in a corner of the room and stared at him and never said anything, even when spoken to. But he got used to me.

Then my lord the Duke decided to go to Outremer; and with him went his seventeen horses, and the horses needed a farrier. The blacksmith of Loucy had a son, a promising young man who was already a master of the trade, and known to be particularly good with horses. He'd already made his mind up to volunteer, he told me, when my lord's man came with the summons. It was an honour and a privilege, and the money was very good, and he'd always had a fancy to travel.

Two days after he told me that, he was dead. I can't remember offhand whether it was cholera or the flux; one of the two. When we were kids, he used to duck my head in the slack bucket, when he was sure nobody was watching, and once he stole my shoes and I had to pretend to my father that I'd lost them crossing the river. When I told his father, I made out that he'd died bravely fighting the heathen; he dashed forward to rescue a fallen comrade, I said, and a savage stabbed him in the back.

So; Garcio and I know each other tolerably well. Which means he knows me well enough to make me show him actual money before I tell him what I want made.

"What in God's name is that supposed to be?" he said.

I'd drawn a sketch in chalk on a roof slate. "It's to scale," I told him. "I measured it with dividers and calipers." He'd taught me to do that, though he hadn't meant to; I'd watched him, with his back to me. Saved my life once, being able to draw up an accurate sketch. I never told him that, of course.

"What is it?"

"It's a trap," I told him.

He peered at the slate. His eyes aren't what they were, on account of staring at white-hot metal for forty years. "What's that supposed to be?"

"That's the sear," I said. "The tripwire disengages the sear from the notch, which releases the shutter."

He looked at me. "What's it a trap for?"

"Lions," I said.

"What do you want to trap lions for?"

"I don't."

Like I said, he was used to me. "How thick's this strut got to be?"

"An inch. Actually, you might get away with seven-eighths, but what the hell."

"Riveted?"

I shook my head. "Welded. Better still, riveted and welded."

He was frowning. "There aren't any lions in these parts," he said.

"Is that right?"

I HAD REASON to believe there'd be a dragon in the caves below Staert, and I was right. They don't exactly conceal their presence.

One of the many things that everybody knows about dragons and that isn't actually true is that they breathe fire. No, of course they don't. But fires start wherever they've been living for any length of time. My friend the lion-catcher in Outremer explained why, or at least he told me what he'd been told. They're desert creatures, he told me. They're what causes deserts.

Which sounds like drivel, until you read old books and look at old maps. From which you learn that once upon a time, hundreds or thousands of years ago, the endless rolling sand dunes of Outremer were once forests and pastures and meadows, quilted with rivers, studded with busy towns and walled cities. Just occasionally you come across them, the corner of a worked stone poking up through the sand, like a bone through the skin. But then, so my friend told me, the dragons came, and something they were or something they did dried up all the water, killed all the trees and the grass. And where you get dead trees and dry grass, you get fires, and before long there's nothing alive at all, which is a pretty good working definition of a desert. Either they poison the water, like the iron ore, or their piss kills the grass, like a sick dog; anyway, you can tell straight away where a dragon lives, because everything round it is dead.

When I was a boy, there was a big stand of ash trees at Staert. My grandfather had them planted the day my father was born, which I always thought was a nice thing to do, and if ever I had a son I'd do the same. All gone. At least, the stub ends of the trunks were still there, charred black, sticking up like the grave markers of a hastily buried army. The ground was black and crunched when you walked on it, all the way from the top of the ridge to the point where the earth becomes rock.

I didn't need to go that far, so I didn't. I stood on top of the Calf, the smaller of the two tall knolls on the other side of the valley cut by the little river that races down from the mountains to join the Blood River at Watersmeet. I don't know that that little river ever had a name, not a proper one. We always called it Calf Water. Anyway, its bed was dry and split with deep cracks, and the withies on what had been its banks were starting to droop. The fire hadn't managed to jump the riverbed, but all the heather on the flanks of the Calf was brown and brittle, and you know what dry heather's like. Breathe on it when you've been eating garlic and you'll have a fire you could weld steel in.

NO HEATHER IN Outremer, naturally. But around the oases they grow marvellous crops of wheat; shorter in the stem than our northern varieties, but with ears as long as your thumb. The enemy used to wait until the corn was just ripening, and then they'd swoop down, drive off the farmers, harvest the corn and cart it back over what we laughingly called the border. Same every year, and the farmers only stayed there because we wouldn't let them leave.

I'd been there two and a half years. I was still alive because I'd been seconded away from my lord the Duke's contingent to serve with one of the emperor's regiments—the locals, in other words, the people who actually lived there and knew what they were doing. They knew about such things as keeping your wounds and water clean, not letting your latrines drain into a river when your allies were camped a mile downstream, that sort of stuff, and they knew about fighting the enemy, which they'd been doing for six hundred years.

The year before, my lord the Duke had been given responsibility for that sector, and he'd tried to forestall the annual invasion by fighting a pitched battle on the border. He lost, needless to say, and seventy knights and five hundred and twelve foot soldiers died, and the enemy went about their business in the usual way. The next year, the rotation meant our lot, the emperor's men, got that sector; and of course, they knew what to do.

Which was nothing. We sat on our horses and watched as the enemy column swaggered (no other word for it) across the little brown river that marked the frontier. We'd already evacuated the locals, so the country was empty for as far as an eagle could fly in a day. We sat and watched them ride down the old Military Road the emperors had built four centuries ago, and we did nothing.

We did nothing while they set about their weary job of *chevauchee*—that's the military word for turning someone else's home into a desert. You trash the houses, cut down the orchards, burn the crops, kill every domesticated animal, and then you move on to the next village. It's hard manual labour, which was why the enemy used prisoners of war—our people—to do the actual work, while they sat in their saddles and made sure they did a proper job. They sat, and we sat, and the chain gangs sweated to death in the blazing sun destroying the livelihoods of their own flesh and blood. Then, when there wasn't anything left, they moved on to the next village, and the next, until they'd finished their allotted sweep and it was time to go home.

The enemy weren't stupid. They sent on the harvested grain ahead in wagons, but they kept back large areas of uncut grain so the army would have something to eat on its way home. The biggest patch was a flat plain, maybe two thousand acres, all rich, fertile land, with the road running straight down the middle.

One of the men in our company was local born and bred. He knew the terrain, and he knew the prevailing winds. So, one night when the enemy were camped in the middle of this enormous cornfield, we crept out and started our fires at carefully chosen points, knowing that the wind was in the right direction and would blow strongly for the next thirty-six hours. Then we split into two, each party blocking one end of the road.

It worked like a charm, though the fighting at the roadblocks was murderous. But we knew we didn't have to prevail, just hold them up long enough for the fire to reach them—and it did, roaring in like waves breaking on a beach, until the smoke was so thick that fighting was irrelevant, and we broke up and got out of there as fast as we possibly could. Of the twenty thousand heathens who marched in, about nine hundred got out. The technical term for that is victory, though of course they were back next year, and the year after that.

We also burned to death about twelve thousand of those prisoners of war, but that couldn't be helped. As my lord the

Duke said later, when claiming the whole thing had been his idea; once captured, those men were assets of the enemy and needed to be dealt with; and besides, better dead than in the hands of the infidel. Actually, he may have been right about that last bit. They had a pretty rough time of it, so I gather. I guess it comes down to a choice, which would you rather die of, fire, torture or starvation?

Also, said my lord the Duke, it's a well known fact that burning the crop actually increases the fertility of the soil, so once this ridiculous war was over and the heathen had been crushed, future generations would bless us. I won't comment on that, if you don't mind.

GARCIO THE BLACKSMITH has always done good work, ever since I've known him. He charged me an angel seventeen for it; extortionate, but it wasn't my money. The change out of the second angel just about paid for the hire of the stonemason's big cart, his big crane and a dozen of his biggest men. Have you noticed that when you're engaged in something truly difficult and dangerous, everybody rips you off?

So; I had a dragon, and a trap. That just left bait.

WHEN I CAME home from Outremer, carrying everything I owned in the world in a hemp sack slung over my shoulder, I hardly knew the place. I looked down from the top of the ridge expecting to see cornfields, neatly laid hedges, a properly made-up road leading through coppiced spinneys to our house. Instead, I saw a wilderness of gorse, briars and nettles. The fields and the hedges and the stumps of the felled trees had vanished, buried like the stones of the ancient cities of Outremer. There was no road, and no house.

Three years after I went away, apparently, there was a fire. The house burnt down; it spread to the spinney, and from there to the fields. My father got out in time, but he was never the same afterwards. He moved to a cottage for a few months but proved entirely incapable of looking after himself, so the monks took him in and gave him a cell, board and lodging in return for a second mortgage on the estate. He died six months later, and they buried him in their own graveyard: something of an honour, apparently, for a layman.

It didn't take long for the tenants to find out that I was home. They sent a deputation to the inn to welcome me, and I had to tell them that not everybody comes home from Outremer leading a string of ponies loaded down with plundered gold. They took it reasonably well. Oh well, they said, and off they went. Later I went to see them each in turn, with some vague idea in my mind of discussing arrears of rent. But it had been hard times all round, they told me, since the old master died, and what I'd seen inclined me to believe them. Three failed harvests in succession, and the grass so bad, they kept the stock alive by cutting hazel branches from the hedges. That's bad, I told them, thinking of the villages in Outremer we'd been sworn to protect (and where one day the corn will grow so high, because of all that ash), and they weren't to worry about rent until they were back on their feet again.

I was still wearing the shoes I'd walked two hundred miles in, from the coast all the way up the Military Road to Loucy. They were good shoes. I took them off a dead heathen in a canyon somewhere, and he'd got them from one of our lot, a rich man's son to judge by shape of the last and the quality of the stitching. They still had a good few miles left in them. A man wearing shoes like that wasn't going to worry too much about sleeping in a barn, or living off unfortunate creatures caught in snares, while he sets about clearing fifty acres of tangled briars with an old hook he found in a fallen-down toolshed.

I was good with cutting tools in Outremer. I could slice a man's arm off with a backhand cut. And the worst a bramble can do is scratch you up a bit. I had energy and motivation; best of all, I was angry (and the greatest of these is anger) But I'd been in the sun too long. I got soaked to the skin by a heavy shower, and next thing I knew I had fever. My friend the lion-catcher had taught me how to cure it, but those herbs don't grow here. I was sick as a dog for a week, and when I snapped out of it, I had no strength left. I limped over to the abbey, where they took me in and gave me bowl after bowl of barley broth with dumplings, and showed me the mortgage deed my father had signed. And that was the end of my crusade to take back my inheritance.

I was twenty-eight years old, and I could see no point in anything. But I was still that crazy kid who'd killed a dragon with his bare hands; so I went south, and signed on with one of the free companies as a mercenary. I found I fitted in well there. I was famous. They called me *ormsbana* and *wurmtoter,* and had a special banner made with a dragon on it, and the enemy ran away as soon as they heard we were coming. We trashed a lot of cottages and burnt a lot of corn, and three years later I'd saved up a hundred angels, which is a lot of money, and I bought a farm, down on the coast, a mile or so from the Straits. From my window, I could see the ships setting sail for Outremer, and very occasionally at night I could see the beacons on the other side, lit to show them the way into harbour.

I HAD A shrewd idea where would be a good place for my trap, if only I could find it again. I was afraid it would all look different, so much else having changed, but when we got there it was exactly as I remembered it. There was a certain tree, under which I'd sat one day after I'd been looking for my brother. It was taller and thicker, but not by very much.

You can't really hide a machine made of iron girders weighing well over a ton, so I told them to put it down anywhere, gave them their money and watched them trundle away. Then I walked round it a few times. A trap is a trap. I could tell what it was and how it was supposed to work just by glancing at it. But Garcio the smith hadn't known until I told him, and a dragon is just a dumb brute.

I wound up the shutters using the winch provided, engaged the sear in the notch, disengaged the hook and chain and hung them back out of the way. There was a pressure plate on the floor. When the dragon stood on it, it would pivot and pull on a cable, which would lift the sear out of battery, and the front and rear shutters would fall simultaneously. There was also a little wicket gate at the back, between the back shutter and the end of the frame. I made sure it opened and shut easily.

The space between the shutter and the wicket was where the bait had to go. I'd thought to bring a little three-legged milking stool. I ducked under the bottom edge of the shutter, and sat down on the stool. Might as well be comfortable while I was waiting.

Not for very long. Dragons have poor eyesight but a marvellous sense of smell. It came, just as I'd anticipated, out of the canopy of that damned tree, unwinding itself like a coil of living rope. Last time I'd been preoccupied; this time I made a point of looking, because a dragon isn't something you see every day. Neck as thick as your waist, head like a pig, tiny black eyes, crest like swordblades, scales like the armour they wear in Outremer, teeth like handspikes. And a voice in my head saying *Run*.

Nice of it to care. But there comes a point in a man's life when he has nowhere left to run to, and a thousand angels is a very great deal of money. I looked into the dragon's eyes, and saw what I'd expected to see.

"Hello, Juifrez," I said.

It lunged at me. I scampered back, fumbling for the wicket catch. As I'd anticipated, it couldn't reach me without sliding into the cage. It arched its spine and slithered forward, and I heard the pressure plate creak. Its head shot forward, just as I threw myself out of the wicket, hit the ground and rolled. I heard the thud as the shutters fell.

The trap was designed to catch lions. It was far too short for twenty feet of dragon. But the shutters were sheet iron, three inches thick; and one had slammed down on its neck, pinning it to the floor, and the other had trapped its tail. It wasn't too happy about that. It shook and wriggled, trying to jackknife, so hard it lifted the whole contraption a handspan off the ground, but it couldn't get free. The shutters were too heavy.

I heard a voice in my head; *let me go. Please.* But even if I'd wanted to, I couldn't. I'd have had to get the hook under the shutters and winch them up, and the winch was buried under the dragon's body. And I knew if I tried to get to it, the dragon would kill me. And what had my lord the Duke had to say on the subject, or something quite similar? Once captured, he was an asset of the enemy and needed to be dealt with. And a thousand angels is a lot of money.

I looked down at my leg and saw a tear in the cloth, tinged with blood. Maybe I'd scratched myself on a sharp edge of the frame, or a thorn, or maybe the dragon's teeth had just nicked me before I got out of its way. Damn, I thought.

"I'm sorry," I said, and walked away.

I WAITED FOR five days. That's what my friend in Outremer had told me, the one who trapped lions for a living. Oh, and dragons too, of course. You leave them in the trap for five days, no food or water, till they're so weak they couldn't hurt a kitten. Then you dose them with a stirrup-pump; distilled essence of poppy, about a gallon, which ought to keep them under for a week at the very least. After that, you can load them onto a boatbuilder's cart and ship them out, and get paid.

So I did that. The prince was as good as his word. I got the mortgage deeds to my land (two thousand acres of brambles and self-seeded withies) and a thousand angels in a linen bag, and he got his dragon. What do you want it for? I asked him. Mind your own damned business, he told me.

An interesting and little-known fact about dragons is that they don't reproduce the same way as other animals. Instead of mating, and bearing and rearing their young, they propagate by contamination, like a disease, like the plague that killed two out of three of the inhabitants of Joiauz Saber the year after I came home, brought there by veterans returning from Outremer. All it takes, so my friend told me, is a little scratch, from its teeth or even just the rough edge of one of its scales. If it draws blood, it infects you.

The incubation period is anything from a few days to ten years. Even being dead won't save you. If a dragon bites a corpse, in due course the corpse becomes a dragon. But they prefer to take their victims alive, like my lord the prince, or the heathens in Outremer who rounded up farmers and marched them back home in chains to burn their cousins' corn.

I've given it some thought over the years, but I honesty can't remember if the dragon I killed when I was nineteen managed to scratch me or not. With every year that passed, I persuaded myself to feel a little safer. And I have no idea whether Juifrez, my poor dear brother Juifrez scratched me, or whether it was a sharp edge on the frame of the trap, or a briar.

It hardly matters. Dragons don't survive here in the north, except in one or two remote places. Their natural habitat is Outremer, where they swarm and proliferate, and even the tiniest scratch turns one of us into one of them, so that the place will never ever be rid of them. It hardly matters because there are far worse things than dragons in Outremer, and the slightest scratch will turn you into one of them; the sort of man who'll burn his own house down, or kill thousands of his own people so as to kill thousands of the enemy, or who'll come home and start doing for money what he hated himself for doing abroad for honour and fealty.

HABITAT

THE PRINCE WANTED a live dragon because he was jealous. He didn't like the fact that a poor knight's son had won imperishable glory by slaying a dragon with his bare hands, and he wanted to emulate the feat, but only after having reduced the concomitant risk to a sensible level. So he had the poor knight's son catch him a dragon, and then he had his people draw the dragon's fangs and dope it with poppy juice until it could barely keep its eyes open. Then he staged a tournament and had the dragon carted into the lists, and rode forth on his white charger to slay the monster. Unfortunately, the dragon fell asleep just as he was about to drive his gauntleted fist into the vulnerable place on top of the monster's head, which his people had sensibly marked for him with bright red paint. It fell asleep and rolled over, and in doing so knocked the prince off his horse and crushed him like an egg. He lived for two days in unspeakable pain and then died. Served him right.

The Big Score

I didn't enjoy my funeral nearly as much as I thought I would. I'd been looking forward to it, but it turned out to be something of a disappointment.

For a start, it rained, and that always takes the edge off a good party. Maybe it was the weather; there were far fewer people there than I'd anticipated, or catered for. I'd spent a lot of money I hadn't really got on good food and fine wine (and I hardly drink at all myself, now I'm dead) and the servants ended up taking most of it home with them. The preacher's eulogy was dreadful, and most of the guests who did turn up proved to be representatives of my creditors or various law-enforcement agencies. Nobody from the universities, the theatres, the Sashan embassy or the imperial court. Instead, there was this granite-faced man with a shiny head and huge eyebrows who buttonholed me as the coffin was lowered into the hole—

"I'm his cousin," I explained. "Only living relative."

He considered me, as though I was a dangerous crack in the wall of his house. "You were close?"

I shook my head. "Hadn't seen him for years."

He had that expression, the one that says, you're about to lie to me. "So you've got no idea where it all is."

"The manuscripts, you mean? The research notes?"

"The money he stole."

"No idea," I lied. "Like I said, we weren't close."

"I never knew he had a cousin."

"On my mother's side," I said. "Twice removed."

ENVIRONMENT AND CIRCUMSTANCE: that's what makes you what you are, not what's inside. The shell, not the egg; the scar, not the wholesome flesh beneath. Take me, for shining example. I have, by universal consensus, the finest mind and the most beautiful soul that ever was. I've written the best plays and poems, the wisest and most perceptive philosophical tracts; I'm the greatest scientist of all time. My name—Saloninus, as though you needed to be told—will live for ever. Nature (as I once put it) might stand up and say to all the world, this was a man.

Quite. And, given such rich and rare gifts, what did I do with them? To which I'm compelled to answer: apart from a few years when I lived quietly and comfortably on the proceeds of my groundbreaking formula for synthetic blue paint, nothing I care to dwell on. Lots of really bad stuff, mostly; thieving and swindling and issuing false coin (I was really good at that) with occasional lapses into the most deplorable kinds of violence. Not because I'm naturally bad and vicious—quite the opposite, since (as I convincingly proved in my Ethical Dialogues) beauty and virtue are essentially the same thing; therefore you can't create a substantial proportion of the beautiful things in the world, as I have, unless you're fundamentally good. No, it was always bad luck, mostly not having any money. And bad luck is just a slovenly way of saying environment and circumstances. If you end up living in Poor Town, always one jump ahead of the authorities, a certain category of things are almost inevitably going to happen to you, all of them miserable. You can call it bad luck if you like, but I'm a scientist.

So: if you take the good man out of the bad place and put him in a good place, where he's got loads of money and nobody knows who he used to be, you give him a chance to be himself;

and that was precisely what I'd planned to do. Just one more little white lie, and everything would be just fine.

At the banquet I gave a little speech. We're here today, I said, to lay to rest Saloninus, the greatest and most original thinker of our time. How will future generations remember him, I wonder? As a scientist—discoverer of the circulation of the blood and the three laws of motion, the man who cured mountain fever and saved countless lives on three continents? Or as a philosopher, probably the greatest there's ever been, author of the *Analects*, the *Ideal Republic* and *Beyond Good and Evil*? As the man who invented the optical telescope, synthetic blue dye, truly functional indoor sanitation and a so far untested but entirely viable flying machine? As a playwright and composer—I give you six words that say it all. *Lycas and Thrasimene*. The Sixth Symphony. How can we truly say that Saloninus is dead when he lives on in every aspect of our daily lives? Half of the expressions we use in our everyday speech are quotations from his plays; and every time we flush a water closet or put on a blue shirt, we honour Saloninus the inventor. To say that a man like that could ever truly die is to anticipate a day when the human race itself will cease to exist—

I looked up and saw a row of blank faces. Not interested. Ah well.

For three days after the funeral, I was aware of deliberately inconspicuous men following me wherever I went. I'm used to that, of course, so I didn't go anywhere.

Just as well that I'd had the opportunities and the foresight to provide for myself during my lifetime, like a loving and dutiful father, so that my afterlife would be entirely different. Poverty, necessity and envy would no longer be the hammer and anvil between which I'd be shaped, and my basically good character wouldn't be warped and subverted into dishonesty and crime. All the sacrifices I'd made when I was alive, just so that I could have a better life after I was gone.

A few words in passing about honesty. It could be argued that the modest sum I bequeathed to myself had not been honestly come by. Fair enough. Now consider the truly inconceivable amount of wealth I've generated in my lifetime, none of which ever came my way. The best-selling book of all time, the Analects; I got sixty stuivers for it from a bookseller in Calyx, just enough to pay my arrears of rent on a damp rabbit-hutch up sixteen flights of stairs. For the plays I got an average of eighty stuivers each; less for the symphonies, and I never actually got the money for the Ninth, because the promoter went bust just before the premiere. True, I did actually get paid for inventing blue paint, but everything else—either someone else got the rights for a pittance, or I had to leave the jurisdiction in a hurry, and so couldn't hang around to argue my case in the civil courts. Now I ask you, is that fair? Is that honest?

Mine is a multifaceted character and I can't credibly deny that a lot of those facets are less than admirable. I became a crook when I was young, impressionable and broke, was forced to carry on being crooked by circumstances beyond my control, and sort of stuck like it thereafter. Another thing I'm forced to admit is that the intelligence, creativity, let's use the word, genius I exhibit in other areas of endeavour hasn't really manifested itself to any marked extent in my criminal activities. The most I can say is, I've made a lot of money and I've never done time. But I've jumped out of a lot of windows and left a lot of towns and cities in a hurry, mostly leaving my ill-gotten gains behind. My biographer says that ninety-six per cent of the money that passed through my hands in my lifetime was dishonestly obtained. Don't know where he came by that figure, but it sounds about right. So? Big deal. I am (to quote me: King

Minax, Act 3, Scene 1) a man more sinned against than sinning, and surely that counts for something.

Or does it? I could argue it conclusively either way, if you paid me for my time. In the absence of financial incentives, I'd say I don't know and I don't really care. All I know for sure is that from time to time I've found myself in dire straits, penniless and on the run, always because of something I did in the last country, or the one before that, and under those oppressive circumstances I've been forced to do things—steal things—that a flawlessly honest man would've left alone. It didn't help that I'm so smart, and honest people are, in comparison, so very stupid.

One of the problems with being dishonest is that you're forced to spend much of your life in the company of very bad people. This isn't as negative as it sounds until you reach the point when you have no choice but to trust them. And then, surprise surprise, they let you down.

"What do you mean," I said, "he's not here?"

She looked at me. She'd been beautiful once, but twenty years of being married to him had scoured her down to bare rock. "He's not here," she said.

"Then where is he?"

"Don't know."

"When will he be back?"

"Don't know."

She was lying, naturally. I could tell, because I saw her brace herself for the slap across the face, the fingers round the neck; I'd rough her up a little and then she'd tell me the second lie, which would send me racing off somewhere while she and he quietly packed up and left town, with all my money. My inheritance, from myself.

"Don't give me that," I pleaded. "Listen, here's the deal. We'll split it, fifty-fifty. That way, you and he will have enough to live on for the rest of your lives, and you won't have to spend every second of every day looking over your shoulder. It's got to be worth it to you. You can't put a price on peace of mind."

Not a flicker. "I'll tell him," she said. "When I see him."

"When might that be?"

"Don't know."

"Fine," I said. "I trusted him. We've been through hell together. I saved him from the gallows, did he ever tell you that?"

"Yes."

"The hell with it," I said, "it's only money. Enjoy it while you can. He'll have gambled it all away in five years."

"Less than that, probably."

I winced. I'd worked hard for that money. Some of it—about 0.01%—was every penny I ever earned from writing *The Consolation of Philosophy, Philemon and Arcite* and *The Principles of Mathematics*. The rest was the haul from the United Sword Blade Bank, where we got in through the roof using a practical application of my discovery of the square on the hypotenuse. Still, it's only money—'twas mine (quoting me again), 'tis his, and shall be slave to thousands. Besides, there was always the other stash.

To reach it meant nine days' walk up the Great East Road, in dead men's shoes; scratch that, worse than dead men's shoes because I'd been buried in my only decent pair, assuming I'd only have a short stroll across the city before inheriting a small fortune. After two days on the road, with nothing to eat except nettles and nothing to drink but rainwater from ditches, I was starting to think mournful thoughts about the two gold angels I'd caused to be laid on my eyes to pay the ferryman, a superstition I've never ever believed in, but you feel the need to do these things properly, don't you, especially when it's for yourself. Two gold angels currently lying in a hole in the ground, when they could be paying my fare to Erech, first class, wine with my dinner. Only a halfwit puts respect for the dead above the needs of the living, particularly when they're both him.

Erech is a miserable place, too hot in summer, freezing cold in winter, and the rest of the year it rains. They make a ridiculous amount of money there growing flax, and a substantial part of the flax-grower's craft consists of leaving the loathsome stuff lying around in heaps until it starts to rot. The resulting perfume hits you just before you get to the Angel of Resilience (assuming you're coming in on the Military Road, from the west) and you don't really get used to it for another seven miles, by which point you're in the outer suburbs. Of course, long-term residents just look at you blankly and say, what smell?

I'd have stopped off at the Angel to rest up and cut the dust if I'd had any money and if I hadn't been barred for life for lewd behaviour (only I was dead now, so presumably that no longer applied); instead I pressed on, hoping to get to the Silver Rose monastery before they locked the gates for the night. But I cleverly put my foot in a rabbit hole and sprained my ankle, which meant another night out in God's clean fresh air, leading to pneumonia. I ended up in the Silver Rose after all; I woke up in the infirmary, looking into the pale blue eyes of a tiny, impossibly ancient monk, who told me I nearly died three times, but he'd prayed for me and now I'd be fine. To which I think I muttered something like, I can't die, I'm dead already, which the monk quite reasonably attributed to me being off my head with fever. Later that day he came back and told me that he'd gone to all that trouble because every human life is precious, even one as pointless and inconsequential as mine. I thanked him and asked him when I could leave. Soon as you like, he told me; I'd served my purpose, enabling him to achieve divine merit by saving my life through prayer, and now I was no further use to him and taking up valuable space.

"Thank you, Father," I said. "If ever I'm rich, I won't forget what you've done."

"Bless you, my son," he said. "But I'm not holding my breath."

In the grounds of the Silver Rose there's a ruined chapel. It's about a thousand years old; the shattered arches are clearly late Mannerist, and when I first went there you could still pick out faint traces of what must have been unbearably lovely frescoes in the Rose Curtain style, though the sheep have rubbed them all away now. The chapel was built to house the tomb of Cassius Cascianus, the second-greatest (guess who's the greatest) alchemist of all time. I'd chosen the tomb to hide my reserve stash in, partly as a gesture of respect to my brother scientist, partly because I know for a fact that nobody ever goes there, because they think Cassius sold his soul to the devil—which I know for a fact isn't true, for what it's worth. They're getting Cassius mixed up with another great alchemist, who did just that. One of my more interesting adventures. Tell you about it some time.

I was almost right. Very, very few people ever went there. Quite probably just me and one other, and him only once, with a sledgehammer and a crowbar. He'd made a real mess, whoever he was; he'd cracked the lid, which I'd been at great pains to lift and slide away, and bashed a hole in the side, which meant the rain had got in and reduced the mortal remains of the Father of Science into stinking grey porridge. Desecrating a tomb, for crying out loud. Some people have no respect.

THEY DO SAY you can't take it with you.

Still, I have to admit, it was one of those low spots, when you can't seem to see your way forward. I guess I allowed anger to cloud my judgement, which is never a good thing. The thought that some thief, some criminal, had coolly helped himself to what I'd spent the best years of my life accumulating, bit by painful bit—grave-robbing, I ask you, stealing from a dead man, how low can you get? I never did anything like that. If only he'd left some clue, I'd have been after him like a shot. But he'd been careful, left no sign or trace. I remember sitting there in the brick-dust, with the sludgy residues of Cassius Cascianus smeared up my arms to the elbows, thinking: all for nothing, all that work, all that pain. An entire life, rich in adventure, achievement and acclaim, and absolutely nothing to show for it.

Also the distressing knowledge that I'd burnt my bridges. True, being me had grown increasingly uncomfortable over the years—it's a big world, but not nearly as big as they'd have you believe, and ever since I published *The Pathology of War* fifteen years ago, there's ever so much more peace and friendly co-operation between nations, which means among other things quicker and easier extradition, so nowhere's really safe any more and it's all my own stupid fault. Even so; when I was alive, there was always some far-flung godforsaken place I could go, hole up in a garret somewhere, write a book or a play, earn a little bit of money, though never enough; always some rustic grand duke willing to keep me in bread and cheese in return for linking his name with the greatest genius who ever lived. Now that I was dead, however—

The Silver Rose gets its name from the spectacular altar piece donated to the monks by Amalrich III (praised by many as the ultimate triumph of Formalist art, though I always reckoned it was gaudy and just a trifle vulgar) which used to adorn the Inner Triclinium before somebody stole it and broke it up for scrap. Not something I'm proud of, but if they couldn't be bothered to keep it secure, they didn't deserve to have it; their pathetic approach to security had cost me everything I had in the world, so I reckon they owed me. It took me nearly a whole night to saw the bloody thing up into sections small enough to carry, and I only got a fraction of its bullion value from a thoroughly dishonest silversmith in Old Town who tried to make me believe it was only sixty-seven parts fine.

It was a good reason for leaving Erech, at any rate, and at least I could afford a ride on the stage as far as Numa, where I forged an imperial travel warrant that got me a berth on a cotton freighter as far as Beloisa. Cotton ships don't move very fast—they don't have to—so I had a bit of time to think.

What I should have been thinking about was what I was going to do next. Instead, I allowed myself to be distracted into contemplation of the question of evil, a topic which I keep coming back to, even though I thought I'd settled it once and for all in Act 2 of *Carausio* and *Reflections On The Abyss*. Apparently not. So I thought about it some more, in the light of my recent experiences, and realised that I was gradually drifting towards a whole new set of conclusions. I remember sitting on deck with my back to the mast and my feet up on a coil of rope, struggling with the realisation that the resolution I thought I'd found ten years earlier, in the magnificently argued third section of *Human, All Too Human*, was actually just plain wrong. I'd contrived to talk myself into believing it, but once you set aside the eloquence and the passion and the sheer poetry of the argument, there was a gaping hole in the hypothesis, bigger than the hole in Cassius' tomb, and look what happened to him.

Nuts, I thought; one of the finest achievements of the human intellect, reduced to grey mush by a little clear thinking. Pity, really; and if word of it ever got out, a lot of people were going to be very disappointed. I got sixteen honorary doctorates from universities right across the world for *Human* (I was stripped of all of them, of course, for being a bad boy, but it's the thought that counts) and nobody would dare to try and pass himself off as educated or enlightened unless he's read it, and at least half a dozen of the associated commentaries; they spend a whole year on it at the Studium, and it's the only foreign language text in the syllabus of the Echmen Imperial Academy. And one of these days, some bright spark will come along, notice what I'd just noticed, and get rich and famous overnight reducing my glorious edifice to rubble. One more nail in my coffin; just what I needed, right then.

It could have been worse. I remember doing more or less the same thing to the celebrated mathematician Proedrus; I disproved the theorem on which his entire reputation was based. Took me about ten minutes, when I should have been working on something else, and because I was young and stupid and not inclined to consider the effects of my actions, I shared my results with the senior tutor, who arranged for them to be published. It destroyed poor Proedrus, a gentle, kind-hearted man who'd spent thirty years working on it. He resigned his lectureship, gave all his money to the university trustees and died two years later of malnutrition and despair. At least that wasn't going to happen to me. I was dead already.

Still: if it wasn't murder, it was manslaughter by reason of criminal recklessness, and trying to blame it all on the truth really doesn't cut it. The truth is a piss-poor excuse for ruining someone's life, your own or somebody else's. What is a truth, a fact, but a hypothesis that hasn't been disproved yet? Until I stuck in my oar, Proedrus' theorem was a fact, true, the truth; likewise the detailed account of the wanderings of the Chosen People in the first five books of Holy Scripture, until some clown (go on, guess) happened to point out on purely philological grounds that they must've been written at least five hundred years later than they claimed to be, and some halfwit (you're way ahead of me) translated the three-thousand-year-old inscriptions on the ruins of Louada which proved that the Children of the Sun never were slaves in Blemmya and far from conquering the Promised Land, they'd been living there all along. That particular snippet of truth started two major wars and deprived countless thousands of people of a faith which was the only thing that made sense of their unbearably miserable lives. Show me a lie that ever did that much damage.

So: I had no duty to the truth; screw it. On the other hand—

"LET'S GET THIS straight," he said. "You claim you've written a book that *disproves* Saloninus' theory of the origins of evil?"

"Yes," I said. "And it's yours for one thousand angels. Cash," I added quickly.

He nodded. "And who are you, precisely?"

"Me? Oh, I'm just a wandering scholar. Just so happens I've devoted my life to the study of this particular area of ethical theory, and—"

"You're a professor? Which university?"

"No, I just said. I'm a wanderer. I move from city to city, consulting all the great libraries."

"How many books have you published?"

"None. None yet. Of course, this book will be—"

He was looking at me. "Just to recap," he said. "You're not a professor, and you haven't published any books. Nobody's ever heard of you. I certainly haven't, and I'm pretty well informed, I have to be, it's my job. That's what you're telling me, isn't it?"

"More or less."

"I thought so. What in God's name makes you think anybody will be interested in anything you have to say?"

I opened my satchel and pulled out the manuscript. "Read it," I said. "It's all in there. Once you've read it—"

He shook his head. "You're nobody anyone's ever heard of and you're asking people to believe you know better than *Saloninus*? Oh, please."

"I knew him," I said.

"Saloninus?"

I nodded. "We were really close."

"Somehow I doubt that."

"I was with him at the end. I paid for his funeral."

He sighed. "It may interest you to know that Saloninus has been dead for seventy years. That's a *fact*. Look it up."

No point arguing, so I left. Nor did I argue with any of the twelve other booksellers I tried to interest in my manuscript, all of whom said the same thing. In the end, I sold the bloody thing to a student I met in a bar; he was out getting drunk, he told me, because he couldn't face the thought of his tutorial with Professor Venhart in two days time, when he'd be forced to admit that he'd been unable to make head nor tail of *Human All Too* bloody *Human* and therefore was in no position to render a reasoned critique. Funny you should say that, I told him, and shortly afterwards a gold angel changed hands. One angel.

("It's sodding long," the student said.

"Value for money."

"I can't copy out all that, I'll sprain my wrist. Can't you sort of cut it down a bit?"

"Every single word in that has been chosen with the utmost care and precision. Take out anything and you'll ruin the structured procession of the argument."

"Oh, balls.")

YOU CAN EXIST for quite some time on one angel, if you don't mind oatmeal porridge. And the porridge life has this to recommend it. You get plenty of time to think.

So I did that; and a fat lot of good it did me. Properly speaking, now that I'd demolished the basic foundations of the modern consensus on the origins and nature of evil, I should've applied my mind to figuring out something to replace it, but I thought, can I be bothered? Answer: no. Instead, I went a certain way towards a scheme for defrauding the Consolidated Goldsmiths' Bank by means of leveraged derivatives based on ultimately worthless mortgages on derelict and abandoned properties. It would probably have worked, at least long enough for me to scoop up the money and run—which was why I didn't bother with it. The thought of the running part of it made me feel tired. The whole point of my death and resurrection was that I wouldn't have to run any more. And since my death, apart from the little matter of the Silver Rose, I'd been as guiltless as a novice in a convent. Did I want to jeopardise all that simply because I was starving and sleeping in doorways?

One such doorway led to the auction rooms in Blind Eye Yard, and I was woken up there very early one morning by a irritable porter who wanted me to move before the bidders started arriving. Turned out that today was a big day for the auctioneers. There was only one lot; the original manuscript of *Philemon and Baucis*—

"By Saloninus."

The porter looked at me. "Fancy you knowing that."

"Everybody knows *Philemon and Baucis.*"

He nodded. "Even the likes of you," he said. "Anyway, they've got hold of it and they're selling it today. Going to be the biggest sale we ever did," he went on. "They're expecting buyers from all over the world, Scheria and Echmen and God only knows where. We had to lay on extra chairs."

"So it's valuable?"

He looked at me as if I was simple. "Half a million angels," he said. "That's the *reserve.*"

I walked away feeling like I'd been run over by a dray. I can clearly remember writing *Philemon and Baucis*—which is, if you ask me, a trivial piece of fluff which flirts with a few interesting issues of identity and integrity but never really addresses them. I dashed it off in a tearing hurry after three months agonising over a much better play which I just couldn't get into (a year later it became *Vetranio,* so I was quite right not to screw it up by writing it when I wasn't ready) and I think the only time I actually read it was when I made the fair copy, which I wrote out on the backs of ninety copies of a proclamation about public sanitation, which some fool carelessly left scattered about the city, nailed to temple doors.

Half a million angels. Five hundred thousand times more valuable than my refutation of Saloninus' doctrine of evil.

(Talking of which, I happened to run into that student again when I was begging on the Priory steps. I want my money back, he said. Really? Yes, he said. That bloody essay you sold me. I got a C. That's impossible. No it bloody isn't, he yelled in my face, and I came this close to getting slung out of the university for presuming to cast doubt on fundamental doctrine. You might have warned me, he said. If I get sent down, my dad'll kill me.)

FIVE HUNDRED THOUSAND angels. And not for the play, just for *one copy* of it.

I tried to remember what had happened to it, after it was grabbed out of my hand by an angry manager, who told me it had better be good since I'd left it so late he hadn't got time to read it. Presumably it ended up on a shelf or in a trunk. Then somebody found it, realised it might be worth money, sold it to someone who sold it to somebody else who sold it to somebody else. Now, with Saloninus dead, the supply cut off for ever and ever, the time had come to realise an exceptionally valuable asset, before the world had had time to consider Saloninus carefully and dispassionately and make up its mind whether he really was such hot stuff after all.

That word valuable. A thing having value. Define value. Value is what, all things being equal, somebody is prepared to pay. And thereby hang all the law and the prophets.

I borrowed some clean clothes from someone's negligently guarded washing line and went to the auction. I sat on my hands in case anyone misconstrued an unguarded flinch as a bid. The room went really quiet when the bidding approached one million, and when the hammer finally fell everyone started to cheer, as though something worthwhile and noble—something valuable—had just been achieved, whereas all that had happened was that a proxy for a very wealthy aristocrat from Choris Seautou had paid a silly price for ninety sheets of stolen Government paper. I felt like I'd been robbed.

TO MARK THE glorious victory of the Choris nobleman, and because the heightened public interest was terrific for business, the Admiral's Men put on a brand new production of *Philemon and Baucis* at the Cockpit, which I duly attended. I'd never actually watched the play before, and my view was a bit circumscribed (I had to prise up a flagstone round the back of Haymarket and crawl through a disused sewer; otherwise they wanted me to pay them three stuivers, just to see my own play) but my original low opinion of the work remained broadly unchanged. I could write something like that standing on my head, I thought—confidently, since I already had.

It had been a while since I'd written a play. Some nations have a rich and vibrant theatrical tradition, others prefer to watch chariot races and bullfights, and in recent years circumstances had landed me in sporting rather than literary jurisdictions—no bad thing; you can wager on fights and races, but nobody's going to bet you money on the outcome of a play. Still, I thought; if I can do it, it can't be that hard. I raised a month's porridge money by selling the clothes I'd borrowed to go to the auction, and fortuitously the city authorities had just issued a new proclamation about grain prices or something such; ink you make from soot, and a pen is just a matter of sneaking up on the nearest goose. I found a shady place under the aqueduct arches where nobody goes because of the smell, and tried to think of something to write about. No dice.

THE PRIORY STEPS is probably the best begging pitch in this man's town. You get people with money and consciences—cause and effect, presumably—delighted to buy a little peace of mind for less than the cost of a cinnamon biscuit. Goes without saying, I had no right to be there. You have to pay the Guild a small fortune for a square yard of the steps, and if I had that kind of money I wouldn't need to beg. But it so happened that the rightful occupant of the fifth step down on the left was indisposed after eating something that disagreed with him (don't look at me, I was the other side of town when he actually ate it) and wasn't able to attend to business for a week, during which time I claimed squatter's rights, so to speak. I got a lot of filthy looks from the other pitch-holders, but since I was being blind from birth for professional reasons, I could quite justifiably pretend not to notice.

To be blind from birth on the Priory steps, you wear a strip of dirty bandage over your eyes. Even so, I really should have seen her coming a mile off.

"Hello," she said, about two feet over my head. Actually, it was hello followed by a name I hadn't heard in a long time, which happens to have belonged to me once. I winced.

"Go away."

I heard a coin clink in my hat. "I've been looking for you. You're hard to find."

"Not hard enough, evidently."

I felt a slight pressure against my shoulder as she sat down next to me. Made my skin crawl. "Everyone thinks you're dead."

I sighed. Prophets and holy men get rich and famous for acts of resurrection, but it's not always a helpful thing to do. "They're right," I said.

"Of course they are." She paused. "Little job I want you to do for me."

THE LAST TIME I saw her, I had this ghastly ringing in my ears, mainly because I'd just combined *sal tonans*, *aqua regia* and *aqua fortis* in a small glass bottle and dropped it off the roof of the sixth precinct Watch house in Beal Defoir—an injudicious thing to do, as you'll know if you've studied alchemy, unless you actually want to blow a hole in a wall big enough to drive a wagon through.

I didn't want to blow holes in the Watch house, not one bit. It's illegal, and it meant I had to leave town in a hurry. She made me do it. She's made me do a lot of things, over the years.

If I hadn't done it, she wouldn't have escaped from her cell, and they'd have taken her out into Cartgate and strung her up; and the world would have been a better place, if a bit less lively. But she'd looked at me with those endless grey eyes and reminded me of various things we'd done together, which (up to then) she'd never told anyone about; in consequence of which, I spent a truly horrible night distilling seven grains of *sal tonans* on makeshift equipment over a charcoal stove; one careless move and they'd have had to redraw all the City maps. It was people like her I'd died to get away from, but apparently, what we had together endured beyond the grave, just like true love is supposed to do.

"Well?" I said.

"Nice to see you too." She scowled at me. "You bastard. I was *heartbroken*."

The thing is, sometimes she tells the truth, and sometimes you believe her. "Not for long."

She shook her head. "I had you dug up."

I opened my mouth but nothing came out.

"Well," she said, "I had to know for sure. Who was he, by the way?"

"No idea. Just someone I found in the river."

"I didn't tell anyone," she said. "Yes, that's him, I told them. He didn't look a bit like you."

"Cremation next time," I said.

"How could you? I cried buckets."

I looked at her. "What exactly do you want?"

"Nothing much. I don't know how I managed to keep going, thinking you'd died. It was like the world had suddenly ended."

"Nothing much?"

"I need you to kill the Lurian ambassador."

SHE'S NOT BEAUTIFUL by any definition, but she's one of those people you can't help looking at when she walks into a room. It's like all the strings were loose until she came along, and just by being there she tightens and tunes them. Please note that I haven't specified the kind of string.

She told me once she comes from Luria, but I don't think it's that simple, because nothing about her ever is. Don't ask me how old she is; I've known her for twenty years, but she hasn't changed a bit. She can't sew a straight line or boil an egg, but she does the very best fake cursive minuscule money can buy, good enough to fool all the scholars in the Studium, as she's proved over and over again. She told me once, a forgery's got to be better than the real thing if you want to fool anyone—painting, coinage, sculpture, manuscript, whatever. I guess that makes her the best creative artist who ever lived, because she's faked them all in her time.

"You must be getting me muddled up with someone else," I said. "I don't kill people."

She smiled.

"Except in the last extremity, in self-defence," I said. "And that was years ago."

That got me her cool look. "Your wife," she said.

"I'd forgotten about her. But that was an accident. Really an accident."

"And then you killed twenty-seven people in an explosion, including the Grand Duke."

"Self-defence."

She didn't actually smile, but her lips warped a little bit. "Well, this'll be self-defence too. Because if you don't do it, I'll turn you in and they'll hang you. Self-defence once removed."

When I first knew her, she made me do dangerous, immoral, illegal things just by being beautiful at me. We'd come a long way since then.

We went to the Sun in Splendour, where they really aren't fussy, and I bought Vesani retsina for her and a small peach tea for myself. There's a sort of balcony on the third floor. You get a breathtaking view out over the Bay, and the only possible eavesdroppers are spiders.

"Why do you want me to kill the Lurian ambassador?"

She smiled at me. "It was a long time ago," she said. "I was fifteen, he was seventeen, we were very much in love. We sat on the beach at twilight. He swore he'd never forget me, as long as he lived."

Starting to make sense. She hasn't changed a bit in all the years I've known her, that's for sure. Good chance, therefore, that her girlhood sweetheart would recognise her if he saw her again; and when I was still alive there were more outstanding warrants against me than her, but not that many. "Why not simply leave town?" I asked her.

She shook her head. "It's the big score," she said, and even though I knew her so well, the low hiss in her voice thrilled me. "Really, it is. The one and only. If it goes through, we'll never have to work again."

OH, THAT.

The big score. The ultimate caper. The very last and the very best. If it actually comes off, all your troubles will be over, money will flow like rivers when the snow melts, the rest of your life will be a symphony of sweetness and joy and you'll have proved beyond a shadow of a doubt that it *was* all worthwhile, that you were right to spend your life and your talents on this side of the fence, that it wasn't all a horrible mistake and a tragic betrayal of everything you might otherwise have been. And it comes only once in a lifetime, until you screw it up and barely escape by the skin on the backs of your heels, and the week after next you start off all over again with another big score or ultimate caper.

But the trouble is, you *have faith*. It's like falling in love. You know full well, when the first poison tendrils hit you and start winding themselves through your heartstrings, that it's all a mistake and it can only end in tears, but what the hell, you can't help it. It's not a rational, informed choice. You see, and you *believe.*

Blessed are those who have seen and yet have not believed; but the blessed in this context are few and far between. Personally, I think the idea of the big score calls out to the inspired part in us, the part wherein dwell all those wonderful wasted gifts and talents we live by perverting and abusing; every master needs a masterpiece. You can spend thirty years painting a hundred and twenty portraits of noblemen's prize racehorses, or you can be Prosper of Schanz and use up the same length of time creating just one colossal bronze horse. The racehorses will pay better, in the long run, but the bronze horse will be a keystone of men's souls until the sun goes cold. Also, with the big score, you get all the money at once, which means you can stash it somewhere safe, turn into a dragon and sprawl all over it till you rot.

"Tell me about it," I said.

She shook her head, which made the ends of her hair swing like bells. "I know you, remember?"

She thought that if I knew what the game was, I'd dart in ahead of her, do the scam myself and cut her out. The thought never crossed my mind, though it may have hung in the air overhead like the sun.

"Fine. You need the ambassador out of the way so he won't recognise you. Does he actually have to be dead?"

"I ask you to do one simple little thing for me, and all I get is attitude."

"Killing people makes things complicated," I said. "More difficult, not less. If an ambassador suddenly drops dead, people ask questions. The whole point, I'd have thought, is to avoid curiosity."

"Not if he dies in his sleep of a heart attack."

Diamonds are proverbially a girl's best friend, but she was also on excellent terms with foxgloves. As well as being an outstanding artist, she has a thorough grasp of practical alchemy, an encyclopedic knowledge of the herbiary and a rock-steady hand. A girl who's never happier than when she's among the flowers.

"All right," I said. "Why me? I don't know the man. I don't mix in those circles. You obviously do, or you wouldn't be scared stiff of bumping into him. You do it."

"I might get caught."

I breathed in deep, then out again slow. "It works both ways, you know. I could tell on you."

She beamed at me. "You'd never do a thing like that."

"Don't be so sure. When they're pulling out my teeth with blacksmith's tongs and asking me who put me up to it, I could say all sorts of things."

"Tell them the Blemmyans paid you to do it. They'd love that."

"You tell them."

"No thanks. Why keep a dog and bark yourself?"

"I don't know the man," I repeated.

"I'll get you an introduction."

"Why me?"

She gave me a smile like a sunrise. "Because this job's really difficult and suicidally dangerous and you're the smartest and most resourceful man who ever lived, of course."

"Ah."

IF YOU WANT to learn a profession, I heartily recommend being on the run from the authorities. You're holed up somewhere, in a derelict barn or an abandoned warehouse, and all you have with you by way of entertainment, spiritual guidance and self-improvement is one book.

In my case, *Principia Medica*, by Aimeric de Poulignac. I stole a luxury edition of it many years ago from the treasury of the Golden

Wing monastery at Scell, along with a sackful of other trifles. During the course of the proceedings, I got in the way of a crossbow bolt loosed off by a careless watchman. I managed to get as far as the harbour, where I had a fishing-boat tied up ready and waiting to take me to Steepholm, a small uninhabited island about three miles off the coast, where there's a ruined priory, an ideal place to stash my modest haul while I made enquiries among wealthy art-lovers. I got to Steepholm, and crawled on my hands and knees to the ruins, and after that things are a bit vague. I remember waking up in a shirt brown and sodden with blood to find eight inches of oak dowel sticking out of me, and not feeling myself.

I hadn't set out to steal the book; it was dark in the treasury and I scooped things up at random and shoved them in the sack, until the barking of unpleasant-sounding dogs made me think it was probably time to go. It was only when I opened the sack, hoping to find something I could use to mop up the blood, that I saw the gold lettering on the gold-and-jewel-encrusted spine. What a pity, I'd been thinking, that there isn't a doctor around, he might possibly have saved my life—and then, lying half-covered by the burlap, not a doctor but the thing that makes doctors; the standard work, the set text, everything you need to know about repairing the human body between two vulgarly ornate covers. It was as though I'd been starving and crying out for bread, and stumbled on a two hundredweight sack of flour.

Poulignac wrote in Old High Scherian and the book has no index, but eventually I found the bit about extracting arrows and more or less figured it out; Old High Scherian isn't that different from Melgoil, and if you can understand Pausanee, you can sort of burst your way through Melgoil, like a pig in an outhouse. In retrospect I realise that I guessed some of the words wrong. I was fine with the introduction (I clearly recall the statement, "arrows inflict wounds with a fatality greater than that of other weapons, particularly when surgical assistance cannot be obtained") but after that it got a bit technical, and I had to keep flicking back to the anatomy section, with my finger between the pages to keep the place. Still, Poulignac saw me through, more or less. He warned me that muscle contraction can be strong enough to bend the point of the arrow, so press down a tad before pulling up—sure enough, he was right; the horrible thing had missed the bone, thank God, but the tip was bent up into a hook, which would've ripped me open if I hadn't disentangled it first. Fortunately I trusted him when he told me to enlarge the wound channel slightly to aid extraction. I really didn't want to, because it meant pushing the pin of a big gold brooch I found in the sack all the way down the wound until I felt the end of the arrowhead, and prising the hole open to make that extra bit of room, but I did it anyway and thereby saved myself from the horrors of pulling out the shaft and leaving the head still in there. All in all, the whole business went surprisingly smoothly, and the worst thing that happened was blood getting all over the exquisitely illuminated pages of the book, thereby significantly reducing its value to collectors.

After that, fever set in, as Dr Aimeric had warned me it would, and after that I was as weak as a kitten for a long time, with nothing to do but lie very still and catch up on my reading. By the time I left the island, I reckon I knew as much about the science of medicine as most of the people who earn their living from it, and very useful that knowledge has been to me over the years. It was only later, during a period of enforced isolation in a condemned foundry in Mesembrocea, that I realised that Poulignac had been wrong about quite a few things, which led me to research this and that, which resulted in my own *Praecepta Medica,* which they tell me has pushed Poulignac out at most of the leading schools, and for which, incidentally, I never got a bent trachy in royalties.

Long story short: I make a pretty convincing doctor when the need arises, so when we were trying to figure out how to worm me into the palace so I could murder the Lurian ambassador, I suggested she introduced me as the learned Dr So-and-So, Professor of Medicine at the Echmen Imperial Academy.

Echmen doctors are the best in the world, and I decided I was one of them. I happen to like the Echmen—pity I can never go back there, really—and their language is actually quite simple when you get into it. She kindly offered to act as my translator—she does actually speak Echmen, believe it or not, one of about twenty people in the West who can; but we had reason to believe that one of the remaining eighteen might be hanging around the Court at that time, so we decided to play it safe. As a doctor, of course, I could poison who the hell I liked, and nobody would be ill-bred enough to comment.

I'd been Professor So-and-So before, so I knew him quite well. I think he actually exists somewhere, hence my reticence with his real name, though if he's still alive he'd be an old man now. The version of him I created was court physician for a while to the Count of Auvade—during which time I took the opportunity to do the research which led to the *Praecepta*—and when he left suddenly the Count was quite upset, though I reckon he had other things on his mind, such as the disappearance of the family collection of Barnasite icons.

Creating a character matters; you need to know your characters inside and out, what they ate for breakfast, what they look for when buying perfume for their mistresses, which diseases they had when they were children, all that sort of thing. I'm lucky; as soon as I think someone up, I know him intimately. I don't have to speculate or ask myself, is this or that right for this person? I just know. Which is why I knew the professor would've bought a wool gown as soon as he got off the boat (the Echmen feel the cold so badly in the West) but would insist on keeping his wooden-soled sandals, because no matter how well made, leather soles never feel right and make his back hurt.

"Where the hell," she wanted to know, "are we going to get Echmen sandals from?"

"Attention to detail," I told her.

"Yes, but who's going to notice?"

"Me."

She argued, but only from force of habit. She knew all about attention to detail. Forgers understand these things. They also know that there's some commodities—the passage of time, for example—that can't be had even for ready money, and you need to find acceptable substitutes. So she made me a pair of Echmen sandals. They were perfect. No good, I told her.

"You what?"

"Too new."

To her credit, I didn't need to explain further. Other men might be prepared to go on a long voyage to a strange land in a new pair of sandals, but not the professor. He'd be set in his ways, and experienced enough to know that no man is more wretched than he who finds himself a long way from home in uncomfortable shoes. He'd have worn his favourite pair, properly broken in, so perfectly adjusted to the shape of his foot that he didn't know he was wearing them.

To simulate the effects of three years of daily wear, she gouged out shallow slots in the soles, soaked and dried them to open the grain, then polished them glassy smooth with ten different grades of carpenter's sand, applied on a wooden strickle, followed by buffing soap. She frayed the leather straps with the edge of a razor, just enough to take the square off the edges, and stained them with vinegar to simulate sweat. In fact, it was her idea to roughen the underside of the soles—which don't show and nobody but me would ever have anything to do with—because an Echmen academic would do a lot of walking on pavements, and in the city the doctor came from, the streets are paved with volcanic tufa. If she wasn't scarier than a cave full of tigers, I'd like her a lot. She has a strain of integrity that I can't help but admire.

THE SCAR LEFT by that stupid arrow is one of my very few distinguishing marks, and of course you have to peel my shirt off to see it. Unfortunately it's recorded in vivid detail in the files of criminal-investigation agencies right across the world, which is why I keep my shirt on even when it's baking hot. Whereby hangs a tale. There was this man in, I think, Mezentia who was pretending to be me in furtherance of some illegal scheme or other—I assume money was involved, but I don't know the details—and he'd read the files and knew about the scar. There was no real need to worry about it. There was an outside chance he'd have to seduce the wife of the Dean of Humanities, but she wasn't likely to know what was in the police files. Aside from that, no real issue. But this man knew about attention to detail and the vital importance of being in character, so he got an arrow, with a bodkin head like the one I'd been shot with, and fixed it to a door pointing out at right angles, and pulled the door towards himself sharply, impaling himself in the precise spot where I'd been hit. He healed up pretty well to begin with, but then something must've got in the wound, because he went down with gangrene and died.

I suppose it's a bit like religion. Perfect virtue, they tell us, can be achieved only by imitating in every detail the life of the Invincible Sun in His human incarnation; which is why nobody can be perfect, since in order to do that you'd need to be able to die for the sins of the people, be resurrected and ascend bodily to Heaven in splendour. Do not try this, as the saying goes, at home. There's a level of perfection that's unattainable *by definition*. He can do it, you can't, so don't bother trying. To which I responded at an early stage by saying: if I can't be perfectly virtuous, I'll always be imperfect, therefore sinful and wicked, and once I've conceded that it's all just a matter of degree, which really doesn't interest me, so why bother at all? My tutors got vexed at me when I pointed this out to them and told me I was missing the point. I got the point all right. When they say, you're missing the point, it means they know their position is logically untenable. The joker who pretended to be me did everything right, in terms of fastidious authenticity, but he died and wasn't able to resurrect himself. I didn't die. And when I did, I rose again from the dead. Not that I'm drawing a parallel. Just something to think about.

I hope you'll understand what I'm getting at when I tell you that the scar on my chest was, as far as I was aware, the only clue I'd left open. Everything else that was possible to cover in advance, we covered. So why omit the scar? I know it sounds stupid, but when I really immerse myself in a character I can go in so deep, I need something—like the golden thread in the Labyrinth myth—to find my way home with. So long as I had the scar, I'd know who I really was.

"That's stupid," she told me.

"I know."

"Something like that could get us both hung."

"Yes."

"It's vanity, that's what it is. It's you saying, I'm so smart, I can leave a bloody great big clue lying about and still you're too dumb to catch me. It'd be like me signing my work on the back in tiny letters."

But she'd done that, several times, and got away with it. Well, I'd noticed, but nobody else. "I agree," I said. "But I'm superstitious."

"The hell you are."

"It's *like* being superstitious," I said. "And anyway, do you know any way to get rid of a twenty-year-old scar?"

"There isn't one."

THE RECTOR OF the University, no less, introduced me to the Duke and his court at a reception for the Lurian ambassador. The Doctor, he explained, had come to town to examine some ancient and incredibly rare medical treatises in the palace library. He'd brought with him letters of introduction and accreditation from his own faculty back in Echmen, together with recommendations and testimonials from a dozen world-famous universities, all of which had been duly lodged and declared acceptable by the Abbot and Chapter, who'd invited him to lecture to them on Saloninus' theory of the circulation of the blood.

The Duke said he'd heard about that, though he had no idea what it meant. I explained it to him. He was shocked. You mean it goes round and round inside you, he said. Yes, I told him, like irrigation channels or the works of a water-clock. But surely you'd feel something, he said, a sort of throbbing, and a sloshing noise. The human body, I told him, is a remarkable thing. Yes, he said. Quite.

Then I was shoved in front of a few more deadheads, and then the Lurian ambassador, who startled the life out of me by greeting me in practically flawless Echmen, though he did get a couple of the tones wrong. His posting before last, he explained, was as diplomatic attaché to Hocha, on the border between the Sashan and the Echmen, and while he was there he learned the language.

You speak it very well, I told him. He was pleased. Do you really think so? he said.

After that, we got on like a house on fire, and since nobody else in the room could understand a word we were saying, we ended up in a corner of the room, quiet so we could hear ourselves think and handy for the food.

"It must be awkward for you," he said. "I mean, there's hardly anything here you can eat."

I smiled. "Our dietary laws aren't nearly as strict as people think. Besides, even if you're ultra-orthodox, you can eat pretty much anything you like so long as you sanctify it first."

"Excuse me?"

"With *cha* powder," I explained.

"I don't think I ever came across—"

"Ah." Mock-furtive. "It's not something we tell foreigners about."

"Oh. So what—?"

"*Cha* powder," I told him, "is the seeds and flowers of a dozen holy herbs, dried and ground and then blessed by the monks of the Crystal Sky monastery, on the slopes of the Holy Mountain. A few specks of *cha* purges all trace of abomination, so you can eat any food that's put in front of you. Provided," I added, "that your motive in doing so is to spare offence to your host, or extreme starvation. Just liking how the stuff tastes won't do, unfortunately."

"That's—ingenious," he said, carefully not grinning.

I shrugged. "As you know," I said, "causing offence to a host or social superior is one of the worst things you can do in our culture. And we found out the hard way, there's few things more likely to upset someone than telling him the delicious food he's prepared for you specially is unclean and an abomination, and just being in the same room with it puts your immortal soul in jeopardy. Also," I added, "our Heavenly Father gave us the Law before we'd made first contact with the Jens Servida."

He nodded gravely. *"Edomi sako."*

"Precisely. But we know that the Heavenly Father is a benevolent god and would never have forbidden us to eat raw fish if He thought that would mean missing out on *edomi sako* marinated in sweet white wine. So, obviously, there must've been a misunderstanding. Our Father's word is immutable, but the human prophets who recorded it were fallible mortals, after all. And the Jens are such touchy people. They take offence at the slightest little thing."

He was looking over my shoulder. The Duke had a Jens chef working for him, and on a silver platter not six feet from my elbow was a whole *edomi* fish, studded with cloves and so far untouched. The Lurians also have a taboo against raw fish.

"I must confess," the ambassador said, in a slightly husky voice, "in the privacy of my own family circle, I have very occasionally... But at a public function, with people watching—"

From my sleeve I took a little ivory box. She'd made it, because you can't buy really good quality Echmen ivory in the West, and the doctor wasn't the sort of man who'd keep his *cha* powder in any old rubbish. A man with few possessions, but those possessions all of the very best. "You put me in a difficult position," I said. "For me to indulge in a delicacy knowing that my host's honoured guest is forbidden to join me would be appallingly bad manners." I twirled the box in my fingers and put it away again.

"That's it, is it? *Cha* powder?"

Portrait of a man to whom an idea has just occurred. "You don't suppose—" I stopped myself. "I'm sorry," I said. "Please ignore me."

It's the colours that make *edomi sako* irresistible: the glistening orange wrapped round the satiny white, and the little yellow and red bits. Personally I can take it or leave it alone, but true connoisseurs of the stuff just can't get enough of it. A fat man, I think he was the Duke's brother-in-law, stopped and hovered round the plate for a moment before helping himself to pigs' knuckles and fermented cabbage. "One of the purposes of my mission to this country is to help foster ecumenical unity and mutual respect and understanding between people of different faiths."

"Is that so?"

"Absolutely. Our Patriarch feels that now is the time for all people of faith to embrace their similarities rather than their differences."

"To reach out, in other words."

"Oh, I think so, don't you?" He watched me take out the box and slide back the lid. "Just a sprinkle on the top?"

"You can barely taste it."

He darted towards the food table like a squirrel chased by a dog and grabbed a plate. I handed him the box. "Is that enough?" he asked.

"Maybe just a trifle more."

The fish looked like it had dandruff. "Not for me," I said, when he waved the platter at me. "Truth is, I love it but it doesn't like me. Too oily. I'd be up half the night."

All the more for me, then, he didn't say. We carried on chatting for a while after that. Apparently, Lurians don't think it's bad manners to talk with your mouth full.

SHE WAS ANGRY with me. I felt hard done by.

"It's not what I told you to do," she said, accurately. "I told you—"

"Same outcome," I argued. "He made an exhibition of himself, throwing up all over the Duke and Duchess, and he's been sent home in disgrace for breaking Lurian dietary law. He's out of your life. No longer a problem."

"I told you to kill him."

"I don't do that."

Not a word about how clever I'd been, dusting the *edomi sako* with a monster emetic rather than poison. The ambassador's violent reaction had been attributed to the raw fish, and the circumstances made it impossible for him to deny that he'd been eating forbidden food, so there was no choice but to send him home. Nobody dead. Nobody under suspicion of murder. And still she was giving me a hard time.

"It was a big risk," she said. "What if he hadn't been a greedy pig with a taste for exotic food?"

"I understood his character."

"You'd never met him."

"No," I told her, "but I'd heard a bit about him. Enough to know that he was the sort of Lurian who likes going abroad because you can do things there which you can't get away with at home. The rest I extrapolated from what I knew. And guess what, I was right. I don't take risks," I added. "I play carefully calculated odds. There's a difference."

She scowled at me. I was in trouble. So what?

"Anyhow," I said, "I've done what you wanted, so that's all right. It's been lovely seeing you again, and now I think I'll be moving on. I rather like the good Doctor and I fancy he might turn out to be lucrative. Don't worry about my share from the scam, whatever it is. You keep it. I have an idea—"

"You're not going anywhere."

That's one of the things about her. You think she's through with you and you're finally free and clear, but there's always one more trivial favour to be done. "Don't be silly," I said. "You wanted me to get rid of the Lurian ambassador—"

"That was just the start," she said. "There's a long way to go yet."

I'd tried to meet her halfway. I'd saved her all the hard work and trouble of double-crossing me and ripping me off for my share by telling her I didn't want it. "There's more."

"Ever such a lot more, yes. All we've done so far is groundwork."

I sighed. "Oh, come on," I said, "be reasonable. You can see I don't want to do this."

"You don't even know what it is yet."

"It's something with you involved. That's enough."

For that I got the sort of look that dissolves the enamel off your teeth, and which I've gotten used to over the years. "That's not a very nice thing to say. And I need you."

"No, you don't."

"Yes, I *do*."

There are ways for a woman to say *I need you, yes I do* to a man that'll break your heart or flood it with joy. And there are other ways. Same words, very different effect.

In case you were wondering, no. Strictly professional, throughout an association going back many years. The way it works is, we bump into each other, we collaborate, she lands me in ghastly trouble and makes off with the proceeds of our joint venture. In the past I worked with her solely because I happened to have a price on my head in the various jurisdictions where we happened to be at the time and she didn't, giving her a certain degree of leverage. Latterly she'd made herself desirable to the authorities in almost as many places as I had, so I'd sort of hoped that her hold over me had dissipated, but apparently not.

"What," I asked her, "could you possibly need me for?"

EVERYTHING IS MY fault.

I started off in the theatre to help out some friends of mine. We were all young and stupid, and they'd pooled what was left of their inheritances to take the lease on the Curtain theatre in Choris Anthropou for the summer season. Dabbling in theatrical management when you don't know exactly what you're doing is the quickest way to get rid of money that doesn't involve fire or deep water, but they thought they'd be fine because one of them was drinking pals with one of the actors in the Duke's Company, and this actor swore blind that he could persuade Theudahad to write a brand new comedy for the Curtain. Put like that it wasn't such a stupid idea. Theudahad had three plays running in Choris that season, all to packed houses, and he'd just fallen out with the Duke's men over who paid what for new rush matting for the floor of the pit.

Sadly, it didn't happen that way. One of the three plays the Great Man had on that year was *The Whore's Tragedy*. Enough said. Theudahad was arrested for sedition and blasphemy, and shortly afterwards drew the biggest house in the shortest run of his career when he starred in his own execution. Which left my pals with an expensive theatre, seventeen actors, forty-six backstage operatives and no play.

So I wrote them one. I did it to help them out, as a bit of fun, because I'd always fancied having a go at it, because I've always felt the drama is the most immediate of the literary genres, because one of the young idiots had a mother who had a particularly valuable piece of jewellery hidden in a chamber pot under her bed (where a thief would never think of looking, her son proudly informed me) and I wanted to be invited to her house, and because I naturally assumed that if the play was a success they would pay me some money. I wanted to call it *The Worms and the Lions*, but one of them thought *Apis and Sophrosyne* was a much better title, and he was quite right.

Ah well. I was talking to a man a year or so back and he told me he was just returned from Chaxaris. There's no reason why you should have heard of the place; it's some way east of the eastern border of the Echmen Empire, and only a few diplomats and very enterprising traders have ever made it out so far. But, this man told me, he went for a stroll round the capital city one evening and what did he find but a theatre playing a Chaxar translation of bloody *Apis and Sophrosyne*, and doing pretty good business too. Every day, in some part of the world or other, someone's staging a production of the wretched thing, and I never see a penny. Personally I think it's a typical young man's play, all rhetoric and tricks and gags, precious little depth or insight into character, but what do I know?

I spent money I hadn't got on lawyers to try and gouge something out of my erstwhile friends, who were now rich enough to afford better lawyers than I could. That got me nowhere, and I never did scrounge that dinner invitation I'd been angling for. On the other hand, every manager in Choris wanted me to write a play for him, and I was only too happy to oblige. It wasn't like it was hard work or anything. All I had to do was choose a plot from some masterpiece I admired by somebody dead, beat it a bit out of shape so that the theft wasn't immediately obvious, decide who the characters were going to be, get to know them, and write down what they wanted to say to each other. That's all there is to it. Anybody who tries to tell you that writing plays constitutes work is lying to you. Essentially all you're doing is eavesdropping on your imaginary friends, pausing now and then to refill your inkwell. Until you've written half a dozen, of course, at which point it all goes blue on you terribly quickly, but I'm getting ahead of myself. For a while there, I honestly believed I'd found my place in the world. True, I wasn't making very much money, about the same per month as a middling-competent plasterer working on a government project, because the managers got all the rights. That's how it goes when you're starting in the profession, until the day comes when your name carries so much weight that you can turn round and say no, from now on it's a share of the gross, plus the rights revert to me at the end of the run. I was just approaching that point when one of my other sidelines suddenly went sideways and I found myself leaving Choris in something of a hurry, on a dung cart, cunningly disguised as part of the dung.

You'd have thought that was the end of my dramatic career, but you know what they say, you can't keep a good man down. Within five years my plays were everywhere, filling theatres in places I daren't set foot, making fortunes for people I'd never met, and a particularly daring and imaginative syndicate of managers from Lonazep City tracked me down—I was living in a semi-derelict croft on the north coast of Aelia, dining on hazelnut stew and crab-apples and putting the finishing touches to *Human, All Too Human*—and suggested that I might care to write them something. There wouldn't be an awful lot of money, they explained, because of all the risks and difficulties; me being a wanted man in practically all the kingdoms of the earth might disincline people to see my plays, and then there were all the associated problems of laundering the money so it could be paid to a convicted criminal in a faraway jurisdiction, stuff like that. They mentioned a figure. It was a week's rent in Lonazep, but in north Aelia, if ever I wanted change they'd have to take on extra staff at the mint. So I wrote them *Evil for Evil,* and *Florian IV parts 1 and 2,* and the rest of the histories, and most of what you would know as the City comedies. They called at intervals to collect the manuscripts, and I asked them how the plays were doing and they shrugged and said business was steady, nothing spectacular, you understand, but building slowly. Any chance, I said tactfully, of a bit more money? And they pulled sad faces and didn't reply, so I didn't push it. Eventually a bounty-hunter got the idea of trailing them, leading to a hectic couple of hours for me, followed by a long sea-voyage and three months in a condemned cell in Paraprosdocia, from which I escaped, I kid you not, thanks to a timely earthquake. But that was the end of what scholars call my Aelian period. I wound up in one of the provincial capitals of the Sashan Empire, where theatre is forbidden by law, and decided to explore other avenues.

The Lonazep syndicate, for what it's worth, decided to invest their profits in real estate and built a chain of cities from Chaon in the north right down to the Blemmyan border. You can if you wish reflect on how their dishonesty did them no good in the long run; after a while their oppressed tenants rose up, lynched them and stuck their heads on pikes, and that's how the Caelian Republic was born, so if you're a Caelian you've got me to thank, in a way. For my part, I never got any of the money but my head's on my shoulders, not a pike. I've done a shedload of stupid things in my time, but I've never gone into theatrical management. Too risky.

"I NEED YOU," she told me, "to write a play."

I closed my eyes. Somewhere, in the streets below our balcony, a flower-seller was yelling about fresh violets. "Oh come on," I said.

It turned out that she'd been at the auction where they sold the manuscript of *Philemon and Baucis* for nearly a million. It had given her ideas.

As a trial run, she sold a simple love sonnet. I was rather touched to find she'd kept it until she explained that she'd used it as a bookmark and forgotten it was there until it suddenly fell out at her. I took it as an omen, she told me, having it turn up like that out of the blue. She put it in an auction in Choris and it made fifty thousand; a nice little score (in her exalted terms), just about right for financing the really big score which had suddenly and unexpectedly manifested itself in her mind like the Transfiguration.

If someone was prepared to pay half a million for *Philemon,* she argued to herself, what wouldn't they pay for a brand new, hitherto undiscovered masterpiece? Especially since the man himself was dead, and so everyone had more or less resigned themselves to there not being any more plays, ever again. Think about it, she urged me. We get two million, at the very least, for the manuscript. On top of that, we reserve fifty per cent of the performing rights for the play itself. It really is the big score, she told me, with what might just possibly have been genuine tears in her eyes; the ultimate, the *ne plus ultra*, the last, best hope for a better tomorrow. And all you have to do—

I held up a hand. "It's a nice idea," I said. "Just one thing. Where do you come into this?"

She looked at me as though I'd just stabbed her. "You what?"

"It's a great idea," I said. "I write a play, in my own handwriting, and I put it up for auction. What do I need you for?"

She breathed out slowly through her nose. "You clown," she explained.

Being Saloninus. What about it?

I have never deliberately been Saloninus. It's something that comes naturally to me, I suppose, something I can't help doing, so that in that sense I can reasonably claim not to be responsible for my actions. I don't get up in the mornings and ask myself, what would Saloninus do next? Which in a way is odd. If it was one of my made-up characters, Philemon or Ardester or that idiotic excuse for a human being Florian IV, I'd have no problem. I ask myself that question, what would Philemon or Florian do next, every time I pick up my pen, and the answer always just comes, like the flowers in spring.

But what would Saloninus do next? You're asking the wrong man. In a way it's like archery. Not something I've ever been much good at, but I've known a few of the really top shots over the years and they've never managed to teach me a damn thing, because when you ask them, how do you do that, they don't know. I just look at the target, they say, really *look* at it, and let go of the string.

In my case, of course, most of the time the string is more or less snatched out of my hand. Someone recognises me, something goes wrong, something is found at the scene that implicates me, and all the ice palaces I've so carefully built up around me shatter and melt, and I'm off on my travels again. I sometimes wonder what would have become of me if only I'd taken to art and science and music and literature before I'd taken to crime. But it didn't happen that way, and I have a nasty feeling that it never could have. If I'd stayed peacefully at home and been very, very good, I suspect the slender golden arrows of inspiration would never have come slanting down out of the sky and hit me. Being Saloninus, thus far at least, has been thirty per cent pure gold and seventy per cent mixed shit, but it seems almost inevitable that the shit had to come first before the gold could begin to crystallise. I speak, mark you, as a leading alchemist.

So: being Saloninus, as far as I'm concerned, is about reacting desperately to desperate situations. I have this theory about, among other things, coal. I believe that what we call coal is in fact the decomposed compost formed by billions and billions of leaves, which fell long ago from forests long since cleared away; coal is just leaf-mould, compressed over inconceivably long periods of time by the weight of the layers of its own self above it, until it's compacted and squashed almost as hard as stone, made brittle, dry and extremely combustible. There's also evidence to suggest, though I won't bore you with the details, that if you compress the compressed coal long enough and hard enough, that's what makes diamonds. It's just a theory, and I don't suppose you're all that interested. I only mention it because, if it's true, it's a good way to describe the process of being Saloninus. A lot of stuff falls on me from a great height, until the sheer weight of fallen stuff concentrates me very hard indeed, and one of the by-products is flawless gems of great value.

"Of course you need me," she told me. "It just won't work otherwise."

It's all a matter, she explained as to an imbecile, of authenticity. You're dead, she pointed out. A freshly written manuscript, with the ink barely dry, would naturally be taken as a forgery, a blatant attempt to cash in on the latest collecting craze—

"But it'd be genuine," I said.

"Being genuine doesn't matter," she said patiently. "You can be as genuine as a new-laid egg and people will just laugh at you. You've got to *look* genuine."

"Ah."

"That's different. That takes a lot of work."

She knows what she's talking about, trust me. So I paid attention.

In order to *look* genuine, she said, a thing's got to be just right. It's got to be written on the right paper in the right ink, with the right amount of fraying and discoloration, with the right number of spelling mistakes, crossings out, illegible words, whatever. It's got to be—well, *right.* And right, in this context, means it's got to be what people expect it to be.

"But I've only been dead, what, nine months. So it doesn't have to be very old—"

She shook her head, and I realised I was being stupid. "It's got to look like the other manuscripts," she said, "the ones that are proved to be genuine, because their provenances are above suspicion. Otherwise the buyers won't want to take the risk."

"But surely," I said, "the actual play. The words themselves."

Uh-huh. "You don't understand," she said. "The thing of it is, Saloninus is a genius, everybody knows that, but nobody really knows why. Or how, rather. Nobody knows how he does it, or else they'd all be doing it themselves. But about a million people have tried to write like him—"

"Excuse me, but what's with the third person?"

She scowled at me. "It's easier for me, with you sitting there. A million people have tried to write like him but they can't quite do it. It's that indefinable something."

"My point exactly."

"No, you're being stupid, you don't get it. Nobody else can quite do it, but about a million people can get very close. It's a tiny margin, thin as a razor, but so's the difference between being alive and being dead. And nobody's going to bet two million angels on their ability to assess a tiny margin. They say, this reads like Saloninus, but what if I'm wrong? What if I'm too stupid to tell the difference? So instead they go by the handwriting and the age of the paper and the composition of the ink, and most of all by the provenance. Which," she added with a sunrise grin, "is why you need me."

The penny dropped. I once calculated that a falling object accelerates by a fixed ratio of thirty-two feet per second per second; so, the farther it falls, the harder it hits when it lands. This penny must've fallen a very long way.

"Oh," I said.

"Exactly. I sold that silly poem of yours and they bought it because everybody knows we used to be lovers—"

"But we—"

"Everybody knows," she repeated firmly. "The provenance was impeccable. So, if you gave me a poem, why not a play?"

Valid point. You know when you're driving a cart through the long grass and you run into a big stone you never guessed was there. She'd got me.

"The reason we're here," she said, in her dove-like cooing voice, "is because— All right. Guess who bought the *Philemon* manuscript."

"No idea."

"The Duke," she said. "Who also bought your crummy sonnet. He's a collector. He's *the* collector. His idea is to build up a massive collection of all the most important manuscripts ever, so that when he's dead people will call him Sighvat the Learned or Sighvat the Wise instead of that bastard Sighvat. We're here so that I can sell him the play. Which he'll buy from me, because he's already bought one absolutely genuine Saloninus manuscript from me, so he knows it's all right."

I felt like I did the first time I saw the pea emerge from under the wrong shell. "I get you," I said.

"Of course," she went on, "before he actually parts with the money he'll have it gone over by experts. Handwriting experts, manuscript experts, historians, scholars and literary critics, the whole nine yards. So it's got to be perfect."

"Well, it will be, won't it?"

She sighed. "You obviously don't understand the first rule of forgery and faking. For a fake to be accepted as genuine, it's got to be better than the original. Not almost as good, not close enough for country music; better. That's always worked for me."

I lifted my head and looked at her. "Better?"

PERFECTION. THAT OLD thing.

We touched on this earlier. Perfection, so they taught me at the seminary, is an attribute unique to the Divine. Only the Invincible Sun is perfect. Our path to salvation is to imitate the divine, but it's an unattainable ambition, a hiding to nothing. So, you can be like me and refuse to play a game where you're not allowed to win, or you can spend your life trying, because success doesn't matter, trying does.

In my defence I've never tried to write the perfect play, symphony, meditation, homily, equation or treatise. I know I can't do it, because it can't be done. I've come close, but so does the man who jumps off a high tower aiming for the three-foot square well of deep water two hundred feet below him. He misses, by a matter of a few inches, and they scrape what's left of him off the flagstones. A nine is a nine is a nine, and when you need to score ten, it's completely useless. The smaller the margin by which you miss, the worse you feel.

I don't aim at the ten. I don't aim at all. I just close my eyes and relax my fingers. And, by and large, I haven't done so terribly badly. With my eyes shut, I outscore everyone else. Comparative merit, as opposed to absolute, is good enough for me. The problem arises when you ask me to compete against myself.

I'd far rather you asked me to create something perfect. At least I'd know what the outcome would be, which would save the anxiety and the stress, and there's always a chance of getting on a side-bet that I'd fail. But ask me to outdo myself—see above, under archery. In order to do that, I'd need to know how I do this stuff in the first place; what that tiny margin between me and everyone else actually is. Know your enemy; it's the golden rule of competition. But the one competitor you can't watch like a hawk is yourself. I can tell you in exquisite detail how Theudahad and Simmacho and Notker and Ellaeus wrote plays, their various tricks and devices, the second-act reveal, Simmacho's jar on the mantelpiece, the double peripateia, the third-act syncopated false ending. Ask me about me; not a clue. I just sit there gnawing the end of my pen and let the characters do the work.

"This is tripe," she told me.

"I know," I said.

She was getting impatient. She was just back from a morning hanging round at the Duke's court, where it was getting harder each day to fend off the Duke's frantic enquiries about the genuine Saloninus manuscript she claimed to have. "If it goes on much longer, he'll send someone to burgle the house," she said.

"Tell him it's in a safe place."

"He knows that's not true. He owns all the safe places, banks, temples, abbey treasuries, he knows it's not in any of them. It's getting embarrassing. He's not the sharpest knife in the drawer, but sooner or later he's going to start suspecting something."

I sighed. The play wasn't going well. I was trying too hard, and I kept getting in the way. There was only one thing I could do, so I did it. I got up, crossed to the fire and shoved my manuscript in among the glowing embers.

"Well, that was melodramatic," she said, as the paper blossomed into flame. "Now what?"

"Now I start again," I said. "New plot, new characters, everything."

"Fine."

I sat down and let my head sink into my hands. "As it happens," I said, "I do have another idea at the back of my mind."

She poured herself a large drink. "Go on."

"There's this prince," I said. "He's lounging about feeling vaguely discontented when suddenly his father's ghost pops up. I was murdered, the ghost said, by my brother; you know, the one who subsequently married your mother and seized the throne. Avenge me."

I looked at her. "And?" she said.

"The prince avenges him."

"And?"

"That's it."

She put down her drink. "That's it?"

"Yes."

"All right, what about the sub-plot?"

"There isn't one."

"Love interest?"

"No."

"Oh come *on,*" she said. "You've got to have a love interest. And a feisty, kick-ass heroine. It's the law."

"No," I said. "There's a girl, but he's not in love with her."

"For crying out loud. So what happens?"

"He sees the ghost. After a while, he kills his uncle. Curtain."

"That's it?"

"There's a certain amount of internal debate about morality and the nature of human existence."

She curled her lip. "Padding."

"You say that like it's a bad thing. It's the stuffing people like, not the chicken."

"Padding," she repeated grimly. "No, what you've got there is Act 1, Scene 1 and Act 5, Scene 6. Now go away and figure out the rest of it."

She was beginning to annoy me. "Who's writing the bloody thing, you or me?"

"You know your trouble? You haven't got a clue. You're not just clueless, you're a bottomless pit down which clues fall and are utterly lost for ever. You can't write that. It's garbage."

It's a problem I have. I tease people.

The problem isn't so much the teasing as the corners I back myself into as a result. Having pitched her the outline of what would obviously turn out to be the worst, most boring play in the history of the drama, I was now committed to writing it, or else face her wrath for wasting precious time by burning two-thirds of a play that could've been fixed with rewrites and judicious cutting. The burning, of course, wasn't the tease. I had to do that, or else I'd have carried on tinkering with the stupid thing when it was obviously dead.

But I've found, on the rare occasions when I'm having difficulties with something, that it often helps to make it harder still. It concentrates the mind, piles on the dead leaves and narrows the focus. Having created for myself the once and future piece of shit, I now began to see its possibilities.

At the very least, I had a character I could listen to. When he first comes on, he's feeling rather like I was feeling at that moment: depressed, miserable, resentful, angry. Then enter the ghost, who immediately multiplies his troubles by a thousand. I paused and listened, and my prince started talking to me.

I listened. I may have chewed the end of my pen a bit. And then it was finished.

As soon as my work ended, hers began. There was nothing I could do to help except keep out of her way, so I sat in a chair and watched. There's something about watching a true master at work that really gets me, especially when I'm not seeing it in a mirror.

We'd figured out that I must have written the play about twelve years earlier, about the same time as the sonnet. In which case, I'd written it in Ap'Escatoy, when I was living in a room over a stable on North Street. Important; because the kind of paper they use in Ap'Escatoy is made from reed pulp, not boiled-rag mush. It's a different colour, the fibres are coarser, and ink doesn't soak into it in the same way. If we used rag paper it wouldn't be absolutely fatal, since it was conceivably possible that I'd written the play on imported paper, maybe a supply I'd brought with me, but it was just the sort of thing that raises an expert's hackles, and once he thinks there's something funny going on, he's apt to pay closer attention.

But it was no big deal. There's only one kind of reed that's suitable for making paper, but fortuitously it was the kind that grows wild along the banks of the river. The actual manufacture makes your arms ache like death but it's scarcely catapult science. Drying the paper once we'd made it was a bit more problematic, since the sun is so much hotter down south; it gives the finished product a crisper feel, and it's shinier. We fixed that by warming it very carefully over a whale-oil stove and burnishing it with a polished steel rod.

Next came the actual writing out—

"What the hell do you think you're doing?" she said.

"Copying—"

"Give me that." She snatched the pen out of my hand. "And get out of my chair. No, don't stand there, you're in my light."

We couldn't use my handwriting. It's always been poor verging on catastrophic, though I'm used to that, but I hadn't realised it had changed over the last twelve years, not till she told me to write something, and then showed me an old letter (the one enclosing the sonnet). I saw what she meant. It was only a slight difference—a bit more rounded, a bit more slipshod—but if you knew what you were looking for, you could see it. And there was no way I'd be able to imitate it. She was going to have to do that. Just as well she's the greatest living expert.

"And I'll do it much faster than you could," she told me, as her hand scuttled sideways across the page like the world's daintiest crab. "That's the trick, go fast. It's when you stop to think that it goes blue on you."

I sat and watched her for a long time. Then she called me over. "I need you to sweat," she said.

"Excuse me?"

"You sweat when you write. Buckets. Didn't you know that?"

No, but I didn't say anything. "So what?"

"I need a couple of drops on this page. And I don't sweat."

Now that I could attest to. "Can't you—?"

"No. You need the real thing. Salt solution ages differently, it's the wrong colour."

So I had to go outside, in the freezing cold, and run round and round the block. "Is that the best you can do?"

"On demand? Yes." I captured a little sweat off my forehead on the tip of my fingernail and trickled it onto the page where she showed me. "That's not quite right," she said. "That's a dribble, not a drop. A drop's round, and that's more pear-shaped. Still, it's done now."

It was strange to see my words being written out in my handwriting by someone else. It would probably have been slightly easier if it had been a stranger rather than someone I knew so well. I offered to dictate to her so she wouldn't have to keep looking from one page to another, but she said no, that would actually make it harder and slow things up. I wasn't sure I liked that. It would have been nice to have played some part in the process. As it was, it felt like I was watching my identical twin brother screwing my wife.

THE THIRD, NO, sorry, the fourth time we worked together, we did what lovers do, up to a point. Between us we created a new life.

The impetus or motivation was a strip of second-rate pasture on the south-facing slopes of the Blackmoor hills, about fifteen miles west of Bine Sauton. When I went to look at it, there was nothing there except a vast, billowing tangle of briars, so tall they choked the few maiden birches and withies; but the underlying soil was sandy loam, and you only get thick briars on good, fertile ground. My guess was that it had once been a vineyard, that if it hadn't it should have been, and that if you found the right buyer, it was worth a great deal of money.

And nobody owned it. I went round asking the locals, and they all shrugged and said, nobody. The district had once been government land, parcelled out to military veterans as their pension, but this particular bit I had my eye on wasn't shown on the government distribution plan in the archive at Bine; nor did it show up on any of the tithe maps at the manor court at Cophis, where the local big house used to be, before it burned down. It quite genuinely didn't belong to anyone.

This sort of thing does happen, very occasionally. Government land gets that way when an estate gets confiscated, for treason or some other major felony; and where you have government action you get government clerks, and for some reason the government doesn't invariably hire the brightest and the best. Mistakes happen, bits get left off, red lines get drawn on plans with a thick brush (and the width of a brush-stroke, to scale, can be as much as a quarter of an acre). My vineyard was probably someone's momentary lapse of attention. It didn't belong to anybody, and Nature abhors a vacuum.

Since I really didn't want to spend the next ten years digging up bramble roots, I decided to sell it. In order to do that, however, I needed to be able to prove legal title. That meant documents. Documents meant a forger. And only the very best would do for the young, stupid Saloninus.

Ownership implies an owner. Abandoned property implies an absentee owner. We conceived and gave birth to one, and then we killed him. Because she insists on doing everything properly, we started with a birth certificate. We decided that our owner had been born in the Sashan Empire (because their documents of record are baked clay tablets rather than bits of paper, and baked clay is the easiest written medium to forge, bar none), which meant he had to be the son of a diplomat, posted abroad at the time of his son's birth. In which case, the grant of government land would have been part of his father's retirement gratuity; so after she'd finished the Treasury conveyance, she forged the old man's will, plus an assent to transfer the land from his executors to his son. After that, she did a lovely job of the owner's own death certificate and will, leaving everything to his beloved niece. I wanted it to be to his beloved niece and nephew, but she pointed out that I was a felon, convicted in absentia, and anything left to me in a will would automatically forfeit back to the Treasury. I hate it when she's right.

We sold the land without any trouble at all, and celebrated our triumph with a bottle of vintage Sauton claret. I woke up three days later with a murderous headache; she, of course, was long gone and so was the money. How she got the knockout drops into the sealed bottle without piercing the pitch I really don't know. I've asked her many times, but she just smiles.

The point being; if you go to Bine and consult the records, you'll find irrefutable evidence of the life and death of one Medeis Oudemia, Vesani citizen, born AUC 1018, died AUC 1061. He's a historical fact, with far more documentation to corroborate his existence than, say, Three-Fingers Speusippa or Volusian the Great. She and I created him, sure, but so what? Your mother and father created you. Not only did he have a verifiable existence, he also lived his life with a definite sense of purpose, which is more than I can say for myself, and even after his death he went on helping people. In my darker moods I like to think of him, contentedly pruning his vines in the cool of the evening, watching the sun go down on another useful and productive day.

Since then, with Oudemia very much in mind, I've tried to reconceive myself, loads of times. Scripture says that the only way to escape death is to be reborn, and I can see the sense in that; it's also a good way of avoiding jail time and substantial accumulated debt. It's never worked, though, and I think I know why. The old saying goes, you can't take it with you. I've come to the conclusion that that's right. And where I screw it all up is trying to take myself with me when I go.

FINISHED, THE MANUSCRIPT looked scruffy; a pile of dog-eared, mildewed paper. The damp had got into it so the pages were slightly crinkled, meaning that when it was stacked up it didn't sit true and square. It was tied up with a bit of green ribbon, faded on one side where it had been exposed to the sunlight. It was the sort of thing you'd put out for the rag-and-bone man, or use to light the fire if you were thriftily inclined. It was her masterpiece, the best thing of its kind ever created, worthy to be displayed in the company of Prasithon's *Sun Ascendant* or the colossal bronze horse of Prosper of Schanz.

The words weren't all that bad, either. I wasn't entirely sure about some of it. I hadn't been in the sunniest of moods, and there were places where I'd let myself go rather, mostly in soliloquy form. I've had a lot of stick about my soliloquies over the years; self-indulgent, breaking dramatic illusion, slows down the action, doesn't advance the plot. Maybe the criticism's valid, I really don't know. Apart from that, though, I was broadly satisfied with the thing, and I reckoned I'd made my point. I'd taken a lousy plot with no dramatic potential and made a drama out of it. That, I felt sure, was exactly the sort of thing Saloninus would've taken great pleasure in doing twelve years ago, when he was experimenting with form versus substance and taking delight in doing things he knew would annoy his more sententious critics.

"We've got a product," I said.

"Don't poke at it," she said. "I've arranged it just right. It looks—"

"Real?"

She wrinkled her nose. "You don't want it looking too real," she said. "Too real is usually fake. What you actually want is nondescript."

The nondescript manuscript. Quite. But I could see what she meant. In context, what we wanted was something that had been mouldering in a windowsill for twelve years, forgotten about and uncared for, a piece of junk. That was what she'd so exactly captured. Only a genius could do that.

I couldn't resist asking. "What did you think of it, by the way?"

"Think of what?"

"The play."

"Oh, that." She pulled a little face. "It's a bit long, and the second act drags, and I don't like *him* at all. And the women weren't convincing. To be honest, you've never been much good at female characters."

"Apart from that?"

"The comic gravedigger was a mistake. And I didn't like the ending much."

"Apart from that."

"I liked your early stuff better."

You can see how I nearly fell in love with her once.

WE FOUND THE perfect bag in the flea market. It was linen, sort of a sandy colour, with brown stains, dust and fluff trapped in the inside seams and the buckle missing. She put the manuscript in the bag and set off for the palace.

Now lettest thou thy servant depart in peace. She had no further use for me, and I've found that if I stay in her company for an extended period of time, bad things tend to happen. My instincts told me to slip away quietly, without leaving a note. She'd left twenty-three angels lying around in a locked drawer where anybody could find them. You can go a long way on twenty-three angels.

On the other hand; the big score. If it worked, two *million* angels. There's no generally established exchange rate, but I've always worked on the principle that a million angels constitutes a flight—two million, one each—flights, to paraphrase slightly what I'd just written, of chunky round golden angels sing thee to thy rest, which in my case was long, long overdue. The big score. That much money, even she couldn't be greedy enough to want it all for herself. Not to mention the income from the rights, which on the least optimistic reckoning was likely to be a sum not much smaller than the annual tax revenue of Coele Moesia. It suddenly struck me that if only I hung around a little longer and held my nerve, there was a chance that for the first time in a long and interesting life, I'd actually get paid proper money for something I'd written.

There's a lot to be said for being sensible and one of these days I owe it to myself to give it a go. But (I said to myself: that soliloquy habit again; no good ever came of it) what did I have to lose by hanging around just a little longer? After all, apart from ripping me off (which I was already resigned to, or I wouldn't be contemplating fading away before the money had even been paid over), what else could she do to me? Amend that; what else would she be motivated to do to me, now that I was of no further use to her? It takes positive action to hurt someone, and she'd always been a great one for economy of effort. And in the other pan of the scale was the slight but tantalising chance that this time she wouldn't screw me to the wall and all my troubles would shortly be over.

Give me the choice between doing the right thing and doing the interesting thing, and I'll do the wrong thing every time.

THE BIG SCORE

SHE CAME BACK looking stunned. I assumed she'd been mugged, only I couldn't see any blood. How did it go, I asked her.

"He wants it," she said.

"How much?"

"Two and a half million."

There was a long, rather sombre silence. Both of us were thinking the same thing. "Did he haggle much?"

She shook her head. "Two and a half million, I told him. Deal, he said. Then we shook hands."

What we were both thinking was: he would probably have given three. It was one of those thoughts best not put into words.

"Subject to verification, of course," she added, giving herself a little shake, like a wet dog. "I left the manuscript with him. He wrote me out a receipt."

We looked at each other. If anything happened to the manuscript while it was in his custody—fire, theft, mice—he'd be honour-bound to pay us two and a half million angels. And say what you like about him (but not when his spies are listening), he's a man of his word.

"It's the sensible thing to do," I said.

"I know."

"Where do you think he's put it?"

"In the Old Library," she said without hesitation. "He told me so himself. It'll be safe there, he said, and it'll be nice and handy for the scholars I've got coming down from the University. They'll be able to check up references and things without having to traipse across the quadrangle."

The Old Library was, as its name hints, old. Timber-framed. Standing on its own in the middle of the South Quadrangle. A bucket of pitch negligently spilt against a wall; a stray spark from a gardener's negligently tended bonfire.

"Only, why bother?" she said, with a sort of brittle casualness in her voice. "It's perfect. His scholars will pass it with flying colours. Why run all the risk of committing half a dozen felonies when all we've got to do is sit tight and wait for them to bring us the money?"

There are some questions that are never intended to be answered. As for the risk, it was pretty negligible. For someone else, maybe. For me—us—a walk in the park. The blind spot on the east wall was there staring you in the face as you crossed the New Bridge into Parktown. A short dash across the grass, one minute to slop round with the pitch, you'd be back over the wall and safe at your usual table in the *Penitence & Grace* before the glow of the fire was even visible. And the Duke's advisers have been nagging him to replace that semi-derelict fire-trap with a purpose-built home for his valuable books for ages, only he doesn't want to spend the money. Everybody would be far too busy smirking and not saying I-told-you-so to suspect foul play.

But: her masterpiece. Destined to be admired and savagely envied by every guest the Duke ever showed round his collection. Destined to be treasured for ever.

There's a fortune to be made insuring the lives of one's children for substantial sums of money and then murdering them. It's money for old rope and practically risk-free, if you take a few minimal precautions. Even so, it doesn't happen very often, and you can understand why. We looked at each other again. Our baby, we didn't need to say.

"Quite," I said. "Why bother?"

(WHICH WAS STRANGE, because I never feel that way about the stuff I do. Well, maybe some of it, very occasionally. But that's rare. Science I do for money. The same goes for music and plays. There's never been any other reason, as far as I'm concerned. Once the money's in my hand (or not in my hand, as is so often the case) that's it, I'm through with it, all passion spent. Once some eager clown came bounding up to me with a whole load of questions about Cerulion's motivation in Act 3 of *King Axio.* I stared at him, trying to remember which king Axio was, and who in God's name was Cerulion? Simple fact is, I only ever read my stuff once, when I'm writing out the fair copy, and that's it. Can you remember the minutiae of a play you read once, twenty years ago? And I never get to see my plays on the stage, because invariably I'm sitting in a draughty room on the other side of town, frantically writing the next one. Or, when they're revived, I can't afford to buy a ticket.

So I could only guess that the new play mattered to me because she and I had created it together. Not that she'd had anything to do with the words or the order they came in; but at least she'd been there, taking an interest, noticing, asking me what the hell was taking so long. I'm not used to that.)

THERE WAS NOTHING more we could do until the Duke's scholars had looked over the manuscript. We didn't have long to wait.

Over the years—you know how a dog starts barking some time before you hear the footsteps in the street or the knock at the door? I'm like that. Don't ask me how I know, I just do. I wake up in a cold sweat, in pitch darkness and dead silence, I roll out of bed, not bothering with shoes, I grab the bag packed with the absolute essentials, which is always ready and handy so I can find it in the dark without thinking, and I sprint for the escape route, which I'd planned the first time I set foot in the place. A couple of minutes later, when I'm outside and crouching in a shady doorway, the Watch or the City Guards or the palace guard come bustling down the street. They pause for a moment to give two or three of their number time to go round and cover the back and sides of the house; then they kick the door in. Once they're all safely inside, I quietly withdraw; walk, don't run, and it always helps if you have at least some idea of where you're headed next. This gift of mine, this sixth sense or whatever, has saved my skin more times than I care to think about, and I've come to rely on it to the point of dangerous complacency.

So imagine my distress when I was jerked out of sleep by someone yelling, *City prefect, open up,* followed by the inimitable sound of splintering wood. I'm not the sort of man who panics, as a rule, but that's because I anticipate, so misfortune rarely catches me unprepared. When it does, I go to pieces, like a covey of partridges all getting up at once.

I slept on the ground floor, under the table she used for work. She slept upstairs, in the bedroom. I knew my escape route wasn't going to be any use to me as soon as I heard the back door yielding to someone's boot. No windows on the ground floor. By the time I'd found my feet, there were steelnecks in the room, waving a lantern around. They saw me. God help me, I froze. I had a nice walnut-sized knob of *gella tonans* in my running-away bag; throw it against a wall and you get a bang, a thick cloud of smoke and a hole big enough to climb through, while the steelnecks are still wondering what hit them. But my bag was on the chair, and there were two guardsmen between it and me. There was nothing I could do. I did it.

"Where is she?" snapped the chief steelneck.

I was debating with myself whether there was any point pretending I didn't know when the lantern lit up the staircase, answering the sergeant's question. Three of them thundered up the stairs. I heard voices, but I couldn't make out the words. Then she came down the stairs, wrapped in a blanket, followed by the guards. She was saying the usual—this is an outrage, the Duke is a personal friend of mine, I'll have your badge for this. The guards were doing the usual, not listening. They formed up round her in the usual formation, marched out through what was left of the doorway and vanished into the darkness. Leaving me behind.

I waited till I couldn't hear footsteps, then five seconds more; then I grabbed my bag and shot out of the back door like a rabbit with a ferret up its tail. Nobody out there. Far away two dogs were barking at each other. It was one of those nights when the moonlight is bright enough to see by even though the sky's overcast—personally I think it's something to do with the light refracting through mist of a certain density, but what the hell—and I had the narrow, high-walled alley entirely to myself. I had no plan of action. Nobody seemed to want me or care about me. I stood there like an idiot until I began to feel the cold, then I went back inside the house and lit a lamp.

I looked at the doors, front and back, but they were both equally beyond repair; the landlord's problem, not mine. I got the charcoal stove going and scrambled a couple of eggs, not that I was hungry but it was something to do. All my instincts were yelling at me to run away, but the idiot who does all the soliloquies kept saying, run away from what? They didn't want you. They had no idea who you are. They think you're dead. Eat your eggs before they go cold.

What was I? Upset? Disappointed? Offended? Nearly the whole of my adult life there have been people only too willing to pay large sums of money for me: for the creations of my brain and hands, for my presence in a locked room, eight feet by six. Actually, no, I wasn't. I was just confused, a rarity for me. Generally speaking, no matter how bad things get, I have some idea of what's going on. At the very least, I know where I need to be, even if it's highly unlikely that I'll get there any time soon. I felt left out, if that makes any sense. I wasn't sure I liked it. It made me feel ordinary.

Cooking isn't one of my talents. The eggs were horrible, like eating that mushy fungus that grows out of rotten trees. I sat down on the chair and waited to see what came next, like a member of the audience.

Some time later, enter her; in a man's coat two sizes too big for her, bags under her eyes, no makeup, white as a sheet and furiously angry. There was no door to slam, a deficiency which clearly annoyed her. She looked at me. "You idiot," she said.

I may have dozed off. I looked up and stared at her. "They let you go," I said.

"You clown. How could you be so stupid?"

"Have you had breakfast?" I asked her.

She sat on the chair. I perched on the edge of the table. She burst into tears.

"What happened?" I asked.

"He doesn't want to buy it," she said.

It wasn't the reply I'd been expecting. "Are we in trouble?" I said.

"He isn't going to press charges, because the attorney general doesn't think there's enough evidence to secure a conviction, but he has serious doubts about my honesty and he'd be obliged if I left the Duchy as quickly as conveniently possible."

At which point I noticed the linen bag, the one we'd bought in the flea market, slung around her neck. She still had the manuscript.

"So we can go," I said.

"What?"

"We're free to leave."

"What? Oh, yes. All that work for *nothing*. And it's all your fault."

Maybe she hasn't spent as much time with steelnecks as I have, I don't know. To me, she sounded a bit like someone who's fallen off a cliff onto a cartful of soft hay, and is yelling at the carter for not taking out a dried thistle. "What happened?" I asked her.

SHE TOLD ME, at length, in detail.

The Duke's experts examined the manuscript. They carefully shredded a tiny sample of the paper, and sure enough, it was reeds, not rags. They tested the ink, which was the basic oak-gall-and-soot mix in which nearly all Saloninus' known manuscripts were written, mixed in the proportions he invariably used. The handwriting man was prepared to pledge his immortal soul that everything was just how it should be—the looped d's, the slanting dots on the i's which characterise Saloninus' middle years (news to me, but then, I'm not an expert), a faint slope of the lines left to right indicative of haste, which you'd expect from a man writing to meet a deadline. Everything—she looked daggers at me at this point—about the manuscript itself was perfect and above reproach. The problem lay with the content.

("Oh come on," I said. "It's probably the best thing I ever—"

"Shut up.")

The difficulties with the metrical form, said the literary experts, weren't insuperable. True, there were seventeen-point-three per cent more lines with feminine endings in this play than in *No Wit Like A Woman's,* its immediate predecessor, but it could be argued that at this point in my career I was being influenced by Macrobian post-realism, and the subsequent decrease in feminine endings merely reflected a rejection of the neo-Classical. Possibly more disturbing was the decline in the number of enjambements—down nineteen per cent from *No Wit,* anticipating the polished fluency of the mature tragedies—

("That's good, surely."

"Be *quiet.")*

Even that (she went on) could perhaps be accounted for by the subject matter, since Saloninus consistently uses enjambement more in the naturalistic dialogue of the City comedies than in the sublime periods of the tragedies. A similar argument could be advanced to account for the comparative infrequency of such devices as paraprosdocia, chiasmus and aposiopesis—

"What the hell," I had to ask, "is paraprosdocia?"

"Interrupt one more time," she said, "and so help me I'll break your arm. Basically, they said, the style was inconclusive.

They reckoned something about it stank, but it could just possibly be explained away. What did it for them was the topical reference."

"What topical reference?"

She quoted;

Approach thou like the rugged Aelian bear,
The armed rhinoceros or the Blemmyan tiger,
Take any shape but that, and my firm nerves
Shall never tremble—

"You halfwit," she added. "What were you thinking of?"

"What bloody topical reference?"

"The Blemmyan tiger, of course, you moron. The first Blemmyan tiger to be exhibited outside of its native country was brought to Choris three years ago and put on public display at the New Palace. Everybody went to see it. For a while you couldn't move for paintings of tigers, statues of tigers, tiger wall-hangings, wine-coolers and samovars in the shape of a crouching tiger—"

"News to me," I said.

"Bullshit."

I shook my head. "Three years ago I was in Permia. Up there, they don't even know where Choris is, let alone the latest fashion craze." I stared at her. "Is that it?"

"Yes."

"They say the play's a fake because of some ludicrous stuff about a tiger?"

"It's an obvious topical reference, according to them."

"Like hell it is," I nearly shouted. "Listen. I nearly made it a wolf, but then I thought, tiger's got that slightly exotic feel about it and the line sounds better with the extra foot. They're *wrong*, dammit."

She gave me a look. "Yes," she said, "but we can hardly tell them so, can we?"

It was enough to reduce a man to tears. "Why the hell," I said, "didn't you pick that up when you were copying it out?"

"I didn't know," she said. "I was in Messagene three years ago. I never heard about any stupid tiger."

There didn't seem to be much else to say.

LATER, I TRIED to make the best of it. We've still got the manuscript, I said. We can put it up for auction, somewhere else.

"Idiot," she said. "You don't suppose these collectors don't talk to each other, do you? By now, every manuscript fancier west of the Maugrat knows about the Blemmyan fucking tiger. No, what we've got here is three hundred sheets of the most expensive arsewipe in literary history. Nine months of my life, planning it all, finding you, making the stupid thing. Not to mention being dragged through the streets wrapped in a blanket, thinking I was off to the gallows. This is the last time I let you talk me into—"

I wasn't listening.

Cast your mind back to the dropping penny. Now imagine that the penny is one of those rocks that comes screaming down out of the sky and digs a crater the size of a village.

"It's all right," I told her.

When you hunt the wild boar (so they tell me) and the loathsome thing charges you, your only chance of getting out of it in one piece is to plant your spear firmly on the ground, the butt end anchored by the side of your back foot, and point the sharp end at the boar. In its rage and fury, the stupid creature will rush straight at you, not noticing or ignoring the lethal spike between you and him, and impale himself to the heart before he realises something is wrong. She stopped in mid-charge and looked at me. Something in my tone of voice, presumably.

"You what?"

"It's all right," I said. "I can see a way round this. Maybe not quite so much money, but maybe even more."

She knows me quite well. She doesn't like me much, but she knows me. "Are you serious?"

"It'll take a bit of time," I said, and I paused to grin, because an essential part of the idea had just dropped elegantly into place, like a component in a beautiful and complex mechanism. "But there's no risk, hardly any additional outlay, and—well, it's perfect, that's all. Actually, genuinely perfect."

It's not a word I use lightly, for reasons touched on above. But I choose my words carefully, always have.

"Well?" she said.

"Well," I said, "I think we've established that this play isn't by Saloninus. Agreed?"

"You bet agreed."

"Fine," I said. "In that case, it needs to be by somebody else." I smiled. "Somebody better."

When I was a student at the University, I knew a man whose father was the leading icon-painter in the whole of the western empire, and he told me a story. His father had been commissioned to paint a small devotional icon for the Duke of Mancalo. The fee was some ridiculous sum, five figures, but my friend's father was the temperamental sort. The agreed subject was the Ascension, but he simply wasn't in the mood. He wanted to paint the Harrowing of Hell, but nobody was in the market for one of those at that precise moment. Never mind, he went ahead and painted it anyway; and meanwhile the Duke's secretary was practically camping out on his doorstep, respectfully clamouring for his master's wretched Ascension.

My friend's father had almost finished his Harrowing, but not quite, and he had a temper and an unconventional sense of humour. He sent his servant down to the Fish Market, where you can always find half a dozen sad-faced men sitting on the ground behind a blanket, on which are spread out a selection of the cheapest, nastiest mass-produced icons money can buy if it's misguided enough to want to do so. Here's twenty stuivers, he said. Buy the first Ascension you see and bring it back here stat.

His servant was an honest man and gave him the five stuivers change. Then, as instructed, he wrapped the icon up in red silk and took it to the Duke. Next day, the secretary called, bringing with him a draft on the Knights of Equity for the five-figure fee (plus a handsome bonus) and a letter—in the Duke's own handwriting, for crying out loud—thanking him for the painting, which was the most beautiful thing he'd ever seen. The only possible thing he could do, the Duke said, was endow a monastery to house it and preserve it for ever.

My friend's father was a bit shaken by this, and he decided to try an experiment. He took down all his very best and finest icons, the ones he hadn't been able to bear to be parted from no matter what he was offered for them. He wrapped them in a blanket and set out for the Fish Market. By the time the sun set he'd sold two icons and made twenty-seven stuivers.

My friend's father originally rose to the top of his profession on account of a simple mistake. Having no commissions, he painted a series of the Hours of the Passion, twelve in all. At that time, the ruling fashion decreed that only icons painted by monks could possibly be any good, so he signed them Brother Modestus, which was not, of course, his name. What he didn't know was that the emperor's youngest nephew had recently retired to a monastery and had taken the name Modestus; furthermore, it was widely known that the young prince had been known to dabble in the fine arts. A high-class society dealer saw the paintings, read the signature, put two and two together, bought the lot and promised to pay silly money for more stuff by the same artist. By the time the dealer realised his mistake, genuine art-lovers had acquired a taste for canvases by Modestus, and my friend's father never looked back.

I rarely if ever look back, because there's always the danger of tripping over your feet while you're running away.

THERE'S A LOT to be said for libraries. Generally they're quiet and restful. You look up from your seat and you see hundreds and thousands of books, each one of them a walled city inhabited by and guarding the informed, the wise, the sympathetic, the understanding. There are friends in books that I've known all my life, with me wherever I go. Libraries are the granary of the spirit, without which we couldn't survive the siege. Some of the books have my name written on the spine or embossed on the brass tube, and because of that I shall never entirely die. Books make you happy, angry, peaceful, discontented, reassured, justified. A book can make me forget who and what I am, for a little while. A book is somewhere I can go and not have to take myself with me. Books say: come to us, all who labour and are heavy laden, and we will give you rest. Books are the islands in the West where good people go when they die. Books are a world apart, yet firmly here and now, written in the moment but eternal; in the beginning was the word, and ever shall be, world without end. Also, some books are very valuable, and the security arrangements in libraries are often woefully lax.

I tried not to think about that. I was in the Old Library of the Studium for a specific purpose, a job to do, no time to be indulging myself and fooling around. I was taking a risk just being there, given that I was dead and buried. I kept a scarf round my face at all times, which itched like buggery and drew unwelcome attention—why would a member of a veiled Order be so interested in modern secular literature?—and whenever I spoke to a librarian I mumbled and avoided eye contact, fortunately not atypical behaviour among scholars. The hell with it. Thirty years since I was here last, and even I'm not that memorable, I hoped.

I have this theory; not one I've ever written up, let alone published, because it's self-evidently false, but that doesn't stop me believing it. I think there are places that are so right for us, at various times of our lives, that we never leave. A small part of us, in my case probably the good part, stays behind, unchanging, for ever. So strongly do I believe this that I was convinced that when I looked up from my desk, I'd catch sight of the young, not-yet-famous, not-yet-fucked-up Saloninus hauling a book down from the open shelves or yawning his way through Priscillian on Oratory. He wasn't there. I can only assume he had a cold that week, or a really bad hangover.

Libraries set me thinking about who the hell I'm supposed to be. They break up the available light like a prism. Who I was; who I am now; who or what, if anything, I shall be. Who I once was but stopped being, who I still am, regardless. Suppose they spread me out on a table and dissected me—a lot of people have wanted to do this—could they identify the various components? A little pile of organs here containing all the bad stuff, the dishonesty, lies, betrayals, cheating, arrogance, cowardice, running away. Another pile next to it; bits containing the science, the philosophy, the plays, the music. Or would they find that the lies and the theories and the tragedies and the thieving were all part of the same thing, impossible to tease apart or smelt or refine with acids; not a library with sections (ground floor, theft, dishonesty and callous treachery; first floor, scientific method and the triumph of reason; art and literature, the mezzanine and the annexe) but all of them words making up one sentence, and if you took any of them out, the whole would no longer make sense? A book can be many things at the same time: a source of enlightenment, a masterpiece of the leather-tooler's art, a handy way to carry two hundred angels in an inside pocket out through the door and down the street to the nearest receiver of stolen goods. You can read me like a book, can't you?

Above all, a library is a place of work. Not much else you can do there. Food, drink, conversation, fornication and falconry not allowed on the premises. A library is a place for diligent study and earnest endeavour. All work and no play makes you a junior assistant lecturer, with tenure.

And libraries don't change all that much, and what they had thirty years ago they probably still have, unless I've stolen it, though they may have forgotten where it's kept. We haven't got that, said the librarians. Yes you have, I told them, go away and look for it, this time properly. They found it. I smiled. Hello, old friend, I muttered under my breath.

THEN IT WAS her turn.

As well as being the best false calligrapher, paper-and-parchment ager, handwriting mimic and bibliophiliac chemist under the sun, she's no slouch at die cutting and seal engraving. We needed a seal; or rather, we needed the impression of a seal, which made life a bit easier.

Your slapdash, born-to-hang cowboy seal-faker gets an impression of the seal he intends to duplicate, usually affixed to a letter or other document. He rolls up a ball of fine-grained clay, presses it onto the seal, peels it off carefully, so as not to distort it, and bakes it in an oven or simply waits for it to dry in the sun. He now has a passable matrix. Press it onto molten wax or lead and you get something that'll fool ninety-nine out of a hundred clerks, jailers and government officials. Any idiot can do it, and most of the people who do it are idiots.

Or you can do it properly. You get a small piece of suitable material. Sandstone is cheap or free, soapstone is the industry standard; she never works in anything but jade. By skill and eye alone you copy the original, chipping and scraping and scribing with tiny steel implements, except that you don't; you make a concave copy of a convex master, which requires powers of visual imagination way beyond anything I could possibly imagine, let alone aspire to. When you've finished, you hold the thing you've made over a candle-flame until its hollow inside is evenly coated with a thin smear of soot. Then you press it down on top of the seal on your letter or document and take it away again. If the original isn't evenly covered in soot, you know you've gone wrong. Probably you have to throw away what you've just made and start again, from scratch. Even if your fake passes the smoke test, there's a fair chance that it'll simply look wrong—identical but different, no bloody use. I've often thought that anyone capable of making a really convincing fake seal must be a fundamentally evil person, because with those skills you could make an absolute fortune doing legitimate work, in which case you're doing bad things for the love of it, not the money.

She's simply the best there is. She has a hollow glass globe about the size of my head, which she fills with water and puts in front of an oil lamp in front of a diptych mirror; the result is fake sunlight, brighter than the actual sun. Most of her scribers and picks are as thin as hairs—she made them all herself—but hard enough to cut stone and tough enough not to bend when she puts her weight behind them. She's got the best eyesight of any living creature, and a lens, which she made by grinding a slab of glass on a potter's wheel covered in sand set in bitumen until it was exactly the right shape; the hardest three days of her life, she told me. I'm amazed she did it so quickly. According to her, with the lens set up just so, the tip of one of those tiny scribers looks as big as a chicken's claw, and as long as you go nice and slow and steady, there's nothing to it, really.

With hindsight, a blob of clay would have done just as well. The clerk who examined the seal in the secretary's office was an old man who had to press his nose against a letter before he could read it, and besides, who on earth would possibly want to fake the seal of the Dean of the Faculty of Secular Literature at the University of Schanz?

I DIDN'T GO to the auction. I'd have liked to, but I'm dead. So I stayed at home and waited.

The final hammer price was four million, two hundred and sixty thousand angels. Just think about that. Enough money to buy all the wheatfields in the Mesoge, or build five thousand ships, or endow fifty monasteries, or fight a land war in Aelia for a week.

Payment was by letter of credit drawn on the Order of the Poor Friars, because there aren't 852,000 gold five-angel coins in existence. The buyer insisted on remaining anonymous, but reliable rumour had it that it was either the Sashan emperor, Luomai Met'Oc or the Mezentine Glassmakers' guild pension fund. Nobody else could possibly have afforded it.

How did I do it? Simple.

Very few of my friends have ever done me any good, but in this case I owe it all to my pal the icon-painter's son. He gave me the idea, in roughly the same way the Invincible Sun gave Man the gift of fire, a glowing ember in a hollow fennel stalk.

The Faculty of Contemporary Letters at the Studium hold an annual seminar, at which papers are presented by or on behalf of the most eminent scholars in the Robur-speaking world. That year, the most exciting and controversial offering was an essay by one Segipert, hitherto unknown but vouched for by the Dean of Faculty at the faraway but prestigious university of Schanz.

The title of the paper was; On The Authorship of The Plays of Saloninus.

Marvellous effort, though I do say so myself. Segipert began by posing the obvious question. Was it really credible that an incorrigible small-time thief and confidence trickster could have written the plays that bear his name, not to mention the philosophical treatises, scientific works and musical compositions? Segipert freely admitted that he wasn't qualified to discuss science, philosophy or music, so he'd concentrated his attention on the plays, a subject he knew something about.

In the first part of the essay, he collated vocabulary and imagery that proved that the author of the plays must have had extensive first-hand knowledge and experience of royal courts, diplomacy and the business of government. Saloninus, he pointed out, had none of these, apart from the circumstances of his disastrous first marriage, which were hardly conducive to absorbing a detailed understanding of such issues.

Next he examined various documents written by what he called the historical Saloninus, the man wanted by the authorities in practically every jurisdiction on earth. To these he applied various philological and metrical tests, from which he drew the inevitable conclusion that Robur wasn't even the historical Saloninus' first language. When he applied the same tests to the plays, he found that not only was the author a native Robur speaker, he was also from one of the three northern provinces of Meturene—the dialectic and syntactical signatures were unmistakeable. Saloninus, the historical Saloninus, had never been anywhere near northern Meturene in his life, as witness the fact that there were no outstanding warrants for his arrest in that jurisdiction.

There followed a summary of the known facts about the life of the historical Saloninus, with particular emphasis on where he was known to have been at the time the plays were composed. In prison; on a prison galley in the middle of the Aelian Sea; a thousand miles away on the borders of the Echmen Empire. Unless he had an identical twin brother or wings like a bird, it was simply impossible for him to have written at least four of the twenty-seven plays attributed to him.

Therefore, Segipert argued, Saloninus did not write the plays. In which case, who did?

I WAITED. THEN I waited a bit more. After that, all I could do was wait.

Four and a quarter million angels. More money than anyone could ever spend, or need, or even want. I could imagine my partner ripping me off if it was just a single lousy million. Suppose you split that fifty-fifty. You might feel that extreme bad luck could intervene and wipe you out of a mere five hundred thousand. You might build a city with it, and then there might be an earthquake, the ground opening and swallowing it up. Stuff happens. You'd want to hang on to the whole million, just in case. But four million; four and a *quarter*. Just the quarter would be a bigger score than anything I'd ever played for in my whole life.

Maybe we should have discussed it before she went to the auction, leaving me behind. I should have said to her, straight out: I know you'll double-cross me, and that's fine. After all, the bare bones of the scam were your idea, you did a lot of the work and I did make one tiny mistake, so it's only fair that you should get, say, sixteen-seventeenths of the take. But would it kill you to spare me just one lousy seventeenth? It would make me so happy, and think how virtuous and honest it'd make you feel.

I waited, but she didn't show. It won't hurt, I told myself, to wait just a little bit longer. That's one thing you learn when you're dead. Patience.

THEREFORE, SEGIPERT ARGUED, Saloninus did not write the plays. In which case, who did?

We have already established, he continued, a number of facts about the true author. He was born and raised in northern Meturene, he was a man of good family, he enjoyed a political or diplomatic career. Already, the field of potential candidates has shrunk to a mere half dozen. Five of them we can safely discount, for a variety of reasons. The sixth—the only possible contender—is Gilifred, Margrave and hereditary Elector of Stammen.

Consider the facts. Gilifred (nicknamed the Frogmouth) was born at the castle of the Stammenburg on the border between the central and eastern provinces of northern Meturene. He was educated at the university of Felsen—of which more later—and thereafter embarked on a period of service as the imperial ambassador to Blemmya. On his return he retired to his extensive estates, where he lived out the rest of his life. He died—coincidence?—six months before the historical Saloninus.

It is regrettable, Segipert went on, that the main thing for which Gilifred is remembered today is his appearance. The Stammen jaw had been a distinguishing feature of his father's family for seven generations. The Lysacht nose, inherited from his mother, Adiol of Lysacht, was always equally prominent. Together, the effect was unfortunate. Fiercely conscious of his disadvantage, Gilifred was throughout his life a solitary, private man, becoming more reclusive as he grew older and the stigmata of his heritage grew more pronounced. He did his duty to his country and his emperor to the best of his abilities as ambassador, but his extreme self-consciousness made him diffident and somewhat remote: a man unable to express himself by conventional means, cut off from the normal society of his equals, perforce an observer rather than a participant; a prisoner of his own body, with no option but to spend most of his life trapped in his own company. He never married. Birth and breeding urged him to distinguish himself, as his forefathers had so spectacularly done in every field of human endeavour. The same thing, the visible legacy of his ancestry, prevented him from doing so. Inevitably, such a man would have to find an outlet, a way of making his mark on the page of history. The desire for fame and glory would have no appeal to a scion of the legendary house of Stammen. Money could not possibly have interested him. But achievement: he would have felt it as a burning physical need. He must achieve, or die. And, since every other avenue was closed to him, where else could he turn but the arts?

Here, once again, his ancestry and family pride at first seemed to thwart him. An Elector of the Empire, writing plays for the public stage: unthinkable. Very well; if he was to fulfil his destiny, he must do so secretly, under an assumed name. Furthermore, there must be no possibility whatever of his secret being revealed. Let it be known that he was dabbling in such things and all his achievements would instantly turn to shame. A dreadful dilemma for a sensitive, tortured man.

At some point, therefore, he will have remembered a chance encounter from his student days. There is firm documentary proof that, while he was a student at Felsen, the historical Saloninus also resided in the town. They both frequented the same inn; we have a sutler's bill, for fortified wine and herrings, addressed to the young margrave; an injunction taken out by the landlord barring the historical Saloninus from his premises on account of breakages and obnoxious behaviour. The two men, therefore, met. Quite possibly, the older man's outrageous conduct, specious glamour and catchpenny wit impressed itself on the impressionable mind of the shy young nobleman. From these facts it is but a short step to an agreement between them, a deadly secret that both would carry to the grave. Gilifred would write plays; Saloninus would pass them off as his own and see that they were produced.

A plausible hypothesis, but can it be proved? Yes, said Segipert, it could, and beyond all reasonable doubt. By good fortune, a number of works from Gilifred's pen survive, preserved in the family archives, which on his death and the extinction of his direct line passed into the custody of the monks of the Studium. They are slight enough, very limited in scope: letters to his father and a cousin; essays on philosophy, theology and the humanities, written while a student; a slim volume, in blank verse, on hare-coursing. But the most rigorous linguistic, grammatical, metrical and stylistic analysis proves beyond any possibility of a question that the man who wrote them *also wrote the plays*. All the most reliable indicia—use of subordinate clauses, incidence of the double caesura, frequency of *hapax legomena* (here followed thirty-six pages of detailed philological evidence, in paralysing detail)—point to the same conclusion: Gilifred of Stammen was the true Saloninus.

We are on firm enough ground when we speculate as to the mechanics of their collaboration. Gilifred sent manuscripts to Saloninus, who copied them out in his own semi-literate handwriting and sold them to theatrical managers. In consequence, Saloninus enjoyed his undeserved moment in the sun, while his noble patron had at least the private satisfaction of knowing that, like his forefathers, he had made no small contribution to the wellbeing of all mankind—

THE BIG SCORE

THE FIRST THING they take you to see in Apaogoa City is the statue. I went there about fifteen years ago, just to see it—mostly to see it (at that time there was no extradition treaty between Apagoa and the empire)—and yes, I was impressed.

The statue is fifty feet tall. A woman stands with her arms by her side, looking down from a mountaintop onto the city below. The locals tell you that they don't know who she is, but she's waiting for the world to end.

Clearly a patient woman, because she was there long before the city, which is relatively recent, though built on ruins built on ruins built on ruins... People have lived there for a very, very long time, but not the same people. When I was there, someone had just dug a well. The story was, the well-sinkers were about a hundred and sixty feet down when they came up against what seemed to be solid rock. It was the flat roof of a building. They broke through and realised that their fragile wicker cage was dangling inside a large chamber. Their lamps flashed off gold and silver, but too far away for them to see. They scrambled back up to the surface, got an armful of better lamps, and went down again. They saw the interior of a vast temple, its walls covered with gilded mosaics, its roof-beams supported by exquisite marble, porphyry and alabaster columns. Above a solid gold altar they saw an icon, ten times life-size; a mother and child of such transfixing beauty that none of them were able to eat or sleep for days afterwards. They saw inscriptions on the walls, in some sort of hieroglyphic script, hundreds of thousands of words miraculously preserved for who knew how many centuries, representing who knew what sublime and ineffable truths. They saw chests, coffers, reliquaries, pyxes and caskets of gold, silver and ivory, all intact, their seals unbroken. Even the silk hangings around the altar and the gorgeous cloth-of-gold hassocks were perfectly preserved. It was, they later agreed, like a vision of Paradise, and worth an absolute fortune.

They hauled up their basket to the place where they'd smashed through the roof, carefully replaced the fragments of slab and sealed them with lead. Then they rushed into the city to tell various business associates of theirs what they'd found.

It took them a while to raise the sort of capital and make the sort of deal that was needed to do their discovery justice, so it was several weeks before they were able to return. They broke the seals, removed the pieces of slab, lit their lamps and lowered their basket. They went down about six feet, and hit water. The whole place had flooded.

Learned men from the university eventually came up with an explanation. It was something to do with air pressure, the weight of a hundred and sixty feet's-worth of stone and rubble, the disturbance caused by breaking the roof, a change in the direction of a subterranean watercourse, a little shifting and settling; at some point since the temple was lost and buried one tiny crack in the temple wall, with all that pressure behind it. All good, valid science, I have no doubt. Anyway, that was that. The short version of the story is that a number of men went to dig a well, and they succeeded. They didn't get to achieve the big score, but then again, nobody ever does.

(THE SCHEME WAS, as I explained to her after the Duke's men had let her go, brilliant, foolproof and simple. If the play wasn't by Saloninus, it had to be by someone else. Someone better. Someone worth even more money.

The problem wasn't with the play, or the manuscript. It was the provenance that was no good. But without a provenance, nobody would give her sixpence for it. So we needed another provenance. She had already committed herself to one version of her dealings with Saloninus, which had been proved to be a lie. So we needed a reason for that lie which would make her a credible witness once again.

Easy as falling off a log.

Bear in mind that I first met her, all those years ago, in the Boar's Head tavern in Schanz, where she was working in the hospitality and entertainment sector. She introduced me to a rich and spectacularly ugly undergraduate who was looking for someone to ghostwrite some things for him—essays, letters home begging for money to pay off his debts, that sort of thing. As it happens, I knew him slightly. Everybody in Meturene (where I was born and grew up; never been back since) knew Pigface by sight, and I'd actually spoken to him, begging him not to send my father to the slate quarries for poaching two rabbits. But I forgave him. I even knocked him up a mock-epic about hunting for some dinner-party entertainment he was organising. He was an idiot but we got on quite well together. He paid my bar bills, and gave her a small gold brooch with a tiny chip of genuine ruby.

All of that is true; but the truth gets lost and buried, and when eventually it's dug up again, sometimes it needs to be cleaned and carefully restored, like a neglected work of art. The bit we restored was the bit where she and Gilifred remained friends throughout his life; she knew his dark secret but wild horses wouldn't have dragged it out of her while he was still alive. So, when desperate poverty forced her to sell her most treasured possession, the play he'd written for her, she kept up the pretence that it was by Saloninus. The mistake she made was trying to give it a fake provenance by linking it to the letter the historical Saloninus had sent her, enclosing a sonnet—by Gilifred, of course, but Saloninus had shamelessly copied it out and passed it off as his own. Quite rightly, her attempt at fraud had been frustrated by the Duke's scholars, though of course they only grazed the surface, so to speak. But when Segipert's paper was published and everybody knew the secret, what possible harm could it do finally to tell the whole, unblemished truth?)

After I'd been waiting for a very long time, some steelnecks came and arrested me, acting on information received from a lady, whose name (quite properly) they declined to reveal. They accused me of being Saloninus. I can't be, I told them, he's dead. Prove you're not him, they said. Prove I am him, I replied. Eventually they let me go. While they were at it, they gave me some very wise, valuable advice. Leave town, they said.

Suicide is getting to be a habit with me. Unlike most habits, though, I believe it's good for me. I killed Saloninus' body to escape my enemies. I killed his immortal soul, his deathless name, his glory, to be rid of her. Small price to pay.

We're bilingual in Mesurene, even the country people. And, before my death, I wrote twenty-three plays. Even when I lie, I tell the truth. And when I'm telling the truth, I'm generally lying.

I'm not sure what I'm going to do with the rest of my life, but at least I have an opportunity I haven't enjoyed before. I can, if I so choose, go away and leave myself behind: crucified, dead and buried. And if that's not the big score, I don't know what is.

Relics

Genseric, *by the grace of the Invincible Sun Archduke of Schanz, Elector, Grand Marshal of the Eastern Command, Precentor of the Holy Diaconate, to Pollio his brother in faith, greetings.*

Thank you ever so much for the shin-bone of Corsellus of Radua, the tibia of Herennius, the three vertebrae of the Blessed Virgin of Ans and the jaw of Rubo the Paraclete. At this rate, pretty soon I shall have enough bits and pieces to build my own saint.

I note that you haven't yet got me any of the stuff I actually asked you to get. I assume that's because you haven't come across it yet, but please keep on looking. And yes, in the meantime, collectable body parts are always welcome. You can't have enough bones, I always say. If it wasn't for bones what would we be? Invertebrates, that's what, and I for one can see no future in that.

Things at this end are the usual sorry mess. My uncle is on the warpath again, God bless him. He's trying to get up a formal motion of censure against me in the synod, and obviously he's not going to get enough votes for that, but even so, it's all trouble for me, and that's what he wants. Meanwhile we've had three grain convoys fail to arrive, two intercepted by pirates and one stopped at Boc Bohec by the imperial governor and sent back, which means I'm going to have to buy most of next month's corn for the city on the open market at Bealregard Fair, and where the money for that's supposed to come from I have no idea. Childegar says put two stuivers on beer and a stuiver on sawn timber, which is clearly impossible—he knows that as well as I do, he's only saying it to make difficulties for me; how I wish we could find a market for difficulties, they're about the only thing we make around here where supply isn't exceeded by domestic demand. Ummerich reckons I should raise a forced loan from the Poor Sisters and confiscate their copper mine at Glimschen. When I tell him that if I did that, it'd be my last official act as Elector because two minutes later I'd be dead, he looks at me as if to say, And that'd be a bad thing because..? Tell you what, Pollio. Why don't you come back here and do the politics, and I'll go round the villages buying up bits of interesting dead people? Seriously. No, I thought not.

How are you doing for money, by the way? I've sent letters of credit to the Knights of Equity at Ruagh and Bartisan, so you can draw up to five thousand at either or both of those if you need to. While you're at it, do get yourself a decent coat and a new pair of boots—I know what you're like. If this reaches you before you get there, give the old place my love.

Wish you were here and I wasn't,

G.

Pollio, pilgrim and slave, to Genseric, Archduke, Elector, Marshal, Precentor, Defender of the Faith, greetings.

Well, here I am again. First thing I did when I got here, I went to the Grace Ascendant and asked, and I'm sorry to have to tell you, you're still barred for life. But he's an Archduke now, I told her. Doesn't matter, she said. After what he did the last time, he's not coming in here again, ever. Then she looked at me closely and I decided it was time to leave. She always did have a wonderful memory for faces. I don't suppose anyone else would recognise me now, but I wouldn't put it past her. And I think I still owe her ninety stuivers for breakages, or was that the Sun in Splendour?

To business. I got here precisely twenty-four hours too late to get the Subelix knuckle. Some high roller from Mezentia showed up and offered silly money for it, presumably for a private collector; I can make enquiries if you like but I don't think it's worth the effort. Bausina—remember him?—has a Prosper icon, except I think it was painted about a month ago, probably that outfit in Auxentia City; it looks too perfect, if you ask me, and the provenance is good but given time I think I could crack it open like an egg. Unless you really want me to I'm not inclined to bother; if you do want me to, let me know at Montresor and I'll drop in on my way back. With any luck Bausina will have sold it to someone else by then, saving us both a lot of aggravation. What I did manage to get was a splinter of the Holy Spear; cheap as chips and a provenance as long as your arm, used to belong to the met'Einai, then when they got sold up for taxes it passed to the abbey at Pelven who traded it for a Hieraticus missal, so on and so forth… Anyway, as far as I can tell it's rock solid and I only paid HA500 for it. I could get you three times that at any fair in the north any day of the week. Poenna was bidding on it for the Sisters, but he was eating a honeycake at the time and a crumb went down the wrong way; by the time he'd finished choking the hammer had gone down and I'd got it, and he was absolutely livid, which is one of the few truly beautiful things that's ever happened to me in my life.

From here, onwards to Naufragia, then a quick trip across the horrible wet sea to New Olbia, where there's rumours of a genuine Sammeticus triptych. If that turns out to be true I'll need money, so get a letter sent to the Knights there; HA3,000 ought to do it but more would be better. I'd hate for something like that to slip through my sweaty paws for want of a little loose change.

Sorry to hear about your uncle. If it wasn't for the mortal-sin aspect, I'd recommend three drops of aconite in his peach tea. Not that you'd ever countenance such a thing, but apparently there's an outfit in New Olbia that brews it so fine, not even a professional taster can pick it up until it's far too late to matter, and if it wasn't for the real and present danger to my immortal soul from even thinking about it, I could pick you up a bottle and send it down along with the splinter. Talking of which, I was planning to wait till Naufragia to mail it, because then it can go on one of the big Scona freighters, and the pirates don't seem to be bothering them at the moment. Up to you; let me know at Montresor.

Stay lucky,

P

Genseric, by the grace of the Invincible Sun Archduke of Schanz, Elector, Grand Marshal of the Eastern Command, Precentor of the Holy Diaconate, to Pollio his brother in faith, greetings.

Oh dear. Off to the wars again.

I hate soldiering. It's wrong at both ends of the scale. I sleep in a tent, for crying out loud, with the rain hammering down and nothing between me and the icy wind but the thickness of a sheet of waxed cloth; there are earwigs in my dinner and my back is killing me from sleeping on a bed consisting of bits of rope stretched tight in a wooden frame... But it's also wrong because outside my tent there are twelve thousand men sleeping in mud on the ground, with the rain soaking into their clothes until they're soaking wet, all the time, and they'd be really glad of earwigs in their food because they haven't seen a shred of meat for days—And the smell, O Invincible Sun, the smell. Twelve thousand men, all with diarrhoea to a greater or lesser extent; sweat and rain-soaked wool and twenty-four thousand feet, and horses and blood and rust and boiled cabbage. I've got a little brazier in my tent and a kid comes in every hour on the hour to burn incense, which is supposed to mask the stench a little bit, but instead I've got frankincense in one nostril and shit in the other, which if you ask me is the worst of both worlds. I don't like soldiering, and that's a fact.

Still, here I am and here we are, and it's my job to look as much as I possibly can like a real fighting soldier, while at the same time not getting under the feet of the generals—because if I think something's a good idea and say so, there's this terrible risk that they might go ahead and do it, with a view to sucking up to the boss, and then twelve thousand human beings would die as a result. Also, strictly between you and me and anyone with half a brain, who can see the obvious for himself without having to read it in secret coded dispatches, three of my five generals aren't the sharpest sabres in the rack; they got to be what they are because they're unimpeachably loyal (for now), not because they can be relied on to distinguishes arses from elbows, even in broad daylight. Well, you know about that, we read the same books and went to the same lectures. You can't trust smart generals; you have to assume they're after your job. I'm running a stupid risk having two of them out of five. Warfare, therefore, is always conducted by second-raters with a proven track record of not being particularly bright. We grinned about that when we were kids, but here it's a horrible cold reality, like rain and fleas and cholera. Not quite so funny when you're living it.

Oh yes, the enemy; nearly forgot about them, since to be perfectly honest they're the least of our problems most of the time. You've probably guessed from passing references to cold and rain that we're in the hill country, God help us; therefore the enemy is my charming brother-in-law. Please don't tell anyone I said so, but I don't like that man. I ought to feel sorry for him, because he's married to my sister and even the most draconian system of retribution can't envision a crime bad enough to merit that kind of punishment. Even so. I only met him once, at the wedding, and I thought to myself, this is a match made in heaven... Wasn't it Saloninus who said that it was perfect that X and Y should get married, because that way they'd only make two people thoroughly unhappy instead of four? But from what I gather, Eucho and Sis are devoted to each other, two twisted minds with but a single thought, two black hearts that beat as one. I don't know. To think that I used to feel sorry for you because you're an orphan with no family. You have no idea how lucky you are.

Anyway; the hell with all that. Thank you for the nice bits and pieces. I happen to think all that stuff is the absolute quintessence of yuck, but you ought to be here and see how much it all means to the soldiers. God knows, it's a big ask, telling a bunch of more or less normal, rational human beings to go and kill a load of perfect strangers, at severe risk of getting killed themselves. I don't think they'd do it, even with the sergeants yelling at them, if it wasn't for the Holy Icons and the Holy Relics. Living in a tent with cloth walls, I can hear every word the men say when they're huddled round the fire at night. It's all right, they keep telling each other, it'll be all right because we've got the shinbone of Respaluus and the Holy Foreskin of Genz; and they really believe it, you can hear it in their voices. Then someone says yes, but those bastards have got the eyelids of Onodia the Protomartyr, and then someone else says yes, but we've got the shoulder-blade of Issadal and two-thirds of the lip of the Blessed Chalice, those fuckers don't stand a chance against that... Faith, God help us; faith is what matters. Faith is what you know, in the teeth of all the evidence.

So keep them coming, for crying out loud. See if you can get me some military saints—Philopoemen or Laza, and a Holy Sword or two would be a godsend, something I could brandish (what exactly is brandishing? I've never actually heard a satisfactory definition) when I'm doing the Big Speech. Money no object. If you have to, use the warrant I gave you. It should be good for up to ten thousand, even with the war and everything—

Talking of which: I think we'll win (see above, under Faith) but you never know, do you? If we lose, I can't really see how I'm going to get home again, assuming I make it through the actual battle; and if I do, home might not be the most sensible place to be, under those circumstances. So this might be my last letter.

Cue sad music and fade out the background lighting—why is it that it's so hard to be serious without also being ridiculous at the same time? Anyway, if bad stuff happens, look after yourself. Be safe. Keep the money. Go a long way away and make sure nobody finds out you ever knew me.

But we're going to win, because we've got the Shinbone and the Holy Foreskin. Foregone conclusion, and the actual fighting's a mere formality.

Wish you were here—actually I don't, because what harm did you ever do me?—and I wasn't,

G

POLLIO, PILGRIM AND slave, to Genseric, Archduke, Elector, Marshal, Precentor, Defender of the Faith, greetings.

Congratulations, you jammy and undeserving bastard, on your famous victory. I'm in Seuva, and you should see the long faces; the end of the world is nigh and we're all going to be raped and murdered in our beds by your ravening hordes. I bet Eucho's wishing he'd never been born or died a bachelor.

You're right, of course. It's all down to the Holy Foreskin, and I'm not going to remind you of the fuss you made because I paid a smidge over the odds for it, because that would be unkind. Let's just agree that you owe it all to me and say nothing more about it.

One unfortunate consequence of your glorious victory—and I bet you never gave it a moment's thought when you sent your dragoons smashing through their over-extended right flank—is that prices are about to go through the roof. I was negotiating for a Segibert icon when the news broke and suddenly the dealer who was handling it started talking silly money, at which point I got up and walked away—no great loss, because I'm forty-nine per cent sure it was a fake, but a good enough fake that it wouldn't have mattered; let's not go there. The point is, people are saying that there's no way in hell you'd have won if it hadn't been for the relics—a valid point, if you ask me; no offence, but what in God's name were you thinking about, marching your infantry through a steep-sided ravine when you didn't know what was at the other end?—and so there's a mad scramble to scarf up anything that might possibly have any spiritual firepower… It's probably not a good time to suggest this, but how about unloading some of the dross you've got locked away in the basilica vault, entirely with a view to getting something really worth having when prices have calmed down a bit?

The really tiresome thing about the sudden shift on the market is that I'm on the track of something really hot. I won't say anything about it now because I'd hate to get your hopes up, and it could turn out to be nothing at all, and if it really is what I think it is, we probably can't afford it anyway—But that's quite enough about that. If it comes off, wonderful; if not, then there's still loads of good stuff around at the moment that we can get, even if we end up paying through the nose for it.

I feel like an absolute arsehole gabbling away at you about this sort of thing when you've just (a) cheated death by the skin of your teeth (b) pulled off a glorious victory that'll have your uncle frothing at the mouth with fear and loathing… I know. It's not your choice and it's not your fault, you were born that way, like a hare lip or an unnaturally elongated skull. I can't possibly understand, because I've never had anyone or anything depending on me. My life is doing deals with unsavoury people for dubious artefacts, while your just-another-day-at-the-office is about hunger and oppression and violence and death, all the stuff we used to pontificate about in the back bar of the King of Beasts—It amazes me to think how stupid we were in those days, so monumentally ignorant, so painfully and unforgivably arrogant. Which are just synonyms for young and over-educated… But the rest of us grew out of it and you got made a Duke. Poor Genseric, you never stood a chance.

So: yes, absolutely. If you need miracle-working foreskins, miracle-working foreskins you shall have, by the bucketful; it's the very least I can do. Meanwhile, for crying out loud, please try and devote at least some of your admittedly limited intelligence to staying alive, and don't go leading any more cavalry charges. Let some other bugger do it; that's what you pay them for.

Cordially,

P

Genseric, by the grace of the Invincible Sun Archduke of Schanz, Elector, Grand Marshal of the Eastern Command, Precentor of the Holy Diaconate, to Pollio his brother in faith, greetings.

Well, I'm back. A certain amount of fun and games at this end—I don't know if you remember me telling you about Theudemar, my second cousin on my mother's side; I don't think you ever met him, and now you'll never get the chance, because his head is stuck up on a pike about forty yards from where I'm writing this; if I look out of the window I can see it plain as anything, cousin Teddy, with a great big crow perched on his forehead picking his eyes out.

It's not an aspect of the job that I particularly relish, slaughtering my relatives, especially the ones I've always got on reasonably well with. If I wasn't a complete halfwit I'd have seen it coming and taken steps to prevent it. I could've appointed him ambassador to Scheria—he'd have liked that, he enjoys, enjoyed, a warm climate—or had a quiet word in his ear or even thrown him in jail; he'd have been as mad as hell about it but at least he'd still be alive, and now he's dead and I've got to watch the local wildlife slowly pecking him down to the bone.

My uncle's fault, needless to say. The idea was, either I'd lose the war, in which case Teddy had to get in quick before anybody else beat him to it, or else I'd win, in which case I (and more important, the army) would be safely out of town and miles away; he'd whip up the mob with fiery rhetoric about bloated aristocrats and evil profiteers grinding the faces of the poor, and away we go—Only, of course, it doesn't work like that, and my stupid uncle ought to know that by now.

Not Teddy's fault, obviously, because he never had a thought in his life, just a big smile and great hair and a rather touching desire to please—He was always pathetically eager to do what he was told, on the rare occasions when anybody thought it'd be worth the effort telling him to do anything. I remember him as a kid, thrilled to bits because my father let him carry his sword in some stupid procession. Of course he dropped the bloody thing, right at a solemn moment when we were all having a two minutes' silence, and you could hear the clatter right across the plaza. I gather that when he was making his impassioned speech, everyone was laughing at him, but he was always a bit deaf (I think he caught something when he was a baby and it screwed up his hearing) and he thought they were cheering, and he didn't realise he was laying an egg until the flying vegetables started hitting him… If he'd had the intelligence of a small rock he'd have got out of town straight away and hidden up somewhere until it was all right for me to forgive him. But Uncle had bought him about five hundred basically-no-good tough guys to give him the illusion of having an army, and of course the stupid idiot had to go and tell them to seize and fortify the Capitol… And obviously they weren't going to do that, because there's no way of slipping away unobtrusively from there when things go wrong; if there's one thing your hired goon insists on, it's a viable exit strategy. So they just left him standing there on an upturned cart in Foregate, and now he's birdfood. Practically the first thing that happened when I got back was the City Prefect bounding up to me and thrusting poor Teddy's oozing head into my arms, like anybody with even a vestigial remnant of a soul could possibly *want* something like that—and I had to grin and pretend I was pleased, like when someone gives you an illuminated psalter for your birthday. God, I hate my uncle. One of these days he'll go a quarter of an inch too far, and then I'll have him.

There I go again, rattling on about my problems. How are things with you? There don't seem to have been any carefully wrapped little packages lately, and to be serious for a moment, I could do with something miraculous right now—for choice, my uncle being eaten by dogs, but I'll settle for a toenail of the Blessed Mother, just so long as I've got something to brandish on the temple steps when we have the thanksgiving service for poor old Teddy getting his head cut off. No pressure or anything.

Wish you were here &c

G

Genseric, by the grace of the Invincible Sun Archduke of Schanz, Elector, Grand Marshal of the Eastern Command, Precentor of the Holy Diaconate, to Pollio his brother in faith, greetings.

You stupid bloody idiot, why didn't you tell me you were sick? But no, I've got to find out from Our Man In New Olbia, who tucks it away in a postscript to some fatuous spiel about salt cod tariffs that I wouldn't have bothered reading, except I was so bored I'd have read anything… Look, as soon as you get this, write to me at once and let me know you're still alive. If you're dead, I shall be seriously annoyed.

G

Pollio, pilgrim and slave, to Genseric, Archduke, Elector, Marshal, Precentor, Defender of the Faith, greetings.

Well, if you must know, I died. Only kidding. It wasn't even close, as it happens; I got a dose of this fever thing they have in these parts, it's very popular with the locals but I can't see much point to it myself; a bit like fermented cabbage, which is the regional delicacy, except that given the choice I know which one I'd choose, and it wouldn't be the fermented cabbage.

You start off feeling like you're burning up, and then you start puking and then you get these perfectly volcanic running shits, you ache all over and your head feels like someone's hammered a wedge in right between your eyes; and it carries on like that for a bit, and then you gradually get better. I spent a ridiculous amount of your money getting prodded and fingered by the local quacks, who wanted to open my veins and stick leeches on me under the curious misapprehension that it would do me good… So I paid them even more money to go away, and the innkeeper's mother, a nice old lady with a moustache, came and fussed round me and made me drink some ghastly form of tea made from tree-bark—I tell you what, they're an odd lot in these parts, with some rather questionable views on what is and isn't appropriate to put in your mouth. Anyhow, panic over, I'm fine now.

But, thanks to all that nonsense, I haven't been getting much work done, for which I apologise. While I was otherwise engaged with the puking and the shits, a very-probably-genuine Sircassio rood-screen came and went, bought for not much money by some knob I've vaguely heard of, on behalf of the Sashan ambassador… Yes, quite. Why are a bunch of fire-worshippers buying up images of the Invincible Sun? Answer: to give to someone as a present. You might want to get one of your people to look into that, when you've got five minutes.

Sorry to hear about your cousin. I have an idea I met him once—didn't he come and visit at the start of Hilary term in Second Year? I vaguely remember a large chap dancing on a table in the Glorious Legacy and falling off and all of us getting thrown out, and then a certain amount of vomiting on the steps of the Hermitage, though I can't recall offhand if that was him or you. Or it could even have been me. If so, I can honestly say that since then, I've really grown and matured as a vomiter. You should've seen me the other day. I nearly broke the bowl.

Also sorry to hear your uncle's being a pest. Changing the subject entirely and à propos of absolutely nothing, there's an outfit in these parts who guarantee to slit the throat of the party of your choice, no mess, no pack drill, for one hundred thalers flat rate plus travel, money back if not entirely satisfied. They've got terrific feedback with the locals and they do overseas work all the time.

Yours for the sanctity of all human life,

P

GENSERIC, BY THE *grace of the Invincible Sun Archduke of Schanz, Elector, Grand Marshal of the Eastern Command, Regent of the Duchy of Selvois, Precentor of the Holy Diaconate, to Pollio his brother in faith, greetings.*

Thanks ever so much for the heads-up about the Sashan. I had the spooks look into it, and yes, they've been scarfing up religious stuff on the sly and handing it out like sweeties to practically everybody except me, ever since we won that stupid battle. It's not a cheerful development and I'd be inclined to worry if it was anyone except the Sashan—but you know what those creeps are like. When they want to make friends, they start off by chumming with all your enemies; that way, when they start sending you flowers and cinnamon-cakes and expressions of undying diplomatic love, you're so relieved that you sign any damn thing they put in front of you without even reading it. Not that I'm convinced I want to be best-buddies with the Sashan. They can be a bit demanding at times, and their definition of a mutual defence pact isn't really like anything we learned about in Third Year. They have this concept of preemptive self-defence that actually sounds quite reasonable until it snaps shut round your ankle, and then suddenly you're comprehensively screwed… But the good thing about the Sashan is that they're patient and they love to flirt—the spooks tell me it's the game they get their kicks from, not the outcome—and they really don't like committing themselves to anything unless they absolutely have to. All that kind of shit gives me a pain in my tummy, but it's a damn sight better than war, so bring it on.

I don't suppose you read all the gammon-and-spinach at the top of the letter, so you probably haven't noticed where it now says *Regent of the Duchy of Selvois;* thought not. Well, anyhow, it's true. My God-knows-how-many-times-removed cousin Grabo finally pegged out, but not before his younger son poisoned his elder son and then got knifed by his sister, who then got bitten by a poisonous spider of a kind not usually encountered in Selvois… Long story short, the shit hit the fan and was promptly deflected onto me, as regent until sister's three-year-old daughter comes of age. Sister was a widow, by the way, her husband died last year from eating a funny mushroom. It amazes me, whenever I contemplate my family, that I haven't turned out even worse than I am.

Anyhow, I now control an additional twelve thousand square miles, though I'm not allowed to touch a bent stuiver of the revenues over and above running expenses, all that's got to be accumulated, for when Her Royal Highness grows up, which is a bitch because I could really use the money right now. Instead, the most contentious buffer state between the Aelian Confederacy and the Olbians is now my responsibility, therefore my fault, and a pretty little nest of vipers it is too.

Selvois is the last place God made, all mountains and rocky outcrops and about two dozen skeletal sheep fighting over three sprigs of heather, but an alarming number of people somehow manage to live there and they've got ridiculously huge deposits of lead in the high mountains, which they mine in a haphazard sort of a way, and as you know, where there's lead there's silver… My people tell me it'd cost about a million gulden to set up a serious mining operation, and obviously I haven't got that sort of money; the Aelians and the Olbians do, it goes without saying, and neither of them can afford to let the other lot get their claws on it, so you'll appreciate that my life suddenly got a whole lot more interesting.

Do you remember when we were in Second Year and we had that long drunken discussion about power and self-interest and the inalienable human right of liberty, and we came to the conclusion that the one absolute criterion for being allowed to have power over other people's lives was not wanting it? Many a true word spoken *in vino veritas,* and all that. Actually, it's the only thing that makes me feel good about myself right now, remembering that conversation. I didn't want this stupid fucking job then and I don't want it now; and I will never, ever forgive my useless, stupid, selfish brother for dying and landing me with it. Note the repetition of the word *stupid,* which is inelegant but fuck it; stupid is precisely what it is: lacking sense, devoid of intellectual input—stupid that things should be allowed to work that way, stupid that my brother should've been stupid enough to go hunting on a lethally dangerous three-year-old stallion, stupid, *stupid*—My entire family are idiots, me included, and we run the stupid country. Why, for crying out loud? It makes absolutely no sense at all.

Sorry. Didn't mean to shout. My secretary is looking at me, and I don't blame him. Talking of which, since when did I have a secretary, sorry, Pila, no, don't write that, you fool—Since I got this ginormous callous on the side of my middle finger from writing all day long, which meant my handwriting got so bad that even I can't read it. So poor Pila has to listen to the sound of my voice from dawn to midnight and pretend he doesn't mind. I feel like I'm slowly but irreparably being diluted, like the wine at the Three Angels. I'd give anything for a day off, but it's not possible. Very few things are when you're doing my job, and the list of possible things gets shorter every day; and by way of compensation they give you the regency of Selvois, which means even fewer things are possible, and so it goes on, like water draining out of a plug-hole.

This is turning into a very long letter, and nearly all of it whining. Sorry about that. Whining and single-source fine white bread with sesame seeds on top are the only two luxuries that remain to me, and sesame seeds give me a rash. Forgive me.

Wish you were here, God knows, and I wasn't,

G

POLLIO, PILGRIM AND slave, to Genseric, Archduke, Elector, Regent, Marshal, Precentor, Defender of the Faith, greetings.

You think you've got problems. You don't know you're born.

Actually, I'm exaggerating slightly. I read somewhere that when you're having a really bad time, nothing cheers you up like hearing about other people having it even worse. I can't really compete with you in the misery stakes so I won't try, but please bear in mind that these things are essentially subjective—my rheumatism hurts me more than your smashed collar-bone, because I'm a sensitive soul and you're as stolid as an ox, and so on. So here goes.

I was in some bar, and I was talking to some clown, and he happened to mention that up in the hills somewhere there's this falling-down old monastery with about half a dozen monks, all of them about ninety years old, and squirrelled away they've got a lock of the hair of Sichelgaita of Chrenz. Well, you know the score. In every hilly region in every province of every country in the world there's a semi-derelict monastery hiding an incredible treasure, and when you eventually get there you find nothing but rocks, or somebody's brother-in-law trying to sell you the Oriaspis Bridge. So I bought this chancer a drink, with your money, and thought nothing of it until the next morning, when I woke up with a mouth like sandpaper and a slight headache and starting thinking about something I'd read somewhere—Which led me to the library of the Silver Rose, which doesn't open till noon, so that was three hours sitting around in the baking hot sun, and then I managed to get hold of a copy of Adelfin's commentary on Bootes, luckily one with the complete scholia, and there it suddenly was, like finding a diamond lodged in a turd.

It was this scholiast moaning about the lies some people tell, including for example those unscrupulous rascals who'd have you believe that the Blessed Sichelgaita didn't die at Oronto, which everybody knows is the truth, but instead she died at some rat-arse little monastery in the hills above Sclim, and the monks there, who are liars, claim to have a lock of her hair encased in amber, though obviously it's no such thing… And the scholiast was writing before the Dissolution, which puts it back eight hundred years at the very least, and four hundred years later Dromius proved beyond a shadow of a doubt that the shrine at Oronto was a fake—

You really need to be careful in this line of work, because ninety-nine times out of a hundred, when you make an amazing discovery like that the morning after some low-life in a bar tells you he knows where something good is, it's because the low-life in the bar has also read the scholiast on Adelfin on Bootes and figured out how to make a buck out of the next sucker he meets. To be painfully frank, I've played that scam myself (not Sichelgaita, obviously, but the same general idea) on rich idiots with more money than sense, back in the days before you rescued me from a life of crime and made me the shining beacon of honesty I am today… But the thing of it is, one time in a hundred it's actually true, and the low-life is just a low-life, and the tumbledown monastery in the armpit of Nowhere really does house a sleeper relic of unimaginable sanctity and value. So of course you've got to go, and so of course I went.

Three days up the sodding mountain; it didn't actually rain, but the air was heavy and wet and all I could hire in Sclim was the skeleton of a donkey, because of the Fair. Anyway I got there and banged on the door, and just when I'd arrived at the conclusion that everybody must've died, a very old man tottered up and opened the door and scowled at me and said, What the hell do you want? It turned out he was the prior (he answers the door because he's the only one fit enough to climb the stairs) and yes, they did have a relic of the Blessed Sichelgaita, did I want to see it? Might as well, I replied, since I'm in the neighbourhood; so off we go, up about a million winding stone stairs to the top of a tower which I swear is only still standing through force of habit; and there in a simple but quite adorable alabaster reliquary is this thing, and—

I think I've been in this business too long. It gets to you after a while. Looked at objectively, I don't suppose it's anything much. It's basically a knob of resin about the size of a plum, a sort of cloudy golden yellow colour, slightly darker than Moschetz honey; there's a couple of air bubbles, and if you look closely, you can see the lock of hair, twisted into a sort of rope and looped over like half a corn dolly. That's it. No big deal—except, it's *genuine*, I can feel it in my water. You develop an eye for these things after a while. You look, and you just know.

Later I was able to rationalise it—like, for example, if it's a fake, then we know it's close on a thousand years old, because of the provenance, and why would anyone have wanted to fake the bloody thing back then, long before bits of the Blessed Sichelgaita were worth money? Also, that technique of sealing things in resin is now a lost art, because the resin only came from one particular species of birch tree that only grew in one region of Permia, and all those trees got cut down for charcoal when the iron mines opened. And stuff like that—which of course is bread and butter to a high-class faker; if you can figure out how to duplicate the unique material and the long-forgotten technique, you can make out like a bandit, because everyone will trust you, et cetera. No, it comes down to instinct and intuition, which is another word for faith, and you get faith where you get the touch of the Divine, just as you get porphyry where you find copper. Call me a halfwit if you like, but that yellow knob spoke to me. I'm real, it said, and what are you going to do about it?

So I said to the prior, how much do you want for it? And he looked at me like I was mad and said, it's not for sale.

Well, of course it wasn't. Nine old men who'd spent their entire lives basically doing nothing but basking in the glow of that little yellow blob; the last thing they'd ever do was exchange it for money. Even if it was all the money in the world (which was essentially what I offered them)—No, absolutely not.

It crossed my mind that I could slaughter the lot of them with my walking stick without breaking into a sweat, and nobody would ever know, and even if they did they wouldn't care... It crossed my mind by the shortest possible route and then it got shown the door. And the same goes for sneaking in at night—they wouldn't hear me, they're all as deaf as posts, and the door to the tower room is so rotten you'd only have to breathe on it... But it doesn't work like that, I'm sorry to say. Besides, without the unimpeachable provenance it'd just be a translucent yellow pebble, so the hell with it. I thanked them all politely, got back on my horrible donkey and lurched my painful way back down the hill to Sclim.

So, like I said, you think you've got problems; spare a thought for me and reflect on how lucky you are. I know where there's a genuine Sichelgaita; and one day quite soon, when the last of the monks drops off the perch, then that amazing artefact will be fair game for the first lucky man who shows up and grabs it. What do I do? Do I camp out on the bare hillside, sniffing the breeze for the scent of putrefying bodies? Or do I shrug my shoulders, remind myself that you can't win 'em all, and ride off into the sunset in search of even greater treasures?

Fuck me if I know. I also have this uneasy feeling that on some level, I'm missing the point. I've seen a relic of the Blessed Sichelgaita. I've held it in my hand; it was smooth and slightly warm. And all I could think about, while all this was going on, was how to obtain possession of it—Daft as a brush. Like marrying the smartest, most beautiful girl in the world because you want someone to clean your shoes for you.

That sort of thing gets to you after a while.

Anyhow, I more than made up for it two days later when I was rummaging about in the junk tray of a dealer in the flea market, and there was this little flat pewter box, and when I opened it there was a tooth... The dealer wanted five groschen but I beat him down to three, and I'm now proud to be sending you a tooth of Gelasian the Stylite, one of only six known. How it got into the dealer's tray I couldn't tell you, but it's the real thing all right. Everything checks out, and I remembered the description from the catalogue of the Imprazia sale. It's all there—the inscription under the lining of the box in teeny tiny letters, three verses from the Nineteenth Psalm; the slightly defective hinge; the damage to one of the roots of the tooth, from when it was ripped out by the torturer with a pair of blacksmith's tongs. If you want me to put a value on it I'd have to say something in excess of HA4,500—that's a conservative valuation, God only knows what it might fetch at auction with a couple of zealots trying to outbid each other. Of course, Gelasian is right up your alley just now, being a high-class military saint and the patron of hereditary authority figures—quite probably more use to you than the Sichelgaita would've been, politically. Even so...I'm sorry. I'd have liked to have sent you something really nice, but I figure the Gelasian will just have to do.

Being ill put me behind schedule on the rather special something I mentioned a while back, but I'm hoping I can get back on track. Wish me luck.

Exultantly yours,

P

GENSERIC, BY THE *grace of the Invincible Sun Archduke of Schanz, Elector, Grand Marshal of the Eastern Command, Regent of the Duchy of Selvois, Precentor of the Holy Diaconate, to Pollio his brother in faith, greetings.*

RELICS

Can you read this? I hope so, but I doubt it, because obviously I'm having to write it myself, my very own fingers holding the pen, which is a pain. But, until they can find me a secretary to replace poor Pila, I'm having to do all my own scribbling. So much for the privileges of high office.

Pila had to go. A pity; I liked him. He had a quiet, understated sense of humour and he didn't take me too seriously. I paid him over the odds, but apparently it wasn't enough—turns out that his father's up to his eyebrows in debt and about to lose the farm. What should have happened is that Pila should've come to me and told me, and I'd have given him the money—it was a trivial sum, a couple of hundred, less than what I give for a new saddle. But instead Pila gets paid a couple of hundred by some very bad people. So what happens is, I've just got out of my bath and I'm sitting there in a towel and the man comes to shave me, only it isn't the man, it's Pila. He grabs my hair and pulls my head back—at which point I realise something's wrong. He's about to slit my throat, but I get both hands round his wrist and there's a sort of idiotic tussle more or less centred around the razor… I got my left hand sliced a bit and a few nicks, and by that time the guards have shown up, and before I can say anything, the sergeant's in there with his sabre and Pila's head is lolling on his left shoulder, only held on by a flap of skin.

I don't blame anyone, except maybe a certain brother of my late father. The sergeant saw a real and present threat and dealt with it, for which I'm profoundly grateful. He told me later, he opted for the quartered descending cut (number two on the diagram) because Pila was in front of me, so a thrust might've gone clean through him and stuck me in the tummy. He had to go for a kill shot, he said, because there was a weapon deployed and in use—the vocabulary soldiers have these days; hooray for education—so the priority was to neutralise the threat. He did that all right, bless him.

And I don't blame Pila. He was the second son, and when he was twelve his father indentured him to a man who trained clerks for the civil service. I've actually taken the trouble to find out what indentures really mean; the way it works is, I pay your dad a chunk of money, and you work for me until your wages have paid off that debt; fair enough. You get valuable training as well as a roof over your head and food to eat and clothes to wear, everybody wins. But when I turn over the flat stone, I find out that all the time you're eating and being sheltered and given clothes and being taught, you're being charged for it—cost of board and lodging and tuition is added to the debt, which increases faster than the carefully calculated wages can pay it off. Now the indentures have a fixed term, five or seven years; but if at the end of that time you still owe me money, I get to keep you till it's all paid off, and so it goes on. My great-grandfather abolished slavery, and everybody said what a wonderful thing that was and how Schanz was a shining beacon of hope in a benighted world, and one thing and another; and a couple of years later, along came the indenture system, which was a good thing because it meant poor kids could learn a trade and get a start in life.

I suppose I ought to do something about it, now that I know what's going on. And yes, I will do something about it; I'm going to set a minimum wage for indentured servants and make it so that a fixed term means a fixed term, no carryover for unpaid board and lodging &c—Complete waste of time, of course, since it won't take them five minutes to drive the proverbial coach and horses through my legislation, and in the meanwhile the honest people who aren't abusing the system (something like sixty per cent, as far as we can tell) won't be able to afford to take on indentured apprentices any more, so a lot of craftsmen won't be able to afford help, and a lot of kids won't have a chance to get out of the slums.

I've noticed this; whenever the Duke steps in to right a wrong, suppress a manifest injustice, do the right thing, what invariably happens is that the wrong doesn't get righted worth a toss, and a whole lot of harmless citizens who were nothing to do with the actual problem get inconvenienced, trodden on or put in jail. But what the hell. It's the hoary old Authoritarian

Syllogism, the one they taught us in First Year. We need to take action. This idea is counterproductive and bloody stupid, but it's unarguably action. So that's what we'll do.

I made sure Pila's dad got to keep the bribe money. His son earned it, even though he bodged the job he was paid to do. Anyway, so here I am, writing my own letters. My finger hurts. Someone ought to invent a new kind of pen with some sort of padding.

I have an idea that my uncle wants my job. I hate my job. Why, therefore, in God's name don't I let my uncle have it? Because I know he'd make an absolute pig's ear of it and thousands of innocent people would suffer? But I'm making an absolute pig's ear of it right now, and thousands of innocent people are suffering—thousands plus one, namely me (except I can hardly claim to be innocent, can I?). I don't know. What do you think? Write and tell me when you've got five minutes, there's a pal.

G

Pollio, pilgrim and slave, to Genseric, Archduke, Elector, Marshal, Regent, Precentor, Defender of the Faith, greetings.

Poor baby. Let me kiss the place and make it better.

You get no sympathy from me, Genseric son of Huneric. Please bear in mind, I know you better than you know yourself. You pretend you haven't got a choice, but of course you have. Look at your great-great-grandfather, or your cousin Bardimer. The day came when they said enough is enough, they packed it in and retired to a monastery and wrote commentaries on the Lives of the Desert Fathers; and then look what happened. Civil war. Thousands dead. Whole provinces deserted and overgrown with brambles, and Bardimer's duchy is now an administrative sub-district of the Sashan Empire. Of course you have a choice, every day of your life. So, every morning, after your bath and your hairdo and your cinnamon rolls, you choose the lesser of two evils. The one you choose is pretty bad. The other one is immeasurably worse, and don't you forget that for one moment.

I imagine there are days when you look out of your oriel window past the peach garden and the arboretum and the statues of the dancing nymphs towards the city, where there are so many desperate, hungry people, and you think: I ought to be doing some good, instead of all this shit. You halfwit. I take it upon myself to forgive you for that. You've clearly got yourself confused with the Invincible Sun—easy mistake to make in your line of work, where you've got so many plausible people trying to persuade you that the Invincible Sun shines out of your arsehole, and you always were a gullible bugger.

Repeat after me. I can only play the cards I've been dealt. I am not God. If I do the best I can, that's all right. If I try to do better than I can, I'm only going to make things horribly worse. Amen.

The immediate problem is clearly your uncle. You know my views on that subject, but you choose—that word again—not to act. Anyway, that's quite enough of that.

Meanwhile, in the real world, some of us have to work for a living, and I've been busy. You remember I told you about the Sichelgaita lock of hair at that monastery, the one I couldn't get them to sell? Well, not long after I went to see it, the monastery was raided. It looks very much like the usual suspects. A couple of fishermen reported seeing a Sherden longship lurking around about a mile out a day or so before it happened, and there were some unsavoury characters out pirating oysters by moonlight, and they reckoned they saw something long and black glide past them in the mouth of the estuary—And the actual attack had Sherden written all over it, the monastery burnt to the ground and the ashes carefully combed through for nails and hinges and pintels and iron fittings of all kinds. The library all went up in smoke, which is a real tragedy, and there was enough paper-ash found on site to make it fairly obvious that whoever it was didn't go there to pinch the books, and then torch the place to make it look like Sherden. But apart from the books there really wasn't anything there worth having, unless you happen to be Sherden and iron's worth its weight in silver where you come from. No survivors, of course, and no witnesses, which is also classic Sherden.

From which you draw the obvious inference that whatever it was the bastards were after, it wasn't the Sichelgaita relic. Like I said earlier, the relic's worthless without the provenance, and the provenance was the monastery. If you're after the relic for what it was and what it represented, the last thing you'd want to do would be to destroy the only agency in all Creation that could authenticate it. All you'd be left with for your trouble would be a knob of synthetic amber. Inference: a wonderful thing, imbued with and marinated in a thousand years of sanctity and grace, has been lost for ever; very sad, oh well, never mind, shit happens.

Which is exactly the sort of thing, as you know, which sets my whiskers twitching. Now I know that this is a point on which you and I differ. You maintain that shit happens. I take the view that people do shit. You, of course, will point out that if people do shit, generally they do it for a reason—that reason is generally money or politics or both, and in this instance there's no money or politics to be made out of taking an object of great potential monetary and political value and destroying it; in consequence of which, there's rather less money and political leverage left in the world than there was previously, and who does that benefit? Nobody. Well, quite, I immediately reply. That's exactly what they *want* you to think.

No, seriously. I honestly believe there's something in this. I show up, people know who I am and who I'm working for, and a few days later the monastery's a smoking ruin. Of course there's the awkward fact that I didn't get the relic. If I'd got it, there would've been no point in torching the monastery. The fact that I didn't get it means that I'd failed, so no action equired on the part of someone resolved that I shouldn't get it. At which point, my head starts hurting—there's no point to any of it, unless it really was just a shipload of Sherden out hunting for nails and door-latches. Which is a real thing, we know, and happens every day.

The answer, I suspect, is something to do with faith. But whose faith? That's what I can't figure out. Anyway, in the meantime I've put in a bid on a recorded icon by the Handless Painter. It's got a rock-solid provenance and the owner wants a bundle for it, but just think how nice it'd look being carried before you in a procession down Foregate. Nobody would dare lay a finger on you, no matter how much money your uncle's offering, not even poor bastards like your late secretary. For what shall it profit a man if he gains the whole world and loses his soul? You'd be as safe as a miser's sixpence. Money well spent. I'll let you know how it goes. Meanwhile, stay safe and don't beat yourself up about things that aren't your fault.

Your friend,

P

Pollio, pilgrim and slave, to Genseric, Archduke, Elector, Marshal, Regent, Precentor, Defender of the Faith, greetings.

You're not going to like this.

I've been lying awake all night agonising about whether to tell you or not. There's absolutely nothing you or I can do about it, so why make you miserable by telling you? But, on the other hand, if I kept it from you you'd never forgive me, and quite right too. So here goes.

Gortilla is dead. She died three days ago. I'm sorry

It's not a nice story. She showed up here about four months ago, in a bit of a mess, same as usual. Apparently she'd been touring with some hayseed company or other; her voice had more or less gone and the booze meant she wasn't quite as decorative as she used to be, but she could still dance and clown about and bring the house down, and thanks to her these no-hopers were packing them in every night, and I guess she was happy, doing the only thing she ever loved. Then she had a bad fall and the quack said her knee was shot so no more dancing. The actors said it didn't matter, they'd still keep her on, but I gather that as far as she was concerned it was the last straw. She crawled further and further into the bottle until they were forced to let her go, and here's where she ended up when the curtain finally fell. I paid for a hole in the ground to put her in, and what she owed around town for booze and breakages. She'd have wanted that. You know how she always hated owing money.

She was dead by the time I got here and I couldn't bring myself to see the body.

You know she was the only thing that ever came between us. I loved her and so did you. You couldn't marry her because of being the son of a duke, and she wouldn't have me because I'm from Poor Town and not worth a bent stuiver. You could never have saved her and made her happy, because of who you are. I could've—maybe—but the opportunity never arose, and now the poor bitch is dead. That needn't have happened. It wasn't inevitable, like so much of the political shit you have to cope with. It wasn't a matter of vast, unstoppable socioeconomic forces or the momentum of centuries of history sweeping us along like driftwood in a tidal wave. It was avoidable and unnecessary and a stupid, stupid waste, and I feel like a light has gone out and I'm left alone in the dark. How you're feeling, now that you've read this, I can easily imagine. I'm not saying I forgive you, I don't think I could ever bring myself to do that, but I know how terribly much it must hurt, and I'm sorry.

I think it's different for you. I think you're luckier than me. Every day, your idiotic job brings you face to face with misery and suffering and disaster, and jams your nose up against it till all the skin's turned to scars, so you can cope. For me, it's not that easy. I had a bad time when my mother died, and then Dad so soon after that; other than that, I haven't had much experience with the sort of pain that makes you want to hang yourself just so it'll stop. I wish now that I could be all calloused and hardened like you are. That's the advantage of being royalty, I guess. You grow up being used to things like this, whereas we commoners get taken completely by surprise and don't have the first idea how to cope.

Sorry. I've probably said more than I should, though I can't actually bring myself to tear up what I've written and start again, because what I've said is true. And you don't need me to tell you how you're feeling right now. Anyway, for what little it's worth, there's one other living creature on this earth who knows what you're going through, and he reckons it's a bad show, and not entirely fair.

Stay safe, old buddy. Just this once, I wish I was there with you.

P

Genseric, by the *grace of the Invincible Sun Archduke of Schanz, Elector, Grand Marshal of the Eastern Command, Regent of the Duchy of Selvois, Precentor of the Holy Diaconate, to Pollio his brother in faith, greetings.*

If it's all right with you, I'm not going to say anything about her. That was all done and finished with years ago.

Instead, guess what, I'm getting married. I imagine the irony of that isn't lost on you. Obviously, I have no choice in the matter. Either I get married or I raise taxes by a minimum of eighteen per cent—no, let's be realistic, more like twenty, actually make that twenty-five. But if I marry Kremild, I get the revenue from the Tuebiga salt pans, which will make all the difference. The plain fact is that everybody in the world needs salt, but nobody except me needs me to be happy. So, the hell with it.

I haven't seen Kremild yet, only a painting of her, six inches by eight inches including the frame, seated under a rose arbour. I have no idea what I'm supposed to say to her when I do meet her. I'm so sorry? It wasn't my idea, it's nothing personal; don't blame me? Of course, even if I do say that, it won't do a blind bit of good, because she won't understand a word of it, she only speaks Permian. For crying out loud.

I know, you have absolutely no sympathy. Why should you? I've known this was coming, all my life, if not Kremild then someone interchangeable with her; it's something I've been conscious of but have avoided thinking about, like death. And no, in practice it's no big deal. She'll have her own wing of the palace, with girls her own age to talk to in Permian; she'll bring her own architect and her own court painters and decorators, and they'll fix her up a tiny bubble of Permia where she won't have to be aware of where she really is or what's really happening to her. She can have the view from her window landscaped to look just like home. Poor kid, living in a bubble is all she's ever known—needlework and harpsichord music and dressing up and never ever being alone. If I had to live like that, I'd go mad inside a week. If she's really lucky she'll have been born too stupid to imagine that there might be more to life than all that. If not—well, I don't suppose I'll be making it significantly worse, at any rate. I've asked the librarian of the Iron Wreath to send me down a Permian grammar and a tutor if they've got one—I don't suppose they have—but you know what a klutz I am about learning languages. I'd have failed Old Aelian if you hadn't done my translations for me. That's me, of course; everything I am is borrowed from someone else or done for me. And everything I do turns out wrong.

When I was a kid—before you knew me—I used to dream about running away. I used to lie in bed staring up at the ceiling, working out the details. For a start I'd have to climb out of the window, which meant rope, and of course I had no way of getting rope; but I'd heard that you could make a rope out of sheets—you twist them, apparently, but I tried it and it didn't look a bit like rope, so then I thought about the bell-pulls, but trying to unhook them made a racket and footmen came running to see what I wanted... I never got out of the window, not even in my imagination. Then I got sent away to Ridichen to learn the sum of human knowledge, with money to spend and nobody to tell me what to do, and I met you and Raffenkel and Auzeil—and Gortilla. And then my stupid brother died, and here I am, back in the cage where I belong, and now I'm going to marry a princess and live happily ever after. You wouldn't do it to a dog, or not a dog you were fond of.

Excuse my ignorance, but who the hell is Sichelgaita? Nobody here has heard of the woman.

Cordially,

G

Pollio, pilgrim and slave, to Genseric, Archduke, Elector, Marshal, Regent, Precentor, Defender of the Faith, greetings.

Oh for fucking out loud. Sichelgaita? Seriously?

Of course I know you're all heretics up there in armpit-of-the-universe Schanz, but even you must have books. Bet you anything you like there's one or two around the place. Try looking on the shelves in the library, or under the legs of formerly wobbly tables. Sichelgaita, you ignorant buffoon, was a major prophet and one of the three human witnesses of the Transfiguration. She's got a list of confirmed accredited miracles as long as your arm. In theological terms, she's so hot you burn your brain just thinking about her.

But not, now I come to think of it, in the Reformed tradition. You savages did away with all that, I seem to recall, sometime around the Great Schism. Why anyone would want to do a thing like that, I really don't know—either you believe in all that stuff or you don't, you don't pick and choose and say yes, I'll take the Ascension and the Parable of the Cherry Stone, but I don't want the Beatitudes or the Dual Procession of the Divine Essence.

No, I tell a lie, you people apparently do. Weird, I call it, but there you go. And presumably you do have books, but your great-grandpa had all the relevant ones burnt. I really wish you'd mentioned all this earlier, before I worked my arse to the bone, but not to worry. It's only me.

About the marriage thing. I'm sorry. If I'd known, I'd have kept my mouth shut about Gortilla. I don't suppose it can have helped, not one tiny bit. If you ask me, the truth has a lot to answer for. It causes most of the unhappiness in this world, and if I had your job the first thing I'd do is have the truth rounded up and stoned to death. Still, there it is. You know now, and I can't do anything about that, I'm afraid.

Being a whole month older than you and immeasurably more intelligent, I suppose I ought to have some good advice to give you about how to handle the marriage thing, but I'm afraid I haven't. I could say, forget about it, it's only politics, it's not a real marriage; but I know you're not like that. Your brother wouldn't have given it a thought, and presumably that's how people like you are supposed to cope. It hadn't occurred to me before, but actually it's obvious. Being insensitive and downright stupid isn't a handicap for you people, it's a survival strategy; because if you actually thought about things, like real people do, you'd all die of guilt, shame and broken hearts. So that's why there's all this interbreeding in royalty and the aristocracy. You're deliberately, and very wisely, breeding men and women who are too dumb to understand. The stupidity doesn't affect their performance in other areas, since they have clever advisers to do everything for them, and the dreadful poverty of their existence never occurs to them, because they lack the intellectual capacity to perceive it. Meanwhile, all the ruling gets done by stolid, unimaginative people, intellectually incapable of idealism or altruistic zeal (neither of which are anybody's friend, as witness the bulk of human history); trained professionals do all the necessary administration, nothing ever really changes and everybody's happy.

It's actually a brilliant system, though it can't be working all that well or why do we have all these tiresome wars? Even so; just because it's not working as well as it ought to doesn't mean it's not better than any of the alternatives. Just because your expensive mechanical clock stops, you don't discard the whole concept of Time and start living your days backwards. The survival of the thickest, the dominion of the not very bright, the apotheosis of the not-the-sharpest-knife-in-the-drawer… I'm guessing you've known about this all long but you're not allowed to mention it to outsiders. Which is only right and proper, after all.

All right, then, I'll forget about the Sichelgaita, much as it pains me to do so. It just so happens that the other thing I mentioned, the really big thing, is hotting up again, so I'll get on it like a mongoose and with any luck I'll have some good news for you soon, for a change. Meanwhile, for God's sake keep an eye on your appalling uncle. It won't have escaped even your snail-paced cognitive processes that if you marry and produce an heir, his chances of getting his arse on the Iron Throne will be significantly prejudiced. Seriously: get yourself a food taster, make your guard sergeant do random rotations of the duty rosters, and buy yourself one of those brigantine coats with all the little steel plates sewn into the lining. I mean it. You know it makes sense.

P

GENSERIC, BY THE grace of the Invincible Sun Archduke of Schanz, Elector, Grand Marshal of the Eastern Command, Regent of the Duchy of Selvois, Precentor of the Holy Diaconate, to Pollio his brother in faith, greetings.

You mean brigandine. A brigantine is a type of ship.

Oddly enough, some of your brilliant insights had also occurred to me. Unfortunately, it's not as easy as that.

Have you ever tried to hire a food taster? It's a real giggle, believe me. It stands to reason it's not something you delegate, so I interviewed the candidates myself. That didn't take very long; it's not exactly a popular job. Consequently, you get mostly deadheads applying. I had three walking skeletons with terminal diseases, two jokers who I knew had been sent along by my uncle even before the spooks reported back, two clowns who couldn't tell aniseed from coriander—I insisted on a practical, which nobody else has ever thought of before; six bowls of nibbles, and they had to tell me what was in them—and a miserable old bugger with body odour issues who'd been taster-in-chief to the Prince of Auzida right up to the time when His late Majesty stopped an arrow at the Battle of Domitz. He got the job, needless to say, and that's a great shame, because he talks with his mouth full and it's very hard to get him to shut up, and he tells the most appalling stories.

The guards' duty roster thing is way more complicated than a mere commoner like you could ever begin to imagine. Basically we've got a pool of a hundred men ready for night guarding duty at any given time, and every evening, just before they lock all the doors, three sergeants huddle round a big silver pot and draw lots, so nobody has a clue who's going to be on duty… Naturally, lot-drawing can be fiddled easy as pie, so if you want to be a sergeant in the palace guard, you have to provide five hostages, to include at least one parent or sibling, spouse and child—If I get murdered in my bed, the hostages get it ten minutes later, and the crazy thing is, the sergeants all put up with that, for the sake of the promotion and the extra fifty gulden a week, and because it's their duty. But that system doesn't actually work; that's what they used to do in Dorland, and you remember what happened to King Torfald. So on top of all that I have a dozen monolithic Rosinholet mercenaries camped outside my bedroom door every night, whose function is basically to guard me against the guards. They're fanatically loyal, they only speak Rosinholet, they cook garlic soup on a little charcoal stove in the corridor, and they flick their dice against my bedroom door, which gets tiresome after a while, and if you ask them not to do it they just look at you and say Ug, which presumably is Rosinholet for something or other, but nobody seems to know what. In consequence I don't sleep much, and as for using my bedroom for any kind of recreational activity, you can forget all about that. A small price to pay for staying alive, maybe, but after a while it gets to you, is all I'm saying.

As for the brigandine, I get through them at a rate of about two a year. It's the sweat; it rusts the steel plates, and by God you sweat in those things, especially with all your goddamned court robes and regalia on top. You know what I fantasise about most of all? Being cool. Not being boiled to death all the bloody time. Being able to spend a whole day wearing just a shirt and a pair of trousers, and taking a piss without having to undo a mile of laces and unhook a discreet little chainmail apron. By the grace of the Divine I'm naturally skinny; just think what it must've been like for Dad, who was as fat as a pig. I remember when I was a small kid, when he'd been sitting in state for any length of time there'd be sweat running down under his cuffs and down his forehead, and when he stood up the back of the chair was sopping wet. The thing is, if you didn't wear all that loathsome clobber, nobody would have a clue who you were.

So: thank you for your concern, but I've got all that covered, and a whole load of other angles you couldn't even imagine. According to the leading technical manual on the subject, there are eighty-six ways to poison a human being besides food and drink; beside poisoning, there's also toxic fumes, asphyxiation from tampered-with stoves, corrosive vitriol in your bathwater, sawn-through floorboards—you didn't think we have all that marble paving because we like the stuff, did you?—snakes, spiders, cisterns of molten lead surreptitiously retro-engineered into the hot water pipes, loosened carriage-wheel cotter pins, chandeliers and priceless works of art falling from a great height, you name it, some bugger's figured out how to adapt it to the purposes of regicide. Also, a note on court ceremonial: we don't do all that shit for fun. If you stick exactly to a preordained routine, you know exactly what His Majesty is going to be doing at all times, day and night, and where he's going to be doing it; you can therefore take steps to ensure that at that time, in that place, he's absolutely safe. Anything spontaneous and unpredictable opens the door on a vast wilderness of assassination opportunities, which the security people quite reasonably refuse to be held accountable for. What that means is that, if I set one pampered foot off the path ordained for me by tradition and the captain of the Guard, I'm liable to be killed, and my own stupid fault for being wilful. I have no option but to take it all very seriously, because if I get the chop, my uncle—well, you know all that. Let's not even think about it.

So: heads of state and maximum security prisoners have a lot in common, except that prisoners can keep pets, if you don't mind rats. I wanted a dog when I first started in this racket. Sure, they said, no problem, it can live in the royal kennels. No, I said, I want it in here, with me. You should have seen the look on their faces, and I never mentioned it again.

Sorry; I'm whining, and I know your views on that. I'll say it and save you the ink; I'm self-centred as a drill bit, all I ever think about is me and my problems, there's a great big world out there crammed to bursting with misery, suffering and injustice and my trivial aches and pains are so insignificant as to be invisible, even under a Mezentine reading-glass. True. No excuses, and saying I was born to it is still just whining. The kid from Poor Town who was born to thieving because he has no other options in life doesn't get spared the noose, and neither should I. Agreed.

I remember going through all of this stuff with you and Raffenkell and Gortilla in the garden of the Sword of Integrity after Prelims. Raffenkell said he'd thought about it and he couldn't see how he could go on associating with someone like me, even though he liked me personally, because of what I represented and what I might become. And I said that was bitterly unfair, and you said tough, life is bitterly unfair... And Gortilla said we were all a bunch of stupid kids, beating up on our friends because of silly things like principles and ideology, and she didn't know why she bothered with any of us. And then you got all stuffy and said principles and ideology were all that mattered in the end; you said something really pompous about the true metal being what was left after all the slag and dross had been burned away, and she burst out giggling, and three seconds later we were all helpless with laughter and the landlord asked us to leave... And then Gortilla solemnly forgave all three of us, for being rich and clever and a cut above; and then Raffenkell forgave her for being beautiful, which was something she hadn't earned, just as we hadn't earned our privileges—and we all decided we ought to be thoroughly ashamed of ourselves, but that was fine, because we'd achieved absolution. And then the proctor's men showed up and you and I and Raffenkell had to run like buggery, and you got away by climbing a tree but Raff and I got hauled up before the Dean and fined for consorting with a lewd woman—

Actually, I don't know if you remember that. You've had plenty of other being-truly-alive moments since then, so probably none of it was any big deal for you. Not me. I remember every minute vividly. I think about them a lot. Foxes have holes and the birds of the air have nests and even the kids in Poor Town have shop doorways and a bit of a ledge under a bridge. The only home I've got is those memories—home as the place you come back to, where you belong. Stupid, really.

Well, this has been a waste of a good sheet of parchment; it looked better, as they say, on the sheep. I had some news I was going to tell you, but I can't remember what it was. Can't have been important.

Cordially,

G

[THE NEXT TWO letters are too fragmentary to be legible]

POLLIO, PILGRIM AND slave, to Genseric, Archduke, Elector, Marshal, Regent, Precentor, Defender of the Faith, greetings.

I trust Your Grace is feeling better now. Your Grace should be aware that there's nothing quite so boring as reminiscences of one's college days, even to those who were there at the time. Your Grace would therefore do well not to unload any of them on anybody important—ambassadors, party leaders and high dignitaries of the church. They may look like they're interested, but they're not, trust me.

While you've been wallowing in self-pity, I've been busy. In fact, I just saved your useless neck.

Nothing to do with relics; I was talking to a man I met in a bar. He was trying to sell me the nose of Vicho of Peguilhan preserved in honey. It was perfect. The jar was exactly right for the period, ditto the label, ditto the writing on the label; the provenance was flawless; the asking price was reassuringly astronomical. I said thanks but no thanks. I didn't point out that there's already one nose of the Blessed Vicho in the treasury of the Blind Angel in Mezentia, because that would've been tantamount to an accusation, which might have caused offence; and I didn't want to offend this character, because as well as peddling dubious noses, he organises half the political assassinations this side of the Friendly Sea, or at least his lords and masters do, but he coordinates it all.

Anyway, he and I were chatting about this and that, and I was taking an interest, and he was probably saying a little more than he'd intended—showing off, the way you do. Of course he wasn't to know about you and me, though on reflection maybe be should've done, if he was as good at his business as he reckoned he was. Anyhow, all he knew about me was that I'm a wandering dealer in holy carrion, with no visible connection to Schanz. So he started dropping hints—dropping; actually, all the emperor's trebuchets never hurled anything with quite so much force—about a really prestigious, one-for-the-CV job he had lined up in one of those dogshit little countries up Permia way; and I said, oh yes? and he said what made it really interesting, from the technical point of view, was that the customer insisted on the mark getting cancelled—that's the in word in assassionation circles, apparently—cancelled at the I-do stage of his wedding at the high altar of the local basilica, with an audience of half the crowned heads of the West, and security like I'd never believe...

A tiny little bell rang inside my head at this point. As you can imagine, I was in a bit of a position. I didn't dare start asking leading questions, for fear of scaring him off and probably getting my throat cut into the bargain. On the other hand, I wanted to be reasonably sure I hadn't got the wrong end of the pointy stick, since I knew you wouldn't be impressed if I laid this sort of thing on you and it all turned out to be a silly mistake. So I played him for an hour and three bottles of genuine imported Echmen rice wine at two gulden a pop—I know you're not a fisherman, it's too cerebral and boring for you, you like chasing things and shooting arrows, not standing dead still up to your waist in cold water. Lucky for you we're different. I played him, trawling flies, spinning out line, making sure he didn't realise he'd taken the hook. I made out that under my cover of mild-mannered art dealer I was also somehow connected with the biz, and all this was very interesting because I had a client who'd approached me with what sounded suspiciously like the same job, but our outfit had turned it down flat because it was too risky... Several times he saw my shadow on the water, so to speak, but I managed to get away with it and keep leading him on; suffice to say, I managed to milk him for enough circumstantial details that I'm personally convinced that you're the mark, and the danger is both real and present.

Now then. If you're sensible, you'll have your uncle arrested and killed, and that'll be the end of that. No uncle, no payment;

no payment, no job. But if you insist on being stupid, then what you've got to look into, urgently, is someone in your ecclesiastical hierarchy who's completely above suspicion and who'll be within arm's reach of you at the point in the service where you're kneeling in front of the altar immediately preceding the exchange of rings. Unfortunately that's all I can tell you; your spooks will have to take it from there, if you can trust them; if not, find someone you *can* trust and let him handle it. All I can say is that the man actually handling the cancellation fully expects to get away with it, because my pal was making an awful fuss about how complex and expensive the extraction process was going to be, but apparently the killer insisted on solid assurances that a rock-solid exit strategy was in place before agreeing to do the job—So it's more than a case of simply being prepared to duck and wearing chainmail under your scarlet and ermine. My guess is that it'll be something really nasty that you eat, drink, kiss or handle, and it won't start taking effect until all the clergy have left the building. That ought to be enough for you to figure it out. If not, for crying out loud make an excuse and cancel the whole show; better still, deal with your bloody uncle.

I'm pissing myself with worry about putting all this in one of our regular letters, because if your uncle intercepts it, you'll never read this and you'll be dead. Trouble is, you're so carefully sewn up that there's no other way to get word to you... Suffice it to say, I won't be getting much sleep until I hear from you again. Quite apart from sentimental considerations, if your uncle reads this I don't suppose he'll like me very much, and thanks to my new pal I've come to understand just how easy it is to get rid of people, and how very often it happens, mostly with nobody suspecting a damn thing. Of course I don't expect the fact that *my* life is now also on the line will carry any weight with you when it comes to deciding what to do about your father's horrible brother. You always were a selfish bastard.

Stay safe, Genseric. Trust me.

P

*G*ENSERIC, BY THE *grace of the Invincible Sun Archduke of Schanz, Elector, Grand Marshal of the Eastern Command, Regent of the Duchy of Selvois, Precentor of the Holy Diaconate, to Pollio his brother in faith, greetings.*

What can I say? You saved my life. Thank you.

The killer was the Dean of the Chapter; seventy years old, blameless life lived in the service of others. They'd got his nephew, the only family the poor bastard has left. The poison was inside the wedding ring. A clever jeweller had raised a tiny little nick on the inside, too small to see without a magnifying-bottle but sharp enough to draw blood. The poison was the venom of some Blemmyan spider, would you believe, and what generally kills you is the convulsions, which cause you to writhe so much you break your own spine.

Anyway: the Dean died on the rack—weak heart, which was a blessing if you ask me. He was chatty enough once they started turning the winch, but he couldn't finger anyone important because he simply didn't know any names. We tried to rescue his nephew but he turned up face down in the river.

We had to tell my prospective in-laws, of course, and they let off a squawk that could probably have been heard in Antecyrene... So the wedding's off for now, until my spooks can satisfy their spooks that they've got a wedding plan that's absolutely guaranteed a hundred-and-fifty-per-cent secure. Trouble is, the plan we were using was a hundred-and-twenty-per-cent... I don't know. I find myself asking myself, exactly what is there that I can actually do? I wasn't allowed to marry the only woman I've ever loved—well, fair enough. But now I can't even marry the woman I'm supposed to marry even though I don't want to. I can't do *anything.*

Talking of which. No, my uncle is still alive and at liberty. He doesn't even know (I don't think) that I know he arranged it all. I shouldn't know, because there's absolutely no proof.

When you know something but there's absolutely no proof… Isn't that what they call faith? I've got a lot of that right now. If I had a quarter of the faith in the Invincible Sun that I have in the fundamental horribleness of my uncle, I'd presumably ascend bodily to heaven.

So why don't I just go ahead and scrag the old bastard anyway? It's what he'd do if he was in my purple ermine-lined buskins of state. That's what you'd be yelling in my face if you were here, and God knows, I can't think what I'd say to you if you were.

The fact is—I love him. He's my nearest, practically my only living relative. When I was a kid, I adored him. He knew how to talk to kids—not baby-talk or talking down at you from an impossibly great height; he was the only member of my family who seemed to *understand*, if you know what I mean. Whenever he came to see us he always brought me something; not a prayer-book or a solid gold spoon or a snow-white goshawk, but something I actually wanted: a horn-handled penknife, a slingshot, Lodian's *Bestiary* with pictures in colour, a pack of cards. He talked to me, just me and a grown-up having a conversation. He listened to me. You have no idea how much that meant to me when I was a kid.

That was when my brother was still alive, of course. Whether Uncle was planning to kill him, I don't know; probably. But at some early stage he'd assessed me and decided I wasn't going to be a threat or an obstacle, and on that basis and strict understanding, I think he actually liked me, for who I was. I've thought about it a lot, and I can't see any percentage for him being nice to me. Easier to kill me and have done with it. But he didn't. And he was never pals with my brother like he was with me. You have no idea what it's like to have someone actually liking you, in the circumstances of my early childhood. I'd more or less reached the conclusion that being liked was something that happened to other people but not to me, because of who I was and how I was situated; and fair enough, because I knew I was Different, it was just one more thing I had to accept. Birds fly over the rainbow, why oh why can't I? Because you're not a bird, stupid. Deal with it. But Uncle showed me that it was possible for me to be liked. That was like being a statue and suddenly coming alive. It was the most wonderful thing ever. I guess it still is.

And now he wants to kill me. Well; nobody's perfect. I guess part of me says, if Uncle wants me dead, it'd be churlish to insist on surviving. It's the only thing he's ever asked of me, after all, and he's given me so much in return. A bit like a lamb. We had some once, when my mother was going through her shepherdess phase, and everbody had to dress up in pastoral-idyll stuff, and the whole of the back lawn was planted out with removable trees hung with silver and gold pears. But the lambs were real, and my brother and I used to feed them, and they gobbled the stuff out of your hand, and they tickled and left your fingers all wet. But then they grew up and weren't cute any more, and in due course they ended up in the kitchen and on our plates—and I thought, well, we were nice to those lambs, we treated them like friends, family even; and all we asked in return was their lives. I decided I could handle that. I think I still can.

I guess it all depends on what value you put on your life. In my case—well. Value depends on what you paid for something. I never paid anything for my life; it was bought for me, given to me, nothing but the very best, nothing ever that I actually wanted. In terms of value, my life's like the illuminated Book of Hours I got for my Ascension; in money it's worth more than a fully equipped warship, but do I value it? No, not really. It's not what I wanted, it's what I got—and I'd part with it without a second thought for even the scintilla of a good reason. Gortilla, on the other hand—all I ever wanted, and precisely what I could never have. Life with her: I'd have fought tooth and nail for that, only somehow I didn't. So, I couldn't have really wanted it—her—happiness—all that much, now could I? And if I don't want happiness, it's no great stretch of the imagination to accept that I don't really want life either. I don't mind having it, but it's no big deal one way or the other.

Fine way to talk to the true friend who made it so that I still have a life, as opposed to a spine broken in three places by my own agonised convulsions. Stupid rich kid, spoilt rotten, doesn't know he's born—go on, say it.

I guess it depends on who gives you the present. The illuminated Hours, coming from my godfather the Margrave, who could afford twenty illuminated books and not notice, was just unwanted stuff. Coming from you, any gift is precious. My mother always used to give me a hard time for not looking after my things. You treat them like so much rubbish, she used to say, justifiably enough. So I'll try and look after this gift you've given me, because of who gave it. Thanks, Pollio. I owe you.

Your friend,

G

PS What exactly were you doing schmoozing with hired killers? I never realised the antiquities trade was quite so interesting.

Pollio, pilgrim and slave, to Genseric, Archduke, Elector, Marshal, Regent, Precentor, Defender of the Faith, greetings.

For God's sake, Genseric.

It's not often that I lose my rag with you, because I have a forgiving, easy-going nature and I make allowances for my friends, even when they're being absolutely fucking insufferable. This time, though, you've gone too far. You've gone so much too far that—if Saloninus is to be believed, and the universe in which we live is not in fact linear but curved, so that time and space are in effect circular—one of these days you're going to meet yourself coming in the other direction. Which will serve both of you right. With knobs on.

Your uncle will be the death of you—literally, not figuratively or tropically; one of these days he's going to kill you, and you'll only have yourself to blame. Can you understand what I'm saying? Sooner or later he'll hire an assassin who gets past all that fancy security of yours, and then you'll die. Everything you are, all the cleverness and sparkle and warmth and wry observation and long-suffering modest good humour and understanding and fun-to-be-with and compassion and (God forgive me for saying this) actual wisdom that make up what you are will be gone, lost for ever—water poured into the sand, smoke dissipated by the wind, sweat evaporated off the forehead of the Universe. One or two people, like me, will remember you to a greater or lesser extent for a little while, and then that'll be it. You'll have gone to waste, like we all do, sooner or later. But entropy is big enough and ugly enough to take care of itself; why help the bastard?

I despair of you, I really do. Also, you simply don't *think*. Try it, just for once. You've just foiled an incredibly sophisticated, deep-laid plot, organised by one of the leading outfits in the business. Now, these people have a living to earn and a reputation to protect. When a job goes inexplicably wrong, like this one did, they don't simply sigh and shake their heads and say, Some you win. They investigate and analyse. There's a leak in our organisation, they say to themselves, and they set out to plug it. They're thorough and painstaking, and their investigators aren't constrained by the usual rules of polite society. They're going to figure out that the leak could only have been my pal the fake nose salesman, and he'll die.

Well, no great loss. But, while they're at it, they'll figure out my part in the debacle, at which point there's something like a sixty per cent chance they'll come after me too—because I fooled them and made them look stupid in front of their potential clients, and we're talking about people who are naturally vindictive.

Fair enough. I knew the risk when I wrote you the letter. Greater love hath no idiot than this, that he lay down his life for his pal. But to take that risk and then have you turn round and say, I like my uncle, I'm going to forgive him and let him carry on trying to kill me until finally he succeeds—Screw you, Genseric. You may not value your life, but I value mine. You rich kids are all the same. You never did a day's work in your life, you never had to earn anything, everything's always been given to you on a silver platter—You don't even value being alive, because all your life it's been easy, spoon-fed, money no object, plenty more where that came from. You treat living and breathing like you treat your expensive clothes or your priceless Echmen porcelain. Use it like it's worthless, and if it gets wasted, so what? Another one will be provided, no big deal. I wouldn't put it past you to believe in the Afterlife; that's the epitome of rich-kid thinking. Doesn't matter what happens to me, you say, to this body; if it gets broken, my Daddy in heaven will buy me a new one even better.

That's just fine for you, Genseric. But where I come from, people have one shirt and one pair of shoes and one spade and one earthenware jug and one life; and if you break it or lose it, it's gone. And the reason why I'm not spending this one life I do have digging ditches and threshing wheat in the Mesoge is that I happened to be born smart, very smart indeed—smart enough to get out of the Mesoge, which is something very few people ever manage to do, which makes me rather special. Now, this smart kid is telling this rich kid not to be so bloody stupid. Pull yourself together, Genseric. Do what you've got to do, get it over with and move on.

P

Pollio, pilgrim and slave, to Genseric, Archduke, Elector, Marshal, Regent, Precentor, Defender of the Faith, greetings.

I take it from the fact that it's been so long since you wrote to me that something I said in my last letter may have offended you. If so, I'm sorry.

If, however, you did write to me and the letter hasn't reached me yet, or the courier got drunk or stabbed or eaten by wolves, then I'm not in the least sorry and everything in my last letter still stands.

But we won't talk about that any more. Instead, I'm going to cheer you up by telling you about the amazing coup I pulled off the day before yesterday, which will live in the annals of my profession until the Sun goes cold and Time itself dies. It was, in fact, pretty smart, though I do say so myself.

Now, one thing everybody in this racket knows is that the One True Robe exists and is a thing, but it's locked up in the treasury of the Grieving Brethren at Opis Olynthia, and all the king's horses and all the king's men couldn't ever get it out of there, because the Brethren don't share their toys with anybody. Which is cool; it's good that there are things in this irredeemably fickle universe that are constant and fixed and unchanging. It's stuff like that that makes it possible to distinguish reality from dreams. If ever we're in doubt, we can ask, is the Robe still at Opis? And the answer comes back, yes, and we know where we are. It's like the old whitewashed shrine at Overstrand, back where I grew up; you can see it for miles around, sitting on top of one of our few-and-far-between hills. You're never lost, my grandfather used to say, if you can see Overstrand church.

And now, here's the thing. Ninety-nine years ago—I've seen the paperwork—the Brethren ran out of money, big time. They had a severe cash-flow crisis, because of the War and a shipping crisis and an earthquake in Blemmya and lots of other horrible things all happening at once. So they took out a loan from the Knights; and for collateral, they gave two square inches of the Robe, carefully and piously snipped from the inside—apparently the Robe has generous seam allowance—which they packed in a solid gold reliquary and shipped off to Scona. Now get this. The two square inches are sealed into the gold box with a sheet of glass, so tight that if you tried to prise it out, it'd break. On the glass, inscribed with a diamond, is the provenance. The first thing the Knights did when they got their paws on it was have Prosper make an exact scale drawing of it, ink on parchment, so that for ever after, everybody would know exactly what the reliquary and the glass and the lettering cut into the glass looks like. The drawing was witnessed and sealed by nine bishops. It's the most rock-solidly authentic thing in the whole wide world, with the possible exception of the Robe itself.

And now the hundred years' term of the loan is almost up and the Brethren haven't got the money to pay, so very soon the Knights will have clear title to the Two Square Inches, and they're prepared to sell…

Now under normal circumstances that would only be of academic interest to a two-bit, poverty-stricken Archduke like yourself. You couldn't possibly afford it, trust me. But there could be—no, strike that, there *is* a way, all thanks to me and my cleverness and my unceasing diligence on your behalf.

(Think, incidentally, of what the Two Square Inches would mean. You could build a cathedral to put it in. You could tell everybody, the city that houses a piece of the One True Robe will never fall, and they'd believe you, right deep down in their hearts where faith happens. Pretty soon it'd be their church at Overstrand—wherever you are, you look up and there it still is, white and shining, and they'd know they aren't lost. They'd love you for it, of course, and then you'd be home and dry, free and clear, and all your troubles would be over—)

I told you before, didn't I, that I had my eye on something really big? Well, this is it, and trust me, they don't come any bigger. And all you have to do is

[The manuscript is damaged at this point]

GENSERIC, BY THE *grace of the Invincible Sun Archduke of Schanz, Elector, Grand Marshal of the Eastern Command, Regent of the Duchy of Selvois, Precentor of the Holy Diaconate, to Pollio his brother in faith, greetings.*

Brilliant. I'm sure we can do that, no problem at all.

I haven't actually seen the bloody thing for years, but I'm more or less certain it's still down there in the treasury somewhere. Who'd have thought something like that would come in useful one day?

We never throw anything out, of course. In fact, it's inconceivable that we could ever get rid of anything. Think about it. The stuff we accumulate—I'm not talking about worn-out bedsheets or broken pottery, consumables; I mean anything that's supposed to last—is inevitably of the highest quality, made by the finest craftsmen; we wouldn't be seen dead with anything less than the best, it goes without saying. So it doesn't wear out in a hurry, and by the time it eventually does it's antique, historical, a slice of our collective heritage. Meanwhile we're constantly acquiring new stuff—gifts mostly, wedding presents and baptism presents and stuff we get given by important visitors, and from time to time we splash out on everything new and shiny when we've got guests we need to impress, a state visit by the emperor, things like that; whereupon yet another generation of surplus-to-requirements treasure gets consigned to long-term storage. We don't sell stuff like that, because of the message that would send—they've run out of money, they're flogging off the family silver. We don't throw it away, because it'd be a crime to dump valuable and irreplaceable antiques. Sometimes we give things away as gifts to our brother heads of state; but you can't go giving the Margrave or the King of Sirupat any old junk you happen to have lying around, you could start a war. If there's a siege, we cut up big silver dishes to mint coins, but there hasn't been a siege for three hundred years.

So it all sits there, in what we euphemistically call the treasury, though in fact it's just a huge, incredibly well-guarded subterranean lumber room. There's a catalogue, naturally, and every now and then someone goes down there with a lamp and a thick wad of paper and makes an inventory, to make sure nobody's been quietly helping himself to our forgotten and obsolete treasures, because that would never do... There was a cook in my grandfather's time who pinched about a quarter of a ton of unwanted cutlery and silverware. He was smart. He didn't try and sell it, he melted it down for bullion. If he hadn't been caught red handed with a whole load of silver knives and spoons stuffed down the front of his apron we'd probably never have found out. I imagine they hanged the poor devil, though I really can't see what harm he did anybody.

Anyway, there you are. Bet you anything you like it's still down there, and because of our magnificently thorough inventory, it shouldn't be a problem laying hands on it straight away. You really are a godsend, Pollio. Thank you, ever so much.

Gratefully,

G

[AT THIS POINT the manuscript becomes too fragmentary to be legible; it is conjectured that at least two letters are missing. It seems probable that one of the missing letters, from Genseric to Pollio, gives an account of Genseric's wedding to the Lady Kremild]

POLLIO, PILGRIM AND slave, to Genseric, Archduke, Elector, Marshal, Regent, Precentor, Defender of the Faith, greetings.

I don't know. Sometimes it makes sense, sometimes it doesn't.

You'd have thought that if it made sense—ie, if it was true, which means susceptible of proof, using an approved scientific method—it'd do so consistently… If a thing's true today, it really ought to be true tomorrow. Likewise with things making sense. If $x–3y(z+3)=4y$ on the third day of the old moon, it ought still to $=4y$ on the second day of the new moon—but it doesn't always, and that bugs me.

Maybe it's all semantics; a degree of sloppiness in the precise definition of y, leading to a blurring of edges, a modest hop-skip-and-jump to unwarranted conclusions, a carelessly assumed assumption or two, with the result that when we say y, what we really mean is b. That's lethally easy to do; especially with language, which is after all a sequence of assumptions… We learn language from eavesdropping on grown-ups; we assume that such and such a noise corresponds with such and such a material thing, but unless the grown-up can peer in through our ear-hole into our brain and see what's going on in there, there's no actual way of knowing we haven't got completely the wrong end of the stick. On arriving at man's estate we assume that we know exactly what the other guy means when he says *y*, because that's what *y* means to us… Words aren't coins, precisely so many grains and scruples of ninety-nine-parts-in-a-hundred pure gold per unit—scrape a bit off and test it with a touchstone to see if it's the prescribed level of fineness, weigh it in a scale against a government-stamped weight. Instead, you have to go by what's stamped on the metal—in your case, *Genseric, by the grace of the Invincible Sun Archduke,* et cetera and so forth; naturally you're the heads, to which I assume I'm the tails. What I mean is, you can't assay a word for purity or weigh it for weight. It passes as currency because everybody thinks they know what it's worth, its value, what it means. Bloody stupid way to do things, if you ask me, but I can't say I can think of a better method offhand.

Anyway; sometimes things make sense, sometimes they don't, that's all I'm saying. I'm considering this, turning on it the full force of my welding-heat intellect, because there are days when I wake up in a strange bed, looking up at the cobwebs draping strange rafters, and ask myself: what the fuck am I doing here? And some days it makes sense and some days it doesn't; hence my quandary.

When it makes sense, I can see clear as day that what I'm doing *matters*. If I can get you various bits of stuff, bits of stuff that matter, you'll be able to survive as Archduke, win your wars, safeguard your people, be great and be happy. This is because, to the vast unwashed mob of superstitious yokels who comprise your people, certain bits of stuff have enormous meaning. They have power. The Black Icon brings victory. The Holy Sandal drives away the plague. Relics of the saints make the wheat grow, keep away the rooks and the pigeons, ensure rain and sun when rain and sun are needed. If some bastard poisons the water-tanks, dip a corner of the shinbone of Respaluus in the polluted water and everything is fine. If the Olbian Confederacy is crossing the border with twenty thousand Aram Chantat horse-archers and a siege train, don't worry about it, because we've got the tooth of Lorica the Protomartyr. What I deal in is, accordingly, faith—than which nothing in the world is more powerful or more precious, or harder to acquire.

Other days, I wake up and it's raining and I know for a fact that the fingernail of Porfax the Stylite I'm going to look at today is as phoney as—well, as I am; but does it really matter, given its flawless provenance? So long as people believe it's the real thing, so what? Old joke in the trade, what has more legs, a millipede or the Blessed Virgin of Procyrene... Because if you gathered up all the guaranteed rock-solid shinbones of the BVP, you'd have enough material to build a small castle. Only two of those shinbones can be genuine, but it's absolutely impossible to prove which ones, so by default they're *all* genuine... Which is a miracle, and that's why they call her the Blessed Virgin, because she can do miracles. Faith, you see.

And in order to work my miracles on your behalf, I need a bit of faith—in you, I guess, in what you're doing, what you want to achieve. Now let's face it, the best you're likely to achieve is making it so that some of the really bad stuff doesn't happen, at the expense of other not-quite-so-bad stuff happening and you getting the blame for it. One of the reasons I believe in you is that you realise this. If you were the sort of leader who hops up on a barrel and yells *I have a dream, yes we can*, I'd yawn and walk away, because I'd know you're full of it and all you'll ever succeed in doing is making things worse. But instead you work quietly and diligently at damage control, making it slightly more difficult for Entropy to weave His insidious form of negative magic... We all know that one day the world will end, civilisation will crumble, brambles and thistles will smother the ruins, everything good and worthwhile will be lost and forgotten—but thanks to you, it'll be the day after tomorrow, or maybe even the day after that.

So far as I know, there isn't a religion anywhere that worships Entropy—which is odd, given that He's real and all-powerful and He's inevitably going to win. Maybe I should start one and get rich. Meanwhile, thank you for keeping the light burning for one more day. I feel it's a good thing that somebody says that, and since nobody else is likely to, I guess it'll have to be me.

So; I have faith, in you. What I need is for you to have faith in me.

What I want you to do is seal what we've been talking about up in a jar—one of those big pointy-ended ones they ship Antecyrenaean wine in will do just fine—and send it to me at the Five Cardinal Virtues in Mi Chanso. Soon as I get it, I can close the deal. Now I can't say fairer than that, can I?

Cheerfully,

P

Genseric, by the grace of the Invincible Sun Archduke of Schanz, Elector, Grand Marshal of the Eastern Command, Regent of the Duchy of Selvois, Precentor of the Holy Diaconate, to Pollio his brother in faith, greetings.

Sent. Thanks.

G.

Pollio, pilgrim and slave, to Genseric, Archduke, Elector, Marshal, Regent, Precentor, Defender of the Faith, greetings

Deal closed. Whoopee.

I—and by extension, you—am/are now the proud owner of two square inches of coarse unbleached linen cloth, and that will make all the difference. I'm happy, you're happy—and for what it's worth, Prince Eutorbida is over the moon, because he's got back the stupid little brass statuette his idiot great-grandfather gave to your idiot great-grandfather, even though it was the Luck of Periboea.

All thanks, I might add, to me. I heard about Eutorbida moving heaven and earth to find the Luck from a contact of mine in Masirene. It rang the faintest of tiny little bells. I think it's because the thing is so phenomenally ugly. You won't remember this, but back in Second Year, when I came to visit you in the long vacation, you took me down to see the junk in your horrible treasury, knowing how scared I am of spiders, and that the biggest, hairiest spiders in the entire world live down there... and while we were scrabbling about among the dusty bling, you pulled something down off a high shelf and said to me, isn't this positively the most hideous artefact you've ever seen in your entire life? And I said yes, because it was.

And I have the most amazing memory for Stuff. Some people remember names, some people remember faces, I remember things. It's why I'm so damned good at this job. I heard the description of the Luck of Periboea—without which the Principality will never prosper and will eventually fall, and so on and so forth—and something went click in my mind, and I just *knew*. So I wrote to a pal of mine in Gamoris, who went and scrabbled about in the archives, and there it was: Trachis III gave the Luck to your great-grandad as collateral for a loan which he never paid back—And of course it was more than his life was worth to confess that he'd pawned the Luck, so he kept quiet about it; and then bad stuff started happening to Periboea and people started saying, This shouldn't be happening, we've got the Luck... And Eutorbida looked for it and guess what, it wasn't there. But Trachis had purged the court archives so nobody would know what he'd done, so there was no record of the loan agreement... But the Knights brokered the deal, and my pal in Gamoris has access to the Knights' archives... God, I'm clever. I wrote to Eutorbida, care of a collector pal of mine in the palace administration, and made him an offer: you buy the two Square Inches, I'll trade them for the Luck. And it actually worked.

I can only assume it worked because I have faith. I can think of no other rational explanation. Anyhow, if I were you I'd start interviewing architects. Cathedrals don't build themselves, you know.

Still cheerfully,

P

Genseric, by the grace of the Invincible Sun Archduke of Schanz, Elector, Grand Marshal of the Eastern Command, Regent of the Duchy of Selvois, Precentor of the Holy Diaconate, to Pollio his brother in faith, greetings.

I am absolutely not building a new cathedral. Those things cost money and we've got a perfectly good basilica already. Instead, we'll rededicate the Silver Horn and call it the True Robe.

The rededication ceremony will, of course, be the biggest thing in any of our lifetimes… I've got the Ceremonies people working on it, three shifts round the clock; they've promised me a draft outline by the end of the month, and I intend to hold them to it. Meanwhile they've cancelled all leave at the Foreign Office—all those kings and princes and heads of state to invite—and General Gordian (remember him?) is having a scale model of the Square built in the parade ground of the Guards barracks so he can play with his painted blocks of wood…

Just one thing. How are we going to get it from where you are to here? Presumably you've been reasonably discreet about all this, but everybody always finds out everything eventually, and meanwhile you're walking around with the most valuable object in the world sewn into your collar or tucked inside the toe of your boot. Should I send a courier? Or the entire navy? Better still, how would it be if you came here yourself?

I'd really like that… And I'll send the navy to fetch you, no problem at all. They're always grumbling about how I never let them go anywhere.

This is of course the most amazing thing, and quite possibly all our troubles really are over. But I'm worried. Write back soon.

G

Gobarzes, commander of the Palace Guard, prisoner of the Royal Clemency and slave, to Genseric, Archduke, Elector, Marshal, Regent, Precentor, Defender of the Faith, greetings.

I have arrived on Scona, which I have chosen as a suitable base of operations, and have interviewed our agents and operatives in the area. I have to report that none of them were able to provide any information about the activities or whereabouts of the wandering scholar, Pollio. I have ordered them to make further enquiries as a matter of urgency, and have briefed my own team of investigators.

You will appreciate that I am hampered in the pursuit of my objective by the need for discretion. If we are seen to be enquiring vigorously for an obscure trader, it cannot fail to excite the interest of the local criminal organisations, not to mention the intelligence agencies of both friendly and unfriendly powers. I have no established network of contacts and informants in this region, and must therefore rely on the goodwill of my counterparts in the Sashan and Olbian administrations. In order to enlist their aid, I have had to tell them a series of lies—the man Pollio, I have told them, is a criminal, wanted for a series of particularly unpleasant murders in Schanz; it is imperative that he be taken alive and unharmed, since his testimony will be vital in convicting his accomplices.

Whether these fictions will prove convincing, I cannot say at this point. Much will depend on how much our rivals already know about Pollio's mission—and his very disappearance would tend to suggest that at least one of them knows all or some of the truth.

If Pollio has been detained by a foreign intelligence service, I have to tell you that it is almost certain that he is either dead or spirited away to a place of confinement. Hostile agents would have no reason to keep him alive, except (a) as a living provenance for the artefact or (b) as a close personal friend of Your Highness, a status easily ascertained from a perusal of your private correspondence; in which case, they may wish to keep him alive to trade for whatever they may want from you.

If he has been detained by local criminals, the same considerations apply, although I would imagine that his chances of survival would be greater in criminal hands, for both the reasons stated above. We would also stand a much better chance of recovering him and/or the artefact. Criminals, after all, are only interested in money, preferably from their point of view money obtained with the minimum of risk and effort.

As your *de facto* head of security I feel it incumbent upon me to point out that in my opinion our chances of success are not great. I appreciate that you have given this mission the highest possible priority. However, I feel it is my duty to mention that the operation as constituted will rapidly deplete the funds available in the covert security budget—indeed, by the time you receive this report it will already have done so; if you wish to continue with this operation, it will be necessary to redirect funds from some other aspect of the defence budget, or to provide additional funds from the Treasury or the Privy Purse. We simply do not have the resources available to, say, the Sashan or the Aelians. Matters of finance are, of course, outside my remit; however, I should be negligent in my duty if I failed to mention the risk to other aspects of our national security should all our resources be devoted to this one object, and I should be obliged if my concerns could be noted in the open file.

As soon as there is anything further to report, I shall of course do so. In the meanwhile, I feel it would be advisable to restrict communications to the bare minimum, for fear of compromising the security of our courier network.

GOBARZES, COMMANDER OF *the Palace Guard, prisoner of the Royal Clemency and slave, to Genseric, Archduke, Elector, Marshal, Regent, Precentor, Defender of the Faith, greetings.*

I have ascertained from members of a local criminal gang that Pollio was intercepted six weeks ago on the road between Doca Votz and Bel Aguida by gang members employed by an unknown patron. He was conveyed unharmed to a ship, the *Hummingbird*, at Liauz and given into the custody of the ship's captain, Thalland. The gang was paid a considerable sum for Pollio's capture, although my informants were unable to tell me the precise sum. Payment was made in Sashan gold coin, which is of course the prevailing hard currency in this region.

My enquiries fall under the following heads;

1. I have assigned investigators to find out as much as possible about the *Hummingbird* and captain Thalland. Obviously I shall make every effort to locate and secure the captain and his ship. I shall also find out the ship's home port (if any), the nature and extent of its usual business, the names and antecedents of its crew &c. I hope thereby to find out where and to whom Pollio was delivered, and when, and who hired Thalland and his men.

2. I have three members of the gang who carried out the abduction in custody, and I shall endeavour to secure members of its senior hierarchy, to extract from them whatever information they may possess. At this stage it would appear that the gang was hired to abduct Pollio, rather than acting on its own initiative as the principal abductor. The information I have about the gang suggests that they are frequently employed to conduct

similar operations by security agencies, wealthy individuals and other criminal organisations. I should mention that the gang is governed by a strong ethic of silence. However, I am reasonably confident that this can be overcome given appropriate handling.

3. I continue to enquire for reports and rumours of the artefact, on the assumption that it has been stolen for resale by criminals. I am now in contact with the leading dealers in stolen goods, who will let me know if any attempt is made to find a buyer.

4. I have activated sleeper contacts inside the Sashan and Mezentine intelligence networks to find out if there has been any mention of the artefact or the abduction within the wider intelligence community. I confess that I have done so reluctantly, as these contacts are hard to come by and can only be used once. However, you have stressed the importance of this mission and I have taken the decision to employ these assets on my own authority.

I must once again reiterate my request that additional funds be made available. The existing operational budget has been exhausted, and at present I am operating on funds borrowed from the Knights, against a forged letter of credit bearing a poor facsimile of the Ducal seal. Fortuitously the Knights' verification protocols appear to be lax. In the interests of future operations, however, I should much prefer to substitute a genuine letter of credit for the forgery. We rely in our work on the trust and goodwill of powerful private sector institutions such as the Knights; should that trust and goodwill be forfeited, it would greatly hamper our activities in the future.

Aloura to Genseric

Well, you've got a nerve, I must say.

Your father—I'm not going to say anything about your father, because what good would it do, after all these years, and besides, you aren't him—something you should be grateful for every day of your life, I might add. But I'll say this for you, you never treated me like rubbish, the way everyone else did. Mind you, you were hardly ever there. As soon as you got back from college, all you did was count the days till you could go back again. I don't blame you for that. The atmosphere in that house was poisonous, and we all know who was to blame for that. The only reason I stuck it out for so long was the money, plain and simple. And I earned every penny, believe me. But let's not go into that.

It's offensive, frankly, that you think I can help you with your problem, because I'm not in that sort of business. Quite apart from anything else, I wouldn't put my girls through what I had to put up with, from men like your precious father. I make discreet introductions for discerning clients, and the welfare of my girls is really important to me. It's different when you've been there and done that yourself, you know what goes on. The business has evolved since I was in there at the sharp end, and high time too.

That said; actually, I think I can help you, though really I don't know why I should. The thing about Scona is, it's a small island, and everybody comes here sooner or later. It so happens that one of my girls—no names, no pack drill—is going with a gentleman who's quite high up in the Friends of the Poor, and she was at his place the other day, being decorative as we say in the trade, and this man was talking with his friends about some deal or other that they were all very excited about. My girl is quite smart and she's got ears like a bat, and obviously she tells me everything. Anyway, they were talking about some sort of relic thing. Apparently one of the other big outfits on Scona has got it, and they're talking to a lot of people about placing it for a lot of money. What made me think of you was, apparently there's a little man who goes with the relic, so to speak. He's the provenance—is that the right word? It's how you know it's genuine. Anyway, he's the witness who can prove it's the real thing, and without him to testify or whatever you'd call it, it's pretty well worthless. Naturally that put me in mind of what you told me about your friend. Anyway, if that's him, then at least he's still alive, at any rate.

Now, then. There are only four outfits on Scona who'd be doing something like this. If one of the smaller ones got hold of something like this relic of yours, they'd pass it on to one of the big firms in return for a percentage, it's more than their lives are worth to try and do anything substantial off their own bat. Now you can rule out the Friends of the Poor, since obviously they haven't got it, from what my girl told me. That leaves the Resurrectionists, the League for Social Justice and the Serpent's Tooth; it'll be one of them, you can bet your life. So I suggest you send one of your spooks to talk to each of them, though from what my girl heard they're already talking to at least one potential buyer.

Anyway, that's what I've heard, for what it's worth. As far as I'm concerned, we're now more than square for anything you may have done for me in the past, and if it's all the same to you I'd rather not hear from you again. You may think you're different but as far as I'm concerned you're your father's son. It's not your fault, but you're more like him than you imagine, and for that reason I want nothing more to do with you.

Please don't reply to this letter.

Aloura.

Genseric, by the grace of the Invincible Sun Archduke of Schanz, Elector, Grand Marshal of the Eastern Command, Regent of the Duchy of Selvois, Precentor of the Holy Diaconate, to Gobarzes his servant, greetings.

I've received information from a reliable source that Pollio is alive and being held by one of the following gangs on Scona—

The Resurrectionists;

The League for Social Justice;

The Serpent's Tooth.

I trust I can leave the rest to you.

In passing, I find it incredibly disappointing that I had to find this out for myself, using a contact that I would have preferred not to involve, and which must surely have been available to you, but which for some reason you neglected to make use of. Saloninus says that one should never attribute to malice anything that can adequately be explained by incompetence or stupidity; accordingly, I'm inclined to believe that you haven't deliberately withheld information or that you are in league with enemies of the state. Should I ever have reason to think otherwise, you may rest assured that there will be consequences.

Please proceed to deal with this matter as quickly as possible.

Genseric.

Pollio, pilgrim and slave, to Genseric, Archduke, Elector, Marshal, Regent, Precentor, Defender of the Faith, greetings.

Well, that was fun.

Your man Gobarzes is unbelievably scary. I really hope he's on your side. If he is, you've got nothing to worry about, believe me.

They'd got me stashed away in a barn on this miserable little island—not that I saw very much of it because as soon as I got off the boat they put a bag over my head. It turns out they'd put me in a hayloft, which would account for me being carried up a ladder over some bugger's shoulder, an interesting experience I'm not anxious to repeat. When your man's goons came charging in, I literally shat myself. There was this man sitting right next to me whose job it was to slit my throat at the first sign of trouble, so when I heard all the yelling I naturally thought, fuck, this is it. And I'd just made my peace with the Divine when the bag came off my head and there was your man Gobarzes standing over me, peering at me as though I was something he'd found in his salad.

Someone had taken a great slice out of his forehead; he was bleeding like the proverbial stuck pig, and it dripped down the side of his face onto his shoulder. I don't think he'd noticed. I guess you have to be pretty focused to do that sort of stuff for a living.

They killed all the Social Justice boys, about twenty of them, in just under two minutes. I don't actually approve of violence, but say what you like about the ethics of it all, it was an amazing performance. Gobarzes told me that these are people you have on the payroll permanently. That's a weird thought. You employ these men who can snuff out human life instantly with incredible skill; did you know that? I don't know whether you do or not. It's an awesome resource to have at your fingertips. Do you think they get to do their stuff often, or just once in a blue moon? Of course that incredible degree of confidence and fluency could just be the result of constant, day-in-day-out training—but does training, no matter how realistic the simulation, prepare you for the real thing, with genuine blood and genuine people dying? I can't see how it possibly could, but what would I know? I can't say I've given much thought to you in your capacity as dispenser of sudden and violent death. It'd be like finding out that Tiamat the Destroyer of Worlds is your aunt. Well, knowing your family, that's not as unlikely as it sounds. But I have to say, I've never really considered you in that light. It's a bit unnerving. Who are you, Genseric? And did it all change when you put on the jewelled hat, or was it always there, tucked away behind the lapel of your coat, like one of those miniature lapdogs?

Not that I'm complaining. Your bloodspattered manslaying employee saved my life, and I won't hear a word against him. Of course, my life wouldn't have needed saving if it hadn't been for you; but if it hadn't been for you, my life probably wouldn't have been worth saving, so it's all as broad as it's long.

The important thing is, the Two Square Inches are now safe with your boy Gobarzes and should be with you shortly. Isn't that nice?

Yours in terror,

P

RELICS

*G*ENSERIC, BY THE *grace of the Invincible Sun Archduke of Schanz, Elector, Grand Marshal of the Eastern Command, Regent of the Duchy of Selvois, Precentor of the Holy Diaconate, to Pollio his brother in faith, greetings.*

Thank you for the nice scrap of cloth, which I've put in a safe place. Why the hell didn't you come with it?

You can be so inconsiderate at times. You realise I've wasted a perfectly good hero's welcome, which hard-working people have worked hard to prepare… Not to mention all the food, and the baskets of rose petals. And the band are going to be insufferable. They were looking forward to playing *See, The Conquering Hero Comes* all the way from the docks to Victory Square. I'll probably have to give them a pay rise, just to stop them whining.

Seriously; why didn't you come back? I assumed you were going to. You've had a rotten time of it, and you've pulled off the most amazing coup; two good reasons why you should be here, putting your feet up, being waited on hand and foot, that sort of thing. Also, it's been nearly two years now. I miss you.

Gobarzes takes some getting used to, I admit. I'd like to say that really he's a sweetheart and he grows roses in his spare time and does conjuring tricks for small children. Unfortunately, not so. When I first took over he scared the life out of me. It came as a shock to be confronted with him, and all the other stuff that goes with him. I suppose I'd always known. The way my father's enemies tended to have fatal freak accidents; that sort of thing. I admit, I never thought about it much. I had enough trouble getting my head around the real soldiers; the army, war, violence as a fundamental part of the political process.

My father tried to prepare me for that, of course. I got my first suit of armour when I was nine—real armour, for crying out loud, your actual steel, but so well made I could walk about and sit down and stand up without being crushed by the weight. And it came with a brigadier-general's sash… I assumed it was just a pretty ribbon, but apparently not. I didn't find out till much later, but at age nine I was a real brigadier-general, entitled to give orders which would've been obeyed without question by real soldiers. In theory at least, I could've ordered the Brigade of Guards to storm the market square or the Hippodrome and slaughter the people… I don't think the colonel would've done it, mind you. It's rather more likely that he'd have made an excuse and checked up with my father first, and I'd have been sent to bed without any supper. But the colonel would probably have faced a court martial, for questioning the orders of a superior officer; he'd have been acquitted, but he'd still have had to stand there for four days while grim-faced men asked him searching questions.

Another reason, you thoughtless bastard, why I'd have liked to have seen you. I worry sometimes. I look in the mirror and ask myself the same question you did in your letter: who are you, Genseric? I worry that I'm turning into my father; into what my father turned into, and his father before him. I didn't actually know my father all that well. There weren't the opportunities. He wasn't a great one for talking about his feelings in any case. I know he loved me and was proud of me; I know he regretted some of the things he'd done. But he never said any of that, out loud. By the time I knew him, the tanning process was well under way, turning his skin to leather.

So far, I still know who I am. At least, I can still remember who I used to be, and I like to think that the person I used to be is still me, or in here somewhere. I can still distinguish between the archduke and the real me. Sometimes he does things and I disapprove—I say to myself, I wouldn't have done that; but of course he's got to, he has no choice. I still don't really believe that he's me. I take the regalia off at night and leave it in a pile on the chair for my valet to deal with—it's creased and quite often it stinks, particulary if the weather's been above freezing—and I stand there in my skin and look at it and feel like I've escaped, or at least been let out for a little while, like a plough-horse at nightfall. I used to hate all the gear but now I think it's really important. The act of putting it on and taking it off gives me a boundary. I can blame the clothes for things I've done—no, things that have been done by the contents of the clothes, but it was the clothes' fault really, not mine. I realise now that that's what the horrible things are for.

And I can say to myself, the army and Gobarzes and the chancellor and the Secretaries of State who raise taxes and the judges who put people in prison are all part of the regalia, and I can take them off at night and they haven't left a mark on my actual skin… So, probably I'm kidding myself, so what? It makes it easier, at any rate.

But it'd have been nice to see you, because you know me, the real me, and I could've been the real me with you. That would be incredibly helpful, like watering a plant when it's all dried up. Why *didn't* you come, you bastard? Was it something I said? We are still all right, aren't we?

G

Pollio, pilgrim and slave, to Genseric, Archduke, Elector, Marshal, Regent, Precentor, Defender of the Faith, greetings.

Yes, Your Grace, we are still all right, or at least I am. I won't say all this stuff hasn't affected me. It's the first time in my life I've been in real danger, the first time I've been scared so much I haven't been able to control my bodily functions, the first time I've been sure I was about to die very soon. People in your line of work probably have to deal with that sort of thing all the time; it's why you get paid the big bucks, presumably. Civilians like me, on the other hand, sort of assume it'll never happen to us, and that we have a right not to have it happen… That's why we get paid the small bucks, presumably. Having had a taste of your lifestyle, I have to say, I don't think I'm too badly off as I am—assuming there won't be too much more of that kind of shit. The shit and the small bucks, on a regular basis, would rapidly become tiresome.

When I was nine I really wanted a suit of armour, but of course I couldn't have one; not even glued-and-painted cloth. You, on the other hand, had real steel. Was that because real steel was cool and stylish, or because, at the age of nine, you were in actual danger of people trying to cut you with weapons? That's an interesting question to which, I suspect, you don't know the answer.

I'm sorry; it didn't actually occur to me to travel to Schanz once your man Gobarzes had sprung me from the Social Justice lot. I was just glad to be alive and out of that horrible barn. And I was really pleased that the deal had come off, and you were going to get the Two Square Inches. Beyond that, I didn't really think at all.

I imagine you're hurt because you assumed that after all that trauma I'd want to to go *home*—home being Schanz. But of course, Schanz isn't home, for me. Home for me is the Mesoge, and as you know, if I never go back there again, that's absolutely fine. Home in the sense you mean it—have I got one? Not sure I have. If home's a place you go back to when you're tired or hurt, I guess it'd be Ridichen and the dear old college, except—strictly between you and me and the doorpost—I never really liked it there. I had a great time, don't get me wrong, but it was in spite of, not because of. I had a great time because of you and Raffenkell and the others, not the geography; certainly not the institution as such, which made it perfectly clear from the outset that it didn't approve of poor people, on principle, and it was doing me a substantial favour letting me be there at all. Still, if I've got to have a home, there it is.

Do you have to have a home? I'm not sure. What's that term the shipping people use, a flag of convenience… That's me, most likely. I got stopped at customs on Scona once, and they wanted to know where I was a citizen of. I had to think about that, which didn't impress the customs goon very much. I told him, the Mesoge, because I was born there, but I haven't been back there in a very long time, the house I grew up in belonged to someone else and nobody who knows my name has lived there for a very long time, I don't own anything in the Mesoge, not so much as a pair of shoes… I imagine my name's written in a ledger somewhere, though I wouldn't be surprised if it wasn't—we weren't exactly punctilious about recording births, since so many kids died in infancy, and if your name got written down they knew you existed, which was a nuisance when the press gangs and the recruiting sergeants came round; the landlord's steward knew your name, of course, and how much you owed each quarter day, and the repairs and delapidations outstanding, but I was never officially a tenant, just a tenant's offspring, part of the live and dead stock, and I don't think our local steward was that organised. In any event, the thought that I'm part of the Mesoge and the Mesoge is part of me makes me feel sick. Can you unilaterally disclaim citizenship? If so, you're my witness that I'm doing so right now, if I haven't already done it by simply not being there, for a very long time.

I know what you're about to say. Just say the word and I can be a fully naturalised son of Schanz, with all the rights and privileges appurtenant thereto. Well, thanks, and if I ever need to be a citizen of anywhere I might well take you up on it, but right now—I prefer not to tell lies unless I have a reason to do so, and it'd be a lie. The truth is, I'm a citizen of a tiny republic composed of you and Raffenkell and about half a dozen people you don't know, scattered carelessly round the shores of the Northern, Middle and Friendly Seas—a republic that has several embassies but no actual territory… Suits me. As far as I'm concerned, home is just one more thing they can take away from you, if you let them. If you haven't got it, it can't be taken away. I imagine that attitude defeats the object of the exercise; but I never claimed to be right about anything in my entire life, now did I?

Except for one thing. Your uncle is a pain in the arse and a threat to navigation, and you really do need to do something about him, before he does something about you. Now I can't offer you a single shred of evidence linking my recent spot of bother with your blasted uncle, but that doesn't mean to say there isn't one—and I have this feeling, that's all. Why not just grit your teeth, send for your boy Gobarzes and get it over with? You know you'll feel better for it.

Cordially,

P

Genseric, by the grace of the Invincible Sun Archduke of Schanz, Elector, Grand Marshal of the Eastern Command, Regent of the Duchy of Selvois, Precentor of the Holy Diaconate, to Pollio his brother in faith, greetings.

It's been a long day, my feet hurt, I'm drenched in sweat and my head isn't everything it ought to be because of all the wine I've had to drink in order to be polite... In spite of all of which, I feel I have to sit down and write to tell you all about a lot of stuff I don't suppose you're really interested in, but what the hell.

We did the Rededication today. It was swell. Some miserable bugger just shoved a piece of paper under my nose, letting me know that thirty-seven of my fellow citizens got squashed or trampled to death in the crowds of happy, cheering people—

Only thirty-seven... Apparently, this was a good result, given the vast size of the crowds who turned out to celebrate the arrival of what we're now officially-unofficially calling the Luck of Schanz. The City Prefect, whose clerk it was who spoiled my moment of bliss after I'd taken my shoes off with that depressing piece of paper, was anticipating deaths in the hundreds, but apparently the City Watch and the guards played a blinder as regards crowd control, and the casualty figures are something to celebrate rather than deplore—

Not how I'd be inclined to see it. What I see is thirty-seven people who set out early this morning to have a good time, and who never came back. Nobody's fault, not even theirs. These things happen. Why these things happen nobody seems able to tell me, but apparently they do.

Calling it the Luck wasn't my idea, in fact I said no, absolutely not, but I was overruled... Of course I wasn't, because my word is law around here, but they all looked at me, so I gave in. They were right, of course, and I was wrong; it's gone down really big with everybody, and I gather legends and prophesies are springing up everywhere, like redshank after a shower of rain. So long as we've got the Luck, the city can never be stormed, we can never be defeated, Schanzers never, never, never will be slaves. As an item of defensive equipment, my chiefs of staff solemnly assure me, it's worth twenty thousand dragoons or a moat. As for my approval ratings, I gather they're through the roof. I also gather that before we got the Two Square Inches they were down somewhere in the cellar, a fact that nobody bothered to tell me at the time and which came as rather a painful surprise, but never mind. I thought I was doing all right. Apparently not.

But that's all fixed now, thanks to you. Now, I know what you're like. You're going to start beating yourself up over the thirty-seven poor buggers who got trodden to death. Actually, that's why I mentioned it, as an experiment, to see how you'd react—and I was right, wasn't I?

Thanks to you, Pollio, my friend. I think I can understand why you didn't come here. You knew it would've been a bad thing. We'd both have been wild with anticipation, before the event. We'd both have pictured the meeting, the big hug, the audible click as we both slotted back into the places in the Great Mechanism we occupied in the old days—and it wouldn't have been like that. We'd have met and then we'd have frozen, because things *have* changed and we *aren't* the same people we used to be... That would have dawned on us as we stood facing each other, with all the joy and excitement draining out of us as though we had spigots in the toecaps of our footwear. There would have been a horrible moment of embarrassment, and disappointment, and terrible loss, and entropy. And then I'd have given you a guided tour of the palace, which is the last thing either of us would have wanted to do. What both of us would've wanted to do was slip away to some bar, drink too much, play knucklebones, talk far too loud and wake up next morning with headaches and diarrhoea—but that wouldn't have been possible, and that would have been heartbreaking.

You realised this before I did, which shows how much smarter you are than me; nothing changes, does it? You realised that the only way we can be ourselves with each other is writing letters—that degree of separation that makes it possible for us still to be together; yes, I get it, you don't need to explain. Ah well.

You're the philosopher, answer me this. Those people, Pollio and Genseric, the ones who used to make a nuisance of themselves in the Flawless Diamonds in Second Year; did they die, or are they still out there somewhere, or in there somewhere, chained to a wall, or hiding from their enemies? I still like to believe that I'm still Genseric, under all the sweat-stained ermine; are you still Pollio, or are you just pretending to be him, to make me happy? I imagine your answer, if you can be bothered to give me one, will involve a reference to Saloninus' observations on the nature of linear time, maybe his Hypothesis of Eternal Recurrence, which I never did get the hang of, and if you hadn't written my essay for me I'd have failed Theory of Ethics...

I don't need to think about stuff like that any more. There are no more essays to write, and if there were, I have people to do that sort of thing for me—But I think about it more now than I ever did back then—cue Saloninus' Third Law: every human being is capable of an infinite quantity of work, so long as it's not the work he's supposed to be doing.

You have no home, so you tell me. I live in the past. I've got a distant cousin who's the Emperor of Mazrhoene—he's got all the papers to prove it, but the Mazrhoene Empire fell to the

Aram Chantat ninety years ago, the city is a bramble thicket and nobody's ever going to drive the savages out and rebuild the Temple, it simply won't happen… I'm a citizen of the past, that's where my home and my allegiance are; a pity, really, that I can never go there ever again; a citizen, in exile. I know it's there, it exists, because all I have to do is close my eyes and I can see it, all clear as day. But it'd be nice, wouldn't it, to have a home I could see with my eyes open. Still, I'm luckier than most, and I ought to be grateful for what I've got, even if it's not what I want—

Sorry. I'm whining. I'll stop now.

For God's sake, write and tell me something about *you*. I'm sick to death of me.

G

Pollio, pilgrim and slave, to Genseric, Archduke, Elector, Marshal, Regent, Precentor, Defender of the Faith, greetings.

How neatly, albeit long-windedly, you evaded my request and my warning. I asked you to do something about your uncle. Not a word about that. So; screw you. On your head, or in your head up to the hilt, be it.

Basically, you haven't got a life, only a heap of duties and responsibilities; therefore you want me to live a life for you. Fine; I can do that. It's not much to ask, for a pal.

I'm writing to you from Cueriz, which is somewhere I've never been before. It's a nice place. You'd like it here. There are mountains wherever you look, so you'd feel at home, but they're—I'm not quite sure how to phrase this—*tidy* mountains: neatly arranged, with rolling green valleys in between them, and picturesque forests of useful timber on their lower slopes; they make a hell of a lot of cheese here, and sausages, and fermented cabbage, which I know isn't your favourite thing in the entire world but they like it—the point being, this is a quiet place where nothing much happens. Also it's easy on the eye, the people are fairly good-natured and friendly, the pace of life is gentle, there's no politics to speak of; I like it here.

Not that I'm here to enjoy myself; perish the thought. It's a nice place, but enjoying yourself is frowned upon. Drinking is what you do when you're thirsty, the women are serious-minded and all spoken for practically from birth, games of chance are entirely legal because nobody wants to play them anyway, the closest they ever get to dissipation and debauchery in Cueriz is the annual Butter Fair, which is when farmers from all over the duchy come together to see who can make the best butter, and there's a small brass cup for the winner... And they have archery contests and a horse race, but only because being able to shoot and ride are useful to the community.

Just because they're serious, though, doesn't mean they're miserable. They get an enormous amount of quiet satisfaction (emphasis on the *quiet*) from religion, though of course the liturgy is pared-to-the-bone simple and there's no colourful vestments or solid silver chalices or any of that nonsense; no music, of course, or religious art—I tried arguing with a couple of old men I met in a bar; what's so bad about making a joyful noise unto the Lord, I said; why not celebrate the Divine with beauty and imagination, instead of sitting on hard benches chanting the same old words over and over? That's silly, they said. Silly? Yes, they said, silly. It's as though you had a really good friend living next door, but instead of talking to him or going to see him, you paint a picture of him and talk to that instead. Why would we want to make do with an imitation when we've got the real thing, right here in the room with us?

Cueriz, in other words, is the ultimate, accept-no-substitute, nine-nine-nine-parts-in-a-thousand-pure hick country—and what, I hear you ask, are you of all people doing there? Answer: I have my reasons, and let's leave it at that.

Oh, all right, then. One small hint. You wouldn't know it just walking around, but this place is still a duchy, meaning they have a duke, who lives in a castle and has rather a lot of nice things he inherited from his great-great-grandfather, who acquired them back when Cueriz wasn't quite such a backwater... You know me, I never could resist a sleeper story. And that's all I'm saying.

Cordially,

P

GENSERIC, BY THE *grace of the Invincible Sun Archduke of Schanz, Elector, Grand Marshal of the Eastern Command, Regent of the Duchy of Selvois, Precentor of the Holy Diaconate, to Pollio his brother in faith, greetings.*

I don't know if you've heard. Presumably you have. My wife is dead.

Poor, poor girl, what sort of a life did she have? Dead at nineteen.

It was murder, of course, though naturally I can't prove a damn thing. Healthy young women don't just die. Apparently her maid came in to wake her up and she was just lying there. She used to sleep on her front, like a baby—one of her ladies-in-waiting told me that, I didn't know, how would I know?—and the maid made the usual it's-morning noise, but she didn't move or wake up, so the maid went away again and came back later—Eventually someone got worried so they tried poking and prodding her, and she was dead.

It'll be a quiet funeral. Her family can't be bothered to come—it's a long way, they have things they need to do at home, there's no political capital to be made burying a dead daughter, as opposed to marrying off a living one. I don't suppose they knew her, any more than I did. She was just this fairly plain, fairly stupid, very quiet young woman who lived with about twenty other young women in the west wing, where nobody ever goes. I know what she looked like, more or less, because a very clever portrait came with her, like a sort of free gift. It's very clever because it looks reasonably like her, but it's cute and sweet—she wasn't, God help her. I had the picture put up opposite where I sit at dinner, so I could look at it. She never joined us; she had all her meals in the west wing, with her ladies-in-waiting and a woman who played the harpischord. One of her women told me she was happy—I don't know if that's true, or if she knew the difference between being happy and being unhappy, it occurs to me that maybe she didn't... If she was happy, I think on balance I'd rather be miserable.

There's a minor diplomatic spat going on between her father's people and mine over who gets the clothes. Apparently she had tons of them—I use a quantitative descriptor involving weight to give you an impression of the sheer scale of the collection, because clothing typically doesn't weigh much in proportion to the amount of space it occupies... That woman had *tons* of clothes, literally. Anyhow, her father's diplomats say the wardrobe reverts to him, and my lawyers reckon it belongs to me. I don't want them, naturally, and I can't imagine he does, either. They were all made to fit her, needless to say, and she was a rather odd shape, poor kid, so I can't begin to imagine they'd be any use to anybody else, and although they cost a ridiculous amount of money it's not like gold or silver, you can't melt clothes down for bullion. I asked the chancellor, why the hell are we arguing the toss like this? It's unfeeling, it's undignified, it's barbaric. It's the principle of the thing, he told me, looking at me as though I'd gone mad. If we're not careful, we could set a precedent. I wanted to have him thrown to the lions, except I haven't got any lions, so I told him to get out of my sight and do his job. And now word is going round the palace that I'm overwrought—wonderful word, that—and everybody's keeping out of my way. Small mercies.

Her life was short and useless, and her death is heartbreaking, but so was her life... I tell myself it wasn't my fault, but I realise that's not the point. If I find out that her death was political, that somebody snuffed out that poor kid in order to send a message or sway some balance of power, I'm going to get seriously angry, and I think people may get hurt.

And that's all wrong, obviously. That's trying to put out a fire with buckets of lamp oil. God almighty, Pollio, what should I do? I can turn Gobarzes loose, and inside of a week he'll have half a dozen poor buggers on the rack, with their bones being dragged out of their sockets, and that'll produce an answer to the question I've asked him to investigate… It may or may not be the right answer, but accuracy is a luxury we can't afford, apparently. So I'll respond to one horrible act of violence and waste with another, and that's what's known as governance.

That's what tends to happen when someone in a position of power feels strongly about something—a bad thing happens, and then governance does something worse—and usually missing the point completely; governance is about doing what we can do, not what we should. It's very easy to torture someone to death; finding out the truth or fixing a complicated problem is much more difficult, and of course it sounds hopelessly weak and uncaring if you tell people we're working on it, we're making investigations, analysing data, weighing up alternatives… But tell them we've had someone hanged, and everybody's satisfied.

I suppose I should've understood all that, growing up with it going on all around me. I should've noticed that that's how we do things; at least then I'd have been prepared for it, I might even have figured out a way of mitigating the hideous effects. But I honestly didn't see it. I saw my father—occasionally—and most of the time I was with him I had to keep still and quiet, be seen and not heard; I knew it was Daddy doing his job, and maybe if I was lucky there'd be time afterwards for me. But my brother was going to be the next duke, so there was no need for me to bother my pretty little head about anything—I guess the worst thing I did wrong was accept that.

Really and truly, Pollio, what *should* I do? We can pass it off as accidental death easy as pie, or we can launch an investigation, which will inevitably mean blood and pain; getting at the truth isn't nearly so inevitable, in fact it's pretty unlikely. For one thing, Gobarzes—Don't get me wrong, he's as loyal as paint. But even he needs to carry round at the back of his mind the fact that nobody lives for ever, not even a healthy Archduke in his late twenties—And if anything happens to me, there will (inevitably) be a new Archduke, who'll hold Gobarzes' life in his hands. It's not sensible to piss off someone who might be your boss this time tomorrow, with the power to stretch you on your own rack and tell your subordinates to start turning the windlass. Which is why there's so much murder around here, I guess; X or Y can't be the next duke if he's dead already, and the final solution is the only one available.

Must stop now, because the Foreign Secretary and the chamberlain and a couple of very important priests are coming to talk to me about my new wife. She's inevitable too, though I don't know who she is; they do, which is all that matters. If you discount the rich food and the soft furnishings, precisely how is my life different from a slave's? Not that I'm complaining.

Pollio, pilgrim and slave, to Genseric, Archduke, Elector, Marshal, Regent, Precentor, Defender of the Faith, greetings.

You ask me what you should do. I've already told you. You won't listen.

How is your life different from a slave's? I can tell you that, no problem.

We could never afford one, but there was an old boy in the next valley who had three, and we all thought he was something special because of it. He bought them when his sons were taken off to the war and didn't come back, but their pals in the regiment sent him their share of the loot from sacking some monastery; HA180, a lot of money, enough to buy three field hands, which is what he did. He got his money's worth out of them, you bet. Mind you, he'd have got his money's worth out of his sons, if they'd lived; we don't fool about in the Mesoge. I can picture them now, three thin, slow-moving, gentle, patient men who never smiled, never complained, never stopped working. What's that line in Saloninus, 'an hour alone is freedom to a slave'? I only saw them when they were out in the fields, of course, but I'm pretty sure they were as happy as any of us—not happy, maybe, content. They had food and clothes and a dry place to sleep and work to do, just like my father and me, and provided that nothing bad happened, it'd be the same tomorrow and the next day. The precise legal status didn't seem to bother them unduly, and it didn't bother anyone else.

I've thought about it since, and I figure it didn't matter because we were all slaves in the Mesoge. What constitutes slavery? Above all, I guess it's lack of choice. Your day is made up of the things you've got to do, plus a few hours' sleep. You can't argue, you can't debate, you just get on with it. If you make trouble, you get twice as much trouble back. And the more I think about it, the more I'm forced to the conclusion that slavery is the natural state of human beings, apart from a very few fortunate individuals—freaks, let's call them, because they're scarcer than unicorns and they don't actually matter worth a damn. You, for example, are the slave of duty. So are most men and women. To be more accurate, slaves of duty and love—when it starts to hurt so much you wonder if you wouldn't be better off opening a vein, it's love that holds you back and tightens the chain; knowing that if you die, the people who love you will be lost and heartbroken and destitute, so you don't even have that choice.

I left the Mesoge. I chose to be free. I recognise only the duties I choose for myself. Nobody loves me or depends on me—you have no idea how liberating that is. I can die tomorrow, and my last thought won't be crushing, agonising guilt. I'm as free as a bird, because like a bird I have nothing.

You know, I don't think men should talk about their feelings, or even write about them in letters. Quite apart from anything else, it sets you thinking, and once you start on that game it's hard to stop, and the secret of happiness in this world, in my not-so-uninformed opinion, is not thinking about the really important stuff.

So: the hell with all that, bring on the trivia. I met this man in a bar, and it turns out he's the brother-in-law of the duke's deputy assistant head groom, so naturally I bought him several drinks, and tomorrow I'm going to be given a tour of the stables. I have no idea where that might lead, but with any luck it'll lead somewhere... I've also been reading up on the history of Cueriz, thanks to a new pal of mine who's a lay archivist in the monastery library. Not so long ago, these people were hot stuff, though they've gone pretty quiet for the last couple of centuries. But once upon a time, Cueriz mercenaries were the best in the world, and mercenaries get paid lots of money, and what do you do with lots of money? You buy things. Therefore, somewhere in this apparent backwater, there are bound to be things which at some point money bought...

The people of Cueriz are slaves too, of course. They're happy slaves, but they wear their chains, just like everybody else. Everybody but me,

Your friend,

P

*G*OBARZES, COMMANDER OF *the Palace Guard, prisoner of the Royal Clemency and slave, to Genseric, Archduke, Elector, Marshal, Regent, Precentor, Defender of the Faith, greetings.*

You have instructed me to investigate the death of Her Grace. My preliminary report is as follows.

1. I have interviewed the members of Her Grace's inner household. There is evidence to suggest that Her Grace was

poisoned, by means of either foxglove or devil's-hood mushroom, introduced into foodstuffs. Since Her Grace habitually ate with her ladies in waiting, and since none of them have shown signs of having been poisoned, I conclude that if Her Grace was indeed poisoned, the toxin must have been administered in some item that only Her Grace consumed—a snack or occasional delicacy. Within the relevant timeframe—that is to say, the period of time within which foxglove or devil's-hood mushroom take effect—Her Grace is known to have eaten two honey cakes and an apple, aside from regular meals shared with others. The honey cakes were procured from a confectioner who has supplied the palace for over thirty years. The apple was taken from a fruit bowl positioned on a windowsill in the main drawing room, from which the ladies of the inner court are at liberty to help themselves at any time. The remaining fruit in the bowl has been secured and analysed and shows no trace of poison. Accordingly, I am inclined to discount the apple.

2. I have interviewed the confectioner, under Schedule Two torture, as is the standard procedure in such cases. I conclude that it would have been possible for either the confectioner or any one of his seven members of staff to have introduced poison into the honey cakes. However, only the confectioner and his eldest son would have been in a position to ensure that a poisoned cake would be included in a consignment intended for the palace.

3. I have interviewed, under Schedule Two torture, as per standard procedure, the members of the palace staff whose duties include taking delivery of the honey cakes and conveying them to Her Grace's apartments. I have identified two women in the Larder and three footmen who could have had unsupervised access to the honey cakes prior to their delivery to the apartment, and the footman who actually took them from the kitchen.

4. I have thoroughly investigated the backgrounds and antecedents of the eight suspects detailed above. Nothing about

them would appear to suggest any contact with known subversive groups, foreign agencies or domestic persons of interest. I am continuing to investigate.

5. I am investigating the movements of the eight suspects during all relevant time periods. Their activities can be accounted for. At all relevant times they were engaged in the performance of their usual duties and cannot be shown to have met with anyone outside their normal spheres of contact.

6. I have commissioned an analysis from the Secretary of Military Intelligence of those parties who are likely to benefit from Her Grace's death, both foreign and domestic.

7. I have in my possession a letter, incomplete and unsigned, which was handed to me by a clerk in the Correspondence Office. He claims to have found it among other routine letters in a folder comprising communications routinely intercepted by his office. These letters are generally sent by or to persons of interest, whose communications we monitor as a matter of course; letters are opened and read, copies are made when deemed necessary or useful, and the original letters are then resealed and sent to the intended recipients. Every letter intercepted in this way should be recorded in the day-books; however, there is no entry relating to the letter in question.

8. The text of the letter is as follows—

"If you can do it, you'd better get on with it straight away. The money's all there, I've seen to that; he's given me loads of money to buy stuff for him and he never asks what I spend it on. I don't see any problems with doing the actual job. The tricky part will be making sure he goes for our girl when the time comes. There's only so much I can do on that score. I can throw out broad hints, but if I start naming names he's going to smell something, and then we're all screwed. The other problem is getting him to scrag his uncle. I keep on about it but he won't play ball—he says he's fond of the old bastard, which I tend to believe, and family is family, and all that stuff. Obviously we need to get him out of the way before we can proceed to the next stage, so really I think the ball's in your court now, not mine. How about a hunting accident, or a fire? Anyway, that's your business. If all else fails—"

—At which point, the text of the letter ends. I should point out that what we have is a copy of the letter, not the letter itself; we cannot therefore trace the handwriting or compare it with any known hands, or acquire any evidence from the paper, parchment or ink. I have asked the chief clerk of the Office to find out, if possible, which of his clerks made the copy, but he states that he does not recognise the hand in which it is written. This, however, is not particularly significant, since all the clerks in the Office have been trained to write in the Office style, in the interests of legibility and consistency, and it is therefore not always possible to distinguish between one clerk's work and another's. I have interviewed all the clerks in the Office, under Schedule Three torture, as per standard procedure, and none of them admits to having made the copy or seen either it or the original from which it was purportedly taken.

I leave it to Your Grace to draw such conclusions as are warranted by the evidence. As regards further action, I suggest that the following options are available;

1. Further interrogation, under Schedule Three torture, of the eight suspects who are known to have had opportunities to adminster poison to Her Grace.

2. Further interrogation, under Schedule Two torture, of the personnel of the Communications Office.

3. The sending of an agent or agents to locate and interview Pollio, who I feel sure you will agree is the person implicated, or intended to be implicated, by the copy of the intercepted letter (if any).

4. Investigation of Pollio's activities, contacts and antecedents.

In view of Your Grace's relationship with Pollio, I shall not proceed with options 3 and 4 until I receive a direct order to do so. I strongly recommend, however, that such authorisation should be forthcoming, and I feel that this is a matter of urgency.

I should point out that there is no conclusive direct evidence that Her Grace was in fact poisoned, only evidence that is consistent with poisoning. The circumstances of her death are also consistent with a number of known medical conditions, although I am assured by the court physicians that all of these are rare and unlikely to cause death in someone so young and healthy. However, it has been known for death to result in cases where the victim is particularly vulnerable as a result of the condition running in the family. I am therefore making enquiries as to whether any of these conditions has been recorded in Her Grace's relatives, though of course sensitive information of this kind relating to members of the aristocracy may not be easy to obtain. I have also not ruled out the possibility of suicide, though as yet there is no evidence whatever to support such a hypothesis.

GENSERIC, BY THE *grace of the Invincible Sun Archduke of Schanz, Elector, Grand Marshal of the Eastern Command, Regent of the Duchy of Selvois, Precentor of the Holy Diaconate, to Gobarzes his servant, greetings.*

Proceed with options 1, 2 and 4. Do not proceed with option 3. Locate a former fellow-student of mine, Raffenkell, last heard of as Dean of Temois. As soon as you have his whereabouts, let me know immediately.

GENSERIC, BY THE *grace of the Invincible Sun Archduke of Schanz, Elector, Grand Marshal of the Eastern Command, Regent of the Duchy of Selvois, Precentor of the Holy Diaconate, to Raffenkell, by the grace of the Invincible Sun Precentor of Scheria, Dean of the College of Saints, greetings.*

I know, I've got a nerve, haven't I? And yes, I want something.

Look, it's about Pollio. And I wouldn't ask, but I've got nobody else I can turn to.

It looks horribly like Pollio's got himself caught up in some ghastly conspiracy against me. It's not an assassination attempt or anything like that; it looks like he's in bed with the people who murdered my wife, and they want me to marry some other princess, and to do in my uncle as well. I haven't got any other details. I'm hoping like mad that this is all a set-up and someone's doing all this to frame Pollio. I can't for one instant imagine that he'd ever do anything to hurt me. By the same token, I can't imagine anyone going to all that trouble to hurt Pollio—after all, apart from being my friend, he's nobody... God, that sounds bad, but I'm not going to cross it out and write something else, that'd be as bad as lying. He's nobody anybody would want to hurt, does that sound any better? Anyhow, you know what I mean.

And you know me, Raff, as well as anyone does, Pollio excepted. You know my faults, my weaknesses, the bad stuff I've done, how thoughtless and selfish I can be. You know how badly I treated you. You also know what Pollio means to me.

I swear to God, if it does turn out he's involved, I won't touch a hair of his head, I promise. But I do need to know; you can understand that, I'm sure. I don't know anybody else I could possibly trust with this. Will you go and find out for me? I know you don't owe me a damn thing and I've got no possible reason to expect you to do anything for me. We used to be friends, that's all I can say.

This thing is tearing me to bits. Look, you're a priest—so am I, of course, but I mean a real one. You believe in all that stuff. Doesn't it say in the Book of Words about mercy being better than justice? I don't deserve any help from you, but you're a better man than I am.

Please?

Genseric.

Raffenkell, &c.

Go fuck yourself, Genseric.

I won't do this for you. I wouldn't piss on you if you were on fire.

I'll do it for Pollio. If I don't, presumably you'll have him killed. If I talk to him and it turns out he's guilty, I'll bring him here, where he'll be safe from you. Even you wouldn't murder someone who's been given sanctuary at Temois. Besides, our security is better than yours. If you send your thugs, you'll get them back shredded in a small box.

I'll let you know what I find out. Never ever write to me again.

Genseric, by the grace of the Invincible Sun Archduke of Schanz, Elector, Grand Marshal of the Eastern Command, Regent of the Duchy of Selvois, Precentor of the Holy Diaconate, to Pollio his brother in faith, greetings.

Well, here we are again. They reckon they've found me a new wife, to love and to cherish, in sickness and in health and all that, and this time we've got everything sorted out well in advance and there aren't any grey areas; as and when she snuffs it, the clothes go back to her father, but he pays the shipping. And now we've got that settled, I guess I can look forward to a long lifetime of connubial bliss.

Her name's Iphianassa and she's the only child of the Cardinal-Margrave of Midons, which means that the next time I write to you, the scrambled-egg at the top of the letter will be longer by the Principality of Totas Parz—in case you've never heard of it (I hadn't), it's a long thin strip of hill country between Selvois and New Scheria: orchards, mostly, and vineyards in the south, ewes'-milk cheese, premium-grade air-dried sausage, and a small but promising lead mine. More to the point, it secures Selvois from the east, which means that if the Sashan decide to expand, that's three buffer states they're going to have to bulldoze through rather than two, which makes it all the less likely that they'll bother. So that massively increases our importance to and leverage with the Aelians, the Mezentines, the Vesani—which means they won't be able to push us around quite so much in trade negotiations, which means prosperity and peace in our time and all sorts of fun stuff.

By all accounts, Iphianassa is an outdoors kind of girl. I buttonholed one of the Midonsois delegates after the talks and more or less threatened him with the rack if he didn't tell me something about her other than her strategic and economic value… He was a bit reluctant, but I insisted. Apparently she likes horses and dogs, she's got a good sense of humour and her favourite food is *glinka*, whatever the hell that is; he'd somehow neglected to bring a portrait of her, but he did have a sample of her embroidery, if I wanted to see it… I told him I was prepared to take her needlework on trust, and we left it at that. Then I got Gobarzes to send one of his people to buy drinks for the delegates' servants, but that was a washout; as soon as my man tried to shift the conversation round to what she looks like and are the rumours about her true, they all clammed up and started staring at their boots—not promising, if you ask me, but what the hell. Segibert—he's the new chancellor and a reasonably good sort, for a politician—reckons that the last quality you want in a duchess is beauty; far better to have one who's fat as a pig and breaks mirrors by looking in them, because then you won't have to worry about lovers hiding in the walk-in closets and your children not looking like you, and all the political problems that sort of thing leads to. Segibert, by the way, is one of my more enlightened and progressive ministers. I really do think I ought to get some lions. If you come across any at a sensible price, let me know.

Your pal,

G

PS I found out what *glinka* is. Apparently, you take two dozen snails, three cloves of garlic, a quart of cream, dried anchovies and a large onion… At which point I put my fingers in my ears and ran away.

POLLIO, PILGRIM AND slave, to Genseric, Archduke, Elector, Marshal, Regent, Precentor, Defender of the Faith, greetings.

Yes, I heard about that. I assumed it couldn't be true. What the hell do you think you're doing?

Funny, you think you know people. If anyone were to ask me, I'd say that by and large you prefer to keep out of trouble, rather than wallowing in it like a pig in shit. Apparently not. You do realise, don't you, that Totas Parz is a deathtrap and a poisoned chalice, and this marriage has been rolling around like a jar full of scorpions for the last three years, with everybody with half a brain climbing trees and jumping out of windows to avoid it?

Use your head, Genseric. Joining Totas Parz to Selvois won't deter the Sashan; quite the opposite. It's the proverbial red rag to a bull. I'd have thought you had people to tell you this sort of thing, but obviously they're not doing their job.

The Sashan Empire—read the books, for crying out loud; you can read, I've seen you do it—doesn't launch wars of aggression in order to acquire new territory. It doesn't want new territory. It's got far more than it can comfortably manage as it is. But the Sashan Empire will go to war at the drop of a very small hat if it believes that its borders or interests are threatened. They call it a strategy of vigorous preemptive defence—anything that looks like it might grow to be a threat, smash it while it's still small and weak, or else you'll have to deal with it later, when it's big and nasty.

The Sashan don't like fighting wars, but it's what they're best at. They're the second biggest empire in the world and they never,

ever lose. And don't for one moment kid yourself that the Aelians and the Vesani will come running to help you. They make a lot of noise and rattle a lot of sabres, but they've spent the last hundred years avoiding a showdown with the east, because they know that if push comes to shove, they'll lose, and that'll be that.

I don't know who's pulling your advisers' strings, but whoever it is, he's not your friend. The way I read it, someone wants to see the Sashan provoked into war. Who that could be I have no idea. I can't imagine whose interests would be served by a million dead, all the cities between the Arba and the Friendly Sea burnt to ashes, the breadbasket of the West overgrown with brambles and thistles because everybody who used to live there is dead or forcibly removed to a Sashan slave plantation—I don't know, presumably there's a way of making money or power out of something like that; I'm glad I don't have the sort of imagination that would enable me to figure it out.

You're making a huge mistake, Genseric. It's the sort of mistake that starts big wars. I know, I keep repeating it, the W word, W-A-R. You don't like looking at it, do you? Well, think what it'd be like if it actually happened. Think how you'd feel if it was all your fault.

Pollio

Genseric, by the grace of the Invincible Sun Archduke of Schanz, Elector, Grand Marshal of the Eastern Command, Regent of the Duchy of Selvois, Prince of Totas Parz, Precentor of the Holy Diaconate, to Pollio his brother in faith, greetings.

Now steady on. I don't mind criticism, so long as it's constructive, and I know I've never been exactly the sharpest arrowhead in the quiver. But I've been in the family business all my life—I may not like it much, but it's what I do and who I am, and even a thicket like me picks up a thing or two over the years.

I'm not that stupid, Pollio. I know about Sashan foreign policy. I grew up with it. I was earwigging on strategy briefings when you were still playing with wooden soldiers. And yes, there's a risk; but there's a hell of a lot more of a risk if we don't secure Totas Parz and Selvois as a single block, because if we don't, it's a practical certainty that Midons is going to get into bed with the Olbians, meaning in reality the Robur, simply because they've got to get into bed with someone, and there isn't anybody else…

You said it yourself; Midons has been hawking that poor unfortunate girl all round the Friendly Sea trying to find someone to offload her onto, and everybody's been ducking out of the way because they don't fancy being at ground zero with the Sashan. Fair enough. That just leaves me. But if I don't step up to the plate and do this ill-advised thing, Midons *will have no choice* but to drop into the lap of the goddamned Robur—and suddenly we're redrawing all the maps, because a balance of power that's been seesawing gently backwards and forwards for a century has just been kicked over, and everything's suddenly become very dangerous indeed.

Yes, obviously the Sashan don't want war. Nobody does. But what do you think is more likely to provoke them: a couple of tinpot duchies coming together to form a slightly larger tinpot duchy, or having the Robur suddenly turn up on their front lawn?

It's not like I've got a choice. I've drawn the short straw. Presumably that's why they poisoned that poor kid, so I'd be available to take the fall. Still, that's why they pay me the big bucks. And having you yelling at me really isn't helping.

Oh God. I've just read what I've written, and it's horrible. I sound like my father, and my grandfather, with a side of my uncle. This is a wedding we're talking about, for crying out loud; and a young woman called Iphianassa, who's going to become my wife, whether you like it or not, in six weeks' time.

It's a terrible thing, Pollio, to find out who you really are. All these years I've been kidding myself. I honestly believed I was good old Genseric, the slightly dim rich kid who was popular because he always paid for the drinks, and his smart, clever friends were good-natured enough to put up with him, because he had money and when you got to know him he wasn't that bad... But guess what, it turns out that I've been Archduke Genseric of the House of Sighvat all along, last of his accursed line, the fulcrum on which the sad history of this deplorable century was fated to swing—

Being good old Genseric was just a hobby, after all. In our family we have hobbies, to help us pretend we're human. My great-grandfather wrote poetry. My great-uncle collected obsolete warships—he had twenty-seven at one point, housed in a vast purpose-built boatshed at Stear Point. My father had the finest and most important archive of pornographic literature this side of Echmen. My hobby is kidding myself I'm an ordinary, decent man overtaken by the family curse.

So please, don't lecture me about politics. I know all about that stuff. Leave it to people like me, for God's sake. Like you said yourself, you're free, free as a bird, and very few people can say that. Realise how lucky you are, keep the hell away from dangerous things you don't understand and stay safe.

Genseric.

Gobarzes, commander of *the Palace Guard, prisoner of the Royal Clemency and slave, to Genseric, Archduke, Elector, Marshal, Prince, Regent, Precentor, Defender of the Faith, greetings.*

You have instructed me to investigate the assassination of your uncle, Rothgar, Marquis of Frael and Archdeacon of the Urban Diaconate.

Having interviewed the relevant witnesses, I can reconstruct the likely sequence of events as follows.

On the evening of the second day of the Feast of the Three Martyrs (the sixteenth day of the eighth month of the third year of your reign), Lord Rothgar dined at home with: Adanaric, canon in residence at the White Eagle temple, and his wife, Schermhild; Helderic, agent of the Knights of Charity trading and banking consortium, and his companion Vorsa, an actress; Tiridates, trade attaché of the Sashan embassy, and his companion Sunigerd, an actress. The meal was of modest proportions and four bottles of wine were consumed. All the guests departed before midnight. Adanaric and his wife and Helderic and his companion returned to their homes, and their presence there until morning has been confirmed by their servants, interrogated under Schedule One torture as per standard procedure. When questioned, Tiridates stated that he returned to his quarters at the embassy; it has not been possible to verify this because of considerations of diplomatic immunity; however, enquiries made through the usual channels appear to confirm his account. The actress Sunigerd, on leaving your uncle's apartments, went by coach to Wallgate where she met Ricebert, a director of the Sword Blade Bank; they proceeded to Ricebert's house in Cornmarket, and their presence there until morning is confirmed by the domestic staff, interrogated under Schedule One torture as per standard procedure.

Lord Rothgar's servants (interrogated, &c) confirm that after the departure of his guests, Lord Rothgar sat reading in his study for approximately half an hour and then retired to his bedchamber. His current companion, the actress Halltraut, was not present; on the night in question she performed the leading role in a burlesque at the Imperial Theatre and thereafter attended a small gathering at the home of the theatre manager; her presence there is vouched for by the nine other guests. The gathering continued until shortly before daybreak, whereupon she went back to the theatre and stayed there until my investigators arrived to question her around noon the next day.

Lord Rothgar's bedroom is located on the second floor of the new extension to the east wing of the palace. The second floor is accessible from above and below by two staircases, the Grand

and Privy Stairs; the latter is used mostly by the domestic staff. Access is also possible through a large window, although this is usually shuttered and bolted from the inside; when the body was discovered in the morning by a maidservant, she asserts that the shutters were closed and bolted as usual.

The maidservant entered to awaken Lord Rothgar approximately half an hour before dawn, in accordance with his standing instructions. She found him lying on the floor on the left side of the bed (facing into the room from the doorway). He was lying on his face. The maidservant withdrew and reported to the Groom of the Chambers, who assembled the staff and entered the room. The Groom (Naches, an Aelian national resident in Schanz for twenty-three years, of good character) examined the body and discovered that the throat had been cut. He sent for me and I attended immediately. I sent for you, and you attended shortly after I reached the scene.

I examined the body, in company with Phraatzes, the court physician. In addition to the total severance of the jugular vein, we found four other wounds; three deep stab-wounds to the abdomen and a long, shallow laceration of the palm of the left hand. Phraatzes agrees with me that these injuries are consistent with Lord Rothgar having been murdered. The angles of penetration and other factors seem to suggest that there were at least two assailants, each of whom stabbed Lord Rothgar; afterwards, one assailant held him down while another cut his throat.

A considerable amount of blood was found on the floor and bedclothes. However, no traces of blood have been found outside the bedroom, although investigations are still proceeding. If no further bloodstains are found, this would strongly suggest the involvement of trained or professional killers. It is the usual practice of such persons to wear additional layers of clothing and footwear, which they remove and bundle up before leaving the scene of a crime, specifically to avoid leaving a trail of blood.

I have interrogated the staff on duty in that part of the palace at the relevant time (under Schedule Two torture &c) and am satisfied that none of them saw or heard any intruders enter or leave the palace. However, a side gate leading from the back yard of the butler's pantry (accessible directly from the Privy Stair) to the mews, which would normally be locked, was found to be unlocked. It is possible to enter and exit the mews via the stable yard, in which there is a drain that connects to an overflow projecting halfway up the outer wall of the palace keep. I examined the overflow and ascertained by experiment that it is possible, though by no means easy, to reach it from the back yard of an adjoining coach house, by means of a ladder.

Alternatively, it is possible that the assailants entered the palace at an earlier time and concealed themselves in one of several empty and unused rooms on the second floor until Lord Rothgar retired for the night; having accomplished the murder, they then concealed themselves in the same or another unused space until considerably later in the day, when they were able to effect their escape without being noticed. I should add that I personally conducted a search of all the rooms in the east-wing extension shortly after examining Lord Rothgar's body, and found no signs of recent occupation in the unused spaces. I also placed guards at all possible exits. However, I cannot rule out the possibility that the intruders were able to evade my search by precise timing, and avoided detection by passing themselves off as security officers, a considerable number of whom were coming to and going from the scene during my investigation.

It is also possible (although, in my view, unlikely) that the murder was carried out by members of the domestic staff, who through prior collusion were able to present me with mutually confirmative alibis when questioned. The character and antecedents of all the domestic staff are, of course, rigorously investigated when they are first hired and periodically thereafter; I have ordered a further investigation, which is proceeding.

I have ordered a full-scale enquiry among our usual sources within the criminal and political-subversive elements, but as yet no firm leads have been established. I have established contact with Your Grace's political and diplomatic advisers, who have agreed to compile detailed reports on considerations relevant to establishing likely motives; once the motive is known, it will of course assist greatly in ascertaining the identity of the perpetrators and their accomplices and instigators.

It remains for me to express my profound condolences on the loss of your uncle.

[THE MANUSCRIPT IS damaged at this point. One or possibly two letters are indecipherable]

RAFFENKELL TO GENSERIC &C.

I went to see Pollio. We talked about old times. He told me about what he's been doing for you.

I made a point of talking about what you did to me, how you treated me. He was sympathetic but tried to make excuses for you. I gave him a lot of opportunities to badmouth you but he didn't.

I told him I'd heard he was in on some scheme to get shot of you. I think he was genuinely offended. He wanted to know what I'd heard and who I'd heard it from. I made up some stuff on the spur of the moment, but Pollio's no fool. It won't take him long to figure out that I was making it up.

I'm pretty sure that if he was involved in something he'd have told me. He seemed genuinely concerned that being in with you and on your payroll was making things bad between him and me. Of course he may have been lying but I don't think so. I know him pretty well, after all.

So you can call off your thugs and leave him alone. And me too.

Pollio, pilgrim and slave, to Genseric, Archduke, Elector, Marshal, Prince, Regent, Precentor, Defender of the Faith, greetings.

The weirdest thing ever. Raffenkell showed up here, out of the blue.

To be honest, I wasn't expecting to see him again; maybe not for a long time, maybe not ever. You know what he's like—he doesn't just bear grudges, he nurtures them like a mother. Last time I spoke to him—not that I got to say very much, mostly I was listening—he told me I was a bastard for taking your side against him, with friends like me who needed enemies, and he never liked me much anyway. For the record, I hadn't taken your side. I agreed with him that you'd behaved extremely badly over the preferment, and if that's what friends are for, give me cholera every time. But I also ventured to suggest that it wasn't entirely your fault that you turned out the way you did—At which point, he let fly at me with that mouth of his, and I though to myself, oh well, that's it, then. And whatever else Raffenkell may be, he's consistent.

And yet suddenly here he was. I was sitting on the terrace outside the Last Hope of Equity in Scutels Town, drinking a beer and reading a book, and I look up and there's this enormously tall fat man in a purple robe embroidered with lions and peacocks... He's started to get thin on top, by the way, I always reckoned he would.

I guess it was the extra weight that threw me off. It took me a long time—two seconds, maybe three—to figure out that the ridiculously tall skinny guy I used to know was now a ridiculously tall fat man. It looked as though someone had bored a hole in the top of the head of the Raffenkell I used to know and filled him up with sand, tamped down hard until the seams stretched. Anyway, it was him.

(I haven't forgotten, by the way, that strictly speaking I'm not talking to you. That letter of yours pissed me off so much I wasn't going to reply. But I can't not share a visit from Raffenkell—a fat, gorgeously dressed Raffenkell who's now a Precentor, for crying out loud—with the only other man I know who'd be capable of appreciating it properly. I tried, but I couldn't bring myself to do it.)

Strange as it may sound, I think he came all the way from Aulida—a boat trip, then two days in a coach—just to bitch about you. I can't tell you exactly what he said because it all kind of surged and frothed around me and over me—from time to time I surfaced and caught my breath, and then another wave broke and washed me away, you know what he's like once he gets going. I have to tell you, he hasn't forgiven you. Not one bit. But then, why should he? You behaved really badly there, and you know it.

And then things got a tad weirder still. I'm not entirely sure what was going on, but I think he was trying to recruit me for some plot or other—which is why I'm telling you all this, in my roundabout, honey-sweetened way; I have a nasty feeling something's going on, and Raffenkell may be involved in it.

Don't whatever you do ask me for details. First, if I had any I wouldn't tell you, naturally—I don't take sides, it's my number-one rule in life. Second, if there were any details buried in that lava-flow of execration and contempt, I'm afraid I must have missed them. I can't tell you what I don't know, and even if I could, I wouldn't.

Suffice it to say—Look, if Raffenkell really is mixed up in some plot against you, please, for my sake if not for his, tell those terrifying people of yours not to hurt him, all right? The thought of our oldest and best friend being chewed up by your man Gobarzes makes me feel sick. Like most people who shout a lot, Raffenkell is soft as butter underneath. He wouldn't survive two minutes in the same room as the rack, let alone on it.

I know: you have a duty to your subjects and the stability of the West. A plot against you is a plot against them. There are certain things you have to do, whether you like it or not. And when push comes to shove you have no choice—except, please, leave Raff out of it. He's noisy and unreasonable and entirely capable of conspiring against you—maybe he's even managed to kid himself that he wants to see you dead, though deep down he doesn't, I know that. But when he gets in a mood he's perfectly capable of doing stupid things he'll spend the rest of his life regretting, we know that. But you're not like him. Please don't hurt him, Genseric. For my sake.

P

POLLIO, PILGRIM AND slave, to Genseric, Archduke, Elector, Marshal, Prince, Regent, Precentor, Defender of the Faith, greetings.

I just heard about your uncle. Was it you?

GOBARZES, COMMANDER OF the Palace Guard, prisoner of the Royal Clemency and slave, to Genseric, Archduke, Elector, Marshal, Prince, Regent, Precentor, Defender of the Faith, greetings.

I have concluded my investigation into the deaths of your first wife and your uncle. My conclusions are as follows.

1. Both your first wife and your uncle were murdered. The murders would appear to be connected, but this cannot be proved.

2. Both murders were politically motivated and would appear to relate to the sequence of events that began when Your Grace acceded to the Regency of Selvois.

3. Once Your Grace took over the government of Selvois, the balance of power between the Western bloc and the Sashan Empire was disturbed. The possibility of joining Selvois and Totas Parz arose; such a union would avoid the necessity for an alliance between Midons and the Olbian/Robur axis, making

a later confontation between the Robur, the Sashan and the Western bloc considerably less likely.

4. Against the advice of your uncle, you opted instead for your first marriage, to the Lady Kremild. In so doing, you intentionally or inadvertently were seen to be siding with the Olbian/Robur axis against the Western bloc. It is not my place to comment on the direction of Your Grace's foreign policy; I refer to it only insofar as it has a bearing on the motivations of the parties involved in this enquiry.

5. At this point, I suspected your uncle's involvement in the Lady Kremild's death. I was quickly able to dismiss that speculation. There is no evidence whatsoever linking your uncle to the murder of the Lady Kremild.

6. Furthermore, I have now identified the parties directly responsible for her murder. She was killed on the orders of the Olbian government, acting through one of its many covert security agencies. Acting on information received, I was able to identify the assassins, freelance operatives known to have been used by the Olbians for similar operations in the past, and who were observed to be in Schanz at the relevant time. The names they were using—Colbias and Orriman—have been shown to be aliases; these individuals were known by many names in different locations. I have not been able to ascertain their true names, nor in my view would that information have any bearing on the investigation.

7. I employed operatives of our own to secure these individuals after they left Schanz and relocated to Scona. My agents forcibly returned them to Schanz, where I interrogated them under Schedule Six torture. I obtained their full confessions.

8. It is, of course, standard procedure to verify confessions obtained under torture from independent outside sources. I therefore used assets of mine in Robur security to confirm that these men were acting on orders issued by the Olbian/Robur regime.

9. I was at a loss to understand why the Olbian/Robur axis would commission the murder of the Lady Kremild, since

her death made possible your subsequent marriage to the Lady Iphianassa, which in turn frustrated Olbian/Robur policy toward Totas Parz. However, as noted above, considerations of foreign policy lie outside my remit, except insofar as they are relevant to motivation.

10. Lord Rothgar was murdered while I was still interrogating the assassins. Since I had the assassins in custody, I assumed that they could not be connected to Lord Rothgar's death. However, I asked them if they knew anything about it. By this stage they were in poor health and in no fit state to give answers to complicated or involved questions. However, I received the impression that Lord Rothgar's death came as no surprise to them. Unfortunately, they died before I could press home this line of enquiry.

11. Their apparent lack of surprise at Lord Rothgar's death put me on notice that the two murders might well be connected. This led me to investigate any further known or suspected Olbian/Robur assets currently present in Schanz.

12. It is a fact of life that the pool of individuals capable of carrying out operations such as the murder of Lord Rothgar is limited. It is specialised work, and as a matter of course I keep a record of persons of interest. I became aware that three such persons had entered Schanz from Scona two days before Lord Rothgar's death. They had adopted carefully prepared false identities, which prevented my agents from identifying them at the time of their arrival. However, my investigations into both murders created an understandable atmosphere of alarm among the criminal element in Schanz; to put it crudely, certain elements were afraid of being blamed for the murders, and were therefore uncharacteristically helpful. They made me aware of the presence of the three foreigners, and assisted me in ascertaining their true identity. They also arranged for my agents to trace and secure them.

13. I interrogated the three suspects under Schedule Six torture. They confirmed that they were guilty of the murder. They

asserted that they were acting on behalf of the Olbian/Robur axis. However, I have not been able to confirm this. I had already expended my assets in Robur security while investigating the murder of Lady Kremild, and I regret to say that I have no other resources inside that regime at the present time. I cannot therefore furnish the objective verification required to corroborate the confession evidence obtained under Schedule Six. Accordingly my identification of the three suspects as the murderers can only be regarded as an unverified hypothesis rather than a proven fact. The suspects did not survive the interrogation and are therefore no longer available for further enquiries.

14. I can therefore summarise as follows.

15. The Lady Kremild was murdered by agents of the Olbian/Robur axis, for reasons that remain obscure

16. Lord Rothgar was murdered, possibly (but this cannot be proved) by agents of the Olbian/Robur axis, for reasons that remain obscure but which might be connected to the murder of the Lady Kremild

17. The immediate perpetrators of the murder of the Lady Kremild are dead. Three men suspected of the murder of Lord Rothgar are also dead. I have referred the conduct of the interrogations of all five men to the Inspectorate of Criminal Procedure; this is standard practice whenever a suspect dies in the course of Schedule Six interrogation and should not be taken to imply any irregularities in the conduct of these particular interrogations.

It remains for me to ask whether you require me to conduct further investigations into these events, with a view to ascertaining or clarifying the motivations for the murders (if possible). If so directed, I anticipate that I would need to interview a number of officers of Your Grace's court and (depending on the direction such enquiries might take) prominent members of Your Grace's council and other public figures and/or individuals known to Your Grace personally. Should you wish me to proceed, I shall be greatly obliged to Your Grace if you would provide me with written instructions to that effect.

Genseric, by the grace of the Invincible Sun Archduke of Schanz, Elector, Grand Marshal of the Eastern Command, Regent of the Duchy of Selvois, Prince of Totas Parz, Precentor of the Holy Diaconate, to Gobarzes his servant, greetings.

Thank you for your report, which I can summarise as follows.

You managed to track down the two hired hands who killed my wife, but you let them die under torture before they were able to tell you anything particularly useful.

You arrested three men who were the sort of people who could've killed my uncle. You tortured them to the point where they'd have said anything to make it stop, and then they died. You haven't been able to come up with any outside evidence, so these men's confessions are essentially useless.

You have arrived at conclusions that make no sense.

Now you want my permission to put my advisers and my friends on the rack, presumably to see if any of them will tell you something helpful.

I confess that I take the view that, aside from routine police investigations, you haven't really achieved anything. Five men are dead. Three of them may well have been innocent. The other two might have told us what we need to know, but now they're not going to.

To say that I'm not impressed would be an understatement. However, I recognise that some investigations are more difficult than others, and I can't expect you to wave a magic wand and pull answers out of a hat. We must also be realistic. Useful information is now out of our reach, but that can't be helped now. I would invite you to learn the lessons from how this investigation has been carried out, but that's a matter for the future.

To be frank, I think you've already done enough damage with the way you've handled this so far. Clearly we need to find out what happened and why, and who's really responsible. I shall therefore be obliged if you'd prepare a detailed proposal setting out how you intend to proceed. Don't take any further action until I've seen and approved the proposal.

*R*AFFENKELL, BY THE *grace of the Invincible Sun Precentor of Scheria, Dean of the College of Saints, to Pollio, his brother in the Divine, greetings.*

I've been thinking about what you said (before I stormed off in a huff) and yes, I suppose it does make sense, though I really wish it didn't.

The trouble is, I've lived all of my adult life in the morality business—manufacturing, marketing and distributing ethics. Like any good salesman, I came to believe in the product.

Having made a careful study of the promotional literature, I started from the premise: wouldn't it be nice if there really was an Invincible Sun, acting as a supreme arbiter of good and bad, actively bringing about the good for those who believe, actively punishing the evildoer?

Then—I can't tell you exactly when, it wasn't one of those lightning-flash moments—the sum of my observations and investigations and analyses led me to the conclusion that my wouldn't-it-be-nice was actually the truth... I reckoned I could indeed detect the workings of the Divine in everything that happened around me—a bit like the bit of string in the neck of a sack, you give it a tug and everything is drawn tightly together. Or a bit like that bilingual inscription they found in the ruins of Ap' Escatoy that made it possible to decipher and translate the Pemari language. So, I came to believe in what I'd been telling everybody for so long. Matter of fact, I still do.

Of course I forgive Genseric. I forgave him long ago, deep down inside where it's dark and hidden and I'm too scared to go. Actually, he only did what I'd have done in his shoes. He had a preferment in his gift and he gave it to the man who he sincerely believed would make the best job of it. That person happened not to be me, his joint-oldest friend, at a time when I really wanted (I almost wrote *needed*, but...) the job. But I wasn't the best man for it. I'd have done it perfectly well, but Genseric was right; that pinhead Ossica was the better candidate, at the time. There was no way Genseric could've known what would happen after that, and the ensuing disaster wasn't his fault. He made the right choice and did the right thing, and I was pissed at him because he put the needs of religion—the thing I believe in most of all in the whole wide world—ahead of me.

So I should forgive him. I do forgive him—deep down. But not on the surface, in the layer of me between my skin and my soul.

In saying that, I freely admit to being an inferior human being. Well, that's hardly news. And yes, before you say it, you're right—A bland admission of fallibility and unworthiness is just a cop-out, and such an easy one... By pretending to a humility you don't in fact possess, you disarm all criticism and end the debate, since there's nothing more to be said. In theological circles we call it the Earthquake Option, and it's deplorably overused. Consequently, nobody believes you when you say it any more. When I say it, I mean it; but I would say that, wouldn't I?

And I really am sorry that I lost my rag with you, just because you don't believe. That was wrong of me, too. It's like being furiously angry with a blind man because he refuses to see.

It took me a long time to tumble to that one, though it really is painfully obvious. You can't make someone believe. Nobody can. It's the one thing even He can't do—if He could, it wouldn't be faith.

I used to spend hours agonising over that—what does He actually want from us? What did He create us for? What good are we to Him? For a while I figured we must be His pets—His beloved dogs, with whom He is well pleased. And He throws sticks for us, not because He wants the sticks brought back (or why did He throw them away in the first place?) but because fetching the sticks and thereby doing our duty gives us—what? Pleasure? Pleasure in knowing that we have fulfilled our duty towards our God. A purpose.

The relationship between owner and pet is a good one. It's not exactly slavery. Both parties to it derive benefits from it, and there's no real exploitation or oppression. Still, it's a disturbing thought. My mother didn't raise me to be no spaniel.

Then I gradually came to see it. What does a dog give you that you can't get anywhere else? Love. What do we give Him that He can't get anywhere else? Faith.

And that's why it's not something He can make us do, and it's not something we can make ourselves do. It happens, or it doesn't.

A very long-winded explanation of why I'm apologising for my crass behaviour. At least you can't accuse me of preaching at you, since preaching is designed to proselytise and convert, and I know I can't convert you, since you—I really feel sorry for you—haven't been blessed with the one gift that really matters. And I can't pray to Him to give it to you, because that's the one blessing He can't confer.

And you're sitting there telling me where to stuff my precious gift—Well, you would say that. There's the parable of the old soldier; you know that one? Sichelgaita was walking through the marketplace and she saw a blind beggar. She said, Your sight is restored to you. No, howled the beggar, don't do that. I was a soldier, I was at the great battle. Before I lost my sight, I saw the most horrible things, and I don't want to see anything like that ever again. Blessed are the blind, Sichelgaita said, for they shall see no evil. But she cured him anyway. To be honest I'm not entirely sure why she did that—it's a hotly debated topic in theological circles. There's a version of the story in which the first thing the soldier sees after he's cured is the Sun, and then he breaks down and thanks her. But it's only in the later manuscripts and it's probably an interpolation.

One of the skills I have and you don't, because you did Logic in Second Year and I did Rhetoric, is the art of the insincere apology. Basically, you start off declaring your intention to apologise, and then you make the actual apology so involved and long-winded that the other guy gets bored and stops listening; at which point, you can subtly backtrack on your apology, and make out that in fact you were right and he was wrong, and he won't even notice… I got an A+ in that module.

Let's agree that we're both right about everything and be friends again. Please?

Yours in His light,

Raff.

PS One thing I do think you're wrong about. Don't tell Genseric what you've done, not ever. He'll never forgive you. He'll understand, sooner or later, but he'll never forgive you. Trust me on this one; I speak from personal experience, see above.

GENSERIC, BY THE *grace of the Invincible Sun Archduke of Schanz, Elector, Grand Marshal of the Eastern Command, Regent of the Duchy of Selvois, Prince of Totas Parz, Precentor of the Holy Diaconate, to Pollio his brother in faith, greetings.*

No, it bloody well wasn't me.

I'm rapidly running out of rope here. Quite apart from everything else, it looks so incredibly bad. In the last six months we've had a war and two high-level political assassinations, to wit, the Duchess and the Duke's uncle. People are starting to say, what sort of a clown have we got running this country?

About the only thing holding us together is the fragment of the One True Robe. If it hadn't been for that, I shudder to think what would've happened. It's the one thing people can turn to and say, yes, but the Holy Robe came to us, that wouldn't have happened if we weren't truly blessed, and therefore all this other stuff must be for a reason and it'll all work out just fine in the end. You know what; if I wasn't college-educated, I'd almost be inclined to believe it myself. The timing, for one thing. It turned up exactly when it was needed, like it was Sent.

You did that for me, and I won't ever forget it. No matter what else you may do or may have done, you saved me and us and for all I know the whole stupid world.

Sorry if I sound rattled. It's because I'm rattled. Everything's coming up dogshit around here, and I don't know how much longer I can cope.

G

GENSERIC, BY THE *grace of the Invincible Sun Archduke of Schanz, Elector, Grand Marshal of the Eastern Command, Regent of the Duchy of Selvois, Prince of Totas Parz, Precentor of the Holy Diaconate, to Gobarzes his servant, greetings.*

I have had an opportunity to study the proposal you submitted to me. Please proceed as advised and report to me daily.

I also note that in order to proceed you require additional resources—which are hereby authorised—and additional powers—which are not. I take the view that it should be possible to conduct an enquiry of this kind without violating the fundamental rights of our citizens. If that is not the case, it would be better for the enquiry not to proceed.

Since the ultimate purpose of this enquiry is to ensure my safety, I feel that I am the only person entitled to assess its value. I am of the opinion that my safety isn't worth that. However, I feel that a competent head of security should be able to do this simple thing without the need for any addition to the already substantial powers at your disposal.

Pollio, pilgrim and slave, to Genseric, Archduke, Elector, Marshal, Prince, Regent, Precentor, Defender of the Faith, greetings.

I hear what you say. My heart bleeds. Deal with it.

What did you see out of your window when you woke up this morning? I saw the sun rise over a snow-capped mountain above a tranquil blue lake. A nice middle-aged lady brought me breakfast in bed: white rolls and honey cakes, fresh blueberries and some of that hard white cheese they do round here, sliced thin as a leaf. Then I got dressed, wandered downstairs, said a few friendly words to some of the other people staying here, and set out into the town, where I saw a man about a toe.

The toe is genuine and enclosed herewith. It's rather a special toe. It used to form part of Edelhild the Anchorite—yes, that Edelhild, the one who wrote the music. There's a strong tradition connecting her to the hot springs here; apparently she built a chapel and a hermitage where the springs flow out into the lake, and people made pilgrimages, and she healed the sick. The toe's been part of the permanent endowment of the local priory ever since; but the priory's endowment turned out not to be quite so permanent after all. The heirs of the local bigwig who did the endowing recently found a loophole in the settlement deed; and now the nuns have been turfed out, the land reverts to the family and they put all the plate and vestments and furnishings and relics on the market. This man I know bought the toe, along with the prettiest provenance certificate you ever saw; rock solid, absolutely hard as nails.

Fortunately, the man I know isn't nearly as smart as he thinks he is. He showed me the certificate. I took a good long look at it, and did that sucking-your-teeth thing and didn't say a word. It's all right, isn't it? he said. I didn't say anything. I'm sure it's all right, he said, it looks just fine to me. I looked at him. Fuck, he said. What's wrong with it?

I didn't lie. Everything I said was true. I pointed out a few things; such as, a certificate of that period, you'd expect the parchment to be white, not sort of off-cream, and usually the ink wouldn't have sunk in quite so far. Stuff like that. I didn't point out that all that could be explained by the parchment having been used before and then sanded down, which was absolutely standard procedure at the time. He should have known that for himself.

Anyway, he spent a minute or so using coarse and unimaginative language. I asked him how much he'd paid for it. He told me; price of a frigate, or building a medium-large manor house on a hilltop. Oh dear, I said; nothing more than that, just Oh dear. Then, it'll be fine, I said, nobody's likely to pick up on it. It's a very recherché thing, parchment science. He looked at me as if to say, You're not helping. Then he gave me a big smile and talked about how long we'd known each other, and various trivial favours he'd done me in the past, though I don't actually remember them the same way as he does. This duke you buy stuff for, he said. Absolutely not, I said. Yes, he said, but he's got loads of money and nobody would ever know. Are you suggesting, I said, that I knowingly deceive my friend by purchasing a fake? He gave me a pleading look. Of course, I went on, I could be wrong about the parchment. It could be, I said, that it was sanded down and reused, and maybe that would account for the discrepancies. He grinned at me. That's the ticket, he said. Go on, be a pal.

I gave him two thirds of what he'd paid for it (which was about a third of what it's worth). He thanked me. He wasn't actually crying, but there were teardrops standing by in the corners of his eyes in case they were needed. And the beautiful thing is, I told him nothing but the truth, at all times. What are friends for?

Anyway, there you go and here it is. It's particularly effective, so they tell me, for headaches. If you feel like some inconsiderate bastard is quarrying slate between your ears, just brush the toe with your lips, very lightly, and you'll be right as rain in two shakes.

Oh, if only it was that easy. Still, what have you got to lose?

P

Genseric, by the grace of the Invincible Sun Archduke of Schanz, Elector, Grand Marshal of the Eastern Command, Regent of the Duchy of Selvois, Prince of Totas Parz, Precentor of the Holy Diaconate, to Pollio his brother in faith, greetings.

Thanks, Pollio. You're at the end of your rope and everything seems hopeless and every man's hand is against you, and then some kind friend sends you an unexpected toe, and suddenly the sun comes out from behind the cloud and everything is all right again.

Actually, it's not all right, but thanks anyway. I gather you're back in Cardai. Nice place. Of course, I can never go there, what with Ducomer being technically at war with Schanz, though since there's fifty miles of mountains between us and them it's not exactly top of either of our to-do lists... Still, it's a bitch. There are quite a few places I can't go, and you're free to float in and out wherever you want to. Like, to take an example at random, a bird.

As regards the money, I think it's only fair that you should keep the difference between the real value of the toe and what you actually paid for it. After all, you were the one who went to all the trouble of gouging and deceiving your pal, who trusted you. Doesn't seem right, somehow, that I should profit by that. Anyway, send me a note of the actual figures and I'll see to it that it gets paid into your account at the Poor Sisters; you know, the one I'm not supposed to know about.

Moving on: unless anything really spectacular comes up, I think I'm basically all right for bits of holy dead people for the time being. After all, it's taxpayers' money and there isn't quite as much of it as we thought there was. Apparently my uncle, rest his soul, got a bit creative with the Treasury paperwork shortly before he died. Gobarzes reckons he can trace some of it and maybe even get it back, but until then things are going to be a bit tight around here. But that's fine, we'll cope; somehow, we always cope, though I have no clear idea how.

Stay safe, Pollio. You can never tell with people.

G

GOBARZES, COMMANDER OF *the Palace Guard, prisoner of the Royal Clemency and slave, to Genseric, Archduke, Elector, Marshal, Prince, Regent, Precentor, Defender of the Faith, greetings.*

You instructed me to analyse the holy relic you recently acquired.

I can confirm that the object, a human toe-bone, has recently been treated with a poisonous substance; namely, an extract prepared by boiling the roots of white hellebore. The poison is sufficiently dilute that merely touching the object with bare skin produces nothing worse than a severe rash, together with stomach cramps and nausea. If ingested, however, even in tiny quantities, it would undoubtedly prove fatal. There is no known antidote and death would be both long drawn out and extremely painful.

GENSERIC, BY THE *grace of the Invincible Sun Archduke of Schanz, Elector, Grand Marshal of the Eastern Command, Regent of the Duchy of Selvois, Prince of Totas Parz, Precentor of the Holy Diaconate, to Gobarzes his servant, greetings.*

Thank you for your report. I am grateful for everything you do for me.

Now I would like you to investigate a friend of mine, Pollio. As you are probably aware, he sent me the poisoned relic. I would quite like to know why.

Please report to me in person. Take no action against him without my specific verbal instruction.

Genseric, by the grace of the Invincible Sun Archduke of Schanz, Elector, Grand Marshal of the Eastern Command, Regent of the Duchy of Selvois, Prince of Totas Parz, Precentor of the Holy Diaconate, to Pollio his brother in faith, greetings.

Since this is likely to be my last letter to you, I thought I'd give you a general all-around update on how things are going.

I guess I'd better start with the political stuff. We rounded up the last of my uncle's people and Gobarzes is talking to them right now. I imagine they'll tell him what he wants to know, sooner or later. I had to speak to him about being overenthusiastic when he talks to people. Dead men tell no tales, I pointed out, and that's counterproductive. I think he's taken that on board.

Do I trust him? I don't know any more. To be honest with you, I'm not entirely sure I care. At the moment—I think—he's the only one I can trust. I could be wrong, and even if I'm not, all that can change. Do I like him? Not really, though that could change, too.

With my uncle's lot out of the way, we can move on, at least until the next thing happens. We can line up our triple alliance of very small, very vulnerable states as a buffer between the Sashan and the Robur. I used to wonder about geography. Why, I used to ask myself, did the Invincible Sun make it that way? He must have realised what a load of problems He was making for people. But He chose to put a vast area of fertile land to the east of a narrow sea, with an apparently limitless steppe due north, and then mountains, only fit for parcelling up into tiny duchies and principalities, and then, due west, more fertile land—making it inevitable that one day there'd be the Sashan Empire in the east, the Robur in the north and the Aelians, the Mezentines and the Vesani in the west—and us, or some poor bastards like us, forming the eternally disputed border between them, an anvil shared between three strikers. Asking for trouble. And then, like a flash, I realised. Asking for trouble is what He does. And we are the anvil on which whatever it is He's up to will one day be made, or is being made right now, or has been made and we're too dumb to realise.

Anyway, things are or soon will be about as stable as they're ever likely to get. There's a fringe benefit for me, namely my new wife. Iffy turns out to be nothing at all like I'd expected, and I have the feeling that if I'm not careful—and why the hell should I want to be careful?—I may end up loving her.

Actually, not quite as surprising as all that. We do have a lot in common, after all. And she's cheerful and funny and so completely thrilled and overjoyed to have got away from Home... I can understand that, at any rate. Also, she's got a natural flair for languages, so quite soon we'll be able to talk to each other, which will be really nice. It's quite possible that by the time she can understand what I'm saying, I'll be ready to say to her things that I'd be embarrassed to communicate via an interpreter... Anyhow, my ministers are delighted that we seem to be getting on so well, since it bodes well for the succession. And I've promised myself that if I do manage to produce a son and heir, I won't make all the mistakes my father made. Yes, well. We'll have to see about that.

I really ought to leave it there, but I don't think I will.

I've told Gobarzes to leave you alone. He says he will, mostly because if his people kill anyone in Ducomer and the Ducomais find out, it could screw things up diplomatically and the fragile balance we're working so hard to build could all come crashing down—Can a balance come crashing down? You know what I mean. So long as you stay in Ducomer, where there's no extradition treaty, you should be pretty safe. If I were you, I'd fake your own death, go away somewhere and reinvent yourself, and then you'll be fine. It's a big world, especially if you've got money.

Talking of which: before you arrange your own funeral, check your balance with the Poor Sisters. It's not wealth beyond the dreams of avarice, but it should be enough to keep you comfortable; or you can use it as working capital for your business, that's entirely up to you. There won't be any more, though, so I would recommend caution. But that's not your way, is it?

You're never going to tell me the truth. What Gobarzes told me is probably as close to the truth as I'll ever get. It'd be nice if you'd write back and correct any details he's got wrong, but I don't for one moment imagine you will.

What Gobarzes told me was this. The Olbians hired you because they knew you were my pal. They didn't ask you to do anything, just kept you on retainer, so that was fine. Then my uncle screwed things up for them by having my first wife killed. His idea all along was to get rid of me, but only once I'd married Iffy and produced an heir—Then he'd kill me and slip in as regent for the kid, which nobody would raise an eyebrow at; whereas if he killed me, his right to succeed simply as my uncle would be decidedly dodgy, and his backers didn't like the odds.

What put us off the scent to begin with was the fact that my uncle and the Olbians looked to be on the same side, as in wanting the same thing. They wanted to sell Schanz out to the Robur. What I was too thick to appreciate was that my uncle wanted it to be *him* who did the selling-out—because then he'd be the one who got paid. If the Olbians succeeded without him, he'd get nothing out of it at all, quite likely he'd be left out in the cold, or be got rid of as an unwelcome loose end. So he killed my first wife and arranged for me to marry Iffy—on the face of it, precisely what the Olbians didn't want—so that later, once I was dead and he was regent and the kid had succumbed to chickenpox or whatever it is babies die of, he'd then be able to strike a really good deal with the Olbians: governor-general or viceroy of the whole region, once they'd annexed it; something like that.

Anyway, the Olbians figured out what he was up to and killed him, and then of course it dawned on them that with him gone, there was no obvious successor to me... So if I died, there'd be chaos and possibly a tiny little civil war, and the Robur could come swooping in while everyone was scratching each others' eyes out, and that'd be that, job done. So they reminded you that they own you, body and soul, and you obligingly sent me a toe.

[At this point in the manuscript approximately five lines are too badly corrupted to be legible]

Certain texts are ambiguous, capable of being interpreted in several different ways. I choose to interpret your last letter to me as conveying a hidden warning. That's how I read it, anyway, which is why I had Gobarzes check the toe for poison. If my interpretation is valid, it suggests that you didn't really want to kill me; presumably you had to try, or else the Olbians would be down on you like a ton of bricks, but you wanted to try and then fail. That's how I'd prefer to see it.

I admit, I'm still a bit confused. If you wanted money, why the hell didn't you embezzle it out of what I sent you? I can't believe it wasn't enough. Your tastes aren't that expensive, and you don't have anyone to provide for except yourself. Or you could just have asked me for it. I'd have given it to you like a shot, and you know that.

My guess is, the Olbians hired you before you started collecting for me, therefore before you had an opportunity to rob me blind... It was only after you'd sold them your soul that I handed you a bottomless purse. Now there's irony. In the twinkling of an eye, you went from being desperate for money to money being the least of your problems—There's a sort of symmetry in that which you generally only find in Dispater or the later plays of Saloninus. I assume it wasn't lost on you. But I guess it didn't seem quite so aesthetically satisfying to you, wriggling about on the sharp end.

You could've come clean, come here and let me protect you from the wrath of the Olbians. That's easy to say; but could I have guaranteed your safety? No, probably not, so you made the right call, in the end. In a way I'm sorry you failed. Now you're going to have one eye over your shoulder for the rest of your life, waiting for the Olbians to catch up with you, because you didn't manage to do what they told you to. Sorry about that. At least you've got enough money to start over, in Echmen or some similarly distant and godforsaken place. Mind you, I don't believe you'll be safe from them in any country you or I have ever heard of. They're persistent bastards.

What I'd really like to say to you is: once you've died and been reborn and settled down, and once all this shit has blown over and it's safe, write to me, not stating your real name but including some detail that only you and I would know, from the old days, and then we can carry on as though none of this had ever happened. I'd like that, really. But I'm not optimistic. By the time all this has blown over—if it ever does—either I'll be assassinated or the Olbians will've found you, or some other variant of the Once and Future Shit will have got in the way, and it probably won't happen. But I prefer to pretend that it's possible. It'll give me something to look forward to.

Stay safe, Pollio, if you possibly can.

Your friend,

Genseric

Copyright Information